XIX - abridgement
62

Clarissa

or the history of a young lady

(1748)

176
85-6
198   80 feather
Belford is the good one
203-hard
204 admonition
223 x fantasy   267 x 5
233
319
340 ; 342
351-2
455 pies Lovelace

Clarissa

or the history
of a young lady

Samuel Richardson

*abridged and edited with an introduction
by Philip Stevick*

RINEHART PRESS
San Francisco

contents

introduction

Some biographical facts must matter to us if we care about an author's works because they are so strikingly germane. We must care that Villon was a thief and Milton was blind; our reading of their works is diminished if we fail to know such irreducible facts. Nothing about Richardson, however, is very striking and, in a sense, nothing in his life is germane to his work. We do not read his life to confirm our impressions of his values; his values are clearly contained in his work. Whether he ever knew a young woman like Clarissa is not likely to strike us as a very interesting or necessary question. Yet in another sense, his life is a complicated and fascinating irony. And his life, as it bears on his works, is relevant to the nature of the novel, the novel's audience, and the cultural setting of the novel ever since.

The facts of his life are easily recorded. Born in Derbyshire in 1689, the son of a joiner, he moved soon after with his family to London. The extent of his early education is uncertain; it is clear that, rather than studying for the ministry, as he had hoped to do, he was apprenticed to a printer. In time, he married the daughter of his master and set himself up as a printer. His first wife died and after two years he married again. Meanwhile his printing business prospered. He became printer to the House of Commons and master of one of the most successful printing houses in London. In 1739 two booksellers proposed that he compile a volume of model letters, illustrating, for the sake of those unskilled in letter writing, how certain social situations could be written about. The book became *Letters Written to and for Particular Friends on the Most Important Occasions* and it was commercially successful. In 1740 and 1741, he published *Pamela*, a work of fiction derivative, to some extent, of his experience in writing the model letters and often regarded as the first novel in English. *Pamela* was followed by *Clarissa* in 1748, undoubtedly his major work of fiction, and in 1754, *Sir Charles Grandison*. With the publication of his novels, he became a celebrity both in his own country and abroad. In 1761 he died in London.

It is a rather dull story of hard work, honesty, sobriety, and duty, all of the usual tradesman's virtues, with an incongruous burst of success at the end—but consider its irony. Scattered through Richardson's life are events that reveal his capacity to listen with patience and understanding to the emotional problems of others and his capacity to set down on paper, if he wished, another person's thoughts and feelings. Certainly that is where all good novels start, with the ability to imagine what it is like to be somebody else. Yet nothing in his early life suggests that this interest in the feelings of others had much more substance to it than such interest has in a back-fence gossip. There is nothing to prevent us from concluding that he had a rather ordinary mind. Yet this apparently dull and uninteresting mind imagined, fleshed out, and projected into his books characters of such power that they shook the emotional life of all Europe. And this seemingly little mind, whom critics in every generation have scorned and patronized, almost singlehandedly created the novel for the English-speaking world.

Or consider the irony of that perfectly amazing burst of creative imagination which Richardson produced in his fifties. The world is full of men with half-finished novels in their desk drawers or men who begin to write a play in middle age. But here is a man who, for fifty years, wrote only for business or his own diversion. And then he found the passion, the imagination, the sheer physical stamina to write one rather long novel of four volumes followed by two of the longest novels in all of world literature, each, in its first edition, seven volumes long.

Or consider the irony of the moral import of his books. It was standard literary doctrine in Richardson's time that a work

of fiction should be "improving," that its only excuse for being
was that it could teach us by examples, good and bad, and help
make us better people. Whether very many writers actually believed such a thing is difficult to surmise. But it is a good guess
that Richardson probably did, for he was a sober, pious, and
humorless man, whose piety is exemplified by his writing a
letter when he was eleven years old to a widow of fifty, a long
letter, full of scripture, admonishing her for her alleged hypocrisy. Yet the first two novels of this pious man have an erotic
power, at times even a voyeuristic perversity, that has startled
readers for two centuries. And they present us not with narrowly
exemplary types of moral and immoral behavior but rather with
characters whose impulses are contradictory, whose motives
are tangled, and whose effect upon us is shifting and ambiguous.

It is almost impossible to overestimate the significance of
Richardson and his books for the course of the novel ever since.
We can almost define the novel by its middle-class orientation.
The novel customarily deals with the wishes and fears of the
middle class; it chronicles details of manners and custom that
are an index of middle-class interests; and it addresses itself
to a large, literate public, the bulk of which is middle class. It
was Richardson who most firmly fixed that class orientation,
and writers even now who might shudder to think of themselves
as being in Richardson's company remain, in the way in which
they extend the bourgeois nature of the novel, in Richardson's
debt.

In his techniques Richardson set numerous important prec-
edents. The novel is quintessentially a temporal art, experienced
by the reader in time and devoted to the portrayal of events
in a time scheme which is, usually, precise, specific, and finely
divided. Other narrative works before Richardson's have time
schemes in the sense of a self-consistent, plausible, and integral
deployment of the narrative according to the author's sense of
duration. But in Richardson the minuteness of the division of
time, the heightened sense of the characters' awareness of the
passage of time—their waiting, and expecting, and hoping, the
interrelatedness of the various characters' different perceptions

of the passage of time made possible by the letters, all of these add up to a treatment of time which is, as Ian Watt has argued, distinctly new.

The novel is also a "point of view" art. We are encouraged, as we read, to see into, almost to share, the consciousness of other people. Any novel gets told to us by a highly specialized "voice," the events having been seen by a highly specialized pair of eyes, and thus point of view is at once the vehicle of a novel's narration and the means by which the novelist is able to give his novel intricacy of meaning and uniqueness of vision. Again, it was Richardson who exploited the possibilities of point of view by means of the letters of his fictive correspondents and established, for the novel ever since, how indistinguishable the teller is from the tale.

Above all, the novel is an art form that properly requires as much formal mastery, as much integrity in its composition as art of any other kind. There is art, no doubt, in earlier prose fiction—wit and style in Nashe, sustained moral power in Bunyan, grace and ingenuity in Congreve. But if we look for a novel that was planned from the beginning as an artistic whole, whose parts were measured and proportioned as carefully as a well-designed building, and whose cumulative effect is overwhelming, the first such novel is *Clarissa*.

The novel occupies a peculiar place in our cultural life because we all imagine we could write one. No one imagines that he could, with a little effort, write symphonic music or design a cathedral. But everyone imagines that he could write a novel and the correspondence schools, the summer camps, the writers' institutes exist to minister to that expectation. It is a strange feeling to find toward one of the major artistic forms, but the feeling does have its reasons for being and, if we trace it back to what must have been its origins, we trace it back to Richardson. For here was a man supremely ordinary, apparently like the rest of us, who really *did* sit down one day in middle age and write a novel, and another, and another. And those novels were not only good; one of them was great. They were not only read; they were adored by some of the finest minds of the French and German Enlightenment and devoured by

Richardson's contemporaries. And in that creative act, Richardson established that special feeling which we have had concerning the novel ever since, a peculiar intimacy based upon the illusion that, although the novel at its best demands skill, endurance, and imagination of a very high order, all of these we could provide if we only wished to.

There is another way in which Richardson's performance establishes the place of the novel in Western culture. Audiences for art have always been saddened and delighted, moved even to tears or laughter, by the experience of the artistic object. But the emotional response to Richardson's novels was qualitatively different from the experience of most art prior to his time. People behaved as if his characters were really alive. As the various segments of his novels appeared, people would meet him in the street or write him letters, imploring, demanding that he not let his characters do so and so. And it is not clear, rereading many such letters now, whether those readers of Richardson were asking him, as author, simply to manage the forthcoming narrative in a way agreeable to them or whether they were asking him to restrain and compel the characters in the way in which one restrains an unruly German shepherd, as if the characters were alive but could be held in check by Richardson's superior will. Certainly the joy of the audience at the marriage of Pamela and the grief of the audience at the death of Clarissa were different from anything that had preceded them. It has been believed, at times, that when the volumes of *Pamela* describing her marriage left the press, church bells in England pealed; and when the final volumes of *Clarissa* were published, describing her final decline and death, church bells tolled. It does not now make much difference whether church bells really did ring or not. What matters is that people have thought that they did, that it has seemed perfectly plausible that a character in a fictional work should have been treated as if she were a living, dying human being.

Even now, reading *Clarissa*, one can feel the immediacy and the power which the book exercised upon its first audience. One lives with the characters, through both the trivialities and the great crises of their lives, and it is difficult not to get caught up in the appearance of life that they generate. Such a quality is especially apparent in books that are both long and great: *War and Peace*, *The Brothers Karamazov*, *Middlemarch*, *Remembrance of Things Past*, perhaps in its way *Moby Dick*, certainly *Ulysses*. But it is a characteristic, in varying degrees, of all good novels, the feeling which they are capable of evoking that reading them is an experience so compelling that it is very like coming to know a group of living persons. And it was Richardson who fully discovered that illusionist power for the novel.

II

In mid-novel, Lovelace sums up the conflict between himself and Clarissa. "This dear creature has too much punctilio: I am afraid, that I have too little. Hence our difficulties." He is right, of course. *Clarissa*, long as it is, is among the easiest of novels to summarize: its action is extremely constricted and, once the Harlowe family recedes from the foreground, the conflict between Clarissa and Lovelace, the differences between their styles, their judgments, their values, their temperaments, and their wills *is* the novel. Yet contained within that opposition of will and temperament is a literary world of many levels and great complication.

Everything in Richardson's novel depends upon everything else. The legacies and codicils, the doweries and marriage licenses, the prohibitions and curses, all of these form a substructure upon which the face-to-face drama is played, and it would be folly to ignore that dense and tangled legalistic level of the book, a level of the characters' existence that heavily restricts their freedom of choice.

When one speaks of the density and complexity with which a fairly simple situation is charged in the pages of Richardson, however, it is the motives of the characters that one most easily and naturally considers. Richardson's characters write endlessly about why they do what they do, why they cannot do what they feel they must not do, how they feel about what someone else has done, how they would feel if they were to do something which they have not yet done and probably will not do. Leslie

Stephen, in his essay on Richardson in *Hours in a Library*,
computes the amount of time that one of Richardson's characters
spends in writing letters. (It is Harriet Byron of *Sir Charles
Grandison* whom he describes but the same computations could
as easily be made with Clarissa.) "Miss Byron, on March 22,
writes a letter of fourteen pages. The same day she follows it up
by two of six and twelve pages respectively. On the 23rd she
leads off with a letter of eighteen pages, and another of ten."
The total comes to ninety-six closely printed pages in three
days. Stephen concludes that she must have written at least
eight hours a day and some days can scarcely have slept at all.
It is amusing to compute the pages of correspondence in this
way and does not really detract from Richardson's fiction.
Stephen admits, and all of us know, that the letter is a conven-
tion, no more silly and improbable than the soliloquy in Shakespeare or the aria in opera. But adding up the letters as Stephen
does reminds us of what we could hardly forget; it reminds us
of the enormous bulk of writing given to a few days and a few
events, the huge proportion of self-analysis in proportion to
action.

What such a large and complicated structure of analysis
makes possible is first of all a series of highly individualized
figures. Everyone in *Clarissa*, except for a few functionaries,
is seen in depth and in all of his special uniqueness. Given an
unidentified paragraph of the novel, most readers could probably guess which character wrote it; in the process of their endless self-analysis, the characters establish themselves as being
different from each other and impossible to confuse with each
other. They have their own voices, their own temperaments,
their own idiosyncratic phrases and rhythms, their own neurotic
compulsions and obsessions. Someone has said that Lovelace
is the most fully realized, most "complete" fictional man before
Joyce's Leopold Bloom. Comparisons are difficult: the reader
of *Ulysses* knows what Bloom eats for breakfast, at what
address, while wearing what clothes, while maintaining what
relation with his cat and his wife. One rarely knows Lovelace,
or any of the figures in Richardson's fiction, with that *kind* of
thoroughness. Still, one sees Lovelace change his mind scores of

times, rationalizing each change with a range of thought extending from mere wish fulfillment to a kind of argument that displays the full resources of a learned and intricate mind. One sees him fluctuate between moods with something rather like a manic-depressive violence. One sees him shift between his authentic self and a large variety of adopted selves, impersonating, taking voices not his own (he even "casts" himself as villain-hero in plays of his own invention). And all of this human amplitude is conveyed with an extraordinary set of verbal resources: Lovelace is master of the Addisonian middle style, cool and detached, fond, at other times, of heroic comparisons, allusions to Milton and the Cavalier poets, given, on other occasions, to a prose style as highly charged and energetic as any other of his century. And with all of this variety, he holds together, remains coherent, a unified image of a single human being. Moreover, the very nature of Richardson's method makes Lovelace more fully realized than he would seem were he standing alone. "Stereoscopic" that method has been called: by means of the interlocking letters we see "around" the characters, in something analogous to a three-dimensional visual effect. Lovelace is the most striking accomplishment in fictional realization that Richardson ever created, but *Clarissa* has two other figures of impressive depth, Clarissa herself and Anna Howe. Even the figures such as Hickman, who, through most of the book, are described and referred to but do not themselves write letters, have a life of their own. If Richardson's book did no more than that, if its only esthetic accomplishment were the presentation of a range of human experience at once unusually various and tightly coherent, a human image, or a group of contrasting human images, more deep and more dense than nearly anything in fiction before or since, if that were the whole substance of Richardson's achievement, it would be a stunning accomplishment in itself. But the prose of Richardson's novel carries layers of assumption and levels of implication which give to the book an unstated power and a complicated mythic resonance.

Dorothy Van Ghent has explored the mythic force of *Clarissa* in what is probably the most brilliant single piece of Richardson criticism. *Clarissa*, she maintains, gathers together a large number of attitudes and feelings common to its time and place and invests its central figures with these beliefs in such a way as to transform the characters from psychological types into symbols. Clarissa both "is" and "stands for," and in the process of coming to stand for those attitudes and feelings, she becomes in effect supernatural, "a fabulous creature of epic stature, clothed with the ideals of a culture and of a race." Part of the complex of symbolic values derives from the Puritan inheritance of Richardson and his audience; part of it derives from the class assumptions of Richardson, assumptions largely shared with the readers of his book. And in the execution of the book these different sources for her mythic power become fused into a kind of all-embracing Clarissa-myth, in which chastity, for example, is both an awesome moral virtue and a commercial value, or in which the fragile whiteness of Clarissa's dress and features are indications both of her repression of the instinctual and her economic gentility.

It is true, as Dorothy Van Ghent maintains, that much of the power of Richardson's novel is hidden and must be, as she puts it herself, "levered up." Yet there is a danger in "levering up" the power of the book from such implicit levels as Puritan repression and bourgeois commercialism, even though such levels of power are certainly there and must be acknowledged. The danger is that Richardson's book may seem more distant than it needs to, a rather repellent curiosity from the past, like a shrunken head in a museum. Dorothy Van Ghent's is a fine and persuasive essay, one of the few pieces of criticism that a student of Richardson must read. But it does not tell us very much about the power of Richardson in the twentieth century. All of us still carry with us, no doubt, a large measure of Puritanism and most of us are members of the middle class. And when Richardson builds his heroine upon the bourgeois ideal of the affectless woman, pale, chaste, expensive, and inaccessible, we know what he means. But the high fashion model is a phenomenon on the fringe of the lives of most of us and her image does not move us. We can afford to hold Dorothy Van Ghent's position in our minds while pursuing a different direction.

What do people do to each other and why? There is something about that question which marks it as a peculiarly twentieth-century object of curiosity. Surprisingly little in pre-twentieth century philosophy or social theory asks the question; very little in early psychology, or even in moral thought, ever gets so close to the human object that it is able to investigate one human being, in relation with one other human being, so as to inquire into what happens between the two of them. There has often been, in the past, a prevailing tendency to draw back from the human object, to generalize and make abstractions. Consider the words we use in the twentieth century, however, to express our curiosity about immediate human relations, our sensitivity to the emotional and moral possibilities of those relations, or our awareness of the pathos and pain in their failure: "compatibility," "defense mechanism," "I and Thou," "games," "manipulative behavior," "confrontation," "interaction ritual," "public image," "divided self." The list could be extended to many times this size, ranging from last week's slang to scientific constructs of the most austere kind, but all of them pointing toward one of our special raw nerves, our sensitivity to our primary interactions with other people. The twentieth century is as brutal and insensitive as any other period but no one can accuse the twentieth century of being unaware of the forms and dimensions of its own brutality, the forms by which we seek to ingratiate ourselves with others, or exploit, persuade, and manipulate others in our direct personal relations, or the sense of possibility which the twentieth century keeps alive, of knowing, seeing, feeling, and understanding between two face-to-face human beings.

Reading Richardson from the twentieth-century perspective I have described, he is likely to seem not only very wise and penetrating, very skillful and imaginative, in his projection of immediate human relationships; he is likely to seem uncompromisingly honest as well. He understands the nature of personal manipulation, the nature of the victim's role, and the ways in which one may use words not as referential symbols, not for communication at all, but as tactics in a game. And his technique gives him an extraordinary opportunity to measure public selves against private selves. But it is in the origins of the pain and exploitation that his characters must endure that his remarkable honesty is evident. For the first third of *Clarissa*, the source of the heroine's agony is not some alien menace but her own family, and the channels through which her family's advantages over her are exerted are the familiar ones of paternal authority and the rivalry of brother and sister. Lovelace creates his own channels through which to press his advantage and they resemble the finest refinement of the eighteenth-century mind, its wit and poise, its facility with language, its logical and analytical methods, its enormous learning, its ability to move with grace between play and irony and earnest partisanship. All of these are the fascinating traits of a brilliant age, mirrored in the figure of Lovelace—and they all become means for the manipulation of Clarissa. Clarissa's own fulfillment of the victim's role grows out of her perfectly conventional reverence for love and obedience, her plausible combination of courage and innocence, her conventional defense of the autonomy of her self, and these again become the means by which she is manipulated and destroyed. In other words, the emotional stress, the exploitation, the pure human viciousness of *Clarissa* comes not from chance or misfortune, not from the introduction into its world of villainous characters and destructive forces, but out of some of the deepest convictions and the most sacred relationships of its culture, and ours.

There are a score of ways to approach *Clarissa*, to clarify its density, to explain it and account for it. Genetically its roots are more firmly in the drama than in previous prose fiction. And a discussion of its use of dramatic conventions can tell us what we could not fully understand on first reading. Richardson did not, as one might expect, invent the epistolary technique by his own synthesis of drama with the model letters. There is a substantial body of fiction in letters before his time and even though such work was not highly influential, it does make another genetic context, one in which Richardson's work can be seen in all of its special novelty against the background of earlier attempts at the same effects. Esthetically, Richardson sought to make *Clarissa* a tragedy. And reading Richardson's own ideas of what he thought tragedy to be can tell us something about the intent of the book. Religiously, *Clarissa* is a Christian tragedy. Clarissa, in dying, is saved. Without under-

standing Richardson's Christianity, the last fourth of the book
seems unduly prolonged and difficult to respond to. Structurally,
the book was shaped by the circumstances of its publication
and the reading tastes of its audience. Mythically, as Dorothy
Van Ghent argues, *Clarissa* is a repository of the cultural attitudes of its time. None of these dimensions of *Clarissa* can be
ignored. Yet none of them does justice to the capacity of the
book to move readers two centuries after its writing. For at
this distance from the writing of *Clarissa*, one must make a
complicated effort to understand the novel in its own cultural
setting; but the art and the urgency of Richardson transcend his
own period so that one is able to feel the power of *Clarissa* as
a living work of art.

III

There is no other novel that one reads for serious purposes
that can be read in shortened form. (There is a shorter *Finnegans
Wake* but that is a special case.) Reading *War and Peace* or
Moby Dick takes endurance and sustained attention; but no
one would dream of cutting them up, throwing out "the dull
parts," and pasting them back together again in half the size for
the convenience of the busy reader. No one would dream of it?
The English novelist Somerset Maugham, a number of years ago,
did just that, cutting and trimming classic novels; the enterprise
was greeted with considerable contempt, not just from academ-
ics, and all of the abridged novels that flowed from Maugham's
blue pencil have long since disappeared, from book stores, from
library shelves, probably even from the homes of those who
once bought them and found that they were no more interested
in reading a short *War and Peace* than they were a long one.
One does not have to be a devotee of Tolstoy or Melville to
respond to the possibility of cutting their work with shock at
the effrontery: How dare anyone take scissors and paste to one
of the enduring works of the human imagination? Well then,
how dare anyone take scissors and paste to Richardson?

First it is useful to realize that Richardson was constantly
aware of his own verbosity. During the composition of *Clarissa*,
he wrote to the poet Edward Young, "—And I have run into

abridgement

such a length!—And am such a sorry pruner, though greatly luxuriant, that I am apt to add three pages for one I take away! Altogether I am frequently out of conceit with it. Then I have nobody that I can presume to advise with on such a subject." Richardson actually wished for someone to cut his growing novel. How serious Richardson was at the moment he wrote the letter is a problem, although he says the same thing in different words again and again. But what he says does make a difference. Despite the art of Richardson's book, despite its carefully adjusted dimensions and its meticulously crafted style, one cannot approach its million words with the same hushed awe with which one approaches the form of the modern art novel.

The primary rationale for abridgment lies, however, not in the troublesome area of our relationship with Richardson but in the perfectly clear area of our relationship with Richardson's book. There are a dozen reasons for not abridging *Clarissa*, one reason *for* abridging it, and that one reason outweighs all the contrary reasons. It is that almost no one would read *Clarissa* if it were unabridged. For it is in a different class from other novels of considerable size. A novel of 600 pages seems long to most of us and one of 800 pages may well seem to demand so much of our time and energy that we put off reading it for a lifetime. If the whole of *Clarissa* were printed in the page format you are now reading, it would extend to something like 2600 pages.

What gets lost in the abridgment *is* quite a bit—The letters in the edition that follows are headed with the dates of their fictive composition. In the full novel, these dates are all plausible and they make, in their interrelation, a time scheme of considerable complexity. Richardson takes into account the time of transmission, the possibility of letters crossing in simultaneous transmission, the time elapsed in composition, the appropriate amount of time required to respond to an especially dramatic, or elliptical, or menacing letter. In an abridgment, most of these nuances disappear. The dates are there but there is no sense in trying to trace them, for the intricacy of their coherence is impossible to represent in an abridgment.

"editor's here"?

The dates are only one of several mechanical aspects of *Clarissa* that are much diminished in abridgment. In the early editions of the full novel, Richardson supplied an elaborate system of cross-referencing by footnote. When a letter refers to an event some time past, Richardson helps us, if we care to look up that past event, by giving us letter and volume number at the bottom of the page. We may think what we will of such cross-referencing, but in a book which the reader must experience at great length it does help to make the book hang together. But in an abridgment it cannot operate and must be edited out.

Every substantial element of the book is different in an abridgment. Its motivational density is thinned out. Its rhythms change. Its scale and structure are shortened. Perhaps most important of all, the time which the reader must spend with the book is altered and the sustained involvement with the characters over an extraordinarily long period of time is not necessary.

It is a mistake, then, not to face quite squarely the consequences of abridging Richardson. The argument that we ought either to read him whole or leave him alone is, in its own way, unanswerable. Yet the contrary argument is just as unanswerable, that to fail to abridge him is virtually to consign him to oblivion. And it is true that of all the classic novelists, Richardson survives abridgment most easily. For despite all that is reduced, much of the power of the original can be retained, even its characteristic expansiveness of style and the effect of its patterned architectonics.

In the abridgment that follows, I have tried to give Richardson's remarkable insight into the pathological a free rein without allowing it to dominate the book. All of the early novelists have had to survive charges of licentiousness. I have assumed that it is not necessary, however, to shield anyone from the more coarse, grotesque, and neurotic aspects of his vision. I have eliminated certain minor elements of the plot and certain minor characters altogether. And in compensation, I have allowed a number of the letters of Clarissa and Lovelace to stand uncut, in all of their original amplitude. Above all, I have tried to be true to the book's own truth, to define and make more prominent, in abridging, Richardson's clear view of human interaction and his complex view of the self, in which we simultaneously love and hate, resist and submit, reason and rationalize, wish to do well and end up doing ill.

IV

Reading a book printed in the eighteenth century is, if one's tastes are at all bookish, a keen pleasure. There is the splendid rag paper, crisp and scarcely yellowed after two hundred years, the hand-made binding, often a tooled calf skin slightly powdery at the joints. There is the pleasure of being in contact not merely with the words of the literary work but with the physical thing itself that moved and excited its audience in its own time. Richardson ends the fourth volume of *Clarissa*, in its first edition, with the words "The Remainder of this Work will be published at once; and that as soon as indispensable avocations will permit." Reading that sentence, one imagines, as one cannot in reading a twentieth-century edition, the extraordinary anxiety that that ending must have provoked, with the later volumes of the novel not yet written and nothing to do but wait. The print in even the best-printed eighteenth-century book is unmistakably set by hand rather than by machine and in the less carefully printed books is a riot of misalignment. It is not only the angles of the type, however, that declare the book to be made by man; it is the punctuation, the indentation, the spelling, all of those mechanical matters that are called "style" in the special sense in which that word is used of printing. To "style" a book nowadays is to make it uniform and standardized in all of those small matters of appearance and we may well become annoyed if we discover inconsistencies as we read through a book. The eighteenth century knew no such concept. Spellings vary, spacing is capricious (by our standards), and punctuation is wildly inconsistent.

Some of this inconsistency is the result of human error, no doubt, the author who forgets what he has written before, the typesetter who makes a mistake. But some of what we would now call inconsistency is, just as surely, a result of deliberate choice. Richardson will enclose a parenthetical phrase within commas sometimes, at other times within brackets, at other

times within dashes; or then again he may leave the phrase
unpunctuated. Each one of these ways of treating such a phrase
looks slightly different, sounds slightly different, means something slightly different from the other ways. And it would be
the utmost folly to assume that Richardson did not know this,
did not know that the rhythm and the sense of any given sentence may be better served by inconsistency than by consistency.
Being a printer, Richardson had a special proximity to the whole
bookmaking process, to the power and force of the way words
look on a page. As a novelist, he used type with an individuality
and virtuosity exceeded in his time only by Sterne and scarcely
equaled since. Only recently have certain experimental writers
attempted to place words on the page with the intent of using
that very placement for its expressive force, something that
Richardson knew two centuries ago.

Thus the inconsistency of a Richardson novel is not merely
quaint and old fashioned. That very inconsistency is an aspect
of its imaginative power and must be preserved, as far as possible, in a modern edition. The ideal modern edition of Richardson would reproduce the rag paper, the calf binding, and the
hand-set type. The next best edition is one that attempts, within
the limits of modern typographical procedures, to reproduce all
of Richardson's "inconsistencies" and that is what the present
edition does, printing the text as it appears in the first edition.
The long *s* has been modernized; apostrophe *d* I have changed to
ed; a very few obvious misprints I have corrected. Otherwise
the text is Richardson's.

It is common editorial practice to construct one's text from
the later editions which an author is known to have had a hand
in. Richardson did, in fact, revise extensively and the later editions do, no doubt, represent his final intentions. Yet there are
good, and to my mind persuasive, reasons for choosing the first
edition over such a more obvious choice as the third for one's
base text.

Measuring the difference between the two versions is
difficult and complicated. Take some small but significant differences. In the third edition, Clarissa customarily refers to her
mother in the early stages of the novel as *Mother*, in the first

edition as *Mamma.* The effect of the *Mamma* is certainly to make Clarissa seem younger, and that is all to the good from our point of view in the twentieth century. She is likely to seem, with her intricate prose style, much older than she is meant to appear. On the other hand, that *Mamma* may seem precious to our ears, a diminutive too childish for her tragic dimensions. Or take those instances in which Richardson clarifies a momentary confusion in pronoun reference by revising so as to make the antecedent clear. It is certainly proper that a novel should be as clear as possible and for that reason it is good to have as few ambiguous he's and she's as possible. On the other hand, writers of letters do not always make their pronoun antecedents perfectly clear. Letters are written in haste, to people one knows. And thus it may be that, although the revised text is better prose, the text in the first edition produces far more successfully the illusion of authentic letters unmediated by a controlling author.

The substantial difference between the two editions, however, lies not in such small and subtle variations but in great blocks of material which were added to the third edition. The nature and apparent intent of this added material is skillfully summarized in an article by M. Kinkead-Weekes in *Review of English Studies* (May, 1959) entitled *"Clarissa* Restored?" The public response to *Clarissa,* as it appeared, was rather different from what Richardson had hoped it would be and was, in fact, profoundly disturbing to him. The contemporary readers of the first edition found Lovelace charming and Clarissa priggish. Or at least enough of them did to convince Richardson that, far from having written a moral book, he was in danger of having written a pernicious one. As a response to such readings, Richardson added italics, notes, and an index, by way of making his intentions more clear. And he added events and descriptions intended to make Clarissa appear more virtuous and Lovelace more contemptible. As a result, the third edition is, although more carefully written, more coarse and heavy-handed in its enlistment of our sympathies. As Professor Kinkead-Weekes poses the textual problem, "All modern editors, regarding the new material as straightforward restoration, have naturally printed the revised version as the author's final intention. But if the changes are proved to be, with relatively few exceptions, the direct result of the misinterpretations of an uncritical audience, the definition of 'intention' becomes less simple. Which represents Richardson's real intention: the novel he wrote expecting an audience capable of appreciating it, or the revision for one he found careless, superficial, and sentimental?"

I have kept one letter of Lovelace's from the "restored" material of the first edition, as an example of the way in which Richardson went about coarsening the character of Lovelace. The letter appears on page 223. Otherwise, the text is that of the first edition of 1748. The first edition is, without much question, less graceful stylistically than the third. But it is morally less crude and truer to his imagination than Richardson allowed himself to be as he revised.

V

It is especially ironic that Richardson, author of some of the world's longest books, has received very little sustained criticism and, in fact, most of the interesting people who have had anything to say about his fiction have delivered themselves in epigrams, or at least in a prose so compressed and witty that it contains epigrams. It is an astonishing contrast, the multivolume novels on the one hand, the one-line judgments on the other. But the epigrams, gathered together, do make an impressive display of critical opinion. There are not many other esthetic objects toward which so much cleverness and insight, intelligence and verbal precision have been directed. Nothing will do, of course, but to quote a fair sample of these judgments.

> Why, Sir, if you were to read Richardson for the story, your impatience would be so much fretted that you would hang yourself. But you must read him for the sentiment, and consider the story as only giving him occasion to the sentiment.
>
> SAMUEL JOHNSON

> Richardson wrote those deplorably tedious lamentations, 'Clarissa', and 'Sir Charles Grandison', which are pictures of high life as con-

ceived by a book-seller, and romances as they would be spiritual-
ized by a Methodist teacher.

HORACE WALPOLE

Any girl that runs away with a young fellow, without intending to
marry him, should be carried to Bridewell or to Bedlam the next
day. Yet the circumstances are so laid, as to inspire tenderness,
notwithstanding the low style and absurd incidents; and I look
upon this and Pamela to be two books that will do more general
mischief than the works of Lord Rochester.

LADY MARY WORTLEY MONTAGU

In the course of a few hours I had run through a larger number of
situations than the longest lifetime is likely to offer. I had heard
the true discourses of the passions; I had seen the springs of self-
interest and self-respect touched upon in a hundred different ways;
I had become a spectator at a multitude of incidents; I felt I had
acquired experience.

DIDEROT

To the letter-writer every event is recent, and is described while
immediately under the eye, without a corresponding degree of
reference to its relative importance to what has past and what is
to come. All is, so to speak, painted in the foreground, and nothing
in the distance. A game at whist, if the subject of a letter, must be
detailed as much at length as a debate in the House of Commons,
upon a subject of great national interest; and hence, perhaps, that
tendency to prolixity, of which the readers of Richardson frequently complain.

SIR WALTER SCOTT

There is a cheerful, sun-shiny, breezy spirit [in Fielding] that prevails every where, strongly contrasted with the close, hot, day-
dreamy continuity of Richardson.

SAMUEL TAYLOR COLERIDGE

[Clarissa] is interesting in her ruffles, in her gloves, her samplers,
her aunts and uncles—she is interesting in all that is uninteresting.

WILLIAM HAZLITT

The plot, as we have seen, is simple, and no underplots interfere with the main design. No digressions, no episodes. It is wonderful that without these helps of common writers, he could support a work of such length. With Clarissa it begins,—with Clarissa it ends. We do not come upon unexpected adventures and wonderful recognitions, by quick turns and surprises: we see her fate from afar, as it were through a long avenue, the gradual approach to which, without ever losing sight of the object, has more of simplicity and grandeur than the most cunning labyrinth that can be contrived by art.

MRS. BARBAULD, *Richardson's biographer*

As I lost this beloved, incomprehensible being but too early [Goethe is speaking of his sister], I felt inducement enough to picture her excellence to myself, and so there arose within me the conception of a poetic Whole, in which it might have been possible to exhibit her individuality: but no other form could be thought of for it than that of the Richardsonian romance. Only by the minutest detail, by endless particularities which all bore vividly the character of the whole, and as they spring up from a wonderful depth give some faint idea of the depth; . . . for the fountain can be examined only while it is flowing.

GOETHE

Of *Clarissa: le premier Roman du Monde.*

ALFRED DE MUSSET

For me, I read Richardson for a hearty and wholesome dose of sentimentality and if one does that one may as well have that quality laid on as thickly as it will go.

FORD MADOX FORD

James has been considering the dullness of naturalistic fiction, particularly the dullness of Zola. *Wilhelm Meister* is not a sprightly composition, and yet *Wilhelm Meister* stands in the front rank of novels. *Romola* is a very easy book to lay down, and yet *Romola* is full of beauty and truth. *Clarissa Harlowe* discourages the most robust persistence, and yet, paradoxical as it seems, *Clarissa Harlowe* is deeply interesting. It is obvious, therefore, that there is something to be said for dullness; and this something is perhaps, primarily, that there is dullness and dullness.

HENRY JAMES

Without *Clarissa* there would have been no *Nouvelle Héloïse*, and had there been no *Nouvelle Héloïse*, everyone of us would have been somewhat different from what we are.

AUGUSTINE BIRRELL

Boccaccio at his hottest seems to me less pornographical than *Pamela* or *Clarissa Harlowe*.

D. H. LAWRENCE

Gide has been writing about the "impurity" of the French novel, the "heterogeneous and inherently indigestible elements" in the fiction of Balzac. It is worthy of note that the English, who have never known how to *purify* their drama in the sense that Racine's tragedy is purified, yet achieved at the very outset a much greater purity in the novels of Defoe, Fielding, and even Richardson.

ANDRÉ GIDE

In the English novel Lovelace is one of the few men of intellect who display an intellect which is their own and not patently an abstract of their author's intellectual interests. . . . Richardson is the least flat, the most stereoscopic novelist of an age which ran the plain or formal statement to death in the end.

V. S. PRITCHETT

Although he squeezes every atom of emotion (and sometimes more) out of every incident, yet because the central conflict is so strong and true and because the scene he has built is so real and solid, the book can in fact, to an astonishing measure, bear such treatment. Hence the paradox that though Richardson is sentimental *Clarissa*, by and large, is not.

ARNOLD KETTLE

Clarissa cannot exist without Lovelace any more than he without her; without him, she is a thematic abstraction awaiting a drama to embody it, a figure of speech in a sermon; without her he is only Don Juan in the world of the bourgeoisie, that is to say, Lord Byron before the fact. Once mutually defined, their futures differ greatly; for Lovelace stands at the end of a tradition, Clarissa at the beginning.

LESLIE FIEDLER

All of these, witty and penetrating as they are, are single visions of Richardson's achievement. It is the nature of epigram that they should be so; epigrams are not balanced and judicious but quick, clever, and rarely fair. It is interesting, all the same, how many of the judgments do look in two directions: Richardson is tiresome and interesting, repugnant and attractive. I see no reason why we should not take a double view, as some of the epigrams begin to do. For they are both right, the critics who disparage Richardson and the critics who adore him. *Clarissa's* world demands an allocation of sympathy, interest, and effort which can only seem grotesque at times. But Richardson's novel can move us and, for all of its distance from us, speak quite powerfully to our sense of who we are; it can, and should, fascinate us as an esthetic object; above all, its definition of its conflict can seem to us, as it does to Arnold Kettle, "strong and true."

Philadelphia
January 1971

P. S.

bibliographical note

The Shakespeare Head Edition of Richardson's novels (Oxford: Blackwell, 1929–31) is the best collected edition and should be consulted for the full text of *Clarissa* using the third edition. There has been no collected edition of Richardson's correspondence since that of Anna Laetitia Barbauld's (London, 1804) but John Carroll has edited a useful selection from the correspondence entitled *Selected Letters of Samuel Richardson* (Oxford: Clarendon, 1964) and the letters between Richardson and his Dutch translator have been edited by William C. Slattery as *The Richardson-Stinstra Correspondence and Stinstra's Prefaces to 'Clarissa'* (Carbondale, Ill.: Southern Illinois University Press, 1969). A useful older biography is Brian Downs' *Richardson* (London: Routledge & Kegan Paul, 1928). The two biographical studies which are now standard for most purposes are W. M. Sale's *Samuel Richardson, Master Printer* (Ithaca: Cornell University Press, 1950) and A. D. McKillop, *Samuel Richardson, Printer and Novelist* (Chapel Hill: University of North Carolina Press, 1936). It is likely that they will be superseded by the biography of T. C. Duncan Eaves and Ben Kimpel soon to be published by the Clarendon Press. Two collections of Richardson's nonfictional prose are especially worth consulting, an edition of the *Familiar Letters*, edited by Brian Downs (London: Routledge, 1928) and *Clarissa: Preface, Hints of Prefaces, and Postscript*, edited by R. F. Brissenden (Los Angeles: Augustan Reprint Society Publication Number 103, 1964).

The best brief critical introduction to Richardson's life and works is the pamphlet by R. F. Brissenden entitled *Samuel Richardson*, Writers and their Work No. 101 (London: Long-

mans, Green, 1958). The volume on Richardson in the Twentieth
Century Views series, *Samuel Richardson: A Collection of Criti-
cal Essays*, ed. John Carroll (Englewood Cliffs, N.J.: Prentice-
Hall, 1969), gathers some important essays along with a good
bibliography of secondary studies; and it can serve as an intro-
duction to the kind of critical work that has been done on
Richardson in the last two decades. Two works helpful in under-
standing the generic setting of Richardson's fiction are John J.
Richetti's *Popular Fiction Before Richardson* (New York: Oxford
University Press, 1969) and Robert Adams Day's *Told in Letters*
(Ann Arbor: University of Michigan Press, 1966). The most
far-ranging work on Richardson is contained in Ian Watt's *The
Rise of the Novel* (London: Chatto and Windus, 1957; Berkeley:
University of California Press, 1957), the one book indispensable
for a consideration of Richardson's significance.

Clarissa

or the history of a young lady

Miss Anna Howe
To Miss Clarissa Harlowe

Jan. 10.

I AM extremely concerned, my dearest friend, for the disturbances that have happened in your family. I know how it must hurt you, to become the subject of the public talk: And yet, upon an occasion so generally known, it is impossible but that whatever relates to a young lady, whose distinguished merits have made her the public care, should engage everybody's attention. I long to have the particulars from yourself; and of the usage I am told you receive upon an accident you could not help; and in which, as far as I can learn, the sufferer was the aggressor.

Mr. Diggs*, whom I sent for at the first hearing of the rencounter, to inquire, for *your* sake, how your brother was, told me, That there was no danger from the wound, if there were none from the fever; which, it seems, has been increased by the perturbation of his spirits.

Mr. Wyerley drank tea with us yesterday; and tho' he is far from being partial to Mr. Lovelace, as it may be well supposed, yet both he and Mr. Symmes blame your family for the treatment they gave him, when he went in person to inquire after your brother's health, and to express his concern for what had happened.

They say, That Mr. Lovelace could not avoid drawing his sword: And that either your brother's unskilfulness or violence left him, from the very first pass, intirely in his power.

This, I am told, was what Mr. Lovelace said upon it; retreating as he spoke: "Have a care, Mr. Harlowe—Your violence puts you out of your defence. You give me too much advantage! For your sister's sake, I will pass by every thing;—if—"

* *Her brother's surgeon.*

1

But this the more provoked his rashness, to lay himself open to the advantage of his adversary—Who, after a slight wound given him in the arm, took away his sword.

There are people who love not your brother, because of his natural imperiousness, and fierce and uncontroulable temper: These say, That the young gentleman's passion was abated, on seeing his blood gush plentifully down his arm; and that he received the generous offices of his adversary, who helped him off with his coat and waistcoat, and bound up his arm, till the surgeon could come, with such patience, as was far from making a visit afterwards from that adversary to inquire after his health, appear either insulting or improper.

Be this as it may, every-body pities you. So steady, so uniform in your conduct: So desirous, as you always said, of sliding through life to the end of it un-noted. How must such a virtue suffer on every hand!—Yet it must be allowed, that your present trial is but proportioned to your prudence!—

As all your friends without doors are apprehensive, that some other unhappy event may result from so violent a contention, in which, it seems, the families on both sides are now engaged, I must desire you to enable me, on the authority of your own information, to do you occasional justice.

My mamma, and all of us, like the rest of the world, talk of nobody but you, on this occasion, and of the consequences which may follow, from the resentments of a man of Mr. Lovelace's spirit; who, as he gives out, has been treated with high indignity by your uncles. My mamma will have it, that you cannot now, with any decency, either see him, or correspond with him. She is a good deal prepossessed by your uncle Antony; who occasionally calls upon us, as you know; and on this rencounter, has represented to her the crime, which it would be in a sister to encourage a man, who is to *wade* into her favour, (this was his expression) thro' the blood of her brother.

Write to me therefore, my dear, the whole of your story, from the time that Mr. Lovelace was first introduced into your family; and particularly an account of all that passed between him and your sister; about which there are different reports; some people supposing that the younger sister (at least by her uncommon merit) has stolen a lover from the elder: And pray write in so full a manner, as may gratify those, who know not so much of your affairs, as I do.

You see what you draw upon yourself, by excelling all your sex. Every individual of it, who knows you, or has heard of you, seems to think you answerable to *her* for your conduct in points so very delicate and concerning.

Every eye, in short, is upon you, with the expectation of an example. I wish to heaven you were at liberty to pursue your own methods: All would then, I dare say, be easy, and honourably ended. But I dread your directors and directresses; for your mamma, admirably well qualified as she is to lead, must submit to be led. Your sister and brother will certainly put you out of your course.

But this is a point you will not permit me to expatiate upon: Pardon me therefore, and I have done. — Yet, why should I say, Pardon me? When your concerns are my concerns? When your honour is my honour? When I love you, as never woman loved another? And when you have allowed of that concern and of that love; and have for years, ranked in the first class of your friends,

Your ever-grateful and affectionate

Anna Howe?

Will you oblige me with a copy of the preamble to the clauses in your grandfather's will in your favour; and allow me to send it to my aunt Harman? — She is very desirous to see it. Yet your character has so charmed her, that, tho' a stranger to you personally, she assents to the preference given you in it before she knows his reasons for that preference.

Miss Clarissa Harlowe
To Miss Howe

Harlowe-Place, Jan. 13.

OUR Family has indeed been strangely discomposed.—
Discomposed!—It has been in *tumults*, ever since the
unhappy transaction; and I have borne all the blame; yet should
have had too much concern, from myself, had I been more
justly spared by every one else.

For, whether it be owing to a faulty impatience, having
been too indulgently treated to be *inured* to blame, or to the
regret I have to hear those censured on my account, whom it
is my duty to vindicate; I have sometimes wished, that it had
pleased God to have taken me in my last fever, when I had
every-body's love and good opinion; but oftener, that I had
never been distinguished by my grandpapa as I was: Which
has estranged from me, I doubt, my brother's and sister's affections; at least, has raised a jealousy, with regard to the apprehended favour of my two uncles, that now-and-then over-
shadows their love.

My brother being happily recovered of his fever, and his
wound, I will be as particular as you desire in the little history
you demand of me.

I will begin, as you command, with Mr. Lovelace's address
to my sister; and be as brief as possible. I will recite facts only;
and leave you to judge of the truth of the report raised, that
the younger sister has robbed the elder.

It was in pursuance of a conference between Lord M. and
my uncle Antony, that Mr. Lovelace (my papa and mamma
not forbidding) paid his respects to my sister Arabella. My
brother was then in Scotland, busying himself in viewing the
condition of the considerable estate which was left him there by
his generous godmother, together with one as considerable in
Yorkshire. I was also absent at my *Dairy-house*, as it is called,[a]

[a] *Her Grandfather, in order to invite her to him, as often as her other friends
would spare her, indulged her in erecting and fitting-up a dairy-house in her own*

4

busied in the accounts relating to the estate which my grandfather had the goodness to bequeath me; and which once a year
are left to my inspection, altho' I have given the whole into my
papa's power.

My sister made me a visit there the day after Mr. Lovelace
had been introduced; and seemed highly pleased with the gentleman. His birth, his fortune in possession, a clear 2000 *l. per
annum*, as Lord M. had assured my uncle; presumptive heir to
that nobleman's large estate: His great expectations from Lady
Sarah Sadleir, and Lady Betty Lawrance; who, with his uncle,
interested themselves very warmly (he being the last of his line)
to see him married.

"So handsome a man!—O her beloved Clary!" (for then
she was ready to love me dearly, from the overflowings of her
good humour on his account!) "He was but *too* handsome a man
for *her!*—Were she but as amiable a *somebody*, there would be a
probability of *holding* his affections!—For he was wild, she
heard; *very* wild, very gay; loved intrigue—But he was young;
a man of sense: Would see his error, could she but have patience with his faults, if his faults were not cured by marriage."

Thus she ran on; and then wanted me "to see the charming
man," as she called him.—Again concerned, "that she was not
handsome enough for him;" With, "A sad thing, that the man
should have the advantage of the woman in that particular."
—But then, stepping to the glass, she complimented herself,
"That she was very *well:* That there were many women deemed
passable, who were inferior to herself: That she was always
thought comely; and, let her tell me, that comeliness having not
so much to lose as beauty had, would hold, when that would
evaporate and fly off:—Nay, for that matter" (and again she
turned to the glass) "her features were not irregular; her eyes
not at all amiss." And I remember they were more than usually
brilliant at that time.

Excuse me, my dear, I never was thus particular before;
no, not to you. Nor would I now have written thus freely of a

---

taste. When finished, it was so much admired for its elegant simplicity and convenience, that the whole seat, before, of old time, from its situation, called The
Grove, was generally known by the name of The Dairy-house; her grandfather,
particularly, was fond of having it so called.

sister; but that she makes a merit to my brother, of disowning that she ever liked him; as I shall mention hereafter: And then you will always have me give you minute descriptions, nor suffer me to pass by the air and manner in which things are spoken, that are to be taken notice of; rightly observing, that air and manner often express more than the accompanying words.

I congratulated her upon her prospects. She received my compliments with a great deal of self-complacency.

She liked the gentleman still more at his next visit: And yet he made no particular address to her; altho' an opportunity was given him for it. This was wondered at, as my uncle had introduced him into our family, declaredly as a visitor to my sister. But as we are ever ready to make excuses, when in good humour with ourselves for the supposed slights of those whose approbation we wish to engage; so my sister found out a reason, much to Mr. Lovelace's advantage, for his not improving the opportunity that was given him.—It was bashfulness, truly, in him. (Bashfulness in Mr. Lovelace, my dear!)—Indeed, gay and lively as he is, he has not the look of an *impudent* man. But I fancy, it is many, many years ago, since he was bashful.

Thus, however, could my sister make it out—"Upon her word, she believed Mr. Lovelace deserved not the bad character he had as to women. He *would* have spoken out, she believed: but once or twice, as he seemed to intend to do so, he was under so *agree*-able a confusion! Such a profound respect he seemed to shew her: A perfect *reverence*, she thought: She loved dearly, that a man in courtship should shew a reverence to his mistress."—So indeed we all do, I believe: And with reason; since, if I may judge from what I have seen in many families, there is little enough of it shewn afterwards.—And she told my aunt Hervey, that she would be a little less upon the reserve next time he came: "She was not one of those *flirts*, not she, who would give pain to a person that deserved to be well-treated; and the more for the greatness of his value for her."

But now she began to be dissatisfied with him: She compared his general character, with This his particular behaviour to her; and, having never been courted before, owned herself puzzled, how to deal with so odd a lover. "What did the man mean! Had not her uncle brought him *declaredly* as a suiter to her?—It could not be bashfulness (now she thought of it), since he might have opened his mind to her *uncle*, if he wanted courage to speak directly to *her*. But it was right, surely, that a woman should be put out of doubt, early, as to a man's intentions, in such a case as This, from his own mouth.—But, truly, she had begun to think, that he was more solicitous to cultivate her *mamma's* good opinion, than *hers!*

How they managed it in their next conversation I know not. One would be tempted to think by the issue, that Mr. Lovelace was ungenerous enough to seek the occasion given, and to improve it. Yet he thought fit to put the question too:—But, she says, it was not till, by some means or other (she knew not how) he had wrought her up to such a pitch of displeasure with him, that it was impossible for her to recover herself, at the instant: Nevertheless he re-urged his question, as expecting a definitive answer, without waiting for the return of her temper, or endeavouring to mollify her: so that she was under a necessity of persisting in her denial: Yet gave him reason to think, she did not dislike his address, only the *manner* of it; his court being rather made to her mamma than to herself, as if he were sure of *her* consent at any time.

A good encouraging denial, I must own:—As was the rest of her plea; to wit, "A disinclination to change her state.—Exceedingly happy as she was: She never could be happier!" And such-like *consenting negatives*, as I may call them; and yet not intend a reflection upon my sister: For what can any young creature, in the like circumstances, say, when she is not sure, but a too ready consent may subject her to the slights of a sex that generally values a blessing, either more or less, as it is obtained with difficulty or ease?

Here I am obliged to lay down my pen. I will soon resume it.

so we know - she is smart
comes from a mean-minded family
- is generous & honest & good

Miss Clarissa Harlowe
To Miss Howe

Jan. 13, 14.

A ND thus, as Mr. Lovelace thought fit to *take it*, had he his answer from my sister. It was with very great regret, as he pretended (I doubt the man is an hypocrite, my dear!), that he acquiesced in it. "So much determinedness; such a noble firmness in my sister; that there was no hope of prevailing upon her to alter sentiments she had adopted on full consideration." He sighed, as Bella told us, when he took his leave of her: "Profoundly sighed; Grasped her hand, and kissed it with *such* an ardor.—Withdrew with *such* an air of solemn respect.—She could almost find in her heart, altho' he had vexed her, to pity him."

He waited on my mamma, after he had taken leave of Bella, and reported his ill success, in so respectful a manner, both with regard to my sister, and to the whole family, and with so much concern that he was not accepted as a relation to it, that it left upon them all (my brother being then, as I have said, in Scotland) impressions in his favour; and a belief, that this matter would certainly be brought on again. But Mr. Lovelace going up directly to town, where he stayed a whole fortnight; and meeting there with my uncle Antony, to whom he regretted his niece's unhappy resolution not to change her state; it was seen that there was a total end put to the affair.

But when Mr. Lovelace returned into the country, he thought fit to visit my papa and mamma; hoping, as he told them, that, however unhappy he had been in the rejection of the wished-for alliance; he might be allowed to keep up an acquaintance and friendship with a family which he should always respect. And then, unhappily, as I may say, was I at home, and present.

It was immediately observed, that his attention was fixed on me.

My aunt Hervey was there; and was pleased to say, We should make the finest couple in England; if my sister had no objection.—No, indeed, with a haughty toss, was my sister's reply!—It would be strange if she had, after the denial she had given him upon full deliberation.

My mamma declared, That her only dislike of his alliance with either daughter, was on account of his reputed faulty morals.

My uncle Harlowe, That his daughter Clary, as he delighted to call me from childhood, would reform him, if any woman in the world could.

My uncle Antony gave his approbation in high terms: But referred, as my Aunt had done, to my sister.

She repeated her contempt of him; and declared, that were there not another man in England, she would not have him. She was ready, on the contrary, she could assure them, to resign her pretensions under hand and seal, if Miss Clary were taken with his tinsel; and if every one else approved of his address to the girl.

My papa, indeed, after a long silence, being urged to speak his mind by my Uncle Antony, said, That he had a letter from his son James, on his hearing of Mr. Lovelace's visits to his daughter Arabella; which he had not shewn to any-body but my mamma, that treaty being at an end when he received it: That in this letter he expressed great dislikes to an alliance with Mr. Lovelace, on the score of his immoralities: That he knew, indeed, there was an old grudge between them: That, being desirous to prevent all occasions of disunion and animosity in his family, he would suspend the declaration of his own mind, till his son arrived, and till he had heard his further objections: That he had heard (So, he supposed, had every-one) that he was a very extravagant man: that he had contracted debts in his travels: And, indeed, he was pleased to say, he had the air of a spendthrift.

But the very next day Lord M. came to Harlowe-Place: I was then absent: and in his nephew's name, made a proposal in form; declaring, That it was the ambition of all his family to be related to ours: And he hoped his kinsman would not have such an answer on the part of the younger sister, as he had had on that of the elder.

In short, Mr. Lovelace's visits were admitted, as those of a man who had not deserved disrespect from our family; but, as to his address to me, with a reservation, as above, on my papa's part, that he would determine nothing without his son. My discretion, as to the rest, was confided in: For still I had the same objections as to the man: Nor would I, when we were better acquainted, hear any-thing but general talk from him; giving him no opportunity of conversing with me in private.

He bore this with a resignation little expected from his natural temper, which is generally reported to be quick and hasty; unused, it seems, from childhood, to check or controul: A case too common in considerable families, where there is an only son: And *his* mother never had any other child. But, as I have heretofore told you, I could perceive, notwithstanding this resignation, that he had so good an opinion of himself, as not to doubt, that his person and accomplishments would insensibly engage me.

Whatever was his motive for a patience so generally believed to be out of his usual character, he certainly escaped many mortifications by it: For while my papa suspended his approbation till my brother's arrival, he received from every-one those civilities which were due to his birth: And altho' we heard, from time to time, reports to his disadvantage with regard to morals; yet could we not question him upon them, without giving him greater advantages than the situation he was in with us would justify to prudence; since it was much more likely, that his address would *not* be allowed of, than that it *would*.

And thus was he admitted to converse with our family, almost upon his own terms; for while my friends saw nothing in his behaviour but what was extremely respectful, and observed in him no violent importunity, they seemed to have taken a great liking to his conversation.

I must break off here. But will continue the subject the very first opportunity. Mean time, I am,

Your most affectionate friend and servant,

Cl. Harlowe

Miss Clarissa Harlowe To Miss Howe

Jan. 15.

THIS, my dear, was the situation Mr. Lovelace and I were in, when my brother arrived from Scotland.

The moment Mr. Lovelace's visits were mentioned to him, he, without either hesitation or apology, expressed his disapprobation of them. He found great flaws in his character; and took the liberty to say in so many words, That he wondered, how it came into the heads of his uncles to encourage such a man for *either* of his sisters: At the same time returning his thanks to my father for declining his consent till *he* arrived, in such a manner, I thought, as a superior would do, when he commended an inferior for having well performed his duty in his absence.

He justified his avowed inveteracy, by common fame, and by what he had known of him at college; declaring, That he had ever hated him; ever should hate him; and would never own him for a brother, or me for a sister, if I married him.

That college-begun antipathy I have heard accounted for in this manner:

Mr. Lovelace was always noted for his vivacity and courage; and no less, it seems, for the swift and surprising progress he made in all parts of literature: For diligence in his studies, in the hours of study, he had hardly his equal. This, it seems, was his general character at the university; and it gained him many friends among the more learned youth; while those who did not love him, feared him, by reason of the offence his vi-

vacity made him too ready to give, and of the courage he
shewed in supporting the offence when given; which procured
him as many followers as he pleased among the mischievous
sort.

But my brother's temper was not happier. His native
haughtiness could not bear a superiority so visible; and whom
we fear more than love, we are not far from hating: And, having
less command of his passions, than the other, was evermore the
subject of his, perhaps *indecent*, ridicule: So that they never
met without quarreling: And every-body, either from love or
fear, siding with his antagonist, he had a most uneasy time of
it, while both continued in the same college.—It was the less
wonder, therefore, that a young man, who is not noted for the
gentleness of his temper, should resume an antipathy early
begun, and so deeply rooted.

He found my sister, who waited but for the occasion, ready
to join him in his resentments against the man he hated. She
utterly disclaimed all manner of regard for him: "Never liked
him at all:—His Estate was certainly much incumbered: It was
impossible it should be otherwise; so intirely devoted as he was
to his pleasures. He kept no house; had no equipage: Nobody
pretended that he wanted pride: The reason therefore was easy
to be guessed at."

I was not solicitous to vindicate him, when I was not joined
in their reflections. I told them, I did not value him enough to
make a difference in the family on his account: And as he was
supposed to have given too much cause for their ill opinion of
him, I thought he ought to take the consequence of his own
faults.

Now-and-then indeed, when I observed, that their vehemence carried them beyond all bounds of probability, I thought
it but justice to put in a word for him. But this only subjected
me to reproach, as having a prepossession in his favour that I
would not own.—So that when I could not change the subject,
I used to retire either to my music, or to my closet.

But Mr. Lovelace is a man not easily brought to give up
his purpose, in a point, especially, wherein he pretends his
heart is so much engaged: And an absolute prohibition not

having been given, things went on for a little while as before:
For I saw plainly, that to have denied myself to his visits (which,
however, I declined receiving, as often as I could) was to bring
forward some desperate issue between the two; since the offence so readily given on one side, was brooked by the other,
only out of consideration to me.

And thus did my brother's rashness lay me under an obligation where I would least have owed it.

I am obliged to break off. But, I believe, I have written
enough to answer very fully all that you have commanded
from me. I will continue to write as I have opportunity, as
minutely as we are used to write to each other. Indeed I have
no delight, as I have often told you, equal to that which I take
in conversing with you:—By *letter*, when I cannot in *person*.

Mean time, I cannot help saying, that I am exceedingly
concerned to find, that I am become so much the public talk as
you tell me, and as *every-body* tells me, I am. Your kind, your
precautionary regard for my fame, and the opportunity you
have given me to tell my own story, previous to any new accident (which heaven avert!) is so like the warm friend I have
ever found in my dear Miss Howe, that, with redoubled obligation, you bind me to be

>Your ever-grateful and affectionate,

>>Clarissa Harlowe

Copy of the requested Preamble to the clauses in her Grandfather's Will: Inclosed in the preceding Letter.

AS the particular estate I have mentioned and described
above is principally of my own raising: As my three sons
have been uncommonly prosperous; and are very rich: The
eldest by means of the unexpected benefits he reaps from his
new-found mines: The second, by what has, as unexpectedly,
fallen in to him, on the deaths of several relations of his present
wife, the worthy daughter by both sides of very honourable

families; over and above the very large portion which he received with her in marriage: My Son Antony, by his East-India traffick, and successful voyages: As furthermore my grandson James will be sufficiently provided for by his god-mother Lovell's kindness to him: For never (blessed be God therefore!) was there a family more prosperous in all its branches: And as my second son James will very probably make it up to my grandson, and also to my grand-daughter Arabella; to whom I intend no disrespect; nor have reason; for she is a very hopeful and dutiful child: And as my sons John and Antony seem not inclined to a married life; so that my son James is the only one who has children, or is likely to have any:—For all these reasons; and because my dearest and beloved grand-daughter Clarissa Harlowe hath been from her infancy a matchless young creature in her duty to me, and admired by all who knew her, as a very extraordinary child; I must therefore take the pleasure of considering her, as my own peculiar child; and this, without intending offence; and I hope it will not be taken as any, since my son James can bestow his favours accordingly, and in greater proportion, upon Miss Arabella, and Master James: —These, I say, are the reasons which move me to dispose of the above described estate in the precious child's favour; who is the delight of my old age: and, I verily think, has contributed, by her amiable duty, and kind and tender regards, to prolong my life.

Wherefore it is my express will and commandment, and I injoin my said three sons John, James, and Antony, and my grandson James, and my grand-daughter Arabella, as they value my blessing, and my memory, and would wish their own last wills and desires to be fulfilled by *their* survivors, that they will not impugn or contest the following bequests and dispositions in favour of my said grand-daughter Clarissa, altho' they should not be strictly conformable to law, or to the forms thereof; nor suffer them to be controverted or disputed on any pretence whatsoever.

And in this confidence, &c. &c. &c.

Miss Clarissa Harlowe
To Miss Howe

I BEG your excuse for not writing sooner. Alas, my dear, I have sad prospects before me! My brother and sister have succeeded in all their views. They have found out another lover for me; an hideous one!—Yet he is encouraged by every-body:—No wonder that I was ordered home so suddenly!—At an hour's warning!—No other notice, you know, than what was brought with the chariot that was to carry me back.—It was for fear, as I have been informed (an unworthy fear!), that I should have entered into any concert with Mr. Lovelace, had I known their motive for commanding me home; apprehending, 'tis evident, that I should dislike the man.

And well might they apprehend so:—For who do you think he is?—No other than that *Solmes!*—Could you have believed it?—And they are all determined too; my mamma with the rest! —Dear, dear excellence! how could she be thus brought over!—when I am assured, that, on his first being proposed, she was pleased to say, That had Mr. Solmes the *Indies* in possession, and would endow me with them, she should not think him deserving of her Clarissa Harlowe.

The reception I met with at my return, convinced me, that I was to suffer for the happiness I had had in your company and conversation for that most agreeable period. I will give you an account of it.

My brother met me at the door, and gave me his hand, when I stepped out of the chariot. He bowed very low:—I thought it in good humour; but found it afterwards mock-respect: And so he led me, in great form, I prattling all the way, inquiring of every-body's health (altho' I was so soon to see them, and there was hardly time for answers), into the great parlour; where were my father, mother, my two uncles, and my sister.

15

I was struck all of a heap as soon as I entered, to see a solemnity which I had been so little used to on the like occasions, in the countenance of every dear relation. They all kept their seats. I ran to my papa, and kneeled: Then to my mamma: And met from both a cold salute: From my papa, a blessing but half-pronounced: My mamma, indeed, called me Child; but embraced me not with her usual indulgent ardor.

After I had paid my duty to my uncles, and my compliments to my sister, which she received with solemn and stiff form, I was bid to sit down. But my heart was full: And I said it became me to stand, if I *could* stand a reception so awful and unusual.

My unbrotherly accuser hereupon stood forth, and charged me with having received no less than *five or six visits* at Miss Howe's from the man they had all so much reason to hate (that was the expression); notwithstanding the commands I had received to the contrary. And he bid me deny it, if I could.

I had never been used, I said, to deny the truth; nor would I now. I owned I had, in the passed three weeks, seen the person I presumed he meant *oftener* than five or six times (Pray hear me out, brother, said I; for he was going to flame).—But he always came and asked for Mrs. or Miss Howe.

I proceeded, That I had reason to believe, that both Mrs. Howe and Miss, as matters stood, would much rather have excused his visits; but they had more than once apologized, that, having not the same reason my papa had, to forbid him their house, his rank and fortune intitled him to civility.

You see, my dear, I made not the pleas I might have made.

My brother seemed ready to give a loose to his passion: My papa put on the countenance, which always portends a gathering storm: My uncles mutteringly whispered: And my sister aggravatingly held up her hands. While I begged to be heard out;—and my mamma said, Let the *child*, that was her kind word, be heard.—

I hoped, I said, there was no harm done: That it became not me to prescribe to Mrs. or Miss Howe who should be their visitors: That Mrs. Howe was always diverted with the raillery that passed between Miss and him: That I had no reason to challenge *her* guest for *my* visitor, as I should seem to have done, had I refused to go into their company, when he was with them: That I had never seen him out of the presence of one or both of those ladies; and had signified to him, once, on his urging for a few moments private conversation with me, that, unless a reconciliation were effected between my family and his, he must not expect, that I would countenance his visits; much less give him an opportunity of that sort.

I told them further, That Miss Howe so well understood my mind, that she never left me a moment, while he was there: That, when he came, if I was not below in the parlour, I would not suffer myself to be called to him: Altho' I thought it would be an affectation, if I had left company when he came in; or refused to enter into it, when I found he would stay any time.

My brother heard me out with such a kind of impatience, as shewed he was resolved to be dissatisfied with me, say what I would. The rest, as the event has proved, behaved as if they *would* have been satisfied, had they not further points to carry, by intimidating me. All this made it evident, as I mentioned above, that they themselves expected not my voluntary compliance; and was a tacit confession of the disagreeableness of the person they had to propose.

I was no sooner silent, than my *brother* swore, altho' in my papa's presence (swore, unchecked either by eye or countenance), That, for his part, he would *never* be reconciled to that libertine: And that he would renounce me for a sister, if I encouraged the addresses of a man so obnoxious to them all.

A man who had like to have been my Brother's murderer, my *sister* said, with a face even bursting with restraint of passion.

The poor Bella has, you know, a plump high-fed face, if I may be allowed the expression. — You, I know, will forgive me for this liberty of speech, sooner than I can forgive myself: Yet, how can one be such a reptile, as not to turn when trampled upon! —

My *papa*, with vehemence both of action and voice (My father has, you know, a terrible voice, when he is angry!), told me, that I had met with too much indulgence, in being allowed to refuse *this* gentleman, and the *other* gentleman; and it was now *his* turn to be obeyed.

Very true, my mamma said:—And hoped his will would not now be disputed by a child so favoured.

To shew they were all of a sentiment, my uncle *Harlowe* said, He hoped his beloved niece only wanted to know her papa's will, to obey it.

And my Uncle *Antony*, in his rougher manner, added, That I would not give them reason to apprehend, that I thought my grandfather's favour to me had made me independent of them all.

I was astonished, you must needs think.—Whose addresses now, thought I, is this treatment preparative to!—Mr. Wyerley's again!—or whose? And then, as high comparisons, where *self* is concerned, sooner than low, come into young peoples heads; be it for whom it will, this is wooing as the English did for the heiress of Scotland in the time of Edward the sixth.—But that it could be for Solmes, how should it enter into my head?

I did not know, I said, that I had given occasion for this harshness: I hoped I should always have a just sense of their favour to me, superadded to the duty I owed as a daughter and a niece: But that I was so much surprised at a reception so unusual and unexpected, that I hoped my papa and mamma would give me leave to retire, in order to recollect myself.

No one gainsaying, I made my silent compliments, and withdrew;—leaving my brother and sister, as I thought, pleased; and as if they wanted to congratulate each other on having occasioned so severe a beginning to be made with me.

I went up to my chamber, and there, with my faithful Hannah, deplored the determined face which the new proposal, it was plain they had to make me, wore.

I had not recovered myself when I was sent for down to tea. I begged, by my maid, to be excused attending: But on the repeated command, went down, with as much chearfulness as I could assume; and had a new fault to clear myself of: For my brother, so pregnant a thing is determined ill-will, by intimations equally rude and intelligible, charged my desire of being excused coming down, to sullens, because a certain person had been spoken against.

I could easily answer you, Sir, said I, as such a reflection deserves: But I forbear. If I do not find a brother in *you*, you shall have a sister in *me*.

Pretty meekness! Bella whisperingly said; looking at my brother, and lifting up her lip in contempt.

He, with an imperious air, bid me *deserve* his love, and I should be sure to *have* it.

As we sat, my mamma, in her admirable manner, expatiated upon brotherly and sisterly love; indulgently blamed my brother and sister for having taken up displeasure too lightly against me; and politically, if I may so say, answered for my obedience to my papa's will.

This was the reception I had on my return from you!

Mr. Solmes came in before we had done tea. My uncle Antony presented him to me, as a gentleman he had a particular friendship for. My uncle Harlowe in terms equally favourable for him. My father said, Mr. Solmes is my friend, Clarissa Harlowe. My mamma looked at him, and looked at me, now-and-then, as he sat near me, I thought with concern.—I at *her*, with eyes appealing for pity.—At *him*, when I could glance at him, with disgust, little short of affrightment. While my brother and sister Mr. *Solmes*'d-him, and *sirr*'d-him up, with high favour. So caressed, in short, by all;—yet such a wretch!

> *Your ever obliged*
>
> Cl. Harlowe

Miss Clarissa Harlowe
To Miss Howe

Feb. 24.

THEY drive on here at a furious rate. The man lives here, I think. He courts them, and is more and more a favourite. Such terms, such settlements! That's the cry.

O my dear, that I had not reason to deplore the family fault, immensely rich as they all are! But this I may the more unreservedly say to you, as we have often joined in the same concern: I, for a father and uncles; you, for a mother; in every other respect faultless.

Hitherto, I seem to be delivered over to my brother, who pretends as great love to me as ever.

You may believe, I have been very sincere with him. But he affects to railly me, and not to believe it possible, the one, so dutiful and so discreet as his sister Clary, can resolve to disoblige all her friends.

Indeed, I tremble at the prospect before me; for it is evident, that they are strangely determined.

My father and mother industriously avoid giving me opportunity of speaking to them alone. They ask not for my approbation, intending, as it should seem, to *suppose* me into their will. And with them I shall hope to prevail, or with no-body. How difficult is it, my dear, to give a negative, where both duty and inclination join to make one wish to oblige!—

I have already stood the shock of three of this man's particular visits, besides my share in his more general ones; and find it is impossible I should ever endure him. He has but a very ordinary share of understanding; is very illiterate; knows nothing but the value of estates, and how to improve them; and what belongs to land-jobbing, and husbandry. Yet am I as one stupid, I think. They have begun so cruelly with me, that I have not spirit enough to assert my own negative.

Help me, dear Miss Howe, to a little of your charming spirit: I never more wanted it.

The man, you may suppose, has no reason to boast of his progress with me. He has not the sense to say anything to the purpose. His courtship, indeed, is to *them*; and my brother pretends to court me as his proxy, truly! I utterly to my brother refuse his application; but thinking a person so well received, and recommended, by all my family, intitled to good manners, all I say against him is affectedly attributed to coyness: And he, not being sensible of his own imperfections, believes that my avoiding him when I can, and the reserves I express, are owing

The siblings resent her for being more loved,
The parents feel guilty for having favoured
her — & now the father wants to assert his
authority

Clarissa or the history of a young lady   21

to nothing else:—For, as I said, all his courtship is to *them*; and I have no opportunity of saying No, to one who asks me not the question. And so, with an air of *mannish* superiority, he seems rather to pity the bashful girl, than apprehend that he shall not succeed.

February 25.

I have had the expected conference with my aunt.

I have been obliged to hear the man's proposals from her; and all their motives for espousing him as they do. I am even loth to mention, how equally unjust it is for him to make such offers, or for those I am bound to reverence to accept of them. I hate him more than before. One great estate is already obtained at the expence of the relations to it, tho' distant relations; my brother's, I mean, by his godmother: And this has given the hope, however chimerical that hope, of procuring others; and that my own, at least, may revert to the family; And yet, in my opinion, the World is but one great family: originally it was so: What then is this narrow selfishness that reigns in us, but relationship remembered against relationship forgot?

But here, upon my absolute refusal of him upon *any* terms, have I had a signification made me, that wounds me to the heart. How can I tell it you? Yet I must. It is, my dear, that I must not, for a month to come, or till licence obtained, correspond with *any*-body out of the house.

Not to Miss Howe? said I.

No, not to Miss Howe, *Madam*, tauntingly: For have you not acknowleged, that Lovelace is a favourite there?

And do you think, brother, this is the way?—

Do *you* look to that.—But your letters will be stopt, I can tell you.—And away he flung.

My sister came to me soon after.—Sister Clary, you are going on in a fine way, I understand. But as there are people who are supposed to harden you against your duty, I am to tell you, that it will be taken well, if you avoid visits or visitings for a week or two, till further order.

Can this be from those who have authority—

Ask them; ask them, child, with a twirl of her finger.—I have delivered my message. Your papa will be obeyed. He is willing to hope you to be all obedience; and would prevent all *incitements* to refractoriness.

Dear Bella, said I! hands and eyes lifted up,—why all this? —Dear, dear Bella, why—

None of your dear, dear Bella's to me.—I tell you, I see thro' your *witchcrafts*.—That was her strange word: And away she flung; adding, as she went,—And so will every-body else very quickly, I dare say.

Bless me, said I to myself, what a sister have I!—How have I deserved this? Then I again regretted my grandfather's too distinguishing goodness to me.

Feb. 25. in the Evening.

What my brother and sister have said against me I cannot tell:—But I am in heavy disgrace with my papa.

I was sent for down to tea. I went with a very chearful aspect: But had occasion soon to change it.

Such a Solemnity in every-body's countenance!—My mamma's eyes were fixed upon the tea-cups; and when she looked up, it was heavily, as if her eyelids had weights upon them; and then not to me. My papa sat half-aside in his elbow-chair, that his head might be turned from me; his hands folded, and waving, as it were, up and down; his fingers, poor dear gentleman! in motion, as if angry to the very ends of them. My sister sat swelling. My brother looked at me with scorn, having measured me, as I may say, with his eyes, as I entered, from head to foot. My aunt was there, and looked upon me, as if with kindness restrained, bending coldly to my compliment to her, as she sat.—Bless me, my dear! that they should choose to intimidate rather than invite a mind, till now, not thought either unpersuadable or ungenerous!—

I took my seat. Shall I make tea, Madam, to my mamma? —I always used, you know, my dear, to make tea.

No! a very short sentence, in one very short word, was the

expressive answer. And she was pleased to take the canister in her own hand.

My sister's Betty attending my brother bid her go:—He would fill her water.

My heart was up at my mouth. I did not know what to do with myself. What is to follow? thought I.

Just after the second dish, out stept my mamma.—A word with you, sister Hervey! taking her in her hand. Presently my sister dropt away. Then my brother. So I was left alone with my papa.

He looked so very sternly, that my heart failed me, as twice or thrice I would have addressed myself to him: Nothing but solemn silence on all hands having passed before.

At last, I asked, if it were his pleasure, that I should pour him out another dish?

He answered me with the same angry monosyllable, which I had received from my mamma before; and then arose, and walked about the room. I arose too, with intent to throw myself at his feet; but was too much overawed by his sternness, even to make such an expression of my duty to him, as my heart overflowed with.

At last, as he supported himself, because of his gout, on the back of a chair, I took a little more courage; and approaching him, besought him to acquaint me, in what I had offended him?

He turned from me, and in a strong voice, Clarissa Harlowe, said he, know, that I will be obeyed.

God forbid, Sir, that you should not!—I have never yet opposed your will—

Nor I your whimsies, Clarissa Harlowe, interrupted he. —Don't let me run the fate of all who shew indulgence to your sex; To be the more contradicted for mine to you.

My papa, you know, my dear, has not (any more than my brother) a kind opinion of our sex; altho' there is not a more condescending wife in the world than my mamma.

I was going to make protestations of duty.—No protestations, girl!—No words.—I will not be prated to!—I will be obeyed!—I have no child.—I will have no child, but an obedient one.

Sir, you never had reason, I hope—

Tell me not what I never *had*, but what I *have*, and what I *shall* have.

Good Sir, be pleased to hear me—My brother and my sister, I fear—

Your brother and sister shall not be spoken against, girl! —They have a just concern for the honour of my family.

And I hope, Sir,—

Hope nothing.—Tell me not of *hopes*, but of *facts*. I ask nothing of you but what is in your power to comply with, and what it is your duty to comply with.

Then, Sir, I will comply with it—But yet I hope from your goodness,—

No expostulations!—No *but's*, girl!—No qualifyings!—I will be obeyed, I tell you!—and chearfully too!—or you are no child of mine!—

I wept.

Let me beseech you, my dear and ever-honoured papa (and I dropt down on my knees) that I may have only yours and my mamma's will, and not my brother's, to obey.—I was going on; but he was pleased to withdraw, leaving me on the floor; saying, That he would not hear me thus by subtilty and cunning aiming to distinguish away my duty; repeating, that he would be obeyed.

My heart is too full;—so full, that it may endanger my duty, were I to try to unburden it to you on this occasion: So I will lay down my pen.—But can—Yet, positively, I will lay down my pen!—

Miss Howe
To Miss Clarissa Harlowe

Feb. 27.

WHAT odd heads some people have!—Miss Clarissa Harlowe to be sacrificed in marriage to Mr. Roger Solmes! Astonishing!

I must not, you say, *give my advice in favour of this man!*
—You now half-convince me, my dear, that you are allied to the
family that could think of so preposterous a match, or you
would never have had the least notion of my advising in his
favour.

Ask me for his picture: You know I have a good hand at
drawing an ugly likeness. But I'll see a little farther first: For
who knows what may happen; since matters are in such a train;
and since you have not the *courage* to oppose so overwhelming
a torrent.

You ask me to help you to a little of my spirit. Are you in
earnest? But it will not now I doubt, do you service.—It will not
sit naturally upon you. You are your mamma's girl, think what
you will, and have violent spirits to contend with. Alas! my
dear, you should have borrowed some of mine a little sooner;
—that is to say, before you had given the management of your
estate into the hands of those who think they have a prior claim
to it.

Now I have launched out a little, indulge me one word
more in the same strain: I will be decent, I promise you. I think
you might have known, that Avarice and Envy are two passions
that are not to be satisfied, the one by *giving*, the other by the
envied person's continuing to *deserve* and *excel*.—Fuel, fuel
both, all the world over, to flames insatiate and devouring.

But you are so tender of some people, who have no tenderness for anybody but themselves, that I must conjure you to
speak out. Remember, that a friendship like ours admits of no
reserves. You may trust my impartiality. It would be an affront
to your own judgment, if you did not: For do you not *ask* my
advice? And have you not taught me, that friendship should
never give a bias against justice?—Justify them therefore, if you
can. Let us see if there be any *sense*, whether sufficient *reason*
or not, in their choice. At present, I cannot (and yet I know
a good deal of your family) have any conception, how *all* of
them, your mamma, in particular, and your Aunt Hervey can
join with the rest against judgments given. As to some of the
others, I cannot wonder at any thing they do, or attempt to do,
where Self is concerned.

You ask, Why may not your brother be first engaged in wedlock?—I'll tell you why: His temper and his arrogance are too well known to induce women he would aspire to, to receive his addresses, notwithstanding his great independent acquisitions, and still greater prospects. Let me tell you, my dear, those acquisitions have given him more pride than reputation. To me he is the most intolerable creature that I ever saw. The treatment you blame, he merited from one whom he would have addressed with the air of a person intending to confer, rather than hoping to receive a favour. I ever loved to mortify proud and insolent spirits. What, think you, makes me bear Hickman near me, but that the man is humble, and knows his distance?

As to your question, Why your elder sister may not be first provided for? I answer, Because she must have no man, but who has a great and clear estate; that's one thing. Another is, Because she has a younger sister:—Pray, my dear, be so good as to tell me, what man of a great and clear estate would think of that elder sister, while the younger were single?

You are all too rich to be happy, child. For must not each of you, by the constitutions of your family, marry to be *still* richer? People who know in what their *main* excellence consists are not to be blamed (are they?) for cultivating and improving what they think most valuable? Is true happiness any part of your family-view?—So far from it, that none of your family, but yourself, could be happy were they not rich. So let them fret on, grumble and grudge, and accumulate; and wondering what ails them that they have not happiness when they have riches, think the cause is want of more; and so go on heaping up, till death, as greedy an accumulator as themselves, gathers them into his garner!

You are pleased to say, and *upon your word too!*—That your *regards* (a mighty quaint word for *affections*) *are not so much engaged, as some of your friends suppose, to another person.* What need you give one to imagine, my dear, that the last month or two has been a period extremely favourable to that *other* person!

But, to pass that by,—*So much* engaged!—*How much*,

my dear? Shall I infer? *Some of your friends* suppose *a great deal.*—You seem to own *a little.*

Don't be angry. It is all fair: Because you have not acknowleged to me That *little.* People, I have heard you say, who affect secrets always excite curiosity.

But you proceed with a kind of drawback upon your averrment, as if recollection had given you a doubt.—*You know not yourself, if they be* [so much engaged]. Was it necessary to say This, to me?—and to say it *upon your word* too?—But you know best.—Yet you don't neither, I believe. For a beginning Love is acted by a subtile spirit; and oftentimes discovers itself to a bystander, when the person possessed (why should I not call it *possessed?*) knows not it has such a demon.

But, O my friend, depend upon it, you are in danger. Depend upon it, whether you know it or not, you are a little in for't. Your native generosity and greatness of mind indanger you: All your friends, by fighting *against* him with impolitic violence, fight *for him.* And Lovelace, my life for yours, notwithstanding all his veneration and assiduities, has seen further than that veneration and those assiduities (so well calculated to your meridian) will let him own he has seen.—Has seen, in short, that his work is doing for him more effectually than he could do it for himself. And have you not before now said, That nothing is so penetrating as the vanity of a lover; Since it makes the person who has it frequently see in his own favour what is *not;* and hardly ever fail of observing what *is.* And who says Lovelace wants vanity?

In short, my dear, it is my opinion, and that from the easiness of his heart and behaviour, that he has seen more than *I* have seen; more than you think *could* be seen;—more than I believe you *yourself* know, or else you would have let *me* know it.

Already, in order to restrain him from resenting the indignities he has received, and which are daily offered him, he has prevailed upon you to correspond with him privately. I know he has nothing to boast of from *what* you have written. But is not his inducing you to receive his letters, and to answer them, a

great point gained?—By your insisting, that he should keep this
correspondence private, it appears, that there is *one secret*,
which you do not wish the world should know: And *he* is master
of that secret. He is indeed *himself*, as I may say, that secret!
—What an intimacy does this beget for the lover!—How is it
distancing the parent!—

Yet who, as things are situated, can blame you?—Your
condescension has no doubt hitherto prevented great mischiefs: It must be continued, for the same reasons, while the
cause remains. You are drawn in by a perverse fate, against
inclination: But custom, with such laudable purposes, will reconcile the inconveniency and *make* an inclination.

It is my humble opinion, I tell you frankly, that, on inquiry
it will come out to be LOVE.—Don't start, my dear!—Has not
your man himself had natural philosophy enough to observe
already to your aunt Hervey, that Love takes the deepest root
in the steadiest minds? The duce take his sly penetration, I was
going to say; for this was six or seven weeks ago.

I have been tinctured, you know. Nor, on the coolest reflection, could I account how, and when, the jaundice began:
But had been over heads and ears, as the saying is, but for some
of that advice from you which I now return you. Yet *my* man
was not half so—So *what*, my dear?—To be sure Lovelace is a
charming fellow.—And were he only—But I will not make you
glow, as you read!—Upon *my word*, I won't.—Yet, my dear,
don't you find at your heart somewhat unusual make it go throb,
throb, throb, as you read just here?—If you do, don't be ashamed
to own it.—It is your *generosity*, my love! that's all.—But, as
the Roman augur said, Caesar, beware of the ides of March!

Adieu, my dearest friend, and forgive; and very speedily,
by the new-found expedient, tell me, that you forgive

Your ever-affectionate

Anna Howe

Miss Clarissa Harlowe
To Miss Howe

Wednesday, March 1.

YOU both nettled and alarmed me, my dearest Miss Howe, by the concluding part of your last. At first reading it, I did not think it necessary, said I to myself, to guard against a critic, when I was writing to so dear a friend. But then recollecting myself, Is there not more in it, said I, than the result of a vein so naturally lively? Surely, I must have been guilty of an inadvertence.—Let me enter into the close examination of myself, which my beloved friend advises.

I did so; and cannot own any of the *glow*, any of the *throbs* you mention.—*Upon my word*, I will repeat, I cannot. And yet the passages in my letter upon which you are so humourously severe, lay me fairly open to your agreeable raillery. I own they do. And I cannot tell what turn my mind had taken, to dictate so oddly to my pen.

But, pray-now—Is it saying so much, when one, who has no very particular regard to *any* man, says, There are *some* who are preferable to *others*? And is it blameable to say, *Those* are the preferable, who are not well used by one's relations; yet dispense with that usage out of regard to one's self, which they would otherwise resent? Mr. Lovelace, for instance, I may be allowed to say, is a man to be preferred to Mr. Solmes; and that I *do* prefer him to that man: But, surely, this may be said without its being a necessary consequence that I must be in love with him.

Indeed I would not be *in love* with him, as it is called, for the world: First, because I have no opinion of his morals; and think it a fault in which our whole family, my brother excepted, has had a share, that he was permitted to visit us with a hope; which, however being distant, did not, as I have observed heretofore, intitle any of us to call him to account for such of his im-

moralities as came to our ears. Next, because I think him to be
a vain man, capable of triumphing, secretly at least, over a person whose heart he thinks he has engaged. And, thirdly, because
the assiduities and veneration which you impute to him, seem to
carry an haughtiness in them, as if his address had a merit in
it, that would be an equivalent for a lady's favour. In short, he
seems to me so to behave, when most unguarded, as if he thought
himself above the very politeness which his birth and education
(perhaps therefore more than his choice) oblige him to shew.
In other words, his very politeness appears to me to be constrained; and, with the most remarkably easy and genteel *person*,
something seems to be behind in his *manner*, that is too studi-
ously kept in.

Indeed, my dear, THIS man is not THE man. I have great
objections to him. My heart throbs not after him. I *glow* not,
but with indignation against myself, for having given room for
such an imputation.—But you must not, my dearest friend,
construe common Gratitude into Love. I cannot bear that you
should. But if ever I should have the misfortune to think it
Love, I promise you, *upon my word*, which is the same as *upon
my honour*, that I will acquaint you with it.

Be satisfied, my dear, mean time, that I am *not* displeased
with you: Indeed I am not: On the contrary, I give you my
hearty thanks for your friendly premonitions. And I charge you,
as I have often done, that if you observe anything in me so very
faulty, as would require, from you to others, in my behalf, the
palliation of friendly and partial love, you acquaint me with it:
For, methinks, I would so conduct myself, as not to give reason
even for an *adversary* to censure me: And how shall so weak
and so young a creature avoid the censure of such, if my *friend*
will not hold a looking-glass before me, to let me see my imperfections?

Judge me then, my dear, as any indifferent person (knowing
what *you* know of me) would do:—I may, at first, be a little
pained; may *glow* a little, perhaps, to be found less worthy of
your friendship, than I wish to be; but assure yourself, that
your kind correction will give me reflection, that shall *amend*
me.

Here I break off; to begin another letter to you; with the assurance, mean time, that I am, and ever will be,

Your equally affectionate and grateful
Cl. Harlowe

Miss Howe
To Miss Clarissa Harlowe

Thursday Morn. March 2.

INDEED you would not be in Love with him for the world! —Your servant, my dear. Nor would I have you. For I think, with all the advantages of person, fortune, and family, he is not by any means worthy of you. And this opinion I give as well from the reasons you mention, which I cannot but confirm, as from what I have heard of him but a few hours ago from Mrs. Fortescue, a favourite of lady Betty Lawrance, who knows him well.—But let me congratulate you, however, on your being the first of our sex, that ever I heard of, who has been able to turn that lion, Love, at her own pleasure, into a lap-dog.

Well but, if you have not the throbs and the glows, you have not: And are not in love; good reason why—because you would not be in love; and there's no more to be said.—Only, my dear, I shall keep a good look-out upon you; and so I hope you will upon yourself: For it is no manner of argument, that because you would not be in love, you are not.—But before I part intirely with this subject, a word in your ear, my charming friend—'Tis only by way of caution, and in pursuance of the general observation, that a stander-by is often a better judge of the game than those that play.—May it not be, that you have had, and have, such cross creatures, and such odd heads, to deal with, as have not allowed you to attend to the throbs?—Or, if you had them a little now and then, whether, having had two accounts to place them to, you have not, by mistake, put them to the wrong one?

But whether you have a value for Lovelace, or not, I know you'll be impatient to hear what Mrs. Fortescue has said of him. Nor will I keep you longer in suspense.

An hundred wild stories she tells of him, from childhood to manhood: for, as she observes, having never been subject to contradiction, he was always as mischievous as a monkey. But I shall pass over these whole hundred of his puerile rogueries to make a few observations upon him and his ways.

Mrs. Fortescue owns, what every-body knows, that he is notoriously, nay, avowedly, a man of pleasure; yet says, that in anything he sets his heart upon, or undertakes, he is the most industrious and persevering mortal under the sun. He rests, it seems, not above six hours in the twenty-four, any more than you. He delights in writing. Whether at his Uncle's, or at Lady Betty's, or Lady Sarah's, he has always, when he retires, a pen in his fingers. One of his companions, confirming his love of writing, has told her, that his thoughts flow rapidly to his pen: And you and I, my dear, have observed that tho' he writes even a fine hand, he is one of the readiest and quickest of writers. He must indeed have had early a very docile genius; since a person of his pleasurable turn, and active spirit, could never have submitted to take long or great pains in attaining the qualifications he is master of; qualifications so seldom attainable by youth of quality and fortune; by such especially of those of either, who, like him, have never known what it was to be controuled.

He had once the vanity, upon being complimented on these talents (and on his surprising diligence, for a man of pleasure) to compare himself to Julius Caesar; who performed great actions by day, and wrote them down at night: And valued himself, that he only wanted Caesar's outsetting, to make a figure among his contemporaries.

That you and I, my dear, should love to write, is no wonder. Our employments are domestic and sedentary; and we can scribble upon twenty innocent subjects, and take delight in them because they *are* innocent; tho' were they to be seen, they might not much profit or please others. But that such a gay, lively young fellow as this, who rides, hunts, travels, frequents the public entertainments, and has *means* to pursue his pleasures, should be able to set himself down to write for hours together, as you and I have heard him say he frequently does, that is the strange thing.

Whatever his other vices are, all the world, as well as Mrs. Fortescue, say, he is a sober man. And among all his bad qualities, *gaming*, that great waster of time, as well as fortune, is not his vice: So that he must have his head as cool, and his reason as clear, as the prime of youth, and his natural gaiety, will permit; and by his early morning hours, a great portion of time upon his hands, to employ in writing, or worse.

A person willing to think favourable of him would hope, that a *brave*, a *learned*, and a *diligent* man, cannot be *naturally* a *bad* man.—But if he be better than his enemies say he is (and, if worse, he is bad indeed), he is guilty of an inexcusable fault, in being so careless as he is of his reputation. I think a man can be so but from one of these two reasons: Either that he is conscious he deserves the evil spoken of him; or, that he takes a pride in being thought worse than he is.—Both very bad and threatening indications: Since the first must shew him to be utterly abandoned; and it is but natural to conclude from the other, that what a man is not ashamed to have imputed to him, he will not scruple to be guilty of, whenever he has opportunity.

Upon the whole, and upon all that I could gather from Mrs. Fortescue, Mr. Lovelace is a very faulty man: You see he never would disguise his natural temper (haughty as it certainly is), with respect to your brother's behaviour to him: Where he thinks a comtempt due, he pays it to the uttermost: Nor has he complaisance enough to spare your uncles.

But were he deep, and ever so deep, you would soon penetrate him, if they would leave you to yourself. His vanity would be your clue. Never man had more: Yet, as Mrs. Fortescue observed, never did man carry it off so happily. There is a strange mixture in it of humourous vivacity:—For but one half of what he says of himself, when he is in the vein, any other man would be insufferable.

Talk *of the devil*, is an old saying.—The lively wretch has made me a visit, and is but just gone away. He is all impatience and resentment, at the treatment you meet with; and full of apprehensions too, that they will carry their point with you.

I told him my opinion, that you will never be brought to think of such a man as Solmes; but that it will probably end in a composition, never to have either.

No man, he said, whose fortunes and alliances are so considerable, ever had so little favour from a lady, for whose sake he had borne so much.

I told him my mind, as freely as I used to do. But who ever was in fault, Self being judge? He complained of spies set upon his conduct, and to pry into his life and morals; and this by your brother and uncles.

I told him, that this was very hard upon him; and the more so, as neither the one nor the other, perhaps, would stand a fair inquiry.

He smiled, and called himself *my servant.*—The occasion was too fair, he said, for Miss Howe, who never spared him, to let it pass.—But, Lord help their shallow souls, would I believe it? they were for turning plotters upon *him.* They had best take care he did not pay them in their own coin. Their *hearts* were better turned for such works, than their *heads.*

I asked him, if he valued himself upon having a head better turned than theirs for *such works*, as he called them?

He drew off: And then ran into the highest professions of reverence and affection for you. The object so meritorious, who can doubt the reality of his professions?

Adieu, my dearest, my noble friend!—I love and admire you for the generous conclusion of your last more than I can express. Tho' I began this letter with impertinent raillery, knowing that you always loved to indulge my mad vein, yet never was there a heart that more glowed with friendly love, than that of

Your own

Anna Howe

Miss Clarissa Harlowe
To Miss Howe

Friday, March 3.

O MY dear friend, I have had a sad conflict! trial upon trial; conference upon conference!—But what law, what ceremony, can give a man a right to a heart which abhors him more than it does any of God Almighty's creatures?

I hope my mamma will be able to prevail for me.—But I will recount all, tho' I sit up the whole night to do it; for I have a vast deal to write; and will be as minute as you wish me to be.

I went down this morning when breakfast was ready, with a very uneasy heart, from what Hannah had told me yesterday afternoon; wishing for an opportunity, however, to appeal to my mamma, in hopes to engage her interest in my behalf, and purposing to try to find one, when she retired to her own apartment after breakfast:—But, unluckily, there was the odious Solmes sitting asquat between my mamma and sister, with *so much* assurance in his looks!—But you know, my dear, that those we love not, cannot do anything to please us.

Had the wretch kept his seat, it might have been well enough: But the bent and broad-shouldered creature must needs rise, and stalk towards a chair, which was just by that which was set for me.

I removed it at a distance, as if to make way to my own: And down I sat, abruptly I believe; what I had heard, all in my head.

But this was not enough to daunt him: The man is a very confident, he is a very bold, staring man!—Indeed, my dear, the man is very confident.

He took the removed chair, and drew it so near mine, squatting in it with his ugly weight, that he pressed upon my hoop. —I was so offended (all I had heard, as I said, in my head), that I removed to another chair. I own I had too little command of myself: It gave my brother and sister too much advantage, I

dare say they took it:—But I did it involuntarily, I think: I could
not help it.—I knew not what I did.

I saw my papa was excessively displeased. When angry, no
man's countenance ever shewed it so much as my papa's. Clarissa Harlowe! said he, with a big voice; and there he stopped.
—Sir! said I, and courtesied.—I put my chair nearer the wretch,
and sat down; my face I could feel all in a glow.

Make tea, child, said my kind mamma: Sit by me, love;
and make tea.

I removed with pleasure to the seat the man had quitted;
and being thus indulgently put into employment, soon recovered
myself; and in the course of the breakfasting officiously asked
two or three questions of Mr. Solmes, which I would not have
done, but to make up with my papa.—*Proud spirits may be
brought to;* whisperingly spoke my sister to me, over her
shoulder, with an air of triumph and scorn: But I did not mind
her.

My mamma was all kindness and condescension. I asked
her once, if she were pleased with the tea? She said, softly, and
again called me *dear*, she was pleased with all I did. I was very
proud of this encouraging goodness: And all blew over, as I
hoped, between my papa and me; for he also spoke kindly to me
two or three times.

Small incidents these, my dear, to trouble you with; only
as they lead to greater; as you shall hear.

Before the usual breakfast-time was over, my papa withdrew with my mamma, telling her he wanted to speak to her.
My sister, and my aunt, who was with us, next dropt away.

My brother gave himself some airs of insult, that I understood well enough; but which Mr. Solmes could make nothing
of:—And at last he arose from his seat—Sister, said he, I have
a curiosity to shew you: I will fetch it: And away he went; shutting the door close after him.

I saw what all this was for. I arose; the man hemming up for
a speech, rising, and beginning to set his splay-feet (indeed, my
dear, the man in all his ways is hateful to me) in an approaching
posture.—I will save my brother the trouble of bringing to me
his curiosity, said I. I courtesied—Your servant, Sir—The man

cried, Madam, Madam, twice, and looked like a fool.—But away I went—to find my brother, to save my word.—But my brother was gone, indifferent as the weather was, to walk in the garden with my sister. A plain case, that he had left his curiosity with me, and designed to shew me no other.

I had but just got into my own apartment, and began to think of sending Hannah to beg an audience of my mamma (the more encouraged by her condescending goodness at breakfast), when Shorey, her woman, brought me her commands to attend her in her closet.

I went down but, apprehending the subject, approached her trembling, and my heart in visible palpitations.

She saw my concern. Holding out her kind arms, as she sat, Come kiss me, my dear, said she, with a smile like a sun-beam breaking through the cloud that overshadowed her naturally benign aspect. Why flutters my jewel so?

This preparative sweetness, with her goodness just before, confirmed my apprehensions. My mamma saw the bitter pill wanted gilding.

O my mamma! was all I could say; and I clasped my arms round her neck, and my face sunk into her bosom.

My child! my child! restrain, said she, your powers of moving!—I dare not else trust myself with you.—And my tears trickled down her bosom, as hers bedewed my neck.

Lift up your sweet face, my best child, my own Clarissa Harlowe!—O my daughter, best-beloved of my heart, lift up a face so ever-amiable to me!—Why these sobs?

Then rising, she drew a chair near her own, and made me sit down by her, overwhelmed as I was with tears of apprehension of what she had to say, and of gratitude for her truly maternal goodness to me; sobs still my only language.

And drawing her chair still nearer to mine, she put her arms round my neck, and my glowing cheek, wet with my tears, close to her own: Let me talk to you, my child; since Silence is your choice, hearken to me, and *be* silent.

You know, my dear, what I every day forego, and undergo, for the sake of peace: Your papa is a very good man, and means well; but he will not be controuled; nor yet persuaded. You have

seemed to pity *me* sometimes, that I am obliged to give up every
point. Poor man! *his* reputation the less for it; *mine* the greater;
yet would I not have this credit, if I could help it, at so dear a
rate to *him* and to *myself*. You are a dutiful, a prudent, and a
wise child, she was pleased to say (in hope, no doubt, to make
me so) You would not add, I am sure, to my trouble: You would
not wilfully break that peace which costs your mamma so much
to preserve. Obedience is better than sacrifice. O my Clary
Harlowe, rejoice my heart, by telling me I have apprehended too
much!—I see your concern! I see your perplexity! I see your
conflict (loosing her arm, and rising, not willing I should see
how much she herself was affected). I will leave you a moment.
—Answer me not (For I was essaying to speak, and had, as soon
as she took her dear cheek from mine, dropt down on my knees,
my hands clasped and lifted up in a supplicating manner): I am
not prepared for your irresistible expostulation, she was pleased
to say.—I will leave you to recollection: And I charge you, on
my blessing, that all this my truly maternal tenderness be not
thrown away upon you.

And then she withdrew into the next apartment; wiping her
eyes, as she went from me; as mine overflowed; my heart taking
in the whole compass of her meaning.

She soon returned, having recovered more steadiness.

Still on my knees, I had thrown my face cross the chair she
had sat in.

Look up to me, my Clary Harlowe—No sullenness, I hope!

She raised me. No kneeling to me, but with knees of duty
and compliance.—Your heart, not your knees, must bend.—It
is absolutely determined.—Prepare yourself therefore to receive
your *papa*, when he visits you by-and-by, as he would wish to
receive *you*. But on this one quarter of an hour depends the
peace of my future life, the satisfaction of all the family, and
your own security from a man of violence: And I charge you
besides, on my blessing, that you think of being Mrs. Solmes.

There went the dagger to my heart, and down I sunk; And
when I recovered, found myself in the arms of my Hannah, my
sister's Betty holding open my reluctantly-opened palm, my

laces cut, my linen scented with hartshorn; and my mamma gone.—Had I been *less* kindly treated, the hated name still forborn to be mentioned, or mentioned with a little more preparation and reserve, I had stood the horrid sound with less visible emotion—But to be bid, on the blessing of a Mother so dearly beloved, so truly reverenced, to think of being Mrs. Solmes, what a denunciation was that!

Shorey came in with a message, delivered in her solemn way: Your mamma, Miss, is concerned for your disorder: She expects you down again in an hour; and bid me say, that she then hopes every thing from your duty.

I made no reply; for what could I say? And leaning upon my Hannah's arm, withdrew to my own apartment. There you will guess how the greatest part of the hour was employed.

Within that time, my Mother came up to *me*. A young creature of your virtuous and *pious* turn, she was pleased to say, cannot surely love a profligate: You love your brother too well, to wish to marry one who had like to have killed him, and who threatened your uncles, and defies us all. You have had your own way six or seven times: We want to secure you against a man so vile. Tell me; I have a right to know; whether you prefer this man to all others?—Yet God forbid, that I should know you do! for such a declaration would make us all miserable. Yet, tell me, are your affections engaged to this man?

I knew what the inference would be, if I had said they were not.

You hesitate: You answer me not: You cannot answer me. —*Rising*—Never more will I look upon you with an eye of favour,—

O Madam, Madam! Kill me not with your displeasure: I would not, I *need* not, hesitate one moment, did I not dread the inference, if I answer you as you wish.—Yet be that inference what it will, your threatened displeasure, will make me speak. And I declare to you, that I know not my own heart, if it be not absolutely free. And pray, let me ask, my dearest mamma, in what has my conduct been faulty, that, like a giddy creature, I must be forced to marry, to save me from—From what?—Let not your Clarissa be precipitated into a state she wishes not to enter into with any man!

I won't be interrupted, Clary.—You have seen in my behaviour to you, on this occasion, a truly maternal tenderness; you have observed that I have undertaken this task with some reluctance, because the man is not everything; and because I know you carry your notions of perfection in a man too high—

Dearest Madam, this one time excuse me!—Is there *then* any danger that I should be guilty of an imprudent thing for the mans' sake you hint at?

Again interrupted!—Am I to be questioned, and argued with? You know this won't do somewhere else. You know it won't. What reason then, ungenerous girl, can you have for arguing with me thus, but because you think from my indulgence to you, you may?

What *can* I say? What *can* I do? What must that cause be that will not bear being argued upon?

Again! Clary Harlowe!—

Dearest Madam, forgive me: It was always my pride and my pleasure to obey you. But look upon that man—see but the disagreeableness of his person—

Should the eye be disgusted, when the heart is to be engaged?—O Madam, who can think of marrying, when the heart must be shocked at the first appearance, and where the disgust must be confirmed by every conversation afterwards?

This, Clary, is owing to your prepossession. Let me not have cause to regret that noble firmness of mind in so young a creature, which I thought your glory, and which was my boast in your character.—Have you not made objections to several—

That was to their *minds*, to their *principles*, Madam—But this man—

Is an honest man, Clary Harlowe. He has a good mind.—He is a virtuous man.

He an honest man! *His* a good mind, Madam! *He* a virtuous man!—

No-body denies him these qualities.

Can *he* be an honest man who offers terms that will rob

ail his own relations of their just expectations?—Can *his* mind be good—

You, Clary Harlowe, for whose sake he offers so much, are the last person that should make this observation.

Just then, up came my Papa, with a sternness in his looks that made me tremble!—He took two or three turns about my chamber.—And then said to my mamma, who was silent as soon as she saw him—

My dear, you are long absent.—Dinner is near ready. Surely, you have nothing to do but to declare *your* will, and *my* will!—But, perhaps, you may be talking of the preparations—Let us have you soon down—Your daughter in your hand, if worthy of the name.

And down he went, casting his eye upon me with a look so stern, that I was unable to say one word to him, or even, for a few minutes, to my mamma.

My mamma, seeing my concern, seemed to pity me. She called me her good child, and kissed me; told me my papa should not know, that I had made such opposition.—Come, my dear,—Dinner will be upon table presently—Shall we go down? —And took my hand.

This made me start: What, Madam, go down, to let it be supposed we were talking of *preparations!*—O my beloved mamma, command me not down upon such a supposition.

You see, child, that to stay longer together, will be owning that you are debating about an absolute duty: And that will not be borne. Did not your papa himself, some days ago, tell you, he would be obeyed? I will a third time leave you. I must say something by way of excuse for you: And that you desire not to go down to dinner—That your modesty on the occasion—

O Madam! say not my modesty on *such* an occasion: For that will be to give hope—

And design you *not* to give hope?—Perverse girl!—*Rising, and flinging from me*, take more time for consideration!—Since it is necessary, *take* more time—And when I see you next, let me know what blame I have to cast upon myself, or to bear from your papa, for my indulgence to you.

She made, however, a little stop at the chamber-door; and

seemed to expect, that I would have besought her to make the gentlest construction for me; for hesitating, she was pleased to say, I suppose, you would not have me make a report—

O Madam, interrupted I, whose favour can I hope for, if I lose my mamma's?

Pray let Robert call every day, if you can spare him, whether I have any thing ready or not.

I should be glad you would not send him empty-handed. What a generosity in you, to write as frequently from friendship, as I am forced to do from misfortune! For I need not say how much I am,

Your sincere and ever-affectionate

Cl. Harlowe

Miss Clarissa Harlowe To Miss Howe

Sat. Night.

I HAVE been down. I *am* to be unlucky in all I do, I think, be my intention ever so good. I have made matters worse instead of better; as I shall now tell you.

I found my mamma and sister together in my sister's parlour.

I came down, I said, to beg of her to forgive me for anything she may have taken amiss in what had passed above respecting herself; and to use her interest to soften my papa's displeasure, when she made the report she was to make to him.

Such aggravating looks; such lifting up of hands and eyes; such a furrowed forehead, in my sister!—

My mamma was angry enough without all that; and asked me, To what purpose I came down, if I were still so untractable?

She had hardly spoken the words, when Shorey came in to tell her, that Mr. Solmes was in the hall, and desired admittance.

Ugly creature! What, at the close of day, quite dark, brought him hither?—But, on second thoughts, I believe it was contrived, that he should be here at supper, to know the result of the conference between my mamma and me; and that my papa, on his return, might find us together.

I was hurrying away; but my mamma commanded me, since I had come down only, as she said, to mock her, not to stir; and at the same time see if I could behave so to him, as might encourage her to make the report to my papa which I had so earnestly besought her to make.

The man stalked in. His usual walk is by pauses, as if (from the same vacuity of thought which made Dryden's Clown whistle) he was telling his steps: and first paid his clumsy respects to my mamma; then to my sister; next to me, as if I were already his wife, and therefore to be last in his notice; and sitting down by me, told us in general what weather it was. Very cold he made it; but I was warm enough. Then addressing himself to me; And how do *you* find it, Miss? was his question; and would have took my hand.

I withdrew it, I believe with disdain enough: My mamma frowned; My sister bit her lip.

I could not contain myself: I never was so bold in my life; for I went on with my plea, as if Mr. Solmes had not been there.

My mamma coloured, and looked at him, looked at my sister, and looked at me. My sister's eyes were opener and bigger than ever I saw them before.

The man understood me. He hemmed, and removed from one chair to another.

I went on, supplicating for my mamma's favourable report: Nothing but invincible dislike—

What would the girl be at? Why, Clary!—Is this a subject!—Is this!—Is this!

I am sorry, on reflection, that I put my mamma into so much confusion.—To be sure it was very saucy in me.

I beg pardon. But my papa would return. I should have no other opportunity. I thought it was requisite, since I was not permitted to withdraw, that Mr. Solmes's presence should not deprive me of an opportunity of such importance for me to

embrace; and at the same time, if he still visited on my account
(looking at him), to shew that it could not possibly be to any
purpose.

Is the girl mad? said my mamma, interrupting me.

My sister, with the affectation of a whisper to my mamma
—This is—This is *spite*, Madam (Very *spitefully* she spoke the
word), because you commanded her to stay.

I only looked at her, and turning to my mamma, Permit
me, Madam, said I, to repeat my request. I have no brother,
no sister!—If I lose my mamma's favour, I am lost for ever!

Mr. Solmes removed to his first seat, and fell to gnawing
the head of his hazel; a carved head, almost as ugly as his own.
I did not think the man was so *sensible*.

My sister rose, with a face all over scarlet, and stepping
to the table, where lay a fan, she took it up, and, altho' Mr.
Solmes had observed that the weather was cold, fanned herself
very violently.

My mamma came to me, and angrily taking my hand, led
me out of that parlour into my own; which, you know, is next
to it—Is not this behaviour very bold, very provoking, think
you, Clary?

I beg your pardon, Madam, if it has that appearance to you.
But indeed, my dear mamma, there seem to be snares laying for
me. Too well I know my brother's drift. With a good word he
shall have my consent for all he wishes to worm me out of.—
Neither he, nor my sister, shall need to take half this pains.—

My mamma was about to leave me in high displeasure.

I besought her to stay: One favour, but one favour, dearest
Madam, said I, give me leave to beg of you—

What would the girl?

I see how every-thing is working about.—I never, never
can think of Mr. Solmes. My papa will be in tumults, when
he is told that I cannot. They will judge of the tenderness of
your heart to a poor child who seems devoted by every-one
else, from the willingness you have already shewn to hearken
to my prayers. There will be endeavours used to confine me,
and keep me out of your presence, and out of the presence of
every one who used to love me—(This, my dear, is threatened)—

If This be effected; if it be put out of my power to plead my own cause, and to appeal to You, and to my uncle Harlowe, of whom only I have hope;—then will every ear be opened against me; and every tale encouraged.—It is, therefore, my humble request, That, added to the disgraceful prohibitions I now suffer under, you will not, if you can help it, give way to my being denied your ear.

Your listening Hannah has given you this intelligence, as she does many others.

My Hannah, Madam, listens not!—My Hannah—

No more in her behalf—She is known to make mischief—She is known—But no more of that busy intermeddler—'Tis true, your father threatened to confine you to your chamber, if you complied not, in order the more assuredly to deprive you of the opportunity of corresponding with those who harden your heart against his will. He bid me tell you so, when he went out, if I found you refractory. But I was loth to deliver so harsh a declaration; being still in hope that you would come down to us in a compliant temper.—And I now assure you, that you will be confined, and prohibited making teazing appeals to any of us: And we shall see who is to submit, You, or every-body to you.

I was ready to sink. She was so good as to lend me her arm to support me.

And this is all I have to hope for from my mamma?

It is. But, Clary, this one further opportunity I give you—Go in again to Mr. Solmes, and behave discreetly to him; and let your papa find you together, upon *civil* terms at least.

My feet moved (of themselves, I think) farther from the parlour where he was, and towards the stairs; and there I stopped and paused.

If, proceeded she, you are determined to stand in defiance of us all—then indeed may you go up to your chamber (as you are ready to do)—And God help you!

God help me indeed! for I cannot give hope of what I cannot intend—But let me have your prayers, my dear mamma!—Those shall have mine, who have brought me into all this distress!

I was moving to go up—

And *will* you go up, Clary?

What can I do, Madam?—What *can* I do?—

Go in again, my child—Go in again, my *dear* child!—repeated she; and let your papa find you together!—

What, Madam, to give *him* hope?—To give hope to Mr. Solmes?

Obstinate, perverse, undutiful Clarissa Harlowe! with a rejecting hand, and angry aspect; then take your own way, and go up!—But stir not down again, I charge you, without leave, or till your papa's pleasure be known concerning you.

She flung from me with high indignation: And I went up with a very heavy heart; and feet as slow as my heart was heavy.

My Father is come home, and my Brother with him. Late as it is, they are all shut up together. Not a door opens; not a soul stirs. Hannah, as she moves up and down, is shunned as a person infected.

The angry assembly is broken up. My two uncles and my aunt Hervey are sent for, it seems, to be here in the morning to breakfast. I shall then, I suppose, know my doom. 'Tis past eleven, and I am ordered not to go to bed.

Twelve o'clock.

This moment the keys of every thing are taken from me. It was proposed to send for me down: But my papa said, he could not bear to look upon me.—Shorey was the messenger. The tears stood in her eyes when she delivered her message.

You, my dear, are happy!—May you always be so!—And then I can never be wholly miserable. Adieu, my beloved friend!

Cl. Harlowe

Miss Clarissa Harlowe
To Miss Howe

Sunday Morning, March 5.

H ANNAH has just brought me, from the private place in the garden-wall, a letter from Mr. Lovelace, deposited last night, signed also by Lord M.

He tells me in it, "That Mr. Solmes makes it his boast, that he is to be married in a few days to one of the shyest women in England: That my brother explains his meaning to be me; assuring every-one, that his younger sister is very soon to be Mr. Solmes's wife. He tells me of the patterns bespoke, which my mamma mentioned to me."

Not one thing escapes him that is done or said in this house!

He knows not what my relations inducements can be, to prefer such a man as Solmes to him. If advantageous settlements be the motive, Solmes shall not offer what he will refuse to comply with.

I suppose, he would have his Lordship's signing to this letter to be taken as a voucher for him.

"He desires my leave, in company with my Lord, in a pacific manner, to attend my father or uncles, in order to make proposals that must be accepted, if they will but see him, and hear what they are: And tells me, that he will submit to any measures that I shall prescribe, in order to bring about a reconciliation."

He presumes to be very earnest with me, "to give him a private meeting some night, in my father's garden, attended by whom I please."

Really, my dear, were you to see his letter, you would think I had given him great encouragement, and were in direct treaty with him; or that he were sure that my friends would drive me into a foreign protection; for he has the boldness to offer, in my Lord's name, an asylum to me, should I be tyrannically treated in Solmes's behalf.

I suppose it is the way of this sex to endeavour to intangle

the thoughtless of ours by bold supposals and offers, in hopes
that we shall be too complaisant or bashful to quarrel with
them; and, if not checked, to reckon upon our silence, as assents
voluntarily given, or concessions made in their favour.

For my own part, I am very uneasy to think how I have
been *drawn* on one hand, and *driven* on the other, into a clandestine, in short, into a mere Lover-like correspondence, which
my heart condemns.

It is easy to see, that if I do not break it off, that Mr. Lovelace's advantages, by reason of my unhappy situation, will every
day increase, and I shall be more and more intangled: Yet if I
do put an end to it, without making it a condition of being freed
from Mr. Solmes's address—May I, my dear, is it best, to continue it a little longer, in hopes, by giving him up to extricate
myself out of the other difficulty?—Whose advice can I now ask
but yours?

All my relations are met. They are at breakfast together.
Mr. Solmes is expected. I am excessively uneasy. I must lay
down my pen.

Sunday Noon.

What a cruel thing is suspense!—I will ask leave to go to
church this afternoon. I expect to be denied: But if I do not ask,
they may allege, that my not going is owing to my self.

I desired to speak with Shorey. Shorey came: I directed
her to carry my request to my mamma, for permission to go
to church this afternoon. What think you was the return? Tell
her, that she must direct herself to her brother for any favour
she has to ask.—So, my dear, I am to be delivered up to my
brother!

I was resolved, however, to ask of *him* this favour. Accordingly, when they sent me up my solitary dinner, I gave the
messenger a billet, in which I made it my humble request to
my papa, thro' him, to be permitted to go to church this afternoon.

This was the contemptuous answer: Tell her, that her request will be taken into consideration *to-morrow.*—My re-

quest to go to church *to-day* to be taken into consideration *to-morrow!*—

Patience will be the fittest return I can make to such an insult. But this method will not do, indeed it will not with your Clarissa Harlowe. And yet it is but the beginning, I suppose, of what I am to expect from my brother, now I am delivered up to him.

On recollection, I thought it best to renew my request. I did. The following is a copy of what I wrote, and what follows that, of the answer sent me.

Sir,

I KNOW not what to make of the answer brought to my request of being permitted to go to church this afternoon. You know, that I never absented myself, when well, and at home, till the two last Sundays; when I was *advised* not to go. My present situation is such, that I never more wanted the benefit of the public prayers. I will solemnly engage only to go thither, and back again. My dejection of spirits will give a too just excuse on the score of indisposition, for avoiding visits. My disgraces, if they are to have an end, need not to be proclaimed to the whole world. I ask this favour, therefore, for my reputation's sake, that I may be able to hold up my head in the neighbourhood, if I live to see an end of the unmerited severities, which seem to be designed for

Your unhappy sister,

Cl. Harlowe

To Miss Clarissa Harlowe

FOR a girl to lay so much stress upon going to church, and yet resolve to defy her parents, in an article of the greatest consequence to them, and to the whole family, is an absurdity.

You are recommended, Miss, to the practice of your *private* devotions: May *they* be efficacious upon the mind of one of the most pervicacious young creatures that ever was heard of! The in-*ten*-tion is, I tell you plainly, to mortify you into a sense of your duty. The neighbours you are so solicitous to appear well with, already know, that you defy *that*. So, Miss, if you have a real value for your reputation, shew it as you ought. It is yet in your own power to establish or impair it.

Ja. Harlowe

Thus, my dear, has my Brother got me into his snares, and I, like a poor silly bird, the more I struggle, am the more intangled.

Miss Clarissa Harlowe
To Miss Howe

Tuesday, March 7.

BY my last deposit, you will see how I am driven, and what a poor prisoner I am: No regard had to my reputation. The whole matter is now before you. Can *such* measures be supposed to soften?—But surely they can only mean to try to frighten me into my brother's views.—All my hope is, to be able to weather this point till my cousin Morden comes from Florence; and he is expected soon. Yet, if they are determined upon a short day, I doubt he will not be here time enough to save me.

It is plain, by my brother's letter, that my mamma has not spared me, in the report she has made of the conferences between herself and me: Yet she was pleased to hint to me, that my brother had views which she would have had me try to disappoint.—But she had engaged to give a *faithful* account of what was to pass between herself and me: And it was doubtless, much more eligible to give up a daughter, than to disoblige a husband, and every other person of the family.

Tuesday Night.

Since I wrote the above, I have ventured to send a letter by Shorey to my mamma. I directed her to give it into her own hand, when no body was by.

I shall enclose the copy of it. You'll see that I would have it thought, that now Hannah is gone, I have no way to correspond out of the house. I am far from thinking all I do, right. I am afraid, this is a little piece of art, that is *not* so. But this is an after-thought: The letter went first.

Honored Madam,

HAVING acknowledged to you, that I had received letters from Mr. Lovelace, full of resentment, and that I answered them purely to prevent further mischief; and having shewn you copies of my answers, which you did not disapprove of, altho' you thought fit, after you had read them, to forbid me any further correspondence with him; I think it my duty to acquaint you, that another letter from him has since come to my hand, in which he is very earnest with me to permit him to wait on my papa, or you, or my two uncles, in a pacific way, accompanied by Lord M.—On which I beg your commands.

I own to you, Madam, that had not the prohibition been renewed, and had not Hannah been so suddenly dismissed my service, I should have made the less scruple to have written an answer, and to have commanded her to convey it to him, with all speed, in order to dissuade him from these visits, lest any thing should happen on the occasion, that my heart akes but to think of.

And here, I cannot but express my grief, that I should have all the punishment, and all the blame, who, as I have reason to think, have prevented great mischief, and have not been the occasion of any. For, Madam, could *I* be supposed to govern the passions of *either* of the gentlemen?—Over the one indeed, I have had some little influence, without giving him hitherto any reason to think he has fastened an obligation upon me for it.—Over the other, Who, Madam, has any?

This communication being as voluntarily made, as dutifully intended; I humbly presume to hope, that I shall not be required to produce the letter itself. I cannot either in honour or prudence do that, because of the vehemence of his style; for having heard [not, I assure you, by my means, or thro' Hannah's] of some part of the harsh treatment I have met with; he thinks himself intitled to place it to his own account, by reason of speeches thrown out by some of my relations, equally vehement.

If I do *not* answer him, he will be made desperate, and think himself justified [tho' I shall not think him so] in resenting the treatment he complains of: If I *do*, and if, in compliment to me, he forbears to resent what he thinks himself intitled to resent; be pleased, Madam, to consider the obligation he will suppose he lays me under.

If I were as strongly prepossessed in his favour as is supposed, I should not have wished this to be considered by you.— And permit me, as a still further proof that I am *not* prepossessed, to beg of you to consider, Whether, upon the whole, the proposal I made of declaring for the Single Life (which I will religiously adhere to) is not the best way, to get rid of his pretensions with honour. To renounce him, and not be allowed to aver, that I will never be the other man's, will make him conclude (driven as I am driven), that I am determined in that other man's favour.

If this has not its due weight, my brother's strange schemes must be tried, and I will resign myself to my destiny, with all the acquiescence that shall be granted to my prayers. And so leaving the whole to your own wisdom, and whether you choose to consult my papa and uncles upon this humble application, or not; or whether I shall be allowed to write an answer to Mr. Lovelace, or not (and if allowed so to do, I beg your direction, by whom to send it); I remain,

Honoured Madam, your unhappy, but ever-dutiful daughter,

Cl. Harlowe

Wednesday Morning.

I have just received an answer to the inclosed letter. My mamma, you'll observe, has ordered me to burn it: But, as you will have it in your safe keeping, and nobody else will see it, her end will be equally answered. It has neither date nor super-scription.

Clarissa,

S AY not all the blame, and all the punishment, is yours. I am as much blamed, and as much punished, as you are; yet am more innocent. When your obstinacy is equal to any other person's passion, blame not your brother. We judged right, that Hannah carried on your correspondencies. Now she is gone, and you cannot write (We *think* you cannot) to Miss Howe, nor she to you, without our knowlege, one cause of uneasiness and jealousy is over.

I had no dislike to Hannah. I did not tell her so; because Somebody was within hearing, when she desired to pay her duty to me at going: I gave her a caution, in a raised voice, To take care, where-ever she went to live next, if there were any young Ladies, how she made parties, and assisted in clandestine correspondencies:—But I slid two guineas into her hand.

I don't know what to write, about your answering that man of violence. What can you think of it, that such a family as ours, should have such a rod held over it? You was once all my comfort: You made all my hardships tolerable:—But now!—However, nothing, it is plain, can move you; and I will say no more on that head: For you are under your papa's discipline now; and he will neither be prescribed to, nor intreated.

As to the rest, you have by your obstinacy put it out of my power to do any-thing for you. Your papa takes upon himself to be answerable for all consequences. You must not therefore apply to me for any favour. I shall endeavour to be only an observer; Happy, if I could be an unconcerned one!—While I had power, you would not let me use it as I *would* have used it. You'll have severe trials. If you have any favour to hope for, it must be from the mediation of your uncles. And yet I believe, they are equally determined: For they make it a principle—(Alas! they never had children!) that that child, who in marriage is not governed by her parents, is to be given up as a lost creature!

I charge you, let not this letter be found. Burn it. There is too much of the *mother* in it, to a daughter so unaccountably obstinate.

Write not another letter to me, I can do nothing for you. But you can do every thing for yourself.

After this letter, you will believe, that I could have very little hopes, that an application directly to my father would stand me in any stead: But I thought it became me to write, were it but to acquit myself *to* myself, that I have left nothing unattempted, that has the least likelihood to restore me to his favour. Accordingly I wrote to the following effect:

"I presume not, I say, to argue with my papa, I only beg his mercy and indulgence in this *one* point, on which depends my present and perhaps my *future* happiness; and beseech him not to reprobate his child for an aversion which it is not in her power to conquer. I beg, that I may not be sacrificed to projects, and remote contingencies: I complain of the disgraces I suffer in this banishment from his presence, and in being confined to my chamber. In every thing but this *one* point, I promise implicit duty and resignation to his will. I repeat my offers of a Single Life; and appeal to him, whether I have ever given him cause to doubt my word. I beg to be admitted to his, and to my mamma's presence, and that my conduct may be under their own eye: And this with the more earnestness, as I have too much reason to believe, that snares are laid for me; and tauntings and revilings used on purpose to make a handle of my words against me, when I am not permitted to speak in my own defence. I conclude with hoping, that my brother's instigations may not rob an unhappy child of her father."

This is the cruel answer, sent without superscription, and unsealed, altho' by Betty Barnes, who delivered it with an air, as if she knew the contents.

reply

Wednesday.

I WRITE, perverse girl, but with all the indignation that your disobedience deserves. To desire to be forgiven a fault you own, and yet resolve to persevere in, is a boldness, no more to be equalled, than passed over. It is *my* authority you defy. Your reflections upon a brother, that is an honour to us all, deserve my utmost resentment. I see how light all relationship sits upon *you*. The *cause* I guess at, too: I cannot bear the reflections that naturally arise from this consideration. Your behaviour to your too indulgent, and too fond mother—But, I have no patience—Continue banished from my presence, undutiful as you are, till you know how to conform to my will. Ingrateful creature! Write no more to me, till you can distinguish better; and till you are convinced of your duty to

A justly incensed Father.

This angry Letter was accompanied with one from my mamma, unsealed, and unsuperscribed also. This letter being a repetition of some of the severe things that passed between my mamma and me, of which I have given you an account, I shall not need to give you the contents—Only thus far, that *she* also praises my brother, and blames me for my freedoms with him.

Miss Howe
To Miss Clarissa Harlowe

Thursday Night, March 9.

I HAVE no patience with any of the people you are with. I know not what to advise you to do. How do you know, that you are not punishable for being the cause, tho' to your own loss, that the will of your grandfather is not complied with?— Wills are sacred things, child. You see, that they, even *they*,

think so, who imagine they suffer by a will, thro' the distinction
paid you in it.

Your grandfather knew the family-failing: He knew what
a noble spirit you had to do good. He himself, perhaps (excuse
me, my dear), had done too little in his lifetime; and therefore
he put it in your power to make up for the defects of the whole
family. Were it to me, I would resume it. Indeed I would.

You will say, You cannot do it, while you are with them.
I don't know that. Do you think they can use you worse than
they do?—And is it not your *right*? And do they not make use
of your own generosity to oppress you? Your uncle Harlowe
is one trustee; your cousin Morden is the other: Insist upon
your right to your uncle; and write to your cousin Morden
about it. This, I dare say, will make them alter their behaviour
to you.

Your insolent brother, what has *he* to do to controul you?
—Were it me (I wish it were for one month, and no more) I'd
shew him the difference. I would be in my own mansion, pursuing my charming schemes, and making all around me happy.
I'd set up my own chariot. I'd visit them when they deserved
it. But when my brother and sister gave themselves airs, I would
let them know, that I was their sister, and not their servant:
And if that did not do, I would shut my gates against them;
and bid them be company for each other.

It must be confessed, however, that this brother and sister
of yours, judging as such narrow spirits will ever judge, have
some reason for treating you as they do. It must have long been
a mortifying consideration to them (set disappointed love on
her side, and avarice on his, out of the question) to be so much
eclipsed by a younger sister.—Such a sun in a family, where
there are none but faint twinklers, How could they bear it!
—Why, my dear, they must look upon you as a prodigy among
them: And prodigies you know, tho' they obtain our admiration,
never attract our love. The distance between you and them is
immense. Their eyes ake to look up at you.

Depend upon it, my dear, you will have more of it, and
more still, as you bear it.

As to this odious Solmes, I wonder not at your aversion to

him. It is needless to say any thing to you, who have so sincere
an antipathy to him, to strengthen your dislike: Yet, who can
resist her own talents? One of mine, as I have heretofore said,
is to give an ugly likeness. Shall I indulge it?—I will. And the
rather, as, in doing so, you will have my opinion in justification
of your aversion to him, and in approbation of a steadiness,
that I ever admired, and must for ever approve of in your temper.

I was twice in this wretch's company. At one of the times
your Lovelace was there. I need not mention to you, who have
such a *pretty curiosity*, tho' at present, *only* a curiosity, you
know! the unspeakable difference!—

Lovelace entertained the company in his lively gay way,
and made every-body laugh at one of his stories. It was before
this creature was thought of for you. Solmes laughed too. It was,
however, *his* laugh: For his first three years, at least, I imagine,
must have been one continual fit of crying; and his muscles
have never yet been able to recover a risible tone. His very
smile (you never saw him smile, I believe; never at least gave
him cause to smile) is so little natural to his features, that it appears in him as hideous as the *grin* of a man in malice.

I took great notice of him, as I do of all the noble Lords of
the creation, in their peculiarities; and was disgusted, nay,
shocked at him even then. I was glad I remember, on that particular occasion, to see his strange features recovering their natural gloominess; tho' they did this but slowly, as if the muscles
which contributed to his distortions, had turned upon rusty
springs.

What a dreadful thing must even the Love of such a husband be! For my part, were I his wife! (—But what have I done
to myself, to make but such a supposition?) I should never have
comfort but in his absence, or when I was quarreling with him.
A splenetic Lady, who must have somebody to find fault with,
might indeed be brought to endure such a wretch: The sight of
him would always furnish out the occasion, and all her servants,
for That reason, and for *That* only, would have cause to bless
their master.

So much for his person: As to the other half of him, he is

said to be an insinuating, creeping mortal to any-body he hopes
to be a gainer by: An insolent, over-bearing one, where he has
no such views: And is not this the genuine spirit of meanness?
—He is reported to be spiteful and malicious, even to the whole
family of any single person, who has once disobliged him; and
to his own relations most of all. I am told, that they are none of
them such wretches as himself. This may be one reason, why
he is for disinheriting them.

My Kitty, from one of his domestics, tells me, that his
tenants hate him: And that he never had a servant who spoke
well of him.

His pockets, they say, are continually crammed with keys:
So that when he would treat a guest (a friend he has not out of
your family), he is half as long puzzling *which* is *which*, as his
niggardly treat might be concluded in.—And if it be wine, he
always fetches it himself: Nor has he much trouble in doing so;
for he has very few visitors—only those, whom business or necessity brings: For a gentleman who can help it, would rather be
benighted, than put up at his house.

Yet this is the man they have found out, for considerations
as sordid as those he is governed by, for a husband (that is to
say, for a Lord and Master) for Miss Clarissa Harlowe!

But perhaps, he may not be quite so miserable as he is
represented. Characters extremely good, or extremely bad, are
seldom justly given. But your uncle Antony has told my mamma, who objected to his covetousness, that it was intended
to tie him up, as he called it, *to your own terms;* which would
be with a hempen, rather than a matrimonial cord, I dare say.
But, is not this a plain indication, that even his own recom-
menders think him a mean creature; and that he must be ar-
ticled with—perhaps for *necessaries?* But enough, and too much,
of such a mortal as this!—You must not have him, my dear—
That I am clear in—tho' not so clear, how you will be able to
avoid it, except you assert the independence to which your
estate gives you a title.

Here my mamma broke in upon me. She wanted to see what

I had written. I was silly enough to read Solmes's character to her.

She owned, that the man was not the most desirable of men; had not the happiest appearance: But what was person in a man? And I was chidden for setting you against complying with your father's will. Then followed a lecture upon the preference to be given in favour of a man who took care to discharge all his obligations to the world, and to keep all together, in opposition to a spendthrift or profligate: A fruitful subject, you know, whether any particular person be meant by it, or not: Why will these wise parents, by saying too much against the persons they dislike, put one upon defending them? Lovelace is not a spendthrift; owes not obligations to the world; tho', I doubt not, profligate enough.—And so we are put, perhaps, upon *curiosities* first, how such a one or his friends may think of one;—And then, but too probably, a distinguishing preference, or something that looks exceedingly like it, comes in.

Your mamma tells you, "That you will have great trials: That you are under your papa's *discipline*." The word's enough for me to despise them who give occasion for its use.—"That it is out of her power to help you!" And again: "That if you have any favour to hope for, it must be by the mediation of your uncles!" I suppose you will write to the oddities, since you are forbid to see them!—But can it be, that such a lady, such a sister, such a wife, such a mother, has no influence in her own family? Who indeed, as you say, would marry, that can live single? My choler is again beginning to rise. RESUME, my dear: —And that is all I will give myself time to say further, lest I offend you, when I cannot serve you—Only this, that I am

Your truly affectionate friend and servant,

Anna Howe

Miss Clarissa Harlowe
To Miss Howe

Sunday Night, March 12.

THIS man, this Lovelace, gives me great uneasiness. He is extremely bold and rash. He was this afternoon at our church: In hopes to see me, I suppose: And yet, if he had such hopes, his usual intelligence must have failed him.

Shorey was at church; and a principal part of her observation was· upon his haughty and proud behaviour, when he turned round in the pew where he sat, to our family-pew.—My papa and both my uncles were there; so were my mamma and sister. My brother happily was not!—They all came home in disorder. Nor did the congregation mind any-body but him; it being his first appearance there, since the unhappy rencounter.

What did the man come for, if he intended to look challenge and defiance, as Shorey says he did, and as others observed it seems as well as she? Did he come for *my* sake; and, by behaving in such a manner to those present of my family, imagine he was doing me either service or pleasure?—He knows how they hate him: Nor will he take pains, would pains do, to obviate their hatred.

Shorey says, that he watched my mamma's eye, and bowed to her: And she returned the compliment. He always admired my mamma. She would not, I believe, have hated *him*, had she not been *bid* to hate him; and had it not been for the rencounter between him and her only son.

My father it seems is more and more incensed against me. And so are my uncles: They had my letters in the morning. Their answers, if they vouchsafe to answer me, will demonstrate, I doubt not, the unseasonableness of this rash man's presence at our church.

They are angry, it seems, with my mamma, for returning his compliment. What an enemy is hatred, even to the common forms of civility! which, however, more distinguish the *payer* of a compliment, than the *receiver*. But they all see, they say,

that there is but one way to put an end to his insults. So I shall
suffer: And in what will the rash man have benefited himself,
or mended his prospects?

I am extremely apprehensive that this worse than ghost-
like appearance of his, bodes some still bolder step. If he come
hither (and very desirous he is of my leave to come), I am afraid
there will be murder. To avoid That, if there were no other way,
I would most willingly be buried alive. *and will be ...*

Cl. H.

Mr. Lovelace — 1st (w abridged)
To John Belford, Esq;

Monday, March 13.

IN vain dost thou[a] and thy compeers press me to go to town,
while I am in such an uncertainty as I am in at present with
this proud Beauty. All the ground I have hitherto gained with
her, is intirely owing to her concern for the safety of people
whom I have reason to hate.

Write then, thou biddest me, if I will not come. That, indeed,
I can do; and as well without a subject, as with one. And what
follows shall be a proof of it.

The Lady's malevolent Brother has now, as I told thee at
M. Hall, introduced another man; the most unpromising in his
person and qualities, the most formidable in his offers, that has
yet appeared.

This man has by his proposals captivated every soul of the
Harlowes—*Soul!* did I say—There is not a soul among them but
my Charmer's: And she, withstanding them All, is actually confined, and otherwise maltreated by a Father the most gloomy
and positive; at the instigation of a Brother the most arrogant

---

[a] *These gentlemen affected, as they called it, the Roman style in their letters:
And it was an agreed rule with them, to take in good part whatever freedoms
they treated each other with, if the passages were written in that style.*

and selfish—But thou knowest their characters; and I will not therefore sully my Paper with them.

But is it not a confounded thing to be in love with one, who is the daughter, the sister, the niece, of a family I must eternally despise? And the devil of it, That Love increasing, with her—What shall I call It?—'Tis not scorn:—'Tis not pride: —'Tis not the insolence of an adored beauty:—But 'tis to *virtue*, it seems, that my difficulties are owing; And I pay for not being a sly sinner, an hypocrite: for being regardless of my reputation; for permitting slander to open its mouth against me. But is it necessary for such a one as I, who have been used to carry all before me, upon my own terms—I, who never inspired a Fear, that had not a discernibly-predominant mixture of Love in it; to be an hypocrite?—Well says the poet:

> He who seems virtuous does but act a part;
> And shews not his own nature, but his art.

Well, but, it seems I must *practise* for This art, if I would succeed with this truly admirable creature! But why *practise* for it?—Cannot I *indeed* reform?—I have but *one* vice;—Have I, Jack?—Thou knowest my heart, if any man living does. As far as I know it myself, thou knowest it. But 'tis a cursed deceiver— For it has many and many a time imposed upon its master— *Master*, did I say? That am I not now: Nor have I been from the moment I beheld this angel of a woman: Prepared indeed as I was by her character, before I saw her: For what a mind must that be, which, tho' not virtuous itself, admires not virtue in another?

I have boasted, that I was once in love before:—And indeed I thought I was. It was in my early manhood—with that Quality-jilt, whose infidelity I have vowed to revenge upon as many of the sex as shall come into my power. I believe, in different climes, I have already sacrificed an hecatomb to my Nemesis, in pursuance of this vow. But upon recollecting what I was *then*, and comparing it with what I find in myself *now*, I cannot say, that I was ever in love before.

What was it then, dost thou ask me, since the disappoint-

ment had such effects upon me, when I found myself jilted, that
I was hardly kept in my senses?—Why, I'll tell thee what, as
near as I can remember; for it was a great while ago:—It was—
egad, Jack, I can hardly tell what it was—But a vehement aspiration after a novelty, I think—Those confounded Poets, with their
celestially-terrene descriptions, did as much with me as the
Lady: They fired my imagination, and set me upon a desire to
become a goddess-maker. I must needs try my new-fledged
pinions in sonnet, elogy, and madrigal. I must have a Cynthia,
a Stella, a Sacharissa, as well as the best of them: Darts, and
flames, and the devil knows what, must I give to my Cupid. I
must create Beauty, and place it where nobody else could find
it: And many a time have I been at a loss for a subject, when my
new-created goddess has been kinder than it was proper for my
plaintive sonnet that she should be.

Then I had a vanity of *another* sort in my passion: I found
myself well-received among the women in general; and I thought
it a pretty *lady-like* tyranny (I was very young then, and very
vain) to single out some *one* of the sex, to make *half a score*
jealous. And I can tell thee, it had its effect: For many an eye
have I made to sparkle with rival indignation: Many a cheek
glow; and even many a fan have I caused to be snapped at a
sister-beauty; accompanied with a reflection, perhaps, at being
seen alone with a wild young fellow, who could not be in private
with both at once.

In short, Jack, it was more Pride than Love, as I now find
it, that put me upon making such a confounded rout about losing
this noble varletess. I thought she loved me at least as well as I
believed I loved her: Nay, I had the vanity to suppose she could
not help it. My friends were pleased with my choice. They
wanted me to be shackled.

I have no notion of playing the hypocrite so egregiously,
as to pretend to be blind to qualifications which every-one sees
and acknowleges.—But yet, shall my vanity extend only to
personals, such as the gracefulness of dress, my debonnaire, and
my assurance?—Self-taught, self-acquired, these!—For my
PARTS, I value not myself upon *them*. Thou wilt say, I have no
cause.—Perhaps not: But if I had any thing valuable as to intel-

lectuals, those are not my own: And to be proud of what a man is answerable for the abuse of, and has no merit in the right use of, is to strut, like the jay, in a borrowed plumage.

But to return to my fair jilt—I could not bear, that a woman, who was the first that had bound me in silken fetters (they were not iron ones, like those I now wear) should prefer a coronet to me: And when the bird was flown, I set more value upon it, than when I had it safe in my cage, and could visit it when I would.

But now am I in-*deed* in love. I can think of nothing, of no-body else, but the divine Clarissa Harlowe.—*Harlowe!*— How that hated word sticks in my throat—But I shall give her for it the name of Love.[a]

> Clarissa!—O there's music in the name,
> That soft'ning me to infant tenderness,
> Makes my heart spring like the first leaps of life!

But couldst thou have thought that I, who think it possible for me to favour as much as I can be favoured; that I, who for this charming creature think of foregoing the *life of honour* for the *life of shackles;* could adopt those over-tender lines of Otway?

I check myself, and leaving the three first lines of the following of Dryden to the family of the whiners, find the workings of the passion in my stormy soul better expressed by the three last:

> Love various minds does variously inspire:
> He stirs in gentle natures gentle fire:
> Like that of incense on the altar laid.
>
> But raging flames tempestuous souls invade:
> A fire, which ev'ry windy passion blows;
> With pride it mounts, and with revenge it glows.

And with Revenge it *shall* glow!—For, dost thou think, that if it were not from the hope, That this stupid family are all com-

---

[a] *Lovelace.*

bined to do my work for me, I would bear their insults?—Is it possible to imagine, that I would be braved as I am braved, threatened as I am threatened, by those who are afraid to see me; and by this brutal brother too, to whom I gave a life (A life, indeed, not worth my taking!); had I not a greater pride in knowing, that by means of his very Spy upon me, I am playing him off as I please; cooling or inflaming, his violent passions, as may best suit my purposes; permitting so much to be revealed of my life and actions, and intentions, as may give him such a confidence in his double-faced agent, as shall enable me to dance his employer upon my own wires?

This it is, that makes my pride mount above my resentment. By this engine, whose springs I am continually oiling, I play them all off.

And what my motive, dost thou ask? No less than this, That my beloved shall find no protection out of my family; for, if I know *hers*, fly she must, or have the man she hates. This, therefore, if I take my measures right, and my Familiar fail me not, will secure her mine, in spite of them all; in spite of her own inflexible heart: Mine, without condition; without reformation-promises; without the necessity of a siege of years, perhaps; and to be even then, after wearing the guise of a merit-doubting hypocrisy, at an uncertainty, upon a probation unapproved of— Then shall I have all the rascals and rascalesses of the family come creeping to me: I prescribing to them; and bringing that sordidly-imperious brother to kneel at the foot-stool of my throne.

But be This as it may, there is a present likelihood of room for glorious mischief. A confederacy had been for *some time* formed against me; but the uncles and the nephew are *now* to be *double*-servanted (*single*-servanted they were before), and those servants are to be *double*-armed when they attend their masters abroad. This indicates their resolute enmity to me, and as resolute favour to Solmes.

The reinforced orders for this hostile apparatus are owing, it seems, to a visit I made yesterday to their church; a good place to begin a reconciliation in, were the heads of the family christians, and did they mean any thing by their prayers. My hopes were to have an invitation (or, at least, to gain a pretence) to accompany home the gloomy sire; and so get an opportunity to see my goddess: For, I believed they durst not but be *civil* to me, at least. But they were filled with terror, it seems, at my entrance; a terror they could not get over. Yet not a hair of any of their stupid heads do I intend to hurt.

Thus, Jack, as thou desirest, have I written: Written upon Something; upon Nothing; upon Revenge, which I love; upon LOVE, which I hate, *heartily* hate, because 'tis my master: And upon the devil knows what besides:—For, looking back, I'm amazed at the length of it. *Thou* may'st read it: *I* would not for a King's ransom—But so as I do *but* write, thou sayest thou wilt be pleased.

Be pleased then. I *command* thee to be pleased: If not for the writer's, or written's sake, for thy word's sake. And so in the royal style (for am I not likely to be thy King and thy Emperor, in the great affair before us?) I bid Thee very heartily

Farewell.

Miss Clarissa Harlowe To Miss Howe

Thursday, March 16.

HAVING met with such bad success in my application to those of my own family, I have taken a step that will surprise you. It is no other than writing a letter to Mr. Solmes himself. I sent it; and have his answer. He had certainly help in it. For I have seen a letter of his; as indifferently worded, as poorly spelt. Yet the superscription is of his dictating, I dare say; for he is a formal wretch. With these, I shall inclose one from my brother to me, on occasion of mine to Mr. Solmes. I did think that it was possible to discourage this man from proceeding; and that it would have answered all my wishes. It was worth the trial. But you'll see nothing will do. My brother has taken his measures too securely.

To Roger Solmes, Esq;

Wednesday, March 15.

Sir,

Y OU will wonder to receive a letter from me, and more still at the uncommon subject of it. But the necessity of the case will justify me, at least in my own apprehension; and I shall therefore make no other apology for it.

When you first came acquainted with my father's family, you found the writer of This one of the happiest creatures in the world; beloved by the best and most indulgent of parents, and rejoicing in the kind favour of two affectionate uncles, and in the esteem of every one.

But how is this happy scene now changed!—You was pleased to cast a favourable eye upon me. You addressed yourself to my friends: Your proposals were approved of by them; approved of without consulting me; as if my choice and happiness were of the least signification. Those who had a right to all reasonable obedience from me, insisted upon it without reserve. I had not the felicity to think as they did; almost the first time my sentiments differed from theirs. I besought them to indulge me in a point so important to my future happiness: But, alas, in vain! And then (for I thought it was but honest) I told you my mind; and even that my affections were engaged. But, to my mortification, and surprize, you persisted, and still persist.

The consequence of all is too grievous for me to repeat: You, who have such free access to the rest of the family, know it too well; too well you know it, either for the credit of your own generosity, or for my reputation. I am used, on your account, as I never before was used, and never before was thought to deserve to be used; and this was the hard, the impossible condition of their returning favour, that I must prefer a man *to* all others, that *of* all others I cannot prefer.

Thus distressed, and made unhappy, and all for your sake, and thro' your cruel perseverance, I write, Sir, to demand of you the peace of mind you have robbed me of: To demand of you the Love of so many dear friends, of which you have deprived me; and, if you have the generosity that should distinguish a man, and a gentleman, to adjure you not to continue an address that has been attended with such cruel effects to the creature you profess to esteem.

If you really value me, as my friends would make me believe, and as you have declared you do, must it not be a mean and selfish value? A value that can have no merit with the unhappy object of it, because it is attended with effects so grievous to her? It must be for *your own sake* only, not for *mine*. And, even in this point you *must* be mistaken; for would a prudent man wish to marry one who has not a heart to give? Who cannot esteem him? Who therefore must prove a bad wife?—And how cruel would it be to make a poor creature a bad wife, whose pride it would be to make a good one?

If I am capable of judging, our tempers and inclinations are vastly different. Any other of my sex will make you happier than I can.

But, if, Sir, you have not so much generosity in your value for me, as to desist for *my own* sake, let me conjure you, by the regard due to *yourself*, and to your own future happiness, to discontinue your suit, and place your affections on a worthier object: For why should you make *me* miserable, and *yourself* not happy? By this means you will do all that is now in your power to restore me to the affection of my friends; and, if That can be, it will leave me in as happy a state as you found me.

Your compliance with this request, will lay me under the highest obligation to your generosity, and make me ever

Your well-wisher, and humble servant,

Clarissa Harlowe

To Miss Clarissa Harlowe

These most humbly present.
Thursday, March 16.

Dearest Miss,

Y OUR Letter has had a very contrary effect upon me, to
what you seem to have expected from it. It has doubly
convinced me of the excellency of your mind, and the honour of
your disposition. Call it *selfish,* or what you please, I must
persist in my suit; and happy shall I be, if by patience and perseverance, and a steady and unalterable devoir, I may at last overcome the difficulty laid in my way.

As your good parents, your uncles, and other friends, are
absolutely determined you shall never have Mr. Lovelace, if
they can help it; and as I presume no other person is in the way;
I will contentedly wait the issue of this matter. And, forgive me,
dearest Miss; but a person should sooner persuade me to give
up to him my estate, as an instance of my generosity, because
he could not be happy without it, than I would a much more
valuable treasure, to promote the felicity of another, and make
his way easier to circumvent myself.

Pardon me, dear Miss; but I must persevere, tho' I am sorry
you suffer on my account, as you are pleased to think; for I
never before saw the Lady I could love: And while there is any
hope, and that you remain undisposed of to some happier man,
I must and will be

Your faithful and obsequious admirer,

Roger Solmes

Mr. James Harlowe
To Miss Clarissa Harlowe

Thursday, March 16.

WHAT a fine whim you took into your head, to write a Letter to Mr. Solmes, to persuade him to give up his pretensions to you!—Of *all* the pretty romantic flights you have delighted in, this was certainly one of the most extraordinary. But to say nothing of what fires us all with indignation against you (your owning your prepossession in a villain's favour, and your impertinence to me, and your sister, and your uncles; how can you lay at Mr. Solmes's door the usage you so bitterly complain of?—You know, little fool, as you are, that it is your fondness for Lovelace that has brought upon you all these things; and which would have happened, whether Mr. Solmes had honoured you with his addresses or not.

As you must needs know This to be true, consider, pretty, witty Miss, if your fond love-sick heart can let you consider, what a fine figure all your expostulations with us, and charges upon Mr. Solmes, make!—With what propriety do you demand of *him* to restore to you your former happiness, as you call it, and *merely* call it, for if you thought our favour so, you would restore it to yourself; since it is yet in your own power to do so. Therefore, Miss Pert, none of your pathetics, except in the right place. Depend upon it, whether you have Mr. Solmes, or not, you shall never have your heart's delight, the vile rake Lovelace, if our parents, if our uncles, if I, can hinder it. No! you fallen angel, you shall not give your father and mother such a *son*, nor me such a *brother*, in giving yourself that profligate wretch for a *husband*. And so set your heart at rest, and lay aside all thoughts of him, if ever you expect forgiveness, reconciliation, or a kind opinion, from any of your family; but especially from him, who, at present, styles himself

Your Brother,

James Harlowe

P.S. I know your knack at letter-writing. If you send me
an answer to this, I'll return it unopened, for I won't
argue with your perverseness in so plain a case—Only
once for all, I was willing to put you right as to Mr.
Solmes; whom I think to blame to trouble his head about
you.

Mr. Lovelace
To John Belford, Esq;

Friday, March 17.

I RECEIVE, with great pleasure, the early and chearful assurances of your loyalty and love. And let our principal and
most trusty friends named in my last know that I do.

I would have thee, Jack, come down, as soon as thou canst.
I believe I shall not want the others so soon. For thyself, thou
must be constantly with me: Not for my *security:* The family
dare do nothing but bully: They bark only at distance: But for
my *Entertainment:* That thou mayst, from the Latin and the
English Classics, keep my love-sick soul from drooping.

Thou hadst best come to me here, in thy old corporal's
coat; thy servant out of livery; and to be upon a familiar foot
with thee, as a distant relation, to be provided for by thy interest above; I mean not in heaven, thou mayst be sure. Thou wilt
find me at a little alehouse; they call it an inn: The White-Hart;
most terribly wounded (but by the weather only) the sign:—In
a sorry village; within five miles from Harlowe-Place. Every-
body knows Harlowe-Place—For, like Versailles, it is sprung up
from a dunghil, within every elderly person's remembrance.
Every poor body, particularly, knows it: But that only for a few
years past, since a certain angel has appeared there among the
sons and daughters of men.

The people here, at the Hart, are poor, but honest; and have
gotten it into their heads, that I am a man of quality in disguise;

and there is no reining-in their officious respect. There is a pretty little smirking daughter; seventeen six days ago. I call her my Rose-bud: Her grandmother (for there is no mother), a good neat old woman, as ever filled a wicker-chair in a chimney-corner, has besought me to be merciful to her.

This simple chit, (for there is a simplicity in her thou wilt be highly pleased with: All humble; all officious; all innocent— I love her for her humility, her officiousness, and even for her *innocence*) will be pretty amusement to thee; while I combat with the weather, and dodge and creep about the walls and purlieus of Harlowe-Place. Thou wilt see in her mind, all that her superiors have been taught to conceal, in order to render themselves less natural, and more undelightful.

I never was so honest for so long together since my matriculation. It behoves me so to be—Some way or other, my recess may be found out; and it will then be thought that my Rose-bud has attracted me. A report in my favour, from simplicities so amiable, may establish me; for the grandmother's relation to my Rose-bud may be sworn to: And the father is an honest poor man: Has no joy, but in his Rose-bud.—O Jack! spare thou therefore (for I shall leave thee often alone with her, spare thou) my Rose-bud!—Let the rule I never departed from, but it cost me a long regret, be observed to my Rose-bud! Never to ruin a poor girl, whose simplicity and innocence was all she had to trust to; and whose fortunes were too low to save her from the rude contempts of worse minds than her own, and from an indigence extreme: Such a one will only pine in secret; and at last, perhaps, in order to refuge herself from slanderous tongues and virulence, be induced to tempt some guilty stream, or seek an end in the knee-incircling garter, that, peradventure, was the first attempt of abandoned Love. Unsuspicious of her danger, the lamb's throat will hardly shun thy knife!—O be not thou the butcher of my lambkin!

The less be thou so, for the reason I am going to give thee— The gentle heart is touched by Love! Her soft bosom heaves with a passion she has not yet found a name for. I once caught her eye following a young carpenter, a widow neighbour's son, living (to speak in her dialect) *at the little white-house over the way:* A gentle youth he also seems to be, about three years older than herself: Play-mates from infancy, till his eighteenth and her fifteenth year furnished a reason for a greater distance in shew, while their hearts gave a better for their being nearer than ever: For I soon perceived the Love reciprocal.

I have examined the little heart: She has made me her confident. She owns, she could love Johnny Barton very well: And Johnny Barton has told her, He could love her better than any maiden he ever saw—But, alas! it must not be thought of. Why not be thought of?—She don't know!—And then she sighed: But Johnny has an aunt, who will give him an hundred pounds, when his time is out; and her father cannot give her but a few things, or so, to set her out with: And tho' Johnny's mother says, she knows not where Johnny would have a prettier, or notabler wife, yet—And then she sighed again—What signifies talking?—I would not have Johnny be unhappy, and poor for me!—For what good would that do *me*, you know, Sir!

What would I give (—By my soul, my angel will indeed reform me, if her friends implacable folly ruin us not both!—What would I give) to have so innocent, and so good a heart, as either my Rose-bud's, or Johnny's!

I have a confounded mischievous one—by *nature* too, I think!—A good motion now-and-then rises from it: But it dies away presently—A love of intrigue!—An invention for mischief!—A triumph in subduing!—Fortune encouraging and supporting!—And a constitution—What signifies palliating? But I believe I had been a rogue, had I been a plough-boy.

But the devil's in this sex! And yet where there is not virtue, which nevertheless we free-livers are continually plotting to destroy, what is there even in the ultimate of our wishes with them?—*Preparation* and *Expectation* are, in a manner, everything: *Reflection*, indeed, may be something, if the mind be hardened above feeling the guilt of a past *trespass:* But the *Fruition*, what is there in that? And yet, That being the end, nature will not be satisfied without it.

See what grave reflections an innocent subject will produce! It gives me some pleasure to think, that it is not out of my *power* to reform: But then, Jack, I am afraid I must keep better

company, than I do at present—For we certainly harden one
another. But be not cast down, my boy; there will be time
enough to give thee, and all thy bretheren, warning to choose
another leader: And I fansy thou wilt be the man.

Mean time, as I make it my rule, whenever I have committed a very capital enormity, to do some good by way of
atonement; and as I believe I am a pretty deal indebted on that
score, I intend, before I leave these parts (successfully shall I
leave them, I hope, or I shall be tempted to double the mischief
by way of revenge, tho' not to my Rose-bud any), to join an
hundred pounds to Johnny's aunt's hundred pounds, to make
one innocent couple happy.

An interruption:—Another letter anon; and both shall go
together.

Mr. Lovelace
To John Belford, Esq;

I HAVE found out by my watchful Spy almost as many of my
charmer's motions, as of those of the rest of her relations.
It delights me to think how the rascal is caressed by the uncles
and nephew; and let into *their* secrets; yet proceeds all the time
by *my* line of direction. I have charged him, however, on forfeiture of his present weekly stipend, and my future favour, to take
care, that neither my beloved, nor any of the family, suspect
him: I have told him, that he may indeed watch her egresses and
regresses; but that only to keep off other servants from her
paths; yet not to be seen by her himself.

The interview I am meditating, will produce her consent,
I hope, to other favours of the like kind: For, should she not
choose the place I am expecting to see her in, I can attend her
any-where in the rambling, Dutch-taste garden, whenever she
will permit me that honour: For my implement, hight Joseph
Leman, has given me the opportunity of procuring two keys
(one of which I have given him, for reasons good) to the garden-

door, which opens to the haunted coppice, as tradition has made the servants think it; a man having been found hanging in it about twenty years ago: And Joseph, upon least notice, will leave it unbolted.

But I was obliged to give him, previously, my honour, that no mischief shall happen to any of my adversaries, from this liberty: For the Fellow tells me, that he loves all his masters; and, only that he knows I am a man of honour; and that my alliance will do credit to the family.

There never was a rogue, who had not a salvo to himself for being so.—What a praise to *honesty*, that every man pretends to it, even at the instant that he knows he is pursuing the methods that will perhaps prove him a knave to the whole world, as well as to his own conscience!

But what this stupid family can mean, to make all this necessary, I cannot imagine. My Revenge and my Love are uppermost by turns. If the latter succeed not, the gratifying of the former will be my only consolation: And, by All that's good, they shall feel it; altho', for it, I become an exile from my native country for ever.

I will throw myself into my charmer's presence. I have twice already attempted it in vain. I shall then see what I may depend upon from her favour. If I thought I had no prospect of that, I should be tempted to carry her off.—That would be a rape worthy of a Jupiter!

But all gentle shall be my movements: All respectful, even to reverence, my address to her!—Her hand shall be the only witness to the pressure of my lip—my trembling lip: I *know* it will tremble, if I do not *bid* it tremble. As soft my sighs, as the sighs of my gentle Rose-bud. By *my* humility will I invite *her* confidence: The loneliness of the place shall give me no advantage: To dissipate her fears, and engage her reliance upon my honour for the future, shall be my whole endeavour.

Miss Clarissa Harlowe
To Miss Howe

Sat. night, Mar. 18.

I HAVE been frighted out of my wits—Still am in a manner out of breath.—Thus occasioned—I went down, under the usual pretence, in hopes to find something from you. Concerned at my disappointment, I was returning from the woodhouse, when I heard a rustling as of somebody behind a stack of wood. I was extremely surprised: But still more, to behold a man coming from behind the furthermost stack. O thought I, at that moment, the sin of a prohibited correspondence!

In the same point of time that I saw him, he besought me, not to be frighted: And, still nearer approaching me, threw open a horseman's coat: And who should it be but Mr. Lovelace! I could not scream out (yet attempted to scream, the moment I saw a man; and again, when I saw who it was) For I had no voice: And had I not caught hold of a prop, which supported the old roof, I should have sunk.

I had hitherto, as you know, kept him at a distance: And now, as I recovered myself, judge of my first emotions, when I recollected his character from every mouth of my family; his enterprising temper; and found myself alone with him, in a place so near a bye-lane, and so remote from the house.

But his respectful behaviour soon dissipated these fears, and gave me others, lest we should be seen together, and information of it given to my brother.

As soon therefore as I could speak, I expressed with the greatest warmth my displeasure; and told him, that he cared not how much he exposed me to the resentments of all my friends, provided he could gratify his own impetuous humour; and I then commanded him to leave the place that moment: And was hurrying from him; when he threw himself in the way at my feet, beseeching my stay for one moment; declaring, that he suffered himself to be guilty of this rashness, as I thought it, to avoid one much greater:—For, in short, he could not bear the hourly insults he received from my family, with the thoughts of having so little interest in my favour, that he could not promise himself, that his patience and forbearance would be attended with any other issue, than to lose me for ever, and be triumphed over and insulted upon it.

This man, you know, has very ready knees. You have said, that he ought, in small points, frequently to offend, on purpose to shew what an address he is master of.

He ran on, expressing his apprehensions, that a temper so gentle and obliging, as he said mine was, to every-body but him, would be wrought upon in favour of a man set up in part to be revenged upon myself, for my grandfather's envied distinction of me; and in part to be revenged upon him, for having given life to one, who would have taken his; and now sought to deprive him of hopes dearer to him than life.

I told him, he might be assured, that the severity and ill-usage I met with would be far from effecting the intended end: That altho' I could, with great sincerity, declare for a Single Life, which had always been my choice; and particularly, that if ever I married, if they would not insist upon the man I had an aversion to, it should not be with the man they disliked—

He interrupted me here: He hoped, I would forgive him for it; but he could not help expressing his great concern, that, after so many instances of his passionate and obsequious devotion—

And pray Sir, said I, let me interrupt you in my turn:—Why don't you assert, in still plainer words, the obligation you have laid me under by this your boasted devotion? Why don't you let me know, in terms as high as your implication, that a perseverance I have not wished for, which has set all my relations at variance with me, is a merit, that throws upon me the guilt of ingratitude, for not answering it as you seem to expect?

I was very uneasy to be gone; and the more as the night came on apace. But there was no getting from him, till I had heard a great deal more of what he had to say.

As he hoped, that I would one day make him the happiest man in the world, he assured me, that he had so much regard for my fame, that he would be as far from advising any step that was likely to cast a shade upon my reputation, (altho' That step was to be ever so much in his own favour) as I would be to follow such advice. But since I was not to be permitted to live single, he would submit it to my consideration, whether I had any way but *one* to avoid the intended violence to my inclinations: My father so jealous of his authority: Both my uncles in my father's way of thinking: My cousin Morden at a distance: My uncle and aunt Hervey awed into *insignificance*, was his word: My brother and sister inflaming every one; Solmes's offers captivating: Miss Howe's mother rather of party with them, for motives respecting example to her own daughter.

He appealed to me, whether ever I knew my papa recede from any resolution he had once fixed; expecially, if he thought either his prerogative, or his authority, concerned in the question.

He was proceeding, as I thought, with reflections of this sort; and I angrily told him, I would not permit my father to be reflected upon; adding, That his severity to me, however unmerited, was not a warrant for me to dispense with my duty to him.

He had no pleasure, he said, in urging any thing that could be *so* construed; for, however well warranted *he* was to make such reflections, from the provocations they were continually giving him, he knew how offensive to *me* any liberties of this sort would be.—And yet he must own, that it was painful to him, who had youth and passions to be allowed for, as well as others; and who had always valued himself upon speaking his mind; to curb himself, under such treatment. Nevertheless, his consideration for me would make him confine himself in his observations, to facts, that were too flagrant, and too openly avowed, to be disputed.

How unhappy, my dear, that there is but too much reason for these observations, and for this inference; made, likewise, with more coolness and respect to my family than one would have apprehended from a man so much provoked, and of passions so high, and generally thought uncontroulable!—

Will you not question me about *throbs* and *glows*, if, from such instances of a command over his fiery temper, for my sake, I am ready to infer, that were my friends capable of a reconciliation with him, he might be affected by arguments apparently calculated for his present and future good?

He represented to me, that my present disgraceful confinement was known to all the world: That neither my sister nor brother scrupled to represent me as an obliged and favoured child, in a state of actual rebellion:—That, nevertheless, everybody who knew me was ready to justify me for an aversion to a man, whom every-body thought utterly unworthy of *me*, and more fit for my *sister:* That unhappy as he was, in not having been able to make any greater impression upon me in his favour, all the world gave me to him:—Nor was there but one objection made to him, by his very enemies (his birth, his fortunes, his prospects all unexceptionable, and the latter splendid); and *that*, he thanked God, and my example, was in a fair way of being removed for ever: Since he had seen his error, and was heartily sick of the courses he had followed; which, however, were far less enormous than malice and envy had represented them to be. But of This he should say the less, as it were much better to justify himself by his actions, than by the most solemn asseverations, and promises. And then complimenting my *person*, he assured me, that he was still more captivated with the graces of my *mind:* And would frankly own, that till he had the honour to know me, he had never met with an inducement sufficient to enable him to overcome an unhappy kind of prejudice to matrimony; which had made him before impenetrable to the wishes and recommendations of all his relations.

You see, my dear, he scruples not to speak of himself, as his enemies speak of him. I can't say, but his openness in these particulars gives a credit to his other professions. I should easily, I think, detect an hypocrite: And *this* man particularly, who is said to have allowed himself in great liberties, were he to pretend to instantaneous lights and convictions—at his time of life too: Habits, I am sensible, are not so easily changed. You have always joined with me in remarking, that he will speak his mind with freedom, even to a degree of unpoliteness sometimes; and that his very treatment of my family is a proof that he cannot make a mean court to anybody for interest sake—What pity, where there are such laudable traces, that they should have been so mired, and choaked up, as I may say!—We have heard, that the man's head is better than his heart: But do you really think Mr. Lovelace can have a *very* bad heart?

I then assured him, that it was with infinite concern, that I had found myself drawn into an epistolary correspondence with him; especially since that correspondence had been prohibited:—And the only agreeable use I could think of making of this unexpected and undesired interview, was, to let him know, that I should from henceforth think myself obliged to discontinue it.

You are to consider, Madam, you have not now an option; and to whom it is owing that you have not; and that you are in the power of those (Parents why should I call them?) who are determined, that you shall *not* have an option. All I propose is, that you will embrace such a protection;—but not till you have tried every way, to avoid the necessity for it.

And give me leave to say, that if a correspondence on which I have founded all my hopes, is, at this critical conjuncture, to be broken off; and if you are resolved not to be provided against the worst; it must be plain to me, that you will at last yield to That worst—Worst to *me* only—It cannot be to *you*—And *then!* (and he put his hand clenched to his forehead) how shall I bear the supposition?—*Then* will you be That Solmes's!—But, by all that's Sacred, neither He, nor your brother, nor your uncles, shall enjoy their triumph:—Perdition seize my soul, if they shall!

The man's vehemence frightened me: Yet, in resentment, I would have left him; but, throwing himself at my feet again, Leave me not thus, I beseech you, dearest Madam, leave me not thus, in despair. I kneel not, repenting of what I have vowed in such a case as That I have supposed. I re-vow it, at your feet! —And so he did. But think not it is by way of menace, or to intimidate you to favour me. If your heart inclines you [and then he arose] to obey your father (your *brother*, rather) and to have Solmes, altho' I shall avenge myself on those who have insulted me, for their insults to myself and family; yet will I tear out my heart from This bosom (if possible, with my own hands), were it to scruple to give up its ardors to a woman capable of such a preference.

I told him, that he talked to me in very high language; but he might assure himself, that I never would have Mr. Solmes (Yet that this I said not in favour to him): and I had declared as much to my relations, were there not such a man as himself in the world.

Would I declare, that I would still honour him with my correspondence?—He could not bear, that, hoping to obtain *greater* instances of my favour, he should forfeit the *only one* he had to boast of.

I bid him forbear rashness or resentment to any of my family, and I would, for some time at least, till I saw what issue my present trials were likely to have, proceed with a correspondence, which, nevertheless, my heart condemned.—

And his spirit him, the impatient creature said, interrupting me, for bearing what he did; when he considered, that the necessity of it was imposed upon him; not by *my* will; for then he would bear it chearfully, and a thousand times more; but by creatures—And there he stopped.

I said, I would try every method, that either my duty or my influence upon any of them should suggest, before I would put myself into any other protection. And, if nothing else would do, would resign the envied estate; and that I dared to say would.

He was contented, he said, to abide that issue. He should be far from wishing me to embrace any other protection, but, as he had frequently said, in the last necessity. But, dearest creature, said he, catching my hand with ardor, and pressing it to his lips, if the yielding up that estate will do—Resign it;—and be mine—And I will corroborate, with all my soul, your resignation!—

I made many efforts to go; and now it was so dark, that I began to have great apprehensions—I cannot say from his behaviour: Indeed, he has a good deal raised himself in my opinion, by the personal respect, even to reverence, which he paid me during the whole conference: For altho' he flamed out once, upon a supposition that Solmes might succeed, it was upon a supposition that would excuse passion, if any thing could, you know, in a man pretending to love with fervor; altho' it was so levelled, that I could not avoid resenting it.

I fansy, my dear, however, that there would hardly be a guilty person in the world, were each *suspected* or *accused* person to tell his or her own story, and be allowed any degree of credit.

I have written a very long letter. To be so particular as you require, in subjects of conversation, it is impossible to be short. I will add to it only the assurance, That I am, and ever will be,

> *Your affectionate and faithful*
> *friend and servant,*

> *Cl. Harlowe*

Miss Howe
To Miss Clarissa Harlowe

Sat. March 25.

MY mamma argues upon this case in a most discouraging manner, for all such of our sex as look forward for happiness in marriage with the *man of their choice*.

Only, that I know, she has a side-view to her daughter; who, at the same time that she now prefers no one to another, values not the man her mamma most regards, of one farthing; or I should lay it more to heart.

What is there in it, says she, that all this bustle is about? Is it such a mighty matter for a young Lady to give up her inclinations to oblige her friends?

Very well, my mamma, thought I! Now, may you ask this— At Forty, you may—But what would you have said at Eighteen, is the question!

Either, said she, the Lady must be thought to have very violent inclinations (and what nice young creature would have That supposed?) which she *could* not give up; or a very stubborn will, which she *would* not; or, thirdly, have parents she was indifferent about obliging.

You know my mamma now-and-then argues very notably: always very warmly at least. I happen often to differ from her; and we both think so well of our own arguments, that we very seldom are so happy as to convince one another.

I pay it off with thinking, that my mamma has no reason to disclaim her share in her Nancy: And if the matter go off with greater severity on her side than I wish for, then her favourite Hickman fares the worse for it, next day.

I know I am a saucy creature: I know, if I do not *say* so, you will *think* so; so no more of This, just now. What I mention it for, is to tell you, that on this serious occasion, I will omit, if I can, all that passed between us, that had an air of flippancy on my part, or quickness on my mamma's, to let you into the *cool* and the *cogent* of the conversation.

"Look thro' the families, said she, which we both know, where the Gentleman and Lady have been said to marry for Love; which, at the time it is so called, is perhaps no more than a passion begun in folly, or thoughtlessness, and carried on from a spirit of perverseness and opposition [Here we had a parenthetical debate, which I omit;] and see, if they appear to be happier than those whose principal inducement to marry, has been convenience, or to oblige their friends; or even whether they are generally *so* happy: For *convenience* and *duty*, where observed, will afford a *permanent* and even an *increasing* satisfaction, as well at the time, as upon the reflection, which seldom fail to reward themselves: While *Love*, if Love *be* the motive, is an idle passion"—[*Idle in* One Sense *my Mother cannot say; for Love is as busy as a Monkey, and as mischievous as a schoolboy*—] "It is a *fervor*, that, like all other *fervors*, lasts but a little while; a bow over-strained, that soon returns to its natural bent.

As it is founded generally upon mere *notional* excellencies,

Love is a temporary aberration.

which were unknown to the persons themselves, till attributed to either by the other; one, two, or three months, usually sets all right on both sides; and then with opened eyes they think of each other—just as everybody else thought of them before.

The lovers *Imaginaries* [Her own word!] are by that time gone off; Nature and Old habits, painfully dispensed with or concealed, return: Disguises thrown aside, all the moles, freckles, and defects in the minds of *each*, discover themselves; and 'tis well if each do not sink in the opinion of the other, as much below the common standard, as the blinded imagination of both had set them above it. And now, said she, the fond pair, who knew no felicity out of each other's company, are so far from finding the never-ending variety each had proposed in an un-restrained conversation with the other (when they seldom were together; and always parted with something *to say;* or, on recol-lection, when parted, wishing they *had* said); that they are con-tinually on the wing in pursuit of amusements out of themselves; and those, concluded my sage Mamma [Did you think her wis-dom so *very* moderne?], will perhaps be the livelier to each, in which the other has no share."

I told my mamma, that if *you* were to take any rash step, it would be owing to the indiscreet violence of your friends: I was afraid, I said, that these reflections upon the conduct of people in the married state, who might set out with better hopes, were but too well grounded: But that this must be allowed me, that if children weighed not these matters so thoroughly as they ought, neither did parents make those allowances for youth, inclination, and inexperience, which were necessary to be made for themselves at their childrens time of life.

She then touched upon the moral character of Mr. Love-lace; and how reasonable the aversion of your relations is, to a man, who gives himself the liberties he is said to take; and who, indeed, himself, denies not the accusation.

A prudent daughter will not wilfully err, because her par-ents err, if they *were* to err: If she *do*, the world, which blames the parents, will not acquit the child. All that can be said, in extenuation of a daughter's error, arises from a kind consideration, which Miss's letter to Lady Drayton pleads for, to be paid to *her* daughter's youth and inexperience. And will such an admirable young person as Miss Clarissa Harlowe, whose prudence, as we see, qualifies her to be an adviser of persons much older than herself, take shelter under so poor a covert?

And thus, my dear, I set my Mother's arguments before you. And the rather, as I cannot myself tell what to advise you to do!—You know best your own heart; and what That will let you do!

Robin undertakes to deposit This very early, that you may receive it by your first morning airing.

Heaven guide and direct you for the best, is the incessant prayer, of

Your ever-affectionate,

Anna Howe

Miss Clarissa Harlowe To Miss Howe

Sunday Afternoon.

I HAD reason to fear, this morning, that a storm was brewing. Mr. Solmes came home this afternoon from church with my brother. Soon after, Betty brought me up a letter, without saying from whom. It was in a cover, and directed by a hand I never saw before; as if it was supposed, I would not have received and opened it, had I known it came from him. These are the contents.

To Miss Clarissa Harlowe

spelling

Dearest Madam,

I THINK myself a most unhappy man, in that I have never yet been able to pay my respects to you with youre consent, for one halfe hour. I have something to communicate to you that concernes you much, if you be pleased to admitt me to youre speech. Youre honour is concerned in it, and the honour of all youre familly. Itt relates to the designes of one whom you are sed to valew more than he deserves; and to some of his reprobat actions; which I am reddie to give you convincing proofes of the truth of. I may appear to be interested in itt: But neverthelesse, I am reddy to make oathe, that every tittle is true: And you will see what a man you are sed to favour. But I hope not so, for youre owne honour.

Pray, Madam, vouchsafe me a hearing, as you valew your honour and family: Which will oblidge, dearest Miss,

Youre most humble and most faithfule Servant,

Roger Solmes

I waite below for the hope of admittance.

I have no manner of doubt, that this is a poor device, to get this man into my company. I would have sent down a verbal answer; but Betty refused to carry any message, which should prohibit his visiting me. So I was obliged either to see him, or to write to him. I wrote, therefore, an answer, of which I shall send you the rough draught. And now my heart akes for what may follow from it; for I hear a great hurry below.

To Roger Solmes, Esq;

Sir,

WHATEVER you have to communicate to me, which concerns my honour, may as well be done by writing, as by word of mouth. If Mr. Lovelace is any of *my* concern, I know not that, *therefore*, he ought to be *yours:* For the usage I receive on *your* account (I *must* think it so!) is so harsh, that were there not such a man in the world as Mr. *Lovelace,* I would not wish to see Mr. *Solmes,* no, not for one half-hour, in the way he is pleased to be desirous to see me. I never can be in any danger from Mr. Lovelace; and, of consequence, cannot be affected by any of your discoveries, if the proposal I made be accepted. You have been acquainted with it, no doubt. If not, be pleased to let my friends know, that if they will rid *me* of my apprehensions of one gentleman, I will rid them of *theirs* of another: And then, of what consequence to *them,* or to *me,* will it be, whether Mr. Lovelace be a good man, or a bad? And, if to neither of *us,* I see not how it can be of any to *you.* But if *you* do, I have nothing to say to That; and it will be a Christian part, if you will expostulate with him upon the errors you have discovered, and endeavour to make him as good a man, as, no doubt, you are *yourself,* or you would not be so ready to detect and expose *him.*

Excuse me, Sir:—But after my former letter to you, and your ungenerous perseverance; and after this attempt to avail yourself at the expence of another man's character, rather than by your own proper merit, I see not that you can blame any asperity in Her, whom you have so largely contributed to make unhappy.

Cl. Harlowe

Miss Clarissa Harlowe
To Miss Howe

Tuesday, Three o'Clock, March 28.

I HAVE mentioned several times the pertness of Mrs. Betty to me; and now, having a little time upon my hands, I will give you a short dialogue that passed just now between us: It may, perhaps, be a little relief to you from the dull subjects with which I am perpetually teazing you.

As she attended me at dinner, she took notice, That Nature is satisfied with a very little nourishment: And thus she complimentally proved it:—For, Miss, said she, you eat nothing; yet never looked more charmingly in your life.

As to the former part of your speech, Betty, said I, you observe well; and I have often thought, when I have seen how healthy the children of the labouring poor *look*, and *are*, with empty stomachs, and hardly a good meal in a week, that Providence is very kind to its creatures, in this respect, as well as in all others, in making *Much* not necessary to the support of life; when three parts in four of its creatures, if it were, would not know how to obtain it.

That she might not be too proud, I told her, I would observe, that the liveliness or quickness she so happily discovered in herself, was not so much an honour to her, as what she owed to her *Sex*; which, as I had observed in many instances, had great advantages over the other, in all the powers that related to imagination: And hence, Mrs. Betty, you'll take notice, as I have of late had opportunity to do, that your own talent at repartee and smartness, when it has *something to work upon*, displays itself to more advantage, than could well be expected from one whose friends, to speak in your own phrase, could not *let go so fast as you pulled*.

The wench gave me a proof of the truth of my observation, in a manner still more alert than I had expected: If, said she, our sex have so much advantage in *smartness*, it is the less to

be wondered at, that *you*, Miss, who have had such an education, should outdo all the men and women too, that come near
you.

Bless me, Betty, said I, what a proof do you give me of
your wit and your courage at the same time! This is outdoing
yourself. It would make young Ladies less proud, and more
apprehensive, were they generally attended by such smart
servants, and their mouths permitted to be unlocked upon them
as yours has lately been upon me!—But, take away, Mrs. Betty.

Why, Miss, you have eat nothing at all:—I hope you are
not displeased with your dinner for any thing I have said.

No, Mrs. Betty, I am pretty well used to your freedoms
now, you know. But tell me, if you can, Is it resolved that I shall
be carried to my uncle Antony's on Thursday?

I was willing to reward myself for the patience she had
made me exercise, by getting at what intelligence I could from
her.

Why, Miss, seating herself at a little distance (excuse my
sitting down), with the snuff-box tapped very smartly, the lid
opened, and a pinch taken with a dainty finger and thumb, the
other three fingers distendedly bent, and with a fine flourish—
I cannot but say, that it is my opinion, you will certainly go
on Thursday; and this *noless foless*, as I have heard my young
Lady say in French.

Whether I am *willing* or *not willing*, you mean, I suppose,
Mrs. Betty?

You have it, Miss.

Well but, Betty, I have no mind to be turned out of doors
so suddenly. Do you think I could not be permitted to tarry
one week longer?

How can I tell, Miss!

O Mrs. Betty, you can tell a great deal, if *you please*. But
here I am forbid writing to any one of my family; none of it
now will come near *me*; nor will any of it permit me to see *them*:
How shall I do to make my request known, to tarry here a week
or fortnight longer!

Why, Miss, I fansy, if you were to shew a compliable tem-

per, your friends would shew a compliable one too. But would
you expect favours, and grant none?

Smartly put, Betty! But who knows what may be the result
of my being carried to my Uncle Antony's?

Who knows, Miss!—Why any-body will guess what may
be the result.

As how, Betty?

As how! repeated the pert wench, Why, Miss, you will
stand in your own light, as you have hitherto done: And your
parents, as such good parents *ought*, will be obeyed.

What will they do, Betty? They won't kill me? What *will*
they do?

Kill you! No!—But you will not be suffered to stir from
thence, till you have complied with your duty. And *no pen
and ink* will be allowed you, as here; where they are of opinion
you make no good use of it: Nor would it be allowed here, only
as they intend so soon to send you away to your uncle's. Nobody will be permitted to see you, or to correspond with you.
What farther will be done, I can't say; and, if I could, it may
not be proper. But you may prevent it all, by One word: And
I wish you would, Miss. All then would be easy and happy. And,
if I may speak my mind, I see not why one man is not as good
as another: Why, especially, a sober man is not as good as a
rake.

Well, Betty, said I, sighing, all thy impertinence goes for
nothing. But I see I am destined to be a very unhappy creature.

Tuesday Night.

I have deposited my letter to Mr. Lovelace. Threatening
as things look against me, I am much better pleased with myself,
than I was before. I suppose he will be a little out of humour
upon it, however. But as I reserved to myself the liberty of
changing my mind; and as it is easy for him to imagine there
may be reasons for it *within*-doors, which he cannot judge of
without; and I have suggested to him some of them; I should
think it strange, if he acquiesces not, on this occasion, with a

chearfulness, which may shew me, that his last letter is the genuine product of his heart: The first step to reformation, as I conceive, is to subdue sudden gusts of passion, from which frequently the greatest evils arise, and to learn to bear disappointments. If the irascible passions cannot be overcome, what opinion can we have of the person's power over those to which bad habit, joined to *greater* temptation, gives stronger force?

Pray, my dear, be so kind, as to make inquiry by some safe hand, after the disguises Mr. Lovelace assumes at the inn he puts up at in the poor village of Neale, he calls it. If it be the same I take it to be, I never knew it was considerable enough to have a name; nor that it has an inn in it.

As he must be much there, to be so constantly near us, I would be glad to have some account of his behaviour; and what the people think of him. In such a length of time, he must give scandal, or hope of reformation. Pray, my dear, humour me in this inquiry. I have reasons for it, which you shall be acquainted with another time, if the result of the inquiry discover them not.

Miss Clarissa Harlowe To Miss Howe

Wednesday Morning, Nine o'Clock.

I AM just returned from my morning walk, and already have received a Letter from Mr. Lovelace in answer to mine deposited last night. He must have had pen, ink, and paper, with him; for it was written in the coppice; with this circumstance; On one knee, kneeling with the other. Not from reverence to the written-to, however, as you'll find.

But here you will be pleased to read his Letter; which I shall inclose.

To Miss Clarissa Harlowe

Good God!

W HAT is now to become of me!—How shall I support
this disappointment!—No new cause!—On one knee,
kneeling with the other, I write!—My feet benumbed with midnight wanderings thro' the heaviest dews, that ever fell: My
wig and my linen dripping with the hoar-frost dissolving on
them!—Day but just breaking—Sun not risen to exhale—May
it never rise again!—Unless it bring healing and comfort to a
benighted soul!—In proportion to the joy you had inspired
(ever lovely promiser!), in such proportion is my anguish!

And *are things drawing towards a crisis between your
friends and you?*—Is not this a reason for me to expect, the
rather to expect, the promised interview?

Can *I write all that is in my mind,* say you?—Impossible!—
Not the hundredth part of what is in my mind, and in my apprehension, can I write!

O the wavering, the changeable sex!—But can Miss Clarissa
Harlowe—

Forgive me, Madam!—I know not what I write!

—Yet, I must, I do, insist upon your promise—Or that you
will condescend to find better excuses for the failure—Or convince me, that stronger reasons are imposed upon *you*, than
those you offer.—A promise *once* given; upon *deliberation*
given!—the promis-*ed* only can dispense with;—or some very
apparent necessity imposed upon the promis-*er*, which leaves
no power to perform it.

You would sooner choose death than Solmes (How my soul
spurns the competition!) O my beloved creature, what are these
but *words!*—*Whose* words?—Sweet and ever-adorable—
What?—Promise-breaker—must I call you?—How shall I believe
the asseveration (your supposed Duty in the question!)

If, my dearest life! you would prevent my distraction, or,

at least distracted consequences, renew the promised hope!—
My *fate* is indeed upon its crisis.

> *Your ever-adoring, yet almost desponding*

Ivy-Cavern, in the
  Coppice—day but
  just breaking.

> *Lovelace!*

This is the Answer I shall return.

> *Wednesday Morning.*

I AM amazed, Sir, at the freedom of your reproaches. Pressed
and teazed, against convenience and inclination, to give you
a private meeting, am *I* to be thus challenged and upbraided,
and my Sex reflected upon, because I thought it prudent to
change my mind?—A liberty I had reserved to myself, when I
made the *appointment*, as you call it. I wanted not instances
of your impatient spirit to other people: yet may it be happy
for me, that I have this new one; which shews, that you can
as little spare *me*, when I pursue the dictates of my own reason,
as you do *others*, for acting up to theirs. Two motives you must
be governed by in this excess. The one *my easiness;* the other
your own presumption. Since you think you have found out the
first, and have shewn so much of the *last* upon it, I am too much
alarmed, not to wish and desire, that your letter of this day
may conclude all the trouble you had from, or for,

> *Your humble Servant,*

> *Cl. Harlowe*

I believe, my dear, I may promise myself your approbation,
whenever I write or speak with spirit, be it to whom it will.
Indeed, I find but too much reason to exert it, since I have to

deal with people, who measure their conduct to me, not by
what is fit or decent, right or wrong, but by what they think
my temper will bear. I have, till very lately, been praised for
mine; but it has always been by those who never gave me opportunity to return the compliment to themselves: Some people
have acted, as if they thought forbearance on *one side* absolutely
necessary for them and me, to be upon good terms together;
and in this case have ever taken care rather to *owe* that obligation than to *lay* it. You have hinted to me, that resentment is
not natural to my temper, and that therefore it must soon sub-
side: It may be so, with respect to my relations: But not to Mr.
Lovelace, I assure you.

> *Adieu, my beloved friend.*

> Cl. Harlowe

Miss Clarissa Harlowe
To Miss Howe

Friday, March 31.

YOU have taught me what to say to, and what to think of,
Mr. Lovelace. You have, by agreeable anticipation, let
me know how it is probable he will apply to me to be excused.
I will lay every thing before you that shall pass on the occasion,
if he does apply, that I may take your advice, when it can come
in time; and when it cannot, that I may receive your correction,
or approbation, as I may happen to merit either.—Only one
thing must be allowed for me; that whatever course I shall be
permitted or be *forced* to steer, I must be considered as a per
son out of her own direction. Tost to and fro, by the high winds
of passionate controul, and, as I think, unreasonable severity,
I behold the desired Port, the *single state,* which I would fain
steer into; but am kept off by the foaming billows of a brother's

extended
Ship mr.

and sister's envy, and by the raging winds of a supposed invaded
authority; while I see in Lovelace, the Rocks on one hand, and
in Solmes, the Sands on the other; and tremble, lest I should
split upon the former, or strike upon the latter.

But you, my better pilot, what a charming hope do you bid
me aspire to, if things come to extremity!—I will not, as you
caution me, too much depend upon your success with your
mamma, in my favour: For well I know her high notions of
implicit duty in a child.—But yet I will *hope* too;—because
her seasonable protection may save me perhaps from a greater
rashness: And, in This case, she shall direct all my ways: I will
do nothing but by her orders, and by her advice and yours:
Not see anybody: Not write to any-body: Nor shall any living
soul, but by her direction and yours, know where I am. In any
cottage place me, I will never stir out, unless, disguised as your
servant, I am now-and-then permitted an evening-walk with
you: And this private protection to be granted for no longer
time than till my cousin Morden comes; which, as I hope, cannot
be long.

I am afraid I must not venture to take the hint you give
me, to deposit some of my cloaths; altho' I will some of my
linen, as well as papers.

I will tell you why. Betty had for some time been very
curious about my wardrobe, whenever I took out any of my
things before her.

Observing this, I once left my keys in the locks, on taking
one of my garden-airings; and on my return, surprised the creature with her hand upon the keys, as if shutting the door.

She was confounded at my sudden coming back. I took no
notice: But, on her retiring, I found my cloaths were not in the
usual order.

I doubted not, upon this, that her curiosity was an effect
of their orders to her; and being afraid they would abridge me
of my airings, if their suspicions were not obviated, it has ever
since been my custom (among other contrivances), not only to
leave my keys in the locks; but to employ the wench now-and
then, in taking out my cloaths, suit by suit, on pretence of
preventing their being rumpled or creased, and to see that the

flowered silver suit did not tarnish; sometimes declaredly as a wile-away-time, having little else to do.

To this, and to the confidence they have in a spy so diligent, and to their knowing, that I have not one confidante in a family, where, I believe, nevertheless every servant in it loves me; nor have attempted to make one; I suppose, I owe the freedom I enjoy of my airings: And, perhaps (finding I make no movements towards going off), they are the more secure, that I shall at last be prevailed upon to comply with their measures: Since they must think, that, otherwise, they give me provocations enough to take some rash step, in order to free myself from a treatment so disgraceful; and which (God forgive me, if I judge amiss!), I am afraid my brother and sister would not be sorry to drive me to take.

If therefore such a step should become necessary (which I yet hope will not!) I must be contented to go away with the cloaths I shall have on at the time. My custom to be dressed for the day, as soon as breakfast is over, when I have had no houshold-employments to prevent me, will make such a step, if I am forced to take it, less suspected.

What a multitude of contrivances may not young people fall upon, if the mind be not engaged by acts of kindness and condescension! I am not used by my friends, of late, as I always used their servants.

Friday Morning, Eleven o' Clock.

I have already made up my parcel of linen; my heart aked all the time I was employed about it; and still akes, at the thoughts of its being a necessary precaution.

When it comes to your hands, as I hope it safely will, you will be pleased to open it. You will find in it two parcels sealed up; one of which contains the letters you have not yet seen; being those written since I left you; in the other are all the letters, and copies of letters that have passed between you and me, since I was last with you; with some other papers, on subjects so much above me, that I cannot wish them to be seen by anybody whose indulgence I am not so sure of, as I am of yours.

If my judgment ripen with my years, perhaps I may review them.

Mrs. Norton used to say, from her reverend Father, that there was one time of life for _imagination_ and _fancy_ to work in: Then, were a writer to lay by his works till _riper years_ and _experience_ should direct the fire rather to _glow_, than to _flame out_; something between both, might, perhaps, be produced, that would not displease a judicious eye.

In a third division, folded up separately, are all Mr. Lovelace's letters, since he was forbidden this house, and copies of my answers to them. I expect that you will break the seals of this parcel, and when you have perused them all, give me your free opinion of my conduct.

By the way, not a line from that man!—Not one line!—Wednesday I deposited mine. It remained there on Wednesday night. What time it was taken away yesterday I cannot tell: For I did not concern myself about it, till towards night; and then it was not there. No return at ten this day. I suppose he is as much out of humour, as I. With all my heart!

Clarissa Harlowe

Miss Howe
To Miss Clarissa Harlowe

Thursday Night, March 30.

THE fruits of my enquiry after your abominable wretch's behaviour and baseness, at the paltry alehouse, which he calls an inn; prepare to hear.

Wrens and Sparrows are not too ignoble a quarry for this villainous goshawk!—His assiduities; his watchings; his nightly risques; the inclement weather he travels in; must not be all placed to _your_ account. He has opportunities of making every thing light to him of that sort. A sweet pretty girl, I am told:

—Innocent till he went thither—Now!—Ah! poor girl!—who knows what?

But just turned of Seventeen!—His friend and brother Rake; a man of humour and intrigue, as I am told, to share the social bottle with. And sometimes another disguised Rake or two. No sorrow comes near their hearts. Be not disturbed, my dear, at his *hoarsenesses*. His pretty Betsey, his Rose-bud, as the vile wretch calls her, can *hear* all he says.

He is very fond of her. They say she is innocent even yet! —Her father, her grandmother, believe her to be so. He is to fortune her out to a young lover!—Ah! the poor young lover! —Ah! the poor simple girl!

Mr. Hickman tells me, that he heard in town, that he used to be often at Plays, and at the Opera, with women; and every time with a different one!—Ah! my sweet friend!—But I hope he is nothing to you, if all this were truth—But this intelligence, in relation to this poor girl, will do his business, if you had been ever so good friends before.

A vile wretch! Cannot such purity in pursuit, in view, restrain him? Yet I wish I may be able to snatch the poor young creature out of his villainous paws. I have laid a scheme to do so; if *indeed* she be hitherto innocent and heart-free.

He appears to the people as a military man, in disguise, secreting himself on account of a duel fought in town; the adversary's life in suspense. They believe he is a great man. His friend passes for an inferior officer; upon a foot of freedom with him. He, accompanied by a third man, who is a sort of subordinate companion to the second. The wretch himself with but one servant. O my dear! How pleasantly can these devils, as I must call them, pass their time, while our gentle bosoms heave with pity for their supposed sufferings for us!

I am just now informed, that, at my desire, I shall see this girl, and her father: I will sift them thoroughly. I shall soon find out such a simple thing as This, if he has not corrupted her already—And if he has, I shall soon find that out too.—If more Art than Nature appears in either her or her father, I shall give them both up—But, depend upon it, the girl's undone.

He is said to be fond of her.—He places her at the upper

end of his table—He sets her a-prattling.—He keeps his friend at a distance from her.—She prates away.—He admires for nature all she says.—Once was heard to call her charming little creature!—An hundred has he called so no doubt.—He puts her upon singing.—He praises her wild note.—O my dear, the girl's undone!—must be undone!—The man, you know, is Lovelace. Let 'em bring Wyerley to you, if they will have you married—Any-body but Solmes and Lovelace be yours!—So advises

Your

Anna Howe

My dearest friend, consider this alehouse as his garrison. Him as an enemy: His Brother-rakes as his assistants and abetters: Would not your brother, would not your uncles, tremble, if they knew how near them, as they pass to and fro?—I am told, he is resolved you shall not be carried to your uncle Antony's.—What can you do, *with* or *without* such an enterprizing—

Fill up the blank I leave.—I cannot find a word bad enough.

Miss Clarissa Harlowe To Miss Howe

Friday, Three o' Clock.

YOU incense, alarm, and terrify me, at the same time! Hasten, my dearest friend, hasten to me, what further intelligence you can gather about this vilest of men!

Fine hopes of such a wretch's reformation!—I would not, my dear, for the world, have any thing to say—But I need not make resolutions.—I have not opened, nor will I open, his letter.—A sycophant creature!—With his hoarsenesses—got, perhaps, by a midnight revel, singing to his wild-note singer.—And only increased in the coppice!

To be already on a foot!—In his esteem, I mean, my dear.—
For myself, I despise him.—I hate myself almost for writing so
much about *him*, and of such a simpleton as *This sweet pretty
girl:* But no-thing can be either *sweet* or *pretty*, that is not modest, that is not virtuous.

This vile Joseph Leman had given a hint to Betty, and she
to me, as if Lovelace would be found out to be a very bad man,
at a place where he had been lately seen in disguise. But he
would see further, he said, before he told her more; and she
promised secrecy, in hope to get at further intelligence. I thought
it could be no harm, to get you to inform yourself, and me, of
what could be gathered. And now I see, his enemies are but too
well warranted in their reports of him: And, if the ruin of this
poor young creature is his aim, and if he had not known her,
but for his visits to Harlowe-place, I shall have reason to be
doubly concerned for her; and doubly incensed against so vile
a man. I think I hate him worse than I do Solmes himself. But
I will not add one other word about him, after I have wished
to know, as soon as possible, what further occurs from your
inquiry;—because I shall not open his letter till then; and because then, if it come out, as I dare say it will, I'll directly put the
letter unopened into the place I took it from, and never trouble
myself more about him. Adieu, my dearest friend.

Cl. Harlowe

Miss Howe
To Miss Clarissa Harlowe

Friday Noon, March 31.

J USTICE obliges me to forward This after my last, on the
wings of the wind, as I may say.—I really believe the man is
innocent. Of this *one* accusation, I think, he must be acquitted;
and I am sorry I was so forward in dispatching away my intelligence by halves.

I have seen the girl. She is really a very pretty, a very neat, and, what is still a greater beauty, a very innocent young creature. He who could have ruined such an undesigning home-bred, must have been indeed infernally wicked. Her father is an honest simple man; intirely satisfied with his child, and with her new acquaintance.

I am almost afraid for your heart, when I tell you, that I find, now I have got to the bottom of this inquiry, something noble come out in this Lovelace's favour.

The girl is to be married next week; and This promoted and brought about by him. He is resolved, her father says, to make one couple happy, and wishes he could make more so [There's for you, my dear!] And having taken a liking also to the young fellow whom she professes to love, he has given her an hundred pounds: The grandmother actually has it in her hands, to answer to the like sum, given to the youth by one of his own relations.

They were desirous, the poor man says, when they first came, of appearing beneath themselves; but now he knows the one (but mentioned it in confidence) to be Colonel Barrow, the other Captain Sloane. The Colonel he owns, was at first very *sweet upon his girl:* But upon her grandmother's begging of him to spare her innocence, he vowed, that he never would offer any thing but good counsel to her; and had kept to his word: And the pretty fool acknowleged, that she never could have been better instructed by the minister himself from the *Bible-Book!*

But what, my dear, will become of us now?—Lovelace not only reformed, but turned preacher!—What will become of us now?—Why, my sweet friend, your *generosity* is now engaged in his favour!—Fie, upon this *Generosity!* I think in my heart, that it does as much mischief to the noble-minded, as *Love* to the ignobler.—What before was only a *conditional liking*, I am now afraid will turn to *liking unconditional.*

Anna Howe

Miss Clarissa Harlowe
To Miss Howe

Saturday, April 1.

HASTY censurers do indeed subject themselves to the charge of variableness and inconsistency in judgment: And so they ought; for, if you, even you, were so loth to own a mistake, as in the instance before us, you pretend to say you were, I believe I should not have loved you so well as I really do love you. Nor could you, my dear, have so frankly thrown the reflection I hint at, upon yourself, had you not had one of the most ingenuous minds that ever woman boasted.

Mr. Lovelace has faults enow to deserve very severe censure, altho' he be not guilty of this. If I were upon such terms with him, as he would wish me to be, I should give him a hint, that this treacherous Joseph Leman cannot be so much his friend, as perhaps he thinks him. If he were, he would not have been so ready to report to his disadvantage (and to Betty Barnes too) this slight affair of the pretty Rustic. Joseph has engaged Betty to secrecy; promising to let her, and her young master too, know more, when he knows the whole of the matter: And this hinders her from mentioning it, as she is nevertheless agog to do, to my sister or brother. And then she does not choose to disoblige Joseph; for altho' she pretends to look above him, she listens, I believe, to some love stories he tells her. Women having it not in their power to *begin* a courtship, some of them very frequently, I believe, lend an *ear* where their *hearts* incline not.

I have another letter from Mr. Lovelace. He is extremely apprehensive of the meeting I am to have with Mr. Solmes tomorrow. He says, "That the airs that wretch gives himself on the occasion, add to his concern; and it is with infinite difficulty that he prevails upon himself not to make him a visit, to let him know what he may expect, if compulsion be used towards me in his favour. He assures me, That Solmes has actually talked with tradesmen of new equipages, and names the people in town, with whom he has treated: That he has even" (Was there ever such a horrid wretch!) "allotted This and That apartment in his house, for a nursery, and other offices."

I have deposited a letter for Mr. Lovelace; in which "I charge him to avoid any rash step, any visit to Mr. Solmes, which may be followed by acts of violence as he would not disoblige me for ever."

I re-assure him, "That I will sooner die than be that man's wife."

Your

Clarissa Harlowe

Miss Clarissa Harlowe To Miss Howe

Tuesday Morning, Six o' clock.

THE day is come!—I wish it were happily over. I have had a wretched night. Hardly a wink have I slept, ruminating upon the approaching interview. The very distance of time which they consented to, has added solemnity to the meeting, which otherwise it would not have had.

A thoughtful mind is not a blessing to be coveted, unless it had such a happy vivacity with it, as yours: A vivacity, which enables a person to enjoy the *present*, without being over-anxious about the *future*.

Tuesday Evening; and continued thro' the Night.

WELL, my dear, I am alive, and here! But how long I shall be either here, or alive, I cannot say!—I have a vast deal to write; and perhaps shall have little time for it. Nevertheless, I must tell you how the saucy Betty again fluttered me, when she came up with this Solmes's message; altho', as you will remember from my last, I was in a way before, that wanted no additional surprizes.

Miss! Miss! Miss! cried she, as fast as she could speak, with her arms spread abroad, and all her fingers distended, and held up, will you be pleased to walk down into your own parlour? —There is every-body, I'll assure you, in full *congregation!*— And there is Mr. Solmes, as fine as a Lord, with a charming white peruke, fine laced shirt and ruffles, coat trimmed with silver, and a waistcoat standing on end with lace!—Quite handsome, believe me!—You never saw such an alteration!—Ah! Miss, shaking her head, 'tis pity you have said so much against him!—But you know how to come off, for all that!—I hope it will not be too late!—

Impertinence! said I—Wert thou bid to come up in this fluttering way?—And I took up my fan, and fanned myself.

Bless me! said she, how soon these fine young Ladies will be put into *flusterations!*—I meant not either to offend or frighten you, I am sure.—

Every-body there, do you say?—Who do you call every-body?—

Why, Miss, holding out her left palm opened, and with a flourish, and a saucy leer, patting it with the forefinger of the other at every mentioned person, There is your papa!—There is your mamma!—There is your uncle Harlowe!—There is your uncle Antony!—Your aunt Hervey!—*My* young Lady!—And my young master!—And Mr. Solmes, with the air of a great courtier, standing up, because he named you:—Mrs. Betty, said he [Then the ape of a wench bowed, and scraped, as awkwardly as I suppose the person she endeavoured to imitate] Pray give my humble service to Miss, and tell her, I wait her commands.

Was not this a wicked wench?—I trembled so, I could hardly stand. I was spiteful enough to say, that her young mistress, I supposed, bid her put on these airs, to frighten me out of a capacity of behaving so calmly, as should procure me my uncle's compassion.

There are two doors to *my* parlour, as I used to call it. As I entered at one, my friends hurried out at the other. I saw just the gown of my sister, the last who slid away. My uncle Antony went out with them; but he staid not long, as you shall hear:

And they all remained in the next parlour, a wainscot-partition only parting the two.

Mr. Solmes approached me as soon as I entered, cringing to the ground; a visible confusion in every feature of his face. After half a dozen choaked-up Madams,—He was very sorry— he was very much concerned—It was his misfortune—And there he stopped, being unable presently to complete a sentence.

This gave me a little more presence of mind. Cowardice in a foe begets courage in one's self:—I see that plainly now;—Yet perhaps, at bottom, the new-made bravo is a greater coward than the other.

I turned from him, and seated myself in one of the fireside chairs, fanning myself. I have since recollected, that I must have looked very saucily. Could I have had any *thoughts* of the man, I should have despised myself for it. But what can be said in the case of an aversion so perfectly sincere?

He hemmed five or six times, as I had done above; and these produced a sentence—That I could not but see his confusion. This sentence produced two or three more. I believe my aunt was his tutoress: For it was his awe, his reverence for so superlative a Lady—[I assure you]—And he hoped—he hoped—Three times he hoped, before he told me what—that I was too generous [Generosity, he said, was my character], to despise him for such—for such—*true* tokens of his love.—

I do indeed see you under some confusion, Sir; and this gives me hope, that altho' I have been compelled, as I may call it, to this interview, it may be attended with happier effects than I had apprehended from it.

He had hemmed himself into more courage.

You could not, Madam, imagine any creature so blind to your merits, and so little attracted by them, as easily to forego the interest and approbation he was honoured with by your worthy family, while he had any hope given him, that one day he might, by his perseverance and zeal, expect your favour.

I am but too much aware, Sir, that it is upon the interest and approbation you mention, that you build such hope. It is impossible, otherwise, that a man, who has any regard for his *own* happiness, would persevere against such declarations as I have made, and think myself obliged to make, in justice to you, as well as to myself.

He had seen many instances, he told me, and had heard of more, where Ladies had seemed as averse, and yet had been induced, some by motives of compassion; others by persuasion of friends, to change their minds; and had been very happy afterwards: And he hoped this might be the case here.

I have no notion, Sir, of compliment, in an article of such importance as this: Yet am I sorry to be obliged to speak my mind so plainly, as I am going to do.—Know then, that I have invincible objections, Sir, to your address. I have declared them with an earnestness that I believe is without example: And why? —Because I believe it is without example, that any young creature, circumstanced as I am, was ever treated as I have been treated on your account.

It is hoped, Madam, that your consent may, in time, be obtained: *That* is the hope; and I shall be a miserable man if it cannot.

Better, Sir, give me leave to say, you were miserable by yourself, than that you should make two so.

You may have heard, Madam, things to my disadvantage. No man is without enemies. Be pleased to let me know *what* you have heard, and I will either own my faults, and amend; or I will convince you, that I am basely *bespattered:* And once I understand you overheard something that I should say, that gave you offence:—Unguardedly, perhaps; but nothing but what shewed my value, and that I would persist so long as I could have hope.

I have indeed heard many things to your disadvantage:— And I was far from being pleased with what I overheard fall from your lips: But as you were not anything to me, and never could be, it was not for me to be concerned about the one or the other.

I am sorry, Madam, to hear this. I am sure you should not tell me of any fault, that I would be unwilling to correct in myself.

Then, Sir, correct *this* fault:—Do not wish to have a young creature compelled in the most material article of her life, for the sake of motives she despises; and in behalf of a person she cannot value: One that has, in her own right, sufficient to set her above all offers, and a spirit that craves no more than what it *has*, to make itself easy and happy.

I don't see, Madam, how you would be happy, if I were to discontinue my address: For—

That is nothing to you, Sir, interrupted I: Do you but withdraw your pretensions: And if it be thought fit to start up another man for my punishment, the blame will not lie at your door. You will be intitled to my thanks; and most heartily will I thank you.

He paused, and seemed a little at a loss: And I was going to give him still stronger and more personal instances of my plaindealing; when in came my uncle Antony!

So, niece, so!—sitting in state like a Queen, giving audience! —*haughty* audience!—Mr. Solmes, why stand you thus humbly? —Why this distance, man? I hope to see you upon a more intimate footing before we part.

I arose, as soon as he entered—and approached him with a bent knee: Let me, Sir, reverence my uncle, whom I have not for so long time seen!—Let me, Sir, bespeak your favour and compassion!

You'll have the favour of every-body, niece, when you know how to deserve it.

If ever I deserved it, I deserve it now.—I have been hardly used—I have made proposals that ought to have been accepted; and such as would not have been *asked* of me. What have I done, that I must be banished and confined thus disgracefully? That I must be allowed to have no free-will, in an article that concerns my present and future happiness?—

Miss Clary, replied my uncle, you have had your will in every-thing till now; and this makes your parents wills sit so heavy upon you.

My will, Sir! Be pleased to allow me to ask, What was my will till now, but my father's will, and yours and my uncle Harlowe's will?—Has it not been my pride to obey and oblige? —I never asked a favour, that I did not first sit down and consider, if it were fit to be granted. And now, to shew my obedi-

ence, have I not offered to live single? Have I not offered to
divest myself of my grandfather's bounty, and to cast myself
upon my papa's; to be withdrawn, whenever I disoblige him?
Why, dear good Sir, am I to be made unhappy in a point so
concerning to my happiness?

Your grandfather's estate is not wished from you. You are
not desired to live a single life. You know *our* motives, and we
guess at *yours*. And let me tell you, well as we love you, we
would much sooner choose to follow you to the grave, than
that *yours* should take place. *&* THEY WILL

I will engage never to marry any man, without my father's
consent, and yours, Sir, and every-body's. Did I ever give you
cause to doubt my word?—And here I will take the solemnest
oath that can be offered me—

That is the matrimonial one, interrupted he, with a big
voice—and to this gentleman.—It shall, it shall, cousin Clary!
—And the more you oppose it, the worse it shall be for you.

This, and before the man, who seemed to assume courage
upon it, highly provoked me.

Then, Sir, you shall sooner follow me to the grave *indeed*.
—I will undergo the cruellest death: I will even consent to enter
into the awful vault of my ancestors, and to have that bricked
up upon me, than consent to be miserable for life.—And, Mr.
Solmes, (turning to him) take notice of what I say: *This*, or *any*
death, I will sooner undergo (That will soon be over), than be
yours, and for *ever* unhappy!

My uncle was in a terrible rage upon this: He took Mr.
Solmes by the hand, shocked as the man seemed to be, and drew
him to the window—Don't be surprised, Mr. Solmes, don't be
concerned at *this*. We know, and rapped out a sad oath, what
women will say: The wind is not more boisterous, nor more
changeable: And again he swore to That! If you think it worth
your while to wait for such an ungrateful girl as This, I'll engage
she'll *veer about*; I'll engage she *shall*: And a third time violently
swore to it.

Then coming up to me (who had thrown myself, very much
disordered by my vehemence, into the contrary window), as if
he would have beat me; his face violently working, his hands

clenched, and his teeth set—Yes, yes, yes, hissed the poor gentleman, you shall, you shall, you shall, cousin Clary, be Mr.
Solmes's; we will see that you shall; and this in one week at
farthest.—And then a fourth time he confirmed it. Poor gentleman, how he swore!

I am sorry, Sir, said I, to see you in such a passion. All This,
I am but too sensible, is owing to my brother's instigation; who
would not himself give the instance of duty that is exacted from
me. It is best for me to withdraw. I shall but provoke you farther, I fear: For though I would gladly obey you, if I could, yet
This is a point determined with me; and I cannot so much as
wish to get it over.

I was going out at the door I came in at; the gentlemen
looking upon one another, as if referring to each other what to
do, or whether to engage my stay, or suffer me to go: And
who should I meet at the door but my brother, who had heard
all that had passed.

Judge my surprize, when he bolted upon me so unexpectedly, and taking my hand, which he grasped with violence,
Return, pretty Miss, said he; return, if you please!—You shall
not yet be *bricked up!*—Your *instigating* brother shall save you
from That!—O thou fallen angel, said he, peering up to my
downcast face,—such a sweetness *here!*—and such an obstinacy
there, tapping my neck!—O thou true woman!—tho' so young
—But you shall not have your Rake: Remember that; in a
loud whisper, as if he would be decently indecent before the
man!—You shall be redeemed, and this worthy gentleman,
raising his voice, will be so good as to redeem you from ruin—
and hereafter you will bless him, or have reason to bless him,
for his *condescension;* that was the brutal brother's word!

He had led me up to meet Mr. Solmes, whose hand he took,
as he held mine. Here, Sir, said he, take the rebel daughter's
hand: I give it you now; She shall confirm the gift in a week's
time; or will have neither father, mother, nor uncles, to boast of.

And how now, Sir—What right have You to dispose of my
hand?—If you govern every-body else, you shall not govern
me; especially in a point so immediately relative to myself, and
in which you neither have, nor ever shall have, any thing to do.

I would have broke from him, but he held my hand too fast.

Let me go, Sir!—Why am I thus treated?—You *design*, I doubt not, with your unmanly gripings, to hurt me, as you do: But again I say, Wherefore is it that I am thus treated by You?

He tossed my hand from him with a whirl, that pained my very shoulder. I wept, and held my other hand to the part.

Mr. Solmes said, He would sooner give up all his hopes of me, than that I should be used unkindly.

But, I said, I am obliged to your intention, Mr. Solmes, to interpose to save me from my brother's violence: But I cannot wish to owe an obligation to a man whose ungenerous perseverance is the occasion, or at least the pretence, of *that* violence, and of all my disgraceful sufferings.

How generous in you, Mr. Solmes, said my brother to him, to interpose in behalf of such an immoveable spirit! I beg of you to persist!—For all our family's sake, and for *her* sake too, if you love her, persist!—Let us save her, if possible, from ruining herself. Look at her person! Think of her fine qualities!—All the world confesses them, and we all gloried in her till now: She is worth saving! And after two or three more struggles, she will be yours, and, take my word for it, will reward your patience! —Talk not therefore, of giving up your hopes, for a little whining folly. She has entered upon a parade, which she knows not how to quit with a *female* grace. You have only her pride and her obstinacy to encounter: And, depend upon it, you will be as happy a man in a fortnight, as a married man *can* be.

Mr. Solmes, said I, if you have any regard for your own happiness [*Mine* is out of the question: You have not generosity enough to make *That* any part of your scheme] prosecute no further your *address*. It is but *just* to tell you, that I could not bring my heart to think of you, without the utmost disapprobation, *before* I was used as I have been:—And can you think I am such a slave, such a *poor* slave, as to be brought to change my mind by the violent usage I have met with?

And you, Sir, turning to my brother, if you think that *meekness* always indicates *tameness*; and that there is no *magnanimity* without *bluster*, own yourself mistaken for once: For you shall have reason to judge from henceforth, that a generous mind is not to be forced; and that—He lifted up his hands and eyes: No more, said the imperious wretch, I charge you!—Then turning to my uncle, Do you hear, Sir? This is your once faultless niece! This is your favourite!

My uncle came up to me, looking up to my face, and down to my feet: And is it possible This can be *you*? All this violence from *you*, Miss Clary?

Yes, it is possible, Sir—And, I will presume to say, this vehemence on my side, is but the natural consequence of the usage I have met with, and the rudeness I am treated with, even in your presence, by a brother, who has no more right to controul me, than I have to controul him.

This usage, cousin Clary, was not till all other means were tried with you.

Tried! to what end, Sir—Do I contend for anything more than a mere negative? You *may*, Sir (turning to Mr. Solmes) *possibly* you may, be induced the *rather* to persevere thus ungenerously, as the usage, I have met with for your sake, and what you have now seen offered to me by my brother, will shew you what I *can* bear, were my evil destiny ever to make me yours!

Lord, Madam, cried Solmes, all this time distorted into twenty different attitudes, as my brother and my uncle were blessing themselves, and speaking only to each other by their eyes, and by their working features; Lord, Madam, what a construction is This!

A fair construction, Sir, interrupted I: For he that can see a person he pretends to value, thus treated, and approve of it, must be capable of treating her thus himself. And that you *do* approve of it, is evident by your declared perseverance, when you know I am confined, banished, and insulted, in order to make me consent to be what I never *can be.*—And this, let me tell you, as I have often told others, not from motives of obstinacy, but *aversion.*

Excuse me, Sir, turning to my uncle!—To you, as to my *papa's* brother, I owe duty. I beg *your* pardon, that I cannot obey you: But as for my *brother*; he is *but* my brother; he shall not constrain me. And, turning to my brother, Knit your brows,

Sir, and frown as you will, I will ask you, Would *you*, in my case, make the sacrifices I am willing to make, to obtain every one's favour? If *not*, what right have you to treat me thus? and to procure me to be treated as I have been, for so long past?

I had put myself by this time into great disorder. They were silent, and seemed to want to talk to one another by their looks, walking about in violent disorders too, between whiles. — I sat down fanning myself (as it happened, against the glass) and I could perceive my colour go and come; and being sick to the very heart, and apprehensive of fainting, I rung. Betty came in. I called for a glass of water, and drank it: — But no-body minded me — I heard my brother pronounce the words, Art! d—d Art! to Solmes; which, I suppose, kept *him* back together with the apprehension, that he would not be welcome, — Else I could see the man was more affected than my brother. And I, still fearing I should faint, rising, took hold of Betty's arm, staggering with extreme disorder, yet courtesying to my uncle, Let me hold by you, Betty, said I: Let me withdraw.

Miss Clarissa Harlowe
To Miss Howe

Wednesday, Eleven o' Clock, April 5.

I MUST write as I have opportunity; making use of my concealed stores: For my pens and ink (all of each, that they could find) are taken from me; as I shall tell you more particularly by-and-by.

About an hour ago, I deposited my long letter to you; as also, in the usual place, a billet to Mr. Lovelace, lest his impatience should put him upon some rashness; signifying, in four lines, "That the interview was over; and that I hoped my steady refusal of Mr. Solmes would discourage any further applications to me in his favour."

Altho' I was unable to deposit my letter to you sooner; yet

I hope you will have it in such good time, as that you will be able to send me an answer to it this night, or in the morning early; which, if ever so short, will inform me, whether I may depend upon your mamma's indulgence, or not. This it behoves me to know as soon as possible; for they are resolved to hurry me away on Saturday next, at farthest; perhaps to-morrow.

I will now inform you of all that happened previous to their taking away my pen and ink, as well as of the manner in which that act of violence, as I may call it, was committed; and this as briefly as I can.

My aunt, (who with Mr. Solmes, and my two uncles) lives here, I think, came up to me, and said, she would fain have me hear what Mr. Solmes had to say of Mr. Lovelace—Only that I might be apprised of some things, that would convince me what a vile man he is, and what a wretched husband he must make. I might give them what degree of credit I pleased.—But it might be of use to me, were it but to question Mr. Lovelace indirectly upon some of them, that related to *myself*.

I was indifferent, I said, about what he could say of me, as I was sure it could not be to my disadvantage; and as *he* had no reason to impute to me the forwardness which my unkind friends had so causlessly taxed me with.

She said, That he gave himself high airs on account of his family; and spoke as despicably of ours, as if an alliance with *us* were beneath him.

I replied, That he was a very unworthy man, if it were true, to speak slightingly of a family, which was as good as his own, 'bating that it was not allied to the peerage: That the dignity itself, I thought, conveyed more shame than honour to descendents, who had not merit to adorn, as well as to be adorned by it: That my brother's absurd pride, indeed, which made him every-where declare, he would never marry but to *quality*, gave a disgraceful preference against ours: But that were I to be assured, that Mr. Lovelace was capable of so mean a pride, as to insult us, or value himself, on such an accidental advantage, I should think as despicably of his sense, as every-body else did of his morals.

She insisted upon it, that he *had* taken such liberties; and

offered to give some instances, which, she said, would surprise
me.

I answered, That were it ever so certain, that Mr. Lovelace
had taken such liberties, it would be but common justice (so
much hated as he was by all our family, and so much inveighed
against in all companies by them) to inquire into the provocation he had to say what was imputed to him. Upon the whole,
Madam, said I, can you say, that the inveteracy lies not as much
on *our* side, as on *his?* Can *he* say anything of *us* more disrespect-
ful than *we* say of *him?*—And as to the suggestion, so often
repeated, that he would make a bad husband, is it possible for
him to use a wife worse than I am used; particularly by my brother and sister?

Wednesday, Four o' Clock in the Afternoon.

I AM just returned from depositing the letter I so lately finished, and such of Mr. Lovelace's letters as I had not sent you.
My long letter I found remaining there.—So you'll have both
together.

I found, in the usual place, another letter from this diligent
man: And by its contents, a confirmation, that nothing passes
in this house, but he knows it; and that, almost as soon as it
passes. For this letter must have been written before he could
have received my billet; and deposited, I suppose, when that was
taken away; yet, he compliments me in it, upon asserting myself, as he calls it, on that occasion, to my uncles and to Mr.
Solmes.

"He assures me, however, that they are more and more
determined to subdue me.

"He sends me the compliments of his family; and acquaints
me with their earnest desire to see me amongst them. Most
vehemently does he press for my quitting This house, while it
is in my power to get away: And again craves leave to order
his uncle's chariot-and-six to attend my orders at the stile leading
to the coppice, adjoining to the paddock.

As to the disgrace a person of my character may be apprehensive of upon quitting my Father's house, he observes, too truly, I doubt, "That the treatment I meet with, is in every one's mouth: Yet, he says, that the public voice is in my favour: My friends themselves, he says, *expect* that I will do myself, what he calls, this justice; Why else do they confine me? He urges, that, thus treated, the independence I have a right to, will be my sufficient excuse, going but from their house to my own, if I choose that measure; or, in order to take possession of my own, if I do not: That all the disgrace I *can* receive, they have already given me: That his concern and his family's concern, *in* my honour, will be equal to my own, if he may be so happy ever to call me his.

"But he repeats, that, in all events, he will oppose my being carried to my uncle's; being well assured, that I shall be lost to him for ever, if once I enter into that house." He tells me, "That my brother and sister, and Mr. Solmes, design to be there to receive me: That my father and mother will not come near me, till the ceremony is actually over: And that then they will appear, in order to try to reconcile me to my odious husband, by urging upon me the obligations I shall be supposed to be under, from a double duty."

How, my dear, am I driven between both!—This last intimation is but a too probable one. All the steps they take, seem to tend to this! And, indeed, they have declared almost as much.

What a dangerous enterprizer, however, is this man!

"He begs a few lines from me, by way of answer to this letter, either This evening, or to-morrow morning. If he be not so favoured, he shall conclude, from what he knows of their fixed determination, that I shall be under a closer restraint than before: And he shall be obliged to take his measures according to that presumption."

You will see by this abstract, as well as by his letter preceding This (for both run in the same strain), how strangely forward the difficulty of my situation has brought him in his declarations and proposals; and in his threatenings too: Which, but for That, I would not take from him.

Something, however, I must speedily resolve upon, or it will be out of my power to help myself.

Trapped

Miss Clarissa Harlowe
To Miss Howe

Thursday, April 6.

ALL my consolation is, as I have frequently said, that I have not, by my own inadvertence or folly, brought myself into this sad situation. If I *had*, I should not have dared to look up to any-body with the expectation of protection or assistance, nor to you, for excuse of the trouble I give you. But, nevertheless we should not be angry at a person's not doing that for ourselves, or for our friend, which thinks she ought *not* to do; and which she has it in her option either to *do*, or to *let alone*. Much less have you a right to be displeased with so prudent a mother, for not engaging herself so warmly in my favour, as you wished she would. If my own aunt can give me up, and that against her judgment, as I may presume to say; and if my father, and mother, and uncles, who onced loved me so well, can join so strenuously against me; can *I* expect, or ought *you*, the protection of your mamma, in *opposition* to them?

Indeed, my dearest Love [Permit me to be *very* serious], I am afraid I am singled out, either for my own faults, or for the faults of my family, or for the faults of both, to be a very unhappy creature!—*signally* unhappy! For see you not how irresistibly the waves of affliction come tumbling down upon me?

We have been till within these few weeks, every-one of us, too happy. No crosses, no vexations, but what we gave ourselves from the *pamperdness*, as I may call it, of our own wills. Surrounded by our heaps and stores, hoarded up as fast as acquired, we have seemed to think ourselves out of the reach of the bolts of adverse fate.

Your partial love will be ready to acquit me of capital and intentional faults:—But oh, my dear! my calamities have humbled me enough, to make me turn my gaudy eye inward; to make me look into myself!—And what have I discovered there?—

116

Why, my dear friend, more *secret* pride and vanity, than I could have thought had lain in my unexamined heart.

If *I* am to be singled out to be the *punisher* of myself, and family, who so lately was the *pride* of it, pray for me, my dear, that I may not be left wholly to myself; and that I may be enabled to support my character, so as to be *justly* acquitted of wilful and premeditated faults. The will of Providence be resigned to in the rest: As *that* leads, let me patiently, and unrepiningly, follow!—I shall not live always!—May but my *closing* scene be happy!—

But I will not oppress you, my dearest friend, with further reflections of this sort. I will take them all into myself. Surely I have a mind, that has room for them. My afflictions are too sharp to last long. The crisis is at hand. Happier times you bid me hope for. I *will* hope!

But yet, I cannot but be impatient at times, to find myself thus driven, and my character so depreciated and sunk, that were all the *future* to be happy, I should be ashamed to shew my face in public, or to look up.

But let me stop: Let me reflect!—Are not these suggestions the suggestions of the *secret* pride I have been censuring? Then, *already* so impatient! But this moment so resigned! so much better disposed for reflection!—Yet 'tis hard, 'tis very hard, to subdue an embittered spirit!—In the instant of its trial too!—I will lay down a pen I am so little able to govern.—And I will try to subdue an impatience, which (if my afflictions are sent me for corrective ends) may otherwise lead me into still more punishable errors!—

I will return to a subject, which I cannot fly from for ten minutes together—called upon especially as I am, by your three alternatives stated in the conclusion of your last.

As to the first; to wit, *Your advice for me to escape to London*—Let me tell you, that that other hint or proposal which accompanies it, perfectly frightens me—Surely, my dear [happy as you are, and indulgently treated as your mamma treats you], you cannot mean what you propose! What a wretch must I be, if I could, for *one* moment only, lend an ear to such a proposal as This!—*I*, to be the occasion of making such a mother's (perhaps *shortened*) life unhappy to the last hour of it!—How must such an enterprize [the rashness *public*, the motives, were they excuseable, *private*] debase you!—But I will not dwell upon the subject.—For your *own* sake I will not.

As to your second alternative, *To put myself into the protection of Lord M. and of the Ladies of that family*, I own to you (as I believe I have owned before), that altho' to do This would be the same thing in the eye of the world, as putting myself into Mr. Lovelace's protection, yet, I think, I would do it rather than be Mr. Solmes's wife, if there were evidently no other way to avoid being so.

Mr. Lovelace, you have seen, proposes to contrive a way to put me into possession of my own house; and he tells me, that he will soon fill it with the Ladies of his family, as my visitors;—upon my invitation, however, to them.—A very inconsiderate proposal I think it to be, and upon which I cannot explain myself to him. What an exertion of independency does it chalk out for me!—For how could I gain possession, but either by legal litigation, which, were I *inclined* to have recourse to it [as I never can be], must take up time; or by forcibly turning out the persons whom my papa has placed there, to look after the gardens, the house, and the furniture—persons intirely attached to himself, and who, as I know, have been lately instructed by my brother?

Your third alternative, *To meet and marry Mr. Lovelace directly:* a man with whose morals I am far from being satisfied —A step, that could not be taken with the least hope of ever obtaining pardon from or reconciliation with, any of my friends; —and against which a thousand objections rise in my mind— That is not to be thought of.

What appears to me upon the fullest deliberation, the most eligible, if I *must* be thus driven, is the escaping to London.— But I would forfeit all my hopes of happiness in this life, rather than you should go off with me, as you rashly propose. If I could get safely thither, and be private, methinks I might remain absolutely independent of Mr. Lovelace, and at liberty, either to make proposals to my friends, or, should they renounce me (and I had no other or better way) to make terms with him;

supposing my cousin Morden, on his arrival, were to join with them. But they would, perhaps, *then* indulge me in my choice of a single life, on giving him up: The renewing to them this offer, when at my own liberty, will at least convince them, that I was in earnest when I made it first: And, upon my word, I *would* stand to it, dear as you seem to think, when you are disposed to railly me, it would cost me, *to* stand to it.

If, my dear, you can procure a conveyance for us *both*, you can, perhaps, procure one for me *singly*; But can it be done without embroiling *yourself* with your mamma, or *her* with our family?—Be it coach, chariot, chaise, waggon, or horse, I matter not, provided You appear not in it. Only, in case it be one of the two latter, I believe I must desire you to get me an ordinary gown and coat, or habit, of some servant; having no concert with any of our own: The more ordinary the better. They may be thrust into the wood-house; where I can put them on; and then slide down from the bank, that separates the wood-yard from the green lane.

But, alas! my dear, this, even *this* alternative, is not without difficulties, which seem, to a spirit so little enterprizing as mine, in a manner insuperable. These are my reflections upon it.

I am afraid, in the first place, that I shall not have time for the requisite preparations for an escape.

Should I be either detected in those preparations, or pursued and overtaken in my flight, and so brought back, then would they think themselves doubly warranted to compel me to have their Solmes: And, conscious, perhaps, of an intended fault, I should be the less able to contend with them.

But were I even to get safely to London, I know nobody there but by name; and those the tradesmen to our family; who, no doubt, would be the first wrote to, and engaged, to find me out. And should Mr. Lovelace discover where I was, and he and my brother meet, what mischiefs might ensue between them, whether I were willing, or not, to return to Harlowe-Place?

But supposing I could remain there concealed, what might not my youth, my sex, and unacquaintedness with the ways of that great, wicked town, expose me to?—I should hardly dare to go to church, for fear of being discovered. People would wonder how I lived. Who knows but I might pass for a kept mistress; and that, altho' nobody came to me, yet, that every-time I went out, it might be imagined to be in pursuance of some assignation?

You, my dear, who alone would know where to direct to me, would be watched in all your steps, and in all your messages; and your mamma, at present not highly pleased with our corre-spondence, would then have reason to be *more* displeased; and might not differences follow between you, that would make me very unhappy, were I to know it?

Were Lovelace to find out where I was; that would be the same thing, in the eye of the world, as if I had actually gone off with him: For (among strangers, as I should be) he would not be prevailed upon to forbear visiting me: And his unhappy character [a foolish man!] is no credit to any young creature, desirous of concealment. Indeed, the world, let me escape whither, and to whomsoever, would conclude *him* to be at the bottom, and the contriver of it.

These are the difficulties which arise to me on revolving this scheme; which, situated as I am, might appear surmountable to a more enterprizing spirit. If you, my dear, think them sur-mountable, in any one of the cases put [and to be sure I can take no course, but what must have *some* difficulty in it], be pleased to let me know your free and full thoughts upon it.

Miss Clarissa Harlowe
To Miss Howe

Thursday Night.

THE alarming hurry I mentioned under my date of last night, and Betty's saucy, dark hints, come out to be owing to what I guessed they were; that is to say to the private intima-tion Mr. Lovelace contrived our family should have of his inso-lent resolution [*insolent* I must call it] to prevent my being carried to my uncle's.

I saw at the time that it was as *wrong*, with respect to answering his own view, as it was *insolent*: For could he think, as Betty (I suppose from her betters) justly observed, That parents would be insulted out of their right to the disposal of their own child, by a violent man, whom they hate?

The rash man has indeed so far gained his point, as to intimidate them from attempting to carry me away: But he has put them upon a surer and a more desperate measure: And this has driven me also into one *as* desperate; the consequence of which, altho' he could not foresee it, may, perhaps, too well answer his great end, little as he deserves to have it answered.

In short, I have done, as far as I know, the rashest thing that ever I did in my life!

About six o'clock this evening, my aunt [who stays here all night; on my account, no doubt] came up, and tapped at my door; for I was writing, and had locked myself in. I opened it; and she entering, thus delivered herself:

I come once more to visit you, my dear; but sorely against my will; because it is to impart to you matters of the utmost concern to You, and to the whole family.

What, Madam, is now to be done with me? said I; wholly attentive.

You will not be hurried away to your uncle's, child; let that comfort you.—They see your aversion to go.—You will not be obliged to go to your uncle Antony's.

How you revive me, Madam! [I little thought what was to follow this supposed condescension] This is a cordial to my heart!

And then I ran over with blessings for this good news [and she permitted me so to do, by her silence]; congratulating myself, that I *thought* my papa could not resolve to carry things to the last extremity.—

Hold, niece, said she, at last.—You must not give yourself too much joy upon the occasion neither.—Don't be surprised, my dear.—Why look you upon me, child, with so affecting an earnestness!—But you must be Mrs. Solmes, for all that.

I was dumb.

She then told me, that they had had undoubted information,

that a certain desperate *ruffian* [I must excuse her that word,
she said] had prepared armed men to waylay my brother and
uncles, and seize me, and carry me off.—Surely, she said, I was
not consenting to a violence, that might be followed by murder
on one side or the other; perhaps on both.—

I was still silent.

That therefore my father (still more exasperated than before) had changed his resolution as to my going to my uncle's;
and was determined next Tuesday to set out thither *himself*
with my mamma; and that on Wednesday I must give my hand
—as they would have me.

I put it to her, in the most earnest manner, to tell me,
whether I might not obtain the favour of a fortnight's respite?

She assured me, It would not be granted.

Would a week? Surely a week would?

She believed a week might, if I would promise two things:
The first, upon my honour, not to write a line out of the house,
in that week: For it was still suspected, she said, that I found
means to write to *some-body*. And, secondly, to marry Mr.
Solmes, at the expiration of it.

Impossible! Impossible! I said with passion.—What! might
I not be obliged with one week, without such a horrid condition
as the last?

She would go down, she said, that she might not seem of
her own head to put upon me what I thought a hardship so
great.

She went down. And came up again.

Did I want, was the answer, to give the vilest of men an
opportunity to put his murderous schemes into execution? And
an end *should* be put on Tuesday or Wednesday next, at farthest;
unless I would give my honour to comply with the condition
upon which my aunt had been *so good* as to allow me a longer
time.

My aunt chid me in a higher strain than ever she did before.

While I, in a half phrensy, insisted upon seeing my Papa:
Such usage, I said, set me above fear. I would rejoice to owe
my death to him, as I did my life.

I did go down half-way of the stairs, resolved to throw

myself at his feet, where-ever he was.—My aunt was frighted.—
Indeed I was quite frenzical for a few minutes.—But hearing
my brother's voice, as talking to some-body, in my sister's
apartment just by, I stopped; and heard the barbarous designer
say, speaking to my sister, This works charmingly, my dear
sister!

It does! It does! said she, in an exulting accent.

My aunt, just then coming down to me, and taking my
hand, led me up; and tried to sooth me.

My raving was turned into sullenness.

She preached patience and obedience to me.

I was silent.

At last she desired me to assure her, that I would offer no
violence to myself.

God, I said, had given me more grace, I hoped, than to be
guilty of so horrid a rashness. I was His creature, and not *my
own*.

I revolved, after she was gone, all that my brother and sister
had said: I dwelt upon their triumphings over me: And found
rise in my mind a rancour, that I think I may say was new to me;
and which I could not withstand.—And putting everything
together, dreading the near day, what could I do?—Am I, in any
manner excuseable for what I *did* do?—If I am condemned by
the world, who know not my provocations, may I be acquitted
by you?—If *not*, I am unhappy indeed.—For This I did.

Having shook off Betty as soon as I could, I wrote to Mr.
Lovelace, to let him know, "That all that was threatened at my
uncle Antony's, was intended to be executed *here*. That I had
come to a resolution to throw myself upon the protection of
either of his two aunts, who would afford it me: In short, that
by endeavouring to obtain leave on Monday, to dine in the ivy-
summerhouse, I would, if possible, meet him without the garden-
door, at two, three, four, or five o'Clock on Monday afternoon,
as I should be able. That in the mean time he should acquaint
me, whether I might hope for either of those Ladies protection:
And if so, I absolutely insisted, that he should leave me with
either, and go to London himself, or remain at his uncle's; nor
offer to visit me, till I were satisfied, that nothing could be done

with my friends in an amicable way; and that I could not obtain possession of my own estate, and leave to live upon it: And particularly, that he should not hint marriage to me, till I consented to hear him upon that subject.—I added, that if he could prevail upon one of the Misses Montague to favour me with her company on the road, it would make me abundantly easier in an enterprize which I could not think of (altho' so driven) without the utmost concern; and which would throw such a slur upon my reputation in the eye of the world, as, perhaps I should never be able to wipe off."

This was the purport of what I wrote; and down into the garden I slid with it in the dark, which at another time I should not have had the courage to do, and deposited it, and came up again, unknown to any-body.

Altho' it is now near Two o'clock, I have a good mind to slide down once more, in order to take back my letter. Our doors are always locked and barred up at eleven; but the seats of the lesser hall windows being almost even with the ground without, and all the shutters not difficult to open, I could easily get out.—

Yet why should I be thus uneasy?—Since, should the letter go, I can but hear what Mr. Lovelace says to it. His aunts live at too great a distance for him to have an immediate answer from them; so I can scruple going off till I have invitation. I can *insist* upon one of his cousins meeting me, as I have hinted, in the chariot; and he may not be able to obtain that favour from either of them. Twenty things may happen to afford me a suspension at least; Why should I be so very uneasy?—When, too, I can resume it early, before it is probable he will have the thought of finding it there. Yet he owns he spends three parts of his days, and has done for this fortnight past, in loitering about in one disguise or other, besides the attendance given by his trusty servant, when he himself is not *in waiting*, as he calls it.

But these strange forebodings! Solicitous for your advice, and approbation too, if I *can* have it, I will put an end to this letter.

Adieu, my dearest friend, adieu!

Miss Clarissa Harlowe
To Miss Howe

Sat. Morn, 8 o'Clock, April 8.

WHETHER you will blame me, or not, I cannot tell, But
I have deposited a letter confirming my former resolution
to leave this house on Monday next, within the hours, if possible,
prefixed in my former. I have not kept a copy of it. But this is
the substance:

I tell him, "That I have no way to avoid the determined
resolution of my friends in behalf of Mr. Solmes; but by aban-
doning this house by his assistance."

I have not pretended to make a merit with him on this score;
for I plainly tell him, "That could I, without an unpardonable
sin, die when I *would*, I would sooner make death my choice,
than take a step, which all the world, if not my own heart, will
condemn me for taking."

I tell him, "That I shall not try to bring any other cloaths
with me, than those I shall have on; and those but my common
wearing-apparel; lest I should be suspected. That I must expect
to be denied the possession of my estate: But that I am determined never to consent to a litigation with my father, were I
to be reduced to ever so low a state: So that the protection I
am to be obliged for, to any one, must be alone for the distress-
sake. That, therefore, he will have nothing to hope for from
this step, that he had not before: And that, in every light, I reserve to myself to accept or refuse his address, as his behaviour,
and circumspection shall appear to me to deserve."

I tell him, "That I think it best to go into a private lodging,
in the neighbourhood of his aunt Lawrance; and not to her
house; that it may not appear to the world, that I have refuged
myself in his family; and that a reconciliation with my friends,
may not, on that account, be made impracticable: That I will
send for thither my faithful Hannah; and apprise only Miss
Howe where I am: That he shall instantly leave me, and go to
London, or to one of his uncle's seats; and (as he had promised)

125

not come near me, but by my leave; contenting himself with a
correspondence by letter only.

That if I find myself in danger of being discovered, and
carried back by violence, I will then throw myself directly into
the protection of either of his aunts, who will receive me: But
This only in case of absolute necessity.

That I must, however, plainly tell him, That if, in this treaty,
my friends insist upon my resolving against marrying him, I
will engage to comply with them; provided they will allow me
to promise him, that I will never be any other man's while he
remains single, or is living. That this is a compliment I am willing
to pay him, in return for the trouble and pains he has taken,
and the usage he has met with, on my account: Altho' I intimate,
that he may, in a great measure, thank himself, and the little
regard he has paid to his reputation, for the slights he has met
with."

I tell him, "That I may, in this privacy, write to my cousin
Morden, and, if possible, interest him in my cause.

I take some brief notice then of his alternatives."

You must think, my dear, that this unhappy force upon me,
and this projected flight, makes it necessary for me to account
to him much sooner than it agrees with my stomach to do, for
every part of my conduct.

O my dear Miss Howe!—what a sad, sad thing is the necessity, forced upon me, for all this preparation and contrivance!—
But it is now too late!—But how!—*Too late*, did I say!—What a
word is *that!*—what a dreadful thing, *were* I to repent, to *find* it
to be too late, to remedy the apprehended evil!

Saturday Afternoon.

A LREADY have I an ecstatic answer, as I may call it, to my
letter.

"He promises compliance in every article with my will:
Approves of all I propose; particularly of the private lodging:
And thinks it a happy expedient to obviate the censures of the
busy and the unreflecting: And yet he hopes, that the putting
myself into the protection of either of his aunts, treated as I

am treated, would be far from being looked upon by any in a disreputable light. But every thing I injoin, or resolve upon, must, he says, be right, not only with respect to my present, but future, honour; with regard to which, he hopes so to behave himself, as to be *allowed* to be, next to myself, more solicitous than any-body. He will only assure me, that his whole family are extremely desirous to take advantage of the persecutions I labour under, to make their court and endear themselves, to me; by their best and most chearful services.

He will this afternoon, he says, write to his uncle, and to both his aunts, that he is now within view of being the happiest man in the world, if it be not his own fault; since the only woman upon earth that can make him so, will be soon out of danger of being another man's.

He had thoughts once, he says, on hearing of his cousin Charlotte's indisposition, to have engaged his cousin Patty's attendance upon me, either at or about the neighbouring village, or at St. Albans: But, he says, she is a low-spirited, timorous girl, who would but the more perplex us."

So, my dear, the enterprize requires courage and high spirits, you see!—And indeed it does!—What am I about to do!—

He himself, it is plain, thinks it necessary that I should be accompanied with one of my own Sex!—He might, at least, have proposed the woman of one of the Ladies of his family.— Lord bless me!—What am I about to do!—

After all, far as I have gone, I know not but I may still recede: And if I do, a mortal quarrel, I suppose, will ensue.— And what if it does?—Could there be any way to escape this Solmes, a breach with Lovelace might make way for the Single Life [so much my preferable wish!] to take place: And then I would defy the Sex. For I see nothing but trouble and vexation that they bring upon ours: And when once entered, one is obliged to go on with them, treading, with tender feet, upon thorns, and sharper thorns, to the end of a painful journey.

What to do I know not. The more I think, the more I am embarassed!—And the stronger will be my doubts as the appointed time draws nearer.

But I will go down, and take a little turn in the garden; and

deposit This, and his letters all but the two last; which I will
inclose in my next, if I have opportunity to write another.

Mean time, my dear friend—But what can I desire you to
pray for?—Adieu then!—Let me only say,—Adieu!—

Miss Howe
To Miss Clarissa Harlowe

Sat. Afternoon.

BY your last date of Ten, in your letter of this day, you could
not long have deposited it, before Robin took it. He rode
hard, and brought it to me just as I had risen from table.

You may justly blame me for sending my messenger empty-
handed, your situation considered; and yet that very situation
[so critical!] is partly the reason for it: For indeed I knew not
what to write, fit to send you.

I had been inquiring privately, how to procure you a conveyance from Harlowe-Place, and yet not appear in it; knowing,
that to oblige in the *fact*, and to disoblige in the *manner*, is but
obliging by halves: My mamma being, moreover, very suspi-
cious, and very uneasy; made more so by daily visits from your
uncle Antony, who tells her, that now every-thing is upon the
point of being determined, and hopes, that her daughter will
not so interfere, as to discourage your compliance with their
wills.

I found more difficulty than I expected, as the time was
confined, and secrecy required, in procuring you a vehicle;
and as you so earnestly forbid me to accompany you in your
enterprize. Had you not obliged me to keep measures with my
mamma, I could have managed it with ease. I could even have
taken our own chariot, on one pretence or other, and put two
horses extraordinary to it, if I had thought fit; and I could have
sent it back from London, and nobody the wiser as to the lodgings we might have taken.

I wish to the Lord, you had permitted This! Indeed I think
you are too punctilious a great deal for your situation. Would
you expect to enjoy yourself with your usual placidness, and
not be ruffled, in an hurricane which every moment threatens
to blow your house down?

Had your distress sprung from yourself, that would have
been another thing. But when all the world knows where to
lay the fault, this alters the case.

How can you say I am happy, when my mamma, to her
power, is as much an abettor of their wickedness to my dearest
friend, as your aunt, or any-body else?—And this thro' the
instigation of that odd-headed and foolish uncle of yours, who
[sorry creature that he is] keeps her up to resolutions, which
are unworthy of her, for an example to me, and please you. Is
not this cause enough for me to ground a resentment upon,
sufficient to justify me for accompanying you; the friendship
between us so well known?

Indeed, my dear, the importance of the case considered,
I must repeat, That you are too nice. Don't they already think,
that your standing-out is owing a good deal to my advice? Have
they not prohibited our correspondence upon that very surmise?
And have I, but on *your* account, reason to value *what* they
think?

I say, and I insist upon it, such a step would *ennoble* your
friend: And if still you will permit it, I will take the office out
of Lovelace's hands; and, to-morrow evening, or on Monday,
before his time of appointment takes place, will come in a chariot, or chaise: And then, my dear, if we get off as I wish, will
we make terms, and what terms we please, with them All. My
mamma will be glad to receive her daughter again, I warrant
ye: And Hickman will cry for *joy* on my return; or he shall for
sorrow.

But you are so very earnestly angry with me for proposing
such a step, and have always so much to say for your side of
any question, that I am afraid to urge it farther.—Only be so
good as to encourage me to resume it, if, upon farther consideration, and upon weighing matters well [and in *this* light, Whether
best to go off with *me*, or with *Lovelace*], you can get over

your punctilious regard for my reputation. A woman going away with a woman is not so discreditable a thing, surely! and with no view, but to avoid the fellows!—I say, only be so good as to *consider* this point; and if you can get over your scruples on *my* account, do.

A time, I hope, will come, that I shall be able to read your affecting narratives, without that impatience and bitterness, which now boils over in my heart, and would flow to my pen, were I to enter into the particulars of what you write. And, indeed, I am afraid of giving you my advice at all, or of telling you what I should do in your case [supposing you will still refuse my offer]; finding too, what you have been brought, or rather driven, to, without it; lest any evil should follow it: In which case, I should never forgive myself. And this consideration has added to my difficulties in writing to you, now you are upon such a crisis, and yet refuse the only method—But I said, I would not for the present touch any more that string.

But one thing, in your present situation, and prospects, let me advise: It is this, That if you *do* go away with Mr. Lovelace, you take the first opportunity to marry. Why should you *not*, when every-body will know by *whose* assistance, and in *whose* company, you leave your father's house, go whithersoever you will?—You may, indeed, keep him at distance, until settlements are drawn, and such-like matters are adjusted to your mind. But even These are matters of less consideration in your particular case, than they would be in that of most others: *Because*, be his other faults what they will, nobody thinks him an ungenerous man: *Because* the possession of your estate must be given up to you, as soon as your cousin Morden comes; who, as your Trustee, will see it done; and done upon proper terms: *Because* there is no want of fortune on his side: *Because* all his family value you, and are extremely desirous that you should be their relation: *Because* he makes no scruple of accepting you without conditions.

For all these reasons, I think, you may the less stand upon previous settlements. It is therefore my absolute opinion, that, if you *do* withdraw with him [And in that case you must let *him*

be judge, when he can leave you with safety, you'll observe
That] you should not postpone the ceremony.

Give this matter your most serious consideration. Punctilio
is out of doors the moment you are out of your father's house.
I know how justly severe you have been upon those inexcuseable
creatures, whose giddiness, and even want of decency, have
made them, in the same hour, as I may say, leap from a parent's
window to a husband's bed—But, considering Lovelace's character, I repeat my opinion, that your Reputation in the eye of the
world requires, that no delay be made in this point, when once
you are in his power.

From this critical and distressful situation, it shall be my
hourly prayers, that you may be delivered without blemish to
that fair fame, which has hitherto, like your heart, been unspotted.

With this prayer, twenty times repeated, concludes

Your ever-affectionate

Anna Howe

Miss Clarissa Harlowe
To Miss Howe

Sunday Morning, April 9.

D O not think, my beloved friend, altho' you have given
me, in yours of yesterday, a *severer* instance of what,
nevertheless, I must call your *impartial* Love, than ever yet I
received from you, that I will be displeased with you for it. That
would be to put myself into the inconvenient situation of Roy-
alty: That is to say, Out of the way of ever being told my faults;
of ever mending them; and In the way of making the sincerest
and warmest friendship useless to me.

And then how brightly, how nobly, burns this sacred flame

in your bosom! that you are ready to impute to the unhappy sufferer a *less degree* of warmth in *her own* cause, than *you* have for her, because she endeavours to divest herself of *Self*, so far as to leave others to the option which they have a right to make? Ought I, my dear, to blame, ought I not rather to admire, you for this ardor?

But now I come to the two points in your letter, which most sensibly concern me: Thus you put them: "Whether I choose not rather to go off with one of my *own Sex*; with my Anna Howe—than with one of the *other*; with Mr. Lovelace?"

And if *not*,

"Whether I should not marry him, as soon as possible?"

You know, my dear, my reasons for rejecting your proposal, and even for being earnest that you should not be *known* to be assisting to me in an enterprize, which a cruel necessity induced *me* to think of engaging; and in which *you* have not the same plea for.—If *I* am hardly excuseable to think of flying from my *unkind* friends, what could *you* have to say for yourself, were you to abandon a mother so *indulgent*? Does she suspect, that your fervent friendship may lead you to a *small* indiscretion? and does this suspicion offend you? And would you, in revenge, shew her and the world, that you can voluntarily rush into the *highest error*, that any of our sex can be guilty of?

I do assure you, that were I to take this step myself, I would run all risques rather than you should accompany me in it. Have I, do you think, a desire to *double* and *treble* my own fault, in the eye of the world? In the eye of that world, which, cruelly as I am used (not knowing all) would not acquit *me*?

But, my dearest, kindest friend, let me tell you, That we will *neither* of us take such a step. The manner of putting your questions, abundantly convinces me, that I ought not, in *your* opinion, to *attempt* it. You, no doubt, intend that I shall *so* take it; and I thank you for the equally polite and forcible conviction.

It is some satisfaction to me, taking the matter in this light, that I had begun to waver before I received your last. And now I tell you, that it has absolutely determined me *not* to go away; at least, not to-morrow.

While I thought only of an escape from *This house*, as an escape from Mr. *Solmes;* that already my reputation suffered by my confinement; and that it would be still in my own option, either to marry Mr. Lovelace, or wholly to renounce him; Bold as the step was, I thought, treated as I am treated, something was to be said in excuse of it — If not to the world, to *myself:* And to be *self*-acquitted, is a blessing to be preferred to the opinion of all the world. But, after I have censured that indiscreet forwardness in some, who (flying from their chamber to the altar) have, without the *least* ceremony, rushed upon the *greatest:* After I have stipulated with him for time, and for an ultimate option, whether to accept or refuse him; and for his leaving me, as soon as I am in a place of safety (which, as you observe, *he* must be the judge of): And after he has complied with these terms; so that I cannot, if I *would*, recall them, and suddenly marry; — You see, my dear, that I have nothing left me, but to resolve, *not* to go away with him.

But, how, on this revocation, shall I be able to pacify him?

Forgive these indigested self-reasonings. I will close here: And instantly set about a letter of revocation to Mr. Lovelace; take it as he will. It will only be another trial of temper to *him*. To *me* of infinite importance. And has he not promised temper and acquiescence, on the supposition of a change in my mind?

Cl. Harlowe

Miss Clarissa Harlowe To Miss Howe

St. Alban's, Tuesday Morn. past One.

O my dearest friend!

AFTER what I had resolved upon, as by my former, what shall I write? What *can* I? With what consciousness, even by *Letter*, do I approach you! — You will soon hear (if already you have not heard from the mouth of common fame), that your Clarissa Harlowe is gone off with a man! —

I am busying myself to give you the particulars at large. The whole twenty-four hours of each day (to begin the moment I can fix) shall be employed in it till it is finished: Every-one of the hours, I mean, that will be spared me, by this interrupting man, to whom I have made myself so foolishly accountable for too many of them. Rest is departed from me. I have no call for That: And That has no balm for the wounds of my mind. So you'll have all those hours without interruption, till the account is ended.

But will you receive, shall you be *permitted* to receive, my letters, after what I have done?

O, my dearest friend!—But I must make the best of it. I hope that will not be very bad! Yet am I convinced, that I did a rash and inexcuseable thing, in meeting him; and all his tenderness, all his vows, cannot pacify my inward reproaches on that account.

The bearer comes to you, my dear, for the little parcel of linen which I sent you with far better and more agreeable hopes.

Send not my letters. Send the linen only: Except you will favour me with one line, to tell me, you will love me still; and that you will suspend your censures, till you have the whole before you. I am the readier to send thus early, because if you have deposited any-thing for me, you may cause it to be taken back, or withhold any-thing you had but intended to send.

Adieu, my dearest friend!—I beseech you to love me still! —But, alas! what will your mamma say?—What will mine?— What my other relations?—and what my dear Mrs. Norton? And how will my brother and sister triumph?—

I cannot at present tell you how, or where, you can direct to me. For very early shall I leave this place; harassed and fatigued to death. But, when I can do nothing else, constant use has made me able to write. Long, very long, has that been all my amusement and pleasure: Yet could not that have been such to me, had I not had you, my best-beloved friend, to write to. Once more adieu. Pity, and pray for,

Your

Cl. Harlowe

Miss Howe
To Miss Clarissa Harlowe

I WRITE, because you enjoin me to do so.—Love you still!—How can I help it, if I would?—You may believe how I stand aghast, your letter communicating the first news—Good God of heaven and earth!—But what shall I say?—I am all impatience for particulars.

Let me now repeat my former advice—If you are *not* married by this time, be sure delay not the ceremony.—Since things are as they are, I wish it were thought, that you were privately married before you went away. If these men plead Authority to our pain, when we are *theirs*—why should we not, in such a case as *this*, make some good out of the hated word, for our reputation, when we are induced to violate a more natural one?

Your brother and sister [that vexes me almost as much as any-thing!] have now their ends. Now, I suppose, will go forward alterations of wills, and such-like spiteful doings.

I send what you write for. If there be any-thing else you want that is in my power, command, without reserve,

Your ever-affectionate

Anna Howe

Miss Clarissa Harlowe
To Miss Howe

Tuesday Night.

I THINK myself obliged to thank you, my dear Miss Howe, for your condescension, in taking notice of a creature, who has occasioned you so much scandal.

135

I am grieved on this account, as much, I verily think, as for the evil itself.

Tell me—But yet I am afraid to know—what your mamma said.

I long, and yet I dread, to be told, what the young ladies my companions, now never more, perhaps, to be so, say of me.

They cannot, however, say worse of me than I will of myself. Self-accusation shall flow in every line of my narrative, where I think I am justly censurable. If anything can arise from the account I am going to give you, for extenuation of my fault, I know I may expect it from your friendship, tho' not from the charity of any other: Since, by this time, I doubt not, every mouth is opened against me; and all that know Clarissa Harlowe, condemn the fugitive daughter.

O my dear! an obliging temper is a very dangerous temper! —By endeavouring to gratify others, it is evermore disobliging itself!

When the bell rang to call the servants to dinner, Betty came to me, and asked, If I had any commands before she went to hers; repeating her hint, that she should be *employed*; adding, that she believed it was expected, that I should not come up till she came down, or till I saw my aunt or Miss Hervey.

I asked her some questions about the cascade, which had been out of order, and lately mended; and expressed a curiosity to see how it played, in order to induce her to go thither, if she found me not where she left me; it being at a part of the garden most distant from the Ivy summerhouse.

She could hardly have got into the house, when I heard the first signal—O how my heart fluttered!—But no time was to be lost. I stept to the garden-door; and, seeing a clear coast, unbolted the ready-unlocked door.—And there was he, all impatience, waiting for me!

A panic, next to fainting, seized me, when I saw him. My heart seemed convulsed; and I trembled so, that I should hardly have kept my feet, had he not supported me.

Fear nothing, dearest creature, said he!—Let us hasten away!—The chariot is at hand!—And, by this sweet condescension, you have obliged me beyond expression, or return.

What is it you mean, Sir!—Let go my hand: For I tell you

[struggling vehemently], that I will sooner die than go with you!—

Good God, said he! with a look of wildness and surprize, what is it I hear!—But [still drawing me after him, as he retreated farther from the door] it is no time to argue—By all that's Good you must go!—Surely you cannot doubt my honour, nor give me cause to question your own.

As you value me, Mr. Lovelace, urge me no farther. I come fixed and resolved. Let me give you the letter I had written. My further reasons shall follow; and they will convince you, that I ought not to go.

All my friends expect you, Madam!—All your own are determined against you!—Wednesday next is the day! the important, perhaps the fatal day! Would you stay to be Solmes's Wife?—Can this be your determination at last?

No, never, never, will I be that man's!—But I will not go with you!—Draw me not thus!—How dare you, Sir?—I would not have seen you, but to tell you so!—I had not met you, but for fear you would have been guilty of some rashness!—And, once more, I will *not* go!—What mean you!—Striving with all my force to get from him.

What can have possessed my angel, quitting my hands, and with a gentler voice, that after so much ill-usage from your relations; vows so solemn on my part; an affection so ardent; you stab me with a refusal to stand by your own appointment!

It is to be their last effort, as I have reason to believe.—And I have reason to believe so too!—Since, if you tarry, you will inevitably be Solmes's wife.

Not so, interrupted I.—I have obliged them in one point—They will be in good humour with me. I shall gain time at least—I am sure I shall—I have several ways to gain time.

And what, Madam, will gaining time do?—It is plain you have not a hope beyond that!—O my dearest, dearest life! let me beseech you not to run a risque of this consequence. I can convince you, that it will be *more* than a risque, if you go back, that you will, on Wednesday next, be Solmes's wife.—Prevent therefore, now that it is in your power to prevent, the fatal mischiefs that will follow such a dreadful certainty.

And then he pathetically enumerated the different instances

of the harsh treatment I had met with; imputing all to the malice
and caprice of a brother, who set everybody against him: And
insisting, that I had no other way to effect a reconciliation with
my father and uncles, than by putting myself out of the power
of my brother's inveterate malice.

Urge me no more, Mr. Lovelace, I conjure you.—You yourself have given me a hint, which I will speak plainer to, than
prudence, perhaps, on any other occasion, would allow me to
speak.—I am convinced, that Wednesday next [if I had time,
I would give you my reasons] is not intended to be the day we
had both so much dreaded: And if, after that day shall be over,
I find my friends determined in Mr. Solmes's favour, I will then
contrive some way to meet you with Miss Howe, who is not
your enemy: And when the solemnity has passed, I shall think
that step a duty, which, *till* then, will be criminal to take: Since
now my father's authority is unimpeached by any greater.

Dearest Madam—

Nay, Mr. Lovelace, if you now dispute!—If, after this
more favourable declaration, than I had the thought of making,
you are not satisfied, I shall know what to think both of your
gratitude and generosity.

The case, Madam, admits not of this alternative. I cannot
express how much I should be delighted with the charming hope
you have given me, were you not next Wednesday, if you stay,
to be another man's. Think, dearest creature! what an heighten-
ing of my anguish the distant hope you bid me look up to, is,
taken in this light!

Depend upon it, I will die sooner than be Mr. Solmes's.
If you would have me rely upon *your* honour, why should you
doubt of *mine*?

I doubt not your *honour*, Madam; your *power* is all I doubt.
You never, never can have such another opportunity.—Dearest
creature, permit me—And he was again drawing me after him.

Let me judge for myself, Sir. Do not you, who blame my
friends for endeavouring to compel me, *yourself* seek to compel
me. I won't bear it.—Your earnestness gives me greater apprehensions, and greater reluctance!—Let me go back, then!—Let
me, before it is too late, go back, that it may not be worse for

both. What mean you by this forcible treatment?—Unhand me this moment, or I will cry out for help.

I will obey you, my dearest creature!—And quitted my hand with a look full of tender despondency, that, knowing the violence of his temper, half-concerned me for him. Yet I was hastening from him, when, with a solemn air, looking upon his sword, but catching, as it were, his hand from it, he folded both his arms, as if a sudden thought had recovered him from an intended rashness.

One word, Madam, however, one word more, approaching me, his arms still folded, as if (as I thought) he would not be tempted to mischief.—Remember only, that I come at your appointment, to redeem you, at the hazard of my life, from your gaolers and persecutors, with a resolution, God is my witness, or may he for ever blast me! [That was his shocking imprecation] to be a father, uncle, brother, and, as I humbly hoped, in your own good time, a *husband* to you, all in one. But since I find you are so ready to cry out for *help* against me, which must bring down upon me the vengeance of all your family, I am contented to run all risques:—I will not ask you to retreat with *me*; I will attend you into the garden, and into the *house*, if I am not intercepted.—Nay, be not surprised, Madam! The help you would have called upon, I will attend you to.—I will face them all: But not as a revenger, if they provoke me not too much. You shall see what I can further bear for your sake. And let us both see, if expostulation, and the behaviour of a gentleman to them, will not procure me the treatment due to a gentleman from them.

Had he offered to draw his sword upon himself, I was prepared to have despised him for supposing me such a poor novice, as to be intimidated by an artifice so common. But this resolution, uttered with so serious an air, of accompanying me in to my friends, made me gasp with terror.

What mean you, Mr. Lovelace, said I?—I beseech you leave me: Leave me, Sir, I beseech you.

Excuse me, Madam! I beg you to excuse me!—I have long enough skulked like a thief about these lonely walls!—Long, too long, have I borne the insults of your brother, and others of

your relations. Absence but heightens malice. I am desperate.
I have but this one chance for it; for is not the day after to-
morrow WEDNESDAY? I have encouraged virulence by my
tameness?—Yet *tame* I will still be!—You shall see, Madam,
what I will bear for your sake. My sword shall be put sheathed
into your hands [And he offered it to me in the scabbard]:—My
heart, if you please, shall afford a sheath to theirs:—Life is nothing, if I lose you.—Be pleased, Madam, to shew me the way into
the garden. I will attend you, tho' to my fate! But too happy,
be it what it will, if I receive it in your presence. Lead on, dear
creature!—You shall see what I can bear for you.—And he
stooped, and took up the key; and offered it to the lock—But
dropped it again, without opening the door, upon my earnest
expostulation to him.

What can you mean, Mr. Lovelace, said I?—Would you
thus expose yourself? Would you thus expose me?—Is this your
generosity?—Is every-body to take advantage thus of the weakness of my temper?

And I wept. I could not help it.

I was sure, I said, of procuring a delay at least. Many ways
I had to procure delay.—Nothing could be so fatal to us both,
as for me now to be found with him.—I should think very hardly
of him, if he sought to detain me longer. But his acquiescence
should engage my gratitude.

And then stooping to take up the key to let myself into the
garden, he started, and looked as if he had heard somebody
near the door, on the inside, clapping his hand on his sword.

This frighted me so, that I thought I should have sunk down
at his feet. But he instantly re-assured me: He thought, he said,
he had heard a rustling against the door: But *had* it been so, the
noise would have been stronger. It was only the effect of his
apprehension for my mind's sake.

And then taking up the key, he presented it to me.—If you
will go, Madam—Yet I cannot, cannot leave you!—Forgive me,
but I *must* enter the garden with you.

And will you, will you, thus ungenerously, Sir, take advantage of my fears!—of my wishes, to prevent mischief?—I,
vain fool, to be concerned for every-one; nobody for me!

And then I again offered the key to the door.

Down the ready kneeler dropt between me and that: And can you, can you, Madam, once more on my knees let me ask you, look with an indifferent eye upon the evils that may follow? Provoked as I have been, and triumphed over as I shall be, if your brother succeeds, my own heart shudders, at times, at the thoughts of what *must* happen: And can *yours* be unconcerned!—My intelligence—

Never, Mr. Lovelace, interrupted I, pin so much faith upon the sleeve of a traitor.—Your base intelligencer is but a servant: He may pretend to know more than he has grounds for, in order to earn the wages of corruption. You know not what contrivances I can find out.

I was once more offering the key to the lock, when, starting from his knees, with a voice of affrightment, loudly whispering, and as if out of breath, *They are at the door, my beloved creature!* And taking the key from me, he fluttered with it, as if he would double-lock it. And instantly a voice from within cried out, bursting against the door, as if to break it open, the person repeating his violent pushes, *Are you there?—Come up this moment!—This moment!—Here they are—Here they are both together!—Your pistol this moment!—Your gun!*—Then another push, and another.—He at the same moment drew his sword, and clapping it naked under his arm, took both my trembling hands in his; and, drawing me swiftly after him, Fly, fly, my charmer; this moment is all you have for it! said he.—Your brother!—Your uncles!—Or this Solmes!—They will instantly burst the door!—Fly, my dearest life! if you would not be more cruelly used than ever!—If you would not see two or three murders committed at your feet, fly, fly, I beseech you!

Now behind me, now before me, now on this side, now on that, turn'd I my affrighted face, in the same moment; expecting a furious brother here, armed servants there, an inraged sister screaming, and a father armed with terror in his countenance, more dreadful than even the drawn sword which I saw, or those I apprehended. I ran as fast as he; yet knew not that I ran; my fears, which at the same time that they took all power of thinking from me, adding wings to my feet: My fears, which probably would not have suffered me to know what course to take, had I not had him to urge and draw me after him: Especially as I beheld a man, who must have come out of the garden-door, keeping us in his eye, running backward and forward, beckoning and calling out to others, whom I supposed *he* saw, altho' the turning of the wall hindered *me* from seeing them; and whom I imagined to be my brother, my father, and their servants.

Thus terrified, I was got out of sight of the door in a very few minutes: And then, altho' quite breathless between running and apprehension, he put my arm under his, his drawn sword in the other hand, and hurried me on still faster: My voice, however, contradicting my action; crying, No, no, no, all the while; straining my neck to look back, as long as the walls of the garden and park were within sight, and till he brought me to his uncle's chariot: Where attending were two armed servants of his own, and two of Lord M's, on horseback.

Here I must suspend my relation for a while: For now I am come to this sad period of it, my indiscretion stares me in the face: And my shame and my grief give me a compunction, that is more poignant, methinks, than if I had a dagger in my heart— To have it to reflect, that I should so inconsiderately give in to an interview, which, had I known either myself or him, or in the least considered the circumstances of the case, I might have supposed, would put me into the power of his resolution, and out of that of my own reason.

But if it shall come out, that the person within the garden was his corrupted implement, employed to frighten me away with him, do you think, my dear, that I shall not have reason to hate him and myself still more? But how came it to pass, that one man could get out at the garden-door, and no more? How, that that man kept aloof, as it were, and pursued us not; nor ran back to alarm the house?—My fright, and my distance, would not let me be certain; but really this single man had the air of that vile Joseph Leman, as I now recollect.

How much more properly had I acted, with regard to that correspondence, had I, once for all, when he was forbid to visit me, and I to receive his visits, pleaded the authority by which

I ought to have been bound by, and denied to write to him!—
But I thought I could proceed or stop as I pleased. I supposed
it concerned me, more than any other, to be the arbitress of the
quarrels of unruly spirits—And now I find my presumption
punished!—Punished, as other sins frequently are, by *itself!*

As to this last rashness; now, that it is too late, I plainly
see how I ought to have conducted myself.—I should not have
been solicitous whether he had got my letter or not: When he
had come, and found I did not answer his signal, he would
presently have resorted to the loose bricks, and there been satisfied by the date of my letter, that it was his own fault, that he
had it not before. But, governed by the same pragmatical motives, which induced me to correspond with him at first, I was
again afraid, truly, with my foolish and busy prescience, that
the disappointment would have thrown him into the way of
receiving fresh insults from the same persons; which might have
made him guilty of some violence to them. And so, to save him
an *apprehended* rashness, I have rushed into a *real* one myself.
And what vexes me more, is, that it is plain to me, now, by all
his behaviour, that he had as great a confidence in my weakness, as I had in my own strength. And so, in a point intirely
relative to my honour, he has triumphed [Can I have patience
to look at him!]; for he has not been mistaken in me, while I
have in myself!

Tell me, my dear Miss Howe, tell me truly, if your unforced
heart does not despise me?—It must! for your mind and mine
were ever *one;* and I despise *myself!*—And well I may: For could
the giddiest and most inconsiderate girl in *England* have done
worse than I shall appear to have done in the eye of the world?

This is the Wednesday morning I dreaded so much, that I
once thought of it as my doomsday: But of the Monday, it is
plain, I ought to have been most apprehensive. Had I stayed,
and had the worst I dreaded happened, my friends would then
have been answerable, if any bad consequences had followed:—
But, now, I have this *only* consolation left me, that I have cleared
them of blame, and taken it all upon *myself!*

You will not wonder to see this narrative so dismally

scrawled. It is owing to different pens and ink, all bad, and written by snatches of time, my hand trembling too with fatigue and grief.

The lodgings I am in, are inconvenient. I shall not stay in them: So it signifies nothing to tell you how to direct to me hither. And where my next may be, as yet I know not.

He knows that I am writing to you; and has offered to send my letter, when finished, by a servant of his. But I thought I could not be too cautious, as I am now situated, in having a letter of this importance conveyed to you. Who knows what such a man may do? So very wicked a contriver! The contrivance, if a contrivance, so insolently mean!—But I hope it is not a contrivance neither! Yet, be that as it will, I must say, that the *best* of him, and of my prospects with him, are bad: And yet, having inrolled myself among the too-late repenters, who shall pity me?

Nevertheless, I will dare to hope for a continued interest in your affections [I shall be miserable indeed, if I may not!], and to be remembered in your daily prayers. I am, my dearest friend,

Your ever-affectionate

Cl. Harlowe

Mr. Lovelace
To Joseph Leman

Sat. April 8.

Honest Joseph,

AT length your beloved young Lady has consented to free herself from the cruel treatment she has so long borne. She is to meet me without the garden-door, at about four o'clock on Monday afternoon; as I told you she had promised. She has confirmed her promise. Thank God, she has confirmed her promise!

I shall have a chariot-and-six ready in the by-road fronting the private path to Harlowe-paddock; and several of my friends and servants not far off, armed to protect her, if there be occasion: But every one charged to avoid mischief. That, you know, has always been my principal care.

All my fear is, that when she comes to the point, the over-niceness of her principles will make her waver, and want to go back: Altho' *her* honour is *my* honour, you know, and *mine* is *hers*. If she should, and I should be unable to prevail upon her, all your past services will avail nothing, and she will be lost to me for ever: The prey, then, of that cursed Solmes, whose vile stinginess will never permit him to do good to any of the servants of the family.

I have no doubt of your fidelity, honest Joseph. You see, by the confidence I repose in you, that I have *not*; more particularly, on this very important occasion, in which your assistance may crown the work: For, if she waver, a little innocent contrivance will be necessary.

Be very mindful, therefore, of the following directions: Take them into your heart. This will probably be your last trouble, until my beloved and I are joined in holy wedlock: And then we will be sure to take care of you.

Contrive to be in the garden, in disguise, if possible, and unseen by your young Lady. If you find the garden-door unbolted, you'll know, that she and I are together, altho' you should not see her go out at it. It will be locked, but my key shall be on the ground, at the bottom of the door, without, that you may open it with yours, as it may be needful.

If you hear our voices parleying, keep at the door till I cry Hem, hem, twice: But be watchful for this signal, for I must not hem very loud, lest she should take it for a signal: Perhaps, in struggling to prevail upon the dear creature, I may have an opportunity to strike the door hard with my elbow, or heel, to confirm you:—Then you are to make a violent burst against the door as if you would break it open, drawing backward and forward the bolt in a hurry: Then, with another push, but with

more noise than strength, lest the lock give way, cry out (as if
you saw some of the family), Come up, come up, instantly!—
Here they are! Here they are! Hasten!—This instant hasten!
And mention swords, pistols, guns, with as terrible a voice as
you can cry out with. Then shall I prevail upon her, no doubt,
if loth before, to fly: If I cannot, I will enter the garden with
her, and the house too, be the consequence what it will. But so
affrighted, there is no question but she will fly.

When you think us at a sufficient distance [and I shall
raise my voice, urging her swifter flight, that you may guess at
that], then open the door with your key: But you must be sure
to open it very cautiously, lest we should not be far enough off.
I would not have her know you have a hand in this matter, out
of my great regard to you.

When you have opened the door, take your key out of the
lock, and put it in your pocket: Then, stooping for mine, put
it in the lock on the *inside*, that it may appear as if the door
was opened by herself, with a key they'll suppose of my procuring (it being new), and left open by us.

They should conclude she is gone off by her own consent,
that they may not pursue us: That they may see no hopes of
tempting her back again. In either case, mischief might happen,
you know.

But you must take notice, that you are only to open the
door with your key, in case none of the family come up to
interrupt us, and before we are quite gone: For, if they do, you'll
find by what follows, that you must not open the door at all.
Let them, on breaking it open, or by getting over the wall, find
my key on the ground, if they will.

If they do not come to interrupt us, and if you, by help of
your key, come out, follow us at a distance, and, with uplifted
hands, and wild and impatient gestures (running backward and
forward, for fear you should come too near us; and as if you
saw somebody coming to your assistance) cry out for Help,
help, and to hasten. Then shall we be soon at the chariot.

Tell the family, that you saw me enter a chariot with her:
A dozen, or more, men on horseback, attending us; all armed;

some with blunderbusses, as you believe; and that we took the quite contrary way to that we shall take.

You see, honest Joseph, how careful I am, as well as you, to avoid mischief.

Observe to keep at such a distance that she may not discover who you are. Take long strides, to alter your gaite; and hold up your head, honest Joseph; and she'll not know it to be you. Mens airs and gaites are as various, and as peculiar, as their faces. Pluck a stake out of one of the hedges; and tug at it, tho' it may come easy: This, if she turn back, will look terrible, and account for your not following us faster. Then returning with it, shouldered, brag to the family, what you would have done, could you have overtaken us, rather than your young Lady should have been carried off by such a—And you may call me names, and curse me. And these airs will make you look valiant, and in earnest. You see, honest Joseph, I am always contriving to give you reputation. No man suffers by serving me.

But, if our parley should last longer than I wish; and if any of her friends miss her before I cry, Hem, hem, twice; then, in order to save yourself (which is a very great point with me, I assure you), make the same noise as above: But, as I directed before, open not the door with your key. On the contrary, wish for a key with all your heart; but for fear any of them should, by accident, have a key about them, keep in readiness half a dozen little gravel-stones, no bigger than peas, and thrust two or three slily into the key-hole; which will hinder their key from turning round. It is good, you know, Joseph, to provide against every accident, in such an important case as this. And let this be your cry, instead of the other, if any of my enemies come in your sight, as you seem to be trying to burst the door open: Sir! or Madam! (as it may prove) O Lord, hasten! O Lord, hasten! Mr. Lovelace!—Mr. Lovelace!—And very loud.—And that shall quicken me more than it shall those you call to.—If it be Betty, and only Betty, I shall think worse of your art of making love, than of your fidelity, if you can't find a way to amuse her, and put her upon a false scent.

You must tell them, that your young Lady seemed to run as fast off with me, as I with her. This will also confirm to them, that all pursuit is in vain. An end will be hereby put to Solmes's hopes: And her friends, after a while, will be more studious to be reconciled to her, than to get her back. So you will be an happy instrument of great good to all round. And This will one day be acknowleged by both families. You will then be every one's favourite: and every good servant, for the future, will be proud to be likened to honest Joseph Leman.

This one time, be diligent, be careful: This will be the crown of all: And, once more, depend for a recompence upon the honour of

Your assured friend,

R. Lovelace

Mr. Lovelace
To John Belford, Esq;

St. Albans, Monday Night.

I SNATCH a few moments, while my Beloved is retired (as I hope, to rest), to perform my promise. No pursuit!—Nor have I apprehensions of any; tho' I must make my charmer dread that there will be one.

And now, let me tell thee, that never was joy so complete as mine!—But let me inquire! Is not the angel flown away?—

O no! She is in the next apartment!—Securely mine!—Mine for ever!

O ecstasy!—My heart will burst my breast,
To leap into her bosom!—

I knew, that the whole stupid family were in a combination

to do my business for me. I told thee, that they were all working for me, like so many underground moles; and still more blind than the moles are said to be, unknowing that they did so.

But did I say, my joy was perfect?—O no!—It receives some abatement from my disgusted pride. For how can I endure to think, that I owe more to her relation's persecutions, than to her favour for me?—Or even as far as I know, to her preference of me to another man?

But let me not indulge this thought. Were I to do so, it might cost my charmer dear.—Let me rejoice, that she has passed the Rubicon: That she cannot return: That, as I have ordered it, the flight will appear to the Implacables to be altogether with her own consent: And that, if I doubt her love, I can put her to trials as mortifying to her niceness, as glorious to my pride.— For, let me tell thee, dearly as I love her, if I thought there was but the shadow of a doubt in her mind, whether she preferred me to any man living, I would shew her no mercy.

Tuesday, Day-dawn.

But, on the wings of love, I fly to my charmer, who, per-haps, by this time, is rising to encourage the tardy dawn. I have not slept a wink of the hour and half I lay down to invite sleep. It seems to me, that I am not so much Body, as to require such vulgar renovation.

But why, as in the chariot, as in the inn, at alighting, all heart-bursting grief, my dearest creature? So persecuted, as thou wert persecuted!—So much in danger of the most abhorred compulsion!

Yet, it must be allowed, that such a sudden transition must affect her—Must ice her over.—When a little more used to her new situation: When her hurries are at an end: When she sees how religiously I shall observe all her Injunctions, she will un-doubtedly have the gratitude to distinguish between the con-finement she has escaped from, and the liberty she has reason to rejoice in.

She comes! She comes!—And the Sun is just rising to attend

her!—Adieu!—Be half as happy as I am [for all diffidences, like night-fogs before the sun, exhale at her approach]; and, next myself, thou wilt be the happiest man in the world.

Miss Clarissa Harlowe
To Miss Howe

Wednesday, April 12.

I WILL pursue my melancholy story.

Being thus hurried to the chariot, it would have been to no purpose to have refused entering into it, had he not, in my fright, lifted me in, as he did: And it instantly drove away a full gallop, and stopt not till it brought us to St. Albans; which was just as the day shut in.

I thought I should have fainted several times by the way. With lifted-up hands and eyes, God protect me, said I often to myself!—Can it be I, that am here!—My eyes running over, and my heart ready to burst with sighs as involuntary as my flight.

How different, how inexpressibly different, the gay wretch; visibly triumphing (as I could not but construe his almost rapturous joy) in the success of his arts! But overflowing with complimental flourishes, yet respectfully distant his address, all the way we *flew;* for that, rather than *galloping,* was the motion of the horses; which took, as I believe, a round-about way, to prevent being traced.

I have reason to think, there were other horsemen at his devotion; three or four different persons, above the rank of servants, galloping by us now-and-then on each side of the chariot: But he took no notice of them; and I had too much grief, mingled with indignation, notwithstanding all his blandishments, to ask any questions about them, or any-thing else.

Think, my dear, what were my thoughts, on alighting from the chariot; having no attendant of my own sex; no cloaths but what I had on, and those little suited for such a journey as I had *already* taken, and was still further to take: Neither hood nor hat, nor any thing but a handkerchief about my neck and shoulders: Fatigued to death: My mind still more fatigued than my body: And in such a foam the horses, that every one in the inn we put up at guessed (they could not do otherwise) that I was a young giddy creature, who had run away from her friends.

The gentlewoman of the inn, whom he sent in to me, shewed me another apartment; and, seeing me ready to faint, brought me hartshorn and water; and then, upon my desiring to be left alone for half an hour, retired: For I found my heart ready to burst, on revolving every thing in my thoughts: And the moment she was gone, fastening the door, I threw myself into an old great chair, and gave way to a violent flood of tears; which a little relieved me.

Mr. Lovelace, sooner than I wished, sent up the gentlewoman, who pressed me, in his name, to admit my Brother, or to come down to him: For he had told her, I was his Sister; and that he had brought me, against my will, and without warning, from a friend's house, where I had been all the winter, in order to prevent my marrying against the consent of my friends; to whom he was now conducting me.

So, my dear, your frank, your open-hearted friend, was forced to countenance this tale; which, indeed, suited me the better, because I was unable, for some time, to talk, speak, or look up; and so my dejection, and grief, and silence, might very well pass before the gentlewoman and her niece who attended me, as a fit of sullenness.

The room I was in being a bed-chamber, I chose to go down, at his repeated message, attended by the gentlewoman of the inn, to that in which he was. He approached me with great respect, yet not exceeding a brotherly politeness, where a brother *is* polite; and, calling me his dearest sister, asked after the state of my mind; and hoped I would forgive him; for never brother half so well loved a sister, as he me.

A wretch!—How naturally did he fall into the character, altho' I was so much out of mine!

But let me give you the particulars of our conversation, a little before and after our supper-time.

When we were alone, he besought me [I cannot say but with all the tokens of a passionate and respectful tenderness] to be better reconciled to myself, and to him: He repeated all the vows of honour, and inviolable affection, that he ever made me: He promised to be wholly governed by me in every future step: He asked me to give him leave to propose, Whether I chose to set out next day to either of his aunts?

I was silent. I knew not what to say, nor what to do.

Whether I chose to have private lodgings procured for me, in either of those ladies neighbourhood, as were once my thoughts?

I was still silent.

Whether I chose to go to either of Lord M's seats; that of Berks, or that in the county we were in?

In lodgings, I said, any-where, where he was not to be.

He had promised This, he owned; and he would religiously keep to his word, as soon as he found all danger of pursuit over; and that I was settled to my mind. —But, if the place were indifferent to me, London was the safest, and the most private: And his relations should all visit me there, the moment I thought fit to admit them. His cousin Charlotte, particularly, should attend me, as my companion, if I would accept of her, as soon as she was able to go abroad. —Mean time, would I go to his aunt Lawrance's (his aunt Sadleir was a melancholy woman)? I should be the most welcome guest she ever received.

I told him, I wished not to go (immediately, however, and in the frame I was in, and likely not to be out of) to any of his relations: That my reputation was concerned to have *him* absent from me: —That, if I were in some private lodging (the meaner the less to be suspected, as it would be known, that I went away by his means; and he would be supposed to have provided me handsome accommodations), it would be most suitable both to my mind and to my situation: That this might be best, I should think, in the country for *me*; in town for *him*.

If he might deliver his opinion, he said, since I declined going to any of his relations, London was the only place in the world to be private in. Every newcomer in a country-town or village excited a curiosity: A person of my figure (and many

compliments he made me) would excite more. Even messages
and letters, where none used to be brought, would occasion
inquiry. He had not provided a lodging any-where, supposing
I would choose to go either to London, where accommodations
of that sort might be fixed upon in an hour's time; or to his
aunt's; or to Lord M's Hertfordshire seat, where was housekeeper an excellent woman, Mrs. Greme, such another as my
Norton.

To be sure, I said, if I were pursued, it would be in their
first passion; and some one of his relations houses would be
the place they would expect to find me at.—I knew not what to
do!

Then he began again to vow the sincerity of his intentions.

But I took him up short; I am willing to *believe* you, Sir.
It would be insupportable but to suppose there were a *necessity*
for such solemn declarations [At this he seemed to collect himself, as I may say, into a little more circumspection]. If I thought
there *were*, I would not sit with you here, in a public inn, I assure
you, altho' *cheated* hither, as far as I know, by methods [You
must excuse me, Sir!] that, the very suspicion that it may be so,
gives me too much vexation, for me to have patience either with
you or with myself.—But no more of this, just now: Let me
but know, I beseech you, *good Sir*, bowing [I was very angry!],
if you intend to leave me; or if I have only escaped from one
confinement to another?—

Cheated hither, as far as you know, madam! Let you *know*
(and with that air too, charming though grievous to my heart!)
if you have only escaped from one confinement to another!—
Amazing! perfectly amazing!—And can there be a necessity for
me to answer this?—You are absolutely your own mistress.—It
were very strange, if you were not. The moment you are in a
place of safety, I will leave you.—One condition only, give
me leave to beg your consent to: It is this: That you will be
pleased, now you are so intirely in your own power, to renew a
promise *voluntarily* made before; for altho' I would not be
thought capable of growing upon concession, yet I cannot bear
to think of losing the ground your goodness had given me room
to hope I had gained; "That, make up how you please with your

relations, you will never marry any other man, while I am living and single, unless I should be so wicked as to give new cause for high displeasure."

I hesitate not to confirm this promise, Sir, upon your *own* condition. In what manner do you expect me to confirm it?—

Only, Madam, by your word.

Then I never will.

I broke from him to write to you my preceding letter; but refused to send it by his servant, as I told you. The gentlewoman of the inn helped me to a messenger, who was to carry what you should give him to Lord M's seat in Hertfordshire, directed for Mrs. Greme the housekeeper there. And early in the morning, for fear of pursuit, we were to set out that way.

I looked over my little stock of money; and found it to be no more than seven guineas and some silver: The rest of my stock was but fifty guineas, and that five more than I thought it was, when my sister challenged me as to the sum I had by me: And those I left in my escritoire, little thinking to be prevailed upon to go away with him.

Indeed my case abounds with a shocking variety of indelicate circumstances. Among the rest, I was forced to account to *him*, who knew I could have no cloaths but what I had on, how I came to have linen with you [for he could not but know I sent for it]; lest he should imagine I had an early design to go away with him, and made that a part of the preparation.

He most heartily wished, he said, for my mind's sake, that your mamma would have afforded me her protection; and delivered himself, upon this subject, with equal freedom and concern.

There are, my dear Miss Howe, a multitude of punctilios and decorums, which a young creature must dispense with, who, in such a situation, makes a man the intimate attendant of her person. I could now, I think, give twenty reasons stronger than any I have heretofore mentioned, why women of the least delicacy should never think of incurring the danger and disgrace of taking the step I have been drawn in to take, but with horror and aversion; and why they should look upon the man who shall tempt them to it, as the vilest and most selfish of seducers.

Mr. Lovelace
To John Belford, Esq;

Tuesday, Wedn. Apr. 11. 12.

Y OU claim my promise, that I will be as particular as possible, in all that passes between me and my goddess. Indeed, I never had a more illustrious subject to exercise my pen upon. And, moreover, I have leisure; for by her good will, my access would be as difficult to her, as that of the humblest slave to an eastern monarch. Nothing, then, but inclination to write, can be wanting: And since our friendship, and thy obliging attendance upon me at the White Hart, will not excuse That, I will endeavour to keep my word.

I parted with thee and thy brethren, with a full resolution, thou knowest, to rejoin ye, if she once again disappointed me, in order to go together, attended by our servants, for shew-sake, to her gloomy father; and demand audience of the tyrant, upon the freedoms taken with my character: And to have tried by fair means, if fair would do, to make them change their resolutions; and treat *her* with less inhumanity, and *me* with more civility.

I told thee my reasons for not going in search of a letter of countermand. I was right; for, if I had, I should have found such a one; and had I received it, she would not have met me. Did she think, that after I had been more than once disappointed, I would not keep her to her promise?

The moment I heard the door unbolt, I was sure of her. That motion made my heart bound to my throat. But when That was followed with the presence of my charmer, flashing upon me all at once in a flood of brightness, sweetly dressed, tho' all unprepared for a journey, I trod air, and hardly thought myself a mortal.

Thou shalt judge of her dress, as, at the moment she appeared to me, and as, upon a nearer observation, she really was. I am a critic, thou knowest, in womens dresses.—Many a one have I taught to dress, and helped to undress. But there is such a native elegance in this lady, that she surpasses all that I could imagine surpassing.

155

Expect therefore, a faint sketch of her admirable person with her dress.

Her wax-like flesh [for, after all, flesh and blood I think she is!] by its delicacy and firmness, answers for the soundness of her health. Thou has often heard me launch out in praise of her complexion. I never in my life beheld a skin so *illustriously* fair. The lily and the driven snow it is nonsense to talk of: Her lawn and her laces one might, indeed, compare to those: But what a whited wall would a woman appear to be, who had a complexion which would justify such unnatural comparisons? But this Lady is all-alive all-glowing, all charming flesh and blood, yet so clear, that every meandring vein is to be seen in all the lovely parts of her, which custom permits to be visible.

Thou hast heard me also describe the wavy ringlets of her shining hair, needing neither art nor powder; of itself an ornament, defying all other ornaments; wantoning in and about a neck that is beautiful beyond description.

Her head-dress was a Brussels-lace mob, peculiarly adapted to the charming air and turn of her features. A sky-blue ribband illustrated that.—But altho' the weather was somewhat sharp, she had not on either hat or hood; for, besides that she loves to use herself hardily (by which means, and by a temperance truly exemplary, she is allowed to have given high health and vigour to an originally tender constitution), she seems to have intended to shew me, that she was determined not to stand to her appointment. O Jack! that such a sweet girl should be a rogue!

Her morning-gown was a pale primrose-coloured paduasoy: The cuffs and robings curiously embroidered by the fingers of this ever-charming Ariadne, in a running pattern of violets, and their leaves; the light in the flowers silver; gold in the leaves. A pair of diamond snaps in her ears. A white handkerchief, wrought by the same inimitable fingers, concealed—O Belford! what still more inimitable beauties did it not conceal!—And I saw, all the way we rode, the bounding heart; by its throbbing motions I saw it! dancing beneath the charming umbrage.

Her ruffles were the same as her mob. Her apron a flowered lawn. Her coat white satten, quilted: Blue satten her shoes, braided with the same colour, without lace, for what need has

the prettiest foot in the world of ornament? Neat buckles in
them: And on her charming arms a pair of black velvet glove-
like muffs, of her own invention; for she makes and gives fash-
ions as she pleases. Her hands, velvet of themselves, thus uncov-
ered, the freer to be grasped by those of her adorer.

I have told thee what were *my* transports, when the un-
drawn bolt presented to me my long-expected goddess.—*Her*
emotions were more sweetly feminine, after the first moments;
for then the fire of her starry eyes began to sink into a less dazling langour. She trembled: Nor knew she how to support the
agitations of a heart she had never found so ungovernable. She
was even fainting, when I clasped her in my supporting arms.

By her dress, I saw, as I observed before, how unprepared
she was for a journey; and not doubting her intention once more
to disappoint me, I would have drawn her after me. Then began
a contention the most vehement that ever I had with lady. It
would pain thy friendly heart to be told the infinite trouble I
had with her. I begged, I prayed; on my knees I begged and
prayed her, yet in vain, to answer her own appointment: And
had I not happily provided for such a struggle, knowing whom
I had to deal with, I had certainly failed in my design.

But my honest agent answering my signal, *tho' not quite
so soon as I expected*, in the manner thou knowest I had laid
down to him, They are coming! They are coming!—Fly, fly, my
beloved creature, cried I, drawing my sword with a flourish,
as if I would have slain half an hundred of them; and, seizing
her trembling hands, I drew her after me so swiftly, that *my*
feet, winged by love, could hardly keep pace with *her* feet, agi-
tated by fear.—And so I became her emperor!

I'll tell thee all, when I see thee: And thou shalt then judge of
my difficulties, and of her perverseness. And thou wilt rejoice
with me, at my conquest over such a watchful and open-eyed
charmer.

But seest thou not now [as I think I do] the wind-out-
stripping fair-one flying *from* her love *to* her love?—Is there
not such a game?—Nay, flying from friends she was resolved not
to abandon, to the man she was determined not to go off with?
—The Sex! The Sex, all over!—Hah, hah, hah, hah!—I must

here—I must here lay down my pen, to hold my sides; for I must have my laugh out, now the fit is upon me!

I believe—I believe—Hah, hah, hah!—I believe, Jack, my dogs conclude me mad: For here has one of them popt in, as if to see what ailed me; or whom I had with me.—The whorson caught the laugh, as he went out.—Hah, hah, hah!—An *impudent* dog!—O Jack, knewest thou my conceit, and were but thy laugh joined to mine, I believe it would hold me for an hour longer.

But, O my best-beloved fair-one, repine not thou at the arts by which thou suspectest thy fruitless vigilance has been over-watched. —If once thy emperor decrees thy fall, thou shalt greatly fall. Thou shalt have cause, if that come to pass which *may* come to pass, to sit down more dissatisfied with thy stars, than with thyself. And come the worst to the worst, glorious terms will I give thee. Thy garison, with general *Prudence* at the head, and governor *Watchfulness* bringing up the rear, shall be allowed to march out with all the honours due to so brave a resistance. And all thy sex, and all mine, that hear of my stratagems, and thy conduct, shall acknowlege the fortress as nobly won, as defended.

Thou wilt not dare, methinks I hear thee say, to attempt to reduce such a goddess as This, to a standard unworthy of her excellencies. It is impossible, Lovelace, that thou shouldst intend to break thro' oaths and protestations so solemn.

That I did *not* intend it, is certain. That I *do* intend it, I cannot (my heart, my reverence for her, will not let me) say. But knowest thou not my aversion to the state of shackles?—And is she not In my Power?

And which I had never taken so much pains to obtain, had I not loved her above all women.—So far upon a par, Jack! —And, if thou pleadest honour, ought not honour to be mutual? If mutual, does it not imply mutual trust, mutual confidence?— And what have I had of *that* from her to boast of?—Thou knowest the whole progress of our warfare: For a warfare it has truly been; and far, very far, from an amorous warfare too. Doubts, mistrusts, upbraidings, on her part: Humiliations the most abject, on mine. Obliged to assume such airs of reformation, that every varlet of ye has been afraid I should reclaim in good earnest. And hadst thou not thyself frequently observed to me, how aukwardly I returned to my usual gaiety, after I had been within a mile of her father's garden-wall, altho' I had not seen her?

Does she not deserve to pay for all this?—To make an honest fellow look like an hypocrite; what a vile thing is that!

Then thou knowest what a false little rogue she has been! How little conscience she has made of disappointing me!—Hast thou not been a witness of my ravings, on this score?—Have I not, in the height of them, vowed revenge upon the faithless charmer?—And, if I *must* be forsworn, whether I answer her expectations, or follow my own inclinations, can I hesitate a moment which to choose?

Then, I fancy, by her circumspection, and her continual grief, that she expects some mischief from me. I don't care to disappoint any-body I have a value for.

But O the noble, the exalted creature! Who can avoid hesitating when he thinks of an offence against her?—Who can but pity—

Yet, on the other hand, so loth at last to venture, tho' threatened to be forced into the nuptial fetters with a man, whom to look upon as a rival, is to disgrace myself!

But I resolve not *any way*. I will see how *her* will works; and how *my* will leads me on. I will give the combatants fair play. And, I find every time I attend her, that she is less in *my* power—I more in *hers.*

Yet, a foolish little rogue! to forbid me to think of marriage till I am a reformed man! Till the Implacables of her family change their natures, and become placable!

It is true, when she was for making those conditions, she did not think, that, without any, she should be cheated out of herself; for so the dear soul, as I may tell thee in its place, phrases it.

How it swells my pride, to have been able to outwit such a vigilant charmer!—I am taller by half a yard, in my imagination, than I was!—I look *down* upon every-body now!—Last night I was still more extravagant.—I took off my hat, as I

walked, to see if the lace were not scorched, supposing it had
brushed down a star; and, before I put it on again, in mere
wantonness, and heart's-ease, I was for buffeting the moon.
In short, my whole soul is joy. When I go to bed, I laugh myself
asleep: And I awake either laughing or singing.—Yet nothing
nearly in view, neither.—For why?—*I am not yet reformed
enough!*

But, ah! Jack, when I see my Angel, when I am admitted
to the presence of this radiant Beauty, what will become of all
this vapouring?—

But, be my end what it may, I am obliged, by thy penetration, fair-one, to proceed by the sap. *Fair and softly.*—A Wife
at any time! That will be always in my power.

But how I ramble!—This it is to be in such a situation, that
I know not what to resolve upon.

I'll tell thee my *inclinings*, as I proceed. The *pro's* and the
con's, I'll tell thee.—But being got too far from the track I set
out in, I will close here. But, perhaps, may write every day something, and send it as opportunity offers.

Regardless, however, in all I write, as I shall be, of connexion, accuracy, or of anything, but of my own imperial will
and pleasure.

Miss Howe
To Miss Clarissa Harlowe

Thursday, April 13.

I HAVE this moment your continuation-letter, and a little
absence of my Argus-eyed mamma.—

Dear creature!—I can account for all your difficulties. A
person of your delicacy!—And with such a man!—I must be
brief—

The man's a fool, my dear, with all his pride, and with all
his complaisance, and affected regards to your injunctions. Yet
his ready inventions—

Sometimes I think you should go to Lady Betty's.—I know not what to advise you to.—I could, if you were not so intent upon reconciling yourself to your relations. But they are implacable, you can have no hopes of them.

You need not to have been afraid of asking me, Whether I thought upon reading your narrative, any extenuation could lie for what you have done. I have told you above my mind as to that—And I repeat, that I think, your *provocations* and *inducements* considered, you are free from blame: At least, the freest, that ever young creature was who took such a step.

But you took it not—You were driven on one side, and, possibly, tricked on the other.—If any young person on earth shall be circumstanced as you were, and shall hold out so long as you did, against her persecutors on one hand, and her seducer on the other, I will forgive her for all the rest.

All your acquaintance, you may suppose, talk of nobody but you. Some, indeed, bring your admirable character against you: But nobody does, or *can*, acquit your father and uncles.

Every-body seems apprized of your brother's and sister's motives. They knew, that if once you were restored to favour, Love suspended would be Love augmented, and that you must defeat and expose them, and triumph by your amiable qualities, and great talents over all their arts.—And now, I hear, they enjoy their successful malice.

Your father is all rage and violence. He ought, I am sure, to turn his rage inward. All your family accuse you of acting with deep art; and are put upon supposing, that you are actually every hour exulting over them, with your man, in the success of it.

They all pretend now, that your trial of Wednesday was to be the last.

They own, however, that a minister was to be present. Mr. Solmes was to be at hand. And your father was previously to try his authority over you, in order to make you sign the settlements.—All of it a romantic contrivance of your wild-headed foolish brother, I make no doubt.—Is it likely, that he and Bell would have given way to your restoration to favour, on any other terms than those their hearts had been so long set upon?

Your Aunt Hervey, it seems, was the first that went down
to the Ivy summer-house, in order to acquaint you, that their
search was over. Betty followed her; and they not finding you
there, went on toward the cascade, according to a hint of yours.

Returning by the garden-door, they met a servant [They
don't say, it was that Joseph Leman; but it is very likely, that
it was he] running, as he said, from pursuing Mr. Lovelace (a
great hedge-stake in his hand, and out of breath) to alarm the
family.

If it were this fellow, and if he were employed in the double
agency of cheating them, and cheating you, what shall we think
of the wretch you are with?—Run away from him, my dear, if
so—No matter to whom—or marry him, if you cannot.

Your aunt and all your family were accordingly alarmed
by this fellow [evidently when too late for pursuit]. They got
together, and, when a posse ran to the place of interview; and
some of them as far as to the tracks of the chariot-wheels, without stopping. And having heard the man's tale, upon the spot,
a general lamentation, a mutual upbraiding, and rage, and grief,
were echoed from the different persons, according to their different tempers and conceptions.

Your brother, at first, ordered horses and armed men, to be
got ready for a pursuit. Solmes and your uncle Tony were to be
of the party. But your mamma and your aunt Hervey dissuaded
them from it, for fear of adding evil to evil; not doubting but
Lovelace had taken measures to support himself in what he had
done; and especially when the servant declared, that he saw you
run with him, as fast as you could set foot to ground; and that
there were several armed men on horseback at a small distance
off.

You have a nice, a very nice part to act with this wretch—
Who yet has, I think, but one plain path before him. I pity you!
—But you must make the best of the lot you have been forced
to draw. Yet I see your difficulties.—But if he do not offer to
abuse your confidence, I would have you *seem*, at least, to place
some in him.

If you think not of marrying soon, I approve of your resolution to fix somewhere out of his reach: And if he know not where

to find you, so much the better. Yet I verily believe, they would force you back, could they but come at you, if they were not afraid of *him*.

I think, by all means, you should demand of both your trustees to be put in possession of your own estate. Mean time I have sixty guineas at your service. I beg you will command them. I don't think you'll have a shilling, or a shilling's worth, of your own, from your relations, unless you extort it from them.

As they believe you went off by your own consent, they are, it seems, surprised, and glad, that you have left your jewels and money behind you, and have contrived for cloaths so ill. Very little likelihood, this shews, of their answering your requests.

Indeed every-body, not knowing what I *now* know, must be at a loss to account for your flight, as they will call it. And how, my dear, can one report it with any tolerable advantage to you?—To say, you did not intend it, when you met him, who will believe it?—To say, that a person of your known steadiness and punctilio was over-persuaded, when you gave him the meeting, how will that sound?—To say you were tricked out of yourself, and people were to give credit to it, how disreputable? —And while unmarried, and yet with him, he a man of such a character, what would it not lead a censuring world to think?

You may depend, I repeat, upon all the little spiteful and disgraceful things they can offer, instead of sending what you write for. So pray accept the Sum I tender. And I will find a way to send you also any of my cloaths and linen for present supply. I beg, my dearest Miss Harlowe, that you will not put your Anna Howe upon a foot with Lovelace, in refusing to accept of my offer. If you do not oblige me, I shall be apt to think, that you rather incline to be obliged to him, than to favour me. And if I find this, I shall not know how to reconcile it with your delicacy in other respects.

Pray inform me of everything that passed between you and him. If anything occur, that you would tell me of if I were present, fail not to put it down in writing, altho', from your natural diffidence, it should not appear to you altogether so worthy of

your pen, or of my knowing. A stander-by may see more of the
game than one that plays. Great consequences, like great folks,
are generally attended, and even *made* great, by small causes,
and little incidents.

I hear, from where I sit, my mamma calling about her, and
putting every-body into motion. She will soon, I suppose, make
me and *my* employment, the subject of her inquiry.

Adieu, my dear. May heaven preserve you, and restore you
with honour as unsullied as your mind, to

> *Your ever-affectionate*
>
> *Anna Howe*

Mr. Lovelace
To John Belford, Esq;

THOU hast heard me often expatiate upon the pitiful figure
a man must make, whose wife *has*, or *believes* she has,
more sense than himself. A thousand reasons could I give, why
I ought not to think of marrying Miss Clarissa Harlowe: At
least till I can be sure, that she loves me with the preference I
must expect from a wife.

I begin to stagger in my resolutions. Ever averse as I was to
the Hymeneal shackles, how easily will old prejudices recur!—
Heaven give me the heart to be honest to her!—There's a prayer,
Jack!—If I should not be heard, what a sad thing would that
be, for the most admirable of women!—Yet, as I do not often
trouble Heaven with my prayers, who knows but this may be
granted?

But there lie before me such charming difficulties, such
scenery for intrigue, for stratagem, for enterprize—What a horrible thing that my talents point all that way!—When I know what
is honourable and just; and would almost wish to be honest?—
Almost I say; for such a varlet am I, that I cannot altogether
wish it, for the soul of me!—Such a triumph over the whole

Sex, if I can subdue this lady!—My maiden vow, as I may call it!—For did not the sex begin with me?—And does this lady spare me?—Thinkest thou, Jack, that I should have spared my Rosebud, had I been set at defiance thus?—Her grandmother besought me, at first, to spare her Rosebud; and when a girl is put, or puts herself, into a man's power, what can he wish for further? while I always considered opposition and resistance as a challenge to do my worst.

Why, why, will the dear creature take such pains to appear all ice to me?—Why will she, by *her* pride, awaken *mine?*—Hast thou not seen, in the above, how contemptibly she treats me? —What have I not suffered *for* her, and even *from* her?—Is it tolerable to be told, that she will despise me, if I value myself above that odious Solmes!—

Then she cuts me short in all my ardors. To vow fidelity, is, by a cursed turn upon me, to shew, that there is reason, in my own opinion, for doubt of it.—The very same reflection upon me, once before. In my power, or out of my power, all one to her.—So, Belford, my poor vows are crammed down my throat, before they can well rise to my lips. And what can a lover say to his mistress, if she will neither let him lye nor swear?

One little piece of artifice I had recourse to: When she pushed so hard for me to leave her, I made a request to her, upon a condition she could not refuse; and pretended as much gratitude upon her granting it, as if it were a favour of the last consequence.

And what was This? but to promise what she had before promised, Never to marry any other man, while I am living, and single, unless I should give her cause for high disgust against me. This, you know, was promising nothing, because she could be offended at any time; and was to be the sole judge of the offence. But it shewed her, how reasonable and just my expectations were; and that I was no encroacher.

She consented; and asked, What security I expected?

Her word only.

She gave me her word: But I besought her excuse for sealing it: And, in the same moment [since to have waited for consent, would have been asking for a denial], saluted her. And, believe me, or not, but, as I hope to live, it was the first time I had the courage to touch her charming lips with mine. And This I tell thee, Belford, that That single pressure (as modestly put too, as if I were as much a virgin as herself, that she might not be afraid of me another time) delighted me more than ever I was delighted by the *Ultimatum* with any other woman.—So precious do awe, reverence, and apprehended prohibition, make a favour!

My charmer has written to her sister for her cloaths, for some gold, and for some of her books. What books can tell her more than she knows? But I can. So she had better study me.

She *may* write. She must be obliged to me at last, with all her pride. Miss Howe will be ready enough, indeed, to supply her; but I question, whether she can do it without her mother, who is as covetous as the grave.

Besides, if Miss Howe has money by her, I can put her mother upon borrowing it of her.—Nor blame me, Jack, for contrivances that have their foundation in generosity. Thou knowest my spirit; and that I should be proud to lay an obligation upon my charmer, to the amount of half my estate. Lord M. has more for me than I can ever wish for. My predominant passion is *Girl*, not *Gold*; nor value I *This*, but as it helps me to *That*, and gives me independence.

Thou wilt think me a sad fellow, I doubt.—But are not all rakes sad fellows?—And thou, to thy little power, as bad as any? If thou dost all that's in thy head and in thy heart to do, thou art worse than I; for I do not, I assure thee.

I proposed, and she consented, that her cloaths, or whatever else her relations should think fit to send her, should be directed to thy cousin Osgood's.—Let a special messenger, at my charge, bring me any letter, or portable parcel, that shall come.—If not portable, give me notice of it. But thou'lt have no trouble of this sort from her relations, I dare be sworn. And, in this assurance, I will leave them, I think, to act upon their own heads. A man would have no more to answer for than needs must.

But one thing, while I think of it [It is of great importance to be attended to]—You must hereafter write to me in character, as I shall do to you. How know we into whose hands our letters may fall? It would be a confounded thing to be blown up by a train of one's own laying.

Another thing remember; I have changed my name: Changed it without an act of parliament. "Robert Huntingford" it is now. Continue *Esquire*. It is a respectable addition, altho' every sorry fellow assumes it, almost to the banishment of the usual travelling one of *Captain*. "To be left till called for, at the posthouse at Hertford."

Upon naming thee, she asked thy character. I gave thee a better than thou deservest, in order to do credit to *myself*. Yet I told her, that thou wert an aukward puppy; and This to do credit to *Thee*, that she may not, if ever she is to see thee, expect a cleverer fellow than she'll find; yet thy *apparent* aukwardness befriends thee not a little: For wert thou a sightly varlet, people would discover nothing extraordinary in thee, when they conversed with thee: Whereas seeing a bear, they are surprised to find in thee any-thing that is like a man.

The lodgings we are in at present are not convenient. I was so delicate as to find fault with them, as communicating with each other, because I knew the lady would; and told her, That were I sure she was safe from pursuit, I would leave her in them, since such was her earnest desire. The devil's in't, if I don't banish even the *shadow* of mistrust from her heart.

Here are two young likely girls, daughters of the widow Sorlings; that's the name of our landlady.

I have only, at present, admired them in their dairy-works. How greedily do the Sex swallow praise!—So pleased was I with the youngest, for the elegance of her works, that I kissed her, and she made me a courtesy for my condescension; and blushed, and seemed sensible all over: Encouragingly, yet innocently, she adjusted her handkerchief, and looked towards the door, as much as to say, She would not tell, were I to kiss her again.

Her elder sister popt upon her. The conscious girl blushed again, and looked so confounded, that I made an excuse for her, which gratified both. Mrs. Betty, said I, I have been so much

pleased with the neatness of your dairy-works, that I could not
help saluting your sister: You have *your* share of merit in them,
I am sure—Give me leave— .

Good souls!—I like them both—She courtesied too!—How
I love a grateful temper! O that my Miss Harlowe were but half
so acknowleging!

I think I must get one of them to attend my charmer, when
she removes.—The mother seems to be a notable woman. She
had not best, however, be *too* notable: For were she by suspicion
to give a face of difficulty to the matter, it would prepare me
for a trial with one or both of the daughters.

Allow me a little rhodomontade, Jack!—But really and
truly my heart is fixed. I can think of no creature breathing
of the sex, but my Gloriana.

Miss Clarissa Harlowe
To Miss Howe

YOU may believe, my dear Miss Howe, that the circumstance of the noise and outcry within the garden-door,
on Monday last, gave me no small uneasiness, to think that I
was in the hands of a man, who could, by such vile premeditation, lay a snare to trick me out of myself, as I have so frequently
called it.

Whenever he came in my sight, the thought of this gave
me an indignation that made his presence disgustful to me; and
the more, as I fansied I beheld in his face a triumph which re-
proached my weakness on that account; altho', perhaps, it was
only the same vivacity and placidness that generally sit upon
his features.

I was resolved to task him upon this subject, the first time
I could have patience to enter upon it with him. For, besides
that it piqued me excessively from the nature of the artifice,
I expected shuffling and evasion, if he were guilty, that would
have incensed me: And, if not confessedly guilty, such unsatis-

factory declarations, as still would have kept my mind doubtful and uneasy.

I have had the opportunity I waited for; and will lay before you the result.

He was making his court to my good opinion in very polite terms, and with great seriousness lamenting that he had lost it; declaring, that he knew not how he had deserved to do so; attributing to me a prejudice, at least an indifference to him, that seemed, to his infinite concern, hourly to increase. And he besought me to let him know my whole mind, that he might have an opportunity either to confess his faults, and amend them, or clear his conduct to my satisfaction, and thereby intitle himself to a greater share of my confidence.

I answered him with quickness—Then, Mr. Lovelace, I will tell you one thing with a frankness, that is, perhaps, more suitable to *my* character, than to *yours*.

I am all attention, Madam.

I never can think tolerably of you, while the noise and voice I heard at the garden-door, which put me into the terror you took so much advantage of, remains unaccounted for. Tell me fairly, tell me candidly, the whole of that circumstance; and of your dealings with that wicked Joseph Leman; and, according to your explicitness in this particular, I shall form a judgment of your future professions.

I will, without reserve, my dearest life, said he, tell you the whole; and hope that my sincerity in the relation will atone for any thing you may think wrong in the fact.

"I knew nothing, *said he*, of this man, this Leman, and should have scorned a resort to so low a method as bribing the servant of any family, to let me into the secrets of that family, if I had not detected him in attempting to corrupt a servant of mine, to inform him of all my motions, of all my supposed intrigues, and, in short, of every action of my private life, as well as of my circumstances and engagements; and this for motives too obvious to be dwelt upon.

My servant told me of his offers, and I ordered him, unknown to the fellow, to let me hear a conversation that was to pass between them.

In the midst of it, and just as he had made an offer of money for a particular piece of intelligence, promising more when procured, I broke in upon them, and by bluster, calling for a knife to cut off his ears (one of which I took hold of), in order to make a present of it, as I said, to his employers, I obliged him to tell me who they were.

Your Brother, Madam, and your Uncle Antony, he named.

It was not difficult, when I had given him my pardon on naming them, after I had set before him the enormity of the task he had undertaken, and the honourableness of my intentions to your dear self, to prevail upon him, by a larger reward, to serve me; since, at the same time, he might keep your uncle and brother's favour; as I desired to know nothing, but what related to myself and to you, in order to guard us both against the effects of an ill-will, which he acknowleged all his fellow-servants, as well as himself, thought undeserved.

I was the more pleased with his services, as, let me acknowlege to you, Madam, they procured to you, unknown to yourself, a safe and uninterrupted egress (which perhaps would not otherwise have been continued to you, so long as it was) to the garden and wood-house: For he undertook to them, to watch all your motions: And the more chearfully (for the fellow loves you), as it kept off the curiosity of others."

So, my dear, it comes out, that I *myself* was obliged to this deep contriver.

I sat in silent astonishment; and thus he went on.

"As to the circumstance, which you, Madam, think so hardly of me for, I do freely confess, that having a suspicion that you would revoke your intention of getting away, and in that case, as I was determined, if possible, to prevail upon you to adhere to your resolution, apprehending that we should not have the time together, that was necessary for that purpose; I had ordered him to keep off every body he *could* keep off, and to be himself within view of the garden-door."—

But pray, Sir, interrupting him, how came you to apprehend that I should revoke my intention? I had indeed deposited a letter to that purpose; but you had it not.

"I will be very ingenuous, Madam: You had made me hope,

that, if you changed your mind, you would give me a meeting, to apprise me of the reasons for it: I went to the loose bricks, and I saw the letter there: And as I knew your friends were immoveably fixed in their schemes, I doubted not but the letter was to revoke or suspend your resolution; and probably to serve instead of a meeting too. I therefore let it lie, that, if you did revoke, you might be under the necessity of meeting me for the sake of the expectation you had given me: And as I came prepared, I was resolved, pardon me, Madam, whatever were your intentions, that you should not go back. Had I taken your letter, I must have been determined by the contents of it, for the present, at least: But not having received it, and you having reason to think I wanted not resolution, in a situation so desperate, to make your friends a personal visit, I depended upon the interview you had bid me hope for."

Wicked wretch! said I; It is my grief, that I gave you opportunity to take so exact a measure of my weakness!—But *would* you have presumed to visit the family, had I not met you?

Indeed I would. I had some friends in readiness, who were to have accompanied me to them. And had they refused to see me, or to give me audience, I would have taken my friends with me to Solmes.

And what did you intend to do to Mr. Solmes?

Not the least hurt, had the man been passive.

But had he *not* been passive, as you call it, what would you have done to Mr. Solmes?

He was loth, he said, to tell me—Yet not the least hurt to his *person*.

I repeated my question.

If he must tell me, he only proposed to carry off the *poor fellow*, and to hide him for a month or two. And this he would have done, let what would have been the consequence.

Was ever such a wretch heard of!—I sighed from the bottom of my heart.—But bid him proceed from the part I had interrupted him at.

"I ordered the fellow, as I told you, Madam, said he, to keep within view of the garden-door: And if he found any parley between us, and any-body coming (before you could retreat undiscovered) whose coming might be attended with violent effects, he would cry out; and this not only in order to save himself from their suspicions of him, but to give me warning to make off, and, if possible, to induce you [I own it, Madam] to go off with me, according to your own appointment. For, had they come, as *I* expected as well as *you*, what a despicable wretch had I been, could I have left you to the insults of a brother and others of your family, whose mercy was cruelty, when they had *not* the pretence which this detected interview would have furnished them with!"

What a wretch, said I!—But if, Sir, taking your *own* account of this strange matter to be fact, any-body were coming, how happened it, that I saw only that man Leman (I *thought* it was he) out of the door, and at a distance, look after us?

Very lucky! said he, putting his hand first in one pocket, then in another.—I hope I have not thrown it away—it is, per-haps, in the coat I had on yesterday—Little did I think it would be necessary to be produced—But I love to come to a demon-stration whenever I can—I *may* be giddy—I *may* be heedless. I *am* indeed—But no man, as to *you*, Madam, ever had a sincerer heart.

He then stepping to the parlour-door, called his servant to bring him the coat he had on yesterday.

The servant did. And in the pocket, rumpled up as a paper he regarded not, he pulled out a letter, written by that Joseph, dated Monday night; in which "he begs pardon for crying out so soon": Says, "That his fears of being discovered to act on both sides, had made him take the rushing of a little dog (that always follows him) thro' the phyllirea-hedge, for Betty's being at hand, or some of his masters: And that, when he found his mistake, he opened the door by his own key [Which the con-triving wretch confessed he had furnished him with] and incon-siderately ran out in a hurry, to have apprised him, that his crying-out was owing to his fright only:" And he added, "that they were upon the hunt for me, by the time he returned."

I shook my head—Deep! deep! deep! said I, at the best!—O Mr. Lovelace! God forgive and reform you!—But you are, I see plainly, upon the whole of your own account, a very artful, a very designing man.

Love, my dearest life, is ingenious, Night and day have I racked my stupid brain [O Sir, thought I, not stupid! 'Twere well perhaps if it were] to contrive methods to prevent the sacrifice designed to be made of you, and the mischief that must have ensued upon it; So little hold in your affections: Such undeserved antipathy from your friends: So much danger of losing you for ever from *both* causes—I have not had, for the whole fortnight before last Monday, half an hour's rest at a time. And I own to you, Madam, that I should never have forgiven myself, had I omitted any contrivance or forethought, that would have prevented your return without me.

Again I blamed myself for meeting him: And justly; for there were many chances to one, that I had *not* met him. And if I had not, all his fortnight's contrivances, as to me, would have come to nothing; and, perhaps, I might nevertheless have escaped Solmes.

Yet, had he resolved to come to Harlowe-Place with his friends, and been insulted, as he certainly would have been, what mischiefs might have followed!

But his resolution to run away with, and to hide the poor Solmes for a month or so, O my dear! what a wretch have I let run away with *me*, instead of *Solmes!*

I asked him, if he thought such enormities as these, such defiances of the laws of society, would have passed unpunished?

He had the assurance to say, with one of his usual gay airs, That he should by this means have disappointed his enemies, and saved me from a forced marriage. He had no pleasure in such desperate pushes. Solmes he would not have *personally* hurt. He must have fled his country for a time at least: And, truly, if he had been obliged to do so, as all his hopes of my favour must have been at an end, he would have had a fellow-traveller of his own sex out of our family, whom I little thought of.

Was ever such a wretch!—To be sure he meant my brother! All that I shall further say on this head, Mr. Lovelace, is this: That as this vile double-faced wretch has probably been the cause of great mischief on both sides, and still continues, as you own, his wicked practices, it is but my duty to have my friends apprised, what a creature he is, whom some of them encourage.

What you please, Madam, as to that—My service and your brother's are now almost over for him. The fellow has made a good hand of it. He does not intend to stay long in his place. He is now actually in treaty for an inn, which will do his business for life. I can tell you further, that he makes love to your sister's Betty: And this by my advice. They will be married, when he is established. An innkeeper's wife is every man's mistress; and I have a scheme in my head, to set some engines at work, to make her repent her saucy behaviour to you to the last day of her life.

What a wicked schemer are you, Sir!—Who shall avenge upon you the still greater evils which *you* have been guilty of?— I forgive Betty with all my heart. She was not my servant; and but too probably, in what she did, obeyed the commands of her, to whom she owed duty, better than I obeyed those, to whom I owed more.

No matter for that, the wretch said [To be sure, my dear, he must design to make me afraid of him] The decree was gone out—Betty must smart—Smart too by an act of her own choice. He loved, he said, to make bad people their own punishers.— Nay, Madam, excuse me; but if the fellow, if this Joseph, in your opinion, deserves punishment, mine is a complicated scheme; a man and his wife cannot well suffer separately, and it may come home to *him* too.—

I had no patience with him. I told him so.—But, Sir, said I, I see what a man I am with. Your *rattle* warns me of the *snake*. And away I flung; leaving him seemingly vexed, and in confusion.

Miss Clarissa Harlowe
To Miss Howe

L ATE as I went to bed, I have had very little rest. Sleep and
I have quarrelled; and altho' I court it, it will not be friends.
I hope its Fellow-irreconcileables at Harlowe-Place, enjoy its
balmy comforts. Else, that will be an aggravation of my fault.
My brother and sister, I dare say, want it not.

Mr. Lovelace, who is an early riser, as well as I, joined me
in the garden about Six; and, after the usual salutations, asked
me to resume our last night's subject. It was upon lodgings at
London, he said.

I think you mentioned one to me, Sir;—Did you not?

Yes, Madam, but (watching the turn of my countenance)
rather as what you would be welcome to, than perhaps approve
of.

I believe so too. To go to town upon an *uncertainty*, I own,
is not agreeable: But to be obliged to any gentleman of your
acquaintance, when I want to be thought independent of you;
and to a gentleman especially, to whom my friends are to direct
to me, if they vouchsafe to take notice of me at all; is an absurd
thing to mention.

Has not your family, Madam, some one tradesman they
deal with, who has conveniences of this kind? I would make
it worth such a person's while, to keep the secret of your being
at his house. Traders are dealers in pins, said he; and will be
more obliged by a peny customer than by a pound present, because it is in their way:—Yet will refuse neither.

My father's tradesmen, I said, would, no doubt, be the
first employed to find me out: So that proposal was as absurd
as the other.

We had a good deal of discourse upon the same topic. But,
at last, the result of all was this—He wrote a letter to one Mr.
Doleman, a married man, of fortune and character, desiring him
to provide decent apartments ready furnished [for I had told

him what they should be] for a single woman; consisting of a
bedchamber; another for a maid-servant, with the use of a
dining-room or parlour. This he gave me to peruse; and then
sealed it up, and dispatched it away in my presence.

I attend the issue of it; holding myself in readiness to set
out for London, unless you advise the contrary.

Mr. Lovelace
To John Belford, Esq;

Thursday, April 20.

H E *begins with communicating to him the letter he wrote
to Mr. Doleman, to procure suitable lodgings in town,
and which he sent away by the Lady's approbation: And then
gives him a copy of the answer to it: Upon which he thus expresses himself:*

Thou knowest the widow; thou knowest her nieces; thou
knowest the lodgings: And didst thou ever read a letter more
artfully couched, than this of Tom Doleman? Every possible
objection anticipated! Every accident provided against! Every
tittle of it plot-proof!

Who could forbear smiling, to see my charmer, like a far-
cical dean and chapter, choose what was before chosen for her;
and sagaciously (as they go in form to prayers, that God would
direct their choice) pondering upon the different proposals, as
if she would make me believe, she had a mind for some other?
The dear sly rogue looking upon me, too, with a view to discover
some emotion in me, that I can tell her, lay deeper than her eye
could reach, tho' it had been a sunbeam.

No confidence in me, fair-one! None at all, 'tis plain. Thou
wilt not, if I were inclined to change my views, encourage me
by a generous reliance on my honour!—And shall it be said, that
I, a master of arts in love, shall be overmatched by so unprac-
tised a novice?

But to see the charmer so far satisfied with my contrivance, as to borrow my friend's Letter, in order to satisfy Miss Howe likewise!

Silly little rogues! to walk out into by-paths on the strength of their own judgments!—When nothing but *experience* can teach them how to disappoint us, and learn them grandmother-wisdom! When they have it indeed, then may they sit down, like so many Cassandra's, and preach caution to others; who will as little mind *them*, as they did *their* instructresses, when-ever a fine handsome confident young fellow, such a one as thou knowest who, comes cross them.

But, Belford, didst thou not mind that sly rogue Doleman's naming Dover-street for the widow's place of abode?—What dost think could be meant by that!—'Tis impossible thou shouldst guess. So, not to puzzle thee about it—Suppose the widow Sinclair's in Dover-street should be inquired after by some officious person, in order to come at characters [Miss Howe is as *sly* as the devil, and as *busy* to the full]; and neither such a name, nor such a house, can be found in that street, nor a house to answer the description, then will not the keenest hunter in England be at a fault?

But how wilt thou do, methinks thou askest, to hinder the Lady from resenting the fallacy, and mistrusting thee the more on that account, when she finds it out to be in another street?

Pho! never mind that: Either I shall have a way for it, or we shall thoroughly understand one another by that time; or, if we don't, she'll know enough of me, not to wonder at *such* a peccadillo.

But how wilt thou hinder the Lady from apprising her friend of the real name?

She must first know it herself, monkey, must she not?

Well, but, how wilt thou do to hinder her from knowing the Street, and her friend from directing letters thither; which will be the same thing as if the name were known?

Let me alone for that too.

If thou further objectest, that Tom Doleman is too great a dunce to write such a letter in answer to mine;—Canst thou not imagine, that, in order to save honest Tom all this trouble,

I, who know the town so well, could send him a copy of what he should write, and leave him nothing to do, but transcribe?

What now sayst thou to *me*, Belford?

This it is to have leisure upon my hands!—What a matchless plotter thy friend!—Stand by, and let me swell!—I am already as big as an elephant; and ten times wiser!—mightier too by far! Have I not reason to snuff the moon with my proboscis?—Lord help thee for a poor, for a very poor creature!—Wonder not, that I despise thee heartily—Since the man who is disposed immoderately to exalt himself, cannot do it but by despising every-body else in proportion.

I shall make good use of the *Dolemanic* hint of being married. But I will not tell thee all at once. Nor, indeed, have I thoroughly digested that part of my plot. When a general must regulate himself by the motions of a watchful adversary, how can he say beforehand what he will, or what he will not, do?

Widow Sinclair!—Didst thou not say, Lovelace?—

Ay, Sinclair, Jack!—Remember the name! Sinclair, I repeat. She *has* no other. And her features being broad, and full-blown, I will suppose her to be of Highland extraction; as her husband the colonel [mind that too] was a Scot, as brave, as honest.

I never forget the *minutiae* in my contrivances. In all *doubtable* matters, the *minutiae* closely attended to, and provided for, are of more service than a thousand oaths, vows, and protestations made to supply the neglect of them, especially when jealousy has made its way in the working mind.

Thou wouldst wonder if thou knewest one half of my *providences*. To give thee but one: I have already been so good as to send up a list of books to be procured for the Lady's closet, mostly at *second-hand*. And thou knowest, that the women there are all well read. But I will not anticipate—Besides, it looks as if I were afraid of leaving anything to my old friend Chance; which has many a time been an excellent second to me; and ought not to be affronted or despised; especially by one, who has the art of making unpromising incidents turn out in his favour.

Miss Clarissa Harlowe
To Miss Howe

Saturday, p.m. April 23.

O MY best, my only friend! Now indeed is my heart broken! —It has received a blow it never will recover! Think not of corresponding with a wretch who now seems absolutely devoted! How can it be otherwise, if a parent's curses have the weight I always attributed to them, and have heard so many instances of their being followed by!—Yes, my dear Miss Howe, superadded to all my afflictions, I have the consequences of a father's curse to struggle with! How shall I support this reflection!

I have, at last, a letter from my unrelenting sister. Would to heaven I had not provoked it, by my second letter to my aunt Hervey. It lay ready for me, it seems. The thunder slept, till I awakened it. I inclose the letter itself. Transcribe it I cannot. There is no bearing the thoughts of it: For (shocking reflection!) the curse extends to the life beyond this.

I am in the depth of vapourish despondency. I can only repeat, Shun, fly, correspond not with a wretch so devoted, as

Your Clarissa Harlowe

To Miss Clarissa Harlowe

To be left at Mr. Osgood's, *near* Soho-Square.

Friday, April 21.

I T was expected you would send again to me, or to my aunt Hervey. The inclosed has lain ready for you therefore by direction. You will have no answer from any-body, write to *whom* you will, and as *often* as you will, and *what* you *will*.

It was designed to bring you back by proper authority, or to send you whither the disgraces you have brought upon us all, should be in the likeliest way, after a while, to be forgotten. But I believe that design is over: So you may *range* securely: Nobody will think it worth while to give themselves any trouble about you. Yet my mamma has obtained leave to send you your cloaths, of all sorts: But your cloaths only. This is a favour you'll see by the within letter not *designed* you: And *now* not granted for *your* sake, but because my poor mother cannot bear in her sight any-thing you used to wear. Read the inclosed, and tremble.

Arabella Harlowe

To the most ungrateful and undutiful of daughters.

Harlowe-Place, Sat. April 15.

Sister that was,

F OR I know not what name you are *permitted*, or *choose* to go by.

You have filled us all with distraction. My father, in the first agitations of his mind, on discovering your wicked, your shameful elopement, imprecated, on his knees, a fearful curse upon you. Tremble at the recital of it!—No less, than "that you may meet your punishment, both *here* and *hereafter*, by means of the very wretch, in whom you have chosen to place your wicked confidence."

Your cloaths will not be sent you. You seem, by leaving them behind you, to have been secure of them, whenever you demanded them. But perhaps you could think of nothing but meeting your fellow:—For every-thing seems to have been forgot, but what was to contribute to your wicked flight.—Yet you judged right, perhaps, that you would have been detected,

had you endeavoured to get off your cloaths.—Cunning creature! not to make *one* step that we could guess at you by!

But does the wretch put you upon writing for your things,
for fear you should be too expensive to him?—That's it, I suppose.

Was there ever a giddier creature?—Yet this is the celebrated, the blazing Clarissa—Clarissa, *what? Harlowe,* no
doubt!—And Harlowe it will be, to the disgrace of us all!

Your drawings and your pieces are all taken down; as is
also your own whole-length picture, in the Vandyke taste, from
your late parlour: They are taken down, and thrown into your
closet, which will be nailed up, as if it were not a part of the
house; there to perish together. For who can bear to see them?
Yet, how did they use to be shewn to every-body; the former,
for the magnifying of your dainty finger-works; the latter, for
the imputed dignity [dignity now in the dust!] of your boasted
figure; and this by those fond parents from whom you have run
away with so *much*, yet with so *little* contrivance!

My brother vows revenge upon your libertine—For the
family's sake he vows it—Not for *yours!*—For he will treat you,
he declares, like a common creature, if ever he sees you: And
doubts not, that this will be your fate.

My uncle Harlowe renounces you for ever.

So does my uncle Antony.

So does my aunt Hervey.

So do *I*, base unworthy creature! the disgrace of a good
family, and the property of an infamous rake, as questionless
you will soon find yourself, if you are not already!

Your books, since they have not taught you what belongs
to your family, to your sex, and to your education, will not
be sent you. Your money neither. Nor yet the jewels so undeservedly made yours! For it is wished you may be seen a beggar
along London-streets!

If all this is heavy, lay your hand to your heart, and ask
yourself, why you have deserved it?

Every gentleman, whom your pride taught you to reject
with scorn (Mr. Solmes excepted, who, however, has reason

to rejoice that he missed you), triumphs in your shameful elopement; and now knows how to account for his being refused.

Every-body, in short, is ashamed of you: But none more
than

Arabella Harlowe

Miss Howe
To Miss Clarissa Harlowe

Tuesday, April 25.

B E comforted; be not dejected; do not despond, my dearest
and best-beloved friend. God Almighty is just and gracious,
and gives not his assent to rash and inhuman curses. If he did,
malice, envy, and the blackest passions, in the blackest hearts,
would triumph, and the best (blasted by the malignity of the
worst) would be miserable in both worlds.

This maledection shews only, what manner of spirit they
are of, and how much their sordid views exceed their parental
love. 'Tis all rage and disappointment, my dear; disappointment
in designs proper to be frustrated; and all you have to grieve
for is, that their own rashness will turn upon their own hearts.
God Almighty cannot succeed a curse so presumptuous, as to
be carried into *his* futurity!

My Mother blames them for this wicked letter; and she
pities you; and, of her own accord, wished me to write to comfort you, for this once: For she says, It is pity your heart, which
was so noble (and when the sense of your fault, and the weight
of a parent's curse, are so strong upon you), should be quite
broken.

I would not have you dwell on the shocking occasion. I
know how it must affect you. But don't let it. Try to make light
of it [Forget it you can't].

Come, my dear, when things are at worst, they must mend.
Good often comes, when evil is expected. Happily improved

upon, this very curse may turn to a blessing.—But if you despond, there can be no hopes of cure.—Don't let them break
your heart; for that, it is plain to me, is now what some people
have in view to do.

How poor, to with-hold from you your books, your jewels,
and your money!—The latter is all you can at present want, since
they will vouchsafe to send your cloaths.—I send fifty guineas
by the bearer, inclosed in single papers in my *Norris's Miscellanies.* I charge you, as you love me, return them not.

I have more at your service. So if you like not your lodgings, or his behaviour when you get to town, leave both out
of hand.

I would advise you to write to Mr. Morden without delay.
If he intends for England, it may hasten him. And you'll do
very well till he can come. But surely Lovelace is bewitched,
if he takes not his happiness from *your consent,* before that of
Mr. Morden's is made needful by his arrival.

If you let not despondency seize you, you will strengthen,
you will add full day to this but glimmering light, from

> *Your ever-affectionate and faithful*
>
> *Anna Howe*

Miss Clarissa Harlowe
To Miss Howe

Wedn. P.M., Apr. 26.

AT length, my dearest Miss Howe, I am in London, and
in my new lodgings. They are neatly furnished, and the
situation, for the town, is pleasant. But, I think, you must not
ask me, how I like the old gentlewoman. Yet she seems courteous
and obliging. Her kinswomen just appeared to welcome me at
my alighting. They seem to be genteel young women. But more
of their aunt and of them, as I shall see more.

As soon as I arrived, I took possession of my apartment. I shall make good use of the light closet in it, if I stay here any time.

And now give me leave to chide you, my dearest friend, for your rash, and I hope revocable resolution, not to make Mr. Hickman the happiest man in the world, while my happiness is in suspense. Suppose I were to be unhappy, what, my dear, would your resolution avail me? Marriage is the highest state of friendship: If happy, it lessens our cares, by dividing them, at the same that it doubles our pleasures by a mutual participation. Why, my dear, if you love me, will you not rather give another friend to one who has not two that she is sure of? — Had you married on your mother's last birth-day, as she would have had you, I should not, I dare say, have wanted a refuge, that would have saved me so many mortifications, and so much disgrace.

Here I was broken in upon by Mr. Lovelace; introducing the widow leading in a kinswoman of hers to attend me, if I approved of her, till my Hannah should come, or till I had provided myself with some other servant. The widow gave her many good qualities; but said, that she had one great defect; which was, that she could not write, nor read writing; that part of her education having been neglected when she was young: But for discretion, fidelity, obligingness, she was not to be outdone by anybody.

As for her defect, I can easily forgive that. She is very likely and genteel; too genteel indeed, I think, for a servant. But what I like least of all in her, she has a strange sly eye. I never saw such an eye: — Half-confident, I think. But indeed Mrs. Sinclair herself (for that is the widow's name) has an odd winking eye; and her respectfulness seems too much studied, methinks, for the London ease and freedom. But people can't help their looks, you know; and after all, she is extremely civil and obliging: And as for the young woman (Dorcas is her name), she will not be long with me.

I accepted her: How could I do otherwise (if I had had a mind to make objections, which in my present situation I had

not), her aunt present, and the young woman also present; and
Mr. Lovelace officious in his introducing of them for my sake?—
But upon their leaving me, I told him, who seemed inclinable
to begin a conversation with me, that I desired that this apartment might be considered as my retirement: That when I saw
him, it might be in the dining-room; and that I might be as little
broken in upon as possible, when I am here. He withdrew very
respectfully to the door; but there stopt; and asked for my company then in the dining-room. If he was about setting out for
other lodgings, I would go with him now, I told him: But if he
did not just then go, I would first finish my letter to Miss Howe.

I see he has no mind to leave me, if he can help it. My
brother's scheme may give him a pretence to try to engage me to
dispense with his promise. But if I now do, I must acquit him of
it intirely.

My approbation of his tender behaviour in the midst of
my grief has given him a right, as he seems to think, of addressing me with all the freedom of an approved lover. I see by this
man, that when once a woman embarks with this sex, there is
no receding. One concession is but the prelude to another with
them. He has been ever since Sunday last continually complain-
ing of the distance I keep him at; and thinks himself intitled now,
to call in question my value for him; strengthening his doubts
by my declared readiness to give him up to a reconciliation
with my friends—And yet has himself fallen off from that
obsequious tenderness, if I may couple the words, which drew
from me the concessions he builds upon.

I have turned over the books I found in my closet; and
am not a little pleased with them; and think the better of the
people of the house for their sakes.

Stanhope's Gospels; Sharp's, Tillotson's, and South's Ser-
mons; Nelson's Feasts and Fasts; a Sacramental piece of the
Bishop of Man, and another of Dr. Gauden, Bishop of Exeter;
and Inett's Devotions; are among the devout books: And among
those of a lighter turn, these not ill-chosen ones: A Telemachus
in French, another in English; Steele's, Rowe's, and Shakespeare's
Plays; that genteel Comedy of Mr. Cibber, The Careless Hus-

band, and others of the same Author; Dryden's Miscellanies; the Tatlers, Spectators, and Guardians; Pope's, and Swift's, and Addison's Works.

In the blank leaves of the Nelson and Bishop Gauden, is Mrs. Sinclair's name; and in those of most of the others, either Sarah Martin, or Mary Horton, the names of the two nieces.

I am exceedingly out of humour with Mr. Lovelace: And have great reason to be so: As you will allow, when you have read the conversation I am going to give you an account of; for he would not let me rest till I gave him my company in the Dining-room.

He began with letting me know, that he had been out to inquire after the character of the widow; which was the more necessary, he said, as he supposed that I would *expect* his frequent absence.

I did, I said; and that he would not think of taking up his lodging in the same house with me. But what was the result of your inquiry?

Why, indeed, the widow's character was, in the main, what he liked well enough. But as it was Miss Howe's opinion, as I had told him, that my brother had not given over his scheme; as the widow lived by letting lodgings; and had others to let in the same part of the house, which might be taken by an enemy; he knew no better way, than for him to take them all, as it could not be for a long time; unless I would think of removing to others.

So far was well enough: But as it was easy for me to see, that he spoke the slighter of the widow, in order to have a pretence to lodge here himself, I asked him his intention in that respect. And he frankly owned, that if I chose to stay here, he could not, as matters stood, think of leaving me for six hours together; and he had prepared the widow to expect, that we should be here but for a few days;—only till we could fix ourselves in a house suitable to our condition; and this, that I might be under the less embarrass, if I pleased to remove.

Fix *our*-selves in a house, and *we* and *our*, Mr. Lovelace— Pray, in what light——

He interrupted me,—Why, my dearest life, if you will hear

me with patience—Yet I am half-afraid, that I have been too forward, as I have not consulted you upon it.—But as my friends in town, according to what Mr. Doleman has written, in the letter you have seen, conclude us to be married—

I perfectly raved at him. I would have flung from him in resentment; but he would not let me: And what could I do? Whither go, the evening advanced?

I am astonished at you! said I:—If you are a man of honour, what need of all this strange obliquity? You delight in crooked ways.—Let me know, since I must stay in your company (for he held my hand), let me know all you have said.—Indeed, indeed, Mr. Lovelace, you are a very unaccountable man.

My dearest creature, need I to have mentioned any thing of this? And could I not have taken up my lodgings in this house, unknown to you, if I had not intended to make you the judge of all my proceedings? But this is what I have told the widow before her kinswomen, and before your new servant,—That indeed we were privately married at Hertford; but that you had preliminarily bound me under a solemn vow, which I am most religiously resolved to keep, to be contented with separate apartments, and even not to lodge under the same roof, till a certain reconciliation shall take place, which is of high consequence to both. And further, that I might convince you of the purity of my intentions, I have acquainted them, that I have solemnly promised to behave to you before every body, as if we were only betrothed, and not married; not even offering to take any of those innocent freedoms which are not refused in the most punctilious loves.

And then he solemnly vowed to me the strictest observance of the same respectful behaviour to me.

What could I say? What could I do?—I verily think, that had he urged me again, in a proper manner, I should have consented (little satisfied as I am with him) to give him a meeting to-morrow morning at a more solemn place than in the parlour below.

But this I resolve, that he shall not have my consent to stay a night under this roof. He has now given me a stronger reason for this determination than I had before.

Alas! my dear, how vain a thing to say, what we will or
what we will not do, when we have put ourselves into the power
of this sex!—He went down to the people below, on my desiring
to be left to myself; and staid till their supper was just ready;
and then, desiring a moment's *audience*, as he called it, he besought my leave to stay that one night, promising to set out
either for Lord M's, or for Edgware, to his friend Belford's,
in the morning after breakfast. But if I were against it, he said,
he would not stay supper; and would attend me about eight
next day.—Yet he added, that my denial would have a very
particular appearance to the people below, from what he had
told them; and the more, as he had actually agreed for all the
vacant apartments (indeed only for a month), for the reason
he had before hinted at: But I need not stay here two days, if,
upon conversing with the widow and her nieces in the morning,
I should have any dislike to them.

This was what I said.—What you *will* do, you *must* do,
I think. You are very ready to promise; very ready to depart
from your promise. You say, however, that you will set out
to-morrow for the country. You know how ill I have been. I
am not well enough now to debate with you upon your in-
croaching ways. I am utterly dissatisfied with the tale you have
told below. Nor will I promise to appear to the people of the
house to-morrow, what I am not.

He withdrew, in the most respectful manner, beseeching
me only to favour him with such a meeting in the morning,
as might not make the widow and her nieces think he had given
me reason to be offended with him.

I retired to my own apartment, and Dorcas came to me soon
after to take my commands. I told her, that I required very
little attendance, and always dressed and undressed myself.

She seemed concerned, as if she thought I had repulsed
her, and said, It should be her whole study to oblige me.

I told her, that I was not difficult to please. And should
let her know from time to time what assistances I should expect
from her. But for that night I had no occasion for her further
attendance.

She is not only genteel, but is well-bred, and well-spoken.—

She must have had what is generally thought to be the polite part of education: But it is strange, that fathers and mothers should make so light, as they generally do, of that preferable part, in girls, which would improve their minds, and give a grace to all the rest.

As soon as she was gone, I inspected the doors, the windows, the wainscot, the dark closet as well as the light one; and finding very good fastenings to the door, and to all the windows, I again had recourse to my pen.

Do you know how my poor Hannah does?

Mr. Lovelace is so full of his contrivances and expedients, that I think it may not be amiss to desire you to look carefully to the seals of my letters, as I shall to those of yours. If I find him base in this particular, I shall think him capable of any evil; and will fly him as my worst enemy.

Miss Howe
To Miss Clarissa Harlowe

Thursday Night, April 27.

I HAVE yours; just brought me. Mr. Hickman has help'd me to a lucky expedient, which, with the assistance of the post, will enable me to correspond with you every day. An honest higgler (Simon Collins his name) by whom I shall send this, and the two inclosed (now I have your direction where), goes to town constantly on Mondays, Wednesdays, and Fridays, and can bring back to me from Wilson's what you shall have caused to be left for me.

I am sorry your Hannah can't be with you. She is very ill still, but not in danger.

I long for your account of the women you are with. If they are not right people, you will find them out in one breakfasting.

I know not what to write upon his reporting to them, that you are actually married. His reasons for it are plausible. But he delights in odd expedients and inventions.

You may depend upon my looking narrowly into the sealings of your letters. If, as you say, he be base in that point, he
will be so in every-thing. But to a person of your merit, of your
fortune, of your virtue, he cannot be base. The man is no fool.
It is his interest, as well with regard to his expectations from
his own friends, as from you, to be honest. Would to heaven,
however, that you were really married! This is now the predominant wish of

Your Anna Howe

Miss Clarissa Harlowe
To Miss Howe

Monday Night, May 1.

I HAVE just escaped from the very disagreeable company I
was obliged, so much against my will, to be in. As a very
particular relation of this evening's conversation would be painful to me, you must content yourself with what you shall be able
to collect from the outlines, as I may call them, of the characters
of the persons, assisted by the little histories Mr. Lovelace gave
me of each yesterday.

The names of the gentlemen are Belton, Mowbray, Tourville, and Belford. These four, with Mrs. Sinclair, Miss Partington, the great heiress mentioned in my last, Mr. Lovelace, and
myself, made up the company.

I gave you before the favourable side of Miss Partington's
character, such as it was given me by Mrs. Sinclair, and her
nieces. I will now add a few words from my own observation
upon her behaviour in *this* company.

In *better* company, perhaps, she would have appeared to
less disadvantage: But, notwithstanding her innocent looks,
which Mr. Lovelace also highly praised, he is the last person
whose judgment I would take upon real modesty. For I observed,
that, upon some talk from the gentlemen, not free enough to be

openly censured, yet too indecent in its implication to come from well-bred persons, in the company of virtuous people, this young lady was very ready to apprehend; and yet, by smiles and simperings, to encourage, rather than discourage, the culpable freedoms of persons, who, in what they went out of their way to say, must either be guilty of absurdity, meaning *nothing;* or, meaning *something*, of rudeness.

But indeed I have seen women, of whom I had a better opinion, than I can say I have of Mrs. Sinclair, who have allowed *gentlemen*, and *themselves* too, in greater liberties of this sort, than I have thought consistent with that purity of manners which ought to be the distinguishing characteristic of our sex: For what are *words*, but the *body* and *dress* of *thought*? And is not the mind indicated strongly by its outward dress?

Monday Midnight.

I AM very much vex'd and disturbed at an odd incident.
Mrs. Sinclair has just now left me, I believe in displeasure, on my declining to comply with a request she made me: Which was, To admit Miss Partington to a share in my bed; her house being crouded by her nieces guests and by their attendants, as well as by those of Miss Partington.

There might be nothing in it; and my denial carried a stiff and ill-natured appearance. But instantly, all at once, upon her making the request, it came into my thought, that I was, in a manner, a stranger to every-body in the house: Not so much as a servant I could call my own, or of whom I had any great opinion: That there were four gentlemen of free manners in the house, avowed supporters of Mr. Lovelace in matters of offence; himself a man of enterprize; all, as far as I knew (and had reason to think by their noisy mirth after I left them), drinking deeply: That Miss Partington herself is not so bashful a lady, as she was represented to me to be: That officious pains were taken to give me a good opinion of her: And that Mrs. Sinclair made a greater parade in prefacing the request, than such a request needed. To deny, thought I, can carry only an appearance of singularity, to people who *already* think me singular. To consent, may possibly, if not probably, be attended with inconveniences.

I told her, that I was writing a long letter: That I should choose to write till I were sleepy: And that Miss would be a restraint upon me, and I upon her.

She was loth, she said, that so delicate a young creature, and so great a fortune, as Miss Partington was, should be put to lie with Dorcas in a press-bed. She should be very sorry, if she had asked an improper thing: She had never been so put to it before: And Miss would stay up with *her*, till I had done writing.

Alarmed at this urgency, and it being easier to persist in a denial *given*, than to give it at *first*, I offered Miss my whole bed, and to retire into the dining-room, and there, locking myself in, write all the night.

The poor thing, she said, was afraid to lie alone. To be sure Miss Partington would not put me to such an inconvenience.

She then withdrew: But returned; begged my pardon for returning: But the poor child, she said, was in tears. Miss Partington had never seen a young lady she so much admired, and so much wished to imitate, as me. The dear girl hoped that nothing had passed in her behaviour, to give me dislike to her. Should she bring her to me?

I was very busy, I said. The letter I was writing was upon a very important subject. I hoped to see Miss in the morning; when I would apologize to her for my particularity. And then Mrs. Sinclair hesitating, and moving towards the door (tho' she turned round to me again) I desired her (lighting her) to take care how she went down.

Pray, Madam, said she, on the stairs head, don't give yourself all this trouble. God knows my heart, I meant no affront: But, since you seem to take my freedom amiss, I beg you will not acquaint Mr. Lovelace with it; for he, perhaps, will think me bold and impertinent.

Now, my dear, is not this a particular incident; either as I have made it, or as it was designed? I don't love to do an uncivil thing. And if nothing were meant by the request, my refusal deserves to be called so. Then I have shewn a suspicion of foul usage by it, which surely dare not be meant. If just, I ought to apprehend every-thing, and fly the house, and the man as I would an infection. If not just, and if I cannot contrive to clear myself of having entertained suspicions, by assigning some other plausible reason for my denial, the very staying here will have an appearance not at all reputable to myself.

I am now out of humour with him, with myself, with all the world but you. His companions are shocking creatures. Why, again I repeat, should he have been desirous to bring me into such company? Once more, I like him not. I am, my dear,

Your affectionate

Cl. Harlowe

Mr. Lovelace
To John Belford, Esq;

Tuesday, May 2.

M ERCURY, as the Fabulist tells us, having the curiosity to know the estimation he stood in among mortals, descended in disguise, and, in a statuary's shop, cheapens a Jupiter, then a Juno, then one, then another, of the *Dii majores;* and, at last, asks, What price that same statue of *Mercury* bore? O, says the artist, buy one of the others, Sir; and I'll throw ye in that for nothing. How sheepish must the god of thieves look, upon this rebuff to his vanity!

So thou!—A thousand pounds wouldst thou give for the good opinion of this single lady: To be only thought tolerably of, and not quite unworthy of her conversation, would make thee happy: And, at parting last night, or rather this morning, thou madest me promise a few lines to Edgware, to let thee know what she thinks of thee, and thy brother varlets.

Thy thousand pounds, Jack, is all thy own: For most heartily does she dislike ye all—Thee as much as any.

I must never talk of reformation, she told me, having such companions, and taking such delight as I seemed to take, in their frothy conversation.

I don't know how it is, Belford; but women think themselves intitled to take any freedoms with *us;* while we are unpolite, forsooth, and I can't tell what, if we don't tell a pack of cursed lyes, and make black white, in *their* favour—teaching us to be hypocrites, yet stigmatizing us, at other times, for deceivers.

Plainly, she said, she neither liked my companions, nor the house she was in.

I liked not the house any more than she: Tho' the people were very obliging, and she had owned they were less exceptionable to herself, than at first: And were we not about another of our own?

She did not like Miss Partington: Let her fortune be what it would, she should not choose an intimacy with her. She thought it was a hardship to be put upon such a difficulty, as she was put upon the preceding night, when there were lodgers in the front-house, whom they had reason to be freer with, than, upon so short an acquaintance, with her.

I pretended to be an utter stranger as to this particular; and, when she explained herself upon it, condemned the request, and called it a confident one.

She, *artfully*, made lighter of her denial of Miss for a bed-fellow, than she *thought* of it, I could see that; for it was plain, she supposed there was room for me to think she had been either *over-nice*, or *over-cautious*.

I offered to resent Mrs. Sinclair's freedom.

No; there was no great matter in it: I was best to let it pass: But as the people below had a large acquaintance, she did not know how often she might have her retirements invaded, if she gave way. And indeed there were levities in Miss's behaviour, which she could not so far pass over as to wish an intimacy with her. But if she were such a vast fortune, she could not but say, that Miss seemed a much more suitable person for me to make my address to, than—

Interrupting her, with gravity, I said, I liked Miss Partington as little as *she could* like her. She was a silly young creature; who seemed too likely to justify her guardians watchfulness over her. But, nevertheless, as to her general conversation and behaviour last night, I must own, that I thought the girl (for girl she was, as to discretion) not exceptionable; only carrying herself like a free good-natured creature, who thought herself secure in the honour of her company.

It was very well said of me, she replied: But, if Miss were so *well* satisfied with her company, she left it to me, whether I was not very kind to suppose her such an *innocent*—For her own part, she had seen nothing of the London world: But thought, she must tell me plainly, that she never was in such company in her life; nor ever again wished to be in it.

There, Belford!—Worse off than Mercury!—Art thou not?

Mr. Belford
To Robert Lovelace, Esq;

plea vi behalf of Cl.

Edgware, Tuesday-night, May 2.

WITHOUT staying for the promised letter from you to inform us what the lady says of *us*, I write to tell you, That we are all of *one* opinion with regard to *her*; which is, that there is not of her age a finer lady in the world, as to her understanding. As for her person, she is at the age of bloom, and an admirable creature; a perfect beauty.

Permit me, dear Lovelace, to be a means of saving this excellent creature from the dangers she hourly runs from the most plotting heart in the world. In a former, I pleaded your own family, Lord M's wishes particularly; and then I had not seen her: But now, I join her sake, honour's sake, motives of justice, generosity, gratitude, and humanity, which are all concerned in the preservation of so fine a creature.—Thou knowest not the anguish I should have had (whence arising, I cannot devise), had I not known before I set out this morning, that the incomparable

creature had disappointed thee in thy cursed view of getting her
to admit the specious Partington for a bedfellow!

There is something so awful, and yet so sweet, in this lady's
aspect, that were I to have the Virtues and the Graces all drawn
in one piece, they should be taken, every one of them, from
different airs and attitudes in her. She was born to adorn the age
she was given to, and would be an ornament to the first dignity.
What a piercing, yet gentle eye, every glance, I thought, mingled
with love and fear of you: What a sweet smile darting through
the cloud that overspread her fair face; demonstrating, that she
had more apprehensions and grief at her heart, than she cared
to express!

You may think what I am going to write too flighty; but, by
my faith, I have conceived such a profound reverence for her
sense and judgment, that, far from thinking the man excuseable
who should treat her basely, I am ready to regret that such an
angel of a lady should even marry. She is, in my eye, all mind:
And were she to meet with a man all mind likewise, why should
the charming qualities she is mistress of, be endangered? Why
should such an angel be plunged so low as into the vulgar offices
of domestic life? Were she mine, I should hardly wish to see her
a mother, unless there were a kind of moral certainty, that
minds like hers could be propagated. For why, in short, should
not the work of bodies be left to *mere* bodies? I know, that you
yourself have an opinion of this lady little less exalted than
mine.

What must that merit and excellence be, that can extort
this from *us*, free livers, like yourself, and all of us your partial
friends, who have joined with you in your just resentments
against the rest of her family, and offered our assistance to
execute your vengeance on them? But we cannot think it reasonable, that you should punish an innocent lady, who loves you so
well; and who is in your protection, and has suffered so much
for you, for the faults of her relations.

And here, let me put a serious question, or two. Thinkest
thou, truly admirable as this lady is, that the end thou proposest
to thyself, if obtained, is answerable to the means, to the trouble
thou givest thyself, and to the perfidies, tricks, stratagems, and

contrivances thou hast already been guilty of, and still medi-
tatest? In every real excellence she surpasses all her sex. But in
the article thou seekest to subdue her for, a mere sensualist, a
Partington, a Horton, a Martin, would make a sensualist a thousand times happier than she either will or can.

Sweet are the joys that come with willingness.

And wouldst thou make *her* unhappy for her whole life, and
thyself not happy for a single moment?

Hitherto, it is not too late; and that, perhaps, is as much as
can be said, if thou meanest to preserve her esteem and good
opinion, as well as person; for I think it is impossible she can get
out of thy hands, now she is in this cursed house: Be honest,
and marry; and be thankful, that she will condescend to have
thee. If thou dost not, thou'lt be the worst of men; and will be
condemned in this world and the next: As I am sure thou ought-
est, and shouldest too, wert thou to be judged by one, who never
before was so much touched in a woman's favour: And whom
thou knowest to be

Thy partial friend,

J. Belford

Our companions consented, that I should withdraw to
write to the above effect. They can make nothing of the
characters we write in; so I read this to them; and they
approve of it; and of their own motion each man would
set his name to it. I would not delay sending it, for fear
of some detestable scheme taking place.

Thomas Belton
Richard Mowbray
James Tourville

Mr. Lovelace
To John Belford, Esq;

Wednesday, May 3.

WHEN I have already taken pains to acquaint thee in full with my views, designs, and resolutions, with regard to this admirable creature, it is very extraordinary, that thou shouldst vapour as thou dost, in her behalf, when I have made no trial, no attempt: And yet, givest it as thy opinion in a former letter, that advantage may be taken of the situation she is in; and that she may be overcome.

I own with thee, and with the poet, *That sweet are the joys that come with willingness*—But is it to be expected, that a woman of education, and a lover of forms, will yield before she is attacked?—And have I so much as summoned This to surrender?—I doubt not but I shall meet with difficulty. I must therefore make my first effort by surprize.—There may possibly be some cruelty necessary: But there may be consent in struggle; there may be yielding in resistance. But the first conflict over, whether the following may not be weaker and weaker, till *willingness* follow, is the point to be tried.—I will illustrate what I have said by the simile of a Bird new-caught. We begin with Birds as boys, and, as men, go on to ladies; and both perhaps, in turns, experience our sportive cruelty.

Hast thou not observed the charming gradations, by which the ensnared volatile has been brought to bear with its new condition? How at first, refusing all sustenance, it beats and bruises itself against its wires, till it makes its gay plumage fly about, and overspread its well-secured cage. Now it gets out its head; sticking only at its beautiful shoulders: Then, with difficulty, drawing back its head, it gasps for breath, and, erectedly perched, with meditating eyes, first surveys, and then attempts, its wired canopy. As it gets breath, with renewed rage, it beats and bruises again its pretty head and sides, bites the wires, and pecks at the fingers of its delighted tamer. Till at last, finding its efforts ineffectual, quite tired and breathless, it lays itself down, and pants at the bottom of the cage, seeming to bemoan its cruel fate, and forfeited liberty. And after a few days, its struggles to escape still diminishing, as it finds it to no purpose to attempt it, its new habitation becomes familiar; and it hops about from perch to perch, resumes its wonted chearfulness, and every day sings a song to amuse itself, and reward its keeper.

Now, let me tell thee, that I have known a bird actually starve itself, and die with grief, at its being caught and caged— But never did I meet with a lady, who was so silly.—Yet have I heard the dear souls most vehemently threaten their own lives on such an occasion. But it is saying nothing in a woman's favour, if we do not allow her to have more sense than a bird. And yet we must all own, that it is more difficult to catch a bird than a lady.

And now, Belford, were I to go no further, how shall I know whether this sweet bird may not be brought to sing me a fine song, and, in time, to be as well contented with her condition as I have brought other birds to be; some of them very shy ones?

The worst, respecting myself, in the case before me, is, that my triumph, when completed, will be so glorious a one, that I shall never be able to keep up to it. All my future attempts must be poor to this. I shall be as unhappy after a while, from my reflections upon this conquest, as Don John of Austria was, in his, on the renowned victory of Lepanto, when he found, that none of his future achievements could keep pace with his early glory.

I am sensible, that my pleas and my reasonings may be easily answered, and perhaps justly censured; but by whom censured? Not by any of the Confraternity, whose constant course of life, even long before I became your general, to this hour, has justified what ye now, in a fit of squeamishness, and thro' envy, condemn.

Be convinced then, that I (according to *our* principles) am right, *thou* wrong; or, at least, be silent. But I command thee to be convinced. And in thy next, be sure to tell me that thou art.

Mr. Belford
To Robert Lovelace, Esq;

Edgware, Thursday, May 4.

I KNOW that thou art so abandoned a man, that to give thee the best reasons in the world against what thou hast once resolved upon, will be but acting the madman, whom once we saw trying to buffet down a hurricane with his hat. I hope, however, that the Lady's merit will still avail her with thee. But if thou persistest; if thou wilt avenge thyself on this sweet lamb, which thou hast singled out from a flock thou hatest, for the faults of the dogs who kept it: If thou art not to be moved by beauty, by learning, by prudence, by innocence, all shining out in one charming object; but she must fall; fall by the man whom she has chosen for her protector; I would not for a thousand worlds have thy crime to answer for.

Upon my faith, Lovelace, the subject sticks with me, notwithstanding I find I have not the honour of the Lady's good opinion. And the more, when I reflect upon her father's brutal curse, and the villainous hard-heartedness of all her family.— But, nevertheless, I should be desirous to know if thou wilt proceed by what gradations, arts, and contriveances, thou effectest thy ingrateful purpose.—If she yield to *fair seduction*, if I may so express myself; if thou canst raise a weakness in her by love, or by arts not inhuman; I shall the less pity her. And shall then conclude, that there is not a woman in the world who can resist a bold and resolute lover.

J. Belford

Miss Clarissa Harlowe
To Miss Howe

Tuesday Night, May 16.

M R. LOVELACE has sent me, by Dorcas, his proposals, as follow:

"To spare a delicacy so extreme, and to obey you, I write: And the rather, that you may communicate this paper to Miss Howe, who may consult any of her friends you shall think proper to have intrusted on this occasion. I say, *intrusted*; because, as you know, I have given it out to several persons, that we are actually married.

In the first place, Madam, I offer to settle upon you, by way of jointure, your whole estate: And moreover to vest in trustees such a part of mine in Lancashire, as shall produce a clear four hundred pounds a year, to be paid to your sole and separate use, quarterly.

My own estate is a clear 2000*l. per annum.* Lord M. proposes to give me possession either of That which he has in Lancashire (to which, by the way, I think I have a better title than he has himself), or That we call *The Lawn* in Hertfordshire, upon my nuptials with a lady whom he so greatly admires; and to make that I shall choose a clear 1000*l. per annum.*

My too great contempt of censure has subjected me to much traduction. It may not therefore be improper to assure you, on the word of a gentleman, that no part of my estate was ever mortgaged: And that altho' I lived very expensively abroad, and made large draughts, yet, that Midsummer-Day next will discharge all that I owe in the world.

If, as your own estate is at present in your father's hands, you rather choose that I should make a jointure out of mine, tantamount to yours, be it what it will, it shall be done. I will engage Lord M. to write to *you*, what he proposes to do on the happy occasion: Not as your desire or expectation, but to demonstrate, that no advantage is intended to be taken of the situation you are in with your own family.

As to cloaths, jewels, and the like, against the time you shall choose to make your appearance, it will be my pride, that you shall not be beholden for such of these as shall be answerable to the rank of both, to those who have had the stupid folly to renounce a daughter they deserved not. You must excuse me, Madam: You would mistrust my sincerity in the rest, could I speak of these people with less asperity, tho' so nearly related to you.

These, Madam, are my proposals. But you have been so determined to try every method for reconciling yourself to your relations, even by giving me absolutely up for ever, that you have seemed to think it but justice to keep me at a distance, till the event of that your *predominant* hope could be seen. It is *now* seen!—And altho' I *have been*, and perhaps still *am*, ready to regret the want of that preference I wished for from you as Miss Clarissa Harlowe; yet I am sure, as the husband of Mrs. Lovelace, I shall be more ready to adore than to blame you for the pangs you have given to a heart, the generosity, or rather *justice* of which, my implacable enemies have taught you to doubt.

I will only add, that if I have omitted any thing, that would have given you further satisfaction; or if the above terms be short of what you would wish; you will be pleased to supply them as you think fit. And when I know your pleasure, I will instantly order articles to be drawn up conformably; that nothing in my power may be wanting to make you happy.

You will now, dearest Madam, judge, how far all the rest depends upon yourself."

You see, my dear, what he offers. You see it is all my fault, that he has not made these offers before.—I am a strange creature! To be to blame in everything, and to every-body! Yet neither intend the ill at the time, nor know it to *be* the ill till too late, or so nearly too late, that I must give up all the delicacy he talks of, to compound for my fault!

I shall now judge how far all the rest depends upon myself! So coldly concludes he such warm, and, in the main, unobjectible proposals! Would you not, as you read, have supposed, that the paper would conclude with the most earnest demand of a day?—I own, I had that expectation so strong, resulting *naturally*, as I may say, from the premises, that without studying for dissatisfaction, I could not help being dissatisfied, when I came to the conclusion.—But you say, there is no help. I must, perhaps, make *further* sacrifices. All delicacy, it seems, is to be at an end with me! But if so, this man knows not what every *wise* man knows, that prudence, and virtue, and delicacy of mind in a *wife*, do the husband more *real* honour, in the eye of the world, than the same qualities (were *she* destitute of them) in *himself*: As the *want* of them in her does him more *dis*-honour: For are not the wife's errors, the husband's reproach? How *justly* his reproach, is another thing.

I will consider this paper; and write to it, if I am able: For it seems *now*, *all the rest depends upon myself*.

Miss Clarissa Harlowe To Miss Howe

Wednesday Morning, May 17.

M R. LOVELACE would fain have engaged me last night. But as I was not prepared to enter upon the subject of his proposals, intending to consider them maturely, and not highly pleased with his conclusion (and then there is hardly any getting from him in tolerable time over-night), I desired to be excused seeing him till morning.

About seven o'clock we met in the dining-room. I find, he was full of expectation that I should meet him with a very favourable, who knows, but with a *thankful* aspect?—And I immediately found by his sullen countenance, that he was under no small disappointment that I did not.

My dearest love, are you well?—Why look you so solemn upon me?—Will your indifference never be over?—If I have proposed terms in any respect *short* of your expectation—

I told him, that he had very considerately mentioned my

shewing his proposals to Miss Howe, and consulting any of her
friends upon them by her means; and I should have an opportunity to send them to her, by Collins, by-and-by; and so insisted
to suspend any talk upon that subject till I had her opinion
upon them.

Thus far, I told him, I could say, That my principal point
was peace and reconciliation with my family. As to other matters, the genteelness of his own spirit would put him upon
doing more for me than I should ask, or expect.

He asked me then, If I would so far permit him to touch
upon the happy day, as to request his uncle's presence on the
occasion, and to be my father?

Father had a sweet and venerable sound with it, I said. I
should be glad to have a father who would own me!

Was not this plain speaking, think you, my dear? Yet it
rather, I must own, appears so to me on reflection, than was
designed freely at the time. For I then, with a sigh from the
bottom of my heart, thought of my *own father*; bitterly regretting, that I am an outcast from him and from my mother.

I am but a very young creature, Mr. Lovelace, said I and
wiped my averted eye, altho' you have *kindly*, and in *love to
me*, introduced so much sorrow to me already: So you must not
wonder, that the word *father* strikes so sensibly upon the heart
of a child, ever dutiful till she knew you, and whose tender
years still require the paternal wing.

He turned towards the window: [Rejoice with me, my dear,
since I seem to be devoted to him, that the man is not absolutely
impenetrable!]—His emotion was visible; yet he endeavoured
to suppress it.

He stopped a moment or two, staring in my downcast face
[Did I not, O my beloved friend, think you, want a father or a
mother just then?] But if he could not, so *soon* as he wished,
procure my consent to a day; in *that* case, he thought the compliment might *as well* be made to Lord M. as *not:*—Since the settlements might be drawn and ingrossed in the intervenient time,
which would pacify his impatience, as no time would be lost.

To be sure, Mr. Lovelace, if this matter is *ever to be*, it must be agreeable to me to have the full approbation of *one* side, since I cannot have that of the *other*.

If this matter be ever to be! Good God! what words are these at this time of day! And full *approbation* of one side! Why that word *approbation?* When the greatest pride of all his family was, That of having the honour of so dear a creature for their relation? Would to Heaven, my dearest life, added he, that, without complimenting *Any*-body, to-morrow might be the happiest day of my life!—What say you, my angel? With a trembling impatience, that *seemed* not affected—What say you for *to-morrow?*

It was likely, my dear, I could say much to it, or name another day, had I been disposed to the latter, with such an hinted delay from him.

Next day, Madam, if not *to-morrow!*—Or the *day after that!*—And taking my two hands, stared me into a half-confusion.

No, no! You cannot think all of a sudden, there should be reason for such a hurry. It will be most agreeable, to be sure, for my Lord to be present.

I am all obedience and resignation, returned the wretch, with a self-pluming air, as if he had acquiesced to a proposal made by me, and had complimented me with a great piece of self-denial.

Modesty, I think, required of me, that it should pass so: Did it not?—I think it did. Would to Heaven—but what signifies wishing?

But when he would have *rewarded himself,* as he had heretofore called it, for this self-supposed concession, with a kiss, I repulsed him with a just and very sincere disdain.

He seemed both vexed and surprised, as one who had made proposals that he had expected every thing from. He plainly said, that he thought our situation would intitle him to such an innocent freedom: And he was both amazed and grieved to be thus scornfully repulsed.

No reply could be made by me. I abruptly broke from him. I recollect, as I passed by one of the pier-glasses, that I saw in it his clenched hand offered in wrath to his forehead: The words, *indifference*, *by his soul*, *next to hatred*, I heard him speak: And something of *ice* he mentioned: I heard not what.

Whether he intends to write to my Lord, or to Miss Montague, I cannot tell. But as all delicacy ought to be over with me *now*, perhaps I am to blame to expect it from a man who may not know *what it is*. If he does *not*, and yet thinks himself very delicate, and intends not to be otherwise, I am rather to be pitied, than he to be censured. And after all, since I *must* take him as I find him, I *must*. That is to say, as a man so vain, and so accustomed to be admired, that, not being conscious of internal defect, he has taken no pains to polish more than his outside: And as his proposals are higher than my expectations; and as in his own opinion, he has a great deal to bear from *me*, I *will* (no new offence preventing) sit down to answer them.

Miss Howe
To Miss Clarissa Harlowe

Thursday, May 18.

I HAVE neither time nor patience, my dear friend, to answer every material article in your last letters, just now received. Mr. Lovelace's proposals are all I like of him. And yet (as you do) I think, that he concludes them not with that warmth and earnestness which we might naturally have expected from him. Never in my life did I hear or read of so patient a man, with such a blessing in his reach. But wretches of his cast, between you and me, my dear, have not, I fancy, the ardors that honest men have. Who knows, as your Bell once spitefully said, but he may have half a dozen creatures to quit his hands of, before he engages for life?—Yet I believe you must not expect him to be honest on this side of his grand climacteric.

He, to suggest delay from a compliment to be made to Lord M. and to give time for settlements!—*He*, a part of whose char-

acter it is, not to know what complaisance to his relations is!—
I have no patience with him!

*Would to Heaven to-morrow, without complimenting any-
body, might be his happy day!*—Villain! After he had himself
suggested the compliment!—And I think he accuses You of
delaying!—Fellow, that he is!—How my heart is wrung—

But, as matters now stand betwixt you, I am very unseason-
able in expressing my resentments against him.—Yet I don't
know whether I am or not, neither; since it is the most cruel
of fates, for a woman to be forced to have a man whom her heart
despises. You must, at *least*, despise him; at times, however.
His clenched fist offered to his forehead on your leaving him
in just displeasure; I wish it had been a pole-ax, and in the hand
of his worst enemy.

I will endeavour to think of some method, of some scheme,
to get you from him, and to fix you safely somewhere, till your
cousin Morden arrives: A scheme to lie by you, and to be pursued as occasion may be given. You are sure, that you can go
abroad when you please; and that our correspondence is safe.
I cannot, however, for the reasons heretofore mentioned, respecting your own reputation, wish you to leave him, while
he gives you not cause to suspect his honour. But your heart,
I know, would be the easier, if you were sure of some asylum,
in case of necessity.

However, since you are thrown upon a fool, marry the
fool, at the first opportunity; and tho' I doubt that this man
will be the most ungovernable of fools, as all witty and vain
fools are, take him as a punishment, since you cannot as a reward. In short, as one given, to convince you, that there is nothing but imperfection in this life.

I shall be impatient till I have your next. I am, my dearest
friend,

Your ever-affectionate and faithful

Anna Howe

Mr. Belford
To Robert Lovelace, Esq;

Wednesday, May 17.

I WOULD conceal nothing from you that relates to yourself so much as the inclosed. You will see what the noble writer apprehends from you, and wishes of you, with regard to Miss Harlowe, and how much at heart all your relations have it, that you do honourably by her. They compliment me with an influence over you, which I wish with all my soul you would let me have in this article.

Let me once more intreat thee, Lovelace, to reflect, before it be too late, before the mortal offence be given, upon the graces and merits of this lady. Let thy frequent remorses at last end in one effectual one. Let not pride and wantonness of heart, ruin thy fairer prospects. By my faith, Lovelace, there is nothing but vanity, conceit, and nonsense, in our wild schemes. As we grow older, we shall be wiser, and looking back upon our foolish notions of the present hour, shall certainly despise ourselves (our youth dissipated) when we think of the honourable engagements we might have made. Thou, more especially, if thou lettest such a matchless creature slide thro' thy fingers. A creature pure from her cradle. In all her actions and sentiments uniformly noble. Strict in the performance of all her even *unrewarded* duties to the most unreasonable of fathers, what a wife will she make the man who shall have the honour to call her his!

Reflect likewise upon her sufferings for thee. Actually at the time thou art forming schemes to ruin her (at least, in *her* sense of the word) is she not labouring under a father's curse laid upon her by thy means, and for thy sake? And wouldst thou give operation and completion to this curse?

Thou knowest, that I have no interest, that I can have no view, in wishing thee to do justice to this admirable creature. For thy own sake, once more I conjure thee, for thy family's sake, and for the sake of our common humanity, let me beseech thee to be just to Miss Clarissa Harlowe.

It is said, that the prince on his throne is not safe, if a mind so desperate can be found, as values not its *own* life. So may it be said, that the most immaculate virtue is not safe, if a man can be met with, who has no regard to his own honour, and makes a jest of the most solemn vows and protestations.

Thou mayest by trick, chicane, and false colours, thou who art worse than a pickeroon in love, overcome a poor lady so intangled as thou hast intangled her; so unprotected as thou hast made her: But consider, how much more generous and just to her, and noble to thyself, it is, to overcome *thyself*.

Whatever the capital devil, under whose banner thou hast listed, will let thee do, with regard to this incomparable woman, I hope thou wilt act with honour, in relation to the inclosed, between Lord M. and me; who, as thou wilt see, desires, that thou mayest not know he wrote on the subject; for reasons, I think, very far from being creditable to thyself: And that thou wilt take as meant, the honest zeal for thy service, of

Thy real friend,

J. Belford

Lord M.
To John Belford, Esq;
[*Inclosed in the preceding*].

M. Hall, *Monday May 15.*

Sir,

I F any man in the world has power over my nephew, it is you. I therefore write this, to beg you to interfere in the affair depending between him and the most accomplished of women, as every one says; and *what every one says, must be true*.

I don't know that he has any bad designs upon her; but I know his temper too well, not to be apprehensive upon such long delays: And the ladies here have been for some time in fear for her; my sister Sadlier, in particular, who (you know) is a wise woman, says, that these delays, in the present case, must be from him, rather than from the lady. He had always indeed a strong antipathy to marriage; and may think of playing his dog's tricks by her, as he has by so many others. If there's any danger of this, 'tis best to prevent it in time: For, *when a thing is done, advice comes too late.*

He has always had the folly and impertinence to make a jest of me for using proverbs: But as they are the wisdom of whole nations and ages, collected into a small compass, I am not to be shamed out of sentences, that often contain more wisdom in them, than the tedious harangues of most of our parsons and moralists. Let him laugh at them, if he pleases: You and I know better things, Mr. Belford.—*Tho' you have kept company with a wolf, you have not learnt to howl of him.*

But nevertheless, you must not let him know that I have written to you on this subject. I am ashamed to say it; but he has ever treated me, as if I were a man of very common understanding. And would perhaps think never the better of the best advice in the world, for coming from me.

This match, however, as the lady has such an extraordinary share of wisdom and goodness, might set all to rights: and if you can forward it, I would enable him to make whatever settlements he could wish; and should not be unwilling to put him in possession of another pretty estate besides: For what do I live for (as I have often said) but to see him and my two nieces well married and settled? May Heaven settle him down to a better mind, and turn his heart to more of goodness and consideration!

If the delays are on his side, I tremble for the lady; and, if on hers (as he tells my niece Charlotte), I could wish she were apprised, that *Delays are dangerous.* Excellent as she is, I can tell her, she ought not to depend on her merits with such a changeable fellow, and such a professed marriage-hater, as he has been. I know you are very good at giving kind hints. *A word to the wise is enough.*

I wish you would try what you can do with him; for I have warned him so often of his wicked practices, that I begin to despair of my words having any effect upon him. But let him remember that *Vengeance, though it comes with leaden feet, strikes with iron hands.* If he behaves ill in this case, he may find it so. What a pity it is, that a man of his talents and learning should be so vile a rake! Alas! alas! *Une poignée de bonne vie vaut mieux que plein muy de clergé*; a handful of good life is better than a whole bushel of learning.

May your good counsels, Mr. Belford, founded upon the hints which I have given, pierce his heart, and incite him to do what will be so happy for himself, and so necessary for the honour of that admirable lady whom I long to see his wife; and, if I may, I will not think of one for myself.

I shall make no apologies for this trouble. I know how well you love him and me; and there is nothing in which you could serve us both more importantly, than in forwarding this match to the utmost of your power. When it is done, how shall I rejoice to see you at M. Hall! Mean time, I shall long to hear, that you are likely to be successful with him; and am,

Dear sir, Your most faithful friend and servant,

M.

Mr. Lovelace
To John Belford, Esq;

Friday Night, May 19.

WHEN I have opened my views to thee so amply, as I have done in my former letters; and have told thee, that my principal design is but to bring virtue to a trial, that, *if* virtue, it need not be afraid of; and that the reward of it will be marriage (that is to say, if, after I have carried my point, I cannot prevail upon her to live with me the Life of Honour; for that thou

knowest is the wish of my heart); I am amazed at the repetition
of thy wambling nonsense.

I am of opinion with thee, that some time hence, when
I am *grown wiser*, I shall conclude, that *there is nothing but
vanity, conceit, and nonsense, in my present wild schemes.*
But what is this saying, but that I must be *first* wiser?

I do *not* intend *to let this matchless creature slide through
my fingers.*

Her gloomy father cursed the sweet creature, because she
put it out of his wicked power to compel her to have the man
she hated. Thou knowest how little merit she has with me on
this score.—And shall I not try the virtue I intend, upon full
proof, to reward, because her father is a tyrant?—Why art thou
thus eternally reflecting upon so excellent a woman, as if thou
wert assured she would fail in the trial?—Nay, thou declarest,
every time thou writest on the subject, that she *will*, that she
must yield, *intangled as she is:* And yet makest her virtue the
pretence of thy solicitude for her.

An instrument of the vile James Harlowe, dost thou call
me?—O Jack! how I could curse thee!—*I* an *instrument* of
that brother! of that sister!—But mark the end—And thou shalt
see what will become of that brother, and of that sister!

If I ruin such a virtue, sayest thou!—Eternal monotonist!—
Again; *The most immaculate virtue may be ruined by men, who
have no regard to their honour, and who make a jest of the
most solemn oaths*, &c. What must be the virtue that will be
ruined without oaths? Is not the world full of these deceptions?
And are not *lovers oaths* a jest of hundreds of years standing?
And are not cautions against the perfidy of our sex, a necessary
part of the female education?

I do intend to endeavour to overcome *myself;* but I must
first try, if I cannot overcome *this lady.* Have I not said, that
the honour of her Sex is concerned that I should *try?*

I am not displeased that thou art so apprehensive of my
resentment, that I cannot miss a day, without making thee
uneasy. Thy conscience, 'tis plain, tells thee, that thou hast
deserved my displeasure.

When a boy, if a dog ran away from me thro' fear, I generally looked about for a stone, a stick, or a brickbat; and if neither offered to my hand, I skimmed my hat after him, to make him afraid for something. What signifies power, if we do not exert it?

Let my Lord know that thou hast scribbled to me. But give him not the contents of thy epistle. Tho' a parcel of crude stuff, *he* would think there was something in it. Poor arguments will do in favour of what we like. But the stupid Peer little thinks, that this lady is a rebel to love. On the contrary, not only he, but all the world, believe her to be a volunteer in his service. — So I shall incur blame, and she will be pitied, if any thing happen amiss.

Since my Lord's heart is so set upon this match, I have written already to let him know, "That my unhappy character has given my beloved an ungenerous diffidence of me. That she is so mother-sick and father-fond, that she had rather return to Harlowe-Place, than marry. That she is even apprehensive, that the step she has taken of going off with me, will make the ladies of a family of such name and rank as ours, think slightly of her. That therefore I desire his Lordship (tho' this hint, I tell him, must be very delicately touched) to write me such a letter as I can shew her. Let him treat me in it ever so freely, I shall not take it amiss, because I know his Lordship takes pleasure in writing to me in a corrective style. That he may make what offers he pleases on the marriage. That I desire his presence at the ceremony; that I may take from his hand the greatest blessing that mortal man can give me."

I have not absolutely told the lady that I would write to his Lordship to this effect; yet have given her reason to think I will. So that without the last necessity I shall not produce the answer I expect from him: For I am very loth, I own, to make use of any of my family's names for the furthering of my designs. And yet I must make all secure, before I pull off the mask. This was my motive for bringing her hither.

Thus, thou seest, that the old Peer's letter came very seasonably. I thank thee for it. But as to his sentences, they cannot possibly do me good. I was early suffocated with his *Wisdom of nations*. When a boy, I never asked any thing of him, but out

flew a *proverb;* and if the tendency of that was to deny me, I
never could obtain the least favour. This gave me so great an
aversion to the very word, that, when a child, I made it a condition with my tutor, who was an honest parson, that I would not
read my Bible at all, if he would not excuse me one of the wisest
books in it: To which, however, I had no other objection, than
that it was called *The Proverbs.* And as for Solomon, he was
then a hated character with me, not because of his polygamy,
but because I had conceived him to be such another musty old
fellow as my uncle.

Well, but let us leave old saws to old men.—What signifies
thy tedious whining over thy departing relation? Is it not generally agreed, that he cannot recover? I hear, that he is pestered
still with visits from doctors, and apothecaries, and surgeons;
that they cannot cut so deep as the mortification has gone; and
that in every visit, in every scarification, inevitable death is
pronounced upon him. Why then do they keep tormenting him?
Is it not to take away more of his living fleece than of his dead
flesh?—When a man is given over, the fee should surely be
refused. Are they not now robbing his heirs?—He sent for thee
[Did he not?] to close his eyes. He is but an *uncle*, is he?

I wish *my* uncle had given *me* the opportunity of setting
thee a better example: Thou shouldst have seen what a brave
fellow I had been. And had I had occasion to write, my conclusion would have been this: "I hope the old Trojan's happy.
In that hope, I am so; and

> *Thy rejoicing friend,*
>
> R. Lovelace"

Miss Clarissa Harlowe
To Miss Howe

Sunday Morning, Seven o'Clock.

I WAS at the Play last night with Mr. Lovelace and Miss Horton. It is, you know, a deep and most affecting Tragedy in the reading. You have my remarks upon it, in the little book you made me write upon the principal acting plays. You will not wonder, that Miss Horton, as well as I, was greatly moved at the representation, when I tell you, and have some pleasure in telling you, that Mr. Lovelace himself was very sensibly touched with some of the most affecting scenes. I mention this in praise of the author's performance; for I take Mr. Lovelace to be one of the most hard-hearted men in the world. Upon my word, my dear, I do.

His behaviour, however, on this occasion, and on our return, was unexceptionable, only that he would oblige me to stay to supper with the women below, when we came back, and to sit up with him and them till near one o'clock this morning. I was resolved to be even with him; and indeed I am not very sorry to have the pretence; for I love to pass the Sundays by myself.

Near Nine o'Clock.

I have your kind letter of yesterday. He knows I have. And I shall expect, that he will be inquisitive next time I see him after your opinion of his proposals. I doubted not your approbation of them, and had written an answer on that presumption; which is ready for him.

He is very importunate to see me. He has desired to attend me to church. He is angry, that I have declined to breakfast with him. I am sure that I should not be at my own liberty, if I had. — I bid Dorcas tell him, that I desired to have this day to myself; I would see him in the morning, as early as he pleased. She says, she knows not what ails him, but that he is out of humour with everybody.

He has just sent me word, that he insists upon supping with me. As we had been in a good train for several days past, I thought it not prudent to break with him, for little matters. Yet, to be, in a manner, threatened into his will, I know not how to bear that.

While I was considering, he came up, and, tapping at my door, told me, in a very angry tone, he must see me this night. He could not rest, till he had been told what he had done to deserve this treatment.

I must go to him. Yet perhaps he has nothing new to say to me.—I shall be very angry with him.

As the Lady could not know what Mr. Love-lace's designs were, nor the cause of his ill humour, it will not be improper to pursue the subject from his letter.

Having described his angry manner of demanding, in person, her company at supper; he proceeds as follows:

'Tis hard, answered the fair Perverse, that I am to be so little my own mistress. I will meet you in the dining-room half an hour hence.

I went down to wait that half-hour. All the women set me hard to give her cause for this tyranny. They demonstrated, as well from the nature of the sex, as of the *case*, that I had nothing to hope for from my tameness, and could meet with no worse treatment, were I to be guilty of the last offence. They urged me vehemently to *try* at least what effect some greater familiarities, than I had ever used with her, would have: And their arguments being strengthened by my just resentments on the discoveries I had made, I was resolved to take some liberties, and, as they were received, to take still greater, and lay all the fault upon her tyranny. In this humour I went up, and never had paralytic so little command of his joints, as I had, as I walked about the dining-room, attending her motions.

With an erect mien she entered, her face averted, her lovely bosom swelling, and the more charmingly protuberant for the erectness of her mien. O Jack! that sullenness and reserve should give this haughty maid new charms! But in every attitude, in every humour, in every gesture, is beauty beautiful.—By her averted face, and indignant aspect, I saw the dear insolent was disposed to be angry—But by the fierceness of mine, as my trembling hands seized hers, I soon made fear her predominant passion. And yet the moment I beheld her, my heart was dastardized, damped, and reverenced over. Surely this is an angel, Jack!—And yet, had she not been known to be a female, they would not from *babyhood* have dressed her as such, nor would she, but upon that conviction, have continued the dress.

Let me ask you, Madam, I beseech you tell me, what I have done to deserve this distant treatment?

And let me ask you, Mr. Lovelace, why are my retirements to be thus invaded?—What can you have to say to me since last night, that I went with you so much against my will to the play? And after sitting up with you, equally against my will, till a very late hour?—

This I have to say, Madam, that I cannot bear to be kept at this distance from you under the same roof. I have a thousand things to say, to talk of, relating to our present and future prospects; but when I want to open my whole soul to you, you are always contriving to keep me at a distance; you make me inconsistent with myself; your heart is set upon delays; you must have views that you will not own. Tell me, Madam, I conjure you to tell me, this moment, without subterfuge or reserve, in what light am I to appear to you in future? I cannot bear this distance; the suspense you hold me in I cannot bear.

In what light, Mr. Lovelace? In no bad light, I hope.—Pray, Mr. Lovelace, do not grasp my hands so hard [endeavouring to withdraw her hands]. Pray let me go—

You hate me, Madam—

I hate nobody, Sir—

You *hate* me, Madam, repeated I.

Instigated and resolved, as I came up, I wanted some new provocation. The devil indeed, as soon as my angel made her appearance, crept out of my heart; but he had left the door open, and was no farther off than my elbow.

You come up in no good temper, I see, Mr. Lovelace—But

pray be not violent—I have done you no hurt—Pray be not violent—

Sweet creature! And I clasped one arm about her, holding one hand in my other—*You have done me no hurt!*—You have done me the greatest hurt!—In what have I deserved the distance you keep me at?—I knew not what to say.

She struggled to disengage herself—Pray, Mr. Lovelace, let me withdraw. I know not why this is—I know not what I have done to offend you. I see you are come with a design to quarrel with me. If you would not terrify me by the ill-humour you are in, permit me to withdraw. I will hear all you have to say another time—To-morrow morning, as I sent you word; but indeed you frighten me.—I beseech you, if you have any value for me, permit me to withdraw.

Night, *mid*-night, *is* necessary, Belford. Surprize, terror, *must* be necessary to the ultimate trial of this charming creature, say the women below what they will—I could not hold my purposes—This was not the first time that I had *intended* to try if she could forgive.

I kissed her hand with a fervor, as if I would have left my lips upon it—Withdraw then, dearest and ever-dear creature— Indeed I entered in a very ill humour: I cannot bear the distance you so causlesly keep me at.—Withdraw, however, Madam, since it is your will to withdraw; and judge me generously; judge me but as I deserve to be judged; and let me hope to meet you to-morrow morning early, in such a temper as becomes our present situation, and my future hopes.

And so saying, I conducted her to the door, and left her there. But instead of going down to the women, went into my own chamber, and locked myself in; ashamed of being awed by her majestic loveliness, and apprehensive virtue, into so great a change of purpose, notwithstanding I had such just provocations from the letters of her saucy friend, founded on her own representations of facts and situations between herself and me.

The Lady writes again on Monday evening;
and gives her friend an account of all that
passed between herself and Mr. Lovelace

that day; and of her being terrified out of her purpose of going. She concludes this letter in these words:

I should say something of your last favour (but a few hours ago received), and of your dialogue with your mother.—Are you not very whimsical, my dear? I have but two things to wish for on this occasion. The one, that your charming pleasantry had a better subject, than that you find for it in this dialogue. The other, that my situation were not such, as must too often damp that pleasantry, and will not permit me to enjoy it, as I used to do. Be, however, happy in yourself, tho' you cannot in

Your Clarissa Harlowe

Mr. Lovelace To John Belford, Esq;

Thursday, May 25.

THOU seest, Belford, how we now drive before the wind.— The dear creature now comes almost at the first word, whenever I desire the honour of her company. I told her last night, that, apprehending delay from Pritchard's slowness, I was determined to leave it to my Lord to make his compliments in his own way; and had actually that afternoon put my writings into the hands of a very eminent lawyer, Counsellor Williams, with directions for him to draw up settlements from my own estate, and conformable to those of my mother; which I put into his hands at the same time. It had been, I said, no small part of my concern, that her frequent displeasure, and our mutual misapprehensions, had hindered me from advising with her before, on this subject. Indeed, indeed, my dearest life, said I, you have hitherto afforded me but a very thorny courtship.

She was silent. *Kindly* silent. For well know I, that she could have recriminated upon me with a vengeance.—I comforted myself, I said, with the hopes, that all my difficulties were over; and that every past disobligation would be buried in oblivion.

I proposed my Lord's chapel for the celebration, where we might have the presence of Lady Betty, Lady Sarah, and my two cousins Montague.

She seemed not to favour a public celebration; and waved this subject for the present. I did suppose, that she would not choose to be married in public, any more than me: So I pressed not this matter farther just then.

But patterns I actually produced; and a jeweller was to bring as this day several sets of jewels, for her choice. But the patterns she would not open. She sighed at the mention of them; The second patterns, she said, that had been offered to her: And very peremptorily forbid the jeweller's coming; as well as declined my offer of getting my own mother's to be new-set; at least for the present.

I do assure thee, Belford, I was in earnest in all this. My whole estate is nothing to me, put in competition with her hoped-for favour.

She then told me, that she had written her opinion of my general proposals; and there had expressed her mind, as to cloaths and jewels:—But on my behaviour to her, for no cause that she knew of, on Sunday night, she had torn the paper in two. I earnestly pressed her to let me be favoured with a sight of this paper, torn as it was. And after some hesitation, she withdrew, and sent it to me by Dorcas.

I perused it again. It was in a manner new to me, tho' I had read it so lately; and by my soul I could hardly stand it. An hundred admirable creatures I called her to myself.—But I charge thee, write not a word to me in her favour, if thou meanest her well; for if I spare her, it must be all *ex mero motu*.

You may easily suppose, when I was re-admitted to her presence, that I ran over in her praises, and in vows of gratitude, and everlasting love. But here's the devil; she still receives all I say with reserve; or if it be not with reserve, she receives it so much as her due, that she is not at all raised by it. Some women are undone by praise, by flattery. I myself am proud of praise.— Perhaps thou wilt say, that those are most proud of it, who least deserve it—As those are of riches and grandeur, who are not born to either. I own, that it requires a soul to be superior to these foibles. Have I not then a soul?—Surely, I have.—Let me then be considered as an exception to the rule.

But yet, what mortifies my pride, is, that this exalted creature, if I were to marry her, would not be governed in her behaviour to me by love, but by generosity merely, or by blind duty; and had rather live single, than be mine.

I cannot bear this. I would have the woman whom I honour with my name, if ever I confer this honour upon any, forego even her superior duties for me. I would have her look after me when I go out, as far as she can see me; and meet me at my return with rapture. I would be the subject of her dreams, as well as of her waking thoughts. I would have her look upon every moment lost, that is not passed with me: Sing to me, read to me, play to me when I pleased; no joy so great as in obeying me. When I should be inclined to love, overwhelm me with it; when to be serious or solitary, if intrusive, awfully so; retiring at a nod; approaching me only if I smiled encouragement: Steal into my presence with silence; out of it, if not noticed, on tip-toe.—Thus of old did the contending wives of the honest patriarchs; each recommending her handmaid to her lord, as she thought it would oblige him, and looking upon the genial product as her own.

The gentle Waller says, *Women are born to be controul'd.* Gentle as he was, he knew that. A tyrant-husband makes a dutiful wife. And why do the Sex love rakes, but because they know how to direct their uncertain wills, and manage them?

Another agreeable conversation. The day of days the subject. As to fixing a particular one, that need not be done till the settlements are completed.

It could not be imagined, I said, but that his Lordship's setting out in a litter, and coming to town, as well as his taste for glare, and the joy he would take to see me married at last, and to her dear self, would give it as much the air of a public marriage, as if the ceremony were performed at his own chapel, all the ladies present.

She could not bear the thoughts of a public day. It would carry with it an air of insult upon her whole family. And, for her part, if my Lord will not take it amiss (and perhaps he will not, as the motion came not from himself, but from me), she would very willingly dispense with his Lordship's presence; the rather, as dress and appearance will then be unnecessary. For she could not bear to think of decking her person, while her parents were in tears.

How excellent this, did not her parents richly deserve to be in tears!

The Sex may say what they will, but a poor innocent fellow had need to take great care of himself, when he dances upon the edge of the matrimonial precipice. Many a faint-hearted man, when he began in jest, or only designed to ape gallantry, has been forced into earnest, by being over-prompt, and taken at his word, not knowing how to own that he meant less than the Lady supposed he meant. I am the better enabled to judge that this must have been the case of many a sneaking varlet; because I, who know the female world as well as any man in it of my standing, am so frequently in doubt of myself, and know not what to make of the matter.

Then these little sly rogues, how they lie couchant, ready to spring upon us harmless fellows, the moment we are in their reach!—When the ice is once broken for them, how swiftly can they make to port!—Meantime, the subject they can least *speak* to, they most *think* of. Nor can you talk of the ceremony before they have laid out in their minds how it is all to be.—Little saucy-face designers! how first they draw themselves in, then us!

Lovelace

The Lady, after having given to Miss Howe the particulars contained in Mr. Lovelace's last letter, thus expresses herself.

A principal consolation arising from these favourable appearances, is, that I, who have now but one only friend, shall most probably, and if it be not my own fault, have as many new ones as there are persons in Mr. Lovelace's family; and this whether Mr. Lovelace treat me kindly, or not. And who knows, but that by degrees, those new friends, by their rank and merit, may have weight enough to get me restored to the favour of my relations? Till which can be effected, I shall not be tolerably easy. Happy I never expect to be. Mr. Lovelace's mind and mine are vastly different; different in *essentials*.

But as matters are at present circumstanced, I pray you, my dear friend, to keep to yourself every thing that might bring discredit to him—Better anybody expose a man than a wife, if I am to be so; and what is said by you will be thought to come from me.

It shall be my constant prayer, that all the felicities which this world can afford, may be yours. And that the Almighty will never suffer you nor yours to the remotest posterity, to want such a friend, as my Anna Howe has been to

Her Clarissa Harlowe

Mr. Lovelace To John Belford, Esq; *

A ND now, that my Beloved seems secure in my net, for my project upon the vixen Miss Howe, and upon her Mother: In which the officious prancer Hickman is to come in for a dash.

But why upon her Mother, methinks thou askest; who,

---

*The following letter does not appear in the first edition. Richardson there gives only a summary of Lovelace's intent. "But as he does not intend to carry it into execution," Richardson concludes, "it [i.e. the implied letter] is omitted." Richardson wrote the letter for inclusion in the revised third edition and I have included it as it appears there for two reasons. First, it is instructive as one of the more obvious and sustained efforts Richardson made, in revising, to darken the character of Lovelace. Second, it is one of the best renderings of Lovelace's fantasy life that Richardson wrote, a beautifully imagined exercise in the pathological.
                                                    —Ed.

unknown to herself, has only acted, by thy impulse, thro' thy agent Joseph Leman, upon the folly of old Tony the Uncle?

No matter for that: She believes she acts upon her own judgment; and deserves to be punished for pretending to judgment, when she has none.—Every living soul, but myself, I can tell thee, shall be punished, that treats either cruelly or disrespectfully so adored a Lady.—What a plague! is it not enough that she is teazed and tormented in person by me?

I have already broken the matter to our three confederates; as a *supposed*, not a *resolved-on* case indeed. And yet they know, that with me, in a piece of mischief, Execution, with its swiftest feet, is seldom three paces behind Projection, which hardly ever limps neither.

Mowbray is not against it. It is a scheme, he says, worthy of us: And we have not done any-thing for a good while, that has made a noise.

Belton indeed hesitates a little, because matters go wrong between him and his Thomasine; and the poor fellow has not the courage to have his sore place probed to the bottom.

Tourville has started a fresh game, and shrugs his shoulders, and should not *chuse* to go abroad at present, *if I please*. For I apprehend that (from the *nature* of the project) there will be a kind of necessity to travel, till all is blown over.

To me, one country is as good as another; and I shall soon, I suppose, chuse to quit this paltry Island; except the mistress of my fate will consent to cohabit at *home*; and so lay me under no necessity of *surprising her into foreign parts*. Traveling, thou knowest, gives the Sexes charming opportunities of being familiar with one another. A very few days and nights must now decide all matters betwixt me and my fair Inimitable.

Doleman, who can act in these causes only as chambercounsel, will inform us by pen and ink [his right hand and right side having not yet been struck, and the other side beginning to be sensible] of all that shall occur in our absence.

As for thee, we had rather have thy company than not; for, altho' thou art a wretched fellow at contrivance, yet art thou intrepid at execution. But as thy present engagements make thy attendance uncertain, I am not for making thy part necessary to our scheme; but for leaving thee to come after us when abroad. I know thou canst not long live without us.

The project, in short, is this:—Mrs. Howe has an elder Sister in the Isle of Wight, who is lately a widow; and I am well informed, that the Mother and Daughter have engaged, before the latter is married, to pay a visit to this Lady, who is rich, and intends Miss for her heiress; and in the interim will make her some valuable presents on her approaching Nuptials; which, as Mrs. Howe, who loves money more than any-thing but herself, told one of my acquaintance, would be *worth fetching*.

Now, Jack, nothing more need be done, than to hire a little trim vessel, which shall sail a pleasuring backward and forward to Portsmouth, Spithead, and the Isle of Wight, for a week or fortnight before we enter upon our parts of the plot. And as Mrs. Howe will be for making the best bargain she can for her passage, the master of the vessel may have orders (as a perquisite allowed him by his owners) to take what she will give: And the Master's name, be it what it will, shall be *Ganmore* on the occasion; for I know a rogue of that name, who is not obliged to be of any country, any more than we.

Well, then, we will imagine them on board. I will be there in disguise. They know not any of ye four—supposing (the scheme so inviting) that thou canst be one.

'Tis plaguy hard, if we cannot *find*, or *make*, a storm.

Perhaps they will be sea-sick: But whether they be or not, no doubt they will keep their Cabin.

Here will be Mrs. Howe, Miss Howe, Mr. Hickman, a Maid, and a Footman, I suppose; and thus we will order it:

I know it will be hard weather: I *know* it will: And before there can be the least suspicion of the matter, we shall be in sight of Guernsey, Jersey, Dieppe, Cherbourg, or any-whither on the French coast that it shall please us to agree with the winds to blow us: And then, securing the footman, and the women being separated, one of us, according to lots that may be cast, shall overcome, either by persuasion or force, the maid-servant: That will be no hard task; and she is a likely wench [I have seen her often]: One, Mrs. Howe; nor can there be much difficulty there; for she is full of health and life, and has been long a

Widow: Another [*That*, says the princely Lion, must be *I!*] the
saucy Daughter; who will be too much frighted to make great
resistance [*Violent* spirits, in that Sex, are seldom *true* spirits—
'Tis but where they *can*—]: And after beating about the coast
for three or four days for recreation's sake, and to make sure
work, and till we see our sullen birds begin to eat and sip, we
will set them all ashore where it will be most convenient; sell
the vessel [To Mrs. Townsend's agents, with all my heart, or
to some other Smugglers] or give it to Ganmore; and pursue
our travels, and tarry abroad till all is hushed up.

Now I know thou wilt make difficulties, as it is thy way;
while it is mine to conquer them. My other vassals made theirs;
and I condescended to obviate them: As thus I will thine, first
stating them for thee according to what I know of thy phlegm.

What, in the first place, wilt thou ask, shall be done with
Hickman? who will be in full parade of dress and primness, in
order to shew the old Aunt what a devilish clever fellow of a
Nephew she is to have.

What!—I'll tell thee—Hickman, in good manners, will
leave the women in their Cabin—and, to shew his courage with
his breeding, be upon deck—

Well, and suppose he is?

Suppose he is!—Why then I hope it is easy for Ganmore,
or any-body else, myself suppose in my pea-jacket and great
watch-coat (if any other make a scruple to do it) while he stands
in the way, gapeing and staring like a novice, to stumble against
him, and push him overboard!—A rich thought!—Is it not,
Belford?—He is certainly plaguy officious in the Ladies correspondence; and, I am informed, plays double between Mother
and Daughter, in fear of both.—Dost not see him, Jack?—I do
—popping up and down, his wig and hat floating by him; and
paddling, pawing, and dashing, like a frighted mongrel—I am
afraid he never ventured to learn to swim.

But thou wilt not drown the poor fellow; wilt thou?

No, no!—That is not necessary to the project—I hate to
do mischief supererogatory. The skiff shall be ready to save
him, while the vessel keeps its course: He shall be set on shore

with the loss of wig and hat only, and of half of his little wits, at the place where he embarked, or anywhere else.

Well, but shall we not be in danger of being hanged for three such enormous Rapes, altho' Hickman should escape with only a bellyful of sea-water?

Yes, to be sure, when caught—But is there any likelihood of that?—Besides, have we not been in danger before now, for worse facts?—And what is there in being only in *danger?*—If we actually were to appear in open day in England before matters are made up, there will be greater likelihood, that these women will *not* prosecute, than that they *will.*—For my own part, I should wish they *may.* Would not a brave fellow chuse to appear in court to such an arraignment, confronting women who would do credit to his attempt? The country is more merciful in *these* cases, than in *any others:* I should therefore like to put myself upon my country.

Let me indulge a few reflections upon what thou mayst think the *worst* that *can* happen. I will suppose that thou art one of us; and that all five are actually brought to tryal on this occasion: How bravely shall we enter a court, *I* at the head of you, dressed out each man, as if to his wedding-appearance!— You are sure of all the women, old and young, of your side.— What brave fellows!—What fine gentlemen!—There goes a charming handsome man!—meaning me, to be sure!—Who could find in their hearts to hang such a gentleman as that! whispers one Lady, sitting perhaps, on the right-hand of the Recorder [I suppose the scene to be in London]: While another disbelieves that any woman could *fairly* swear against me. All will croud after *me:* It will be each man's happiness (if ye shall chance to be bashful) to be neglected: I shall be found to be the greatest criminal; and my safety, for which the general voice will be engaged, will be yours.

But then comes the triumph of triumphs, that will make the accused look up, while the accusers are covered with confusion.

Make room there!—Stand by!—Give back!—One receiving a rap, another an elbow, half a score a push apiece!—

Enter the slow-moving, hooded-faced, down-looking Plain-tiffs.—

And first the Widow, with a sorrowful countenance tho' half-veil'd, pitying her Daughter more than herself. The people, the women especially, who on this occasion will be five-sixths of the spectators, reproaching her—You'd have the conscience, would you, to have five such brave gentlemen as these hanged for you know not what?

Next comes the poor maid—who perhaps had been ravished twenty times before; and had not appeared now, but for com-pany-sake; mincing, simpering, weeping, by turns; not knowing whether she should be sorry or glad.

But every eye dwells upon Miss!—See, see, the handsome gentleman bows to her!

To the very ground, to be sure, I shall bow; and kiss my hand.

See her confusion! See! She turns from him!—Ay! that's because it is in open court, cries an arch one!—While others admire her—Ay! that's a girl worth venturing one's neck for!

Then we shall be praised—Even the Judges, and the whole crouded Bench, will acquit us in their hearts; and every single man wish he had been me!—The women, all the time, disclaim-ing prosecution, were the case to be their own. To be sure, Belford, the sufferers cannot put half so good a face upon the matter as we.

Then what a noise will this matter make!—Is it not enough, suppose us moving from the Prison to the Sessions-house[a], to make a noble heart thump it away most gloriously, when such an one finds himself attended to his tryal by a parade of guards and officers, of miens and aspects warlike and unwar-like; himself their whole care, and their business!—weapons in their hands, some bright, some rusty, equally venerable for their antiquity and inoffensiveness! others, of more authorita-tive demeanour, strutting before with fine painted staves! shoals

[a] Within these few years past, a passage has been made from the Prison to the Sessions-house, whereby malefactors are carried into court without going thro' the street. Lovelace's triumph on their supposed march shews the wisdom of this alteration.

of people following, with a Which is he whom the *young* Lady appears against?—Then, let us look down, look up, look round, which way we will, we shall see all the doors, the shops, the windows, the sign-irons and balconies (garrets, gutters, and chimney-tops included) all white-capt, black-hooded, and peri-wigg'd, or crop-ear'd up by the *Immobile Vulgus:* While the floating *street-swarmers*, who have seen us pass by at one place, run with stretched-out necks, and strained eye-balls, a round-about way, and elbow and shoulder themselves into places by which we have not passed, in order to obtain another sight of us; every street continuing to pour out its swarms of late-comers, to add to the gathering snowball; who are content to take de-scriptions of our persons, behaviour, and countenances, from those who had the good fortune to have been in time to see us.

Let me tell thee, Jack, I see not why (to judge according to our principles and practices) we should not be as much elated in our march, were this to happen to us, as others may be upon any other the most *mob-attracting* occasion—Suppose a Lord-Mayor on his *Gawdy;* suppose a victorious General, or Embas-sador, on his public Entry—Suppose (as I began with the *lowest*) the *grandest* parade that can be supposed, a Coronation—For, in all these, do not the royal guard, the heroic trained-bands, the pendent, clinging throngs of spectators, with their waving heads rolling to-and-fro from house-tops to house-bottoms and street-ways, as I have above described, make the principal part of the Raree-shew?

Well, but suppose, after all, we are convicted; what have we to do, but in time make over our estates, that the sheriffs may not revel in our spoils?—There is no fear of being hanged for such a crime as this, while we have *money* or *friends.*— And suppose even the worst, that two or three were to die, have we not a chance, each man of us, to escape? The devil's in them, if they'll hang Five for ravishing Three!

I know I shall get off for one—were it but for family sake: And being a handsome fellow, I shall have a dozen or two of young maidens, all dressed in white, go to Court to beg my life—And what a pretty shew they will make, with their white hoods, white gowns, white petticoats, white scarves, white gloves, kneeling for me, with their white handkerchiefs at their eyes, in two pretty rows, as Majesty walks thro' them, and nods my pardon for their sakes!—And, if once pardoned, all is over: For, Jack, in a crime of this nature there lies no appeal, as in a murder.

So thou seest the worst that can happen, should we *not* make the Grand Tour upon this occasion, but stay and take our tryals. But it is most likely, that they will not prosecute at all. If not, no risque on our side will be run; only taking our pleasure abroad, at the worst; leaving friends tired of us, in order, after a time, to return to the same friends endeared to us, as we to them, by absence.

This, Jack, is my scheme, at the first running. I know it is capable of improvement—For example: I can land these Ladies in France; whip over before they can get a passage back, or before Hickman can have recovered his fright; and so find means to entrap my Beloved on board—And then all will be right; and I need not care if I were never to return to England.

Memorandum, To be considered of—Whether, in order to complete my vengeance, I cannot contrive to kidnap away either James Harlowe or Solmes? or both? A man, Jack, would not go into exile for nothing.

Mr. Lovelace
To John Belford, Esq;

IF, Belford, thou likest not my plot upon Miss Howe, I have three or four more as good in my own opinion; better, perhaps, they will be in thine: And so 'tis but getting loose from thy present engagement, and thou shalt pick and choose. But as for thy three brethren, they must do as I'd have them: And so, indeed, must thou:—Else why am I your general?—But I will refer this subject to its proper season. Thou knowest, that I never absolutely conclude upon a project, till 'tis time for execution: And then lightning strikes not quicker than I.

And now, Jack, what dost think?

That thou art a cursed fellow, if —

If! No If's — But I shall be very sick to-morrow. I shall, 'faith.

Sick! — Why sick? — What a devil shouldst thou be sick for?

For more good reasons than one, Belford.

I should be glad to hear but one. — Sick, quotha! Of all thy roguish inventions, I should not have thought of this.

Perhaps thou thinkest my view to be, to draw the lady to my bedside: That's a trick of three or four thousand years old; and I should find it much more to my purpose, if I could get to hers. However, I'll condescend to make thee as wise as myself.

And what will being sick do for thee?

Have patience. I don't intend to be so very bad as Dorcas shall represent me to be. But yet I know I shall reach confoundedly, and bring up some clotted blood. To be sure, I shall break a vessel: There's no doubt of that; and a bottle of Eaton's styptic shall be sent for; but no doctor. If she has *humanity*, she will be concerned. But if she has *love*, let it have been pushed ever so far back, it will, on this occasion, come forward, and shew itself; not only in her eye, but in every line of her sweet face.

I will be very intrepid. I will not fear death, or any thing else. I will be sure of being well in an hour or two, having formerly found great benefit by this balsamic medicine, on occasion of an inward bruise by a fall from my horse in hunting, of which, perhaps this malady may be the remains. And this will shew her, that tho' those about me may make the most of it, I don't; and so can have no design in it.

What then, thou egregious contriver?

Why then I shall have the less remorse, if I am to use a little violence: For can she deserve compassion, who shews none?

And what if she shew a great deal of concern?

Then shall I be in hope of building on a good foundation. Love hides a multitude of faults, and diminishes those it cannot hide. Love, when found out, or acknowleged, authorizes freedom; and freedom begets freedom; and I shall then see how far I can go.

Well but, Lovelace, how the duce wilt thou, with that full health and vigour of constitution, and with that bloom in thy face, make any-body believe thou art sick?

How!—Why take a few grains of Ipecacuanha; enough to make me reach like a fury.

Good!—But how wilt thou manage to bring up blood, and not hurt thyself?

Foolish fellow! Are there not pigeons and chickens in every poulterer's shop?

Cry thy mercy.

But then I will be persuaded by Mrs. Sinclair, that I have of late confined myself too much; and so will have a chair called, and be carried to the Park; where I will try to walk half the length of the Mall, or so; and in my return, amuse myself at White's or the Cocoa.

And what will this do?

Questioning again?—I am afraid thou'rt an infidel, Belford. —Why then shall I not know if my beloved offers to go out in my absence?—And shall I not see whether she receives me with tenderness at my return? But this is not all: I have a foreboding that something affecting will happen while I am out. But of this more in its place.

And now, Belford, wilt thou, or wilt thou not, allow, that it is a right thing to be sick?—Lord, Jack, so much delight do I take in my contrivances, that I shall be half-sorry, when the occasion for them is over; for never, never shall I again have such charming exercise for my invention.

Mr. Lovelace
To John Belford, Esq;

Cocoa-tree, Saturday, May 27.

THIS Ipecacuanha is a most disagreeable medicine! That these cursed physical folks can find out nothing to do us good, but what would poison the devil! In the other world,

were they only to take physic, it would be punishment enough
of itself for a mis-spent life. A doctor at one elbow, and an
apothecary at the other, and the poor soul labouring under their
prescribed operations, he need no worse tormentors.

But now this was to take down my countenance. It has
done it: For, with violent reachings, having taken enough to
make me sick, and not enough water to carry it off, I presently
looked as if I had kept my bed a fortnight. *Ill-jesting*, as I thought
in the midst of the exercise, *with edgetools*, and worse with
physical ones.

Two hours it held me. I had forbid Dorcas to let my beloved
know anything of the matter; out of tenderness to her; being
willing, when she knew my prohibition, to let her see that I
expected her to be concerned for me:—What a worthless fellow
must *he* be, whose own heart gives him up, as deserving of no
one's regard!

Well, but Dorcas nevertheless is a *woman*, and she can
whisper to her lady the secret she is injoined to keep!

Come hither, you toad (sick as a devil at the instant); Let
me see what a mixture of grief and surprize may be beat up
together in thy pudden-face.

That won't do. That dropt jaw, and mouth distended into
the long oval, is more upon the Horrible, than the Grievous.

Nor that pinking and winking with thy *odious eyes*, as my
charmer once called them.

A little better *That*; yet not quite right: But keep your
mouth closer. You have a muscle or two which you have no
command of, between your cheek-bone and your lips, that
should carry one corner of your mouth up towards your crow's-
foot, and that down to meet it.

There! Begone! Be in a plaguy hurry running up stairs and
down, to fetch from the dining-room what you carry up on
purpose to fetch, till motion extraordinary put you out of breath,
and give you the sigh-natural.

What's the matter, Dorcas?

Nothing, Madam.

My beloved wonders she has not seen me this morning, no
doubt; but is too shy to say she wonders. Repeated What's the

matter's, however, as Dorcas runs up and down stairs by her door, bring on, Oh! Madam, my master!—my master!

What! How! When!—And all the monosyllables of surprize.

[Within Parenthesis let me tell thee, that I have often thought, that the little words in the republic of letters, like the little folks in a nation, are the most significant. The *trisyllables*, and the *rumblers* of syllables more than *three*, are but the good for little *magnates*.]

I must not tell you, Madam—My master ordered me not to tell you—But he is in a worse way than he thinks for!—But he would not have *you* frighted.

High concern took possession of every sweet feature. She pitied me!—By my soul, she pitied me!

Where is he?

At last, O Lord! let Mrs. Lovelace know!—There is danger, to be sure! whispered from one nymph to another, in her hearing; but at the door, and so loud, that my listening fair one might hear.

Out she darts.—As how! as how, Dorcas!

O Madam—A vomiting of blood! A vessel broke, to be sure!

Down she hastens; finds every one as busy over my blood in the entry, as if it were that of the Neapolitan Saint.

In steps my charmer! with a face of sweet concern.

How do you, Mr. Lovelace?

O my best Love!—Very well!—Very well!—Nothing at all! Nothing of consequence!—I shall be well in an instant!—straining again; for I was indeed plaguy sick, tho' no more blood came.

In short, Belford, I have gained my end. I see the dear soul loves me. I see she forgives me all that's past. I see I have credit for a new score.

Miss Howe, I defy thee, my dear—Nor will the choicest of my fair-one's favours be long prohibited goods to me!

Every one now is sure, that she loves me. Tears were in her eyes more than once for me. She suffered me to take her hand,

and kiss it as often as I pleased. On Mrs. Sinclair's mentioning, that I too much confined myself, she pressed me to take an airing; but obligingly desired me to be careful of myself. Wished I would advise with a physician. *God made physicians*, she said.

I did not think That, Jack. God indeed made us All. But I fansy she meant *physic* instead of *physicians;* and then the phrase might mean what the vulgar phrase means;—*God sends meat, the devil cooks.*

I was well already, on taking the styptic from *her* dear hands.

On her requiring me to take the air, I asked, if I might have the honour of her company in a coach; and This, that I might observe if she had an intention of going out in my absence.

If she thought a chair were not a more proper vehicle for my case, she would with all her heart!

I kissed her hand again! She was all goodness!—Would to Heaven I better deserved it, I said!—But all were golden days before us!—Her presence and generous concern had done everything. I was well! Nothing ailed me. But since my beloved will have it so, I'll take a little Airing!—Let a chair be called!—O my charmer! were I to have owed this indisposition to my late harasses, and to the uneasiness I have had for disobliging you; all is infinitely compensated by your goodness—All the art of healing is in your smiles!—Your late displeasure was the only malady!

While Mrs. Sinclair, and Dorcas, and Polly, and even poor silly Mabell (for Sally went out, as my angel came in) with up-lifted hands and eyes, stood thanking Heaven that I was better, in audible whispers: See the power of love, cried one!—What a charming husband, another!—Happy couple, all!

O how the dear creature's cheek mantled!—How her eyes sparkled!—How sweetly acceptable is praise to conscious merit, while it but reproaches when applied to the undeserving!

And now, Belford, was it not worth while to be sick? And yet I must tell thee, that too many pleasanter expedients offer themselves, to make trial any more of this confounded Ipeca-cuanha.

Miss Clarissa Harlowe
To Miss Howe

Saturday, May 27.

MR. LOVELACE, my dear, has been very ill. Suddenly taken. With a vomiting of blood in great quantities. Some vessel broken. He complained of a disorder in his stomach overnight. I was the more affected with it, as I am afraid it was occasioned by the violent contentions between us.—But was I in fault?

How lately did I think I hated him!—But hatred and anger, I see, are but temporary passions with me. One cannot, my dear, hate people in danger of death, or who are in distress or affliction. My heart, I find, is not proof against kindness, and acknowledgement of errors committed.

He took great care to have his illness concealed from me as long as it could. So tender in the violence of his disorder!—So desirous to make the best of it!—I wish he had not been ill in my sight. I was too much affected—Every-body alarming me with his danger—The poor man, from such high health, so *suddenly* taken!—And so unprepared!—

He is gone out in a chair. I advised him to do so. I fear that my advice was wrong; since Quiet in such a disorder must needs be best. We are apt to be so ready, in cases of emergency, to give our advice, without judgment, or waiting for it!—I proposed a physician indeed; but he would not hear of one. I have great honour for the faculty; and the greater, as I have always observed, that those who treat the professors of the art of healing contemptuously, too generally treat higher institutions in the same manner.

I am really very uneasy. For I have, I doubt, exposed myself to him, and to the women below. *They* indeed will excuse me, as they think us married. But if he be not generous, I shall have cause to regret this surprize; which has taught me more than I knew of myself; as I had reason to think myself unaccountably treated by him.

Nevertheless let me tell you that if again he give me cause to resume distance and reserve, I hope my reason will gather strength enough from his imperfections to enable me to keep my passions under.—What can we do more than govern ourselves by the temporary lights lent us?

But I will not add another word, after I have assured you, that I will look still more narrowly into myself: And that I am

Your equally sincere and affectionate

Cl. Harlowe

Mr. Lovelace
To John Belford, Esq;

Friday, June 2.

NOTWITHSTANDING my studied-for politeness and complaisance for some days past; and though I have wanted courage to throw the mask quite aside; yet I have made the dear creature more than once look about her, by the warm, tho' decent expressions of my passion. I have brought her to own, that I am *more* than indifferent to her: But as to Love, which I pressed her to acknowlege, *What need of acknowlegements of that sort, when a woman consents to marry?*—And once repulsing me with displeasure, *The proof of the true love I was vowing for her, was* respect, *not* freedom.

I endeavoured to justify my passion, by laying over-delicacy at her door. That was *not*, she said, *my* fault, if it were *hers*. She must plainly tell me, that I appeared to her incapable of distinguishing what were the requisites of a pure mind. Perhaps, had the *libertine* presumption to imagine, that there was no difference in *heart*, nor any but what proceeded from *education* and *custom*, between the pure and the impure—And yet custom *alone*, as she observed, would make a second nature, as well in good as in bad habits.

I have just now been called to account for some innocent liberties which I thought myself intitled to take before the women; as they suppose us married, and now within view of consummation.

I took the lecture very hardly; and with impatience wished for the happy day and hour, when I might call her all my own, and meet with no check from a niceness that had no example.

She looked at me with a bashful kind of contempt. I thought it *contempt*, and required the reason for it; not being conscious of offence, as I told her.

This is not the first time, Mr. Lovelace, said she, that I have had cause to be displeased with you, when *you*, perhaps, have not thought yourself exceptionable.—But, Sir, let me tell you, that the married state, in my eye, is a state of purity, and (I think she told me) not of *licentiousness;* so at least, I understood her.

Marriage-purity, Jack!—Very comical, 'faith—Yet, sweet dears, half the female world ready to run away with a rake, *because* he is a rake; and for no *other* reason; nay, every other reason *against* their choice.

But have not you and I, Belford, seen young wives, who would be thought modest; and when maids, were fantastically shy; permit freedoms in public from their *lambent* husbands, which have shewn, that they have forgot what belongs either to prudence or decency? While every modest eye has sunk under the shameless effrontery, and every modest face been covered with blushes for those who could not blush.

I once, upon such an occasion, proposed to a circle of a dozen, thus scandalized, to withdraw; since they must needs see that as well the *lady*, as the gentleman, wanted to be in private. This motion had its effect upon the amorous pair; and I was applauded for the check given to their licentiousness.

But, upon another occasion of this sort, I acted a little more in character.—For I ventured to make an attempt upon a bride, which I should not have had the courage to make, had not the unblushing passiveness with which she received her fond husband's public toyings (looking round her with triumph rather than with shame, upon every lady present), incited my curiosity to know if the same complacency might not be shewn to a private friend. 'Tis true, I was in honour obliged to keep the secret. But I never saw the turtles bill afterwards, but I thought of Number Two to the same female; and in my heart thanked the fond husband for the lesson he had taught his wife.

From what I have said, thou wilt see, that I approve of my beloved's exception to *public* loves. That, I hope, is all the charming Icicle means by *marriage-purity*.

From the whole of the above, thou wilt gather, that I have not been a mere dangler, a Hickman, in the passed days, though not absolutely active, and a Lovelace.

The dear creature now considers herself as my wife-elect. The *unsaddened* heart, no longer prudish, will not now, I hope, give the sable turn to every action of the man she dislikes not. And yet she must keep up so much reserve, as will justify past inflexibilities. But should she resent ever so strongly, she cannot now break with me; since, if she does, there will be an end of the family reconciliation; and that in a way highly discreditable to herself.

Sat. June 3.

Just returned from Doctors-Commons. I have been endeavouring to get a licence. Very true, Jack. I have the mortification to find a difficulty in obtaining this *all-fettering* instrument, as the Lady is of rank and fortune, and as there is no consent of father or *next friend*.

I made report of this difficulty. It is very right, she says, that such difficulties should be made. But not to a man of my known fortune, surely, Jack, tho' the woman were the daughter of a duke.

I asked, If she approved of the settlements? She said, She had compared them with my mother's, and had no objection. She had written to Miss Howe upon the subject, she owned; and to inform her of our present situation.

Just now, in high good-humour, my beloved returned me the draughts of the settlements; a copy of which I had sent to Captain Tomlinson. She complimented me, that she never had any doubt of my honour in cases of this nature.—In matters between man and man nobody ever had, thou knowest. I had need, thou'lt say, to have some good qualities.

Mr. Lovelace
To John Belford, Esq;

Monday, June 5.

I AM now almost in despair of succeeding with this charming frost-piece by love or gentleness.—A copy of the draughts, as I told thee, has been sent to Captain Tomlinson; and that by special messenger. Ingrossments are proceeding with. I have been again at the Commons. Should in all probability have procured a licence by Mallory's means, had not Mallory's friend the proctor been suddenly sent for to Cheshunt, to make an old lady's will.—Yet with all these favourable appearances no conceding moment to be found, no improveable tenderness to be raised.

Twice indeed with rapture, which once she called rude, did I salute her; and each time, resenting the freedom, did she retire; tho', to do her justice, she favoured me again with her presence at my first intreaty, and took no notice of the cause of her withdrawing.

Is it policy to shew so open a resentment for innocent liberties, which, in her situation, she must so soon forgive?

Yet the woman who resents not initiatory freedoms must be lost. For Love is an incroacher. Love never goes backward. Love is always aspiring. Always must aspire. Nothing but the highest act of Love can satisfy an indulged Love. And what advantages has a lover, who values not breaking the peace, over his mistress, who is solicitous to keep it!

I have now at this instant wrought myself up, for the dozenth time, to a half-resolution. A thousand agreeable things I have to say to her. She is in the dining-room. Just gone up. She always expects me when there.

High displeasure!—followed by an abrupt departure.

I sat down by her. I took both her hands in mine. I would *have* it so. All gentle my voice.—Her father mentioned with respect. Her mother with reverence. Even her brother amicably spoken of. I never thought I could have wished so ardently, as I told her I did wish, for a reconciliation with her family.

A sweet and grateful flush then overspread her fair face; a gentle sigh now-and-then heaved her handkerchief.

I perfectly longed to hear from Captain Tomlinson. It was impossible for her uncle to find fault with the draught of the settlements. I would not, however, be understood, by sending them down, that I intended to put it in her uncle's power to delay my happy day. When, when, was it to be?

It was time enough to name the day, when the settlements were completed, and the licence obtained. Happy should she be, could the kind Captain Tomlinson obtain her uncle's presence privately!

A good hint!—It may perhaps be improved upon—Either for a *delay*, or a *pacifier*.

No new delays, for heaven's sake, I besought her; reproaching her gently for the past. Name but the day—(an early day, I hoped in the following week)—that I might hail its approach, and number the tardy hours.

My cheek reclined on her shoulder—kissing her hands by turns. Rather bashfully than angrily reluctant, her hands sought to be withdrawn; her shoulder avoiding my reclined cheek—Apparently loth and more loth to quarrel with me; her downcast eye confessing more than her lips could utter.—Now surely, thought I, is my time to try if she can forgive a still bolder freedom than I had ever yet taken.

I then gave her struggling hands liberty. I put one arm round her waist: I imprinted a kiss on her sweet lips, with a *Be quiet* only, and an averted face, as if she feared another.

Encouraged by so gentle a repulse, the tenderest things I said; and then, with my other hand, drew aside the handkerchief that concealed the beauty of beauties, and pressed with my burning lips the most charming breast that ever my ravished eyes beheld.

A very contrary passion to that which gave her bosom so delightful a swell, immediately took place. She struggled out of my incircling arms with indignation. I detained her reluctant hand. Let me go, said she. I see there is no keeping terms with you. Base incroacher! Is this the design of your flattering speeches?—Far as matters have gone, I will for ever renounce you. You have an odious heart. Let me go, I tell you.—

I was forced to obey, and she flung from me, repeating *base*, and adding *flattering*, incroacher.

In vain have I urged by Dorcas for the promised favour of dining with her. She would not dine *at all*. She *could not*.

But why makes she every inch of her person thus sacred?— So near the time too, that she must suppose, that all will be my own, by deed of purchase and settlement?

She has read, no doubt, of the art of the Eastern monarchs, who sequester themselves from the eyes of their subjects, in order to excite their adoration, when, upon some solemn occasions, they think fit to appear in public.

But let me ask thee, Belford, whether (on these solemn occasions) the preceding cavalcade; here a great officer, and there a great minister, with their satellites, and glaring equipages; do not prepare the eyes of the wondering beholders, by degrees, to bear the blaze of canopy'd majesty (what tho' but an ugly old man perhaps himself? yet) glittering in the collected riches of his vast empire?

And should not my beloved, for her own sake, descend, by *degrees*, from *goddess-hood* into *humanity*? If it be *pride* that restrains her, ought not that pride to be punished? If, as in the Eastern emperors, it be *art* as well as *pride*, *art* is what she of all women need not use. If *Shame*, what a shame to be ashamed to communicate to her adorer's sight the most admirable of her personal graces?

Let me perish, Belford, if I would not forego the brightest diadem in the world, for the pleasure of seeing a Twin-Lovelace at each charming breast, drawing from it his first sustenance; the pious task continued for one month, and no more!

I now, methinks, behold this most charming of women in

this sweet office pressing with her fine fingers the generous flood into the purple mouths of each eager hunter by turns: Her conscious eye now dropt on one, now on the other, with a sigh of maternal tenderness; and then raised up to my delighted eye, full of wishes, for the sake of the pretty varlets, and for her own sake, that I would deign to legitimate; that I would condescend to put on the nuptial fetters.

Mr. Lovelace
To John Belford, Esq;

Wednesday Night, 11 o' Clock.

F AITH, Jack, thou hadst half undone me with thy nonsense. So near to execution my plot! So near springing my mine! All agreed upon between the women and me, or I believe thou hadst overthrown me.

I have time for a few lines preparative to what is to happen in an hour or two; and I love to write to the moment.—

We have been extremely happy. How many agreeable days have we known together! What may the next two hours produce!—

When I parted with my charmer (which I did with infinite reluctance, half an hour ago), it was upon her promise, that she would not sit up to write or read. For so engaging was the conversation to me (and, indeed, my behaviour throughout the whole of it, was confessedly agreeable to her), that I insisted, if she did not directly retire to rest, that she should add another happy hour to the former.

To have sat up writing or reading half the night, as she sometimes does, would have frustrated my view, as thou wilt observe, when my little plot unravels.

What—What—What now!—Bounding villain! wouldst thou choak me!—

I was speaking to my heart, Jack!—It was then at my throat.
—And what is all this for?—These shy ladies, how, when a man
thinks himself near the mark, do they tempest him!—

Is all ready, Dorcas? Has my beloved kept her word with
me?—Whether are these billowy heavings owing more to Love
or to Fear? I cannot tell for the soul of me, of which I have most.
If I can but take her before her apprehension, before her eloquence, is awake—

Limbs, why thus convulsed!—Knees, till now so firmly
knit, why thus relaxed? Why beat ye thus together? Will not
these trembling fingers, which twice have refused to direct the
pen, and thus curvedly deform the paper, fail me in the arduous
moment?

Once again, Why and for what all these convulsions? This
project is not to end in matrimony surely!

But the consequences must be greater than I had thought
of till this moment—My beloved's destiny or my own may
depend upon the issue of the two next hours!

I will recede, I think!—

Soft, O virgin saint, and safe as soft, be thy slumbers!—

I will now once more turn to my friend Belford's letter.
Thou shalt have fair play, my charmer. I will reperuse what
thy advocate has to say for thee. Weak arguments will do, in
the frame I am in!—

But, what the matter!—What's the matter!—What a
double—But the uproar abates!—What a *double coward* am I?
—Or is it that I am taken in a cowardly minute? for heroes have
their fits of *fear*; cowards their *brave* moments: And virtuous
ladies, all but my Clarissa, their moment *critical*—

But thus coolly enjoying thy reflections in a hurricane!—
Again the confusion's renewed!—

What! where!—How came it!—

Is my beloved safe?—

O wake not too roughly my beloved!—

Mr. Lovelace
To John Belford, Esq;

Thursday Morning, Five o' clock, June 8.

NOW is my reformation secured; for I never shall love any other woman!—O she is all variety! She must be ever new to me! *Imagination* cannot form; much less can the pencil paint; nor can the soul of painting, *poetry*, describe an angel so exquisitely, so elegantly lovely!—But I will not by anticipation pacify thy impatience. Altho' the subject is too hallowed for profane contemplation; yet shalt thou have the whole before thee as it passed: And this not from a spirit wantoning in description upon so rich a subject; but with a design to put a bound to thy roving thoughts.—It will be iniquity greater than a Lovelace ever was guilty of, to carry them farther than I shall acknowlege.

Thus then, connecting my last with the present, I lead to it.

Didst thou not, by the conclusion of my former, perceive the consternation I was in, just as I was about to reperuse thy letter, in order to prevail upon myself to recede from my purpose of awaking in terrors my slumbering charmer? And what dost think was the matter?

I'll tell thee—

At a little after two, when the whole house was still, or seemed to be so, and, as it proved, my Clarissa abed, and fast asleep; I also in a manner undressed, for an hour before, and in my gown and slippers, tho' to oblige thee, writing on;—I was alarmed by a trampling noise over head, and a confused buz of mix'd voices, some louder than others, like scolding, and little short of screaming all raised to vocatives, as in a fright: And while I was wondering what could be the matter, down stairs ran Dorcas, and at my door, in an accent rather frightedly and hoarsly inward, than shrilly clamorous, cried out Fire! Fire! And this the more alarmed me, as she seemed to endeavour to cry out louder, but could not.

My pen (its last scrawl a benediction on my beloved) dropt

from my fingers; and up started I; and making but three steps to the door, opening it, and cried Where! Where! almost as much terrified as the wench. While she, more than half-undrest, her petticoats in her hand, unable to speak distinctly, pointed up stairs.

I was there in a moment, and found all owing to the careless-ness of Mrs. Sinclair's cook-maid, who, having sat up to read the simple history of Dorastus and Faunia, when she should have been in bed, had set fire to an old pair of callico window-cur-tains.

She had had the presence of mind, in her fright, to tear down the half-burnt vallens, as well as curtains, and had got them, tho' blazing, into the chimney, by the time I came up; so that I had the satisfaction to find the danger happily over.

Mean time Dorcas, after she had directed me up stairs, not knowing the worst was over, and expecting every minute the house would be in a blaze, out of tender regard for her lady [I shall for ever love the wench for it] ran to her door, and rapping loudly at it, in a recovered voice, cried out, with a shrillness equal to her love, Fire! Fire!—The house is on fire!—Rise, Madam!—This instant rise—if you would not be burnt in your bed!

No sooner had she made this dreadful outcry, but I heard her lady's door, with hasty violence, unbar, unbolt, unlock, and open, and my charmer's voice sounding like that of one going into a fit.

You may believe how much I was affected. I trembled with concern for her, and hastened down faster than the alarm of fire had made me run up, in order to satisfy her, that all the danger was over.

When I had *flown down* to her chamber-door, there I beheld the charmingest creature in the world, supporting herself on the arm of the gasping Dorcas, sighing, trembling, and ready to faint, with nothing on but an under-petticoat, her lovely bosom half-open, and her feet just slipt into her shoes. As soon as she saw me, she panted, and struggled to speak; but could only say, Oh, Mr. Lovelace! and down was ready to sink.

I clasped her in my arms with an ardor she never felt before:

My dearest life! fear nothing: I have been up—The danger is over—The fire is got under—And how (foolish devil! to Dorcas) could you thus, by your hideous yell, alarm and frighten my angel!

Oh Jack! how her sweet bosom, as I clasped her to mine, heaved and panted! I could even distinguish her dear heart flutter, flutter, flutter against mine; and for a few minutes, I feared she would go into fits.

Lest the half-lifeless charmer should catch cold in this undress, I lifted her to her bed, and sat down by her upon the side of it, endeavouring with the utmost tenderness, as well of action as expression, to dissipate her terrors.

But what did I get by this my generous care of her, and by my *successful* endeavour to bring her to herself?—Nothing, ungrateful as she was! but the most passionate exclamations: For we had both already forgotten the occasion, dreadful as it was, which had thrown her into my arms: I, from the joy of incircling the almost disrobed body of the loveliest of her sex; she, from the greater terrors that arose from finding herself in my arms, and both seated on the bed, from which she had been so lately frighted.

And now, Belford, reflect upon the distance the watchful charmer had hitherto kept me at. Reflect upon my love, and upon my sufferings for her: Reflect upon her vigilance, and how long I had lain in wait to elude it; the awe I had stood in, because of her frozen virtue and over-niceness; and that I never before was so happy with her; and then think how ungovernable must be my transports in those happy moments!—And yet, in my own account, I was both decent and generous.

But, far from being affected by an address so fervent (although from a man she had so lately owned a regard for and with whom, but an hour or two before, she had parted with so much satisfaction), that I never saw a bitterer, or more moving grief, when she came fully to herself.

She appealed to Heaven against my *treachery*, as she called it; while I, by the most solemn vows, pleaded my own equal fright, and the reality of the danger that had alarmed us both.

She conjured me, in the most solemn and affecting manner,

by turns threatening and soothing, to quit her apartment, and permit her to hide herself from the light, and from every human eye.

I besought her pardon; yet could not avoid offending; and repeatedly vowed, that the next morning's sun should witness our espousals: But taking, I suppose, all my protestations of this kind, as an indication that I intended to proceed to the last extremity, she would hear nothing that I said; but, redoubling her struggles to get from me, in broken accents, and exclamations the most vehement, she protested, that she would not survive, what she called a treatment so disgraceful and villainous; and, looking all wildly round her, as if for some instrument of mischief, she espied a pair of sharp-pointed scissars on a chair by the bed-side, and endeavoured to catch them up, with design to make her words good on the spot.

Seeing her desperation, I begged her to be pacified; that she would hear me speak but one word, declaring that I intended no dishonour to her: And having seized the scissars, I threw them into the chimney; and she still insisting vehemently upon my distance, I permitted her to take the chair.

But, O the sweet discomposure!—Her bared shoulders and arms, so inimitably fair and lovely: Her spread hands crossed over her charming neck; yet not half concealing its glossy beauties: The scanty coat, as she rose from me, giving the whole of her admirable shape, and fine-turn'd limbs: Her eyes running over, yet seeming to threaten future vengeance: And at last her lips uttering what every indignant look, and glowing feature, portended; exclaiming as if I had done the worst I could do, and vowing never to forgive me; wilt thou wonder, that I could avoid resuming the incensed, the already too-much-provoked fair-one?

I did; and clasped her once more to my bosom: But, considering the delicacy of her frame, her force was amazing, and shewed how much in earnest she was in her resentment; for it was with the utmost difficulty that I was able to hold her: Nor could I prevent her sliding through my arms, to fall upon her knees: Which she did at my feet: And there, in the anguish of her soul, her streaming eyes lifted up to my face with supplicating softness, hands folded, dishevelled hair; for her night head-dress having fallen off in her struggling, her charming tresses fell down in naturally shining ringlets, as if officious to conceal the dazling beauties of her neck and shoulders; her lovely bosom too heaving with sighs, and broken sobs, as if to aid her quivering lips, in pleading for her—In this manner, but when her grief gave way to her speech, in words pronounced with that emphatical propriety, which distinguishes this admirable creature in her elocution from all the women I ever heard speak; did she implore my compassion, and my honour.

"Consider me, *dear* Lovelace," were her charming words! "on my knees I beg you to consider me, as a poor creature who has no protector but you; who has no defence but your honour: By that Honour! By your Humanity! By all you have vowed! I conjure you not to make me abhor myself!—Not to make me vile in my own eyes!"

I mentioned the morrow as the happiest day of my life.

Tell me not of to-morrow; if indeed you mean me honourably, *Now*, This very instant NOW! you must shew it, and begone! You can never in a whole long life repair the evils you may NOW make me suffer!

Wicked wretch!—Insolent villain!—[Yes, she called me insolent villain, altho' so much in my power! And for what?—only for kissing with passion indeed her inimitable neck, her lips, her cheeks, her forehead, and her streaming eyes, as this assemblage of beauties offered itself at once to my ravished sight; she continuing kneeling at my feet, as I sat].

If I *am* a villain, Madam—And then my grasping, but trembling hand—I hope I did not hurt the tenderest and loveliest of all her beauties—If I am a villain, Madam—

She tore my ruffle, shrunk from my happy hand, with amazing force and agility, as with my other arm I would have incircled her waist.

Indeed you are!—The worst of villains!—Help! dear blessed people! and screamed—No help for a poor creature!—

Am I then a villain, Madam?—*Am* I then a villain, say you?—and clasped both my arms about her, offering to raise her to my bounding heart.—

O no!—And yet you are!—And again I was her *dear* Lovelace!—Her hands again clasped over her charming bosom:—Kill me! Kill me!—If I am odious enough in your eyes, to deserve this treatment; and I will thank you!—Too long, much too long, has my life been a burden to me!—Or, wildly looking all around her, give me but the means, and I will instantly convince you, that my honour is dearer to me than my life!

Then, with still folded hands, and fresh-streaming eyes, I was her *blessed* Lovelace; and she would thank me with her latest breath, if I would permit her to make that preference, or free her from farther indignities.

I sat suspended for a moment: By my soul, thought I, thou art, upon full proof, an angel and no woman! Still, however, close clasping her to my bosom, as I had raised her from her knees, she again slid through my arms, and dropt upon them:—"See, Mr. Lovelace!—Good God! that I should live to see this hour, and to bear this treatment!—See, at your feet, a poor creature, imploring your pity, who, for your sake, is abandoned of all the world! Let not my father's curse thus dreadfully operate! Be not *you* the inflicter, who have been the *cause* of it! But spare me! I beseech you spare me!—For how have I deserved this treatment from you?—For your own sake, if not for my sake, and as you would that God Almighty, in your last hour, should have mercy upon you, spare me!"—

What heart but must have been penetrated?

I would again have raised the dear suppliant from her knees; but she would not be raised, till my softened mind, she said, had yielded to her prayer, and bid her rise to be innocent.

Rise then, my angel, rise, and be what you are, and all you wish to be! Only pronounce me pardoned for what has passed, and tell me, you will continue to look upon me with that eye of favour and serenity, which I have been blessed with for some days past, and I will submit to my beloved conqueress, whose power never was at so great an height with me, as now; and retire to my apartment.

God Almighty, said she, hear your prayers in your most arduous moments, as you have heard mine! And now leave me, this moment leave me, to my own recollection: In *that* you will leave me to misery enough, and more than you ought to wish to your bitterest enemy.

Impute not every thing, my best Beloved, to design; for design it was not—

O Mr. Lovelace!—

Upon my Soul, Madam, the fire was real—(And so it was, Jack!)—The house might have been consumed by it, as you will be convinced in the morning by ocular demonstration.

O Mr. Lovelace!—

Excuse me, dearest creature, for those liberties, which, innocent as they were, your too great delicacy may make you take amiss—

No more! No more!—Leave me, I beseech you! Again looking upon herself, and around her, in a sweet confusion.—Begone! Begone!—Then weeping, she struggled vehemently to withdraw her hands, which all the while I held between mine.—Her struggles!—O what additional charms, as I now reflect, did her struggles give to every feature, every limb, of a person so sweetly elegant and lovely!

Impossible, my dearest life, till you pronounce my pardon! —Say but you forgive me!—Say you do!

I beseech you, begone! Leave me to myself, that I may think what I *can* do, and what I *ought* to do.

That, my dearest creature, is not enough. You must tell me, that I am forgiven; that you will see me to-morrow, as if nothing had happened.

And then, clasping her again in my arms, hoping she would not forgive me—

I will—I do forgive you—Wretch that you are!

Nay, my Clarissa! And is it such a reluctant pardon, mingled with a word so upbraiding, that I am to be put off with, when you are thus (clasping her close to me) in my power?

I do, I *do* forgive you!

Heartily?

Yes, heartily!

And freely?

Freely!

And will you look upon me to-morrow, as if nothing had passed?

Yes, yes!

I cannot take these peevish affirmatives, so much like intentional negatives!—Say you will, upon your honour.

Upon my honour, then—O now, begone! begone!—And never—

What, never, my angel!—Is this forgiveness?

Never, said she, let what has passed be remembered more!

I insisted upon one kiss to seal my pardon—And retired like a fool, a woman's fool, as I was!—I sneakingly retired!—Couldst thou have believed it?

But I had no sooner entered my own apartment, than, reflecting upon the opportunity I had lost, and that all I had gained was but an increase of my own difficulties; and upon the ridicule I should meet with below, upon a weakness so much out of my usual character; I repented, and hastened back, in hope, that through the distress of mind which I left her in, she had not so soon fastened her door; and I was fully resolved to execute all my purposes, be the consequence what it would; for, thought I, I have already sinned beyond *cordial* forgiveness, I doubt; and if fits and desperation ensue, I can but marry at last, and then I shall make her amends.

But I was justly punished;—for her door was fast: And hearing her sigh and sob, as if her heart would burst, My beloved creature, said I, rapping gently, and her sobbings ceasing, I want but to say three words to you, which must be the most acceptable you ever heard from me. Let me see you but for one moment.

I thought I heard her coming to open the door, and my heart leapt in that hope; but it was only to draw another bolt, to make it still the faster, and she either could not, or would not, answer me, but retired to the further end of her apartment, to her closet, probably: And more like a fool than before, again I sneaked away.

This was mine, my plot!—And this was all I made of it!

I love her more than ever!—And well I may!—Never saw

I such polished ivory as her arms and shoulders seemed to be; never touched I velvet so soft as her skin: Then such an elegance! O Belford, she is all perfection! Her pretty foot, in her struggling, losing her shoe, but just slipped on, as I told thee, equally white and delicate as the hand of any other lady, or even as her own hand!

But seest thou not, that I have a claim of merit for a grace that every-body hitherto had denied me? And that is, for a capacity of being moved by prayers and tears: Where, where, on this occasion, was the *callus*, where the flint, that my heart was said to be surrounded by?

This, indeed, is the first instance, in the like case, that ever I was wrought upon. But why? Because I never before encountered a resistance so much in earnest: A resistance, in short, so irresistible.

But if she can *now* forgive me—Can!—She *must*. Has she not upon her honour already done it?—But how will the dear creature keep that part of her promise, which engages her to see me in the morning, as if nothing had happened?

She would give the world, I fancy, to have the first interview over!—She had not best reproach me:—Yet *not* to reproach me!—What a charming puzzle!—Let her break her word with me at her peril. Fly me she cannot: No appeals lie from my tribunal.—What friend has she in the world, if my compassion exert not itself in her favour?—And then the worthy Captain Tomlinson, and her Uncle Harlowe, will be able to make all up for me, be my next offence what it will.

As to thy apprehensions of her committing any rashness upon herself, whatever she might have done in her passion, if she could have seized upon her scissars, or found any other weapon, I dare say, there is no fear of that from her *deliberate* mind. A man has trouble enough with these truly pious, and truly virtuous girls [Now I believe there are such]; he had need to have some benefit *from*, some security *in*, the rectitude of their minds.

In short, I fear nothing in this lady but grief; yet that's a slow worker, you know; and gives time to pop in a little joy between its sullen fits.

Mr. Lovelace
To John Belford, Esq;

HER chamber-door has not yet been opened. I must not expect she will breakfast with me: Nor dine with me, I doubt. A little silly soul, what troubles does she make to herself by her over-niceness!—All I have done to her, would have been looked upon as a frolick only, a romping-bout, and laughed off by nine parts in ten of the sex accordingly. The more she makes of it, the more painful to herself, as well as to me.

But perhaps I am more afraid than I need. I believe I am. From her *over*-niceness arises my fear, more than from any extraordinary reason for resentment. Next time, she may count herself very happy, if she come off no worse.

The dear creature was so frightened, and so fatigued last night, no wonder she lies it out this morning.

I hope she has had more rest than I have had: Soft and balmy, I hope, have been her slumbers, that she may meet me in tolerable temper. All sweetly blushing and confounded—I *know* how she will look!—But why should she, the *sufferer*, be ashamed, when I, the *trespasser*, am not?

But custom is a prodigious thing. The ladies are told how much their blushes heighten their graces: They practise for them therefore: Blushes come as readily when they call for them, as their tears: Aye, that's it! While we men, taking blushes for a sign of guilt or sheepishness, are equally studious to suppress them.

By my troth, Jack, I am half as much ashamed to see the women below, as my fair one can be to see me. I have not yet opened my door, that I may not be obtruded upon by them.

After all, what devils may one make of the Sex! To what a height of—What shall I call it?—must those of it be arrived, who once loved a man with so much distinction, as both Polly

254

and Sally loved me, and yet can have got so much above the pangs of jealousy as to wish for, and promote a competitorship in his love, and make their supreme delight consist in reducing others to their level!—For thou canst not imagine, how even Sally Martin rejoiced last night in the thought that the lady's hour was approaching.

Past Ten o' clock.

I never longed in my life for any-thing with so much impatience, as to see my charmer. She has been stirring, it seems, these two hours.

Dorcas just now tapped at her door, to take her morning commands.

She had none for her, was the answer.

She desired to know, If she would not breakfast?

A sullen and low-voiced *negative* she received.

I will go myself.

Three different times tapped I at the door, but had no answer.

Permit me, dearest creature, to inquire after your health. As you have not been seen to-day, I am impatient to know how you do.

Not a word of answer; but a deep sigh, even to sobbing.

Let me beg of you, Madam, to accompany me up another pair of stairs—You'll rejoice to see what a happy escape we have all had.

A happy escape, indeed, Jack!—For the fire had scorched the window-board, sindged the hangings, and burnt through the slit-deal lining of the window-jambs.

No answer, Madam!—Am I not worthy of one word?—Is it thus you keep your promise with me?—Shall I not have the favour of your company for two minutes, only for two minutes, in the dining-room?

Hem!—And a deep sigh!—were all the answer.

Answer me, but how you do! Answer me but that you are

well! Is this the forgiveness that was the condition of my obedience?

Then, in a faintish but angry voice, Begone from my door!—
Wretch, inhuman, barbarous, and all that's base and treacherous!—Begone from my door! Nor teaze thus a poor creature,
intitled to protection, not outrage.

Well, Madam, I see, how you keep your word with me!—
If a sudden impulse, the effects of an unthought-of accident,
cannot be forgiven—

O the dreadful weight of a father's curse, thus in the letter
of it.

And then her voice dying away into inarticulate murmurs,
so likely to be fulfilled! I looked through the key-hole, and saw
her on her knees, her face, tho' not towards me, lifted up, as
well as hands, and these folded, deprecating, I suppose, that
gloomy tyrant's curse.

I could not help being moved.

My dearest life! admit me to your presence, but for two
minutes, and confirm your promised pardon; and may lightning
blast me on the spot, if I offer any thing but my penitence, at a
shrine so sacred!—I will afterwards leave you for the whole
day; and till to-morrow morning; then to attend, with writings,
all ready to sign, a licence obtained, or, if it cannot, a minister
without one. This once believe me.

I cannot see you! Would to heaven I never had! If I write,
that's all I can do.

Let your writing then, my dearest life, confirm your promise. And I will withdraw in expectation of it.

Past Eleven o' clock.

S HE rung her bell for Dorcas; and, with her door in her hand,
only half-opened, gave her a billet for me.

How did the dear creature look, Dorcas?

She was dressed. She turned her face quite from me. Sighed,
as if her heart would break.

Sweet creature!—I kissed the wet wafer, and drew it from
the paper with my breath.

These are the contents.—No inscriptive Sir! No Mr. Lovelace!

I cannot see you: Nor will I, if I can help it. Words cannot express the anguish of my soul on your baseness and ingratitude.

If the circumstances of things are such, that I can have no way for reconciliation with those who would have been my natural protectors from such outrages, but through *you* (the only inducement I can have to stay a moment longer in your knowlege), pen and ink must be, at present, the only means of communication between us.

Vilest of men! and most detestable of plotters! how have I deserved from you the shocking indignities—But no more— Only for your own sake, wish not, at least for a week to come, to see

The undeservedly injured and insulted,

Clarissa Harlowe

But not to see her for a week!—Dear pretty soul! how she anticipates me in the every thing! The counsellor will have finished the writings, ready to sign, to-day, or to-morrow, at furthest: The licence with the parson, or the parson without the licence, must be also procured within the next four-and-twenty hours: Pritchard is as good as ready with his indentures tripartite: Tomlinson is at hand, with a favourable answer from her Uncle— *Yet not to see her for a week!*—Dear sweet soul!—Her good angel is gone a journey: Is truanting at least. But nevertheless, in thy week's time, or in much less, my charmer, I doubt not to have completed my triumph!

But what vexes me of all things, is, that such an excellent creature should break her word.—Fie, fie, upon her!—But nobody is absolutely perfect! *'Tis human to err*, but *not to persevere*—I hope my charmer cannot be inhuman!

Mr. Lovelace
To John Belford, Esq;

Thursday Evening, June 8.

O FOR a curse to kill with!—Ruined! Undone! Outwitted! Tricked!—Zounds, man, the lady is gone off!—Absolutely gone off!—Escaped!—

Thou knowest not, nor canst conceive, the pangs that wring my heart!—What can I do!—O Lord, O Lord, O Lord!

And thou, too, who hast endeavoured to weaken my hands, wilt but clap thy dragon's wings at the tidings!—

Yet I must write, or I shall go distracted. Little less have I been these two hours; dispatching messengers to every stage; to every inn; to every waggon or coach, whether flying or creeping, and to every house with a bill up, for five miles round.

The little hypocrite, who knows not a soul in this town [*I thought I was sure of her at any time*], such an unexperienced traitress; giving me hope too, in her first billet, that her expectation of the family-reconciliation would with-hold her from taking such a step as this—Curse upon her contrivances!—I thought, that it was owing to her bashfulness, to her modesty, that, after a few innocent freedoms, she could not look me in the face; when, all the while, she was impudently [yes, I say *impudently*, though she be Clarissa Harlowe]; contriving to rob me of the dearest property I had ever purchased—Purchased by a painful servitude of many months; fighting thro' the wild beasts of her family for her, and combating with a wind-mill virtue, that hath cost me millions of perjuries only to attempt; and which now, with its damn'd air-fans, has tost me a mile and an half beyond hope!—And this, just as I had arrived within view of the consummation of all my wishes!

O Devil of Love! God of Love no more!—How have I deserved this of thee!—Never before the friend of frozen virtue! —*Powerless* demon, for powerless thou must be, if thou meanedst not to play me booty; who shall henceforth kneel at thy altars!—May every enterprizing heart abhor, despise, execrate, renounce thee, as I do.—But what signifies cursing now!

How she could effect this her wicked escape, is my astonishment; the whole sisterhood having charge of her:—For, as yet, I have not had patience enough to inquire into the particulars, nor to let a soul of them approach me.

Of this I am sure, *or I had not brought her hither,* There is not a creature belonging to this house, that could be corrupted either by virtue or remorse: The highest joy every infernal nymph of this worse than infernal habitation, *could* have known, would have been to reduce this proud Beauty to her own level.—And as to my villain, who also had charge of her, he is such a seasoned varlet, that he delights in mischief for the sake of it: No bribe could seduce him to betray his trust, were there but wickedness in it!—'Tis well, however, he was out of my way, when the cursed news was imparted to me!—Gone, the villain! in quest of her: Not to return, nor to see my face (so it seems he declared), till he has heard some tidings of her.

I am mad, stark mad, by Jupiter, at the thoughts of this!—Unprovided, destitute, unacquainted—some villain, worse than myself, who adores her not as I adore her, may have seized her, and taken advantage of her distress!—Let me perish, Belford, if a whole hecatomb of *innocents*, as the little plagues are called, shall atone for the broken promise and wicked artifices of this cruel creature.

Coming home with resolutions favourable to her, judge thou of my distraction, when her escape was first hinted to me, although but in broken sentences. I knew not what I said, nor what I did; I wanted to kill somebody. I flew out of one room into another, while all avoided me but the veteran Betty Carberry, who broke the matter to me: I charged bribery and corruption, in my first fury, upon all; and threatened destruction to old and young, as they should come in my way.

Dorcas continues *locked* up from me: Sally and Polly have not yet dared to appear: The vile Sinclair—

But here comes the odious devil: She taps at the door,
though that's only a-jar, whining and snuffling, to try, I suppose,
to coax me into temper.

What a helpless state, where a man can only execrate himself and others; the occasion of his rage remaining; the evil increasing upon reflection; time itself conspiring to deepen it!—O
how I curs'd her!

I have her now, methinks, before me blubbering—How
odious does sorrow make an ugly face!—Thine, Jack, and this
old beldam's, in penitentials, instead of moving compassion,
must evermore confirm hatred; while Beauty in tears, is beauty
heightened, and what my heart has ever delighted to see.—

What excuse!—Confound you, and your cursed daughters,
what excuse can you make! Is she not gone!—Has she not
escaped!—But before I am quite distracted! before I commit
half an hundred murders, let me hear how it was.

I have heard her story!—Art, damn'd, confounded, wicked,
unpardonable Art, in a woman of her character—But shew me
a woman, and I'll shew thee a plotter!—

This is the substance of the old wretch's account.

She told me, "That I had no sooner left the vile house, than
Dorcas acquainted the Syren" [Do, Jack, let me call her names!—
I beseech thee, Jack, to permit me to call her names!] "than Dor-
cas acquainted her lady with it; and that I had left word, that
I was gone to Doctors-Commons, and should be heard of for
some hours at the Horn there, if inquired after by the counsellor,
or any-body else: That afterwards I should be either at the
Cocoa-Tree, or King's-Arms, and should not return till late.
She then urged her to take some refreshment.

She was in tears when Dorcas approached her; her saucy
eyes swelled with weeping: She refused either to eat or drink;
sighed as if her heart would break." False, devilish grief! not the
humble, silent grief, that only deserves pity!—Contriving to
ruin me, to despoil me of all that I held valuable, in the very
midst of it.

"Nevertheless, being resolved not see me for a week at least,
she ordered her to bring her up three or four French rolls, with

a little butter, and a decanter of water; telling her, she would dispense with her attendance; and that should be all she would live upon in the interim. So, artful creature! pretending to lay up for a week's siege."—For, as to substantial food, she, no more than other angels—Angels, said I!—The devil take me, if she shall be any more an angel!—For she is odious in my eyes; and I hate her mortally!—

But oh! Lovelace, thou lyest!—She is all that is lovely! All that is excellent!

But *is* she, *can* she, be gone!—O how Miss Howe will triumph!—But if that little Fury receive her, Fate shall make me rich amends; for then will I contrive to have them both.

"Dorcas consulted the old wretch about obeying her: O yes, by all means, for Mr. Lovelace knew how to come at her at any time; and directed a bottle of sherry to be added.

This chearful compliance so obliged her, that she was prevailed upon to go up, and look at the damage done by the fire; and seemed not only shocked at it, but satisfied it was no trick, as she owned she had at first apprehended it to be. All this made them secure; and they laughed in their sleeves, to think what a childish way of shewing her resentment, she had found out."

Now this very childishness, as *they* thought it, in such a genius, would have made *me* suspect either her head, after what had happened the night before; or her intention, when the marriage was, so far as she knew, to be completed within the week she was resolved to secrete herself from me in the same house.

"She sent Will. with a Letter to Wilson's, directed to Miss Howe, ordering him to inquire if there were not one for her there.

He only pretended to go, and brought word there was none; and put her letter in his pocket for me.

She then ordered him to carry another (which she gave him) to the Horn-Tavern to me.—All this done without any seeming hurry; yet she appeared to be very solemn; and put her handkerchief frequently to her eyes.

Will. pretended to come to me, with this letter. But tho' the dog had the sagacity to mistrust something, on her sending him out a second time (and to *me*, whom she had refused to see);

which he thought extraordinary; and mentioned his mistrusts
to Sally, Polly, and Dorcas; yet they made light of his suspicions;
Dorcas assuring them all, that her Lady seemed more stupid with
her grief, than active; and that she really believed she was a
little turned in her head, and knew not what she did.—But all of
them depended upon her inexperience, her open temper, and
upon her not making the least motion towards going out, or to
have a coach or chair called, as sometimes she had done; and
still more upon the preparations she had made for a week's
siege, as I may call it.

Will. went out, pretending to bring the letter to me; but
quickly returned; his heart still misgiving him; on recollecting
my frequent cautions, that he was not to judge for himself, when
he had *positive* orders; but if any doubt occurred, from circumstances I could not foresee, literally to follow them, as the only
way to avoid blame.

But it must have been in this little interval, that she escaped;
for soon after his return, they made fast the street-door and
hatch, the mother and the two nymphs taking a little turn into
the garden; Dorcas going up stairs, and Will. (to avoid being seen
by his lady, or his voice heard) down into the kitchen.

About half an hour after, Dorcas, who had planted herself
where she could see her Lady's door open, had the curiosity to
go to look through the key-hole, having a misgiving, as she
said, that her Lady might offer some violence to herself, in the
mood she had been in all day; and finding the key in the door,
which was not very usual, she tapped at it three or four times,
and having no answer, opened it, with Madam, Madam, did you
call?—Supposing her in her closet.

Having no answer, she stept forward, and was astonished
to find she was not there: She hastily ran into the dining-room,
then into my apartments, searched every closet; dreading all the
time to behold some sad catastrophe.

Not finding her any-where, she ran down to the old creature, and her nymphs, with a Have you seen my Lady?—Then
she's gone!—She's no-where above!

They were sure she could not be gone out.

The whole house was in an uproar in an instant; some run-

ning up stairs, some down, from the upper rooms to the lower;
and all screaming, How should they look me in the face!

Will. cried out, he was a dead man! *He* blamed *them;
They, him;* and every one was an *accuser*, and an *excuser* at the
same time.

When they had searched the whole house, and every closet
in it, ten times over, to no purpose: They took it into their heads
to send to all the porters, chairmen, and hackney-coachmen,
that had been near the house for two hours past, to inquire if
any of them saw Such a young Lady; describing her.

This brought them some light: The only dawning for hope,
that I can have, and which keeps me from absolute despair. One
of the chairmen gave them this account: That he saw such a
one come out of the house a little before four (in a great hurry,
and as if frighted), with a little parcel tied up in an handkerchief, in her hand: That he took notice to his fellow, who plied
her, without her answering, that she was a fine young lady:
That he'd warrant, she had either a bad husband, or very cross
parents; for that her eyes seemed swelled with crying.

From these appearances, the fellow who gave this information, had the curiosity to follow her, unperceived. She often
looked back. Every-body who passed her, turned to look after
her; passing their verdicts upon her tears, her hurry, and her
charming person; till coming to a stand of coaches, a coachman
plied her; was accepted; alighted, opened the coach-door in a
hurry, seeing *her* hurry; and in it she stumbled for haste; and
the fellow believed, hurt her shins with the stumble.

The devil take me, Belford, if my generous heart is not
moved for her, notwithstanding her wicked deceit, to think
what must be her reflections and apprehensions at the time!
—A mind so delicate, heeding no censures; yet, probably, afraid
of being laid hold of by a Lovelace in every-one she saw! At
the same time, not knowing to what dangers she was going to
expose herself; nor of whom she could obtain shelter; a stranger
to the town, and to all its ways; the afternoon far gone; but
little money; and no cloaths but those she had on.

"The fellow heard her say, Drive fast! Very fast! Where,
Madam?—To Holborn Bars, answered she; repeating, Drive

very fast!—And up she pulled both the windows: And he lost sight of the coach in a minute.

Will. as soon as he had this intelligence, speeded away in hopes to trace her out; declaring, that he would never think of seeing me, till he had heard some tidings of his lady."

And now, Belford, all my hope is, that this fellow (who attended us in our airing to Hampstead, to Highgate, to Muzzle-hill, to Kentish-Town) will hear of her at some one or other of those places.—And on this I the rather build, as I remember, she was once, after our return, very inquisitive about the stages, and their prices; praising the conveniency to passengers in their going off every hour.

I have been traversing her room, meditating, or taking up every-thing she but touched or used: The glass she dressed at, I was ready to break, for not giving me the personal image it was wont to reflect, of *her*, whose idea is for ever present with me. I call for her, now in the tenderest, now in the most reproachful terms, as if within hearing: Wanting *her*, I want my own soul, at least every-thing dear to it. What a void in my heart! what a chilness in my blood, as if its circulation were arrested!

But when in my first fury, at my return, I went up two pair of stairs, resolved to find the locked-up Dorcas, and beheld the vainly-burnt window-board, and recollected my baffled contrivances, baffled by my own weak folly, I thought my distraction completed, and down I ran as one frighted at a spectre, ready to howl for vexation; my head and my temples shooting with a violence I had never felt before; and my back aching as if the vertebrae were disjointed, and falling in pieces.

But now that I have heard the mother's story, and contemplated the dawning hopes given by the chairman's information, I am a good deal easier, and can make cooler reflections. Most heartily pray I for Will.'s success, every four or five minutes. If I lose her, all my rage will return with redoubled fury. The disgrace to be thus outwitted by a novice, an infant, in stratagem and contrivance, added to the violence of my passion for her, will either break my heart, or (what saves many an heart in evils insupportable) turn my brain. And as the sting of this reflection will sharpen upon me if I recover her not, how shall I be able to bear it?

If ever—

Here Mr. Lovelace lays himself under a curse, too shocking to be repeated, if he revenge not himself upon the Lady, should he once more get her into his hands.

I have collected, from the result of the inquiries made of the chairman, and from Dorcas's observations before the cruel creature escaped, a description of her dress; and am resolved, if I cannot otherwise hear of her, to advertise her in the Gazette, as an eloped wife, both by her maiden and acknowleged name; for her elopement will soon be known by every *Enemy*, why then should not my *Friends* be made acquainted with it, from whose inquiries and informations I may expect some tidings of her?

She had on a brown lustring night-gown, fresh, and looking like new, as every thing she wears does, whether new or not, from an elegance natural to her. A beaver hat, a black ribband about her neck, and blue knots on her breast. A quilted petticoat of carnation-coloured satten; a rose-diamond ring, supposed on her finger; and in her whole person and appearance, as I shall express it, a dignity, as well as beauty, that commands the repeated attention of every one who sees her.

The description of her person, I shall take a little more pains about. My mind must be more at ease, before I can undertake that. And I shall threaten, that if, after a certain period given for her voluntary return, she be not heard of, I will prosecute any person, who presumes to entertain, harbour, abett, or encourage her, with all the vengeance that an injured gentleman and husband may be warranted to take by Law, or otherwise.

Fresh cause of aggravation!—But for this scribbling vein, or I should still run mad.

Again going into her chamber, because it was hers, and

sighing over the bed, and every piece of furniture in it, I cast my eye towards the drawers of the dressing-glass, and saw peep out, as it were, in one of the half-drawn drawers, the corner of a letter. I snatched it out, and found it superscribed, by her, *To Mr. Lovelace.* The sight of it made my heart leap, and I trembled so, that I could hardly open the seal.

How does this damn'd Love unman me!—But nobody ever loved as I love!—It is even increased by her unworthy flight, and my disappointment.

I will not give thee a copy of this letter. I owe her not so much service.

Mr. Lovelace
To John Belford, Esq;

A LETTER is put into my hands by Wilson himself—Such a Letter!

A Letter from Miss Howe to her cruel friend!—

I made no scruple to open it.

It is a miracle, that I fell not into fits at the reading of it; and at the thought of what might have been the consequence, had it come to the hands of *this Clarissa Harlowe.* Let my justly-excited rage excuse my irreverence.

O this devilish Miss Howe!—Something must be resolved upon, and done with that little Fury!

Thou wilt see the margin of this cursed letter crouded with indices [☞]. I put them to mark the places devoted for vengeance, or requiring animadversion. Return thou it to me the moment thou hast it.

Read it here; and avoid trembling for me, if thou canst.

To Miss Laetitia Beaumont

My dearest friend,

YOU will perhaps think, that I have been too long silent. But I had begun two letters at different times since my last, and written a great deal each time; and with spirit enough, I assure you; incensed as I was against the abominable wretch you are with; particularly on reading yours of the 21st of the past month.

But I must stop here, and take a little walk, to try to keep down that just indignation which rises to my pen, when I am about to relate to you what I must communicate.

I am not my own mistress enough—Then my mother—Always up and down—And watching as if I were writing to a fellow—But I will try if I can contain myself in tolerable bounds—

The women of the house where you are—O my dear—The women of the house—But you never thought highly of them—So it cannot be very surprising—Nor would you have staid so long with them, had not the notion of removing to one of your own, made you less uneasy, and less curious about their characters, and behaviour. Yet I could *now* wish, that you had been less reserved among them—But I teaze you—In short, my dear, you are certainly in a devilish house!—Be assured, that the woman is one of the vilest of women!—Nor does she go to you by her right name—Very true—Her name is *not* Sinclair—Nor is the Street she lives in, Dover-street.—Did you never go out by yourself, and discharge the coach or chair, and return by another coach or chair? If you did (yet I don't remember that you ever wrote to me, that you did), you would never have found your way to the vile house, either by the woman's name, *Sinclair*, or by the street's name, mentioned by that Doleman in his letter about the lodgings.

The wretch might indeed have held out these false lights a little more excuseably, had the house been an honest house; and had his end only been to prevent mischief from your brother.—But this contrivance was antecedent, as I think, to your brother's project: So that no excuse can be made for his intentions at the *time*—The man, whatever he may *now* intend, was certainly then, even *then*, a villain in his heart!

I write, perhaps, with too much violence, to be clear. But I cannot help it. Yet I lay down my pen, and take it up every ten minutes, in order to write with some temper—My mother too in and out—What need I (she asks me) lock myself in, if I am only reading past correspondencies?—for that is my pretence, when she comes poking in with her face sharpened to an edge, as I may say, by a curiosity that gives her more pain than pleasure—The Lord forgive me; but I believe I shall huff her next time she comes in.

Do *You* forgive me too, my dear. My mother *ought*; because she says, I am my father's girl; and because I am sure I am *hers*. I don't know what to do—I don't know what to write next—I have so much to write, yet have so little patience, and so little opportunity.

But I will tell you how I came by my intelligence.

Thus then it came about—"Miss Lardner (whom you have seen at her Cousin Biddulph's) saw you at St. James's church on Sunday was fortnight. She kept you in her eye during the whole time; but could not once obtain the notice of yours, tho' she courtesied to you twice. She thought to pay her compliments to you when the Service was over; for she doubted not but you were married—and for an odd reason—*because you came to church by yourself.*—Every eye, as usual, she said, was upon you; and this seeming to give you hurry, and you being nearer the door than she, you slid out, before she could get to you. But she ordered her servant to follow you till you were housed. This servant saw you step into a chair, which waited for you; and you ordered the men to carry you to the place where they took you up.

The next day, Miss Lardner sent the same servant, out of mere curiosity, to make private inquiry whether Mr. Lovelace were, or were not, with you there. And this inquiry brought out, from *different* people, that the house was suspected to be one of those genteel wicked houses, which receive and accommodate fashionable people of both sexes.

Miss Lardner, confounded at this strange intelligence, made further inquiry; injoining secrecy to the servant she had sent, as well as to the gentleman whom she employed: Who had it confirmed from a rakish friend, who knew the house; and told him, that there were two houses; the one, in which all decent appearances were preserved, and guests rarely admitted, the other, the receptacle of those who were absolutely engaged, and broken to the vile yoke."

Say—my dear creature—say—Shall I not execrate the wretch?—But words are weak—What can I say, that will suitably express my abhorrence of such a villain as he must have been, when he meditated to bring a Clarissa Harlowe to such a place!

"Miss Lardner kept this to herself some days, not knowing what to do; for she loves you, and admires you of all women. At last, she revealed it, but in confidence, to Miss Biddulph, by letter. Miss Biddulph, in like confidence, being afraid it would distract *me*, were I to know it, communicated it to Miss Lloyd; and so, like a whispered scandal, it passed through several canals; and then it came to me. Which was not till last Monday."

I thought I should have fainted upon the surprising communication. But rage taking place, it blew away the sudden illness. I besought Miss Lloyd to re-injoin secrecy to every-one. I told her, that I would not for the world, that my mother, or any of your family, should know it. And I instantly caused a trusty friend to make what inquiries he could about Tomlinson.

I had thoughts to have done it before: But not imagining it to be needful, and little thinking that you could be in such a house, and as you were pleased with your changed prospects, I forbore. And the rather forbore, as the matter is so laid, that Mrs. Hodges is supposed to know nothing of the projected treaty of accommodation; but, on the contrary, that it was designed to be a secret to her, and to every-body but immediate parties; and it was Mrs. Hodges that I had proposed to sound by a *second* hand.

Now, my dear, it is certain, without applying to that too-much favoured housekeeper, that there is not such a man within ten miles of your Uncle. Very true! One *Tomkins* there is, about four miles off; but he is a day-labourer: And one *Thompson*, about five miles distant the other way; but he is a parish-schoolmaster, poor, and about seventy.

Yet, methinks, the story is so plausible: Tomlinson, as you describe him, is so good a man, and so much of a gentleman; the end to be answered by his being an impostor, so much *more than necessary*, if Lovelace has villainy in his head; and as you are in such a house—

But this is what I am ready to conjecture, that Tomlinson, specious as he is, is a machine of Lovelace; and that he is employed for some end, which has not yet been answered.

But can I think (you will ask, with indignant astonishment), that Lovelace can have designs upon your honour?

That such designs he *has had*, if he *still* hold them not, I can have no doubt, now that I know the house he has brought you to, to be a vile one. This is a clue that has led me to account for all his behaviour to you ever since you have been in his hands.

Allow me a brief retrospection of it all.

We both know, that Pride, Revenge, and a delight to tread in unbeaten paths, are principal ingredients in the character of this finished libertine.

He hates all your family, yourself excepted; and I have several times thought, that I have seen him stung and mortified, that Love has obliged him to kneel at your footstool, because you are a *Harlowe*.—Yet is this wretch a Savage in Love.—Love that humanizes the fiercest spirits, has not been able to subdue his.

Let me stop to admire, and to bless my beloved friend, who, unhappily for herself, at an age so tender, unacquainted as she was with the world, and with the vile arts of libertines, having been called upon to sustain the hardest and most shocking trials, from persecuting Relations on one hand, and from a villainous Lover on the other, has been enabled to give such an illustrious example of fortitude and prudence, as never woman gave before her; and who, as I have heretofore observed, has made a far greater figure in adversity, than she possibly could have made, had all her shining qualities been exerted in their full force and power, by the continuance of that prosperous run of fortune, which attended her for Eighteen years of life out of Nineteen.

But now, my dear, do I apprehend, that you are in greater danger than ever yet you have been in; if you are not married in a week; and yet stay in this abominable house. For were you out of it, I own, I should not be much afraid for you.

If you do not fly the house upon reading of this, or some way or other get out of it, I shall judge of his power over you, by the little you will have over either him or yourself.

I shall send this long letter by Collins, who changes his day to oblige me; and that he may try (now I know where you are), to get it into your own hands. If he cannot, he will leave it at Wilson's. As none of our letters by that conveyance have miscarried, when you have been in more *apparently* disagreeable situations than you are in at present, I hope that This will go safe, if Collins should be obliged to leave it there.

One word more. Command me up, if I can be of the least service or pleasure to you. I value not fame; I value not censure; nor even life itself, I verily think, as I do your honour, and your friendship—For, is not your honour my honour? And is not your friendship the pride of my life?

May heaven preserve you, my dearest creature, in honour and safety, is the prayer, the hourly prayer, of

Your ever-faithful and affectionate

Anna Howe

Thursday Morn. 5. I have written all night.

To Miss Howe

My dearest creature,

HOW you have shocked, confounded, surprised, astonished me, by your dreadful communication!—My *heart is too weak* to bear up against such a stroke as this!—When all hope was with me! When my prospects were so much mended!—But can there be such villainy in men, as in this vile principal, and equally vile agent!

I am really ill—Very ill—Grief and surprize, and, now I will say, despair, have overcome me!—All, all, you have laid down as conjecture, appears to me now to be *more* than conjecture!

O that your mother would have the goodness to permit me the presence of the only comforter that my afflicted, my half-broken heart, could be raised by! But I charge you, think not of coming up without her indulgent permission.—I am too ill, at present, my dear, to think of combating with this dreadful man; and of flying from this horrid house!—My bad writing will shew you this.—But my illness will be my present security, should he indeed have meditated villainy.—Forgive, O forgive me, my dearest friend, the trouble I have given you!—All must soon—But why add I grief to grief, and trouble to trouble?—But I charge you, my beloved creature, not to think of coming up, without your mother's leave, to the truly desolate, and broken-spirited

Clarissa Harlowe

Well, Jack!—And what thinkest thou of this last letter? Miss Howe values not either *fame* or *censure;* and thinkest thou, that this letter will not bring the little fury up, tho' she could procure no other conveyance than her higgler's paniers, one for herself, the other for her maid?—She knows where to come now!—Many a little villain have I punished for knowing more than I would have her know; and that by adding to her knowlege and experience.—What thinkest thou, Belford, if by getting

272

hither this virago, and giving *cause* for a lamentable letter from her to the fair fugitive, I should be able to recover *her*?—Would she not visit that friend in *her* distress, thinkest thou, whose intended visit to her in *hers*, brought her into the condition she herself had so perfidiously escaped from?

Let me enjoy the thought!

Shall I send this letter?—Do they not both deserve it of me? —Seest thou not how the raveing girl threatens her mother?— Ought she not to be punished?—And can I be a worse devil, or villain, or monster, than she calls me in this letter; and has called me in her former letters; were I to punish them both, as my vengeance urges me to punish them. And when I have executed That my vengeance, how charmingly satisfied may they both go down into the country, and keep house together, and have a much better reason than their pride could give them, for living the Single-life they have both seemed so fond of?

I will set about transcribing it this moment, I think. I can resolve afterwards. I am on tiptoe, Jack, to enter upon this project.—Is not one country as good to me as another, if I should be obliged to take another tour upon it?

But the principal reason that withholds me (for 'tis a tempting project!) is, for fear of being utterly blown up, if I should not be quick enough with my letter, or if Miss Howe should deliberate on setting out, or try her mother's consent first; in which time, a letter from my frighted beauty might reach her; for I have no doubt, where-ever she has refuged, but her first work was to write to her vixen friend. I will therefore go on patiently; and take my revenge upon the little fury at my leisure.

But, in spite of my compassion for Hickman, whose better character is sometimes my envy, and who is one of those mortals that bring clumsiness into credit with the *mothers*, to the disgrace of us clever fellows, and often to our disappointment, with the *daughters*; and who has been very busy in assisting these double-armed beauties against me; I swear by all the *Dii Majores*, as well as *Minores*, that I will have Miss Howe, if I cannot have her more exalted friend!—And then, if there be as much flaming love between these girls as they pretend, what will my charmer profit by her escape?

But this, Belford, I hope—that if I can turn the poison of this letter into wholesome aliment; that is to say, if I can make use of it to my advantage; I shall have *thy* free consent to do it.

I am always careful to open covers cautiously, and to preserve seals intire. I will draw out from this cursed letter an alphabet. Nor was Nick Rowe ever half so diligent to learn Spanish, at the Quixote recommendation of a certain Peer, as I will be to gain a mastery of this vixen's hand.

Miss Clarissa Harlowe To Miss Howe

Thursday Evening, June 8.

AFTER my last, so full of other hopes, the contents of This will surprise you. O my dearest friend, the man has at last proved himself to be a villain!

It was with the utmost difficulty last night, that I preserved myself from the vilest dishonour. He extorted from me a promise of forgiveness; and that I would see him next day, as if nothing had happened: But if it were possible to escape from a wretch, who, as I have too much reason to believe, formed a plot to fire the house, to frighten me, almost naked, into his arms, how could I see him next day?

I have escaped, Heaven be praised, I have! And have now no other concern, than that I fly from the only hope that could have made such an husband tolerable to me; The reconciliation with my friends, so agreeably undertaken by my uncle.

All my present hope is, To find some reputable family, or person of my own Sex, who is obliged to go beyond sea, or who lives abroad; I care not whither; but if I might choose, in some one of our American colonies—Never to be heard of more by my relations, whom I have so grievously offended.

Impute not this scheme, my beloved friend, either to dejection on one hand, or to that romantic turn on the other, which we have supposed generally to obtain with our Sex, from Fifteen to Twenty-two: For, be pleased to consider my unhappy situation, in the light in which it really must appear to every considerate person, who knows it. In the first place, the man, who has had the assurance to think me, and to endeavour to make me, his *property*, will hunt me from place to place, and search after me as an estray: And he knows he may do so with impunity; for whom have I to protect me from him?

This wicked man knows I have no friend in the world but you: Your neighbourhood therefore would be the first he would seek for me in, were you to think it possible for me to be concealed in it: And in this case You might be subjected to inconveniences greater even than those which you have already sustained on my account.

From my cousin Morden, were he to come, I could not hope protection; since, by his letter to me, it is evident, that my brother has engaged him in his party: Nor would I, by any means, subject so worthy a man to danger; as might be the case, from the violence of this ungovernable spirit.

These things considered, what better method can I take, than to go abroad to some one of the English Colonies; where nobody but yourself shall know any-thing of me; nor You, let me tell you, presently, nor till I am fixed, and, if it please God, in a course of living tolerably to my mind. For it is no small part of my concern, that my indiscretions have laid so heavy a tax upon You, my dear friend, to whom, once, I hoped to give more pleasure than pain.

I am at present at one Mrs. Moore's at Hampstead. My heart misgave me at coming to this village, because I had been here with him more than once: But the coach hither was so ready a conveniency, that I knew not what to do better.

O why was the great fiend of all unchained, and permitted to assume so specious a form, and yet allowed to conceal his feet and his talons, till with the one he was ready to trample upon my honour, and to strike the other into my heart!—And what had I done, that he should be let loose particularly upon me!

Forgive me this murmuring question, the effect of my impatience, my *guilty* impatience, I doubt: For, as I have escaped with my honour, and nothing but my worldly prospects, and my pride, my ambition, and my vanity, have suffered in this wreck of my hopefuller fortunes, may I not still be more happy than I deserve to be? And is it not in my own power still, by the divine favour, to secure the great stake of all? And who knows, but that this very path into which my inconsideration has thrown me, strew'd as it is with briars and thorns, which tear in pieces my gaudier trappings, may not be the right path to lead me into the great road to my future happiness; which might have been endangered by evil communication?

When I began, I thought to write but a few lines. But, be my subject what it will, I know not how to conclude, when I write to you. It was *always* so: It is not therefore owing peculiarly to that most interesting and unhappy situation, which you will allow, however, to engross, at present, the whole mind of,

> Your unhappy, but ever-affectionate,
>
> Clarissa Harlowe

Mr. Lovelace
To John Belford, Esq;

Friday Morning, past Two o' Clock.

I O *Triumphe!* Io Clarissa, sing!—Once more, what a happy man thy friend!—A silly dear novice, to be heard to tell the coachman whither to carry her!—And to go to *Hamstead*, of all the villages about London!—The place where we had been together more than once!

Methinks I am sorry she managed no better!—I shall find the recovery of her too easy a task, I fear! Had she but known, how much difficulty enhances the value of any thing with me, and had she had the least notion of obliging me, she would never have stopt short at *Hamstead*, surely.

Well, but after all this exultation, thou wilt ask, If I have already got back my charmer?—I have not.—But knowing where she is, is almost the same thing as having her in my power: And it delights me to think, how she will start and tremble, when I first pop upon her! How she will look with conscious guilt, that will more than wipe off my guilt of Wednesday night, when she sees her injured lover, and acknowleged husband, from whom, the greatest of felonies, she would have stolen herself.

But thou wilt be impatient to know how this came about. Read the inclosed here, and remember the instructions, which, from time to time, I have given my fellow, in apprehension of such an elopement; and that will tell thee all, and what I may reasonably expect from the rascal's diligence and management, if he wishes ever to see my face again.

I received it about half an hour ago, just as I was going to lie down in my cloaths: And it has made me so much alive, that, midnight as it is, I have sent for a Blunt's chariot, to attend me here by day-peep, with *my usual coachman*, if possible; and knowing not else what to do with myself, I sat down, and, in the joy of my heart, have not only wrote thus far, but have concluded upon the measures I shall take when admitted to her presence: For well am I aware of the difficulties I shall have to contend with from her perverseness.

Honnored Sur,

T HIS is to sertifie your honner, as how I am heer at Hamestet, wher I have found out my Lady to be in logins at one Mrs. Moore's, near upon Hamestet hethe. And I have so ordered matters, that her Ladiship cannot stur but I must have notice of her goins and comins. As I knowed I dursted not look into your Honner's fase, if I had not found out my Lady, thoff she was gone off the prems's in a quarter off an hour, as a man may say; so I knowed you would be glad at heart to know I had found her out: And so I send thiss Petur Partrick, who is to have 5 shillins, it being now nere 12 of the clock at nite; for he would not stur without a hartie drinck too besides: And I was willing all shulde be snug likeways at the logins befoer I sent.

My Lady knows nothing of my being hereaway. But I thoute it best not to leve the plase, because she has tacken the logins but for a fue nites.

If your Honnor come to the Upper Flax, I will be in site all the day about the Tapp-house or the Hethe; I have borroued an othir cote, instead off your Honnor's liferie, and a blacke wigge; so cannot be knoen by my Lady, iff as howe she shuld see me.

The tow inner Letters I had from my Lady, before she went off the prems's. One was to be left at Mr. Wilson's for Miss Howe. The next was to be for your Honner. But I knew you was not at the plase directed; and being afear'd of what fell out, so I kept them for your Honner, and so could not give um to you, until I seed you. Miss How's I only made belief to her Ladiship as I carred it, and sed as how there was nothing left for hur, as shee wished to knoe: So here they be bothe.

I am, may it plese your Honner,

Your honner's most dutiful, and, wonce more, happy servant,

Wm. Summers

The two *inner* Letters, as Will. calls them, 'tis plain, were written for no other purpose, but to send him out of the way with them, and one of them to amuse me. That directed to Miss Howe is only this:

Thursday, June 8.

I WRITE this, my dear Miss Howe, only for a feint, and to see if it will go current. I shall write at large very soon, if not miserably prevented!!!

Cl. H.

Now, Jack, will not her feints justify *mine?* Does she not invade my province, thinkest thou? And is it not now fairly come to *Who shall most deceive and cheat the other?* So, I thank my stars, we are upon a par, at last, as to this point—Which is a great ease to my conscience, thou must believe. And if what Hudibras tells us is true, the dear fugitive has also abundance of pleasure to come.

> Doubtless the pleasure is as great
> In being cheated, as to cheat.
> As lookers-on find most delight,
> Who least perceive the juggler's sleight;
> And still the less they understand,
> The more admire the sleight of hand.

This is my dear juggler's letter to me; the other *inner* letter sent by Will.

Thursday, June 8.

Mr. Lovelace,

D O not give me cause to dread your return. If you would not that I should hate you for ever, send me half a line by the bearer, to assure me that you will not attempt to see me for a week to come. I cannot look you in the face without equal confusion and indignation. The obliging me in This is but a poor atonement for your last night's vile behaviour.

You may pass this time in a journey to your uncle's; and I cannot doubt, if the Ladies of your family are as favourable to me, as you have assured me they are, but that you will have interest enough to prevail with one of them, to oblige me with her company. After your baseness of last night, you will not wonder, that I insist upon this proof of your future honour.

If Captain Tomlinson comes mean time, I can hear what he has to say, and send you an account of it.

But in less than a week, if you see me, it must be owing to a fresh act of violence, of which you know not the consequence.

Send me the requested line, if ever you expect to have the forgiveness confirmed, the promise of which you extorted from

The unhappy

Cl. H.

Now, Belford, what canst thou say in behalf of this sweet rogue of a Lady? What *canst* thou say for her? 'Tis apparent, that she was fully determined upon an elopement, when she wrote it: And thus would she make me of party against myself, by drawing me in to give her a week's time to complete it in: And, more wicked still, send me upon a fool's errand to bring up one of my cousins:—When we came, to have the satisfaction of finding her gone off, and me exposed for ever!—What punishment can be bad enough for such a little villain of a Lady!

The chariot is not come; and if it were, it is yet too soon for every-thing but my impatience. And as I have already taken all my measures, and can think of nothing but my triumph, I will resume her violent letter, in order to strengthen my resolutions against her. I was *before* in too gloomy a way to proceed with it: But now the subject is all alive to me, and my gayer fancy, like the sun-beams, will irradiate it, and turn the solemn deep green into a brighter verdure.

Suffice it at present to tell thee, in the first place, that *she is determined never to be my wife.*—To be sure, there ought to be no compulsion in so material a case. Compulsion was her parents fault, which I have censured so severely, that I shall hardly be guilty of the same. And I am glad I know her mind as to this essential point.

I have *ruined* her, she says!—Now that's a fib, take it in her own way:—If I had, she would not perhaps have run away from me.

She is *thrown upon the wide world:* Now I own, that Hamstead-Heath affords very pretty, and very *extensive* prospects; but 'tis not the *wide world* neither: And suppose *that* to be her grievance, I hope soon to restore her to a *narrower*.

I am the *enemy of her soul, as well as of her honour!*—Confoundedly severe! Nevertheless, another fib!—For I love her soul very well; but think no more of it in this case than of my own.

She is to be *thrown upon strangers!*—And is not that her own fault?—Much against my will, I am sure!

She is cast from a state of *independency* into one *of obliga-*

tion. She never was in a state of *independency;* nor is it fit a woman should, of any age, or in any state of life. And as to the state of obligation, there is no such thing as living without being beholden to some-body. Mutual obligation is the very essence and soul of the social and commercial life:—Why should *she* be exempt from it?—I am sure the person she raves at, desires not such an exemption;—has been long *dependent* upon her; and would rejoice to owe *further obligations* to her than he can boast of hitherto.

She talks of her *father's curse*—But have I not repaid him for it an hundred-fold in the same coin? But why must the faults of other people be laid at my door? Have I not enow of my own?

But the grey-eyed dawn begins to peep—Let me sum up all.

In short, then, the dear creature's letter is a collection of invectives not very new to *me;* though the occasion for them, no doubt, is new to *her.* A little sprinkling of the romantic and contradictory runs thro' it. She loves, and she hates: She encourages me to pursue her, by telling me I safely may; and yet she begs I will not: She apprehends poverty and want, yet resolves to give away her estate: To gratify whom?—Why, in short, those who have been the cause of her misfortunes. And finally, tho' she resolves never to be mine, yet she has some regrets at leaving me, because of the opening prospects of a reconciliation with her friends.

But never did morning dawn so tardily as this!—The chariot not yet come neither.

And now (all around me so still, and so silent) the rattling of the chariot-wheels at a street's distance do I hear!—And to this angel of a Lady I fly!

Reward, O God of Love (the cause is thy own); reward thou, as it deserves, my suffering perseverance!—Succeed my endeavours to bring back to thy obedience, this charming fugitive!—Make her acknowlege her rashness; repent her insults; implore my forgiveness; beg to be reinstated in my favour, and that I will bury in oblivion the remembrance of her heinous offence against thee, and against me, thy faithful votary.

The chariot at the door!—I come! I come—
I attend you, good Captain—
Indeed, Sir—
Pray, Sir—Civility is not ceremony.

And now, dressed like a Bridegroom, my heart elated
beyond that of the most desiring one (attended by a foot-man
whom my Beloved never saw), I am already at Hamstead!

Mr. Lovelace
To John Belford, Esq;

Upper-Flask, Hamstead, (June 9) Friday morn. 7 o'clock

I AM now here, and here have been this hour and half. What
an industrious spirit have I! Nobody can say, that I eat the
bread of idleness. I take true pains for all the pleasure I enjoy.
I cannot but to admire myself strangely; for, certainly, with
this active soul, I should have made a very great figure in whatever station I had filled. But had I been a prince!—To be sure
I should have made a most *noble* prince! I should have led up a
military dance equal to that of the great Macedonian. I should
have added kingdom to kingdom, and robbed all my neighbour-
sovereigns, in order to have obtained the name of *Robert the
Great*. And I would have gone to war with the Great Turk, and
the Persian, and the Mogholl, for their Seraglios; for not one of
those Eastern Monarchs should have had a pretty woman to
bless himself with, till I had done with her.

All Will's account, from the Lady's flight to his finding her
again, all the accounts of the people of the house, the coachman's
information to Will, and so forth, collected together, stand thus.

"The Hamstead coach, when the lady came to it, had but
two passengers in it. But she made the fellow go off directly,
paying for the vacant places.

The two passengers directing the coachman to set them
down at the Upper-Flask, she bid him set her down there also.

They took leave of her (very respectfully no doubt), and she went into the house, and asked, If she could not have a dish of tea, and a room to herself for half an hour?

They shewed her up to the very room where I now am. She sat at the very table I now write upon; and, I believe, the chair I sit in was hers." O Belford, if thou knowest what Love is, thou wilt be able to account for these *minutiae*.

"She seemed spiritless and fatigued. The gentlewoman herself chose to attend so genteel and lovely a guest. She asked her, If she would have bread and butter to her tea? No. She could not eat. They had very good biscuits. As she pleased. The gentlewoman stept out for some; and returning on a sudden, she observed the sweet fugitive endeavouring to restrain a violent burst of grief, which she had given way to, in that little interval.

However, when the tea came, she made her sit down with her, and asked her abundance of questions about the villages and roads in that neighbourhood.

The gentlewoman took notice to her, *that she seemed to be troubled in mind*.

Tender Spirits, she replied, could not part with *dear* friends without concern."

She meant *me*, no doubt.

"She made no inquiry about a lodging, tho' by the sequel, thou'lt observe, that she seemed to intend to go no farther that night than Hamstead. But after she had drank two dishes, and put a Biscake in her pocket—[Sweet soul, to serve for her supper perhaps—] she laid down half-a-crown; and refusing change, sighing, took leave, saying, she would proceed towards Hendon; the distance to which had been one of her questions.

They offered to send to know, if a Hamstead coach were not to go to Hendon that evening.

No matter, she said—Perhaps she might meet the chariot." Another of her *feints*, I suppose; for how, or with whom, could any thing of this sort have been concerted since yesterday morning?

"She had, as the people took notice to one another, something so uncommonly noble in her air, and in her person and behaviour, that they were sure she was of quality. And having

no servant with her of either sex, her eyes [her fine eyes, the
gentlewoman called them, stranger as she was, and a woman!]
being swelled and red, they were sure there was an elopement
in the case, either from parents or guardians; for they supposed
her too young and too maidenly to be a married lady: And were
she married, no husband would let such a fine young creature
be unattended and alone; nor give her cause for so much grief,
as seemed to be settled in her countenance. Then, at times, she
seemed to be so bewildered, they said, that they were afraid she
had it in her head to make away with herself.

All these things put together, excited their curiosity; and
they engaged a *peery* servant, as they called a footman who was
drinking with Kit the hostler at the tap-house, to watch all her
motions. This fellow reported the following particulars, as they
were re-reported to me.

She indeed went towards Hendon, passing by the sign of
the Castle on the heath; then, stopping, looked about her, and
down into the valley before her. Then, turning her face towards
London, she seemed, by the motion of her handkerchief to her
eyes, to weep; repenting (who knows?) the rash step she had
taken, and wishing herself back again—"

"She then saw a coach and four driving towards her empty.
She crossed the path she was in, as if to meet it; and seemed to
intend to speak to the coachman, had he stopt or spoke first.
He, as earnestly, looked at *her*. Every one did so, who passed
her (so the man who dogged her was the less suspected)"—
Happy rogue of a coachman, hadst thou known whose notice
thou didst engage, and whom thou mightest have obliged!—
It was the divine Clarissa Harlowe at whom thou gazedst!—My
own Clarissa Harlowe!—But it was well for me that thou wert
as undistinguishing as the beasts thou drovest; otherwise, what
a wild-goose chace had I been led?

"By this time she had reached the houses. She looked up at
every one, as she passed; now-and-then breathing upon her
bared hand, and applying it to her swelled eyes, to abate the
redness, and dry the tears. At last, seeing a bill up for letting
lodgings, she walked backwards and forwards half a dozen
times, as if unable to determine what to do. And then went

farther into the town; and there the fellow being spoken to by
one of his familiars, lost her for a few minutes: But he soon saw
her come out of a linen-drapery shop, attended with a servant-
maid, having, as he believed, bought some little matters, and,
as it proved, got that maid-servant to go with her to the house
she is now at.

The fellow, after waiting about an hour, and not seeing her
come out, returned, concluding that she had taken lodgings
there."

And here, supposing my narrative of the dramatic kind,
ends Act the First. And now begins,

Act II.

Scene, Hamstead Heath continued.

Enter my rascal.

WILL. having got at all these particulars, by exchanging
others as frankly against them, which I had formerly
prepared him with, both verbally and in writing; I found the
people already of my party, and full of good wishes for my
success, repeating to me all they told him.

But he had first acquainted me with the accounts he had
given them of his lady and me. It is necessary that I give thee
the particulars of his tale—And I have a little time upon my
hands; for the maid of the house, who had been out of an errand,
tells us, that she saw Mrs. Moore (with whom must be my first
business) go into the house of a young gentleman, within a few
doors of her, who has a maiden sister, Miss Rawlins by name,
so notify'd for prudence, that none of her acquaintance undertake anything of consequence, without consulting her.

Mean while my honest coachman is walking about Miss
Rawlins's door, in order to bring me notice of Mrs. Moore's
return to her own house. I hope her gossips-tale will be as soon
told as mine. Which take as follows.

Will. told them, before I came, "That his lady was but lately married to one of the finest gentlemen in the world. But that, he being very gay and lively, she was *mortal* jealous of him; and in a fit of that sort, had eloped from him. For altho' she loved him dearly, and he doated upon her (as well he might, since, as they had seen, she was the finest creature *that ever the sun shone upon*), yet she was apt to be very wilful and sullen, if he might take the liberty to say so—but truth was truth;—and if she could not have her own way in every thing, would be for leaving him. That she had three or four times played his master such tricks; but with all the virtue and innocence in the world; running away to an intimate friend of hers, who, tho' a young lady of honour, was but too indulgent to her in this her *only* failing; for which reason his master had brought her to London-lodgings; their usual residence being in the country."

When I came, my person and dress having answered Will's description, the people were ready to worship me. I now-and-then sighed, now-and-then put on a lighter air; which, however, I designed should shew more of vexation ill-disguised, than of real chearfulness: And they told Will, It was a thousand pities so fine a lady should have such *skittish tricks*; adding, that she might expose herself to great dangers by them; for that there were Rakes every-where [*Lovelace's in every corner, Jack!*], and many about that town, who would leave nothing un-attempted to get into her company: And altho' they might not prevail upon her, yet might they nevertheless hurt her reputa-tion; and, in time, estrange the affections of so fine a gentleman from her.

Good sensible people, these!—Hay, Jack!

Here, landlord; one word with you.—My servant, I find, has acquainted you with the reason of my coming this way. An unhappy affair, landlord! A very unhappy affair! But never was there a more virtuous woman.

So, Sir, she seems to be. A thousand pities her ladyship has such ways—And to so good-humoured a gentleman as you seem to be, Sir.

Mother-spoilt, landlord!—Mother-spoilt! that's the thing!—But, sighing, I must make the best of it. What I want *you* to do for me, is to lend me a great coat. I care not what it is. If my spouse should see me at a distance, she would make it very difficult for me to get at her speech. A great coat with a cape, if you have one. I must come upon her before she is aware.

I am afraid, Sir, I have none fit for such a gentleman as you.

O, any thing will do!—The worse the better.

Exit Landlord. Re-enter with two great coats.

Ay, landlord, This will be best; for I can button the cape over the lower part of my face. Don't I look devilishly down and concerned, landlord?

I never saw a gentleman with a better-natured look. 'Tis pity you should have such tryals, Sir.

I must be very unhappy, no doubt of it, landlord. And yet I am a little pleased, you must needs think, that I have found her out before any great inconvenience has arisen to her. However, if I cannot break her of these freaks, she'll break my heart; for I do love her with all her failings.

Pray, your honour, said she, if I may be so bold, was Madam ever a mamma?

No!—and I sighed—We have been but a little while married; and, as I may say to *you*, it is her own fault that she is not in that way [Not a word of a lye in this, Jack]. But to tell you truth, madam, she may be compared to the dog in the manger—

I understand you, Sir (simpering)—She is but young, Sir. I have heard of one or two such skittish young ladies in my time, Sir.—But when madam is in that way, I dare say, as she loves you (and it would be strange if she did not!), all this will be over, and she may make the best of wives.

That's all my hope.

All this time, I was adjusting my horseman's coat, and Will was putting in the ties of my wig, and buttoning the cape over my chin.

I asked the gentlewoman for a little powder. She brought me a powder-box, and I lightly shook the puff over my hat, and flapt one side of it, tho' the lace looked a little too gay for my covering; and slouching it over my eyes, Shall I be known, think you, Madam?

Your Honour is so expert, Sir!—I wish, if I may be so bold, your lady has not some *cause* to be jealous. But it will be impossible, if you keep your laced cloaths covered, that any-body should know you in that dress to be the same gentleman—

And now I am going to try, if I can't agree with goody Moore for lodgings and other conveniencies for my sick wife.

Wife, Lovelace! methinks thou interrogatest.

Yes, *wife*; for who knows what cautions the dear fugitive may have given in apprehension of me?

But has goody Moore any other lodgings to lett?

Yes, yes; I have taken care of that; and find, that she has just such conveniencies as I want. And I know that my wife will like them. For, altho' married, I can do every thing I please; and that's a bold word, you know. But had she only a garret to let, I would have liked it; and been a poor author afraid of arrests, and made that my place of refuge; yet would have made shift to pay before-hand for what I had. I can suit myself to any condition, that's my comfort.

Mr. Lovelace
To John Belford, Esq;

Hamstead, Friday Night, June 9.

NOW, Belford, for the narrative of narratives. I will continue it, as I have opportunity; and that so dextrously, that if I break off twenty times, thou shalt not discern where I piece my thread.

Although grievously afflicted with the gout, I alighted out of my chariot (leaning very hard on my cane with one hand, and on my new servant's shoulder with the other) the same instant almost that he had knocked at the door, that I might be sure of admission into the house.

I took care to button my great coat about me, and to cover with it even the pommel of my sword; it being a little too gay for my years. I knew not what occasion I might have for my sword. I stooped forward; blinked with my eyes to conceal their lustre [No vanity in saying that, Jack!]; my chin wrapt up for the tooth-ach; my slouched, laced hat, and so much of my wig as was visible, giving me, all together, the appearance of an antiquated beau.

The maid came to the door. I asked for her mistress. She shewed me into one of the parlours; and I sat down, with a gouty Oh!—

Enter goody Moore.

Your servant, Madam—But you must excuse me; I can not well stand.—I find by the bill at the door, that you have lodgings to lett [Mumbling my words as if, like my man Will, I had lost some of my fore-teeth]: Be pleased to inform me what they are; for I like your situation:—And I will tell you my family—I have a wife, a good old woman—Older than myself, by the way, a pretty deal. She is in a bad state of health, and is advised into the Hamstead air. She will have two maid-servants and a foot-man. The coach or chariot (I shall not have them up both to-gether), we can put up any-where, and the coachman will be with his horses.

When, Sir, shall you want to come in?

I will take them from this very day; and, if convenient, will bring my wife in the afternoon.

Perhaps, Sir, you would board, as well as lodge?

That as you please. It will save me the trouble of bringing my cook, if we do. And I suppose you have servants who know how to dress a couple of dishes. My wife must eat plain food, and I don't love kickshaws.

You shall see what accommodations I have, if you please, Sir. But I doubt, you are too lame to walk up stairs.

I can make shift to hobble up, now I have rested a little. I'll just look upon the apartment my wife is to have. Any thing may do for the servants.

She led the way; and I, leaning upon the banisters, made shift to get up with less fatigue than I expected from ancles so

weak. But oh! Jack, What was Sixtus the Vth's artful depression
of his natural powers to mine, when, as the half-dead Montalto,
he gaped for the pretendedly unsought Pontificate, and, the
moment he was chosen, leapt upon the prancing beast, which it
was thought, by the amazed conclave, he was not able to mount
without help of chairs and men? Never was there a more joyous
heart and lighter heels than mine, joined together, yet both
denied their functions; the one fluttering in secret, ready to burst
its bars for relief-ful expression, the others obliged to an hobbling
motion; when, unrestrained, they would, in their master's imagination, have mounted him to the lunar world without the help of
a ladder.

I liked the lodgings well; and the more, as she said the third
room was still handsomer. I must sit down, Madam (and chose
the darkest part of the room): Won't you take a seat yourself?
No price shall part us. But I will leave the terms to you and my
wife, if you please: And also whether for board or not. Only
please to take This for earnest, putting a guinea into her hand.—
And one thing I will say; My poor wife loves money; but is not
an ill-natured woman. She was a great fortune to me: But if she
make too close a bargain with you, tell *me*; and, unknown to *her*,
I will make it up.

She said, I was a very considerate gentleman; and, upon the
condition I had mentioned, she was content to leave the terms
to my lady.

But, Madam, cannot a-body just peep into the other apartment, that I may be more particular to my wife in the furniture
of it?

The lady desires to be private, Sir—But—And was going
to ask her leave.

I caught hold of her hand—However, stay, stay, Madam:
It mayn't be proper, if the lady loves to be private. Don't let
me intrude upon the lady—

No intrusion, Sir, I dare say: The lady is good-humoured.
She will be so kind as to step down into the parlour, I dare say.
As she stays so little a while, I am sure she will not wish to stand
in my way.

No, Madam, that's true, if she be good-humoured, as you say—Has she been with you long, Madam?

But yesterday, Sir—

I believe I just now saw the glimpse of her. She seems to be an elderly lady.

No, Sir; you're mistaken. She's a young lady; and one of the handsomest I ever saw.

Cot so, I beg her pardon! Not but that I should have liked her the better, were she to stay longer, if she had been elderly. I have a strange taste, Madam, you'll say; but I really, for my wife's sake, love every elderly woman: Indeed I ever thought age was to be reverenced, which made me (taking the fortune into the scale too, *that* I own) make my addresses to my present dear.

Very good of you, Sir, to respect age: We all hope to live to be old.

Right, Madam. But you say the lady is beautiful. Now you must know, that tho' I chuse to converse with the elderly, yet I love to see a beautiful young woman, just as I love to see fine flowers in a garden. There's no casting an eye upon her, is there? without her notice? For in this dress, and thus muffled up about my jaws, I should not care to be seen, any more than she, let her love privacy as much as she will.

I will go ask, if I may shew a gentleman the apartment, Sir; and, as you are a married gentleman, and not *over*-young, she'll perhaps make the less scruple.

I appeared, upon the whole, so indifferent about seeing the room, or the lady, that the good woman was the more eager I should see both. And the rather, as I, to stimulate her, declared, that there was more required in my eye to merit the character of a handsome woman, than most people thought necessary; and that I had never seen six truly lovely ladies in my life.

To be brief, she went in; and after a little while came out again. The lady, Sir, is retired to her closet. So you may go in and look at the room.

I hobbled in, and stumped about, and liked it very much; and was sure my wife would. I begged excuse for sitting down,

and asked, Who was the minister of the place? If he were a good
preacher? Who preached at the chapel? And if *he* were a good
preacher, and good *liver* too, Madam—I must inquire after *That*:
For I love, I must needs say, that the Clergy should practise what
they preach.

Very right, Sir; but that is not so often the case, as were to
be wished.

More's the pity, Madam. But I have a great veneration for
the Clergy in general. It is more a satire upon Human nature,
than upon the Cloth, if we suppose those who have the *best*
opportunities to be good, less perfect than other people.—But
I keep the lady in her closet. My gout makes me rude.

Then stumping towards the closet, over the door of which
hung a picture—What picture is that—Oh! I see: A St. Caecilia!

A common print, Sir!—

Pretty well, pretty well! It is after an Italian master.—I
would not for the world turn the lady out of her apartment.
We can make shift with the other two, repeated I, louder still:
But yet mumblingly hoarse: for I had as great regard to unifor-
mity in accent, as to my words.

O Belford! to be so near my angel, think what a painful
constraint I was under—

I was resolved to fetch her out, if possible: And pretending
to be going—You can't agree as to any *time*, Mrs. Moore, when
we can have this third room, can you?—Not that (whispered I,
loud enough to be heard in the next room; Not that) I would
incommode the lady: But I would tell my wife *when* abouts—
And women, you know, Mrs. Moore, love to have every thing
before them of this nature.

Mrs. Moore, says my charmer (and never did her voice
sound so harmonious to me: Oh how my heart bounded again!
It even talked to me, in a manner; for I thought I *heard*, as well
as *felt*, its unruly flutters; and every vein about me seemed a
pulse: Mrs. Moore], you may acquaint the gentleman, that I
shall stay here only for two or three days, at most, till I receive
an answer to a letter I have written into the country; and rather
than be your hindrance, I will take up with any apartment a
pair of stairs higher.

Not for the world!—Not for the world, young lady, cried
I!—My wife, well as I love her, should lie in a garret, rather
than put such a considerate lady as you seem to be, to the least
inconvenien-cy.

She opened not the door yet; and I said, But since you have
so much goodness, Madam, if I could but just look into the
closet as I stand, I could tell my wife whether it is large enough
to hold a cabinet she much values, and will have with her where-
ever she goes.

Then my charmer opened the door, and blazed upon me, as it
were, in a flood of light, like what one might imagine would
strike a man, who, born blind, had by some propitious power
been blessed with his sight, all at once, in a meridian sun.

Upon my soul, I never was so strangely affected before.
I had much ado to forbear discovering myself that instant: But,
hesitatingly, and in great disorder, I said, looking into the closet,
and around it, There is room, I see, for my wife's cabinet; and it
has many jewels in it of high price; but, upon my soul (for I could
not forbear swearing, like a puppy:—Habit is a cursed thing,
Jack—) Nothing so valuable as the lady I see, can be brought
into it.

She started, and looked at me with terror. The truth of the
compliment, as far as I know, had taken dissimulation from my
accent.

I saw it was impossible to conceal myself longer from her,
any more than (from the violent impulses of my passion) to
forbear manifesting myself. I unbuttoned therefore my cape,
I pulled off my flapt, slouched hat; I threw open my great coat,
and, like the devil in Milton (an odd comparison tho'!),

> I started up in my own form divine,
> Touch'd by the beam of her celestial eye,
> More potent than Ithuriel's spear!—

Now, Belford, for a similitude—Now for a likeness to
illustrate the surprising scene, and the effect it had upon my
charmer, and the gentlewoman!—But nothing *was* like it, or
equal to it. The plain fact can only describe it and set it off. Thus
take it.

She no sooner saw who it was, than she gave three violent screams; and, before I could catch her in my arms (as I was
about to do the moment I discovered myself), down she sunk at
my feet, in a fit; which made me curse my indiscretion for so
suddenly, and with so much emotion, revealing myself.

The gentlewoman, seeing so strange an alteration in my
person, and features, and voice, and dress, cried out, Murder,
help! Murder, help! by turns, for half a dozen times running.
This alarmed the house, and up ran two servant maids, and *my*
servant after them. I cried out for water and hartshorn, and
every one flew a different way, one of the maids as fast down as
she came up; while the gentlewoman ran out of one room into
another, and by turns up and down the apartment we were in,
without meaning or end, wringing her foolish hands, and not
knowing what she did.

Up then came running a gentleman and his sister, fetched,
and brought in by the maid who had run down; and who having
let in a cursed crabbed old wretch, hobbling with his gout, and
mumbling with his hoarse broken-toothed voice, was metamor-
phosed all at once into a lively gay young fellow, with a clear
accent, and all his teeth; and she would have it, that I was neither
more nor less than the devil, and could not keep her eye from my
foot; expecting, no doubt, every minute to see it discover itself
to be cloven.

For my part, I was so intent upon restoring my angel, that I
regarded nobody else. And at last, she slowly recovering motion, with bitter sighs and sobs (only the whites of her eyes however appearing for some moments), I called upon her in the
tenderest accent, as I kneeled by her, my arm supporting her
head; My angel! My charmer! My Clarissa! look upon me, my
dearest life!—I am not angry with you!—I will forgive you, my
best beloved!—

The gentleman and his sister knew not what to make of all
this: And the less, when my fair-one, recovering her sight,
snatched another look at me; and then again groaned, and
fainted away.

I threw up the closet-sash for air, and then left her to the
care of the young gentlewoman, the same notable Miss Rawlins,

whom I heard of at the Flask; and to that of Mrs. Moore; who by this time had recovered herself; and then retiring to one corner of the room, I made my servant pull off my gouty stockens, brush my hat, and loop it up into the usual smart cock.

I then stept to the closet to Mr. Rawlins, whom, in the general confusion, I had not much minded before.—Sir, said I, you have an uncommon scene before you. The lady is my wife, and no gentleman's presence is necessary here but my own.

I beg pardon, Sir; *If* the lady is your wife, I have no business here. *But*, Sir, by her concern at seeing you—

Pray, Sir, none of your *if's*, and *but's*, I beseech you: Nor *your* concern about the *lady's* concern. You are a very unqualified judge in this cause; and I beg of you, Sir, to oblige me with your absence. The ladies only are proper to be present on this occasion, added I; and I think myself obliged to them for their care and kind assistance.

'Tis well he made not another word: For I found my choler begin to rise. I could not bear, that the finest neck, and arms, and foot, in the world, should be exposed to the eyes of any man living but mine.

I withdrew once more from the closet, finding her beginning to recover, lest the sight of me too soon, should throw her back again.

The first words she said, looking round her with great emotion, were, O hide me! Hide me! Is he gone!—O hide me! Is he gone!

Sir, said Miss Rawlins, coming to me with an air somewhat peremptory and assured, This is some surprising case. The lady cannot bear the sight of you. What you have done, is best known to yourself. But another such fit will probably be her last. It would be but kind, therefore, for you to retire.

It behoved me to have so notable a person of my party; and the rather, as I had disobliged her impertinent brother.

The dear creature, said I, may *well* be concerned to see me. If *you*, Madam, had a husband who loved you, as I love her, you would not, I am confident, fly from him, and expose yourself to hazards, as she does whenever she has not all her way— And yet with a mind not capable of intentional evil—But,

mother-spoilt! This is her fault, and All her fault: And the more
inexcuseable it is, as I am the man of her choice, and have reason
to think she loves me above all the men in the world.

You *speak* like a gentleman; you *look* like a gentleman,
said Miss Rawlins—But, Sir, this is a strange case; the lady
seems to dread the sight of you.

No wonder, Madam; taking her a little on one side, nearer
to Mrs. Moore. I have three times already forgiven the dear
creature.—But this *jealousy*—There is a spice of *that* in it—and
of *phrensy* too (whispered I, that it might have the face of a
secret, and, of consequence, the more engage their attention)—
But our story is too long—

I then made a motion to go to the lady. But they desired,
that I would walk into the next room; and they would endeavour
to prevail upon her to lie down.

I begged that they would not suffer her to talk; for that she
was accustomed to fits, and would, when in this way, talk of
anything that came uppermost: and the more she was suffered
to run on, the worse she was; and if not kept quiet, would fall
into ravings; which might possibly hold her a week.

They promised to keep her quiet; and I withdrew into the
next room; ordering every one down but Mrs. Moore and Miss
Rawlins.

She was full of exclamations. Unhappy creature! miserable!
ruined! and undone! she called herself; wrung her hands, and
begged they would assist her to escape from the terrible evils
she should otherwise be made to suffer.

They preached patience and quietness to her; and would
have had her to lie down; but she refused; sinking, however,
into an easy chair; for she trembled so, she could not stand.

By this time, I hoped, that she was enough recovered to
bear a presence, that it behoved me to make her bear; and fearing she would throw out something in her exclamations, that
would still more disconcert me, I went into the room again.

O there he is! said she, and threw her apron over her face—
I cannot see him!—I cannot look upon him!—Begone! begone!
touch me not!—

For I took her struggling hand, beseeching her to be pacified; and assuring her, that I would make all up with her, upon her own terms and wishes.

Base man! said the violent lady, I have no wishes, but never to behold you more! Why must I be thus pursued and haunted? Have you not made me miserable enough already?

She started up with a trembling impatience, her apron falling from her indignant face—Now, said she, that thou darest to call the occasion *slight* and *accidental*, and that I am happily out of thy vile hands, and out of a house I have reason to believe *as* vile, traitor and wretch that thou art, I will venture to cast an eye upon thee—And O that it were in my power, in mercy to my sex, to look thee first into shame and remorse, and then into death!

This violent tragedy-speech, and the high manner in which she uttered it, had its desired effect. I looked upon the women, and upon her, by turns, with a pitying eye; and they shook their wise heads, and besought *me* to retire, and *her* to lie down to compose herself.

This hurricane, like other hurricanes, was presently allayed by a shower. She threw herself once more into her armed chair—And begged pardon of the women for her passionate excess; but not of me: Yet I was in hopes, that when compliments were stirring, I should have come in for a share.

I thought then, that the character of a husband obliged me to be angry.

You may one day, Madam, repent this treatment:—By my soul you may. You know I have not deserved it of you—You *know* I have not.

Do I know you have not?—Wretch! Do I know—

You do, Madam—And never did man of my figure and consideration [I thought it was proper to throw that in] meet with such treatment. [She lifted up her hands: Indignation kept her silent.]—But all is of a piece with the charge you bring against me of *despoiling you of all succour and help*, of making you *poor* and *low*, and with other unprecedented language. I will only say, before these two gentlewomen, that since it *must* be so, and since your former esteem for me is turned into so riveted an aversion, I will soon, *very* soon, make you intirely

easy. I *will* be gone:—I *will* leave you to *your own fate*, as you
call it; and may That be happy!—Only, that I may not appear
to be a spoiler, a robber indeed, let me know whither I send
your apparel, and every thing that belongs to you, and I *will*
sent it.

Send it to this place; and assure me, that you will never
molest me more; never more come near me; and that is all I ask
of you.

I *will* do so, Madam, said I, with a dejected air. But did I
ever think I should be so indifferent to you?—However, you
must permit me to insist on your reading this letter; and on your
seeing Captain Tomlinson, and hearing what he has to say from
your uncle. He will be here by-and-by.

Don't trifle with me, said she, in an imperious tone—Do
as you offer. I will not receive any letter from your hands. If
I see Captain Tomlinson, it shall be on his *own* account; not on
yours. You tell me you will send me my apparel: If you would
have me believe any thing you say, let This be the test of your
sincerity—Leave me *now*, and send my things.

The women stared. They did nothing but stare; and appeared to be more and more at a loss what to make of the matter
between us.

I pretended to be going from her in a pet: But when I had
got to the door, I turned back; and, as if I had recollected myself,
One word more, my dearest creature!—Charming even in your
anger!—O my fond soul! said I, turning half-round, and pulling
out my handkerchief.

I believe, Jack, my eyes did glisten a little. I have no
doubt but they did.—The women pitied me. Honest souls!
—They shewed, that they had each of them a handkerchief
as well as I. So, hast thou not observed (to give a familiar
illustration) every man in a company of a dozen, or more,
obligingly pull out his watch, when some one has asked,
What's o'clock?

One word only, Madam, repeated I, as soon as my voice
had recovered its tone—I have represented to Captain Tomlinson in the most favourable light the cause of our present misunderstanding. You know what your uncle insists upon; and
which you have acquiesced with. The letter in my hand [and

again I offered it to her] will acquaint you with what you have
to apprehend from your brother's active malice.

She was going to speak in a high accent, putting the letter
from her, with an open palm—Nay, hear me out, Madam—The
Captain, you know, has reported our *marriage* to two different
persons. It is come to your brother's ears. My own relations have
also heard of it. Letters were brought me from town this morning, from Lady Betty Lawrance and Miss Montague. Here they
are [I pulled them out of my pocket, and offered them to her,
with That of the Captain; but she held back her still open palm,
that she might not receive them]: Reflect, Madam, I beseech you
reflect, upon the fatal consequences which this your high resentment may be attended with.

Ever since I knew you, said she, I have been in a wilderness
of doubt and error. I bless God that I am out of your hands. I
will transact for myself what relates to myself. I dismiss all your
solicitude for me. Am I not my own mistress!—Am I not—

The women stared [The devil stare ye, thought I! can ye
do nothing but stare?]. It was high time to stop her here.

I raised my voice to drown hers—You used, my dearest
creature, to have a tender and apprehensive heart—You never
had so much reason for such a one as now.

Let me judge for myself, upon what I shall *see*, not upon
what I shall *hear*—Do you think I shall ever—

I dreaded her going on—I *must* be heard, Madam, raising
my voice still higher. You must let me read one paragraph or two
of This Letter to you, if you will not read it yourself—

She was just going to speak—If we are to *separate for ever*,
in a strong and solemn voice, proceeded I, this island shall not
long be troubled with me.—Mean time, only be pleased to give
these letters a perusal, and consider what is to be said to your
uncle's friend; and what he is to say to your uncle.—Any thing
will I come into (renounce me if you will), that shall make for
your peace, and for the reconciliation your heart was so lately
set upon. But I humbly conceive, that it is necessary, that you
should come into better temper with me, were it but to give a
favourable appearance to what *has passed*, and weight to any
future application to your friends, in whatever way you shall
think proper to make it.

I then put the letters into her lap, and retired into the next apartment with a low bow, and a very solemn air.

I was soon followed by the two women. Mrs. Moore withdrew to give the fair Perverse time to read them: Miss Rawlins for the same reason; and because she was sent for home.

Here therefore thou mayest read that Letter of Captain Tomlinson, which I had left with the lady. And a charming letter to my purpose, if thou givest the least attention to its contents, wilt thou find it to be.

To Robert Lovelace, Esq;

Wedn. June 7.

Dear Sir,

ALTHO' I am obliged to be in town to-morrow, or next day at farthest, yet I would not dispense with writing to you, by one of my servants (whom I send up before me upon a particular occasion) in order to advertise you, *that it is probable you will hear from some of your own relations on your [supposed*[*] nuptials*. One of the persons (Mr. Lilburne by name) to whom I hinted my belief of your marriage, happens to be acquainted with Mr. Spurrier, Lady Betty Lawrance's steward; and (not being under any restriction) mentioned it *to* Mr. Spurrier, and he to Lady Betty, as a thing certain.

Her ladyship, it seems, has *business that calls her to town;* [and you will possibly choose to put her right. If you do, it will, I presume, *be in confidence;* that nothing may perspire from your own family to contradict what I have given out.]

[I have ever been of opinion, *That truth ought to be strictly adhered to on all occasions:* And am concerned that I have departed (tho' with so good a view) from my old maxim. But my dear friend Mr. John Harlowe would have it so. Yet I never knew a departure of this kind a *single* departure. But, to make

---

*What is between hooks [ ] thou mayest suppose, Jack, I sunk upon the women, in the account I gave them of the contents of this letter.

the best of it now, allow me, Sir, once more to beg the lady, as soon as possible, to authenticate the report given out.] When you both join in the acknowlegement, it will be impertinent in any one to be inquisitive as to the *day or week*.

And yet it is very probable, that minute inquiries will be made; and this is what renders precaution necessary. For Mr. James Harlowe will not believe that you are married; and is sure, he says, that you both lived together when Mr. Hickman's application was made to Mr. John Harlowe: And if you lived together *any* time unmarried, he infers from *your* character, Mr. Lovelace, that it is not probable, that you would ever marry. And he leaves it to his two uncles to decide, if you even *should be* married, whether there be not room to believe, that his sister was first dishonoured; and if so, to judge of the title she will have to their favour, or to the forgiveness of any of her family. I believe, Sir, this part of my letter had best be kept from the lady.

What makes young Mr. Harlowe the more earnest to find this out (and find it out he is resolved, and to come at his sister's speech too; and for that purpose sets out to-morrow, as I am well-informed, with a large attendance, armed, and Mr. Solmes is to be of the party) is this: Mr. John Harlowe has told the whole family, that he will alter and new-settle his will. Mr. Antony Harlowe is resolved to do the same by his; for, it seems, he has now given over all thoughts of changing his condition; *having lately been disappointed in a view he had of that sort with Mrs. Howe.* These two brothers generally act in concert; and Mr. James Harlowe dreads (and let me tell you, that he has reason for it, on *my* Mr. Harlowe's account), that his younger sister will be, at last, more benefited than he wishes for, by the alteration intended. He has already been endeavouring to sound his uncle Harlowe on this subject; and wanted to know whether any new application had been made to him on his sister's part. Mr. Harlowe avoided a direct answer, and expressed his wishes for a general reconciliation, and his hopes that his niece was married. This offended the furious young man, and he reminded his uncle of engagements they had all entered into at his sister's going away, *not to be reconciled but by general consent.*

Mr. John Harlowe complains to me often, of the uncontroulableness of his nephew; and says, that now, that the young man has not any-body of whose superior sense he stands in awe, he observes not decency in his behaviour to any of them. And this makes *my* Mr. Harlowe still more desirous than ever of bringing his younger niece into favour again. I will not say all I might of this young man's extraordinary rapaciousness:—But one would think, *that these grasping men expect to live for ever!*

Mr. Harlowe hopes, Sir, that you will rather take pains to *avoid*, than to *meet* this violent young man. He has the better opinion of you, let me tell you, Sir, from the account I gave him of your moderation and politeness; neither of which are qualities with his nephew. *But we have all of us something to amend.*

I will put an end to this long epistle. Be pleased to make my compliments acceptable to the most excellent of women; as well as believe me to be,

Dear sir, Your faithful friend, and humble servant,

Antony Tomlinson

During the conversation between me and the women, I had planted myself at the further end of the apartment we were in, over-against the door; which was open; and opposite to the lady's chamber-door, which was shut. I spoke so low, that it was impossible, at that distance, that she should hear what we said; and in this situation I could see if her door opened.

I told the women, that what I had mentioned of Lady Betty's and her niece's coming to town, and of their intention to visit my spouse, whom they had never seen, nor she them, was real; and that I expected news of their arrival every hour. I then shewed them copies of the other two letters, which I had left with her; the one from lady Betty, the other from my cousin Montague.

The women having read the copies of these two letters, I thought that I might then threaten and swagger—"But very little heart have I, said I, to encourage such a visit from Lady Betty and Miss Montague to my spouse. For after all, I am tired out with her strange ways. She is not what she was, and (as I told her in your hearing, ladies) I will leave this plaguy island, tho' the place of my birth, and tho' the stake I have in it is very considerable; and go and reside in France or Italy, and never think of myself as a married man, *nor live like one.*"

O dear! said one.

That would be a sad thing! said the other.

'Tis an unheard-of case, ladies—Had she not preferred me to all mankind—There I stopped—And that, resumed I, feeling for my handkerchief, is, what staggered Captain Tomlinson, when he heard of her flight; who, the last time he saw us together, saw the most affectionate couple on earth!—The most affectionate couple on earth!—in the accent-grievous, repeated I.

Out then I pulled my handkerchief, and putting it to my eyes, arose, and walked to the window—It makes me weaker than a woman!—Did I not love her, as never man loved *his wife* [I have no doubt but I do, Jack]—

There again I stopt; and resuming—Charming creature, as you see she is, I wish I had never beheld her face!—Excuse me, ladies; traversing the room. And having rubbed my eyes till I supposed them red, I turned to the women; and, pulling out my letter-case, I will shew you one letter—Here it is—Read it, Miss Rawlins, if you please—It will confirm to you, how much all my family are prepared to admire her. I am freely treated in it;—so I am in the two others: But after what I have told you, nothing need be a secret to you two.

She took it, with an air of eager curiosity, and looked at the seal, ostentatiously coronetted; and at the superscription, reading out, *To Robert Lovelace, Esq;*—Ay Madam—Ay, Miss—that's my name (giving myself an air, tho' I had told it to them before) I am not ashamed of it. My wife's maiden name—*Un-married* name, I should rather say—fool that I am!—and I rubbed my cheek for vexation [Fool enough in conscience, Jack!] was Harlowe—Clarissa Harlowe—You heard me call her *My Clarissa.*—

I did—but thought it to be a feigned or love name, said Miss Rawlins.

I wonder what is Miss Rawlins's love-name, Jack. Most of

the fair Romancers have in their early womanhood chosen Love-names. No parson ever gave more *real* names, than I have given *fictitious* ones. And to very good purpose: Many a sweet dear has answered me a letter for the sake of owning a name which her godmother never gave her.

No—It was her real name, I said.

I bid her read out the whole letter. If the spelling be not exact, Miss Rawlins, said I, you will excuse it; the writer is a Lord. But, perhaps, I may not shew it to my spouse; for if those I have left with her have no effect upon her, neither will this: And I shall not care to expose my Lord M. to her scorn.

Miss Rawlins, who could not but be pleased with this mark of my confidence, looked as if she pitied me.

And here thou mayest read the Letter, No. III.

To Robert Lovelace, Esq;

M. Hall, Wedn. June 7.

Cousin Lovelace,

I THINK you might have found time to let us know of your nuptials being actually solempnized. I might have expected this piece of civility from you. But perhaps the ceremony was performed at the very time that you asked me to be your lady's Father—But I shall be angry if I proceed in my guesses—And *little said is soon amended.*

May this marriage be crowned with a great many fine boys (I desire no girls) to build up again a family so antient! The first boy shall take my surname by act of parliament. That is in my will.

Lady Betty and niece Charlotte will be in town about business *before you know where you are.* They long to pay their compliments to your fair bride. I suppose you will hardly be at the Lawn when they get to town; because Greme informs me, you have sent no orders there for your lady's accommodation.

My most affectionate compliments and congratulations to
my new niece, conclude me, for the present, in violent pains,
that with all your heroicalness would make you mad,

   Your truly affectionate uncle,

                                        M.

   This Letter clench'd the nail. Not but that, Miss Rawlins
said, she saw I had been a wild gentleman; and, truly, she
thought so, the moment she beheld me.
   Ladies, you are exceedingly good to us both. I should have
some hopes, if my unhappily-nice spouse could be brought to
dispense with the unnatural oath she has laid me under. You
see what my case is. Do you think I may not insist upon her
absolving me from this abominable oath? Will you be so good,
as to give your advice, that one apartment may serve for a man
and his wife at the hour of retirement?—Modestly put Belford!
   They both simpered, and looked upon one another.
   These subjects always make women simper, at least. No
need but of the most delicate hints to *them.* A man who is gross
in a woman's company, ought to be knocked down with a club:
For, like so many musical instruments, touch but a single wire,
and the dear souls are sensible all over.
   To be sure, Miss Rawlins learnedly said, playing with her
fan, a casuist would give it, that the matrimonial vow ought to
supersede any other obligation.
   Mrs. Moore, for her part, was of opinion, that, if the Lady
owned herself to be a Wife, she ought to behave *like* one.
   Whatever be my luck, thought I, with this *all-eyed* fair-one,
any other woman in the world, from fifteen to five-and-twenty,
would be mine upon my own terms before the morning.
   And now, that I may be at hand to take all advantages, I
will endeavour, said I to myself, to make sure of good quarters.

Mr. Lovelace
To John Belford, Esq;

I THOUGHT it was now high time to turn my whole mind to my beloved; who had had full leisure to weigh the contents of the letters I had left with her.

I therefore requested Mrs. Moore to step in, and desire to know, whether she would be pleased to admit me to attend her in her apartment, on occasion of the letters I had left with her; or whether she would favour me with her company in the dining-room?

Mrs. Moore desired Miss Rawlins to accompany her in to the lady. They tapped at her door, and were both admitted.

I will now give thee the substance of the dialogue that passed between the two women and the lady.

Wonder not, that a perverse wife makes a listening husband. The event, however, as thou wilt find, justified the old observation, *That listeners seldom hear good of themselves*. There is something of sense, after all, in these proverbs, in these phrases, in this *wisdom of nations*.

Mrs. Moore was to be the messenger; but Miss Rawlins began the dialogue.

Your Spouse, Madam—[Devil!—Only to fish for a negative or affirmative declaration.]

Cl. My *Spouse*, Madam—

Miss R. Mr. Lovelace, Madam, averrs, that you are married to him; and begs admittance, or your company in the Dining-room, to talk upon the subject of the letters he left with you.

Cl. He is a poor wicked wretch. Let me beg of you, Madam, to favour me with your company as often as possible while he is hereabouts, and I remain here.

As to the Letters he has left with me, I know not what to say to *them:*—But am resolved never to have anything to say to *him*.

Miss R. If, Madam, I may be allowed to say so, I think you carry matters very far. He has owned, that an accidental fire had frightened you very much on Wednesday night—And that—

306

And that—And that—an accidental fire had frightened you—
Very much frightened you—last Wednesday night!—

Then, after a short pause—In short, He owned, That he had
taken some innocent liberties, which might have led to a breach
of the oath you had imposed upon him: And that This was the
cause of your displeasure.

I would have been glad to see how my charmer then looked.
—She hesitated—Did not presently speak—When she did, she
wished, That she, Miss Rawlins, might never meet with any
man who would take such innocent liberties with *her*.

Cl. You have heard *his* Story. Mine, as I told you before, is
too long, and too melancholy; my disorder on seeing the wretch
is too great; and my time here is too short, for me to enter upon
it. And if he has any end to serve by his own vindication, in
which I shall not be a *personal* sufferer, let him make himself
appear as white as an angel; with all my heart.

Cl. Let me look out—[I heard the sash lifted up] Whither
does that path lead? Is there no possibility of getting to a coach?
—Surely, he must deal with some fiend, or how could he have
found me out?—Cannot I steal to some neighbouring house,
where I may be concealed till I can get quite away?—You are
good people!—I have not been always among such!—O help
me, help me, ladies (with a voice of impatience), or I am ruined!

Miss R. On the side of the heath is a little village called
North-end. A kinswoman of mine lives there. But her house is
small. I am not sure she could accommodate such a lady.

Cl. A barn, an outhouse, a garret, will be a palace to me,
if it will but afford me a refuge from *this man!*—

Her senses, thought I, are much livelier than *mine*. What a
devil have I done, that she should be so *very* implacable!—I
told thee, Belford, All I did: Was there any thing in it so *very*
much amiss!—Such prospects of family-reconciliation before
her too!—To be sure she is a very *sensible* lady!—

Miss Rawlins said something; but so low, that I could not
hear what it was. Thus it was answered.

Cl. I am greatly distressed! I know not what to do!—But,
Mrs. Moore, be so good as to give his letters to him—Here they
are.—Be pleased to tell him, That I wish him and his aunt and

cousin a happy meeting. He never can want excuses to them for what has happened, any more than pretences to those he would delude. Tell him, That he has ruined me in the opinion of my own friends. I am for that reason the less solicitous how I appear to his.

Mrs. Moore then came to me; and being afraid that something would pass mean time between the other two, which I should not like, took the letters, and entered the room, and found them retired into the closet; my beloved whispering with an air of earnestness to Miss Rawlins, who was all attention.

Her back was towards me; and Miss Rawlins, by pulling her sleeve, giving intimation of my being there, Can I have no retirement uninvaded, Sir, said she, with indignation, as if she were interrupted in some talk her heart was in?—What business have you here, or with me?—You have your letters, han't you?

Lovel. I have, my dear; and let me beg of you to consider what you are about. I every moment expect Captain Tomlinson here. Upon my soul, I do. He has promised to keep from your uncle what has happened.—But what will he think, if he finds you hold in this strange humour?

Cl. I will endeavour, Sir, to have patience with you for a moment or two, while I ask you a few questions before this lady and Mrs. Moore [who just then came in], both of whom you have prejudiced in your favour by your specious stories:— Will you say, Sir, that we are married together? Lay your hand upon your heart, and answer me, Am I your wedded wife?

I am gone too far, thought I, to give up for such a push as this—home-one as it is.

My dearest soul! how can you put such a question?—Is it either for *your* honour or *my own*, that it should be doubted?— Surely, surely, Madam, you cannot have attended to the contents of Captain Tomlinson's letter.

You and I! *Vilest of men*—

My name is Lovelace, Madam—

Therefore it is, that I call you the *vilest of men* [Was this pardonable, Jack?] *You* and *I* know the truth, the *whole* truth—I want not to clear up my reputation with these gentlewomen:— That is already lost with every one I had most reason to value:

But let me have this *new* specimen of what you are capable of—Say, wretch (say, Lovelace, if thou hadst rather), Art thou really and truly my wedded husband?—Say! answer without hesitation!—

Lovel. My dearest Love, how wildly you talk! What would you *have* me answer? Is it necessary that I *should* answer? May I not re-appeal this to your own breast, as well as to Captain Tomlinson's treaty and letter? You know yourself how matters stand between us.—And Captain Tomlinson—

Cl. O wretch! Is this an answer to my question? Say, Are we married, or are we not?

Lovel. What *makes a marriage*, we all know. If it be the union of two hearts [There was a turn, Jack!] to my utmost grief, I must say we are *not;* since now I see you hate me. If it be the completion of marriage, to my confusion and regret, I must own we are *not.* But, my dear, will you be pleased to consider what answer half a dozen people whence you came, could give to your question? And do not now, in *the disorder of your mind,* and in the height of passion, bring into question before these gentlewomen a point you have acknowleged before those who know us better.

By my Soul, Belford, the little witch with her words, but more by her manner, moved *me!* Wonder not then, that her action, her grief, her tears, set the women into the like compassionate manifestations.

I took this opportunity to step to the women, to keep them steady.

You see, ladies (whispering), what an unhappy man I am! You see what a spirit this dear creature has!—All, all owing to her implacable relations, and to her father's curse.—A curse upon them all; they have turned the head of the most charming woman in the world.

Ah! Sir, Sir, replied Miss Rawlins, whatever be the fault of her relations, all is not as it should be between you and her. 'Tis plain she does not think herself married: 'Tis *plain* she does not: And if you have any value for the poor lady, and would not totally deprive her of her senses, you had better withdraw, and leave to time and cooler consideration the event in your favour.

She will compel me to this at last, I fear, Miss Rawlins; I *fear* she will; and then we are both undone: For I cannot live without her; she knows it too well:—And she has not a friend who will look upon her: This also she knows. Our marriage, when her uncle's friend comes, will be proved incontestably. But I am ashamed to think I have given her room to believe it no marriage: That's what she harps upon!

Well, 'tis a strange case, a very strange one, said Miss Rawlins; and was going to say further, when the angry Beauty, coming towards the door, said, Mrs. Moore, I beg a word with you. And they both stepped into the dining-room.

Mr. Lovelace

In Continuation.

W E had at dinner, besides Miss Rawlins, a young widow-niece of Mrs. Moore, who is come to stay a month with her aunt—*Bevis* her name; very forward, very lively, and a great admirer of *me*, I assure you;—hanging smirkingly upon all I said; and prepared to approve of every word before I spoke: And who, by the time we had half-dined (by the help of what she had collected before) was as much acquainted with our Story, as either of the other two.

As it behoved me to prepare them in my favour against whatever might come from Miss Howe, I improved upon the hint I had thrown out above-stairs against that mischief-making Lady. I represented her to be an arrogant creature, revengeful, artful, enterprizing, and one who, had she been a man, would have sworn and cursed, and committed rapes, and played the devil, as far as I knew [and I have no doubt of it, Jack]: but who, nevertheless, by advantage of a female education, and pride, and insolence, I believed was *personally* virtuous.

And yet nobody (added I) has more reason than she to

know by *experience* the force of a hatred founded in envy; as I hinted to *you* above, Mrs. Moore, and to *you*, Miss Rawlins, in the case of her sister Arabella.

I had compliments made to my person and talents on this occasion; which gave me a singular opportunity of displaying my modesty, by disclaiming the merit of them, with a *No, indeed!—I should be very vain, Ladies, if I thought so.* While thus abasing myself, and exalting Miss Howe, I got their opinion both for modesty and generosity; and had all the graces which I disclaimed, thrown in upon me, besides.

In short, they even oppressed that modesty, which (to speak modestly of myself) their praises *created*, by disbelieving all I said against myself.

And, truly, I must needs say, they have almost persuaded even me myself, that Miss Howe is actually in love with me. I have often been willing to hope this. And who knows but she may? The Captain and I have agreed, that it shall be so insinuated *occasionally*—And what's thy opinion, Jack? She certainly hates Hickman: And girls who are *disengaged* seldom *hate*, tho' they may not *love:* And if she had rather have *another*, why not that *other* me? For am I not a smart fellow, and a rake? And do not your sprightly Ladies love your smart fellows, and your rakes?

Nor accuse thou me of singular vanity in this presumption, Belford. Wert thou to know the secret vanity that lurks in the hearts of those who *disguise* or *cloak it best*, thou wouldst find great reason to acquit, at least, to allow for, *me*.

But now I have appealed this matter to thee, let me use another argument in favour of my observation, that the Ladies generally prefer a rake to a sober man; and of my presumption upon it, that Miss Howe is in love with me: It is this: Common fame says, That Hickman is a very virtuous, a very innocent fellow—a *male-virgin*, I warrant!—An odd dog I always thought him.—Now women, Jack, like not novices. They are pleased with a Love of the Sex that is founded in the knowlege of it.

Mr. Lovelace

In Continuation.

I T was now high time to acquaint my spouse, that Captain Tomlinson was come. And the rather, as the maid told us, that the lady had asked her, If such a gentleman (describing him) was not in the parlour?

Mrs. Moore went up, and requested, in my name, that she would give us audience.

But she returned, with a desire, that Captain Tomlinson would excuse her for the present. She was very ill. Her spirits were too weak to enter into conversation with him; and she must lie down.

I was vexed, and, at first extremely disconcerted. The Captain was vexed too. And my concern, thou mayest believe, was the greater on his account.

She had been very much fatigued, I own. Her fits in the morning must have weakened her: And she had carried her resentment so high, that it was the less wonder she should find herself low, when her raised spirits had subsided. *Very* low, I may say; if sinkings are proportioned to risings; for she had been lifted up above the standard of a common mortal.

I would have had the Captain lodge there that night, as well in compliment to him, as introductory to my intention of entering my self upon my new-taken apartment. But his hours were of too much importance to him to stay the evening.

It was indeed very inconvenient for him, he said, to return in the morning; but he was willing to do all in his power to heal this breach, and that as well for the sakes of me and my lady, as for that of his dear friend Mr. John Harlowe; who must not know how far this misunderstanding had gone. He would there-fore only drink one dish of tea with the ladies and me.

And accordingly, after he had done so, and I had had a little private conversation with him, he hurried away.

I had hardly taken leave of the Captain, and sat down again with the women, when Will. came; and calling me out, "Sir, Sir," said he, grinning with a familiarity in his looks as if what

he had to say intitled him to take liberties; "I have got the fellow
down!—I have got old Grimes—Hah, hah, hah, hah—He is at
the Lower-Flask—Almost in the condition of *David's sow*, and
please your Honour—[The dog himself not much better] Here
is his letter—from—from Miss Howe—Ha, ha, ha, ha," laughed
the varlet; holding it fast, as if to make conditions with me,
and to excite my praises, as well as my impatience.

I was once thinking to rumple up this billet till I had broken
the seal. *Young* families (Miss Howe's is not an antient one) love
ostentatious sealings: And it might have been supposed to have
been squeezed in pieces, in old Grimes's breeches pocket. But I
was glad to be *saved* the guilt as well as suspicion of having a
hand in so dirty a trick; for thus much of the contents (enough
for my purpose) I was enabled to scratch out in character, without it; the folds deprieving me only of a few connecting words;
which I have supplied between hooks.

" I CONGRATULATE you, my dear, with all my heart and
soul, upon [your escape] from the villain. [I long] for the
particulars of all. [My mamma] is out: But expecting her return
every minute, I dispatched [your] messenger instantly. [I will
endeavour to come at] Mrs. Townsend without loss of time;
and will write at large in a day or two, if in that time I can see
her. [Mean time I] am excessively uneasy for a letter I sent you
yesterday by Collins, [who must have left it at] Wilson's after
you got away. [It is of very] great importance. [I hope the]
villain has it not. I would not for the world [that he should.]
Immediately send for it, if by so doing, the place you are at
[will not be] discovered. If he has it, let me know it by some
way [out of] hand. If not, you need not send.

Ever, ever yours,

June 9.

A. H."

O Jack, what heart's-ease does this *interception* give me!—
I sent the rascal back with the letter to old Grimes, and charged

him to drink no deeper. He owned, that he was *half seas over*, as he phrased it.

Away, villain!—Let old Grimes come; and on horseback, too, to the door—

He shall, and please your Honour, if I can get him on the saddle, and if he can sit—

And charge him not to have alighted, nor to have seen *any*-body—

Enough, Sir! familiarly nodding his head, to shew he took me. And away went the villain: Into the parlour, to the women, I.

In a quarter of an hour came old Grimes on horseback, waving to his saddle-bow, now on this side, now on that; his head, at others, joining to that of his more sober beast.

It looked very well to the women, that I made no effort to speak to old Grimes (tho' I wished *before them*, that I knew the contents of what he brought); but, on the contrary, desired that they would instantly let my spouse know, that her messenger was returned.

Down she flew, violently as she had the head-ach!

O how I prayed for an opportunity to be revenged of her, for the ingrateful trouble she had given to her uncle's friend!

She took the letter from old Grimes with her own hands, and retired to an inner parlour to read it.

She presently came out again to the fellow, who had much ado to sit his horse—Here is your money, friend. I thought you long. But what shall I do to get somebody to go to town immediately for me? I see *you* cannot.

Old Grimes took his money; let fall his hat in d'offing it; had it given him; and rode away; his eyes ising-glass, and set in his head, as I saw thro' the window; and in a manner speechless; all his language hiccoughs. My dog need not to have gone so deep with this *tough* old Grimes.—But the rascal was in his kingdom with him.

The lady applied to Mrs. Moore: She mattered not the price. Could a man and horse be engaged for her?—Only to go for a letter left for her, at one Mr. Wilson's in Pall-mall.

A poor neighbour was hired. A horse procured for him. He had his directions.

In vain did I endeavour to engage my Beloved, when she was below. Her head-ach, I suppose, returned. She, like the rest of her sex, can be ill or well when she pleases.—

I see her drift, thought I: It is to have all her lights from Miss Howe before she resolves; and to take her measures accordingly.

Saturday, One o' clock.

Tomlinson at last is come. Forced to ride five miles about (tho' I shall impute his delay to great and important business) to avoid the sight of two or three impertinent rascals, who, little thinking whose affairs he was employed in, wanted to obtrude themselves upon him. I think I will make this fellow easy, if he behave to my liking in this affair.

I sent up the moment he came.

She desired to be excused receiving his visit till four this afternoon.

Intolerable!—No consideration!—None at all in this sex, when their cursed humours are in the way!

The Captain is in a pet. Who can blame him? Even the women think a man of his consequence, and generously coming to serve *us*, hardly used.

My beloved has not appeared to any-body this day, except to Mrs. Moore. Is, it seems, extremely low: Unfit for the interesting conversation that is to be held in the afternoon. Longs to hear from her dear friend Miss Howe—Yet cannot expect a letter for a day or two. Has a bad opinion of all mankind.—No wonder!—Excellent creature as she is! with such a *father*, such *uncles*, such a *brother*, as she has!

How does she look?

Better than could be expected from yesterday's fatigue, and last night's ill-rest.

These tender doves know not, till put to it, what they can bear; especially when engaged in love-affairs; and their atten-

tion wholly engrossed. But the sex love busy scenes. Still-life is
their aversion. A woman will *create* a storm, rather than be
without one. So as they can preside in the whirlwind, and direct
it, they are happy.—But my beloved's misfortune is, that she
must live in tumults; yet neither raise them herself, nor be able
to controul them.

Mr. Lovelace
To John Belford, Esq;

Sat. Night, June 10.

W HAT will be the issue of all my plots and contrivances,
devil take me if I am able to divine! But I will not, as
Lord M. would say *forestall my own market.*

At four, the appointed hour, I sent up, to desire admittance
in the Captain's name and my own.

She would wait upon the *Captain* presently [Not upon
me!]; and in the parlour, if it were not engaged.

The dining-room being *mine*, perhaps that was the reason
of her naming the parlour—Mighty nice again, if so!—No good
sign for me, thought I, this stiffness.

The conversation between the Captain and the Lady, when
we were retired, was to the following effect: They both talked
loud enough for me to hear them: The Lady from anger, the
Captain with design; and thou mayst be sure, there was no lis-
tener but myself. What I was imperfect in was supplied afterwards; for I had my vellom-leaved book, to note all down.—If
she had known this, perhaps she would have been more sparing
of her invectives—and but *perhaps* neither.

He told her, that as her brother was absolutely resolved to
see her; and as he himself, in compliance with her uncle's expedient, had reported her marriage; and as that report had
reached the ears of Lord M. Lady Betty, and the rest of my

relations; and as he had been obliged, in consequence of his first report, to vouch it; and as her brother might find out where she was, and apply to the women here, for a confirmation or refutation of the marriage; he had thought himself obliged to countenance the report before the women: That this had embarrassed him not a little, as he would not for the world that she should have cause to think him capable of prevarication, contrivance, or double-dealing: And that this made him desirous of a private conversation with her.

It was true, she said, she *had* given her consent to such an expedient, believing it was her *Uncle's;* and little thinking, that it would lead to so many errors. Yet she might have known, that one error is frequently the parent of many. Mr. Lovelace had made her sensible of the truth of that observation, on more occasions than one.

He then told her, that her uncle had already made some steps towards a general reconciliation. The moment, Madam, that he knows you are really married, he will enter into conference with your *father* upon it; having actually expressed his desire to be reconciled to you, to your *mother*.

And what, Sir, said my mother? What said my *dear* mother?

Your mother, Madam, burst into tears upon it: And your uncle was so penetrated by *her* tenderness, that he could not proceed with the subject. But he intends to enter upon it with her in form, as soon as he hears that the Ceremony is over.

By the tone of her voice she wept. The dear creature, thought I, begins to relent!—And I grudged the dog his eloquence. I could hardly bear the thought, that any man breathing should have the power, which I had lost, of persuading this high-souled lady, tho' in my own favour. And, wouldst thou think it? this reflection gave me more uneasiness at the moment, than I felt from her reproaches, violent as they were; or than I had pleasure in her supposed relenting. For there is beauty in everything she says and does: Beauty in her passion: Beauty in her tears!—Had the Captain been a young fellow, and of rank and fortune, his throat would have been in danger; and I should have thought very hardly of her!

Cl. Well, Sir, I can only say, I am a very unhappy creature!

—I must resign to the will of Providence, and be patient under evils, which *that* will not permit me to shun. But I have taken my measures. Mr. Lovelace can never make *me* happy, nor I *him*. I wait here only for a letter from Miss Howe. That must determine me—

Determine you as to Mr. Lovelace, Madam? interrupted the Captain.

Cl. I am already determined as to him.

Capt. If it be not in his favour, I have done. I cannot use stronger arguments than I have used, and it would be impertinent to repeat them.—If you cannot forgive his offence, I am sure it must have been much greater than he has owned to me.—If you are absolutely determined, be pleased to let me know what I shall say to your uncle?

Here I entered with a solemn air.

Lovel. Mr. Tomlinson, I have heard a great part of what has passed between you and this unforgiving, however otherwise excellent lady. I am cut to the heart to find the dear creature so determined. I could not have believed it possible, with such prospects, that I had so little a share in her esteem. Nevertheless I must do myself justice with regard to the offence I was so unhappy as to give, since I find you are ready to think it much greater than it really was.

Cl. I hear not, Sir, your recapitulations. I am, and ought to be, the sole judge of insults offered to my person. I enter not into discussion with you, nor hear you on the shocking subject. And was going.

I put myself between her and the door—You *may* hear all I have to say, Madam. My *fault* is not of such a nature, but that you *may*. I will be a just accuser of myself; and will not wound your ears.

I then protested that the fire was a real fire [So it was]. I disclaimed [less truly indeed] premeditation. I owned that I was hurried on by the violence of a youthful passion, and by a sudden impulse, which few other persons, in the like situation, would have been able to check: That I withdrew, at her command and intreaty, on the promise of *pardon*, without having offered the least indecency, or any freedom, that would not have been forgiven by persons of delicacy, surprised in an attitude so charming—Her terror, on the alarm of fire, calling for a soothing behaviour, and personal tenderness, she being ready to fall into fits: My hoped-for happy day so near, that I might be presumed to be looked upon as a betrothed lover.

High indignation filled her disdainful eye, eye-beam after eye-beam flashing at me. Every feature of her sweet face had soul in it. Yet she spoke not. Perhaps, Jack, she had a thought, that this *plea for the women* accounted for my contrivance to have her pass to them as married, when I *first carried her thither.*

She was going to speak; but, not liking the turn of her countenance (altho', as I thought, its severity and indignation seemed a little abated), I said, and had like to have blown myself up by it—One expedient I have just thought of—

Cl. None of your expedients, Mr. Lovelace! I abhor your expedients, your inventions—I have had too many of them.

Lovel. See, Capt. Tomlinson!—See, Sir—O how we expose ourselves to you!—Little did you think, I dare say, that we have lived in such a continued misunderstanding together! But you will make the best of it all. We may yet be happy. O that I could have been assured, that this dear creature loved me with the hundredth part of the Love I have for her!—Our diffidences have been mutual. This dear creature has too much punctilio: I am afraid, that I have too little. Hence our difficulties. But I have a heart, Capt. Tomlinson, a heart, that bids me hope for her love, because it is resolved to deserve it, as much as man *can* deserve it.

Capt. I am indeed surprised at what I have seen and heard. I defend not Mr. Lovelace, Madam, in the offence he has given you—As a father of daughters myself, I *cannot* defend him; tho' his fault seems to be lighter than I had apprehended—But in my conscience I think, that you, Madam, carry your resentment too high.

Cl. Too high, Sir!—Too high, to the man that might have been happy if he would!—Too high to the man that has held *my soul in suspense* an hundred times, since (by artifice and deceit) he obtained a power over me!—Say, Lovelace, thyself say, Art thou not the *very* Lovelace, who by insulting *me,* hast

wronged thine *own hopes?*—The wretch that appeared in vile
disguises, personating an old lame creature, seeking for lodgings
for thy sick wife?—Telling the gentlewomen here, stories all of
thine own invention; and asserting to them an husband's right
over me, which thou hast not?—And is it (turning to the Captain) to be expected, that I should give credit to the protestations
of such a man?

Lovel. Treat me, dearest creature, as you please, I will bear
it: And yet your scorn and your violence have fixed daggers
in my heart—But was it possible, without those disguises, to
come at your speech?—And could I lose you, if study, if invention, would put it in my power to arrest your anger, and give me
hope to engage you to confirm to me the *promised pardon?*

Cl. O thou strange wretch, how thou talkest!—But, Captain Tomlinson, give me leave to say, that, were I inclined to
enter farther upon this subject, I would appeal to Miss Rawlins's
judgment (Whom else have I to appeal to?); she seems to be a
person of prudence and honour; but not to any *man's* judgment,
whether I carry my resentment beyond fit bounds, when I resolve—

Capt. Forgive, Madam, the interruption—But I think there
can be no reason for this. You ought, as you said, to be the *sole
judge* of indignities offered you. The gentlewomen here are
strangers to you. You will perhaps stay but a little while among
them. If you lay the state of your case before any of them, and
your brother come to inquire of them, your uncle's intended
mediation will be discovered, and rendered abortive—*I* shall
appear in a light that I never appeared in, in my life—for these
women may not think themselves obliged to keep the secret.

Cl. O what difficulties has one fatal step involved me in!—
But there is no necessity for such an appeal. I am resolved on
my measures.

Capt. Absolutely resolved, Madam?

Cl. I am.

Capt. What shall I say to your Uncle Harlowe, Madam?—
Poor gentleman! how will he be surprised!—You see, Mr. Lovelace—You see, Sir—turning to me, with a flourishing hand—But
you may thank yourself—And admirably stalked he from us.

She had thrown herself into a chair; her eyes cast down: She was motionless, as in a profound study.

The Captain bowed to her again: But met with no return to his bow. *Mr. Lovelace,* said he (with an air of equality and independence) *I am Yours.*

Still the dear unaccountable sat as immoveable as a statue; stirring neither hand, foot, head, nor eye—I never before saw any one in so profound a reverie, in so waking a dream.

He passed by her to go out at the door she sat near, tho' the other door was his direct way; and bowed again. She moved not. I will not disturb the lady in her meditations, Sir—Adieu, Mr. Lovelace—*No farther, I beseech you.*

She started, sighing—Are you going, Sir?

Capt. I am, Madam. I could have been glad to do you service: But I see it is not in my power.

She stood up, holding out one hand, with inimitable dignity and sweetness—I am sorry you are going, Sir—I can't help it—I have no friend to advise with—Mr. Lovelace has the art (or good-fortune, perhaps, I should call it) to make himself many. —Well, Sir—If you will go, I can't help it.

Capt. I will *not* go, Madam, his eyes twinkling. [Again seized with a fit of humanity!]. I will *not* go, if my longer stay can do you either service or pleasure. What, Sir (turning to me), what, Mr. Lovelace, was your expedient?—Perhaps something may be offered, Madam—

She sighed, and was silent.

Revenge, *invoked I to myself, keep thy throne in my heart. —If the usurper Love once more drive thee from it, thou wilt never regain possession!*

Lovel. What I had thought of, what I had intended to propose, and I sighed—was this, That the dear creature, if she will not forgive me, as she promised, will suspend the displeasure she has conceived against me, till Lady Betty arrives.—That lady may be the mediatrix between us. This dear creature may put herself into *her* protection, and accompany her down to her Seat in Oxfordshire. It is one of her Ladyship's purposes to prevail on her supposed new niece to go down with her. It may pass to every one but to Lady Betty, and to you, Capt. Tomlin-

son, and to your friend Mr. Harlowe (as he desires), that we
have been some time married: And her being with my relations,
will amount to a proof to James Harlowe, that we *are;* and our
nuptials may be privately, and at this beloved creature's pleasure, solemnized; and your report, Captain, authenticated.

Capt. Upon my honour, Madam, clapping his hand upon
his breast, a charming expedient!—This will answer every end.

She mused—She was greatly perplexed—At last, God direct
me! said she: I know not what to do—A young unfriended
creature, whom have I to advise with?—Let me retire, if I *can*
retire.

She withdrew with slow and trembling feet, and went up
to her chamber.

For Heaven's sake, said the penetrated varlet, his hands
lifted up, for Heaven's sake, take compassion upon this admirable lady!—I cannot proceed—I cannot proceed—She deserves all things—

Softly!—damn the fellow!—The women are coming in.

He sobbed up his grief—turn'd about—hemm'd up a more
manly accent—Wipe thy cursed eyes—He did. The sunshine
took place on one cheek, and spread slowly to the other, and
the fellow had his whole face again.

Mr. Lovelace
To John Belford, Esq;

Sat. Midnight.

N O Rest, says a text that I once heard preached upon, *to
the wicked*—And I cannot close my eyes; yet wanted only
to compound for half an hour in an elbow-chair. So must scribble on.

I parted with the Captain, after another strong debate with
him in relation to what is to be the fate of this lady. I had a good
deal of difficulty with him; and at last brought myself to promise, that if I could prevail upon her generously to forgive me,

and to reinstate me in her favour, I would make it my whole endeavour to get off of my contrivances, as happily as I could; and then, substituting him for her uncle's proxy, take shame to myself, and marry.

But if I should, Jack (with the strongest antipathy to the state that ever man had), what a figure shall I make in rakish annals? And can I have taken all this pains for nothing? Or for a wife only, that, however excellent (and *any* woman, do I think, I could make good, because I could make any woman *fear* as well as *love* me), might have been obtained without the plague I have been at, and much more reputably than with it? And hast thou not seen, that this haughty lady knows not how to forgive with graciousness? Indeed has not at all forgiven me? But holds my soul in a *suspense*, which has been so grievous to her own.

It is my intention, in all my reflections, to avoid repeating, at least dwelling upon, what I have before written to thee, tho' the state of the case may not have varied; so I would have thee re-consider the *old* reasonings (particularly those contained in my answer to thy last expostulatory nonsense); and add the *new*, as they fall from my pen; and then I shall think myself invincible;—at least, as arguing rake to rake.

I take the gaining of this lady to be essential to my happiness: And is it not natural for *all men* to aim at obtaining whatever they think will make them happy, be the object more or less considerable in the eyes of others?

As to the manner of endeavouring to obtain her, by falsification of oaths, vows, and the like—Do not the poets of two thousand years and upwards tell us, that Jupiter laughs at the perjuries of lovers?

Do not the mothers, the aunts, the grandmothers, the governesses of the pretty innocents, always, from their very cradles to riper years, preach to them the deceitfulness of men?—That they are not to regard their oaths, vows, promises?—What a parcel of fibbers would all these reverend matrons be, if there were not now-and-then a pretty credulous rogue taken in for a justification of their preachments, and to serve as a beacon lighted up for the benefit of the rest?

Do we not then see, that an honest prowling fellow is a

necessary evil on many accounts? Do we not see, that it is highly requisite that a sweet girl should be now-and-then drawn aside by him?—And the more eminent the lady, in the graces of person, mind, and fortune, is not the example likely to be the more efficacious?

If these *postulata* be granted me, who, I pray, can equal my charmer in all these? Who therefore so fit for an example to the rest of the Sex?—At worst, I am intirely within my worthy friend Mandeville's rule, *That private vices are public benefits.*

Well then, if this sweet creature must *fall*, as it is called, for the benefit of all the pretty fools of the Sex, she *must*; and there's an end of the matter. And what would there have been in it of uncommon or rare, had I not been so long about it?—And so I dismiss all further argumentation and debate upon the question: And I impose upon thee, when thou writest to me, an eternal silence on this head.

Mr. Lovelace
To John Belford, Esq;

Sunday Morning.

I HAVE had the honour of my charmer's company for two complete hours. We met before six in Mrs. Moore's garden: A walk on the heath refused me.

The sedateness of her aspect, and her kind compliance in this meeting, gave me hopes. And all that either the Captain or I had urged yesterday to obtain a full and free pardon, that re-urged I; and I told her, besides, that Capt. Tomlinson was gone down with hopes to prevail upon her uncle Harlowe to come up in person, in order to present me with the greatest blessing that man ever received.

But the utmost I could obtain was, That she would take no resolution in my favour, till she received Miss Howe's next letter.

She had considered of every thing, she told me. My whole

conduct was before her. The house I carried her to, must be a vile house. The people early shewed what they were capable of, in the earnest attempt made to fasten Miss Partington upon her; as she doubted not, with my approbation.—[Surely, thought I, she has not received a duplicate of Miss Howe's letter of detection!] They heard her cries. My insult was undoubtedly premeditated. I had the vilest of views, no question. And my treatment of her put it out of all doubt.

Soul all over, Belford! she seems sensible of liberties, that my passion made me insensible of having taken.

She besought me to give over all thoughts of her. Sometimes, she said, she thought herself cruelly treated by her nearest and dearest relations: At *such* times, a spirit of repining, and even of resentment, took place; and the reconciliation, at other times so desirable, was not then so much the favourite wish of her heart, as was the scheme she had formerly planned—of taking her good Norton for her directress and guide, and living upon her own estate in the manner her grandfather had intended she should live.

This scheme, she doubted not, that her cousin Morden, who was one of her trustees for that estate, would enable her to pursue. And if he can, and does, what, Sir, let me ask you, said she, have I seen in your conduct, that should make me prefer to it an union of interests, where there is such a disunion in minds?

So thou seest, Jack, there is *reason*, as well as *resentment*, in the preference she makes against me!—Thou seest, that she presumes to think, that she can be happy *without* me; and that she must be unhappy *with* me!

I had besought her, in the conclusion of my re-urged arguments, to write to Miss Howe before Miss Howe's answer could come, in order to lay before her the present state of things.

So I would, Mr. Lovelace, was the answer, if I were in doubt myself, which I would prefer; marriage, or the scheme I have mentioned. You cannot think, Sir, but the latter must be my choice.

She frankly owned, that she had once thought of embarking *out of all our ways* for some one of our American colonies: But now that she had been *compelled* to see me (which had been her greatest dread, and which she would have given her life to avoid), she thought she might be happiest in the resumption of her former favourite scheme, if Miss Howe could find her a reputable and private asylum, till her cousin Morden could come. But if he came not soon, and if she had a difficulty to get to a place of refuge, whether from her brother or from *any-body else* (meaning me, I suppose) she might yet perhaps go abroad: For, to say the truth, she could not think of returning to her father's house; since her brother's rage, her sister's upbraidings, her father's anger, her mother's still more-affecting sorrowings, and her own consciousness under them all, would be insupportable to her.

O Jack! I am sick to death, I pine, I die, for Miss Howe's next letter! I would bind, gag, strip, rob, and do any thing but murder, to intercept it.

Mr. Lovelace
To John Belford, Esq;

Sunday afternoon.

O BELFORD! what a hair's-breadth escape have I had!— Such an one, that I tremble between terror and joy, at the thoughts of what *might* have happened, and did not.

What a perverse girl is this, to contend with her fate; yet has reason to think, that her very stars fight against her! I am the luckiest of men!—But my breath almost fails me, when I reflect upon what a slender thread my destiny hung.

But not to keep thee in suspense; I have, within this half-hour, obtained possession of the expected letter from Miss Howe.

Here read the letter, if thou wilt. But thou art not my friend, if thou offerest to plead for either of the saucy creatures, after thou *hast* read it.

To Mrs. Harriot Lucas

at Mrs. Moore's, at Hamstead.

AFTER the discoveries I had made of the villainous machinations of the *most abandoned of men*, particularized in my long letter of Wednesday last, you will believe, my dearest friend, that my surprize upon perusing yours of Thursday evening from Hamstead was not so great as my indignation. Had the *villain* attempted to fire a city instead of an house, I should not have wondered at it. All that I am amazed at, is, that he (whose boast, as I am told, it is, that no woman shall keep him out of her bedchamber, when he has made a resolution to be in it) did not discover *his foot* before. And it is as strange to me, that, having got you at such a shocking advantage, and in such an horrid house, you could, at the time, *escape dishonour*, and afterwards get from such a set of *infernals*.

I gave you, in my long letter of Wednesday and Thursday last, reasons why you ought to mistrust that specious Tomlinson. That man, my dear, must be a solemn villain. *May lightning from Heaven blast the wretch, who has set him, and the rest of his* Remorsless Gang, *at work, to endeavour to destroy the most consummate virtue!* Heaven be praised! you have escaped from all their snares, and *now are out of danger.*—So I will not trouble you at present with the particulars that I have further collected relating to this abominable imposture.

Your thought of going abroad, and your reasons for so doing, most sensibly affect me. But, be comforted, my dear; I hope you will not be under a necessity of quitting your native country. Were I sure, that That must be the cruel case, I would abandon all my own better prospects, and soon be with you. And I would accompany you whithersoever you went, and share fortunes with you: For it is impossible that I should be happy, if I knew that you were exposed not only to the perils of the sea, but to the attempts of other vile men; your personal graces attracting every eye, and exposing you to those hourly dangers, which others, less distinguished by the gifts of nature, might avoid.

327

O, my dear, were I ever to marry, and to be the mother
of a Clarissa (*Clarissa* must be the name, if promisingly lovely!)
how often would my heart ake for the dear creature, as she grew
up, when I reflected, that a prudence and discretion unexampled
in woman, had not, in *you*, been a sufficient protection to that
beauty, which had drawn after it as many admirers as beholders!

Sat. Afternoon.

I have just parted with Mrs. Townsend. I thought you had
once seen her with me: But, she says, she never had the honour
to be personally known to you. She has a *manlike spirit*. She
knows the world. And her two brothers being in town, she is
sure she can engage them, in so good a cause, and (if there should
be occasion) *both their ships crews*, in your service.

Give your consent, my dear; and the *horrid villain* shall be
repaid with *broken bones*, *at least*, for all his vileness!

Mrs. Townsend will in person attend you—She *hopes*, on
Wednesday.—Her brothers, and some of their people, will
scatteringly, and as if they knew nothing of you (so we have
contrived), see you safe not only to London, but to her house at
Deptford.

She has a kinswoman, who will take your commands there,
if she herself be obliged to leave you. And there you may stay,
till the wretch's fury on losing you, and his search, are over.

He will very soon, 'tis likely, enter upon some *new villainy*,
which may engross him: And it may be given out, that you are
gone to lay claim to the protection of your cousin Morden at
Florence.

Possibly, if he can be made to believe it, he will go over in
hopes to find you there.

After a while, I can procure you a lodging in one of our
neighbouring villages; where I may have the happiness to be
your daily visiter.

As to your estate, since you are resolved not to litigate for
it, we will be patient, either till Col. Morden arrives, or till
shame compels some people to be just.

Upon the whole, I cannot but think your prospects *now*

much happier, than they could have been, had you been actually married to such a man as this. I must therefore congratulate you upon your escape, not only from an *horrid libertine*, but from so vile a husband, as he *must* have made to any woman; but more especially to a person of your virtue and delicacy.

You hate him, heartily hate him, I hope, my dear—I am sure you do. It would be strange, if so much purity of life and manners were not to abhor what is so repugnant to itself.

I shall long to hear how you and Mrs. Townsend order matters. I wish she could have been with you sooner. But I have lost no time in engaging her, as you will suppose. I refer to *her*, what I have further to say and advise. So shall conclude with my prayers, that Heaven will direct, and protect, my dearest creature, and make your future days happy!

Anna Howe

Mr. Lovelace
To John Belford, Esq;

Sunday Night—Monday Morning.

I WENT down with revenge in my *heart*; the contents of Miss Howe's letter almost engrossing me, the moment that Miss Harlowe and Mrs. Moore, accompanied by Miss Rawlins, came in: But in my countenance all the gentle, the placid, the serene, that the glass could teach; and in my behaviour all the polite, that such an unpolite creature, as she has often told me I am, could put on.

She had vouchsafed, I should tell thee, with eyes turned from me, and in an *half-aside* attitude, to sip two dishes of tea in my company—Dear soul!—How anger *unpolishes* the most polite! for I never saw Miss Harlowe behave so aukwardly. I imagined she knew not how to be aukward.

When we were in the garden, I poured my whole soul into her attentive ear; and besought for returning favour.

She told me, that she had formed her scheme for her future life: That, vile as the treatment was which she had received from me, that was not all the reason she had for rejecting my suit: But that, on the maturest deliberation, she was convinced, that she could neither be happy with me, nor make me happy; and she injoined me, for both our sakes, to think no more of her.

The Captain, I told her, was rid down post in a manner, to forward my wishes with her uncle.

Lady Betty and Miss Montague were undoubtedly arrived in town by this time.

I would set out early in the morning to attend them.

They adored her. They longed to see her. They *would* see her.—They would not be denied her company into Oxfordshire.

Where could she better go, to be free from her brother's insults?—Where, to be absolutely made unapprehensive of any-body else?—Might I have any hopes of her returning favour, if Miss Howe could be prevailed upon to intercede for me?

Miss Howe prevailed upon to intercede for you! repeated she, with a scornful bridle, but a very pretty one.—And there she stopt.

Don't tell me, that virtue and principle are her guides on this occasion!—'Tis *pride*, a greater pride than my own, that governs her. Love, she has none, thou seest; nor ever had; at least not in a superior degree.—Love never was under the do-minion of *prudence*, or of any *reasoning* power.—She cannot bear to be thought a *woman*, I warrant! And if, in the last at-tempt, I find her *not* one, what will she be the worse for the trial?—No one is to blame for suffering an evil he cannot shun or avoid.

Were a general to be overpowered, and robbed by a high-wayman, would he be less fit for the command of an army on that account?—If indeed the general, pretending great valour, and having boasted, that he never would be robbed, were to make but faint resistance, when he was brought to the test, and to yield his purse when he was master of his own sword, then indeed will the highwayman, who robs him, be thought the braver man.

Thou seest at bottom, that I am not an abandoned fellow;

and that there is a mixture of gravity in me. This, as I grow older, may increase; and when my active capacity begins to abate, I may sit down with the Preacher, and resolve all my past life into vanity and vexation of spirit.

This is certain, that I shall never find a woman so well suited to my taste, as Miss Clarissa Harlowe. I only wish (if I live to see that day), that I may have such a lady as her to comfort and adorn my setting-sun. I have often thought it very unhappy for us both, that so excellent a creature sprung up a little too late for my *setting-out*, and a little too early in my *progress*, before I can think of *returning*. And yet, as I have picked up the sweet traveller in my way, I cannot help wishing, that she would bear me company in the *rest* of my journey, altho' she were to step out of her own path to oblige me. And then, perhaps, we could put up in the *evening* at the same *inn*; and be very happy in each other's conversation; recounting the difficulties and dangers we had passed in our way to it.

And now, Belford, I set out upon business.

Mr. Lovelace
To John Belford, Esq;

Monday, June 12.

DIDST ever see a Licence, Jack?
  N.N., *by divine permission, Lord Bishop of London, To our well-beloved in Christ Robert Lovelace* [Your servant, my good Lord! What have I done to merit so much goodness, who never saw your Lordship in my life?], *of the parish of St. Martin's in the Fields, Batchelor, and Clarissa Harlowe of the same parish, Spinster, sendeth greeting.—Whereas ye are, as is alleged, determined to enter into the holy state of matrimony* [This is only alleged, thou observest], *by and with the consent of, &c. &c. &c. and are very desirous of obtaining your marriage to be solemnized in the face of the church: We are willing, that such your honest desires* [Honest desires, Jack!] *may more speedily*

*have their due effect: And therefore, that ye may be able to
procure such marriage to be freely and lawfully solemnized in
the parish-church of St. Martin in the Fields, or St. Giles's in
the Fields, in the county of Middlesex, by the rector, vicar, or
curate thereof, at any time of the year* [At any time of the year,
Jack!], *without publication of banes: Provided, that by reason of
any precontract* [I verily think, that I have had three or four
precontracts in my time; but the good girls have not claimed
upon them of a long time], *consanguinity, affinity, or any other
lawful cause whatsoever, there be no lawful impediment in this
behalf; and there be not at this time any action, suit, plaint,
quarrel, or demand, moved or depending before any judge
ecclesiastical or temporal, for or concerning any marriage contracted by or with either of you; and that the said marriage be
openly solemnized in the church above-mentioned, between
the hours of eight and twelve in the forenoon; and without
prejudice to the minister of the place where the said woman is
a parishioner: We do hereby, for good causes* [It cost me—Let
me see, Jack—What did it cost me?], *give and grant our licence,
or faculty, as well to you the parties contracting, as to the rector,
vicar, or curate of the said church, where the said marriage is
intended to be solemnized, to solemnized the same in manner and
form above-specified, according to the rites and ceremonies
prescribed in the Book of Common-prayer in that behalf published by authority of parliament. Provided always, That if
hereafter any fraud shall appear to have been committed, at the
time of granting this licence, either by false suggestions, or
concealment of the truth* [Now this, Belford, is a little hard upon
us: For I cannot say, that every one of our suggestions is literally
true:—So, in good conscience, I ought not to marry under this
licence], *the licence shall be void to all intents and purposes,
as if the same had not been granted. And in that case, we do
inhibit all ministers whatsoever, if any thing of the premises
shall come to their knowlege, from proceeding to the celebration
of the said marriage, without first consulting Us, or our Vicar-
general. Given, &c.*

Then follow the Register's name, and a large pendent seal,

with these words round it—Seal of the Vicar-General and Offi-
cial-Principal of the diocese of London.

A good whimsical instrument, take it all together!—But
what, thinkest thou, are the arms to this matrimonial harbinger?
—Why, in the first place, *Two crossed swords;* to shew, that
marriage is a state of offence as well as defence: *Three lions;*
to denote, that those who enter into the state, ought to have a
triple proportion of courage. And (couldst thou have imagined,
that these priestly fellows, in so solemn a case, would cut their
jokes upon poor souls, who come to have their *honest desires*
put in a way to be gratified?) there are *three crooked horns,*
smartly top-knotted with ribbands; which being the Ladies wear,
seem to indicate, that they may very probably adorn, as well
as bestow, the bull's feather.

To describe it according to heraldry-art, if I am not mistaken—Gules, two swords, saltire-wise, Or; second coat, a
coat, a chevron sable between three bugle-horns, Or [*So it ought
to be*]: On a chief of the second, three lions rampant of the first—
But the devil take them for their hieroglyphics, should I say,
if I were determined in good earnest to marry!   ✓

Mr. Lovelace
To John Belford, Esq;

WELL, but now my plots thicken; and my employment of
writing to thee on this subject will soon come to a conclusion. For now, having got the licence; and Mrs. Townsend,
with her tars being to come to Hamstead next Wednesday or
Thursday; and another letter possibly, or message, from Miss
Howe, to inquire how Miss Harlowe does, upon the rustic's
report of her ill health, and to express her wonder that she has
not heard from her, in answer to hers on her escape;—I must
soon blow up the lady, or be blown up myself. And so I am
preparing, with Lady Betty and my cousin Montague, to wait

upon my Beloved with a coach and four, or a set; for Lady Betty
will not stir out with a pair, for the world; tho' but for two or
three miles. And this is a well-known part of her character.

Thou hast seen Lady Betty Lawrance several times—Hast
thou not, Belford?

No, never in my life.

But thou hast; and lain with her too; or fame does thee
more credit than thou deservest—Why, Jack, knowest thou not
Lady Betty's other name?

Other name!—Has she two?

She has. And what thinkest thou of Lady Bab. Wallis?

O the devil!

Now thou hast it. Lady Barbara, thou knowest, lifted up
in circumstances, and by pride, never appears, or produces
herself, but on occasions special—To pass to men of quality or
price, for a duchess, or countess, at least. She has always been
admired for a grandeur in her air, that few women of quality
can come up to: And never was supposed to be other than what
she passed for; tho' often and often a paramour for Lords.

And who, thinkest thou, is my cousin Montague?

Nay, how should I know?

How indeed! Why, my little Johanetta Golding, a lively,
yet modest-looking girl, is my Cousin Montague.

There, Belford, is an aunt!—There's a cousin! Both have
wit at will. Both are accustomed to ape quality. Both are gen-
teelly descended. Mistresses of themselves; and well educated—
Yet past pity.

And how dost think I dress them out?—I'll tell thee.

Lady Betty in a rich gold tissue, adorned with jewels of high
price.

My cousin Montague in a pale pink, standing an end with
silver flowers of her own working. Charlotte, as well as my
Beloved, is admirable at her needle. Not quite so richly jewel'd
out as Lady Betty; but ear-rings and solitaire very valuable,
and infinitely becoming.

Johanetta, thou knowest, has a good complexion, a fine
neck, and ears remarkably fine.—So has Charlotte. She is nearly
of Charlotte's stature too.

Thou canst not imagine what a sum the loan of the jewels cost me; tho' but for three days.

This sweet girl will half ruin me. But seest thou not by this time, that her reign is short?—It must be so. And Mrs. Sinclair has already prepared every-thing for her reception once more.

Here come the ladies—Attended by Susan Morrison, a tenant-farmer's daughter, as Lady Betty's woman; with her hands before her, and thoroughly instructed.

How dress advantages women!—especially those, who have naturally a genteel air and turn, and have had education!

Hadst thou seen how they paraded it—Cousin, and Cousin, and Nephew, at every word; Lady Betty bridling, and looking haughtily-condescending: Charlotte galanting her fan, and swimming over the floor without touching it.

How I long to see my niece-elect! cries one—For they are told, that we are not married; and are pleased, that I have not put the slight upon them, that they had apprehended from me.

How I long to see my dear cousin that is to be, the other!

Curse those eyes!—Those glancings will never do. A down-cast bashful turn, if you can command it—Look upon me. Suppose me now to be my Beloved.

Sprightly, but not confident, cousin Charlotte!—Be sure forget not to look down, or aside, when looked at. When eyes meet eyes, be yours the retreating ones. Your face will bear examination.

O Lord! O Lord! that so young a creature can so soon forget the innocent appearance she first charmed by; and which I thought born with you all!—Five years to ruin what Twenty had been building up! How natural the latter lesson! How difficult to regain the former!

Have I not told you, that my Beloved is a great observer of the eyes? She once quoted upon me a text[a], which shewed me how she came by her knowlege.—Dorcas's were found guilty of treason the first moment she saw her.

[a] Ecclus. xxvi. *The whoredom of a woman may be known in her haughty looks and eye-lids. Watch over an impudent eye, and marvel not if it trespass against thee.*

Once more, suppose me to be my charmer.—Now you are
to encounter my *examining* eye, and my *doubting* heart—

That's my dear!
Study that air in the pier-glass!—

Charming!—Perfectly right!
Your honours, now, devils!—

Pretty well, cousin Charlotte, for a young country lady!—
Till form yields to familiarity, you *may* courtesy low. You must
not be supposed to have forgot your boarding-school airs.

Graceful ease, conscious dignity, like that of my charmer,
O how hard to hit!

Both together now—

Charming!—That's the air, Lady Betty!—That's the cue,
cousin Charlotte, suited to the character of each!—But, once
more, be sure to have a guard upon your eyes.

Never fear, nephew!—
Never fear, cousin.
A dram of Barbados each—
And now we are gone—

Mr. Lovelace
To John Belford , Esq;

At Mrs. Sinclair's, Monday Afternoon.

ALL'S right, as heart can wish!—In spite of all objection—
in spite of a reluctance next to fainting—In spite of all
foresight, vigilance, suspicion, once more is the charmer of my
soul in her old lodgings!

But I have not time for the particulars of our management.
My Beloved is now directing some of her cloaths to be

packed up—Never more to enter this house! Nor ever more will she, I dare say, when once again out of it!

Yet not so much as a condition of forgiveness!—The Harlowe-spirited Fair-one will not *deserve* my mercy!—She will wait for Miss Howe's next letter; and then, if she find a *difficulty in her new schemes* [Thank her for nothing]—will—Will what? —Why even *then* will take time to consider, whether I am to be forgiven, or for ever rejected. An indifference that revives in my heart the remembrance of a thousand of the like nature.— And yet Lady Betty and Miss Montague [One would be tempted to think, Jack, that they wish her to provoke my vengeance] declare, that I ought to be satisfied with such a proud suspension!

They are intirely attached to her. Whatever she says, *is, must be*, gospel!—They are guarantees for her return to Hamstead this night. They are to go back with her. A supper bespoke by Lady Betty at Mrs. Moore's. All the vacant apartments there, by my permission (for I had engaged them for a month certain), to be filled with them and their attendants, for a week at least, or till they can prevail upon the dear Perverse, as they hope they shall, to restore me to her favour, and to accompany Lady Betty to Oxfordshire.

In short, we are here, as at Hamstead, all joy and rapture: All of us, except my beloved, in whose sweet face [her almost fainting reluctance to re-enter these doors not overcome] reigns a kind of anxious serenity!—But how will even *that* be changed in a few hours!

Methinks I begin to pity the half-apprehensive Beauty!— But avaunt, thou unseasonably-intruding pity! Thou hast more than once, already, well nigh undone me!—And, Adieu reflection! Begone consideration! and commiseration! I dismiss ye all, for, at least, a week to come!—Be remembred her broken word! Her flight, when my fond soul was meditating mercy to her!—What is it she ought not to expect from an unchained Beelzebub, and a plotting villain?

Be her preference of the single life to *me*, also remembred!— That she despises me!—That she even refuses to be my WIFE!— A proud Lovelace to be denied a *Wife!*—To be more proudly rejected by a daughter of the *Harlowes!*—The ladies of my own family [She thinks them the ladies of my family] supplicating in vain for her returning favour to their despised kinsman, and taking laws from her still prouder punctilio!

Is not *this* the crisis for which I have been long waiting? Shall Tomlinson, shall these women, be engaged; shall so many engines be set at work, at an immense expence, with infinite contrivance; and all to no purpose?

Is not *this* the hour of her trial—And in *her*, of the trial of the virtue of her whole Sex, so long premeditated, so long threatened?—Whether her frost is frost indeed? Whether her virtue is principle? Whether, if *once subdued, she will not be always subdued?* And will she not want the very crown of her glory, the proof of her till now all-surpassing excellence, if I stop short of the ultimate trial?

Abhorred be force!—Be the thoughts of force! There's no triumph over the will in force! This I know I have said. But would I not have avoided it, if I could?—Have I not tried every other method? And have I any other recourse left me? Can she resent the *last outrage* more than she has resented a *fainter effort?*—And if her resentments run ever so high, cannot I repair by matrimony?—She will not refuse me, I know, Jack; the haughty Beauty will not refuse me, when her pride of being corporally inviolate is brought down; when she can tell no tales, but when (be her resistance what it will) even her own sex will suspect a yielding in resistance; and when that modesty, which may fill her bosom with resentment, will lock up her speech.

What shall we do now!—We are immersed in the depth of grief and apprehension!—How ill do women bear disappointment!—Set upon going to Hamstead, and upon quitting for ever a house she re-entered with infinite reluctance; what things she intended to take with her, ready pack'd up; herself on tip-toe to be gone; and I prepared to attend her thither; she begins to be afraid, that she shall not go this night; and in grief and despair, has flung herself into her old apartment; locked herself in; and, thro' the key-hole, Dorcas sees her on her knees—praying, I suppose, for a safe deliverance.

And from what?—And wherefore these agonizing apprehensions?

Why, here, this unkind Lady Betty, *with* the dear creature's knowlege, tho' to her concern, and this mad-headed cousin Montague *without* it, while she was employ'd in directing her package, have hurried away in the coach to their own lodgings —Only, indeed, to put up some night-cloaths, and so forth, in order to attend their sweet cousin to Hamstead; and, no less to my surprize than hers, are not yet returned.

I have sent to know the meaning of it.

In a great hurry of spirits, she would have had me gone myself. Hardly any pacifying her!—The girl! God bless her! is wild with her own idle apprehensions!—What is she afraid of?

Oh! here's my aunt's servant, with a billet.

To Robert Lovelace, Esq;

Monday Night.

EXCUSE us, dear Nephew, I beseech you, to my dearest kinswoman. One night cannot break squares. For here Miss Montague has been taken violently ill with three fainting fits, one after another. The hurry of her joy, I believe, to find your dear lady so much surpass all expectation (Never did family-love, you know, reign so strong, as among us), and the too eager desire she had to attend her, have occasioned it: For she has but weak spirits, poor girl! well as she looks.

If she be better, we will certainly go with you to-morrow morning, after we have breakfasted with her, at your lodgings. But, whether she be, or not, I will do myself the pleasure to attend your lady to Hamstead; and will be with you for that purpose, about nine in the morning. With due compliments to your most worthily beloved, I am

Yours affectionately,

Elizab. Lawrance

Faith and troth, Jack, I know not what to do with myself:
For here, just now, having sent in the above note by Dorcas,
out came my beloved with it in her hand: In a fit of phrensy!—
True, by my soul!

She had indeed complained of her head all the evening.

Dorcas ran to me, out of breath, to tell me, that her lady
was coming in some strange way: But she followed her so quick,
that the frighted wench had not time to say in what way.

It seems, when she read the billet—Now indeed, said she,
am I a lost creature! O the poor Clarissa Harlowe!

She tore off her head-cloaths; inquired where I was: And in
she came, her shining tresses flowing about her neck; her ruffles
torn, and hanging in tatters about her snowy hands; with her
arms spread out; her eyes wildly turned, as if starting from their
orbits—Down sunk she at my feet, as soon as she approached
me; her charming bosom heaving to her uplifted face; and,
clasping her arms about my knees, Dear Lovelace, said she, if
ever—if ever—if ever—And, unable to speak another word,
quitting her clasping hold, down prostrate on the floor sunk
she, neither in a fit nor out of one.

I was quite astonished.—All my purposes suspended for a
few moments, I knew neither what to say, nor what to do. But,
recollecting myself, Am I *again*, thought I, in a way to be overcome, and made a fool of!—If I now recede, I am gone for ever.

I lifted her, however, into a chair; and in words of disordered passion, told her, All her fears were needless: Wondered
at them: Begged of her to be pacified: Besought her reliance on
my faith and honour: And revowed all my old vows, and poured
forth new ones.

At last, with an heart-breaking sob, I see, I see, Mr. Lovelace, in broken sentences she spoke—I see, I see—that at last—
at last—I am ruined!—Ruined, if *your* pity—Let me implore
your pity!—And down on her bosom, like a half-broken-stalked
lily, top-heavy with the over-charging dews of the morning,
sunk her head, with a sigh that went to my heart.

All I could think of to re-assure her, when a little recovered,
I said.

Why did I not send for their coach, as I had intimated? It
might return in the morning for the ladies.

I had actually done so, I told her, on seeing her strange uneasiness. But it was then gone to fetch a doctor for Miss Montague, lest his chariot should not be so ready.

Ah! Lovelace! said she, with a doubting face; anguish in her imploring eye.

Let her go to Lady Betty's lodgings, then; *directly* go; if the person I called Lady Betty was really Lady Betty.

If, my dear! Good Heaven! What a villain does that If shew you believe me to be!

I cannot help it—I beseech you once more, Let me go to Mrs. Leeson's, if *that* If ought not to be said.

Then assuming a more resolute spirit—I will go! I will inquire my way!—I will go by myself!—And would have rushed by me.

I folded my arms about her to detain her; pleading the bad way I heard poor Charlotte was in; and what a farther concern her impatience, if she went, would give her.

She would believe nothing I said, unless I would instantly order a coach (since she was not to have Lady Betty's, nor was permitted to go to Mrs. Leeson's), and let her go in it to Hamstead, late as it was; and all alone; so much the better.

Dreading what might happen as to her intellects, and being very apprehensive, that she might possibly go thro' a great deal before morning (tho' more violent she could not well be with the worst she dreaded), I humoured her, and ordered Will. to endeavour to get a coach directly, to carry us to Hamstead; I cared not at what price.

Robbers, whom I would have terrified her with, she feared not—*I* was all her fear, I found; and this house her terror: For I saw plainly, that she now believed, that Lady Betty and Miss Montague were both impostors.

But her mistrust is a little of the latest to do her service.

And, O Jack, the rage of Love, the rage of Revenge, is upon me! By turns they tear me!—The progress already made!—The womens instigations!—The power I shall have to try her to the utmost, and still to marry her, if she be not to be brought to cohabitation!—Let me perish, Belford, if she escape me now!

Will. is not yet come back.—Near eleven.—

Will. is this moment returned.—No coach to be got, *for love or money*.

Once more, she urges—To Mrs. Leeson's let me go! Lovelace! What is Miss Montague's illness to my terror?—For the Almighty's sake, Mr. Lovelace!—her hands clasped—

O my angel! What a wildness is this!—Do you know, do you see, my dearest life, what appearance your causeless apprehensions have given you?—Do you know it is past eleven o' clock?

Twelve, one, two, three, four—any hour—I care not—If you mean me honourably, let me go out of this hated house!

Thou'lt observe, Belford, that tho' this was written afterwards, yet (as in other places) I write it as it was spoken, and happened; as if I had retired to put down every sentence as spoken. I know thou likest this lively *present-tense* manner, as it is one of my peculiars.

Just as she had repeated the last words, *If you mean me honourably, let me go out of this hated house*, in came Mrs. Sinclair, in a great ferment.—And what, pray, Madam, has *this house* done to you?—Mr. Lovelace, you have known me some time; and, if I have not the niceness of this lady, I hope I do not deserve to be treated thus!

She set her huge arms a-kembo: *Hoh!* Madam, let me tell you, I am amazed at your freedoms with my character! And, Mr. Lovelace (holding up, and violently shaking, her head), if you are a gentleman, and a man of honour—

Having never before seen anything but obsequiousness in this woman, little as she liked her, she was frighted at her masculine air, and fierce look—God help me! cried she—What will become of me now! Then, turning her head hither and thither, in a wild kind of amaze, Whom have I for a protector! What will become of me now!

I will be your protector, my dearest love!—But indeed you are uncharitably severe upon poor Mrs. Sinclair! Indeed you are!—She is a gentlewoman born, and the relict of a man of honour; and tho' left in such circumstances as oblige her to let lodgings, yet would she scorn to be guilty of a wilful baseness.

I hope so—It may be so—I may be mistaken—But—But

there is no crime, I presume, no treason, to say I don't like her house.

The old dragon straddled up to her, with her arms kemboed again—Her eye-brows erect, like the bristles upon a hog's back, and, scouling over her shortened nose, more than half-hid her ferret eyes. Her mouth was distorted. She pouted out her blubber-lips, as if to bellows up wind and sputter into her horse-nostrils; and her chin was curdled, and more than usually prominent with passion.

With two *Hoh-Madams* she accosted the frighted fair-one; who, terrified, caught hold of my sleeve.

I feared she would fall into fits; and, with a look of indignation, told Mrs. Sinclair, that these apartments were mine; and I could not imagine what she meant, either by listening to what passed between me and my spouse, or to come in, uninvited; much less to give herself these violent airs.

I may be to blame, Jack, for suffering this wretch to give herself these airs; but her coming in was without my orders.

The old Beldam, throwing herself into a chair, fell a blubbering and exclaiming. And the pacifying of her, and endeavouring to reconcile the lady to her, took up till near one a clock.

And thus, between terror and the late hour, and what followed, she was diverted from the thoughts of getting out of the house to Mrs. Leeson's, or any-where else.

Mr. Lovelace
To John Belford , Esq;

Tuesday Morn. June 13.

AND now, Belford, I can go no farther. The affair is over. Clarissa lives. And I am

Your humble servant,

R. Lovelace.

*The whole of this black transaction is given
by the injured lady, to Miss Howe, in her
subsequent letters, dated Thursday July 6.
To which the reader is referred.*

Mr. Belford
To Robert Lovelace, Esq;

Watford, Wedn. June 14.

O THOU savage-hearted monster! What work hast thou
made in *one guilty hour*, for a *whole age* of repentance!

I am inexpressibly concerned at the fate of this matchless
lady! She could not have fallen into the hands of any other man
breathing, and suffered as she has done with thee.

Poor, poor lady! It is a pain to me, that I ever saw her. Such
an adorer of virtue to be sacrificed to the vilest of her sex; and
thou their implement in the devil's hands, for a purpose so base,
so ungenerous, so inhumane!—Pride thyself, O cruellest of men,
in this reflection; and that thy triumph over a lady, who for thy
sake was abandoned of every friend she had in the world, was
effected, not by advantages taken of her weakness and credulity;
but by the blackest artifice.

I can tell thee, it is well either for thee or for me, that I am
not the brother of the lady. Had I been her brother, her violation
must have been followed by the blood of one of us.

Clarissa lives, thou sayst. That she does, is my wonder; and
these words shew, that thou thyself (tho' thou couldst, nevertheless, proceed) hardly expectedst she would have survived the
outrage. What must have been the poor lady's distress (watchful
as she had been over her honour), when dreadful certainty took
place of cruel apprehension!—And yet a man may guess what it
must have been, by that which thou paintest, when she suspected
herself tricked, deserted, and betrayed, by the pretended aunt
and cousin.

That thou couldst behold her phrensy on this occasion, and her half-speechless, half-fainting prostration at thy feet, and yet retain thy evil purposes, will hardly be thought credible, even by those who know *thee*, if they have seen *her*.

This melancholy occasion may possibly have contributed to humanize me: But surely I never could have been so remorseless a caitiff as *thou* hast been, to a woman of *half* this lady's excellence.

Thou art desirous to know what advantage I reap by my uncle's demise. I do not certainly know; for I have not been so greedily solicitous on this subject, as some of the kindred have been, who ought to have shewn more decency, as I have told them, and suffered the corpse to have been cold before they had begun their hungry inquiries. But, by what I gathered from the poor man's talk to me, I deem it will be upwards of 5000*l*. in cash, and in the funds, after all legacies paid, besides the real estate, which is a clear 500*l*. a year.

Were the estate to be of double the value, thou shouldst have it every shilling; only upon one condition—That thou would permit me the honour of being this fatherless lady's *Father*, as it is called, at the altar.

Think of this! my dear Lovelace: Be honest: And let me present thee with the brightest jewel that man ever possessed; and then, body and soul, wilt thou bind to thee for ever, thy

Belford

Mr. Lovelace
To John Belford, Esq;

Thursday, June 15.

LET me alone, you great dog, you!—Let me alone!—have I heard a lesser boy, his coward arms held over his head and face, say to a bigger, who was pummeling him, for having run away with his apple, his orange, or his ginger-bread.

So say I to thee, on occasion of thy severity to thy poor friend, who, as thou ownest, has furnished thee (ungenerous as thou art!) with the weapons thou brandishest so fearfully against him.—And to what purpose, when the mischief is done; when, of consequence, the affair is irretrievable? and when a Clarissa could not move me?

Well, but, after all, I must own, that there is something very singular in this lady's case: And, at times, I cannot help regretting, that I ever attempted her; since not one power either of body or soul could be moved in my favour.

But peoples extravagant notions of things alter not facts, Belford: And, when all's done, Miss Clarissa Harlowe has but run the fate of a thousand others of her Sex—Only that they did not set such a romantic value upon what they call their *honour;* that's all.

And yet I will allow thee this—That if a person sets a high value upon any-thing, be it ever such a trifle in itself, or in the eye of others, the robbing of that person of it is *not* a trifle to *him.* Take the matter in this light, I own I have done wrong, great wrong, to this admirable creature.

But have I not known twenty and twenty of the sex, who have seemed to carry their notions of virtue high; yet, when brought to the test, have abated of their severity? And how should we be convinced that *any* of them are proof, till they are tried?

A thousand times have I said, that I never yet met with such a woman as this. If I *had*, I hardly ever should have attempted Miss Clarissa Harlowe. Hitherto she is all angel: And was not that the point which at setting out I proposed to try? And was not *cohabitation* ever my darling view? And am I not now, at last, in the high-road to it?—It is true, that I have nothing to boast of as to her Will. The very contrary. But now are we come to the test, whether she cannot be brought to make the best of an irreparable evil?—If she exclaim (She has reason to exclaim, and I will sit down with patience, by the hour together, to hear her exclamations, till she is tired of them), she will then descend to expostulation perhaps: Expostulation will give me hope: Expostulation will shew, that she hates me not. And if she hate me not, she will forgive: And if she *now* forgive; then will all be over; and she will be mine upon my own terms: And it shall then be the whole study of my future life to make her happy.

So, Belford, thou seest, that I have journeyed on to this stage (indeed, thro' infinite mazes, and as infinite remorses) with one determined point in view, from the first. To thy urgent supplication then, that I will do her grateful justice by marriage, let me answer in Matt. Prior's two lines on his hoped-for Auditorship; as put into the mouths of his St. John and Harley;

> —Let that be done, which Matt. doth say.
> Yea, quoth the Earl—but not to-day.

Thou seest, Jack, that I make no resolutions, however, against doing her, one time or other, the wished-for justice, even were I to succeed in my principal view, *cohabitation*. And of this I do assure thee, that, if I ever marry, it must, it shall be Miss Clarissa Harlowe.—Nor is her honour at all impaired with *me*, by what she has *so far* suffered: But the contrary. She must only take care, that, if she be at last brought to forgive me, she shew me, that her Lovelace is the only man on earth, whom she could have forgiven on the like occasion.

But, ah, Jack! what, in the mean time, shall I do with this admirable creature? At present—I am loth to say it—But, at present, she is quite stupefied.

I had rather, methinks, she should have retained all her active powers, tho' I had suffered by her nails and her teeth, than that she should be sunk into such a state of absolute—insensibility (shall I call it), as she has been in ever since Tuesday morning. Yet, as she begins a little to revive, and now-and-then to call names, and to exclaim, I dread almost to engage with the anguish of a spirit that owes its extraordinary agitations to a niceness that has no example either in antient or modern story.

But I will leave this subject, lest it should make me too grave.

Mr. Lovelace
To John Belford, Esq;

CAESAR never knew what it was to be *hypped*, I will call it, till he came to be what Pompey was; that is to say, till he arrived at the height of his ambition: Nor did thy Lovelace know what it was to be gloomy, till he had completed his wishes upon the charming'st creature in the world, as the other did upon the most potent republic that ever existed.

And yet why say I, *completed?* when the *will*, the *consent*, is wanting—And I have still views before me of obtaining that?

Yet I could almost join with thee in the wish, which thou sendest me up by thy servant, unfriendly as it is, that I had had thy misfortune before Monday night last: For here, the poor lady has run into a contrary extreme to that I told thee of in my last: For now is she as much too lively, as before she was too stupid; and, 'bating that she has pretty frequent lucid intervals, would be deemed raving mad, and I should be obliged to confine her.

I am most confoundedly disturbed about it: For I begin to fear, that her intellects are irreparably hurt.

Who the devil could have expected such strange effects from a cause so common, and so slight?

But these high-souled and high-sensed girls, who had set up for shining lights and examples to the rest of the sex, are with such difficulty brought down to the common standard, that a wise man, who prefers his peace of mind to his glory in subduing one of that exalted class, would have nothing to say to them.

I do all in my power to quiet her spirits, when I force myself into her presence.

I go on, begging pardon one minute; and vowing truth and honour another.

I would at first have persuaded her, and offered to call

witnesses to the truth of it, that we were actually married. Tho'
the licence was in her hands, I thought the assertion might go
down in her disorder; and charming consequences I hoped would
follow. But this would not do—

I therefore gave up that hope: And now I declare to her,
that it is my resolution to marry her, the moment her uncle
Harlowe informs me, that he will grace the ceremony with his
presence.

But she believes nothing I say; nor (whether in her senses,
or not) bears me with patience in her sight.

I pity her with all my soul; and I curse myself, when she is
in her wailing fits, and when I apprehend, that intellects, so
charming as hers, are for ever damped.—But more I curse these
women, who put me upon such an expedient!—Lord! Lord! what
a hand have I made of it!—And all for what?

Last night, for the first time since Monday last, she got to
her pen and ink: But she pursues her writing with such eagerness
and hurry, as shew too evidently her discomposure.

I hope, however, that this employment will help to calm
her spirits.

Just now Dorcas tells me, that what she writes she tears,
and throws the paper in fragments under the table, either as not
knowing what she does, or disliking it: Then gets up, wrings
her hands, weeps, and shifts her seat all round the room: Then
returns to her table, sits down, and writes again.

One odd Letter, as I may call it, Dorcas has this moment
given me from her—Carry this, said she, to the vilest of men.
Dorcas, a toad! brought it, without any further direction, to
me.—I sat down, intending (tho' 'tis pretty long) to give thee a
copy of it: But, for my life, I cannot; 'tis so extravagant. And
the original is too much an original to let it go out of my hands.

But some of the scraps and fragments, as either torn
through, or flung aside, I will copy, for the novelty of the thing,
and to shew thee how her mind works, now she is in this whimsical way. Yet I know I am still furnishing thee with new wea-

pons against myself. But spare thy comments. My own reflections render them needless. Dorcas thinks her Lady will ask for
them: So wishes to have them to lay again under her table.

By the first thou'lt guess, that I have told her, that Miss
Howe is very ill, and can't write; that she may account the
better for not having received the letter designed for her.

Paper One.

(Torn in two pieces.)

My dearest Miss Howe!

O! WHAT dreadful, dreadful things have I to tell you!
But yet I cannot tell you neither. But say, Are you really
ill, as a vile, vile creature informs me you are?

But he never yet told me truth, and I hope has not in this:
And yet, if it were not true, surely I should have heard from you
before now!—But what have I to do, to upbraid?—You may
well be tired of me!—And if you are, I can forgive you; for I
am tired of myself: And all my own relations were tired of me
long before you were.

How good you have always been to me, mine own dear
Anna Howe!—But how I ramble!

I sat down to say a great deal—My heart was full—I did
not know what to say first—And thought, and grief, and confusion, and (O my poor head!) I cannot tell what—And thought,
and grief, and confusion, came crouding so thick upon me; *one*
would be first, *another* would be first, *all* would be first; so I
can write nothing at all.—Only that, whatever they have done
to me, I cannot tell; but I am no longer what I was in any one
thing.—In any one thing did I say? Yes, but I am; for I am still,
and I ever will be,

Your true—

Plague on it! I can write no more of this eloquent nonsense myself; which rather shews a raised, than a quenched, imagination: But Dorcas shall transcribe the others in separate papers, as written by the whimsical charmer: And some time hence, when all is over, and I can better bear to read them, I may ask thee for a sight of them. Preserve them therefore; for we often look back with pleasure even upon the heaviest griefs, when the cause of them is removed.

Paper Two.
(Scratch'd thro', and thrown under the Table.)

A ND can you, my dear honoured papa, resolve for ever to reprobate your poor child?—But I am sure you would not, if you knew what she has suffered since her unhappy —And will nobody plead for your poor suffering girl?— No one good body?—Why, then, dearest Sir, let it be an act of your own innate goodness, which I have so much experienced, and so much abused.—I don't presume to think you should receive me—No, indeed—my name is—I don't know what my name is!—I never dare to wish to come into your family again! —But your heavy curse, my papa—Yes, I *will* call you papa, and help yourself as you can—for you are my own dear papa, whether you will or not—And tho' I am an unworthy child— yet I *am* your child—

Paper Three.

A LADY took a great fancy to a young Lion, or a Bear, I forget which—But a Bear, or a Tyger, I believe, it was. It was made her a present of, when a whelp. She fed it with her own hand: She nursed up the wicked cub with great tenderness; and would play with it, without fear or apprehension of danger: And it was obedient to all her commands: And its tameness, as she used to boast, increased with its growth; so that, like a lap-dog, it would follow her all over the house. But mind what followed: At last, some-how, neglecting to satisfy its hungry maw, or having other-wise disobliged it on some occasion, it resumed its nature; and on a sudden fell upon her, and tore her in pieces.—And who was most to blame, I pray? The brute, or the lady? The lady, surely!—For what *she* did, was *out* of nature, *out* of character, at least: What *it* did, was *in* its own nature.

Paper Four.

HOW art thou now humbled in the dust, thou proud Clarissa Harlowe! Thou that never steppedst out of thy father's house, but to be admired! Who wert wont to turn thine eye, sparkling with healthful life, and self-assurance, to different objects at once, as thou passedst, as if (for so thy penetrating sister used to say) to plume thyself upon the expected applauses of all that beheld thee! Thou that usedst to go to rest satisfied with the adulations paid thee in the past day, and couldst put off everything but thy vanity!—

Paper Five.

REJOICE not now, my Bella, my sister, my friend; but pity the humbled creature, whose foolish heart you used to say you beheld thro' the thin veil of humility, which covered it.

It must have been so! My fall had not else been permitted—

You penetrated my proud heart with the jealousy of an elder sister's searching eye.

You knew me better than I knew myself.

Hence your upbraidings, and your chidings, when I began to totter.

But forgive now those vain triumphs of my heart.

I thought, poor proud wretch that I was, that what you said was owing to your envy.

I thought I could acquit my intention of any such vanity.

I was too secure in the knowlege I thought I had of my own heart.

My supposed advantages became a snare to me.

And what now is the end of all?—

Paper Six.

WHAT now is become of the prospects of a happy life, which once I thought opening before me?—Who now shall assist in the solemn preparations? Who now shall provide the nuptial ornaments, which soften and divert the apprehensions of the fearful virgin? No court now to be paid to my smiles! No encouraging compliments to inspire thee with hope of laying a mind not unworthy of thee under obligation! No elevation now for conscious merit, and applauded purity, to look down from on a prostrate adorer, and an admiring world, and up to pleased and rejoicing parents and relations!

Paper Seven.

THOU pernicious caterpiller, that preyest upon the fair leaf of virgin fame, and poisonest those leaves which thou canst not devour!

Thou fell blight, thou eastern blast, thou overspreading mildew, that destroyest the early promises of the shining year!

that mockest the laborious toil, and blastest the joyful hopes, of the painful husbandman!

Thou fretting moth, that corruptest the fairest garment!

Thou eating canker-worm, that preyest upon the opening bud, and turnest the damask rose into livid yellowness!

If, as Religion teaches us, God will judge us, in a great measure, by our benevolent or evil actions to one another—O wretch! bethink thee, in time bethink thee, how great must be thy condemnation!

Paper Eight.

AT first, I saw something in your air and person that displeased me not. Your birth and fortunes were no small advantages to you.—You acted not ignobly by my passionate brother. Every-body said you were brave: Every-body said you were generous. A *brave* man, I thought, could not be a *base* man: A *generous* man could not, I believed, be *ungenerous*, where he acknowleged *obligation*. Thus prepossessed, all the rest, that my soul loved, and wished for, in your reformation, I hoped!—I knew not, but by report, any flagrant instances of your vileness. You seemed frank, as well as generous: Frankness and generosity ever attracted me: Whoever kept up those appearances, I judged of their hearts by my own; and whatever qualities *I wished* to find in them, I was *ready* to find; and, *when* found, I believed them to be natives of the soil.

My fortunes, my Rank, my Character, I thought a further security. I was in none of those respects unworthy of being the niece of Lord M. and of his two noble sisters.—Your vows, your imprecations—But, Oh! you have barbarously and basely conspired against that honour, which you ought to have protected: And now you have made me—What is it of vile, that you have *not* made me?—

Yet, God knows my heart, I had no culpable inclinations!

—I honoured virtue!—I hated vice!—But I knew not, that you were vice itself!

Paper Nine.

HAD the happiness of any the poorest outcast in the world, whom I had never seen, never known, never before heard of, lain as much in *my* power, as my happiness did in *yours*, my benevolent heart would have made me fly to the succour of such a poor distressed—With what pleasure would I have raised the dejected head, and comforted the desponding heart!—But who now shall pity the poor wretch, who has increased, instead of diminished, the number of the miserable!

After all, Belford, I have just skimmed over these transcriptions of Dorcas; and I see there is method and good sense in some of them, wild as others of them are; and that her memory, which serves her so well for these poetical flights, is far from being impaired. And this gives me hope, that she will soon recover her charming intellects—Tho' I shall be the sufferer by their restoration, I make no doubt.

But, in the letter she wrote to me, there are yet greater extravagancies; and tho' I said, It was too affecting to give thee a copy of it, yet, after I have let thee see the loose papers inclosed, I think I may throw in a transcript of that. Dorcas, therefore, shall here transcribe it: *I* cannot. The reading of it affected me ten times more, than the severest reproaches of a regular mind.

To Mr. Lovelace

I NEVER intended to write another line to you. I would not see you, if I could help it. O that I never had!

But tell me of a truth, Is Miss Howe really and truly ill?—

Very ill?—And is not her illness poison? And don't *you* know who gave it her..

What you, or Mrs. Sinclair, or somebody, I cannot tell who, have done to my poor head, you best know: But I shall never be what I was. My head is gone. I have wept away all my brain, I believe; for I can weep no more. Indeed I have had my full share; so it is no matter.

But, good now, Lovelace, don't set Mrs. Sinclair upon me again! I never did her any Harm. She *so* affrights me, when I see her!—Ever since—When was it? I cannot tell. *You* can, I suppose. She may be a good woman, as far as I know. She was the wife of a man of honour—Very likely!—Tho' forced to lett lodgings for her livelihood. Poor gentlewoman! Let her know I pity her: But don't let her come near me again—Pray don't!

Yet she may be a very good woman—

What would I say!—I forget what I was going to say.

O! Lovelace! If you could be sorry for yourself, I would be sorry too—But when all my doors are fast, and nothing but the key-hole open, and the key of late put into that, to be where you are, in a manner without opening any of them—O wretched, wretched Clarissa Harlowe!

For I never will be Lovelace—let my uncle take it as he pleases.

Well, but now I remember what I was going to say—It is for *your* good—not *mine*—For nothing can do me good now!— O thou villainous man! thou hated Lovelace!

But Mrs. Sinclair may be a good woman—If you love me— But that you don't—But don't let her bluster up with her worse than mannish airs to me again! O she is a frightful woman! If she *be* a woman!—She needed not to put on that *fearful mask* to scare me out of my poor wits.

Alas! you have killed my head among you—I don't say who did it!—God forgive you all!—But had it not been better to have put me out of all your ways at once? You might safely have done it! For nobody would require me at your hands—No, not a soul—Except, indeed, Miss Howe would have said, when she should see you, What, Lovelace, have you done with Clarissa

Harlowe?—And then you could have given any slight gay answer—Sent her beyond sea; or, she has run away from me, as
she did from her parents. And this would have been easily
credited; for you know, Lovelace, she that could run away from
them, might very well run away from *you*.

But this is nothing to what I wanted to say. Now I have
it.

I have lost it again—This foolish wench comes teazing me—
For what purpose should I eat! For what end should I wish to
live?—I tell thee, Dorcas, I will neither eat nor drink. I cannot
be worse than I am.

I will do as you'd have me—Good Dorcas, look not upon
me so fiercely—But thou canst not look so bad as I have seen
somebody look.

Mr. Lovelace, now that I remember what I took pen in
hand to say, let me hurry off my thoughts, lest I lose them
again.

I must needs be both a trouble and an expence, to you.
And here my uncle Harlowe, when he knows how I am, will
never wish any man to have me: No, not even *you*, who have
been the occasion of it—Barbarous and ungrateful!—A less
complicated villainy cost a Tarquin—But I forget what I would
say again—

Then *this* is it: I never shall be myself again: I have been a
very wicked creature—a vain, proud, poor creature—full of
secret pride—which I carried off under an humble guise, and
deceived every-body—My sister says so—And now I am punished—so let me be carried out of this house, and out of your
sight; and let me be put into that Bedlam privately, which once
I saw: But it was a sad sight to me then! Little as I thought what
I should come to *myself!*—That is all I would say: This is all I
have to wish for—Then I shall be out of all your ways; and I
shall be taken care of; and bread and water, without your
tormentings, will be dainties; and my straw bed the easiest I
have lain in—for—I cannot tell how long!—

My cloaths will sell for what will keep me there, perhaps,
as long as I shall live. But, Lovelace, *dear* Lovelace I will call
you; for you have cost me enough, I'm sure!—don't let me be

made a shew of, for my *family's* sake; nay, for your *own sake*,
don't do that—

So, suppose, instead of Bedlam, it were a private madhouse,
where nobody comes!—That will be better a great deal.

But, another thing, Lovelace: Don't let them use me cruelly
when I am there—*You* have used me cruelly enough, you know!
—Don't let them use me cruelly; for I will be very tractable;
and do as any-body would have me do—Except what you would
have me do—for that I never will.—Another thing, Lovelace:
Don't let this *good* woman; I was going to say *vile* woman; but
don't tell her that—Because she won't let you send me to this
happy refuge perhaps, if she were to know it—

A little interval seems to be lent me. I had begun to look
over what I have written. It is not fit for any one to see, so far
as I have been able to re-peruse it: But my head will not hold,
I doubt, to go through it all. If therefore I have not already mentioned my earnest desire, let me tell you, it is this: That I may
be sent out of this abominable house without delay, and locked
up in some private madhouse about this town; for such, it seems,
there are; never more to be seen, or to be produced to any-body,
except in your own vindication, if you should be charged with
the murder of my person; a much lighter crime, than that of my
honour, which the greatest villain on earth has robbed me of.
And deny me not this my last request, I beseech you; and one
other, and that is, Never to let me see you more! This surely
may be granted to

   The miserably abused

                        Clarissa Harlowe

I will not hear thy heavy preachments, Belford, upon this
plaguy letter. So, not a word of that sort! The paper, thou'lt
see, is blister'd with the tears even of the harden'd transcriber;
which has made her ink run here-and-there.

Mrs. Sinclair is a true heroine, and, I think, shames us all.
And she is a *woman* too! Thou'lt say, The best things corrupted

become the worst. But this is certain, that whatever the sex set their hearts upon, they make thorough work of it. And hence it is, that a mischief which would end in simple robbery among men-rogues, becomes murder, if a woman be in it.

I know thou wilt blame me for having had recourse to *art.* But do not physicians prescribe opiates in acute cases, where the violence of the disorder would be apt to throw the patient into a fever or delirium? I averr, that my motive for this expedient was *mercy;* nor could it be anything else.

Mean time I have a little project come into my head, of a *new* kind; just for amusement-sake, that's all: Variety has irresistible charms. I cannot live without intrigue. My charmer has no passions; that is to say, none of the passions that I want her to have. She engages all my reverence. I am at present more inclined to regret what I have done, than to proceed to new offences: And shall regret it till I see how she takes it when recovered.

Shall I tell thee my project? 'Tis not a high one—'Tis this— To get hither Mrs. Moore, Miss Rawlins, and my Widow Bevis; for they are desirous to make a visit to my spouse, now we are so happy together. And, if I can order it right, Belton, Mowbray, Tourville, and I, will shew them a little more of the ways of this wicked town, than they at present know. Why should they be *acquainted* with a man of my character, and not be the *better* and *wiser* for it?

This moment Dorcas tells me, she believes she is coming to find me out. She asked her after me: And Dorcas left her, drying her red-swoln eyes at her glass [No design of moving me by her tears!]; sighing too sensibly for my courage. But to what purpose have I gone thus far, if I pursue not my principal end?—Niceness must be a little abated. She knows the worst. That she cannot fly me; that she must see me; and that I can look her into a sweet confusion; are circumstances greatly in my favour. What can she do, but rave and exclaim? I am used to raving and exclaiming— But, if recovered, I shall see how she behaves upon this our first sensible interview after what she has suffered.

Here she comes!—

Mr. Lovelace
To John Belford , Esq;

Sunday Night.

NEVER blame me for giving way to have Art used with this admirable creature. All the princes of the air, or beneath it, joining with me, could never have subdued her while she had her senses.

I will not anticipate—Only to tell thee, that I am too much awakened by her to think of sleep, were I to go to bed; and so shall have nothing to do, but to write an account of our odd conversation, while it is so strong upon my mind that I can think of nothing else.

She was dressed in a white damask night-gown, with less negligence than for some days past. I was sitting with my pen in my fingers; and stood up when I first saw her, with great complaisance, as if the day were still her own. And so indeed it is.

She entered with such dignity in her manner, as struck me with great awe, and prepared me for the poor figure I made in the subsequent conversation. A poor figure indeed!—But I will do her justice.

She came up with quick steps, pretty close to me; a white handkerchief in her hand; her eyes neither fierce nor mild, but very earnest; and a fixed sedateness in her whole aspect, which seemed to be the effect of deep contemplation.

You see before you, Sir, the wretch, whose preference of you to all your Sex you have rewarded—as it indeed deserved to be rewarded. My father's dreadful curse has already operated upon me in the very letter of it, as to This life; and it seems to me too evident, that it will not be your fault, that it is not intirely completed in the loss of my soul, as well as of my honour— Which you, villainous man! have robbed me of, with a baseness so unnatural, so inhuman, that, it seems, you, even *you*, had not the heart to attempt it, till my senses were made the previous sacrifice.

360

Here I made an hesitating effort to speak, laying down my pen.—But she proceeded:—Hear me out, guilty wretch!—abandoned man!—*Man* did I say?—Yet what name else can I? since the mortal worryings of the fiercest beast would have been more natural, and infinitely more welcome, than what you have acted by me; and that with a premeditation and contrivance worthy only of that single heart, which now, *base* as well as ingrateful as thou art, seems to quake within thee.

By my Soul, Belford, my whole frame was shaken: For not only her looks, and her action, but her voice, so solemn, was inexpressibly affecting: And then my cursed guilt, and her innocence, and merit, and rank, and superiority of talents, all stared me at that instant in the face so formidably, that my present account, to which she unexpectedly called me, seemed, as I then thought, to resemble that general one, to which we are told we shall be summoned, when our conscience shall be our accuser.

My dear—My love—I—I—I never—No never—Lips trembling, limbs quaking, voice inward, hesitating, broken—Never surely did miscreant look so *like a* miscreant! While thus she proceeded, waving her snowy hand, with all the graces of moving oratory.

I have no pride in the confusion visible in thy whole person. I have been all the day praying for a composure, if I could not escape from this vile house, that should once more enable me to look up to my destroyer with the consciousness of an innocent sufferer.—Thou seest me, since my wrongs are beyond the power of *words to express*, thou seest me, *calm enough* to wish, that thou may'st continue harassed by the workings of thy own conscience, till effectual repentance take hold of thee, that so thou may'st not forfeit all title to *that* mercy, which thou hast not shewn to the poor creature now before thee, who had so well deserved to meet with a faithful friend, where she met with the worst of enemies.

But tell me (for no doubt thou hast *some* scheme to pursue), Tell me, since I am a prisoner, as I find, in the vilest of houses, and have not a friend to protect or save me, what thou intendest shall become of the remnant of a life not worth the keeping? Tell me, if yet there are more evils reserved for me; and if the ruin of my soul, that my father's curse may be fulfilled, is to complete the triumphs of so vile a confederacy?—Answer me!—Say, if thou hast courage to speak out to her whom thou hast ruined, tell me, what *further* I am to suffer from thy barbarity?

She stopped here; and, sighing, turned her sweet face from me, drying up with her handkerchief those tears which she endeavoured to restrain; and, when she could not, to conceal from my sight.

She then called upon her cousin Morden's name, as if he had warned her against a man of free principles; and walked towards the window; her handkerchief at her eyes: But, turning short towards me, with an air of mingled scorn and majesty—[*What, at the moment, would I have given never to have injured her!*] What amends hast *thou* to propose!—What amends can such a one as Thou make to a person of spirit, or common sense, for the evils thou hast so inhumanly made me suffer?

As soon, Madam—As soon—as—As soon as your uncle—or—not waiting—

Thou wouldst tell me, I suppose—I know what thou wouldst tell me—But thinkest thou, that marriage will satisfy for a guilt like thine? Destitute as thou hast made me both of friends and fortune, I too much despise the wretch, *who could rob himself of his wife's virtue*, to endure the thoughts of thee, in the light thou seemest to hope I will accept thee in!—

I hesitated an interruption: But my meaning died away upon my trembling lips. I could only pronounce the word *marriage*—And thus she proceeded:

Let me therefore know, whether I am to be controuled in the future disposal of myself? Whether, in a country of liberty, as *this*, where the Sovereign of it must not be guilty of *your* wickedness, and where *you* neither durst have attempted it, had I one friend or relation to look upon me, I am to be kept here a prisoner, to sustain fresh injuries? Whether, in a word, you intend to hinder me from going whither my destiny shall lead me?

After a pause; for I was still silent;

Can you not answer me this plain question?—I quit all

claim, all expectation, upon you—What right have you to detain me here?

I could not speak. What could I say to such a question?

Mr. Lovelace To John Belford, Esq;

Monday Morn. 5 o'clock, June 19.

I MUST write on. Nothing else can divert me.

Now indeed do I from my heart wish, that I had never known this lady. But who would have thought there had been such a woman in the world? Of all the sex I have hitherto known, or heard, or read of, it was *once subdued, and always subdued.* The *first* struggle was generally the *last;* or, at least, the subsequent struggles were so much fainter and fainter, that a man would rather have them, than be without them. But how know I yet—

It is now near six—The sun has been illuminating, for several hours, every-thing about me: For that impartial orb shines upon mother Sinclair's house, as well as upon any other: But nothing within me can it illuminate.

At day-dawn I looked thro' the key-hole of my Beloved's door. She had declared she would not put off her cloaths any more in this house. There I beheld her in a sweet slumber, which I hope will prove refreshing to her disturbed senses; sitting in her elbow-chair, her apron over her head, and that supported by one sweet hand, the other hand hanging down upon her side, in a sleepy lifelessness; half of one pretty foot only visible.

See the difference in our cases, thought I! She, the charming injured, can sweetly sleep, while the varlet-injurer cannot close his eyes; and has been trying to no purpose, the whole night, to divert his melancholy, and to fly from himself!

Six o'clock.

Just now Dorcas tells me, that her lady is preparing openly, and without disguise, to be gone. Very probable. The humour she flew away from me in last night, has given me expectation of such an enterprize.

Now, Jack, to be thus hated, and despised!—And if I *have* sinned beyond forgiveness—

But she has sent me a message by Dorcas, that she will meet me in the dining-room; and desires [Odd enough!] that the wench may be present at the conversation that shall pass between us. This message gives me hope.

Nine o'clock.

Confounded art, cunning, villainy!—By my soul, she had like to have slipt thro' my fingers. She meant nothing by her message, but to get Dorcas out of the way, and a clear coast. Is a fancied distress sufficient to justify this lady for dispensing with her principles? Does she not shew me, that she can wilfully deceive, as well as I?

Had she been in the fore-house, and no passage to go thro' to get at the street-door, she had certainly been gone. But her haste betrayed her: For Sally Martin happening to be in the fore-parlour, and hearing a swifter motion than usual, and a rustling of silks, as if from somebody in a hurry, looked out; and seeing who it was, stept between her and the door, and set her back against it.

You must not go, Madam. Indeed you must not.

By what right?—And how dare you?—And such like imperious airs the dear creature gave herself.—While Sally called out for her aunt; and half a dozen voices joined instantly in the cry, for me to hasten down, to hasten down, in a moment.

I was gravely instructing Dorcas above-stairs, and wondering what would be the subject of the conversation which she was to be a witness to, when these outcries reached my ears. And down I flew.—And there was the charming creature, the sweet deceiver, panting for breath, her back against the partition, a parcel in her hand [Women make no excursions without their parcels] Sally, Polly (but Polly obligingly pleading for her) the Mother, Mabell, and Peter (the footman of the house), about her; all, however, keeping their distance; the Mother and Sally between her and the door—In her soft rage the dear Soul repeating, I *will* go!—Nobody has a right—I *will* go!—If you kill me, women, I won't go up again!

As soon as she saw me, she stept a pace or two towards me; Mr. Lovelace, I *will* go! said she—Do you authorize these women—What right have they, or *you* either, to stop me?

I desired them to leave us, all but Dorcas, who was down as soon as I. I then thought it right to assume an air of resolution, having found my tameness so greatly triumphed over. And now, my dear, said I (urging her reluctant feet) be pleased to walk into the fore-parlour. Here, since you will not go up stairs; here, we may *hold our parley:* and Dorcas *be witness to it.*—And now, Madam, seating her, and sticking my hands in my sides, your pleasure!

Insolent Villain! said the furious lady. And, rising, ran to the window, and threw up the sash [She knew not, I suppose, that there were iron rails before the windows]. And, when she found she could not get out into the street, clasping her uplifted hands together—having dropt her parcel—For the Love of God, good honest man!—For the Love of God, mistress—to two passers-by—a poor, poor creature, said she, ruined!—

I clasped her in my arms, people beginning to gather about the window: And then she cried out, Murder! Help! help!—And carried her up to the dining-room, in spite of her little plotting heart (as I may now call it), altho' she violently struggled, catching hold of the banisters here and there, as she could. I would have seated her there; but she sunk down half-motionless, pale as ashes. And a violent burst of tears happily relieved her.

Dorcas wept over her. The wrench was actually moved for her!

This attempt, so resolutely made, alarmed me not a little.

Mrs. Sinclair, and her Nymphs, are much more concerned; because of the reputation of their house, as they call it, having received some insults (broken windows threatened), to make them produce the young creature who cried out.

While the mobbish inquisitors were in the height of their office, the women came running up to me, to know what they should do; a constable being actually fetched.

Get the constable into the parlour, said I, with three or four of the forwardest of the mob, and produce one of the nymphs, onion-eyed, in a moment, with disordered head-dress and handkerchief, and let her own herself the person: The occasion, a female skirmish; but satisfied with the justice done her. Then give a dram or two to each fellow, and all will be well.

Mr. Lovelace
To John Belford, Esq;

THERE is certainly a good deal in the observation, *That it costs a man ten times more pains to be wicked, than it would cost him to be good.* What a confounded number of contrivances have I had recourse to, in order to carry my point with this charming creature; and, after all, how have I puzzled myself by it; and yet am near tumbling into the pit, which it was the end of all my plots to shun! What a happy man had I been with such an excellence, could I have brought my mind to marry when I first prevailed upon her to quit her father's house! But *then*, as I have often reflected, how had I *known*, that a but blossoming beauty, who could carry on a private correspondence, and run such risques with a notorious wild fellow, was not prompted by inclination, which one day might give such a free liver as myself, as much pain to reflect upon, as, at the time, it gave me pleasure?

Monday Night.

How determined is this lady!—Again had she like to have escaped us!—What a fixed resentment!—She only, I find, assumed a little calm, in order to quiet suspicion. She was got down, and actually had unbolted the street-door, before I could get to her; alarmed as I was by Mrs. Sinclair's cookmaid, who was the only one that saw her fly thro' the passage: Yet lightning was not quicker than I.

Again I brought her back to the dining-room, with infinite reluctance on her part. And before her face, ordered a servant to be placed constantly at the bottom of the stairs for the future.

She seemed even choaked with grief and disappointment.

I see, I see, said she, when I had brought her up, what I am to expect from your new professions, O vilest of men!—

Have I offered to you, my beloved creature, any thing that can justify this impatience after a more hopeful calm?

She wrung her hands. She disordered her head-dress. She tore her ruffles. She was in a perfect phrensy.

I dreaded her returning malady: But intreaty rather exasperating, I affected an angry air.—I bid her expect the worst she had to fear—And was menacing on, in hopes to intimidate her, when, dropping down at my feet,

'Twill be a mercy, said she, the highest act of mercy you can do, to kill me outright upon this spot—This happy spot, as I will, in my last moments, call it!—Then, baring, with a still more frantic violence, part of her inchanting neck—Here, here, said the soul-harrowing beauty, let thy pointed mercy enter! And I will thank thee, and forgive thee for all the dreadful past! —With my latest gasp will I forgive and thank thee!—Or help *me* to the means, and I will myself put out of thy way so miserable a wretch! And bless thee for those means!

Why all this extravagant passion, why all these exclamations? Have I offered any new injury to you, my dearest life! What a phrensy is this! Am I not ready to make you all the reparation that I *can* make you? Had I not reason to hope—

No, no, no, no—half a dozen times, as fast as she could speak.

Had I not reason to hope, that you were meditating upon the means of making me happy, and yourself not miserable, rather than upon a flight so causeless and so precipitate?—

No, no, no, no, as before, shaking her head with wild impatience, as resolved not to attend to what I said.

My resolutions are so honourable, if you will permit them

to take effect, that I need not be solicitous whither you go, if you will but permit my visits, and receive my vows. And, God is my witness, that I bring you not back from the door with any view to your dishonour, but the contrary: And this moment I will send for a minister to put an end to all your doubts and fears.

Say this, and say a thousand times more, and bind every word with a solemn appeal to that God, whom thou art accustomed to invoke to the truth of the vilest falshoods, and all will still be short of what thou *hast* vowed and promised to me. And, were *not* my heart to abhor thee, and to rise against thee, for thy *perjuries*, as it *does*, I would not, I tell thee once more, I would not, bind my soul in covenant with such a man, for a thousand worlds!

Compose yourself, however, Madam; for *your own sake*, compose yourself. Permit me to raise you up; *abhorred* as I am of your soul!—

Nay, if I must not touch you; for she wildly slapt my hands; but with such a sweet passionate air, her bosom heaving and throbbing as she looked up to me, that altho' I was most sincerely enraged, I could with transport have pressed her to mine.

If I must not touch you, I will not.—But depend upon it (and I assumed the sternest air I could assume, to try what *that* would do), depend upon it, Madam, that this is not the way to avoid the evils you dread. Let me do what I will, I cannot be used worse!—Dorcas, be gone!

She arose, Dorcas being about to withdraw, and wildly caught hold of her arm: O Dorcas! If thou art of mine own Sex, leave me not, I charge thee!—Then quitting Dorcas, down she threw herself upon her knees, in the furthermost corner of the room, clasping a chair with her face laid upon the bottom of it!—O where can I be safe?—Where, where can I be safe, from this man of violence?—

This gave Dorcas an opportunity to confirm herself in her lady's confidence: The wench threw herself at my feet, while I seemed in violent wrath; and, embracing my knees, Kill me, Sir, kill me, Sir, if you please!—I must throw myself in your way, to save my lady.

This, humoured by me, Begone, devil!—Officious devil, begone!—startled the dear creature; who, snatching up hastily her head from the chair, and as hastily popping it down again in terror, hit her nose, I suppose, against the edge of the chair; and it gushed out with blood, running in a stream down her bosom; she herself too much affrighted to heed it!—

Never was mortal man in such terror and agitation as I; for I instantly concluded, that she had stabbed herself with some concealed instrument.

I ran to her in a wild agony—For Dorcas was frighted out of all her mock interposition—

What have you done!—O what have you done!—Look up to me, my dearest life!—Sweet injured innocence, look up to me! What have you done!—Long will I not survive you!—And I was upon the point of drawing my sword to dispatch myself, when I discovered—[What an unmanly blockhead does this charming creature make me at her pleasure!] that all I apprehended was but a bloody nose, which, as far as I know (for it could not be stopped in a quarter of an hour), may have saved her head, and her intellects.

But I see by this scene, that the sweet creature is but a pretty coward at bottom; and that I can terrify her out of her virulence against me, whenever I put on sternness and anger: But then, as a qualifier to the advantage this gives me over her, I find myself to be a coward too, which I had not before suspected, since I was capable of being so easily terrified by the apprehensions of her offering violence to herself.

Mr. Lovelace
To John Belford, Esq;

BUT, with all this dear creature's resentment against me, I cannot, for my heart, think but she will get all over, and consent to enter the pale with me. Were she even to die to-morrow, and to know she should, would not a woman of her sense, of her punctilio, and in her situation, and of so proud a family, rather die married, than otherwise?—No doubt but she would; altho' she were to hate the man ever so heartily. If so, there is now but one man in the world whom she can have—And that is *Me.*

Now I talk [*familiar writing* is but *talking*, Jack] thus glibly of entering the pale, thou wilt be ready to question me, I know, as to my intentions on this head.

As much of my heart, as I know of it myself, will I tell thee. —When I am *from* her, I cannot still help hesitating about marriage, and I even frequently resolve against it; and am resolved to press my favourite scheme for cohabitation. But when I am *with* her, I am ready to say, to swear, and to do, whatever I think will be most acceptable to her: And were a parson at hand, I should plunge at once, no doubt of it, into the state.

A wife at any time, I used to say. I had ever confidence and vanity enough, to think, that no woman breathing could deny her hand, when I held out mine. I am confoundedly mortified to find, that this lady is able to hold me at bay, and to refuse all my *honest* vows.

The lady tells Dorcas, that her heart is broken; and that she shall live but a little while. I think nothing of that, if we marry. In the first place, she knows not what a mind unapprehensive will do for her, in a state to which all the sex look forward with high satisfaction. A few months heart's-ease will give my charmer a quite different notion of things: And I dare say, as I have heretofore said, once married, and I am married for life.

I will allow, that her pride, in *one* sense, has suffered abasement: But her triumph is the greater in every other. And while I can think that all her trials are but additions to her honour, and that I have laid the foundations of her glory in my own shame, can I be called cruel, if I am *not* affected with her grief, as some men would be?

And for what should her heart be broken? Her will is unviolated:—At *present*, however, her will is unviolated. The destroying of good habits, and the introducing of bad, to the corrupting of the whole heart, is the violation. That her will is not to be corrupted, that her mind is not to be debased, she has hitherto unquestionably proved.

What nonsense then to suppose, that such a mere notional violation as she has suffered, should be able to cut asunder the strings of life?

O Jack! had I an imperial diadem, I swear to thee, that I would give it up, even to my *enemy*, to have one charming boy by this Lady. And should she *escape me*, and no such effect follow, my revenge on her family, and, in *such* a case, on herself, would be incomplete, and I should reproach myself as long as I lived.

Were I to be sure, that this foundation is laid [And why may I not hope it is?], I should not doubt to have her still (should she withstand her day of grace) on my own conditions: Nor should I, if it were so, question that *revived* affection in *her*, which a woman seldom fails to have for the father of her first child, whether born in wedlock, or out of it.

And pr'ythee, Jack, see in this *aspiration*, let me call it, a distinction in my favour from other rakes; who almost to a man follow their inclinations, without troubling themselves about consequences. In imitation, as one would think, of the strutting villain of a bird, which from feathered lady to feathered lady pursues his imperial pleasures, leaving it to his sleek paramours to hatch the genial product, in holes and corners of their own finding out.

Mr. Lovelace
To John Belford, Esq;

Thursday Night.

CONFOUNDEDLY out of humour with this perverse lady. Nor wilt thou blame me, if thou art my friend.

With great difficulty I prevailed upon her to favour me with her company for one half-hour this evening. The necessity

I was under to go down to M. Hall, was the subject I wanted to talk to her upon.

I told her, that as she had been so good as to promise, that she would endeavour to make herself easy till she saw the Thursday in next week over,—I hoped, that she would not scruple to oblige me with her word, that I should find her here, at my return from M. Hall.

Indeed she would make me no such promise. Nothing of *this house* was mentioned to me, said she: You know it was not. And do you think that I would have given *my consent to my imprisonment in it?*

I was plaguily nettled, and disappointed too. If I go not down to M. Hall, Madam, you'll have no scruple to stay here, I suppose, till Thursday is over?

If I cannot help myself, I must.—But I insist upon being permitted to go out of this house whether *you* leave it or not.

Well, Madam, then I will comply with your commands. And I will go out this very evening, in quest of lodgings that you shall have no objection to.

I will have no lodgings of your providing, Sir—I will go to Mrs. Moore's at Hamstead.

Mrs. Moore's, Madam?—I have no objection to Mrs. Moore's.—But will you give me your promise, to admit me there to your presence?

As I do here—When I cannot help it.

Do you think yourself in my power, Madam?

If I were not—And there she stopt—

Dearest creature, speak out—I beseech you, dearest creature, speak out.—

She was silent; her charming face all in a glow.

Have you, Madam, any reliance upon my honour?

Still silent.

You hate me, Madam. You despise me more than you do the most odious of God's creatures.

She arose. I beseech you, let me withdraw.

I snatched her hand, rising, and pressed it first to my lips, and then to my heart, in wild disorder. She might have felt the bounding mischief ready to burst its bars—You *shall* go—To

your own apartment, if you please—But, by the great God of
Heaven, I will accompany you thither.

She trembled—Pray, pray, Mr. Lovelace, don't terrify me
so!

Be seated, Madam! I beseech you be seated!—

I will sit down—

Do then, Madam—Do then—All my soul in my eyes, and
my heart's blood throbbing at my finger ends.

I will—I will—You hurt me—Pray, Mr. Lovelace, don't—
don't frighten me so—And down she sat, trembling; my hand
still grasping hers.

I hung over her throbbing bosom, and putting my other
arm round her waist—And you say, you hate me, Madam—And
you say, you despise me!—And you say, you promised me
nothing—

Yes, yes, I did promise you—Let me not be held down thus
—You see I sat down when you bid me—Why (struggling) need
you hold me down thus?—I did promise *to endeavour to be
easy till Thursday was over!* But you won't let me!—How can
I be easy?—Pray, let me not be thus terrified.

And what, Madam, *meant* you by your promise? Did you
mean any-thing in my favour?—You designed, that I should,
at the time, *think* you did. Did you mean anything in my favour,
Madam?—Did you intend, that I should *think* you did?

Let go my hand, Sir—Take away your arm from about me,
struggling, yet trembling—*Why do you gaze upon me so?*

Then pausing, and gaining more spirit, Let me go, said she;
I am but a woman—but a weak woman—But my life is in my
own power, tho' my person is not—I will not be thus constrained.

You shall not, Madam, quitting her hand, bowing, but my
heart at my mouth, and hoping farther provocation.

She arose, and was hurrying away.

I pursue you not, Madam—I will try your generosity.—
Stop—Return—This moment stop, return, if, Madam, you
would not make me desperate.

She stopt at the door; burst into tears—O Lovelace!—How,
how, have I deserved—

Be *pleased*, dearest angel, to return.

She came back—But with declared reluctance; and imputing her compliance to terror.

Terror, Jack, as I have heretofore found out, tho' I have so little benefited by the discovery, must be my resort, if she make it necessary—Nothing else will do with the inflexible charmer.

She seated herself over-against me; extremely discomposed. —But indignation had a visible predominance in her features.

I was going towards her, with a countenance intendedly changed to love and softness: Sweetest, dearest angel, were my words, in the tenderest accent:—But, rising up, she insisted upon my being seated at distance from her.

I obeyed—and begged her hand over the table, to my extended hand; to see, as I said, if in any thing she would oblige me—But nothing gentle, soft, or affectionate would do. She refused me her hand!—Was she wise, Jack, to confirm to me, that nothing but terror would do?

Do you intend, Madam, to honour me with your hand, in your uncle's presence, or do you not?

My heart and my hand shall never be separated. Why, think you, did I stand in opposition to the will of my best my natural friends?

I know what you mean, Madam—Am I then as hateful to you as the vile Solmes?

Ask me not such a question, Mr. Lovelace.

I *must* be answered. Am I as hateful to you, as the vile Solmes?

Why do you call Mr. Solmes vile?

Don't *you* think him so, Madam?

Why should I? Did Mr. Solmes ever do vilely by me?

Dearest creature! don't distract me by hateful comparisons! And perhaps by a more hateful preference.

Don't you, Sir, put questions to me, that you know I will answer truly, tho' my answer were ever so much to enrage you.

My heart, Madam, my soul is all yours at present. But you *must* give me hope, that your promise, in your own construction, binds you, no *new cause* to the contrary, to be mine on Thursday. How else can I leave you?

Let me go to Hamstead; and trust to my favour.

May I trust to it?—Say, only, *May* I trust to it?

How will you trust to it, if you extort an answer to this question?

Say only, dearest creature, say only, *may* I trust to your favour, if you go to Hamstead?

How *dare* you, Sir, if I must speak out, expect a promise of favour from me?—What a mean creature must you think me, after your ingrateful baseness to me, were I to give you such a promise?

Then standing up, Thou hast made me, O vilest of men! (her hands clasped, and a face crimsoned over with indignation) an inmate of the vilest of houses—Nevertheless, while I am in it, I shall have a heart incapable of any thing but abhorrence of *that* and of *thee!*

And round her looked the angel, and upon me, with fear in her sweet aspect of the consequence of her free declaration.—But what a devil must I have been, I, who love bravery in a man, had I not been more struck with admiration of her fortitude at the instant, than stimulated by revenge?

If you have any intention to oblige me, leave me at my own liberty, and let me not be detained in this abominable house. To be constrained as I have been constrained! To be brought up by force, and to be bruised, in my own defence against such illegal violence!—I dare to die, Lovelace—And the person that fears not death is not to be intimidated into a meanness unworthy of her heart and principles!

Wonderful creature! But why, Madam, did you lead me to hope for something favourable for next Thursday?—Once more, make me not desperate—You *may,* you *may*—But do not, do not make me brutally threaten you!—Do not, do not make me desperate!

My aspect, I believe, threatened still more than my words. I was rising—She arose—Mr. Lovelace, be pacified—You are even more dreadful than the Lovelace I have long dreaded—Let me retire—I ask your *leave* to retire—You really frighten me—Yet I give you no hope—From my heart I ab—

Say not, Madam, you *abhor* me. You must, for your own

sake, conceal your hatred—At least not avow it.—I seized her hand.

Let me retire—Let me retire, said she—in a manner out of breath.

I will only say, Madam, that I refer myself to your generosity. My heart is not to be trusted at this instant. As a mark of my submission to your will, you shall, *if you please*, withdraw.—But I will not go to M. Hall—Live or die my Lord M. I will not go to M. Hall.—But will attend the effect of your promise. Remember, Madam, you have promised *to endeavour to make yourself easy, till you see the event of next Thursday*— Next Thursday, remember, your uncle comes up, to see us married.—*That's the event*—You think ill of your Lovelace— Do not, Madam, suffer your own morals to be degraded by the *infection*, as you called it, of his example.

Away flew the charmer, with this half-permission—And no doubt thought, that she had an escape—nor without reason.

I knew not for half an hour what to do with myself. Vexed at the heart, nevertheless, now she was from me, when I reflected upon her hatred of me, and her defiances, that I suffered myself to be so over-awed, checked, restrained—

But I will go down to these women—and perhaps suffer myself to be laughed at by them.

Mr. Lovelace
To John Belford, Esq;

JUST come from the women.

"Have I gone so far, and am I afraid to go farther?—Have I not already, as it is evident by her behaviour, sinned beyond forgiveness?—A woman's tears used to be to me but as water sprinkled on a glowing fire, which gives it a fiercer and brighter blaze: What defence has this lady, but her tears and her eloquence? She was before taken at *no weak* advantage. She was *insensible* in her moments of trial. *Had* she been sensible, she *must* have been sensible. So they say. The methods taken with her have augmented her glory and her pride. She has now a tale to tell, that she *may* tell, with honour to herself. She can look me into confusion, without being conscious of so much as a *thought*, which she need to be ashamed of."

This, Jack, is the substance of my conference with the women.

And yet I have promised, as thou seest, that she shall set out to Hamstead as soon as she pleases in the morning, and that without condition on her side.

Dost thou ask, What I meant by this promise?

No *new cause* arising, was the proviso on my side, thou'lt remember. But there *will be* a new cause.

Suppose Dorcas should drop the promisory-note given her by her Lady? Servants, especially those who cannot read or write, are the most careless people in the world of written papers. Suppose I take it up?—At a time, too, that I was determined that the dear creature should be her own mistress?—Will not this detection be a *new cause?*—A cause that will carry against her the appearance of ingratitude with it!

That she designed it a *secret to me*, argues a *fear of detection*, and indirectly a *sense of guilt*. I wanted a pretence. Can I have a better? If I am in a violent passion upon the detection, is not passion an universally allowed extenuator of violence?

Mr. Lovelace To John Belford , Esq;

JUST come from my charmer. She will not suffer me to say half the obliging, the tender things, which my honest heart is ready to overflow with. A confounded situation, that, when a man finds himself in humour to be eloquent, and pathetic at the same time; yet cannot engage the mistress of his fate to lend an ear to his fine speeches.

She claimed the performance of my promise, the moment

she saw me, of *permitting* her (haughtily she spoke the word) to go to Hamstead, as soon as I were gone to Berks.

Most chearfully I renewed it.

She desired me to give orders in her hearing.

I sent for Dorcas and Will. They came.—Do you both take notice (But, perhaps, Sir, I may take *you* with me), that your lady is to be obeyed in all her commands. She purposes to return to Hamstead as soon as I am gone—

And then (the servants being withdrawn) I urged her again for the assurance, that she would meet me at the altar on Thursday next. But to no purpose. May she not thank herself for all that may follow?

One favour, however, I would not be denied; to be admitted to pass the evening with her.

All sweetness and obsequiousness will I be on this occasion. My whole soul shall be poured out to move her to forgive me. If she will not, and if the promisory-note should fall in my way, my revenge will doubtless take total possession of me.

Mr. Lovelace
To John Belford, Esq;

Friday Night, or rather Sat. Morn. 1 o'Clock.

I THOUGHT I should not have had either time or inclination to write another line before I got to M. Hall. But have the first; must find the last; since I can neither sleep, nor do anything but write, if I can do that. I am most *confoundedly* out of humour. The reason let it follow; if it will follow—No preparation for it, from me.

I tried by gentleness and love to soften—What?—Marble. A heart incapable either of love or gentleness. Her past injuries for ever in her head. Ready to receive a favour; the permission to go to Hamstead; but neither to deserve it, nor return any. So my scheme of the gentle kind was soon given over.

I then wanted her to provoke me: Like a coward boy, who waits for the first blow, before he can persuade himself to fight, I half-challenged her to challenge or defy me: She seemed aware of her danger; and would not directly brave my resentment: But kept such a middle course, that I neither could find a pretence to offend, nor reason to hope: Yet she believed my tale, that her uncle would come to Kentish Town; and seemed not to apprehend, that Tomlinson was an impostor.

She was very uneasy, upon the whole, in my company: Wanted often to break from me: Yet so held me to my promise of permitting her to go to Hamstead, that I knew not how to get off it; altho' it was impossible, in my precarious situation with her, to think of performing it.

Poke thy damn'd nose forward into the event, if thou wilt—Curse me if thou shalt have it, till its proper time and place—And too soon then.

She had hardly got into her chamber, but I found a little paper, as I was going into mine; which I took up; and, opening it (for it was carefully pinned in another paper), what should it be, but a promisory note, given as a bribe, with a further promise of a diamond ring, to induce Dorcas to favour her mistress's escape?

How my temper changed in a moment!—Ring, ring, ring, ring, my bell, with a violence enough to break the string, and as if the house were on fire.

Every devil frighted into active life: The whole house in an uproar: Up runs Will.—Sir—Sir—Sir!—Eyes goggling, mouth distended—Bid the damn'd toad Dorcas come hither (as I stood at the stair-head) in a horrible rage, and out of breath, cried I.

In sight came the trembling devil—but standing aloof, from the report made her by Will. of the passion I was in, as well as from what she heard.

Flash came out my sword immediately; for I had it ready on—Cursed, confounded, villainous, bribery and corruption!—

Up runs she to her lady's door, screaming out for safety and protection.

Good your honour, interposed Will. for God's sake!—O Lord, O Lord!—receiving a good cuff.—

Take that, varlet, for saving the ungrateful *wretch* from my vengeance!—

Up ran two or three of the sisterhood, What's the matter! What's the matter!

The matter! (for still my beloved opened not her door; on the contrary, drew another bolt) This *abominable* Dorcas!— (Call her aunt up!—Let her see what a traitress she has placed about me!—And let her bring the toad to answer for herself)— has taken a bribe, a provision for life, to betray her trust; by that means to perpetuate a quarrel between a man and his wife, and frustrate for ever all hopes of reconciliation between us!

Let me perish, Belford, if I have patience to proceed with the farce!

Up came the aunt puffing and blowing!—She never knew such a plotting perverse lady in her life!—Well might servants be at the pass they were, when such ladies as Mrs. Lovelace made no conscience of corrupting them. For *her* part, she desired no mercy for the wretch: No niece of hers, if she were not faithful to her trust!—But what was the proof?—

She was shewn the paper—

But too evident!—Cursed, cursed Toad, Devil, Jade, passed from each mouth:—And the vileness of the *corrupted*, and the unworthiness of the *corruptress*, were inveighed against.

Up we all went, passing the lady's door into the dining-room, to proceed to tryal—

Stamp, stamp, stamp up, each on her heels; Rave, rave, rave, every tongue!—

Up was brought Dorcas (whimpering) between two, both bawling out—You must go!—You shall go!—'Tis fit you should answer for yourself!—You are a discredit to all worthy servants!—as they pulled and pushed her up stairs.—She whining, I cannot see his honour!—I cannot look so good and so generous a gentleman in the face!—O how shall I bear my aunt's ravings!—

Come up, and be d—n'd—Bring her forward, her imperial judge!—What a plague, it is the *detection*, not the *crime*, that confounds you. You could be quiet enough for days together, as I see by the date, under the villainy. Tell me ingrateful devil, tell me, who made the first advances.

Ay, disgrace to my family and blood, cried the old one! —Tell his Honour! Tell the truth;—Who made the first advances!—

Ay, cursed creature, cried Sally, Who made the first advances?

I have betrayed one trust already!—O let me not betray another!—My lady is a good lady!—O let not *her* suffer!—

But suppose, Sir, said Sally, you have my lady and the wench face to face! You see she cares not to confess.

O my *carelessness!* cried Dorcas—Don't let my poor lady suffer!—Indeed if you all knew what I know, you would say, Her ladyship has been cruelly treated—

Your Lady *won't*, she *dare* not come out to save you, cried Sally; tho' it is more his Honour's mercy, than your desert, if he does not cut your vile throat this instant.

Say, repeated Polly, was it your lady, that made the first advances, or was it you, you creature?—

Just then, we heard the lady's door unbar, unlock, unbolt—

Now, Sir!

Now, Mr. Lovelace!

Now, Sir! from every encouraging mouth!—

But, O Jack, Jack, Jack! I can write no more!

If you must have it all you must!

Now, Belford, see us all sitting in judgment resolved to punish the fair briberess—I, and the mother, the hitherto *dreaded* mother, the nieces Sally, Polly, the traitress Dorcas, and Mabell, a guard, as it were, over her, that she might not run away, and hide herself:—All pre-determined, and of *necessity* pre-determined, from the journey I was going to take, and my precarious situation with her:—And hear her *unbolt, unlock, unbar,* the door; then, as it proved afterwards, put the key into the lock on the outside, lock the door, and put it in her pocket; Will. I knew, below, who would give me notice, if, while we were all above, she should mistake her way, and go down stairs, instead of coming into the dining-room: The street-doors also doubly secured, and every shutter to the windows round the house fastened, that no noise or screaming should be heard [Such was the brutal preparation]—And then *hear* her step towards us, and instantly *see* her enter among us, confiding in her own innocence; and with a majesty in her person and manner, that is *natural* to her; but which then shone out in all its glory!—Every tongue silent, every eye awed, every heart quaking, mine, in a particular manner, sunk, throbless, and twice below its usual region, to once at my throat:—A shameful recreant!—She silent too, looking round her, first on Me; then on the mother, as no longer fearing her; then on Sally, Polly; and the culprit Dorcas!—Such the glorious power of innocence exerted at that awful moment!

She would have spoken, but could not, looking down my guilt into confusion. A mouse might have been heard passing over the floor, her own light feet and rustling silks could not have prevented it; for she seemed to tread air, and to be all soul—She passed to the door, and back towards me, two or three times, before speech could get the better of indignation; and at last, after twice or thrice hemming, to recover her articulate voice—O thou contemptible and abandoned Lovelace, thinkest thou that I see not thro' this poor villainous plot of thine, and of these thy wicked accomplices?

Thou, woman, looking at the mother, once my terror! always my dislike! but now my detestation! shouldst once more (for thine perhaps was the preparation) have provided for me intoxicating potions, to rob me of my senses—

And then, *turning to me*, Thou, wretch, mightest more securely have depended upon such a low contrivance as this!—

And ye, vile women, who perhaps have been the ruin, body and soul, of hundreds of innocents (you shew me *how*, in full assembly), know, that I am not married—ruined as I am, by your helps, I bless God, I am *not* married, to this miscreant—And I have friends that will demand my honour at your hands!—And to whose authority I will apply; for none has this man over me. Look to it then, what further insults you offer me, or incite him to offer me. I am a person, tho' thus vilely betrayed, of rank and fortune. I never will be his; and, to your utter ruin, will find friends to pursue you: And now I have this full proof of your detestable wickedness, and have heard your base incitements, will have no mercy upon you!

They could not laugh at the poor figure I made.—Lord! how every devil, conscience-shaken, trembled!—

And as for thee, thou vile Dorcas! Thou *double* deceiver!— whining out thy pretended love for me!—Begone, wretch!— Nobody will hurt thee!—Begone, I say!—Thou hast too well acted thy part to be blamed by *any* here but myself—Steal away into darkness! No inquiry after this will be made, whose the first advances, thine or mine.

And, as I hope to live, the wench, confoundedly frightened, slunk away; so did her centinel Mabell; tho' I, endeavouring to rally, cried out for Dorcas to stay: But I believe the devil could not have stopt her, when an angel bid her begone.

Madam, said I, let me tell you; and was advancing towards her, with a fierce aspect, most cursedly vexed, and ashamed too—

But she turned to me; Stop where thou art, O vilest and most abandoned of men!—Stop where thou art!—Nor, with that determined face, offer to touch me, if thou wouldst not that I should be a corpse at thy feet!

To my astonishment, she held forth a penknife in her hand, the point to her own bosom, grasping resolutely the whole handle, so that there was no offering to take it from her.

I offer not mischief to any-body but myself. You, Sir, and ye, women, are safe from every violence of mine. The Law shall be all my resource: The LAW, and she spoke the word with emphasis, that to such people carries natural terror with it, and now struck a panic into them.

No wonder, since those who will damn themselves to procure ease and plenty in this world, will tremble at every thing that seems to threaten their methods of obtaining that ease and plenty.—

"The LAW only shall be my refuge!—"

The infamous mother whispered me, that it were better to *make terms* with this *strange* lady, and let her go.

Sally, notwithstanding all her impudent bravery at other times, said, *If* Mr. Lovelace had told *them* what was *not true* of her being his wife—

And Polly Horton: That she must *needs* say, the lady, if she were *not* my wife, had been very much injured; that was all.

That is not now a matter to be disputed, cried I: You and I know, Madam—

We do,—said she; and I thank God, I am *not* thine:—*Once more*, I thank God for it! I have no doubt of the further baseness that thou hadst intended me, by this vile and low trick: But I have my Senses, Lovelace: And from my heart, I despise thee, thou very poor Lovelace!—How canst thou stand in my presence!—Thou, that—

Madam, Madam, Madam—These are insults not to be borne—And was approaching her. She withdrew to the door, and set her back against it, holding the pointed knife to her heaving bosom; while the women held me, beseeching me not to provoke the violent lady—For their *house* sake, and be curs'd to them, they besought me—and all three hung upon me—While the truly-heroic lady braved me, at that distance:

Approach me, Lovelace, with resentment, if thou wilt. I dare die. It is in defence of my honour. God will be merciful to my poor soul! I expect no mercy from thee! I have gained this distance, and two steps nearer me, and thou shalt see what I dare do!—

Leave me, women, to myself, and to my angel!—They retired at a distance—O my beloved creature, how you terrify me!—Holding out my arms, and kneeling on one knee—Not a step, not a step further, except to receive my death at that injured hand that threatens its own.—I am a villain! the blackest of villains!—Say you will sheath your knife in the injurer's, not the injured's, heart; and then will I indeed approach you, but not else.

Unawares to myself, I had moved onward to my angel—And dost thou, dost thou, *still* disclaiming, *still* advancing—

Dost thou, dost thou, *still* insidiously move towards me; and her hand was extended I dare—I dare—Not rashly neither—My heart from *principle* abhors the act, which *thou* makest *necessary!*—God, in thy mercy!—Lifting up her eyes, and hands— God, in thy mercy!—

I threw myself to the farther end of the room. An ejaculation, a silent ejaculation, employing her thoughts that moment; Polly says the whites of her lovely eyes were only visible: And, in the instant that she extended her hand, *assuredly* to strike the fatal blow [How the very recital terrifies me!], she cast her eye towards me, and saw me at the utmost distance the room would allow, and heard my broken voice [My voice was utterly broken; nor knew I what I said, or whether to the purpose or not]: And her charming cheeks, that were all in a glow before, turned pale, as if terrified at her own purpose; and lifting up her eyes—Thank God!—Thank God! said the angel—Delivered *for the present;* for the *present* delivered from myself!—Keep, Sir, keep that distance (looking down towards me, who was prostrate on the floor, my heart pierced, as with an hundred daggers!): That distance has saved a life; to what reserved, the Almighty only knows!—

To *be* happy, Madam; and to *make* happy!—And O let me but hope for your favour for to-morrow—I will put off my journey till then—And may God—

This I say, of This you may assure yourself, I never, never *will be yours.*—And let me hope, that I may be intitled to the performance of your promise, to permit me to leave this *innocent* house, as one called it (but long have my ears been accustomed to such inversions of words) as soon as the day breaks.

Did my perdition depend upon it, that you cannot, Madam, but upon terms. And I hope you will not terrify me—Still dreading the accursed knife.

Nothing less than an attempt upon my honour shall make me desperate.—I have no view, but to defend my honour: With such a view only I entered into treaty with your infamous agent below. The resolution you have seen, I trust, God will give me again upon the same occasion. But for a *less,* I wish not for it. Only take notice, women, that I am no wife of *this man:* Basely as he has used me, I am not his wife. He has no authority over me. If he go away by-and-by, and you act by his authority to detain me, look to it.

Then, taking one of the lights, she turned from us; and away she went, unmolested.—Not a soul was *able* to molest her.

Mabell saw her, tremblingly, and in a hurry, take the key of her chamber-door out of her pocket, and unlock it; and, as soon as she entered, heard her double lock, bar, and bolt it.

By her taking out her key, when she came out of her chamber to us, she no doubt suspected my design: Which was, to have carried her in my arms thither, if she made such force necessary, after I had intimidated her; and to have been her companion for that night.

She was to have had several bedchamber-women to assist to undress her upon occasion: But, from the moment she entered the dining-room with so much intrepidity, it was absolutely impossible to think of prosecuting my villainous designs against her.

This, This, Belford, was the hand I made of a contrivance from which I expected so much!—And now am I ten times worse off than before.

Thou never sawest people in thy life look so like fools upon one another, as the mother, her partners, and I, did for a few minutes. And at last, the two devilish Nymphs broke out into insulting ridicule upon me; while the old wretch was concerned for her house, the reputation of her house. I cursed them all together; and, retiring to my chamber, locked myself in.

And now it is time to set out: All I have gained, detection, disgrace, fresh guilt by repeated perjuries, and to be despised by her I *doat upon;* and, what is still worse to a proud heart, by *myself.*

Success, success in projects, is every thing. What an admirable fellow did I think myself till now! Even for this scheme among the rest! But how pitifully foolish does it appear to me now!—Scratch out, erase, never to be read, every part of my preceding letters, where I have boastingly mentioned it.—And never presume to railly me upon the cursed subject: For I cannot bear it.

But for the lady, by my soul I love her, I admire her, more than ever!—I *must* have her. I *will* have her still—*With* honour, or *without*, as I have often vowed.—My cursed fright at her accidental bloody nose, so lately, put her upon improving upon me thus: Had she threatened ME, I should soon have been master of *one* arm, and *in both!*—But for so sincere a virtue to threaten *herself*, and not offer to intimidate *any other*, and with so much presence of mind, as to distinguish, in the very passionate intention, the necessity of the act in defence of her *honour*, and so *fairly* to disavow *lesser* occasions; shewed such a deliberation, such a choice, such a principle; and then keeping me so watchfully at a distance, that I could not seize her hand, so soon as she could have given the fatal blow; how impossible not to be subdued by so *true* and so *discreet* a magnanimity!

But she is not *gone;* shall not go. I will press her with letters for the Thursday—She shall yet be mine, legally mine. For, as to cohabitation, there is now no such thing to be thought of.

The Captain shall give her away, as proxy for her uncle. My Lord will die. My fortune will help my *will*, and set me above every-thing and every-body.

But here is the curse:—She despises me, Jack!—What man, as I have heretofore said, can bear to be despised—especially by his wife?—O Lord! O Lord! What a hand, what a cursed hand, have I made of this plot!—And here ends

The history of the Lady and the Penknife!!!—The devil take the penknife!—It goes against me to say,

God bless the Lady!

Near 5, Sat. Morn.

Mr. Lovelace
To Miss Clarissa Harlowe

Superscribed, To Mrs. Lovelace.

M. Hall, Sunday Night, June 25.

My dearest Love,

I CANNOT find words to express how much I am mortified at the return of my messenger, without a line from you.

Thursday is so near, that I will send messenger after messenger every four hours, till I have a favourable answer; the one to meet the other, till its eve arrives, to know if I may venture to appear in your presence, with the hope of having my wishes answered on that day.

Your love, Madam, I neither expect, nor ask for; nor will, till my future behaviour gives you cause to think I deserve it. All I at present presume to wish, is, To have it in my power to do you all the justice I can now do you: And to your generosity will I leave it, to reward me, as I shall merit, with your affection.

At present, revolving my poor behaviour of Friday night before you, I think I should sooner choose to go to my last audit, unprepared for it as I am, than to appear in your presence, unless you give me some hope, that I shall be received as your elected husband, rather than (however deserved) as a detested criminal.

Let me therefore propose an expedient, in order to spare my own confusion; and to spare you the necessity for that soul-harrowing recrimination, which I cannot stand, and which must be disagreeable to yourself—To name the church, and I will have every thing in readiness; so that our next interview will be, in a manner, at the very altar; and then you will have the kind husband to forgive for the faults of the ingrateful lover. If your resentment be still too high to write more, let it only be, in your own dear hand, these words, St. Martin's church,

Thursday—or these, St. Giles's church, Thursday; nor will I insist upon any inscription, or subscription, or so much as the initials of your name. This shall be all the favour I will expect, till the dear hand itself is given to mine, in presence of that Being whom I invoke as a witness of the inviolable faith and honour of

Your adoring

Lovelace

Mr. Lovelace To Miss Clarissa Harlowe

Superscribed, To Mrs. Lovelace.

M. Hall, Wedn. Morn. One o'Clock, June 28.

NOT one line, my dearest life, not one word, in answer to three letters I have written! The time is now so short, that this *must* be the last letter that can reach you on this side of the important hour that might make us legally one.

My friend Mr. Belford is apprehensive, that he cannot wait upon you in time, by reason of some urgent affairs of his own.

I the less regret the disappointment, because I have procured a *more* acceptable person, as I hope, to attend you; Captain Tomlinson I mean: To whom I had applied for this purpose, before I had Mr. Belford's answer.

I was the more solicitous to obtain this favour from him, because of the office he is to take upon him, as I humbly presume to hope, to-morrow. I acquainted him with my unhappy situation with you; and desired, that he would shew me, on this occasion, that I had as much of his favour and friendship, as your uncle had; since the whole treaty must be broken off, if he could not prevail upon you in my behalf.

I ought not (but cannot help it) to anticipate the pleasure

Mr. Tomlinson proposes to himself, in acquainting you with the likelihood there is of your mother's seconding your uncle's views. For, it seems, he has privately communicated to her his laudable intentions: And *her* resolution depends, as well as *his*, upon what to-morrow will produce.

Disappoint not then, I beseech you, for an hundred persons sakes, as well as for mine, *that* uncle, and *that* mother, whose displeasure I have heard you so often deplore.

You may think it impossible for me to reach London by the canonical hour. If it should, the ceremony may be performed in your own apartment, at any time in the day, or at night: So that Captain Tomlinson may have it to aver to your uncle, that it was performed on his anniversary.

Tell but the Captain, that you *forbid me not* to attend you: And that shall be sufficient for bringing to you, on the wings of Love,

> *Your ever-grateful and affectionate*
>
> > > *Lovelace*

Mr. Mowbray
To Robert Lovelace, Esq;

> Wednesday, 12 o'clock.

Dear Lovelace,

I HAVE plaguy news to acquaint thee with. Miss Harlowe is gon off!—Quite gon, by my soul!—I have not time for particulars, your servent being going off. But iff I had, we are not yet come to the bottom of the matter. The ladies here are all blubbering like devils, accusing one another most confoundedly: Whilst Belton and I damn them all together in thy name.

If thou shouldst hear that thy fellow Will. is taken dead out of some horse-pond, and Dorcas cutt down from her bed's teaster, from dangling in her own garters, be not surprized. Here's the devill to pay. No-body serene but Jack Belford, who is taking minnutes of examminations, accusations, and confessions, with the signifficant air of a Middlesex Justice.

I heartily condole with thee: So does Belton. But it may turn out for the best: For she is gone away with thy marks, I understand. A foolish little devill! Where will she mend herself? For no-body will look upon her. And they tell me, that thou wouldst certainly have married her, had she staid.—But I know thee better.

Dear Bobby, adieu. If thy uncle will die now, to comfort thee for this loss, what a *seasonable* exit would he make! Let's have a letter from thee. Pr'ythee do. Thou canst write devill-like to Belford, who shews us nothing at all.

Thine heartily,

Rd. Mowbray

Miss Clarissa Harlowe To Miss Howe

Wednesday Night, June 28.

O my dearest Miss Howe!

ONCE more have I escaped—But, alas! *I*, my *best self*, have not escaped!—Oh! your poor Clarissa Harlowe! *You* also will hate me, I fear!—Yet you won't, when you know All!—

But no more of my self! My *lost* self. You that can rise in a morning, to be blest, and to bless; and go to rest delighted with your own reflections, and in your unbroken, unstarting slumbers, conversing with saints and angels, the former only more pure than yourself, as they have shaken off the incumbrance of body; You shall be my subject, as you have long, long, been my only pleasure. And let me, at awful distance, revere my

beloved Anna Howe, and in *her* reflect upon what her Clarissa
Harlowe once was!—

Forgive, O forgive, my rambling. My peace is destroyed.
My intellects are touched. And what flighty nonsense must you
read, if now you will vouchsafe to correspond with me, as
formerly!—

O my best, my dearest, my *only* friend! What a tale have
I to unfold!—But still upon *Self*, this vile, this hated *Self!*—I
will shake it off, if possible; and why should I not, since I think,
except one wretch, I hate nothing so much? Self, then, be banished from *Self* one moment (for I doubt it *will* for no longer) to
inquire after a *dearer* object, my beloved Anna Howe!—Whose
mind, all robed in spotless white, charms and irradiates—But
what would I say?—

And how, my dearest friend, after this rhapsody, which,
on re-perusal, I would not let go, but to shew you what a distracted mind dictates to my trembling pen; *How do you?* You
have been very ill, it seems. That you are *recovered*, my dear,
let me hear. That your mamma is well, pray let me hear, and
hear quickly!—This comfort, surely, is owing to me; for if life
is no *worse* than chequer-work, I must now have a little white
to come, having seen nothing but black, all unchequered dismal
black, for a great, great while.

And what is all this wild incoherence for? It is only to beg
to know how you have been, and how you now do, by a line
directed for Mrs. Rachel Clark, at Mr. Smith's, a glove-shop,
in King-street, Covent-garden; which (altho' my abode is secret
to everybody else) will reach the hands of—*Your unhappy*—but
that's not enough—

Your miserable

Clarissa Harlowe

Miss Howe
To Miss Clarissa Harlowe

(Superscribed, as directed in the preceding.)

Friday, June 30.

Miss Clarissa Harlowe,

YOU will wonder to receive a letter from me. I am sorry
for the great distress you seem to be in. Such a hopeful
young lady as you were!—But see what comes of disobedience
to parents!

For my part; altho' I pity you, yet I much more pity your
poor father and mother. Such education as they gave you!
such improvements as you made! and such delight as they took
in you!—And all come to this!—

But pray, Miss, don't make my Nancy guilty of your fault;
which is that of disobedience. I have charged her over and over
not to correspond with one who has made such a giddy step. It
is not to her reputation, I am sure. You *know* that I so charged
her; yet you go on corresponding together, to my very great
vexation; for she has been very perverse upon it, more than
once. *Evil communication*, Miss—You know the rest.

Here, people cannot be unhappy by themselves, but they
must involve their friends and acquaintance, whose discretion
has kept them clear of their errors, into near as much unhappi-
ness as if they had run into the like of their own heads. Thus
my poor daughter is always in tears and grief. And she has post-
poned her own felicity truly, because *you* are unhappy!

If people, who seek their own ruin, could be the only sufferers by their headstrong doings, it were something: But, O
Miss, Miss! what have *you* to answer for, who have made as
many grieved hearts, as have known you! The whole sex is indeed wounded by you: For, who but Miss Clarissa Harlowe was
proposed by every father and mother for a pattern for their
daughters?

393

I write a long letter, where I proposed to say but a few words; and those to forbid you writing to my Nancy: And this as well because of the false step you have made, as because it will grieve her poor heart, and do you no good. If you love her, therefore, write not to her. Your sad Letter came into my hands, Nancy being abroad; and I shall not shew it her: For there would be no comfort for her, if she saw it, nor for me, whose delight she is—As you once was to your parents—

But you seem to be sensible enough of your errors now! So are all giddy girls, when it is too late—And what a crest-fallen figure then does their self-willed obstinacy and head-strongness compel them to make!

I may say too much: only as I think it proper to bear that testimony against your rashness, which it behoves every careful parent to bear: And none more than

Your *compassionating well-wisher,*

Annabella Howe

Miss Clarissa Harlowe
To Mrs. Howe

Saturday, July 1.

PERMIT me, Madam, to trouble you with a few lines, were it only to thank you for your reproofs; which have nevertheless drawn fresh streams of blood from a bleeding heart.

My story is a dismal story. It has circumstances in it, that would engage pity, and possibly a judgment not altogether unfavourable, were those circumstances known. But it is my business, and shall be *all* my business, to repent of my failings, and not endeavour to extenuate them.

Nor will I seek to distress your worthy mind. If *I cannot suffer alone*, I will make as few parties as I can in my sufferings. And, indeed, I took up my pen with this resolution when I wrote the letter which has fallen into your hands: It was only to know, and that for a very particular reason, as well as for affection unbounded, if my dear Miss Howe, from whom I had not heard of a long time, were ill; as I had been told she was; and if so, how she now does. But my injuries being recent, and my distresses having been exceeding great, *Self* would croud into my letter. When distressed, the human mind is apt to turn itself to every one in whom it imagined or wished an interest, for pity and consolation—Or, to express myself better and more concisely, in your own words, *Misfortune makes people plaintive: And to whom, if not to a friend, can the afflicted complain?*

Miss Howe being abroad, when my letter came, I flatter myself that she is recovered. But it would be some satisfaction to me to be informed, if she *has been ill.* Another line from *your* hand would be too great a favour. But, if you will be pleased to direct any servant to answer *yes,* or *no,* to that question, I will not be farther troublesome.

Nevertheless, I must declare, that my Miss Howe's friendship was all the comfort I had or expected to have, in this world; and a line from her would have been a cordial to my fainting heart. Judge then, dearest Madam, how reluctantly I must obey your prohibition—But yet, I will endeavour to obey it; altho' I should have hoped, as well from the tenor of all that has passed between Miss Howe and me, as from *her* established virtue, that she could not be tainted by *Evil communication,* had one or two letters been permitted. This, however, I ask not for, since I think I have nothing to do, but to beg of God to give me a truly broken spirit, if it be not already broken enough, and then to take to his mercy.

The unhappy

Clarissa Harlowe

Miss Clarissa Harlowe
To Miss Howe

Thursday, July 6.

FEW young persons have been able to give more convincing proofs than myself, how little true happiness lies in the enjoyment of our own wishes.

But how to defend myself in every-thing that has happened, I cannot tell: Since in some part of the time, in which my conduct appears to have been censurable, I was not myself; and to this hour know not all the methods taken to deceive and ruin me.

You tell me, that in your first letter you gave me such an account of the vile house I was in, and such cautions about that Tomlinson, as make you wonder how I could think of going back.

Alas, my dear! I was tricked, most vilely tricked back, as you shall hear in its place.

Without *knowing* the house was so very *vile* a house from your *intended* information, I disliked the people too much, ever *voluntarily* to have returned to it. But had you really written such cautions about Tomlinson, and the house, as you seem to have *purposed* to do, they must, had they come in time, have been of infinite service to me. But not one word of either, whatever was your *intention*, did you mention to me, in that *first* of the *three* letters you so warmly tell me you *did* send me. *I will inclose it to convince you.*[a]

But your account of your messenger's delivering to me your second letter, and the description he gives of me, as *lying upon a couch, in a strange way, bloated, and flush-coloured, you don't know how,* absolutely puzzles and confounds me.

Lord have mercy upon the poor Clarissa Harlowe! What can this mean!—*Who* was the messenger you sent? Was *he* one of Lovelace's creatures too!—Could nobody come near me but that man's confederates, either *setting out so,* or *made so?*

---

[a] The letter she incloses was Mr. Lovelace's forged one.

396

Let me see. You say, this was *before* I went from Hamstead! My intellects had not then been touched!—Nor had I ever been surprised by wine (strange if I had!): How then could I be found in such a *strange way, bloated, and flush-coloured; you don't know how!*—Yet what a vile, what a hateful figure has your messenger represented me to have made!

But indeed, I know nothing of any messenger from you.

Believing myself secure at Hamstead, I staid longer there than I would have done, in hopes of the letter promised me in your short one of the 9th, brought me by my own messenger, in which you undertake to send for and engage Mrs. Townsend in my favour.

I wondered I heard not from you: And was told you were sick; and, at another time, that your mother and you had had words on my account, and that you had refused to admit Mr. Hickman's visits upon it: So that I supposed at one time, that you were not *able* to write; at another, that your mother's prohibition had its *due* force with you. But now I have no doubt, that the wicked man must have intercepted your letter; and I wish he found not means to *corrupt your messenger* to tell you so strange a story.

It was on Sunday June 11. you say, that the man gave it me. I was at church twice that day with Mrs. Moore. Mr. Lovelace was at her house the while, where he boarded, and wanted to have lodged; but I would not permit that, tho' I could not help the other. In one of these spaces *it must be* that he had time to work upon the man.

Had any-body seen me afterwards, when I was betrayed back to the vile house, struggling under the operation of wicked potions, and robbed *indeed* of my intellects (for this, as you shall hear, was my dreadful case!), I might then, perhaps, have appeared *bloated*, and *flush-coloured*, and *I know not how myself.*

In a word, it could not be *me* your messenger saw; nor (if any-body) who it was can I divine.

I will now, as *briefly* as the subject will permit, enter into the darker part of my sad story: And yet I must be somewhat circumstantial, that you may not think me capable of *reserve* or *palliation*. The *latter* I am not conscious that I need. I should be utterly inexcuseable, were I guilty of the *former* to you. And yet, if you knew how my heart sinks under the thoughts of a recollection so painful, you would pity me.

As I shall not be able, perhaps, to conclude what I have to write in even two or three letters, I will begin a new one with my story; and send the whole of it together, altho' written at different periods, as I am able.

Allow me a little pause, my dear, at this place; and to subscribe myself

Your ever-affectionate and obliged
Clarissa Harlowe

Miss Clarissa Harlowe To Miss Howe

Thursday Night.

HE had found me out at Hamstead: Strangely found me out; for I am still at a loss to know by what means.

I was loth, in my billet of the 9th, to tell you so, for fear of giving you apprehensions for me; and besides, I hoped then to have a shorter and happier issue to account to you for, thro' your assistance, than I met with.

> *She then gives a narrative of all that passed at Hamstead between herself, Mr. Lovelace, Capt. Tomlinson and the women there, to the same effect with that given by Mr. Lovelace.*

Mr. Lovelace, finding all he could say, and all Capt. Tomlinson could urge, ineffectual, to prevail upon me to forgive an outrage so flagrantly premeditated; rested all his hopes on a visit which was to be paid me by Lady Betty Lawrance and Miss Montague.

In my uncertain situation, my prospects all so dark, I knew not to whom I might be obliged to have recourse in the last resort: And as those ladies had the best of characters, insomuch that I had reason to regret, that I had not from the first thrown myself upon their protection (when I had forfeited *that* of my own friends), I thought I would not *shun* an interview with them.

On Monday the 12th of June, these pretended ladies came to Hamstead; and I was presented to them, and they to me, by their kinsman.

They were richly dressed, and struck out with jewels; the pretended Lady Betty's were particularly very fine.

I had heard, that Lady Betty was a fine woman, and that Miss Montague was a beautiful young lady, genteel, and graceful, and full of vivacity—Such were these impostors; and having never seen either of them, I had not the least suspicion, that they were not the ladies they personated; and being put a little out of countenance by the richness of their dresses, I could not help, fool that I was! to apologize for my own.

The pretended Lady Betty then told me, that her nephew had acquainted them with the situation of affairs between us. And altho' she could not but say, that she was very glad that he had not put such a slight upon his Lordship and them, as report had given them cause to apprehend; yet it had been matter of great concern to her, to find so great a misunderstanding subsisting between us, as, if not made up, might distance all their hopes.

She could easily tell who was in fault, she said.—And gave him a look both of anger and disdain; asking him, How it was possible for him to give an offence of *such* a nature to so charming a lady (so she called me), as should occasion a resentment so strong?

He pretended to be awed into shame and silence.

My dearest niece, said she, and took my hand (I *must* call you niece, as well from love, as to humour your uncle's laudable expedient), permit me to be, not an advocate, but a mediatrix for him; and not for his sake, so much as for my own, my Charlotte's, and all our family's. The indignity he has offered to you, may be of too tender a nature to be inquired into. But as he declares, that it was not a premeditated offence; whether, my dear (for I was going to rise upon it in my temper), it were or not; and as he declares his sorrow for it (and never did creature express a deeper sorrow for any offence than he!); and as it is a reparable one; let *Us*, for this one time, forgive him; and thereby lay an obligation upon this man of errors—Let US, I say, my dear: For, Sir (turning to him), an offence against such a peerless lady as This, must be an offence against *me*, against your *cousin*, here, and against *all the virtuous* of our Sex.

See, my dear, what a creature he had picked out! Could you have thought there was a woman in the world who could thus express herself, and yet be vile? But she had her principal instructions from him, and those written down too, as I have reason to think: For I have recollected since, that I once saw this Lady Betty (who often rose from her seat, and took a turn to the other end of the room with such emotion as if the joy of her heart would not let her sit still) take out a paper from her stays, and look into it, and put it there again.

The wretch himself then came forward. He threw himself at my feet. How was I beset!—The women grasping one my right hand, the other my left: The pretended Miss Montague pressing to her lips more than once the hand she held: The wicked man on his knees, imploring my forgiveness; and setting before me my happy and my unhappy prospects, as I should forgive or not forgive him. All that he thought would affect me in his former pleas, and those of Capt. Tomlinson, he repeated. He vowed, he promised, he bespoke the pretended ladies to answer for him; and they engaged their honours in his behalf.

Indeed, my dear, I was distressed, perfectly distressed. I was sorry that I had given way to this visit. For I knew not how, in tenderness to relations (as I thought them) so worthy, to treat so freely as he deserved, a man nearly allied to them.

I pleaded, however, my application to you. I expected every

hour, I told them, an answer from you to a letter I had written, which would decide my future destiny.

They offered to apply to you themselves in person, in *their own behalf*, as they politely termed it. They besought me to write to you to hasten your answer.

But as to the success of their requests in behalf of their kinsman, That depended not upon the expected answer; for *that*, I begged their pardon, was out of the question. I wished him well. I wished him happy. But I was convinced, that I neither could make *him* so, nor he *me*.

Then! how the wretch promised!—How he vowed!—How he intreated!—And how the women pleaded!—And they engaged themselves, and the honour of their whole family, for his just, his kind, his tender behaviour to me.

In short, my dear, I was so hard set, that I was obliged to come to a more favourable compromise with them, than I had intended. I would wait for your answer to my letter, I said: And if that made doubtful or difficult the change of measures I had resolved upon, and the scheme of life I had formed, I would then consider of the matter; and, if they would permit me, lay all before them, and take their advice upon it, in conjunction with yours.

They shed tears upon this—Of joy they called them—But since, I believe, to their credit, bad as they are, that they were tears of temporary remorse; for the pretended Miss Montague turned about, and, as I remember, said, There was no standing it.

But Mr. Lovelace was not so easily satisfied. He was fixed upon his villainous measures perhaps; and so might not be sorry to have a pretence against me. He bit his lip—He had been but too much used, he said, to such indifference, such coldness, in the very midst of his happiest prospects.—I had on twenty occasions, shewn him, to his infinite regret, that any favour I was to confer upon him was to be the result of—There he stopt—And not of my choice.

They then engaged me in a more agreeable conversation— The pretended Lady declared, that she, Lord M. and Lady

Sarah, would directly and personally interest themselves to bring about a general reconciliation between the two families, and this either in open or private concert with my uncle Harlowe, as should be thought fit. Animosities on one side had been carried a great way, she said; and too little care had been shewn on the other to mollify or heal. My father should see that they could treat him as a brother and a friend; and my brother and sister should be convinced, that there was no room either for the jealousy or envy they had conceived from motives too unworthy to be avowed.

Could I help, my dear, being pleased with them?—

Permit me here to break off. The task grows too heavy, at present, for the heart of

> Your
>
> *Clarissa Harlowe*

Miss Clarissa Harlowe

In Continuation.

I WAS very ill, and obliged to lay down my pen. I thought I should have fainted. But am better now—So will proceed.

The pretended Ladies, the more we talked, seemed to be the fonder of me. And *The* Lady Betty had Mrs. Moore called up; and asked her, If she had accommodations for her niece and self, her woman, and two menservants, for three or four days?

Mr. Lovelace answered for her, that she had.

She would not ask her dear niece Lovelace [*Permit me, my dear*, whispered she, *this charming style before strangers!—I will keep your uncle's secret*] whether she should be welcome or not to be so near her. But for the time she should stay in these parts, she would come up every night—What say *you*, Niece Charlotte?

The pretended Charlotte answered, she should like to do so, of all things.

The Lady Betty called her an obliging girl. She liked the place, she said. Her cousin Leeson would excuse her. The air, and my company, would do her good. She never chose to lie in the smoky town, if she could help it. In short, my dear, said she to me, I will stay till you hear from Miss Howe; and till I have your consent to go with me to Glenham-Hall. Not one moment will I be out of your company, when I can have it. Niece Charlotte, one word with you, child.

They retired to the farther end of the room, and talked about their night-dresses.

The Miss Charlotte said, Morrison might be dispatched for them.

True, said the other—But she had some letters in her private box, which she must have up. And you know, Charlotte, that I trust nobody with the keys of that.

Could not Morrison bring up that box?

No. She thought it safest where it was. She had heard of a robbery committed but two days ago at the foot of Hamstead-hill; and she should be ruined, if she lost her box.

Well then, it was but going to town to undress, and she would leave her jewels behind her, and return; and should be easier a great deal on all accounts.

The grand deluder was at the farther end of the room, another way; probably to give me an opportunity to hear these preconcerted praises—looking into a book, which, had there not been a preconcert, would not have taken his attention for one moment. It was *Taylor's Holy Living and Dying.*

When the pretended ladies joined me, he approached me, with it in his hand—A smart book, This, my dear!—This old divine affects, I see, a mighty flowery stile upon a very solemn subject. But it puts me in mind of an ordinary country funeral, where the young women, in honour of a defunct companion, especially if she were a virgin, or *passed for such*, make a flower-bed of her coffin.

And then, laying down the book, turning upon his heel, with one of his usual airs of gaiety, And are you determined, Ladies, to take up your lodgings with my charming creature?

Indeed they were.

Never were there more cunning, more artful impostors, than these women. Practised creatures, to be sure: Yet genteel; and they must have been well-educated—Once, perhaps, as much the delight of their parents, as I was of mine.

Mr. Lovelace carried himself to his pretended aunt with high respect, and paid a great deference to all she said. He permitted her to have all the advantage over him in the repartees and retorts that passed between them.

The pretended Miss Montague was still more reverent in her behaviour to her pretended aunt. While the aunt kept up the dignity of the character she had assumed, raillying both of them with the air of a person who depends upon the superiority which years and fortune give over younger persons; who might have a view to be obliged to her, either in her life, or at her death.

The severity of her raillery, however, was turned upon Mr. Lovelace, on occasion of the character of the people who kept the lodgings, which, she said, I had thought myself so well warranted to leave privately.

He seemed abashed. But how was it possible, that even that florid countenance of his should enable him to command a blush at his pleasure? For blush he did, more than once: And the blush, on this occasion, was a deep-dyed crimson, unstrained-for, and natural, as I thought—But he is so much of the actor, that he seems able to enter into any character; and his muscles and features appear intirely under obedience to his wicked will.

The pretended Lady went on, saying, She had taken upon herself to inquire after the people, on hearing that I had left the house in disgust; and tho' she heard not anything much amiss, yet she heard enough to make her wonder, that he would carry his spouse, a person of so much delicacy, to a house, that, if it had not a *bad* fame, had not a *good* one.

You must think, my dear, that I liked the pretended Lady Betty the better for this. I suppose it was designed I should.

He was surprised, he said, that her Ladyship should hear a bad character of the people. It was what he had never before heard that they deserved. It was easy, indeed, to see, that they had not very great delicacy, tho' they were not indelicate. The nature of their livelihood, letting lodgings, and taking people to board, led them to aim at being free and obliging.

He wished, however, that her Ladyship would tell *what* she had heard: Altho' now it signified but little, because he would never ask me to set foot within their doors again: And he begged she would not mince the matter.

Nay, no great matter, she said. But she had been informed, that there were more women-lodgers in the house than men: Yet that their visitors were more men than women. And this had been hinted to her (perhaps by ill-willers, she could not answer for that) in such a way, as if somewhat further were meant by it than was spoken.

Women, he owned, ought to be more scrupulous than men needed to be where they lodged. Nevertheless, he wished, that fact, rather than surmise, were to be the foundation of their judgments, especially when they spoke of one another.

The pretended Lady Betty said, All who knew her, would clear her of censoriousness: That it gave her some opinion, she must needs say, of the people, that he had continued there so long with me; that I had rather *negative* than *positive* reasons of dislike to them; and that so shrewd a man, as she heard Capt. Tomlinson was, had not objected to them.

They then fell into family-talk; Family-happiness on my hoped-for accession into it. They mentioned Lord M's and Lady Sarah's great desire to see me. How many friends and admirers, with up-lift hands, I should have! [*O my dear, what a triumph must these creatures, and he, have over the poor devoted all the time!*]—What a happy man he would be.

They then talked again of reconciliation and intimacy with every one of my friends; with my mother particularly; and gave the dear good lady the praises that every one gives her, who has the happiness to know her.

Ah, my dear Miss Howe! I had almost forgot my resentments against the pretended nephew!—So many agreeable things said, made me think, that, if you should advise it, and if I could bring my mind to forgive the wretch for an outrage so *premeditatedly* vile, and could forbear despising him for that

and his other ingrateful and wicked ways, I might not be unhappy in an alliance with such a family.

But amidst all these delightful prospects, I must not, said
The Lady Betty, forget that I am to go to town.

She then ordered her coach to be got to the door—We will
all go to town together, said she, and return together. My cousin
Leeson's servants can do all I want to be done with regard to my
night-dresses, and the like. And it will be a little airing for you,
my dear, and a good opportunity for Mr. Lovelace to order what
you want of your apparel to be sent from your former lodgings
to Mrs. Leeson's; and we can bring it up with us from thence.

I had no intention to comply. But as I did not imagine that
she would insist upon my going to town with them, I made no
answer to that part of her speech.

I must here lay down my tired pen!

Recollection! Heart-affecting Recollection! How it pains
me!

Miss Clarissa Harlowe
To Miss Howe

IN the midst of these agreeablenesses, the coach came to the
door. The pretended Lady Betty besought me to give them my
company to their cousin Leeson's. I desired to be excused: Yet
suspected nothing. She would not be denied. How happy would
a visit so condescending make her cousin Leeson!—Her cousin
Leeson was not unworthy of my acquaintance: And would take
it for the greatest favour in the world.

I objected my dress. But the objection was not admitted.
She bespoke a supper of Mrs. Moore to be ready at nine.

Mr. Lovelace, vile hypocrite, and wicked deceiver, seeing,
as he said, my dislike to go, desired her Ladyship not to insist
upon it.

Fondness for my company was pleaded. She begged me to

oblige her: And, in short, was so very urgent, that my feet complied against my speech, and my mind: And, being in a manner,
led to the coach by her, and made to step in first, she followed
me; and her pretended niece, and the wretch, followed her: And
away it drove.

Nothing but the height of affectionate complaisance passed
all the way: Over and over, What a joy would this unexpected
visit give her cousin Leeson! What a pleasure must it be to such
a mind as mine, to be able to give so much joy to every-body I
came near!

But think, my dear, what a dreadful turn all had upon me,
when, through several streets and ways I knew nothing of, the
coach, slackening its pace, came within sight of the dreadful
house of the dreadfullest woman in the world; as she proved
to me.

Lord be good unto me! cry'd the poor fool, looking out of
the coach—Mr. Lovelace!—Madam! turning to the pretended
aunt—Madam! turning to the niece, my hands and eyes lifted
up—Lord be good unto me!

What! What! What! my dear!

He pulled the string—What need to have come this way?
said he.—But since we are, I will ask a question—My dearest
life, *why* this apprehension?

The coachman stopped: *His* servant, who, with one of hers
was behind, alighted—Ask, said he, if I have any letters? Who
knows, my dearest creature, turning to me, but we may already
have one from the Captain?—We will not go out of the coach!—
Fear nothing—Why so apprehensive?

Dreadfully did my heart then misgive me: I was ready to
faint. Why this terror, my life?—You shall not stir out of the
coach!—But one question, now the fellow has drove us this
way!

Your lady will faint, cried the execrable Lady Betty, turning
to him.—My dearest niece! I *will* call you, taking my hand, we
must alight, if you are so ill.—Let us alight—Only for a glass
of water and hartshorn—Indeed we must alight.

No, no, no—I am well—Quite well—Won't the man drive
on?—I am well—quite well—Indeed I am.—*Man*, drive on,

putting my head out of the coach—*Man*, drive on!—tho' my voice was too low to be heard.

The coach stopped at the door. How I trembled!

Dorcas came to the door, on its stopping.

My dearest creature, said the vile man, gasping, as it were for breath, you shall *not* alight—Any letters for me, Dorcas?

There are two, Sir. And here is a gentleman, Mr. Belton, Sir, waits for your Honour; and has done so above an hour.

I'll just speak to him. Open the door—You sha'n't step out, my dear—A letter, perhaps, from the captain already!—You sha'n't step out, my dear.

I sighed, as if my heart would burst.

But we *must* step out, nephew: Your lady will faint. Maid, a glass of hartshorn and water!—My dear, you *must* step out.—You will faint, child—We must cut your laces.—[I believe my complexion was all manner of colours by turns]—Indeed, you must step out, my dear.

He knew, he said, I should be well, the moment the coach drove from the door. I should *not* alight. By his soul, I should not.

Lord, Lord, nephew, Lord, Lord, cousin, both women in a breath, What ado you make about nothing! You *persuade* your lady to be afraid of alighting!—See you not, that she is just fainting?

Indeed, Madam, said the vile seducer, my dearest love must not be moved in this point against her will!—I beg it may not be insisted upon.

Fiddle-faddle, foolish man!—What a pother is here!—I guess how it is: You are ashamed to let us see, what sort of people you carried your lady among!—But do you go out, and speak to your friend, and take your letters.

He stept out; but shut the coach-door after him, to oblige me.

The coach may go on, Madam, said I.

The coach *shall* go on, my dear life, said he—But he gave not, nor intended to give, orders that it should.

Let the coach go on! said I—Mr. Lovelace may come after us.

Indeed, my dear, you are ill!—Indeed you must alight—
Alight but for one quarter of an hour!—Alight but to give
orders yourself about your things. Whom can you be afraid of
in my company, and my niece's? These people must have behaved shockingly to you! Please the Lord, I'll inquire into it!
—I'll see what sort of people they are!

Immediately came the old creature to the door. A thousand
pardons, dear Madam, stepping to the coachside, if we have
any-way offended you—Be pleased, Ladies (to the other two),
to alight.

I was afraid I should have fallen into fits: But still refused
to go out—Man!—Man!—Man! cried I, gaspingly, my head out
of the coach and in, by turns, half a dozen times running, drive
on!—Let us go!

My heart misgave me beyond the power of my own accounting for it; for still I did not suspect these women. But the
antipathy I had taken to the vile house, and to find myself so
near it, when I expected no such matter, with the sight of the
old creature, all together, made me behave like a distracted
person.

The hartshorn and water was brought. The pretended lady
Betty made me drink it. Heaven knows if there were any-thing
else in it!

Besides, said she, whisperingly, I must see what sort of
creatures the *nieces* are. Want of delicacy cannot be hid from
me. You could not surely, my dear, have this aversion to re-
enter a house, for a few minutes, in our company, in which you
lodged and boarded several weeks, unless these women could
be so presumptuously vile, as my nephew ought not to know.

Out stept the pretended lady; the servant, at her command,
having opened the door.

Dearest Madam, said the other, let me follow you (for I
was next the door). Fear nothing: I will not stir from your presence.

Come, my dear, said the pretended Lady: Give me your
hand; holding out hers. Oblige me this once!

I will bless your footsteps, said the old creature, if once
more you honour my house with your presence.

A croud by this time was gathered about us; but I was too much affected to mind that.

Again the pretended Miss Montague urged me (standing up as ready to go out if I would give her room). Lord, my dear, said she, who can bear this croud?—What will people think?

The pretended Lady again pressed me, with both her hands held out—Only, my dear, to give orders about your things.

And thus pressed, and gazed at (for then I looked about me), the women so richly dressed, people whispering; in an evil moment, out stepped I, trembling, forced to lean with both my hands (frighted too much for ceremony) on the pretended Lady Betty's arm—O that I had dropped down dead upon the guilty threshold!

We shall stay but a few minutes, my dear!—but a few minutes! said the same specious jilt—out of breath with her joy, as I have since thought, that they had thus triumphed over the unhappy victim!

Come, Mrs. Sinclair, I think your name is, shew us the way— following her, and leading me. I am very thirsty. You have frighted me, my dear, with your strange fears. I must have tea made, if it can be done in a moment. We have further to go, Mrs. Sinclair, and must return to Hamstead this night.

It shall be ready in a moment, cried the wretch. We have water boiling.

Hasten, then.—Come, my dear, to me, as she led me through the passage to the fatal inner house—Lean upon me— How you tremble!—how you faulter in your steps!—Dearest niece Lovelace (the old wretch being in hearing), why these hurries upon your spirits?—We'll begone in a minute.

And thus she led the poor sacrifice into the old wretch's too well-known parlour.

Never was any-body so gentle, so meek, so low-voiced, as the odious woman; drawling out, in a puling accent, all the obliging things she could say: Awed, I then thought, by the conscious dignity of a woman of quality; glittering with jewels.

The called-for tea was ready presently.

I was made to drink two dishes, with milk, complaisantly urged by the pretended Ladies helping me each to one. I was stupid to their hands; and, when I took the tea, almost choaked with vapours; and could hardly swallow.

I thought, *transiently* thought, that the tea, the last dish particularly, had an odd taste. They, on my palating it, observed, that the milk was *London milk*; far short in goodness of what they were accustomed to from their own dairies.

I have no doubt, that my two dishes, and perhaps my hartshorn, were prepared for me; in which case it was more proper for their purpose, that *they* should help me, than that I should help *myself*. Ill before, I found myself still more and more disordered in my head; a heavy torpid pain increasing fast upon me. But I imputed it to my terror.

Nevertheless, at the pretended Ladies motion, I went upstairs, attended by Dorcas; who affected to weep for joy, that once more she saw my *blessed* face; and immediately I set about taking out some of my cloaths, ordering what should be put up, and what sent after me.

While I was thus employed, up came the pretended Lady Betty, in a hurrying way—My dear, you won't be long before you are ready. My Nephew is very busy in writing answers to his letters: So, I'll just whip away, and change my dress, and call upon you in an instant.

O Madam!—I *am* ready! I am *now* ready!—You must not leave me here: And down I sunk, affrighted, into a chair.

This instant, this instant, I will return—Before you can be ready—Before you can have packed up your things—We would not be late—The robbers we have heard of may be out—Don't let us be late.

And away she hurried before I could say another word. Her pretended niece went with her, without taking notice to me of her going.

It cannot *be*, thought I, that *such* Ladies will abet treachery against a poor creature they are so fond of. They must undoubtedly *be* the persons they *appear* to be—What folly to doubt it! The air, the dress, the dignity, of women of quality.— How unworthy of them, and of my charity, concluded I, is this ungenerous shadow of suspicion!

So, recovering my stupefied spirits, as well as they could

be recovered (for I was heavier and heavier; and wondered to
Dorcas, what ailed me; rubbing my eyes, and taking some of her
snuff, pinch after pinch, to very little purpose), I pursued my
employment: But when that was over, all packed up that I designed to be packed up; and I had nothing to do but to *think*;
and found them tarry so long; I thought I should have gone distracted. I shut myself into the chamber that had been mine; I
kneeled, I prayed, yet knew not what I prayed for: Then ran out
again: It was almost dark night, I said: Where, where, was Mr.
Lovelace?

He came to me, taking no notice at first of my consternation and wildness: All goes well, said he, my dear!—A line from
Captain Tomlinson!

All indeed did go well for the villainous project of the most
cruel and most villainous of men!

I *demanded* his aunt!—I *demanded* his cousin!—The evening, I said, was closing!—My head was very, *very* bad, I remember, I said.—And it grew worse and worse.—

Terror, however, as yet kept up my spirits; and I insisted
upon his going himself to hasten them.

He called his servant. He raved at the *sex* for *their* delay:
'Twas well that business of consequence seldom depended upon
such parading, unpunctual triflers!

His servant came.

He ordered him to fly to his cousin Leeson's; and to let his
aunt and cousins know how uneasy we both were at their delay:
Adding, of his own accord, Desire them, if they don't come
instantly, to send their coach, and we will go without them.
Tell them I wonder they'll serve me so!

I thought this was considerately and fairly put. But now,
indifferent as my head was, I had a little time to consider the
man, and his behaviour. He terrified me with his looks, and with
his violent emotions, as he gazed upon me. Evident _joy-sup-_
pressed emotions, as I have since recollected. His sentences short,
and pronounced as if his breath were touched. Never saw I his
 abominable eyes look, as then they looked—Triumph in them!
—Fierce and wild; and more disagreeable than the womens at
the vile house appeared to me when I first saw them. Yet his

behaviour was decent—A decency, however, that I might have seen to be struggled for—For he snatched my hand two or three times, with a vehemence in his grasp that hurt me; speaking words of tenderness through his shut teeth, as it seemed; and let it go with a beggar-voiced humble accent, like the vile woman's just before; half-inward; yet his words and manner carrying the appearance of strong and almost convulsed passion!

I complained once or twice of thirst. My mouth seemed parched. At the time, I supposed, that it was my terror (gasping often as I did for breath) that parched up the roof of my mouth. I called for water: Some table-beer was brought me: Beer, I suppose, was a better vehicle (if I were not dosed enough before) for their potions. I told the maid, That she knew I seldom tasted malt-liquor: Yet, suspecting nothing of this nature, being extremely thirsty, I drank it, as what came next: And instantly, as it were, found myself much worse than before; as if inebriated, I should fancy: I know not how.

His servant was gone twice as long as he needed: And just before his return, came one of the pretended Lady Betty's, with a letter for Mr. Lovelace.

He sent it up to me. I read it: And then it was that I thought myself a lost creature; it being to put off her going to Hamstead that night, on account of violent fits which Miss Montague was pretended to be seized with: For then immediately came into my head his vile attempt upon me in this house; the revenge that my flight might too probably inspire him with on that occasion, and because of the difficulty I made to forgive him; his very looks wild and dreadful to me; and the women of the house such as I had more reason than ever to be afraid of: All these crouding together in my apprehensive mind, I fell into a kind of phrensy.

I have not remembrance how I was, for the time it lasted: But I know, that in my first agitations, I pulled off my headdress, and tore my ruffles in twenty tatters, and ran to find him out.

When a little recovered, I insisted upon the hint he had given of their coach. But the messenger, he said, had told him, that it was sent to fetch a physician, lest his chariot should be put up, or not ready.

I then insisted upon going directly to Lady Betty's lodgings.

Mrs. Leeson's was now a crouded house, he said: And as my earnestness could be owing to nothing but groundless apprehension he hoped I would not add to their present concern. Charlotte, indeed, was used to fits, he said, upon any great surprizes, whether of joy or grief; and they would hold her for a week together, if not got off in a few hours.

You are an *observer of eyes*, my dear, said the villain; perhaps in secret insult: Saw you not in Miss Montague's now-and-then at Hamstead, something wildish?—I was afraid for her then—Silence and quiet only do her good: Your concern for *her*, and her love for *you*, will but augment the poor girl's disorder, if you should go.

All impatient with grief and apprehension, I still declared myself resolved not to stay in that house till morning. All I had in the world, my rings, my watch, my little money, for a coach! or, if one were not to be got, I would go on foot to Hamstead that night, tho' I walked it by myself.

A coach was hereupon sent for, or pretended to be sent for. Any price, he said, he would give to oblige me, late as it was; and he would attend me with all his soul.—But no coach was to be got.

Let me cut short the rest. I grew worse and worse in my head; now stupid, now raving, now senseless. The vilest of vile women was brought to frighten me. Never was there so horrible a creature as she appeared to me at the time.

I remember, I pleaded for mercy.—I remember that I said *I would be his—Indeed I would be his*—to obtain his mercy—But no mercy found I!—My strength, my intellects, failed me—And then such scenes followed—O my dear, such dreadful scenes!—Fits upon fits (faintly indeed, and imperfectly remembred) procuring me no compassion—But death was with-held from me. That would have been too great a mercy!

Thus was I tricked and deluded back by blacker hearts of my own sex, than I thought there were in the world; who appeared to me to be persons of honour: And, when in his power, thus barbarously was I treated by this villainous man!

I was so senseless, that I dare not averr, that the horrid creatures of the house were personally aiding and abetting: But some visionary remembrances I have of female figures, flitting, as I may say, before my sight; the wretched woman's particularly. But as these confused ideas might be owing to the terror I had conceived of the worse than masculine violence she had been permitted to assume to me, for expressing my abhorrence of her house; and as what I suffered from his barbarity wants not that aggravation; I will say no more on a subject so shocking as this must ever be to my remembrance.

I never saw the personating wretches afterwards. He persisted to the last (dreadfully invoking heaven as a witness to the truth of his assertion), that they were really and truly the Ladies they pretended to be; declaring, that they could not take leave of me, when they left the town, because of the state of senselessness and phrensy I was in. For their intoxicating, or rather stupefying, potions had almost deleterious effects upon my intellects, as I have hinted; insomuch that, for several days together, I was under a strange delirium; now moping, now dozing, now weeping, now raving, now scribbling, tearing what I scribbled, as fast as I wrote it: *Most* miserable when now-and-then a ray of reason brought confusedly to my remembrance what I had suffered.

Miss Clarissa Harlowe

In Continuation.

THE *Lady next gives an account,*
Of her recovery from her phrensical and sleepy disorders:
Of her attempt to get away in his absence:
Of the conversations that followed, at his return, between
  them:
Of the guilty figure he made:
Of her resolution not to have him:

Of her several efforts to escape:

Of her treaty with Dorcas, to assist her in it:

Of Dorcas's dropping the promisory note, undoubtedly, as she says, on purpose to betray her:

Of her triumph over all the creatures of the house, assembled to terrify her; and perhaps to commit fresh outrages upon her:

Of his setting out for M. Hall:

Of his repeated letters to induce her to meet him at the altar, on her uncle's Anniversary:

Of her determined silence to them all:

Of her second escape, effected, *as she says*, contrary to her own expectation: That attempt being at first but the intended prelude to a more promising one, which she had formed in her mind:

And of other particulars; which being to be found in Mr. Lovelace's preceding letters, and that of his friend Belford, are omitted. She then proceeds:

The very hour that I found myself in a place of safety, I took pen to write to you. When I began, I designed only to write six or eight lines, to inquire after your health: For, having heard nothing from you, I feared *indeed*, that you *had been*, and *still were*, too ill to write. But no sooner did my pen begin to blot the paper, but my sad heart hurried it into length. The apprehensions I had lain under, that I should not be able to get away; the fatigue I had in effecting my escape: the difficulty of procuring a lodging for myself; having disliked the people of two houses, and those of a third disliking me; for you must think I made a frighted appearance—These, together with the recollection of what I had suffered from him, and my farther apprehensions of my insecurity, had so disordered me, that I remember I rambled strangely in that letter.

How have I been led on!—What will be the end of such a false and perjured creature; Heaven not less profaned and defied by him, than myself deceived and abused! This, however, against myself I must say, That if what I have suffered is the natural consequence of my first error, I never can forgive *myself*, although you are so partial in my favour, as to say, that I was not censurable for what passed before my first escape.

Miss Howe To Miss Clarissa Harlowe

Sunday, July 9.

MAY heaven signalize its vengeance, in the face of all the world, upon the most abandoned and profligate of men! —And in its own time, I doubt not but it will.—And we must look to a world beyond this for the reward of your sufferings!—

Another shocking detection, my dear!—How have you been deluded!—Very watchful I have thought you; very sagacious:— But, alas! not watchful, not sagacious enough, for the horrid villain you have had to deal with!—

The letter you sent me inclosed as mine, of the 7th of June, is a villainous forgery. The hand, indeed, is astonishingly like mine; and the cover, I see, is actually my cover: But yet the letter is not so exactly imitated, but that (had you had any suspicions about his vileness at the time) you, who so well know my hand, might have detected it.

In short, this vile forged letter, tho' a long one, contains but a few extracts from mine. Mine was a *very* long one. He has omitted everything, I see, in it, that could have shewn you what a detestable house the house is; and given you suspicions of the vile Tomlinson.

Apprehensive for *both* our safeties, from such a daring and profligate contriver, I must call upon you, my dear, to resolve upon taking legal vengeance of the infernal wretch. And this not only for our own sakes, but for the sakes of innocents, who otherwise may yet be deluded and outraged by him.

'Tis my opinion, my dear, that you will be no longer safe where you are, than while the V. is in the country. Words are poor!—or how could I execrate him! I have hardly any doubt,

that he has sold himself for a time. O may the time be short!—
Or may his infernal prompter no more keep covenant with him,
than he does with others!

   With what comfort must those parents reflect upon these
things, who have happily disposed of their daughters in marriage to a virtuous man! And how happy the young women,
who find themselves safe in a worthy protection!—If such a
person, as Miss Clarissa Harlowe could not escape, who can be
secure?—Since, tho' every rake is not a Lovelace, neither is every
woman a Clarissa: And his attempts were but proportioned to
your resistance and vigilance.

   My mother has commanded me to let you know her
thoughts upon the whole of your sad story. I beseech you, my
dearest creature, to believe me to be,

   Your truly sympathizing and unalterable friend,

                                 Anna Howe

Mr. Lovelace
To John Belford, Esq;

                                 Wedn. July 12.

So, Jack,

L OVE (like some self-propagating plants or roots, which
     have taken strong hold in the earth), when once got deep into
the heart, is hardly ever *totally* extirpated, except by Matrimony
indeed, which is the Grave of Love, because it allows of the End
of Love. Then these ladies, all advocates *for* herself, *with* herself, Miss Howe at their head, perhaps—Not in favour to me—I
don't expect That from Miss Howe.—But perhaps in favour to
herself: For Miss Howe has reason to apprehend vengeance from
me, I ween.—The lady's case desperate with her friends too;
and likely to be so, while single, and her character exposed to
censure.

A husband is a charming cloak; a fig-leafed apron for a wife: And for a lady to be protected in liberties, in diversions, which her heart pants after—and all her faults, even the most criminal, were she to be detected, to be thrown upon the husband, and the ridicule too; a charming privilege for a wife!

But I shall have one comfort, if I marry, which pleases me not a little. If a man's wife has a dear friend of her sex, a hundred liberties may be taken with that friend, which could *not* be taken, if the *single lady* (knowing what a title to freedoms marriage has given him with her *friend*) was not less scrupulous with him than she ought to be, as to *herself*. Then there are *broad* freedoms (shall I call them?) that may be taken by the husband with his wife, that may not be *quite* shocking, which if the wife *bears before her friend*, will serve for a lesson to *that friend*; and if that friend *bears* to be present at them without check or bashfulness, will shew a sagacious fellow, that she can bear as much herself, at *proper time* and *place*. *Chastity*, Jack, like *Piety*, is an uniform thing. If in *look*, if in *speech*, a girl gives way to undue levity, depend upon it, the devil has got one of his cloven feet in her heart already—So, Hickman, take care of thyself, I advise thee, whether I marry or not.

But after all, It would be very whimsical, would it not, if all my plots and contrivances should end in wedlock? What a punishment would this come out to be, upon myself too, that all this while I have been plundering my own treasury?

But, Jack, two things I must insist upon with thee, if this is to be the case.—Having put secrets of so high a nature between me and my spouse into thy power, I must, for my own honour, and for the honour of my wife and my illustrious progeny, first oblige thee to give up the letters I have so profusely scribbled to thee; and, in the next place, do by thee, as I have heard whispered in France was done by the *true* father of a certain monarque; that is to say, cut thy throat, to prevent thy telling of tales.

Now pry'thee, dear Jack, since so many good consequences are to flow from these our nuptials; and since there may be room to fear, that Miss Howe will not give us her help; I pr'ythee now exert thyself to find out my Clarissa Harlowe, that I may make

a Lovelace of her. Set all the city bellmen, and the country
criers, for ten miles round the metropolis, at work, with their
"O yes's! and if any man, woman, or child, can give tale or
tidings"—Advertise her in all the news-papers; and let her
know, "That if she will repair to Lady Betty Lawrance, or to
Miss Charlotte Montague, she may hear of something greatly
to her advantage."

My two Cousins Montague are actually to set out to-
morrow, to Mrs. Howe's, to engage her vixen daughter's interest
with her friend. They will flaunt it away in a chariot and six,
for the greater state and significance.

Confounded mortification to be reduced thus low!—My
pride hardly knows how to brook it.

Miss Howe
To Miss Charlotte Montague

Tuesday Morning, July 18.

Madam,

I TAKE the liberty to write to you, by this special messenger:
In the phrensy of my soul, I write to you, to demand of you,
and of any of your family who can tell, news of my beloved
friend; who, I doubt, has been spirited away by the base arts of
one of the blackest—O help me to a name bad enough to call
him by!—Her piety is proof against self-attempts: It must, it
must be Him, the only Him, who could injure such an innocent;
and now—who knows what he has done with her!

If I have patience, I will give you the occasion of this distracted vehemence.

I wrote to her the very moment you and your sister left
me. But being unable to procure a special messenger, as I intended, was forced to send by the post. I urged her with earnest-

ness, to comply with the desires of all your family. Having no answer, I wrote again on Sunday night; and sent it by a particular hand, who travelled all night; chideing her for keeping a heart so impatient as mine in such cruel suspense, upon a matter of so much importance to her; and therefore to me.

But, judge my astonishment, my distraction, when last night, the messenger, returning post-haste, brought me word, that she had not been heard of since Friday morning! And that a letter lay for her at her lodgings, which came by the post; and must be mine.

She went out about six that morning; only intending, as they believe, to go to morning prayers at Covent-garden church, just by her lodgings, as she had done divers times before: Went on foot!—Left word she should be back in an hour—Very poorly in health!

Lord, have mercy upon me! What shall I do!—I was a distracted creature all last night!

O Madam! You know not how I love her!—She was my earthly saviour, as I may say!—My own soul is not dearer to me, than my Clarissa Harlowe!—Nay, she *is* my soul—For I now have none!—Only a miserable one, however!—For she was the joy, the stay, the prop of my life! Never woman loved woman as we love one another!—But now!—Who knows, whether the dear injured has not all her woes, her undeserved woes, completed in death; or is not reserved for a worse fate!—This I leave to your inquiry—For—your—(shall I call the man—your) relation, I understand, is still with you.

Surely, my good Ladies, you were well authorized in the proposals you made in presence of my mother! Surely he dare not abuse your confidence, and the confidence of your noble relations. I make no apology for giving you this trouble, nor for desiring you to favour with a line by this messenger.

Your almost distracted

Anna Howe

Mr. Lovelace
To John Belford, Esq;

M. Hall, Sat. Night, July 15.

ALL undone, undone, by Jupiter!—Zounds, Jack, what shall I do now! A curse upon all my plots and contrivances! —But I have it!—In the very heart and soul of me, I have it!

Thy assistance I bespeak: The moment thou receivest this, I bespeak thy assistance. This messenger rides for life and death!—And I hope he'll find you at your town-lodgings.

This cursed, cursed woman, on Friday dispatched man and horse with the joyful news that she had found out my angel as on Wednesday last; and on Friday morning, after she had been at prayers at Covent-garden church—praying for my reformation, perhaps!—got her arrested by two sheriffs officers, as she was returning to her lodgings, who put her into a chair they had in readiness, and carried her to one of the cursed fellows houses.

She has arrested her for 150*l*. pretendedly due for board and lodgings: A sum, besides the low villainy of the proceeding, which the dear soul could not possibly raise; all her cloaths and effects, except what she had on and with her, when she went away, being at the old devil's!

Hasten, hasten, dear Jack; for the love of God, hasten to the injured charmer! My heart bleeds for her!—She deserved not This!—I dare not stir!—It will be thought done by my contrivance:—And if I am absent from this place, that will confirm the suspicion.

Damnation seize quick this accursed woman!—Yet she thinks she has made no small merit with me!—Unhappy, thrice unhappy circumstance!—At a time too, when better prospects were opening for the sweet creature!

Set her free, the moment you see her: Without conditioning, free!—On your knees, for me, beg her pardon: And assure her, that, where-ever she goes, I will not molest her: No, nor come near her, without her leave: And be sure allow not any of the

422

damned crew to go near her—Only, let her permit *you* to receive her commands from time to time: You have always been her friend and advocate. What would I now give, had I permitted you to have been a successful one!

Let her have all her cloaths and effects sent her instantly, as a small proof of my sincerity. And force upon the dear creature, who must be moneyless, what sums you can get her to take. Let me know how she has been treated: If roughly, woe be to the guilty!

The great devil fly away with them all, one by one, thro' the roof of their own cursed house, and dash them to pieces against the tops of chimneys, as he flies; and let the lesser devils collect their scattered scraps, and bag them up, in order to put them together again in their alloted place, in the element of fire, with cements of molten lead.

A line! A line! A kingdom for a line! with tolerable news, the first moment thou canst write!—This fellow waits to bring it!

Miss Charlotte Montague To Miss Howe

M. Hall, *Tuesday afternoon.*

Dear Miss Howe,

Y OUR letter has infinitely disturbed us all.
This wretched man has been half distracted ever since Saturday night.

We knew not what ailed him, till your letter was brought.

Vile wretch, as he is, he is however innocent of this new evil.

Indeed he is, he *must* be; as I shall more at large acquaint you.

But will not now detain your messenger.

Only to satisfy your just impatience, by telling you, that the dear young lady is safe, and, we hope, well.

A horrid mistake of his general orders has subjected her to the terror and disgrace of an arrest.

Poor dear Miss Harlowe! her sufferings have endeared her to us, almost as much as her excellencies can have done to you.

But she must be now quite at liberty.

He has been a distracted man, ever since the news was brought him; and we knew not what ailed him.

But that I said before.

I know not what I write.

But you shall have all the particulars, just, and true, and fair, from,

> Dear madam,
> Your most faithful and obedient servant,
>
> Ch. Montague

Mr. Belford
To Robert Lovelace, Esq;

Sunday night, July 16.

WHAT a cursed piece of work hast thou made of it, with the most excellent of women! Thou mayest be in earnest, or in jest, as thou wilt; but the poor lady will not be long either thy sport, or the sport of fortune!

I will give thee an account of a scene that wants but her affecting pen to represent it justly; and it would wring all the black blood out of thy callous heart.

Thou only, who art the author of her calamities, shouldst have attended her in her prison. I am unequal to such a task: Nor know I any other man but would.

Your messenger found me at Edgware, expecting to dinner with me several friends, whom I had invited three days before. I sent apologies to them, as in a case of life and death; and speeded to town to the wicked woman's: For how knew I but shocking attempts might be made upon her by the cursed wretches; perhaps by thy contrivance, in order to mortify her into thy measures?

Finding the lady not there, I posted away to the officer's, altho' Sally told me, that she had been just come from thence; and that she had refused to see her, or, as she sent down word, any-body else; being resolved to have the remainder of that Sunday to herself, as it might, perhaps, be the last she should ever see.

I sent up to let her know, that I came with a commission to set her at liberty. I was afraid of sending up the name of a man known to be your friend. She absolutely refused to see *any man*, however, for that day, or to answer further to anything said from me.

Having therefore informed myself of all that the officer, and his wife, and servant, could acquaint me with, as well in relation to the horrid arrest, as to her behaviour, and the womens to her; and her ill state of health; I went back to Sinclair's, as I will still call her, and heard the three womens story.

Thy villain it was that set the poor lady, and had the impudence to appear, and abet the sheriff's officers in the cursed transaction. He thought, no doubt, that he was doing the most acceptable service to his blessed master. They had got a chair; the head ready up, as soon as service was over. And as she came out of the church, at the door fronting Bedford-street, the officers, stepping to her, whispered, that they had an action against her.

She was terrified, trembled, and turned pale.

Action! said she. What is that?—I have committed *no bad action!*—Lord bless me! Men, what mean you?

That you are our prisoner, Madam.

Prisoner, Sirs!—What—How—Why—What have I done?

You must go with us. Be pleased, Madam, to step into this chair.

With *you!*—With *men!* Must go with *men!*—I am not used to go with *strange men!*—Indeed you must excuse me!

We can't excuse you: We are sheriff's officers.—We have a Writ against you. You *must* go with us, and you shall know at whose Suit.

Suit! said the charming innocent; I don't know what you mean. Pray, men, don't lay hands upon me!—They offering to put her into the chair. I am not used to be thus treated!—I have done nothing to deserve it.

She then spied thy villain—O thou wretch, said she, where is thy vile master?—Am I again to be *his prisoner?* Help, good people!

A croud had before begun to gather.

The people were most of them struck with compassion. A fine young creature!—A thousand pities! cried some.—While some few threw out vile and shocking reflections: But a gentleman interposed, and demanded to see the fellows authority.

They shewed it. Is your name Clarissa Harlowe, Madam? said he.

Yes, yes, indeed, ready to sink, my name *was* Clarissa Harlowe:—But it is now *Wretchedness!*—Lord be merciful to me! what is to come next?

You *must* go with these men, Madam, said the gentleman: They have authority for what they do. He pitied her, and retired.

She heard not this—But said, Well, if I must go, I must!—I cannot resist—But I will not be carried to the woman's!—I will rather die at your feet, than be carried to the woman's!

You won't be carried there, Madam, cried thy fellow.

Only to *my* house, Madam, said one of the officers.

Where is that?

In High-Holborn, Madam.

I know not where High-Holborn is: But any-where, except to the woman's.—But am I to go with *men* only?

Looking about her, and seeing the three passages, to wit, that leading to Henrietta-street, that to King-street, and the fore-right one, to Bedford-street, crouded, she started—Any-where—Any-where, said she, but to the woman's! And stepping into the chair, threw herself on the seat, in the utmost distress and confusion—Carry me, carry me out of sight—Cover me—Cover me up—forever!—were her words.

Thy villain drew the curtains: She had not power; and they went away with her through a vast croud of people.

Here I must rest. I can write no more at present. Only, Lovelace, remember, *All this was to a Clarissa!!!*

The unhappy lady fainted away when she was taken out of the chair at the officer's house.

Several people followed the chair to the very house, which is in a wretched court. Sally was there; and satisfied some of the inquirers, that the young gentlewoman would be exceedingly well used: And they soon dispersed.

Dorcas was also there; but came not in her sight. Sally, as a favour, offered to carry her to her former lodgings: But she declared, they should carry her thither a corpse, if they did.

Very gentle usage the women boast of: So would a vultur, could it speak, with the entrails of its prey upon its rapacious talons. Of this thou'lt judge, from what I have to recite.

She asked, What was meant by this usage of her? People told me, said she, that I *must* go with the men!—That they had authority to take me: So I submitted. But now, what is to be the end of this disgraceful violence?

The end, said the vile Sally Martin, is, for honest people to come at their own.

Bless me! have I taken away anything that belongs to those who have obtained this power over me?—I have left very valuable things behind me; but have taken nothing away, that is not my own.

And who do you think, *Miss Harlowe*, for I understand, said the cursed creature, you are not married; who do you think is to pay for your board and your lodgings; such handsome lodgings! for so long a time as you were at Mrs. Sinclair's?

Lord have mercy upon me! Miss Martin (I think you are Miss Martin)!—And is this the cause of such a disgraceful insult upon me in the open streets?

And cause enough, *Miss Harlowe* (fond of gratifying her

jealous revenge, by calling her *Miss*)—One hundred and fifty guineas, or pounds, is no small sum to lose—And by a young creature, who would have bilked her lodgings!

You amaze me, Miss Martin!—What language do you talk in?—*Bilk my lodgings!*—What is that?

She stood astonished, and silent for a few moments.

But recovering herself, and turning from her to the window, she wrung her hands; and lifting them up—O my sister!—O my brother!—Tender mercies were your cruelties to *this!*

After a pause, her handkerchief drying up her falling tears, she turned to Sally! *Now*, have I nothing to do but acquiesce— Only let me say, That if this aunt of yours, This Mrs. Sinclair; or This man, This Mr. Lovelace, come near me; or if I am carried to the horrid house (for that I suppose is the design of this new outrage); God be merciful to the poor Clarissa Harlowe! —Look to the consequence!—Look, I charge you, to the consequence!

The vile wretch told her, It was not designed to carry her any-whither against her will: But, if it were, they should take care not to be frighted again by a *penknife.*

Sally inquired, in her presence, whether she had eat or drank any-thing; and being told by the woman, that she could not prevail upon her to taste a morsel, or drink a drop, she said, This is wrong, *Miss Harlowe!* Very wrong!—Your religion, I think, should teach you, that starving yourself is self-murder.

She answered not.

Am I not worth an answer, *Miss Harlowe?*

I would answer you (said the sweet sufferer, without any emotion), if I knew how.

I have ordered pen, ink, and paper, to be brought you, *Miss Harlowe.* There they are. I know you love writing. You may write to whom you please. Your friend Miss Howe will expect to hear from you.

I have no friend, said she. I deserve none.

Rowland, for that is the officer's name, told her, She had friends enow to pay the debt, if she would write.

She would trouble nobody; she had no friends; was all they could get from her.

About six in the Evening, Rowland's wife pressed her to drink tea. She said, She had rather have a glass of water; for her tongue was ready to cleave to the roof of her mouth.

The woman brought her a glass, and some bread and butter. She tried to taste the latter; but could not swallow it: But eagerly drank the water; lifting up her eyes in thankfulness for that!!!

The divine Clarissa, Lovelace—reduced to rejoice for a cup of cold water!—By whom *reduced!*

About nine o'clock she asked, If any-body were to be her bedfellow?

Their maid, if she pleased; or, as she was so weak and ill, the girl should sit up with her; if she chose she should.

She chose to be alone both night and day, she said. But might she not be trusted with the keys of the room where she was to lie down; for she should not put off her cloaths!

That, they told her, could not be.

She was afraid not, she said.—But indeed she would not get away, if she could.

They told me, that they had but one bed, besides that they lay in themselves; which they would fain have had her accept of; and besides *that* their maid lay in, in a garret, which they called a hole of a garret: And that *that* one bed was the prisoner's bed; which they made several apologies to me about. I suppose it is shocking enough.

But the lady would not lie in theirs. Was she not a prisoner, she said?—Let her have the prisoners room.

Yet they owned that she started, when she was conducted thither. But recovering herself, Very well, said she—Why should not my wretchedness be complete?

She found fault, that all the fastenings were on the outside, and none within; and said, She could not trust herself in a room, where others could come in at their pleasure, and she not go out. She had not *been used* to it!!!

Dear, dear soul!—My tears flow as I write.—Indeed, Lovelace, she had not been used to such treatment!

They assured her, that it was as much their duty to protect her from other persons insults, as from escaping herself.

Then they were people of more honour, she said, than she had of late been used to!

She asked, If they knew Mr. Lovelace?

No, was their answer.

Have you heard of him?

No.

Well then, you may be good sort of folks in your way.

Again they asked her, If they should send any word to her lodgings?

These are my lodgings now; are they not?—was all her answer.

She sat up in a chair all night, the back against the door; having, it seems, thrust a broken piece of a poker thro' the staples where a bolt had been on the inside.

At twelve Saturday night, Rowland sent to tell them, that she was so ill, that he knew not what might be the issue; and wished her out of his house.

And this made them as heartily wish to hear from you. For their messenger, to their great surprize, was not then returned from M. Hall. And they were sure he must have reached that place by Friday night.

Early on Sunday morning, both devils went to see how she did. They had such an account of her weakness, lowness, and anguish, that they forbore, out of compassion, they said, finding their visits so disagreeable to her, to see her.

They sent for the apothecary Rowland had had to her, and gave him, and Rowland, and his wife and maid, paradeful injunctions for the utmost care to be taken of her: No doubt, with an Old-Bailey forecast. And they sent up to let her know what orders they had given: But that, understanding she had taken something to compose herself, they would not disturb her.

She had scrupled, it seems, to admit the apothecary's visit over-night, because he was a MAN.—Nor could she be prevailed upon, till they pleaded *their own safety* to her.

When I first came, and told them of thy execrations for what they had done, and joined my own to them, they were astonished. The mother said, she had thought she had known Mr. Lovelace better; and expected thanks, and not curses.

While I was with them, came back halting and cursing, most horribly, their messenger; by reason of the ill-usage he had received from you, instead of the reward he had been taught to expect, for the supposed good news that he carried down of the lady's being found out, and secured.—A pretty fellow! art thou not, to abuse people for the consequences of thy own faults?

Under what shocking disadvantages, and with this addition to them, that I am thy friend and intimate, am I to make a visit to this unhappy lady to-morrow morning: In thy *name* too!—Enough to be refused, that I am of a *sex*, to which, for *thy* sake, she has so justifiable an aversion: Nor, having such a tyrant of a father, and such an implacable brother, has she reason to make an exception in favour of *any* of it on *their* accounts.

It is three o'clock. I will close here; and take a little rest: What I have written will be a proper preparative for what shall offer by-and-by.

J. Belford

Mr. Belford
To Robert Lovelace, Esq;

Monday, July 17.

ABOUT Six this morning I went to Rowland's. Mrs. Sinclair was to follow me, in order to dismiss the action; but not to come in sight.

Rowland, upon inquiry, told me, that the lady was extremely ill; and that she had desired, not to let anybody but his wife or maid come near her.

I said, I *must* see her. I had told him my business overnight; and I *must* see her.

His wife went up: But returned presently, saying, She could not get her to speak to her; yet that her eyelids moved; tho' she either would not, or could not, open them, to look up at her.

A horrid hole of a house, in an alley they call a court; stairs wretchedly narrow, even to the first-floor rooms: And into a den they led me, with broken walls, which had been papered, as I saw by a multitude of tacks, and some torn bits held on by the rusty heads.

The floor indeed was clean, but the ceiling was smoked with variety of figures, and initials of names, that had been the woful employment of wretches who had no other way to amuse themselves.

A bed at one corner, with coarse curtains tacked up at the feet to the ceiling; because the curtain rings were broken off; but a coverlid upon it with a cleanish look, tho' plaguily in tatters, and the corners tied up in tassels, that the rents in it might go no farther.

The windows dark and double-barred, the tops boarded up to save mending; and only a little four-paned eyelet-hole of a casement to let in air; more, however, coming in at broken panes, than could come in at That.

Four old turkey-worked chairs, bursten-bottomed, the stuffing staring out.

An old, tottering, worm-eaten table, that had more nails bestowed in mending it to make it stand, than the table cost fifty years ago, when new.

On the mantle-piece was an iron shove-up candlestick, with a lighted candle in it, twinkle, twinkle, twinkle, four of them, I suppose, for a peny.

Near that, on the same shelf, was an old looking-glass, cracked thro' the middle, breaking out into a thousand points; the crack given it, perhaps, in a rage, by some poor creature, to whom it gave the representation of his heart's woes in his face.

To finish the shocking description, in a dark nook stood an old, broken-bottomed cane couch, without a squab, or coverlid, sunk at one corner, and unmortised by the failing of one of its worm-eaten legs, which lay in two pieces under the wretched piece of furniture it could no longer support.

And This, thou horrid Lovelace, was the bedchamber of the divine Clarissa!!!

I had leisure to cast my eye on these things: For, going up softly, the poor lady turned not about at our entrance; nor, till I spoke, moved her head.

She was kneeling in a corner of the room, near the dismal window, against the table, on an old bolster, as it seemed to be, of the cane couch, half-covered with her handkerchief; her back to the door; which was only shut to (No need of fastenings!); her arms crossed upon the table, the fore-finger of her right-hand in her bible. She had perhaps been reading in it, and could read no longer. Paper, pens, ink, lay by her book, on the table. Her dress was white damask, exceeding neat; but her stays seemed not tight-laced. I was told afterwards, that her laces had been cut, when she fainted away at her entrance into this cursed place; and she had not been solicitous enough about her dress, to send for others. Her head-dress was a little discomposed; her charming hair, in natural ringlets, as you have heretofore described it, but a little tangled, as if not lately comb'd, irregularly shading one side of the loveliest neck in the world; as her dis-ordered, rumpled handkerchief did the other. Her face [O how altered from what I had seen it! Yet lovely in spite of all her griefs and sufferings!] was reclined, when we entered, upon her crossed arms; but so, as not more than one side of it to be hid.

When I survey'd the room around, and the kneeling lady, sunk with majesty too in her white flowing robes [for she had not on a hoop], spreading the dark, tho' not dirty, floor, and illuminating that horrid corner; her linen beyond imagination white, considering that she had not been undressed ever since she had been here; I thought my concern would have choaked me. Something rose in my throat, I know not what, which made me, for a moment, guggle, as it were, for speech: Which, at last, forcing its way, Con—Con—Confound you both, said I to the man and woman, is this an apartment for such a lady? And could the cursed devils of her own sex, who visited this suffering angel, see her, and leave her, in so damn'd a nook?

Up then raised the charming sufferer her lovely face; but with such a significance of woe overspreading it, that I could not, for the soul of me, help being visibly affected.

She waved her hand two or three times towards the door, as if commanding me to withdraw; and displeased at my intrusion; but did not speak.

Permit me, Madam—I will not approach one step farther

without your leave—Permit me, for one moment, the favour of
your ear!

No—No—Go, go; MAN, with an emphasis—And would
have said more; but, as if struggling in vain for words, she
seemed to give up speech for lost, and dropped her head down
once more, with a deep sigh, upon her left arm; her right, as if
she had not the use of it (numbed, I suppose) self-moved, dropping down on her side.

I dare not approach you, dearest Lady, without your leave:
But on my knees I beseech you to permit me to release you from
this damn'd house, and out of the power of the accursed woman,
who was the occasion of your being here!

She lifted up her sweet face once more, and beheld me on
my knees. Never knew I before what it was to pray so heartily.

Are you not—Are you not Mr. Belford, Sir? I think your
name is Belford?

It is, Madam, and I ever was a worshipper of your virtues,
and an advocate for you; and I come to release you from the
hands you are in.

And in whose to place me? O leave me, leave me! Let me
never rise from this spot! Let me never, never more believe in
man!

This moment, dearest Lady, this very moment, if you please,
you may depart whithersoever you think fit. You are absolutely
free, and your own mistress.

I had now as lieve die here in this place, as any-where. I will
owe no obligation to any friend of *him* in whose company you
have seen me. So, pray, Sir, withdraw.

Then turning to the officer, Mr. Rowland I think your
name is? I am better reconciled to your house than I was at first.
If you can but engage, that I shall have nobody come near me but
your wife; no *Man!* and neither of those women, who have
sported with my calamities; I will die with you, and in this very
corner. And you shall be well satisfied for the trouble you have
had with me.—I have value enough for that—for, see, I have a
diamond ring; taking it out of her bosom; and I have friends
will redeem it at a high price, when I am gone.

But for *you*, Sir, looking at me, I beg you to withdraw. If you mean me well, God, I hope, will reward you for your good meaning; but to the friend of my *destroyer* will I not owe an obligation.

You will owe no obligation to me, nor to any-body. You have been detained for a debt you do not owe. The action is dismissed; and you will only be so good as to give me your hand into the coach, which stands as near to this house as it could draw up. And I will either leave you at the coach-door, or attend you whithersoever you please, till I see you safe where you would wish to be.

Will you then, Sir, *compel* me to be beholden to you?

You will inexpressibly oblige me, Madam, to command me to do you either service or pleasure.

Why then, Sir—looking at me—But why do you mock me in that humble posture! Rise, Sir! I cannot speak to you else.

I arose.

Only, Sir, take this ring. I have a sister, who will be glad to have it, at the price it shall be valued at, for the *former* owner's sake!—Out of the money she gives, let this man be paid; handsomely paid: And I have a few valuables more at my lodging (Dorcas, or the Man William, can tell where that is); let them, and my cloaths at the wicked woman's, where you have seen me, be sold, for the payment of my lodging first, and next of your *friend's* debts, that I have been arrested for; as far as they will go; only reserving enough to put me into the ground, any-where, or any-how, no matter.—Tell your friend, I wish it may be enough to satisfy the whole demand; but if it be not, he must make it up himself; or if he think fit to draw for it on Miss Howe, she will repay it, and with interest, if he insist upon it.

I approached her, and was going to speak—

Don't speak, Sir: Here's the ring.

I stood off.

And won't you take it? Won't you do this last office for me?—I have no other person to ask it of; else, believe me, I would not request it of *you*. But take it or not, laying it upon the table—you must withdraw, Sir: I am very ill. I would fain get a little rest, if I could. I find I am going to be bad again.

And offering to rise, she sunk down thro' excess of weakness and grief, in a fainting fit.

The maid coming in just then, the woman and she lifted her up on the decrepit couch; and I withdrew with this Rowland; who wept like a child, and said, he never in his life was so moved.

They recovered her by harts-horn and water: I went down mean while; for the detestable woman had been below some time. O how did I curse her! I never before was so fluent in curses.

I sent up again, by Rowland's wife, when I heard that the lady was recovered, beseeching her to quit that devilish place; and the woman assured her, that she was at full liberty to do so; for that the action was dismissed.

But she cared not to answer her: And was so weak and low, that it was almost as much out of her power as inclination, the woman told me, to speak.

I would have hastened away for my friend doctor H. but the house is such a den, and the room she was in such a hole, that I was ashamed to be seen in it by a man of his reputation, especially with a woman of such an appearance, and in such uncommon distress; and I found there was no prevailing on her to quit it for the peoples bedroom, which was neat and lightsome.

And here being obliged to give way to an indispensable avocation, I will make thee taste a little in thy turn, of the plague of suspense; and break off, without giving thee the least hint of the issue of my further proceedings.

Another letter, however, shall be ready, send for it as soon as thou wilt. But, were it not, have I not written enough to convince thee, that I am

Thy ready and obliging friend,

J. Belford?

Mr. Belford
To Robert Lovelace, Esq;

Monday-night, July 17.

ON my return to Rowland's, I found that the Apothecary was just gone up. Mrs. Rowland being above with him, I made the less scruple to go up too, as it was probable, that to ask for leave would be to ask to be denied.

I represented to her, that she would be less free where she was, from visits she liked not, than at her own lodging. I told her, that it would probably bring her, in particular, *one visitor*, who, otherwise, I would engage, should not come near her, without her consent. And I expressed my surprize, that she should be unwilling to quit such a place as this; when it was more than probable, that some of her friends, when it was known how bad she was, would visit her.

She said, the place, when she was first brought into it, was indeed very shocking to her: But that she had found herself so weak and ill, and her griefs had so sunk her, that she did not expect to have lived till now: That therefore all places had been alike to her; for to die in a prison, *was* to die; and equally eligible as to die in a palace (palaces, she said, could have no attractions for a dying person): But that, since she feared she was not so soon to be released, as she had hoped; since she was suffered to be so little mistress of herself *here:* and since she might, by removal, be in the way of her dear friend's letters; she would hope, that she might depend upon the assurances I gave her, of being at liberty to return to her last lodgings (otherwise she would provide herself with new ones, out of my knowlege as well as out of yours).

I assured her, in the strongest terms (*but swore not*), that you were resolved not to molest her: And, as a proof of the sincerity of my professions, besought her to give me directions (in pursuance of my friend's express desire) about sending all her apparel, and whatever belonged to her, to her new lodgings.

She seemed pleased; and gave me instantly out of her pocket her keys; asking me, If Mrs. Smith, whom I had named, might not attend me; and she would give *her* further directions? To which I chearfully assented; and then she told me, that she would accept of the chair I had offered her.

I withdrew; and took the opportunity to be civil to Rowland and his maid; for she found no fault with their behaviour, for what they *were*; and the fellow seems to be miserably poor.

She gave the maid something; probably, the only half-guinea she had: And then, with difficulty, her limbs trembling under her, and supported by Mrs. Rowland, got down stairs.

I offered my arm: She was pleased to lean upon it. I doubt, Sir, said she, as she moved, I have behaved rudely to you: But, if you knew all, you would forgive me.

I ordered my servant (whose mourning made him less observable as such, and who had not been in the lady's eye) to keep the chair in view; and to bring me word, how she did, when set down. The fellow had the thought to step into the shop just before the chair entered it, under pretence of buying snuff; and so enabled himself to give me an account, that she was received with great joy by the good woman of the house; who told her, she was but just come in; and was preparing to attend her in High-Holborn.—O Mrs. Smith, said she, as soon as she saw her, did you not think I was run away?—You don't know what I have suffered since I saw you. I have been in a prison!—Arrested for debts I owe not!—But, thank God, I am here!

Will you let Katharine assist me to bed?—I have not had my cloaths off since Thursday night.

What she further said the fellow heard not, she leaning upon the maid, and going up-stairs.

'Tis a cursed thing, after all, that such a woman as this should be treated as she has been treated. Hadst thou been a king, and done as thou hast done by such a meritorious innocent, I believe in my heart, it would have been adjudged to be a national sin, and the sword, the pestilence, or famine, must have atoned for it!—But, as thou art a private man, thou wilt

certainly meet with thy punishment, as she will her reward,
Hereafter.

It must be so, if there be really such a thing as *future
Remuneration;* as now I am more and more convinced there
must:—Else, what a hard fate is hers, whose punishment, to
all appearance, has so much exceeded her fault? And, as to
thine, how can *temporary* burnings, wert thou by some accident
to be consumed in thy bed, expiate for thy abominable vileness
to her, in breach of all obligations moral and divine?

I was resolved to lose no time in having every-thing which
belonged to the lady at the cursed woman's sent her. Accordingly, I took coach to Smith's, and procured the lady to give
proper directions to Mrs. Smith: Whom I took with me to
Sinclair's; and who saw every-thing looked out, and put into the
trunks and boxes they were first brought in, and carried away
in two coaches.

Had I not been there, Sally and Polly would each of them
have taken to herself something of the poor Lady's spoils. This
they declared: And I had something to do to get from Sally
a fine Brussels-lace head, which she had the confidence to say
she would wear for *Miss Harlowe's* sake.

I ordered the abandoned women to make out your account.
They answered, *That* they would do with a *vengeance.* Indeed
they breathe nothing but revenge. For now they say, you will
assuredly marry; and your example will be followed by all your
friends and companions—As the old one says, to the utter ruin
of her poor house.

Mr. Belford
To Robert Lovelace, Esq;

Wednesday, July 19.

THIS morning I took chair to Smith's; and, being told, that
the lady had a very bad night, but was up, I sent for her
worthy apothecary; who, on his coming to me, approving of my

proposal of calling in Dr. H. I bid the women acquaint her with the designed visit.

Having been told, I was below with Mr. Goddard, she desired to speak one word with me, before she saw the Doctor.

She was sitting in an elbow-chair, leaning her head on a pillow; Mrs. Smith and the widow on each side her chair; her nurse, with a phial of harts-horn, behind her; in her own hand, her salts.

Raising her head at my entrance, she inquired, If the Doctor knew Mr. Lovelace?

I told her, No; and that I believed you never saw him in your life.

Was the Doctor my friend?

He was; and a very worthy and skilful man. I named him for his eminence in his profession: And Mr. Goddard said, he knew not a better physician.

I have but one condition to make before I see the gentleman; that he refuse not his fees from me. If I am poor, Sir, I am proud. I will not be under obligation. You may *believe*, Sir, I will not. I suffer this visit, because I would not appear ungrateful to the few friends I have left, nor obstinate to such of my relations, as may some time hence, for their private satisfaction, inquire after my behaviour in my sick hours. So, Sir, you know the condition. And don't let me be vexed: I am very ill; and cannot debate the matter.

Seeing her so determined, I told her, If it must be so, it should.

Then, Sir, the gentleman may come. But I shall not be able to answer many questions. Nurse, you can tell him, at the window there, what a night I have had, and how I have been for two days past. Pray let me be as little questioned, as possible.

He took her hand, the lily not of so beautiful a white: Indeed, Madam, you are very low, said he: But, give me leave to say, That you can do more for yourself, than all the faculty can do for you.

He then withdrew to the window. And, after a short conference with the women, he turned to me, and to Mr. Goddard, at the other window: We can do nothing here, speaking low, but by cordials and nourishment. What friends has the lady? She seems to be a person of condition; and, ill as she is, a very fine woman.—A single lady, I presume?

I whisperingly told him she was. That there were extraordinary circumstances in her case; as I would have apprised him, had I met with him yesterday. That her friends were very cruel to her; but that she could not hear them named, without reproaching herself; tho' they were much more to blame than she.

I knew I was right, said the Doctor. A love-case, Mr. Goddard! A love-case, Mr. Belford! There is one person in the world, who can do her more service, than all the faculty.

Mr. Goddard said, he had apprehended her disorder was in her mind; and had treated her accordingly: And then told the Doctor what he had done: Which he approving of, again taking her charming hand, said, My good young lady, you will require very little of our assistance. You must, in a great measure, be your own doctress. Come, *dear* Madam, chear up your spirits. Resolve to do all in your power to be well; and you'll soon grow better.

You are very kind, Sir, said she. I will take whatever you direct. My spirits have been hurried. I shall be better, I believe, before I am worse. The care of my good friends here, looking at the women, shall not meet with an ingrateful return.

The Doctor wrote. He would fain have declined his fee. As her malady, he said, was rather to be relieved by the soothings of a friend, than by the prescriptions of a physician, he should think himself greatly honoured to be admitted rather to *advise* her in the *one* character, than to *prescribe* to her in the *other*.

She answered, That she should be always glad to see so humane a gentleman: That his visits would *keep her in charity with his sex*: But that, were she to *forget* that he was her *physician*, she might be apt to abate of the confidence in his skill, which might be necessary to effect the amendment that was the end of his visits.

We all withdrew together; and the Doctor and Mr. Goddard having a great curiosity to know something more of her story, at the motion of the latter we went into a neighbouring coffeehouse, and I gave them, in confidence, a brief relation of it; making all as light for you as I could; and yet you'll suppose, that, in order to do but common justice to the lady's character, heavy must be that light.

Mr. Belford
To Robert Lovelace, Esq;

Friday Noon, July 21.

THIS morning I was admitted, as soon as I sent up my name, into the presence of the divine lady. Such I may call her; as what I have to relate will fully prove.

She had had a tolerable night, and was much better in spirits; though weak in person; and visibly declining in looks.

Mrs. Lovick and Mrs. Smith were with her; and accused her, in a gentle manner, of having applied herself too assiduously to her pen for her strength, having been up ever since five.

She had been writing, she said, a letter to her sister: But had not pleased herself in it; tho' she had made two or three essays: But that the last must go.

By hints I had dropt from time to time, she had reason, she said, to think that I knew every-thing that concerned her and her family; and, if so, must be acquainted with the heavy curse her father had laid upon her; which had been dreadfully fulfilled in one part, as to her temporary prospects, and that in a very short time; which gave her great apprehensions of the other. She had been applying herself to her sister, to obtain a revocation of it. I hope my father will revoke it, said she, or I shall be very miserable.—Yet (and she gasped as she spoke, with apprehension)—I am ready to tremble at what the answer may be; for my sister is hard-hearted.

I said something reflecting upon her friends; as to what they would deserve to be thought of, if the unmerited imprecation were not withdrawn.—Upon which she took me up, and talked in such a dutiful manner of her parents, as must doubly condemn them (if they remain implacable), for their inhuman treatment of such a daughter.

She said, I must not blame her parents: It was her dear Miss Howe's fault. But what an enormity was there in her crime, which could set the best of parents (as they had been to her, till she disobliged them) in a bad light, for resenting the rashness of a child, from whose education they had reason to expect better fruits! If they had any fault, it was only, that they would not inform themselves of some circumstances, which would alleviate a little her misdeed; and that, supposing her a guiltier creature than she was, they punished her without a hearing.

Lord!—*I was going to curse thee, Lovelace! How every instance of excellence, in this all-excelling creature, condemns thee!—Thou wilt have reason to think thyself of all men most accursed, if she die!*

I then besought her, while she was capable of such glorious instances of generosity and forgiveness, to extend her goodness to a man whose heart bled in every vein of it, for the injuries he had done her; and who would make it the study of his whole life to repair them.

The women would have withdrawn when the subject became so particular. But she would not permit them to go. She told me, that if, after this time, I was for entering, with so much earnestness, into a subject so very disagreeable to *her*, my visits must not be repeated. Nor was there occasion, she said, for my friendly offices in your favour; since she had begun to write her whole mind upon that subject to Miss Howe, in answer to letters from her, in which Miss Howe urged the same arguments, in compliment to the wishes of your noble and worthy relations.

Mean time, you may let him know, said she, That I reject him with my whole heart:—Yet that, altho' I say this with such a determination as shall leave no room for doubt, I say it not however with passion. On the contrary, tell him, that I am trying to bring my mind into such a frame, as to be able to *pity* him; and that I shall not think myself qualified for the state I am aspiring to, if, after a few struggles more, I cannot *forgive*

him too: And I hope, clasping her hands together, uplifted, as
were her eyes, my dear *earthly* father will set me the example
my *heavenly* one has already set us all; and, by forgiving his
fallen daughter, teach her to forgive the man, who then, I hope,
will not have destroyed my eternal prospects, as he has my
temporal!

*Stop here, thou wretch!—But I need not bid thee!—For I
can go no farther!*

Mr. Belford

In Continuation.

YOU will imagine how affecting her noble speech and behaviour was to me, at the time, when the bare recollection
and transcription obliged me to drop my pen. The women had
tears in their eyes. I was silent for a few moments.—At last,
Matchless excellence! inimitable goodness; I called her, with
a voice so accented, that I was half-ashamed of myself, as it was
before the women.—Methinks, said I (and I really, in a manner
involuntarily, bent my knee), I have before me an angel indeed.

She was going to interrupt me, with a prohibitory kind of
earnestness in her manner—

I beg leave to proceed, Madam: I have cast about twenty
ways how to mention this before, but never dared till now.
Suffer me, now that I have broken the ice, to tender myself—
as your banker only.—I know you will not be obliged: You
need not. You have sufficient of your own, if it were in your
hands: and from *that*, whether you live or die, will I consent
to be reimbursed. I do assure you, that the unhappy man shall
never know either *my* offer, or *your* acceptance—Only permit
me this small—

And down behind her chair I dropt a Bank note of 100*l.*
which I had brought with me, intending some how or other to
leave it behind me: Nor shouldst thou ever have known it, had
she favoured me with the acceptance of it; as I told her.

You give me great pain, Mr. Belford, said she, by these instances of your humanity. And yet, considering the company I have seen you in, I am not sorry to find you capable of such.— But as to your kind offer, whatever it be, if you take it not up, you will greatly disturb me. I have no need of your kindness. I have effects enough, which I never can want, to supply my present occasions; and, if needful, can have recourse to Miss Howe. I have promised that I would—So, pray, Sir, urge not upon me this favour.

I beg, Madam, but one word—

Not one, Sir, till you have taken back what you have let fall. I doubt not either the *honour*, or the *kindness*, of your offer; but you must not say one word more on this subject. I cannot bear it.

She was stooping, but with pain. I therefore prevented her; and besought her to forgive me for a tender, which, I saw, had been more discomposing to her than I had hoped (from the purity of my intentions), it would be. But I could not bear to think, that such a mind as hers should be distressed.

You are very kind to me, Sir, said she, and very favourable in your opinion of me. But I hope, that I cannot now be easily put out of my present course. My declining health will more and more confirm me in it. Those who arrested and confined me, no doubt, thought they had fallen upon the ready method to distress me so, as to bring me into all their measures. But I presume to hope, that I have a mind that cannot be debased, in *essential instances*, by temporal calamities.

She then turned from me towards the window, with a dignity suitable to her words; and such as shewed her to be more of soul than of body, at that instant.

I repeated my offers to write to any of her friends; and told her, that, having taken the liberty to acquaint Dr. H. with the cruel displeasure of her relations, as what I presumed lay nearest her heart, he had proposed to write himself, to acquaint her friends how ill she was, if she would not take it amiss.

It was kind in the *Doctor*, she said: But begged, that no step of that sort might be taken without her knowlege and consent. She would wait to see what effects her letter to her sister

would have. All she had to hope for, was, <u>that her father would</u>
<u>revoke his malediction.</u>

Mrs. Smith went down; and, soon returning, asked, If the
lady and I would not dine with her that day: For it was her
wedding-day. She had engaged Mrs. Lovick, she said; and should
have nobody else, if we would do her that favour.

The charming creature sighed, and shook her head.—
Wedding-day, repeated she!—I wish you, Mrs. Smith, many
happy wedding-days!—But you will excuse *me*.

She then desired they would all sit down. You have several
times, Mrs. Lovick and Mrs. Smith, hinted your wishes, that
I would give you some little history of myself: Now, if you are
at leisure, that this gentleman, who, I have reason to believe,
knows it all, is present, and can tell you if I give it justly, or
not, I will oblige your curiosity.

They all eagerly, the man Smith too, sat down; and she
began an account of herself, which I will endeavour to repeat,
as nearly in her own words, as I possibly can: For I know you
will think it of importance to be apprised of her manner of
relating your barbarity to her, as well as what her sentiments
are of it.

At first when I took these lodgings, said she, I thought
of staying but a short time in them; and so, Mrs. Smith, I told
you: I therefore avoided giving any other account of myself,
than that I was a very unhappy young creature, seduced from
good friends, and escaped from very vile wretches.

This account I thought myself obliged to give, that you
might the less wonder at seeing a young body rushing thro'
your shop, into your back apartment, all trembling, and out
of breath; an ordinary garb over my own; craving lodging and
protection; only giving my bare word, that you should be handsomely paid: All my effects contained in a pocket-handkerchief.

My sudden absence, for three days and nights together,
when arrested, must still further surprise you: And altho' this
gentleman, who, perhaps, knows more of the darker part of
my story, than I do myself, has informed you (as you, Mrs.
Lovick, tell me) that I am only an *unhappy*, not a *guilty* creature;

yet I think it incumbent upon me not to suffer honest minds to
be in doubt about my character.

I was visited (at first, with my friends connivance) by a
man of birth and fortune, but of worse principles, as it proved,
than I believed any man could have. My brother, a very headstrong young man, was absent at that time; and, when he returned (from an old grudge, and knowing the gentleman, it is
plain, better than I knew him), intirely disapproved of his visits:
And, having a great sway in our family, brought other gentlemen to address me: And at last (several having been rejected)
he introduced one extremely disagreeable: In every *indifferent*
body's eyes disagreeable. I could not love him. They all joined
to compel me to have him; a rencounter between the gentleman
my friends were set against, and my brother, having confirmed
them all his enemies.

To be short: I was confined, and treated so very hardly,
that, in a rash fit, I appointed to go off with the man they hated.
A wicked intention, you'll say: But I was greatly provoked:
Nevertheless, I repented; and resolved not to go off with him;
yet I did not mistrust his honour to me neither; nor his love;
because nobody thought me unworthy of the latter, and my
fortune was not to be despised. But foolishly (wickedly, as my
friends still think, and contrivingly, with a design, as they
imagine, to abandon them) giving him a private meeting, I was
tricked away.

After remaining some time at a farm-house in the country,
behaving to me all the time with honour, he brought me to
handsome lodgings in town, till still better provision could be
made for me. But they proved to be, as he indeed knew and
designed, at a vile, a very vile creature's; tho' it was long before
I found her to be so; for I knew nothing of the town, or its ways.

There is no repeating what followed: Such unprecedented
vile arts!—For I gave him no opportunity to take me at any
disreputable advantage.—

And here (half covering her sweet face, with her handkerchief put to her tearful eyes) she stopt.

Hastily, as if she would fly from the hateful remembrance,

she resumed:—"I made my escape afterwards from the abominable house in his absence, and came to yours: And this gentleman
has almost prevailed on me to think, that the ingrateful man
did not connive at the vile arrest: Which was made, no doubt,
in order to get me once more to those wicked lodgings: For
nothing do I owe them, except I were to pay them"—(she sighed,
and again wiped her charming eyes—adding in a softer, lower
voice)—"*for being ruined!*"—

My real name you now know to be Harlowe: *Clarissa*
Harlowe. I am not yet twenty years of age.

I have an excellent mother, as well as father; a woman of
family, and fine sense—Worthy of a better child!—They both
doated upon me.

In short, I was beloved by every-body. The Poor—I used
to make glad *their* hearts: I never shut my hand to any distress,
where-ever I was—But now I am poor myself!

So, Mrs. Smith, so, Mrs. Lovick, I am *not* married. It is
but just to tell you so. And I am now, as I ought to be, in a state
of humiliation and penitence for the rash step which has been
followed by so much evil.

I see, continued she, that I, who once was every one's
delight, am now the cause of grief to every-one—You, that are
strangers to me, are moved for me! 'Tis kind!—but 'tis time to
stop. Your compassionate hearts, Mrs. Smith, and Mrs. Lovick,
are too much touched. My hopes, like opening buds or blos-
soms in an over-forward spring, have been nipt by a severe
frost!—Blighted by an eastern wind!—But I can but *once die*;
and if life be spared me, but till I am discharged from a heavy
malediction, which my father in his wrath laid upon me, and
which is fulfilled literally in every article relating to this world,
it is all I have to wish for; and death will be welcomer to me,
than rest to the most wearied traveller, that ever reached his
journey's-end.

And then she sunk her head against the back of her chair,
and, hiding her face with her handkerchief, endeavoured to
conceal her tears from us.

Not a soul of us could speak a word. Thy presence, perhaps,
thou hardened wretch, might have made us ashamed of a weak-

ness, which, perhaps, thou wilt deride *me* in particular for, when thou readest this!—

She retired to her chamber soon after, and was forced, it seems, to lie down. We all went down together; and, for an hour and half, dwelt upon her praises; Mrs. Smith and Mrs. Lovick repeatedly expressing their astonishment, that there could be a man in the world capable of offending, much more of wilfully injuring, such a lady; and repeating, that they had an angel in their house.—I thought they had; and that as assuredly as there is a devil under the roof of good Lord M.

I hate thee heartily!—By my faith I do!—Every hour I hate thee more than the former!—

J. Belford

Mr. Lovelace
To John Belford, Esq;

Sat. July 22.

WHAT dost hate me for, Belford?—And why more and more?—Have I been guilty of any offence thou knewest not before?—If *pathos* can move such a heart as thine, can it alter facts?—Did I not always do this incomparable creature as much justice as thou canst do her for the heart of thee, or as she can do herself?—What nonsense then thy hatred, thy *augmented* hatred, when I still persist to marry her, pursuant to word given to thee, and to faith plighted to all my relations? But hate, if thou wilt, so thou dost but write. Thou canst not hate me so much as I do myself: And yet I know, if thou really hatedst me, thou wouldst not venture to tell me so.

Well, but after all, what need of her history to these women? She will certainly repent, some time hence, that she has thus needlessly exposed us both.

Sickness palls every appetite, and makes us hate what we loved: But renewed health changes the scene; disposes us to be pleased with ourselves; and then we are in a way to be pleased with every-one else. Every hope, then, rises upon us: Every hour presents itself to us on dancing feet: And what Mr. Addison says of Liberty, may, with still greater propriety, be said of *Health (For what is Liberty itself without Health?):*

> It makes the gloomy face of nature gay;
> Gives beauty to the sun, and pleasure to the day.

And I rejoice that she is already so much better, as to hold, with strangers, such a long and interesting conversation.

Strange, confoundedly strange, and as perverse (that is to say, as *womanly*) as strange, that she should refuse, and sooner choose to die—[O the obscene word! and yet how free does thy pen make with it to me!], than be mine, who offended her by acting *in* character, while her parents acted shamefully *out of theirs*, and when I am now willing to act *out of my own* to oblige her: Yet I not to be forgiven! *They* to be faultless with her!—And marriage the only medium to repair all breaches, and to salve her own honour!—Surely thou must see the inconsistence of her *forgiving* unforgivingness, as I may call it!—Yet, heavy varlet as thou art, thou wantest to be drawn up after her!

But the prettiest whim of all was, to drop the bank note behind her chair, instead of presenting it on thy knees to her hand!—To make such a lady as this *doubly* stoop—By the acceptance, and to take it from the ground!—What an ungraceful *benefit-conferrer* art thou! How aukward, to take it into thy head, that the best way of making a present to a lady, was to throw the present behind her chair!

I am very desirous to see what she has written to her sister; what she is about to write to Miss Howe; and what return she will have from the Harlowe-Arabella. Canst thou not form some scheme to come at the copies of these letters, or at the substance of them at least, and of that of her other correspondencies?

But one consolation arises to me, from the pretty regrets which this admirable creature seems to have, in indulging reflections on the peoples wedding-day.

What once a lady hopes, in love-matters, she always hopes,

while there is room for hope: And are we not both single? Can
she be any man's but mine? Will I be any woman's but hers?

I never will! I never can!—And I tell thee, that I am every
day, every hour, more and more in love with her: And, at this
instant, have a more vehement passion for her than ever I had
in my life!—And that with views absolutely honourable, in *her
own sense* of the word: Nor have I varied, so much as in *wish*,
for this week past; firmly fixed, and wrought into my very
nature, as the *life of honour*, or of generous confidence in me,
was, in preference to the life of *doubt* and *distrust*.

I shall go on Monday morning to a kind of Ball, to which
Colonel Ambrose has invited me. It is given on a family account.
I care not on what: For all that delights me in the thing, is, that
Mrs. and Miss Howe are to be there; Hickman, of course; for the
old lady will not stir abroad without him. The Colonel is in
hopes, that Miss Arabella Harlowe will be there likewise; for all
the fellows and women of fashion round him are invited.

I fell in by accident with the Colonel, who, I believe, hardly
thought I would accept of the invitation. But he knows me not,
if he thinks I am ashamed to appear at any place, where ladies
dare shew their faces. Yet he hinted to me, that my name *was
up*, on Miss Harlowe's account. But, to allude to one of my
uncle's phrases, if it be, I will not *lie abed* when any-thing joyous
is going forward.

As I shall go in my Lord's chariot, I would have had one
of my cousins Montague to go with me: But they both refused:
And I sha'n't choose to take either of thy brethren. It would
look as if I thought I wanted a body guard: Besides, one of them
is too rough, the other too smooth, and too great a fop for some
of the staid company that will be there; and for *me* in particular.

I remember, when I first saw thee, my mind laboured with
a strong puzzle, whether I should put thee down for a great
fool, or a smatterer in wit: Something I saw was wrong in thee,
by thy *dress*. If this fellow, thought I, delights not so much in
ridicule, that he will not spare *himself*, he must be plaguy silly
to take so much pains to make his ugliness more conspicuous
than it would otherwise be.

Plain dress, for an ordinary man or woman, implies at

least *modesty*, and always procures kind quarter from the
censorious. Who will ridicule a personal imperfection in one
that seems conscious that it *is* an imperfection? *Who ever said,
an anchoret was poor?* But to such as appear proud of their
deformity, or bestow tinsel upon it in hopes to set it off, who
would spare so very absurd a wrong head?

But, altho' I put on these lively airs, I am sick at my soul!—
My whole heart is with my charmer! With what indifference
shall I look upon all the assemblée at the Colonel's, my Beloved
in my ideal eye, and engrossing my whole heart?

Miss Howe
To Miss Arabella Harlowe

Thursday, July 20.

Miss Harlowe,

I CANNOT help acquainting you (however it may be received,
coming from *me*) that your poor sister is dangerously ill,
at the house of one Smith, who keeps a glover's and perfume-
shop, in King-street, Covent-Garden. She knows not that I write.
Some violent words, in the nature of an imprecation, from her
father, afflict her greatly in her weak state. I presume not to
direct to you what to do in this case. You are her sister. I therefore could not help writing to you, not only for her sake, but
for your own.

I am, Madam, Your humble servant,

Anna Howe

Miss Arabella Harlowe
In Answer.

Thursday, July 20.

Miss Howe,

I HAVE yours of this morning. All that has happened to the unhappy body you mention, is what we foretold, and expected. Let *him*, for whose sake she abandoned us, be her comfort. We are told he has remorse, and would marry her. We don't believe it, indeed. She *may* be very ill. Her disappointment may make her so, or ought. Yet is she the only one I know, who is disappointed.

I cannot say, Miss, that the notification from you is the *more* welcome for the liberties you have been pleased to take with our whole family, for resenting a conduct, that it is a shame any young lady should justify. Excuse this freedom, occasioned by greater.

I am, Miss, Your humble servant,

Arabella Harlowe

Miss Howe
In Reply.

Friday, July 21.

Miss Arabella Harlowe,

I F you had half as much sense as you have ill-nature, you would (notwithstanding the exuberance of the latter) have been able to distinguish between a kind intention to you all (that you might have the less to reproach yourselves with, if a deplorable case should happen), and an officiousness I owed you not, for the *unhappy body's* sake, as you call a sister you

453

have helped to make so, say all that I *could* say. If what I fear happen, you shall hear (whether desired or not) all the mind of

Anna Howe

Miss Arabella Harlowe To Miss Howe

Friday, July 21.

Miss Ann Howe,

Y OUR pert letter I have received. You, that spare no-body, I cannot expect should spare me. You are very happy in a prudent and watchful mother—But else—Mine cannot be exceeded in prudence: But we had all too good an opinion of Somebody, to think watchfulness needful. There may possibly be some reason why *you* are so much attached to her, in an error of this flagrant nature.

I help to make a sister unhappy!—It is false, Miss!—It is all her own doings!—Except, indeed, what she may owe to Somebody's advice—You know who can best answer for that.

Let us *know your mind* as soon as you please: As we shall know it to be *your* mind, we shall judge what attention to give it. That's all, from, &c.

Ar. H.

Mr. Lovelace To John Belford, Esq;

Friday, July 28.

H OW often have I ingenuously confessed my sins against this excellent creature?—Yet thou never sparest me, altho' as bad a man as myself. Since then I get so little by my confessions, I had a good mind to try to defend myself; and that not only from antient and modern story, but from common practice; and yet avoid repeating anything I have suggested before in my own behalf.

I am in a humour to play the fool with my pen: Briefly then, from antient story first:—Dost thou not think, that I am as much intitled to forgiveness on Miss Harlowe's account, as Virgil's hero was on Queen Dido's? For what an ungrateful varlet was that vagabond to the *hospitable* princess, who had *willingly* conferred upon him the last favour?—Stealing away (whence, I suppose, the ironical phrase of *Trusty Trojan* to this day) like a thief; pretendedly indeed at the command of the gods; but could that be, when the errand he went upon was to rob other princes, not only of their dominions, but of their lives?— Yet this fellow is, at every word, the *pius* AEneas, with the immortal bard who celebrates him.

Should Miss Harlowe even break her heart (which Heaven forbid!) for the usage she has received (to say nothing of her disappointed pride, to which her death would be attributable, more than to reason) what comparison will *her* fate hold to Queen Dido's? And have I half the obligation to her, that AEneas had to the Queen of Carthage? The latter placing a confidence, the former none, in her man?—Then, whom *else* have I robbed? Whom *else* have I injured? Her brother's worthless life I gave him, instead of taking any man's; while the Trojan vagabond destroyed his thousands. Why then should it not be the *pius* Lovelace, as well as the *pius* AEneas?

But for a more modern instance in my favour—Have I used Miss Harlowe, as our famous Maiden-Queen, as she was called, used one of her own blood, a Sister-Queen; who threw herself into her protection from her rebel-subjects; and whom she detained prisoner eighteen years, and at last cut off her head? Yet do not honest Protestants pronounce *her* pious too?— And call her particularly *their* Queen?

As to *common practice*—Who, let me ask, that has it in his power to gratify a predominant passion, be it what it will, denies himself the gratification?—Leaving it to cooler deliberation; and, if he be a great man, to his flatterers; to find a reason for it afterwards?

Then, as to the worst part of my treatment of this lady—
How many men are there, who, as well as I, have sought, by
intoxicating liquors, first to inebriate, then to subdue? What
signifies what the *potations* were, when the same end was in
view?

Let me tell thee, upon the whole, that neither the Queen
of Carthage, nor the Queen of Scots, would have thought they
had any reason to complain of cruelty, had they been used no
worse than I have used the Queen of my heart: And then do I
not aspire with my whole soul to repair by marriage? Would the
pius AEneas, thinkest thou, have done such a piece of justice
by Dido, had she lived?

Come, come, Belford, let people run away with notions
as they will, I am *comparatively* a very innocent man. And if
by these, and other like reasonings, I have quieted my own
conscience, a great end is answered. What have I to do with the
world?

This cursed arrest, because of the ill effects the terror might
have had upon her, in that hoped-for circumstance, has concerned me more than on any other account. It would be the pride
of my life to prove, in this charming frost-piece, the triumph
of nature over principle, and to have a young Lovelace by such
an angel: And then, for its sake, I am confident she will live,
and will legitimate it. And what a meritorious little cherub
would it be, that should lay an obligation upon both parents
before it was born, which neither of them would be able to
repay!—Could I be sure it is so, I should be out of all pain for
her recovery: *Pain*, I say; since, were she to *die*—(*Die!* abominable word! how I hate it!) I verily think I should be the most
miserable man in the world.

As for the earnestness she expresses for death, she has
found the words ready to her hand in honest Job; else she would
not have delivered herself with such strength and vehemence.

Her innate piety (as I have more than once observed) will
not permit her to shorten her own life, either by violence or
neglect. She has a mind too noble for that; and would have
done it before now, had she designed any such thing.

Then, as I observed in a like case, a little while ago, the

distress, when this was written, was strong upon her; and she saw no end of it: But all was darkness and apprehension before her. Moreover, has she it not in her power to *disappoint*, as much as she has been *disappointed*? Revenge, Jack, has induced many a woman to cherish a life, which grief and despair would otherwise have put an end to.

Miss Clarissa Harlowe To Miss Howe

Sunday, July 30.

YOU have given me great pleasure, my dearest friend, by your approbation of my reasonings, and of my resolution founded upon them, never to have Mr. Lovelace. This approbation is so *right* a thing, give me leave to say, from the nature of the case, and from the strict honour and true dignity of mind, which I always admired in my Anna Howe, that I could hardly tell to what, but to my evil destiny, which of late would not let me please any-body, to attribute the advice you gave me to the contrary.

But let not the ill state of my health, and what that may naturally tend to, sadden you. I have told you, that I will not run away from life, nor avoid the means that may continue it, if God see fit: And if he do *not*, who shall repine at his will?

If it shall be found, that I have not acted unworthy of your love, and of my own character, in my greater trials, that will be a happiness to both on reflection.

I am more grieved (at times however) for *others*, than for *myself*. And so I *ought*. For as to *myself*, I cannot but reflect, that I have had an escape, rather than a loss, in missing Mr. Lovelace for a husband: Even had he *not* committed the vilest of all outrages.

Let any one, who knows my story, collect his character from his behaviour to *me*, *before* that outrage; and then judge, whether it was in the least probable for such a man to make me happy. But to collect his character from his principles, with regard to the *Sex in general*, and from his enterprizes upon many of them, and to consider the cruelty of his nature, and the sportiveness of his invention, together with the *high opinion he has of himself*, it will not be doubted, that a wife of his must have been miserable; and more miserable if she loved him, than if she could have been indifferent to him.

Had I been his but a *month*, he must have possessed the estate on which my relations had set their hearts; the more to their regret, as they hated *him* as much as he hated *them*.

Have I not reason, these things considered, to think myself happier without Mr. Lovelace, than I could have been with him?—My will too unviolated; and very little, nay, not anything as to him, to reproach myself with?

But with my *relations* it is *otherwise*. They indeed deserve to be pitied. They are, and no doubt will long be, unhappy.

To judge of their resentments, and of their conduct, we must put ourselves in their situation:—And while *they* think me more in fault than themselves (whether my favourers are of their opinion, or not) and have a right to judge for themselves, they ought to have great allowances made for them; my parents especially. They stand at least *self*-acquitted (that cannot I); and the rather, as they can recollect, to their pain, their past indulgencies to me, and their unquestionable love.

Now Mr. Belford knows, as I have already mentioned, every-thing that has passed. He is a man of spirit, and, it seems, as fearless as the other, with more humane qualities. You don't know, my dear, what instances of sincere humanity this Mr. Belford has shewn, not only on occasion of the cruel arrest, but on several occasions since. And Mrs. Lovick has taken pains to inquire after his general character; and hears a very good one of him, for justice and generosity in all his concerns of *Meum* and *Tuum*, as they are called: He has a knowlege of law-matters; and has two executorships upon him at this time, in the discharge of which his honour is unquestioned.

But, after all, I know not, if it were not more eligible by far, that my story should be forgotten as soon as possible. And of this I shall have the less doubt, if the character of my parents cannot be guarded (You will forgive me, my dear) from the unqualified bitterness, which, from your affectionate zeal for me, has sometimes mingled with your ink.

If you set out to-morrow, this letter cannot reach you till you get to your Aunt Harman's. I shall therefore direct it thither, as Mr. Hickman instructed me.

I hope you will have met with no inconveniences in your little journey and voyage; and that you will have found in good health all whom you wish to see well.

Your ever-faithful and affectionate

Cl. Harlowe!

Mr. Lovelace
To John Belford , Esq;

Sat. Aug. 5.

THOU runnest on with thy cursed nonsensical *reformado-rote*, of dying, dying, dying! and, having once got the word by the end, canst not help foisting it in at every period! The devil take me, if I don't think thou wouldst give her poison with thy own hands, rather than she should recover, and rob thee of the merit of being a conjurer!

But no more of thy cursed knell; thy changes upon death's candlestick turned bottom-upwards: She'll live to bury me; I see that: For, by my soul, I can neither eat, drink, nor sleep; nor, what is still worse, love any woman in the world but her. Nor care I to look upon a woman now; on the contrary, I turn my head from every one I meet; except by chance an eye, an air, a feature, strikes me resembling hers in some glancing-by face; and then I cannot forbear looking again; tho' the second look recovers me; for there can be nobody like her.

But surely, Belford, the devil's in this lady! The more I think
of her nonsense and obstinacy, the less patience I have with
her. Is it possible she can do herself, her family, her friends, so
much justice any *other* way, as by marrying me? Were she sure
she should live but a day, she ought to die a wife. If her *Christian revenge* will not let her wish to do so for her *own* sake,
ought she not for the sake of her family, and of her sex, which
she pretends sometimes to have so much concern for? And if
no *sake* is dear enough to move her Harlowe-spirit in my favour,
has she any title to the pity thou so pitifully art always bespeak-
ing for her?

I have one half of the house to myself; and that the best;
for the Great enjoy that least which costs them most: *Grandeur*
and *Use* are two things: The common part is theirs; the state
part is mine: And here I lord it, and *will* lord it, as long as I
please; while the two pursy sisters, the old gouty brother, and
the two musty nieces, are stived up in the other half, and dare
not stir for fear of meeting me. Pretty dogs and doggesses, to
quarrel and bark at me, and yet, whenever I appear, afraid to
pop out of their kennels; or if out before they see me, at the
sight of me run growling in again, with their flapt ears, their
sweeping dewlaps, and their quivering tails curling inwards.

And here, while I am thus worthily waging war with beetles,
drones, wasps, and hornets, and am all on fire with the rage of
slighted love, thou art regaling thyself with phlegm and rock-
water, and art going on with thy reformation-scheme, and thy
exultations in my misfortunes!

The devil take thee for an insensible dough-baked varlet:
I have no more patience with thee, than with the lady; for thou
knowest nothing either of love or friendship, but art as unworthy of the one, as incapable of the other; else wouldst thou
not rejoice, as thou dost under the *grimace of pity*, in my disappointments.

And thou art a pretty fellow, art thou not? to engage to
transcribe for her some parts of my letters written to thee in
confidence? Letters that thou shouldst sooner have parted with
thy cursed tongue, than have owned thou ever hadst received

such: Yet these are now to be communicated to *her!* But I charge thee, and woe be to thee if it be too late! that thou do not oblige her with a line of mine.

If thou *hast* done it, the least vengeance I will take, is to break thro' *my* honour given to thee not to visit her, as thou wilt have broken thro' *thine* to me, in communicating letters written under the seal of friendship.

I am now convinced, too sadly for my hopes, by her letter to my cousin Charlotte, that she is determined never to have me.

Unprecedented wickedness, she calls mine to her. But how does *she* know what the ardor of flaming love will stimulate? How does *she* know the requisite distinctions of the words she uses in this case?—To think the *worst*, and to be able to *make comparisons* in these *very* delicate situations, must she not be less delicate than I had imagined her to be?—But she has heard, that the devil is black; and having a mind to make one of me, brays together, in the mortar of her wild fancy, twenty chimney-sweepers, in order to make one sootier than ordinary rise out of the dirty mass.

But what a whirlwind does she raise in my soul, by her proud contempts of me! Never, never, was mortal man's pride so mortified. How does she sink me, even in my own eyes!— *Her heart* sincerely repulses me, she says, for my Meanness— Yet she intends to reap the benefit of what she calls so!—Curse upon her *haughtiness*, and her *meanness*, at the same time!

I will venture one more letter to her, however; and if that don't do, or procure me an answer, then will I endeavour to see her, let what *will* be the consequence. If she get out of my way, I will do some noble mischief to the vixen girl whom she most loves, and then quit the kingdom for ever.

And now, Jack, since thy hand is in at communicating the contents of private letters, tell her this, if thou wilt. And add to it, That if She abandon me, GOD will; and it is no matter *then* what becomes of

Her Lovelace!

Mr. Lovelace
To Miss Clarissa Harlowe

Monday, Aug. 7.

LITTLE as I have reason to expect either your patient ear,
or forgiving heart, yet cannot I forbear to write to you once
more (as a more pardonable intrusion, perhaps, than a visit
would be), to beg of you to put it in my power to atone, as far
as it is possible to atone, for the injuries I have done you.

Your angelic purity, and my awakened conscience, are
standing records of your exalted merit, and of my detestable
baseness: But your forgiveness will lay me under an eternal
obligation to you—Forgive me then, my dearest life, my earthly
good, the visible anchor of my future hope! As you (who believe you have something to be forgiven for) hope for pardon
yourself, forgive me, and consent to meet me, upon your own
conditions, and in whose company you please, at the holy altar,
and to give yourself a title to the most repentant and affectionate
heart that ever beat in a human bosom.

But, perhaps, a time of probation may be required. It may
be impossible for you, as well from *indisposition* as *doubt*, so
soon to receive me to absolute favour as my heart wishes to be
received. In this case, I will submit to your pleasure; and there
shall be no penance which you can impose, that I will not chearfully undergo, if you will be pleased to give me hope, that, after
an expiation, suppose of months, wherein the regularity of my
future life and actions shall convince you of my reformation,
you will at last be mine.

Let me beg the favour then of a few lines, encouraging me
in this *conditional* hope, if it must not be a still *nearer* hope, and
a more generous encouragement.

If you refuse me This, you will make me desperate. But
even then I must, at all events, throw myself at your feet, that
I may not charge myself with the omission of any earnest, any
humble effort, to move you in my favour: For in You, Madam,
in your *forgiveness*, are centred my hopes as to *both worlds*:

Since to be reprobated finally by *You*, will leave me without expectation of mercy from *Above!*—For I am now awakened enough to think, that to be forgiven by injured innocents is *necessary* to the Divine pardon; the Almighty putting into the power of such (as is reasonable to believe) the wretch who causlesly and capitally offends them. And *who* can be intitled to this power, if You are not?

Your cause, Madam, in a word, I look upon to be the *cause of Virtue*, and, as such, the *cause of God*. And may I not expect, that He will assert it in the perdition of a man, who has acted by a person of the most spotless purity, as I have done, if *you*, by rejecting me, shew that I have offended beyond the possibility of forgiveness?

I *repeat*, that all I beg for the present, is a few lines, to guide my doubtful steps; and (if possible for you so far to condescend) to encourage me to hope, that, if I can justify my present vows by my future conduct, I may be permitted the honour to style myself

Eternally yours,

R. Lovelace

Miss Cl. Harlowe To Robert Lovelace, Esq;

Friday, Aug. 11.

'T IS a cruel alternative to be either forced to see you, or to write to you. But a will of my own has been long denied me; and to avoid a greater evil, nay, now I may say, the greatest, I write.

Were I capable of disguising or concealing my real sentiments, I might safely, I dare say, give you the remote hope you request, and yet keep all my resolutions. But I must tell you, Sir; it becomes my character to tell you; that, were I to live more

years than perhaps I may weeks, and there were not another
man in the world, I could not, I would not, be yours.

There is no *merit* in performing a *duty*.

Religion enjoins me, not only to forgive injuries, but to
return good for evil. It is all my consolation, and I bless God
for giving me That, that I am now in such a state of mind with
regard to you, that I can chearfully obey its dictates. And accordingly I tell you, that, where-ever you go, I wish you happy.
And in This I mean to include every good wish.

And now having, with great reluctance, I own, complied
with one of your compulsatory alternatives, I expect the fruits
of it.

Clarissa Harlowe

Miss Clarissa Harlowe To Miss Howe

I WILL send you a large pacquet, as you desire and expect;
since I can do it by so safe a conveyance: But not all that is
come to my hand—For I must own, that my friends are very
severe; too severe for any-body who loves them not, to see their
letters. You, my dear, would not call them my *friends*, you said,
long ago; but my *relations:* Indeed I cannot call them my *relations*, I think!—But I am ill; and therefore, perhaps, more peevish
than I should be. It is difficult to go out of ourselves to give a
judgment against ourselves; and yet, oftentimes, to pass a *just*
judgment, we ought.

I thought I should alarm you in the choice of my Executor.
But the sad necessity I am reduced to must excuse me.

As I have the accompanying transcripts from Mr. Belford
in confidence from his friend's letters to him, I must insist, that
you suffer no soul but yourself to peruse them; and that you
return them by the very first opportunity; that so no use may
be made of them that may do hurt either to the original writer,

or to the communicator. You'll observe I am bound by promise to this care. If thro' *my* means any mischief should arise, between this *humane* and that *inhuman* libertine, I should think myself utterly inexcuseable.

I subjoin a list of the Papers or Letters I shall inclose. You must return them all when perused.

I am very much tired and fatigued—with—I don't know what—with writing, I think—But most with myself, and with a situation I cannot help aspiring to get out of, and above!

O, my dear, the world we live in is a sad, a very sad world! —While under our parents protecting wings, we know nothing at all of it. Book-learned and a scribbler, and looking at people as I saw them as visitors or visiting, I thought I knew a great deal of it. Pitiable ignorance!—Alas! I knew nothing at all!

With zealous wishes for your happiness, and the happiness of every one dear to you, I am, and will ever be,

Your gratefully-affectionate

Cl. Harlowe

Mr. Antony Harlowe
To Miss Cl. Harlowe

Aug. 12.

Unhappy girl!

AS your Uncle Harlowe chooses not to answer your pert letter to him; and as mine written to you before was written as if it were in the spirit of prophecy, as you have found to your sorrow; and as you are now making yourself worse than you are in your health, and better than you are in your penitence, *as we are very well assured*, in order to move compassion; which you do not deserve, having had so much warning: For all these reasons, I take up my pen once more; tho' I had told your *brother, at his going to Edinburgh,* that I would not

write to you, even were you to write to me, without letting him
know. So indeed *had we all;* for he prognosticated what would
happen, as to your applying to us, when you knew not how to
help it.

Brother John has hurt your niceness, it seems, by asking
you a plain question, which your mother's heart is too full of
grief to let her ask; and modesty will not let your sister ask,
tho' but the consequence of your actions—And yet it *must* be
answered, before you'll obtain from your father and mother,
and us, the notice you hope for, I can tell you that.

You lived several guilty weeks with one of the vilest fellows that ever drew breath, at bed as well as board, no doubt
(for is not his character known?); and pray don't be ashamed
to be asked after what may naturally come of such free living.
This modesty, indeed, would have become you for eighteen
years of life—You'll be pleased to mark that—but makes no
good figure compared with your behaviour since the beginning
of April last. So pray don't take it up, and wipe your mouth
upon it, as if nothing had happened.

But, may be, I likewise am too shocking to your niceness!—
O, girl, girl! your modesty had better been shewn at the right
time and place!—Every-body, but you, believed what the Rake
was: But you would believe nothing bad of him—What think
you now?

Your folly has ruined all our peace. And who knows where
it may yet end?—Your poor father but yesterday shewed me
this text: With bitter grief he shewed it me, poor man! And do
you lay it to your heart:

"A father waketh for his daughter, when no man knoweth;
and the care for her taketh away his sleep—When she is young,
lest she pass away the flower of her age *(and you know what
proposals were made to you at different times):* And, being
married, lest she should be hated: In her virginity, lest she
should be defiled, and gotten with child in her father's house
(I don't make the words, mind that): And, having an husband,
lest she should misbehave herself." *And what follows?* "Keep a
sure watch over a shameless daughter *(yet no watch could hold
you!),* lest she make thee a laughing-stock to thine enemies *(as*

you have made us all to this cursed Lovelace), and a bye-word in the city, and a reproach among the people, and make thee ashamed before the multitude." *Ecclus.* xlii. 9, 10, &c.

Now will you wish you had not written pertly. Your sister's severities!—Never, girl, say that is *severe,* that is *deserved.* You know the meaning of words. No-body better. Would to the Lord you had acted up but to one half of what you know. Then had we not been disappointed and grieved, as we all have been: And no-body more than him who was

> *Your loving uncle,*
>
> > *Antony Harlowe*

Miss Cl. Harlowe
To Mr. Ant. Harlowe, Esq;

Sunday, Aug. 13.

Honoured sir,

I AM very sorry for my pert letter to my Uncle Harlowe. Yet I did not intend it to be pert. People *new* to misfortune may be too easily moved to impatience.

The fall of a regular person, no doubt, is dreadful and inexcuseable. It is like the sin of apostasy. Would to Heaven, however, that I had had the circumstances of mine inquired into!

If, Sir, I make myself worse than I am in my health, and better than I am in my penitence, it is fit I should be punished for my double dissimulation: And *you* have the pleasure of being one of my punishers. My sincerity in both respects will, however, be best justified by the event. To *that* I refer.—May Heaven give you always as much comfort in reflecting upon the reprobation I have met with, as you seem to have pleasure in mortifying a poor creature, *extremely* mortified; and that from a *right* sense, as she presumes to hope, of her own fault!

What you have *heard of me* I cannot tell. When the nearest and dearest relations give up an unhappy wretch, it is not to be wondered at, that those who are *not* related to her are ready to take up and propagate slanders against her. Yet I think I may defy calumny itself, and (excepting the fatal, tho' involuntary step of *April* 10.) wrap myself in my own innocence, and be easy. I thank you, Sir, nevertheless, for your *caution*, mean it what it will.

As to the question required of me to answer, and which is allowed to be too shocking either for a mother to put to a daughter, or a sister to a sister; and which however, *you* say, I *must* answer.—O Sir!—And *must* I answer?—This then be my answer:—"A *little* time, a much *less* time than is imagined, will afford a more satisfactory answer to my whole family, and even to my *brother* and *sister*, than I can give in words."

Nevertheless, be pleased to let it be remembred, that I did not petition for a restoration to favour. I could not hope for that. Nor yet to be put in possession of any part of my own estate. Nor even for means of necessary subsistence from the produce of that estate—But only for a blessing; for a *last* blessing!

And this I will further add, because it is *true*, that I have no wilful crime to charge against myself: No free living at bed and at board, as you phrase it!

Why, why, Sir, were not *other* inquiries made of me, as well as this shocking one?—Inquiries that modesty *would* have permitted a mother or a sister to make; and which, if I may be excused to say so, would have been still *less* improper, and *more* charitable, to have been made by *uncles* (were the Mother *forbid*, or the Sister *not inclined*, to make them) than those they have made.

God almighty bless, preserve, and comfort my dear sorrowing and grievously offended father and mother!—And continue in honour, favour, and merit, my happy sister!—May God forgive my brother, and protect him from the violence of his own temper, as well as from the destroyer of his sister's honour!—And may you, my dear uncle, and your no less now than ever dear brother, my second papa, as he used to bid me call him, be

blessed and happy in them, and in each other!—And, in order
to this, may you all speedily banish from your remembrance
for ever

The unhappy Clarissa Harlowe!

Mr. Lovelace
To John Belford, Esq;

Wednesday Morn. Aug. 23.

A LL alive, dear Jack, and in ecstasy! Likely to be once more
a happy man! For I have received a Letter from my beloved
Miss Harlowe; in consequence, I suppose, of advices which I
mentioned in my last from her sister. And I am setting out for
Berks directly, to shew the contents to my Lord M. and to receive
the congratulations of all my kindred upon it.

I went, last night, as I intended, to Smith's: But the dear
creature was not returned at near ten o'clock. And, lighting
upon Tourville, I took him home with me, and made him sing
me out of my megrims. I went to bed tolerably easy at two; had
bright and pleasant dreams, not such a frightful one as that I
gave thee an account of: and at eight this morning, as I was
dressing, I had this Letter brought me by a chairman.

To Mr. Robert Lovelace, Esq;

Tuesday Night, 11 o'clock (Aug. 22.)

Sir,

I HAVE good news to tell you. I am setting out with all diligence for my father's house. I am bid to hope that he will
receive his poor penitent with a goodness peculiar to himself;
for I am overjoyed with the assurance of a thorough reconcilia-

tion, thro' the interposition of a dear blessed friend, whom I
always loved and honoured. I am so taken up with my preparation for this joyful and long-wished-for journey, that I cannot
spare one moment for any other business, having several matters
of the last importance to settle first. So, pray, Sir, don't disturb
or interrupt me—I beseech you don't.—You may, in time, possibly, see me at my father's; at least, if it be not your own fault.

I will write a letter, which shall be sent you when I am got
thither and received: Till when, I am, &c.

Clarissa Harlowe

I dispatched instantly a Letter to the dear creature, assuring
her, with the most thankful joy, "That I would directly set out
for Berks, and wait the issue of the happy reconciliation, and the
charming hopes she had filled me with. I poured out upon her a
thousand blessings. I declared, that it should be the study of my
whole life to merit such transcendent goodness. And that there
was nothing which her father or friends should require at my
hands, that I would not for *her* sake comply with, in order to
promote and complete so desirable a reconciliation."

I hurried it away without taking a copy of it; and I have
ordered the chariot-and-six to be got ready; and hey for M.
Hall!—I hope a letter from thee is on the road. And if the poor
fellow can spare thee, make haste, I advise thee, to attend this
truly divine lady. Thou mayest not else see her of months perhaps; at least, not while she is Miss Harlowe. And favour me
with one letter before she sets out, if possible, confirming to me
and accounting for, this generous change.

But what accounting for it is necessary? The dear creature
cannot receive consolation herself but she must communicate
it to others. How noble! She would not see me in her adversity:
but no sooner does the sun of prosperity begin to shine upon
her, than she forgives me.

I know to whose mediation all this is owing. It is to Col.
Morden's. She always, as she says, loved and honoured him:
And he loved her above all his relations.

I shall now be convinced that there is something in dreams.

L's dream

The ceiling opening is the reconciliation in view. The bright form, lifting her up through it to another ceiling stuck round with golden cherubims and seraphims, indicates the charming little boys and girls, that will be the fruits of this happy reconciliation. The welcomes, thrice repeated, are those of her family, now no more to be deemed implacable. Yet are they a family too, that my soul cannot mingle with.

But then what is my tumbling over and over, thro' the floor, into a frightful hole, _descending_ as she _ascends_? Ho! only This; it alludes to my disrelish to matrimony: Which is a bottomless pit, a gulph, and I know not what. And I suppose, had I not awoke, in such a plaguy fright, I had been soused into some river at the bottom of the hole, and then been carried (mundified or purified from my past iniquities) by the same bright form (waiting for me upon the mossy banks) to my beloved girl; and we should have gone on cherubiming of it and carolling to the end of the chapter.

But what are the black sweeping mantles and robes of Lord M. thrown over my face, and what are those of the Ladies? Oh, Jack! I have these too: They indicate nothing in the world but that my Lord will be so good as to die, and leave me all he has. So, rest to thy good-natured soul, honest Lord M.

Lady Sarah Sadleir and Lady Betty Lawrance, will also die, and leave me swindging legacies.

Miss Charlotte and her sister — what will become of them? — O! they will be in mourning of course for their uncle and aunts — That's right!

As to Morden's flashing through the window, and crying, Die, Lovelace, and be damned, if thou wilt not repair my cousin's wrongs! That is only, that he would have sent me a challenge, had I not been disposed to do the lady justice.

All I dislike is This part of the dream: For, even in a dream, I would not be thought to be threatened into any measure, though I liked it ever so well.

And so much for my prophetic dream.

Dear charming creature! What a meeting will there be between her and her father and mother and uncles! What transports, what pleasure, will this happy, long-wished-for reconciliation give her dutiful heart! And indeed, now, methinks, I am glad she *is* so dutiful to them; for her duty to parents is a conviction to me, that she will be *as* dutiful to her husband: Since duty upon principle is an uniform thing.

Why, pr'ythee, now, Jack, I have not been so much to blame, as thou thinkest: For had it not been for me, who have led her into so much distress, she could neither have *received* nor *given* the joy that will now overwhelm them all. So here rises great and durable good out of temporary evil!

I knew they loved her (the pride and glory of their family) too well to hold out long!

I wish I could have seen Arabella's letter. She has always been so much eclipsed by her sister, that, I dare say, she has signified this reconciliation to her with intermingled phlegm and wormwood; and her invitation most certainly runs all in the rock-water style.

I shall long to see the promised letter too when she is got thither, which I hope will give an account of the reception she will meet with.

There is a solemnity, however, I think, in the style of her letter, which pleases and affects me at the same time. But as it is evident she loves me still, and hopes soon to see me at her father's, she could not help being a little solemn, and half-ashamed, (dear blushing pretty rogue!) to own her love, after my usage of her.

And then her subscription: *Till when, I am* Clarissa Harlowe: As much as to say, *After that,* I shall be, if not *your own fault,* Clarissa Lovelace!

O my best Love! My ever-generous and adorable creature! How much does this thy forgiving goodness exalt us both!— I, for the occasion given thee! Thee for turning it so gloriously to thy advantage, and to the honour of both!

And if, my beloved creature, you will but connive at the imperfections of your adorer, and not play the *Wife* upon me, I shall get above sense; and then, charmed by thy soul-attracting converse, and brought to despise my former courses, what I now, at distance, consider as a painful duty, will be my joyful choice, and all my delight will centre in thee!

Miss Arabella Harlowe
To Miss Clarissa Harlowe

Monday, Aug. 21.

Sister Clary,

I FIND by your letters to my uncles, that they, as well as I, are in great disgrace with you for writing our minds to you.

We can't help it, sister Clary.

You don't think it worth your while, I find, to press for the blessing you pretend to be so earnest about, a second time. You think, no doubt, that you have done your duty in asking for it: So you'll sit down satisfied with That, I suppose, and leave it to your wounded parents to repent hereafter that they have not done *Theirs*, in giving it to you, at the *first* word; and in making such enquiries about you, as you think ought to have been made. Fine encouragement to inquire after a run-away daughter! living with her fellow, as long as he would live with her! You repent also, (with your *full mind*, as you modestly call it) that you wrote to me.

So we are not likely to be applied to any more, I find, in this way.

Well then, since This is the case, sister Clary, let me, *with all humility*, address myself with a proposal or two to you; to which you will be *graciously* pleased to give an answer.

Now you must know, that we have had hints given us from several quarters, that you have been used in such a manner by the villain you ran away with, that his life would be answerable for his crime, if it were fairly to be proved. And, by your own hints, something like it appears to us.

If, Clary, there be any-thing but jingle and affecting period in what proceeds from your *full mind*, and your *dutiful consciousness*; and if there be truth in what Mrs. Norton and Mrs. Howe have acquainted us with; you may yet justify your character to us, and to the world, in every thing but your scandalous elopement; and the Law may reach the villain: And, could we

but bring him to the gallows, what a meritorious revenge would
that be to our whole injured family, and to the innocents he has
deluded, as well as the saving from ruin many others!

Let me, therefore, know (if you please) whether you are
willing to appear to do *Yourself*, and *Us*, and your *Sex*, this
justice? If *not*, sister Clary, we shall know what to think of you;
for neither *you* nor *we* can suffer more than we have done from
the scandal of your fall: And, if *you will*, Mr. Ackland and
Counsellor Derham will both attend you to make *proper inquiries*, and to take Minutes of your story, to found a process
upon, if it will bear one, with as great a probability of success,
as we are told it may be prosecuted with.

But, by what Mrs. Howe intimates, this is not likely to be
complied with; for it is what she hinted to you, it seems, by her
lively daughter, but without effect; and then, again, possibly,
you may not at present behave so prudently in some certain
points, as to intitle yourself to public justice; which if true, the
Lord have mercy upon you!

But if you will not agree to this, I have another proposal to
make to you, and that in the name of every one in the family;
which is, that you will think of going to Pensylvania to reside
there for some few years till all is blown over; And, if it please
God to spare you, and your unhappy parents, till they can be
satisfied, that you behave like a true and uniform penitent; at
least till you are one-and-twenty; you may then come back to
your own estate, or have the produce of it sent you thither, as
you shall choose.

Mr. Hartley has a Widow-Sister at Pensylvania, with whom
he will undertake you may board, and who is a sober, sensible,
and well read woman. And if you were once well there, it would
rid your father and mother of a world of cares, and fears, and
scandal; and I think is what you should wish for of all things.

Mr. Hartley will engage for all accommodations in your
passage suitable to your rank and fortune; and he has a concern in a ship, which will sail in a month; and you may take your
secret-keeping Hannah with you, or whom you will of your
newer acquaintance. 'Tis presumed that your companions will
be of your own sex.

These are what I had to communicate to you; and if you'll oblige me with an answer (which the hand that conveys this will call for on Wednesday Morning) it will be very condescending.

Arabella Harlowe

Miss Clarissa Harlowe To Miss Arabella Harlowe

Tuesday, Aug. 22.

W RITE to me, my hard-hearted sister, in what manner you please, I shall always be thankful to you for your notice. But (think what you will of me) I cannot see Mr. Ackland and the Counsellor on such a business as you mention.

The Lord have mercy upon me indeed? For none else will.

Surely I am believed to be a creature past all shame, or it could not be thought of sending two *gentlemen* to me on such an errand.

Had my mother required of me (or would *modesty* have permitted you to enquire into) the particulars of my sad story, or had *Mrs.* Norton been directed to receive them from me, methinks it had been more fit; and, I presume to think, that it would have been more in every one's character too, had they been required of me before such heavy judgment had been passed upon me, as has been passed.

To your other proposal, of going to Pensylvania; this is my answer:—If nothing happen within a month which may full as effectually rid my parents and friends of that world of cares, and fears, and scandals, which you mention, and if I am *then* able to be carried on board of ship, I will chearfully obey my father and mother, altho' I were sure to die in the passage.

I am equally surprised and concerned at the hints which both you and my Uncle Antony give of *new* points of misbehaviour in me!—What can be meant by them?

I will not tell you, Miss Harlowe, how much I am afflicted at your severity, and how much I suffer by it, and by your hard-hearted levity of style, because what I shall say may be construed into *jingle* and *period*, and because I know it is *intended* (very possibly for *kind* ends) to mortify me. All I will therefore say, is, That it does not lose its end, if that be it.

But, nevertheless, (divesting myself as much as possible of all resentment) I will only pray, that heaven will give you, for *your own* sake, a kinder heart, than at present; since a kind heart, I am convinced, is a greater blessing to its possessor, than it can be to any other person. Under this conviction I subscribe myself, my dear Bella,

Your ever-affectionate sister,

Cl. Harlowe

Mr. Belford
To Robert Lovelace, Esq;

Tuesday, Aug. 29.

I WAS at Smith's at half an hour after seven. They told me, that the lady was gone in a chair to St. Dunstan's; but was better than she had been in either of the two preceding days; and that she said to Mrs. Lovick and Mrs. Smith, as she went into the chair, I have a good deal to answer for to you, my good friends, for my vapourish conversation of last night.

If, Mrs. Lovick, said she smiling, I have no new matters to discompose me, I believe my spirits will hold out purely.

She returned immediately after prayers.

I told her I was sorry to hear she had been so ill since I had the honour to attend her; but rejoiced to find, that now she seemed a good deal better.

It will be sometimes better, and sometimes worse, replied she, with poor creatures, when they are balancing between life and death. But no more of these matters just now. I hope, Sir, you'll breakfast with me. I was quite vapourish yesterday. I had a very bad spirit upon me. Had I not, Mrs. Smith? But I hope I shall be no more so. And to-day I am perfectly serene. This day rises upon me as if it would be a bright one.

She desired me to walk up, and invited Mr. Smith and his wife, and Mrs. Lovick also, to breakfast with her. I was better pleased with her liveliness than with her looks.

The good people retiring after breakfast, the following conversation passed between us.

Pray, Sir, let me ask you, said she, if you think I may promise myself that I shall be no more molested by your friend?

I hesitated: For how could I answer for such a man?

What shall I do, if he comes again?—You see how I am.—I cannot fly from him now—If he has any pity left for the poor creature whom he has thus reduced, let him not come.—But have you heard from him lately? And will he come?

I hope not, Madam; I have not heard from him since Thursday last, that he went out of town, rejoicing in the hopes your letter gave him of a reconciliation between your friends and you, and that he might in good time see you at your father's; and he is gone down to give all his friends joy of the news, and is in high spirits upon it.

Alas for me! I shall then surely have him come up to persecute me again! As soon as he discovers that That was only a stratagem to keep him away, he will come up; and who knows but even *now* he is upon the road? I thought I was so bad, that I should have been out of his and every-body's way before now; for I expected not, that this contrivance would serve me above two or three days; and by this time he must have found out, that I am not so happy as to have any hope of a reconciliation with my family; and then he will come, if it be only in revenge for what he will think a deceit.

I believe I looked surprised to hear her confess that her letter was a stratagem only; for she said, You wonder, Mr. Belford, I observe, that I could be guilty of such an artifice. I doubt it is not right: But how could I see a man who had so mortally injured me; yet, pretending sorrow for his crimes, and wanting to see me, could behave with so much shocking levity, as he did to the honest people of the house? Yet, 'tis strange too, that neither you nor he found out my meaning on perusal of my letter. You have seen what I wrote, no doubt?

I have, Madam. And then I began to account for it, as an *innocent* artifice.

Thus far indeed, Sir, it is *innocent*, that I meant him no hurt, and had a right to the effect I hoped for from it; and he had none to invade me. But have you, Sir, that letter of his in which he gives you (as I suppose he does) the copy of mine?

I have, Madam. And pulled it out of my letter-case: But hesitating—Nay, Sir, said she, be pleased to read my letter to yourself—I desire not to see *his*—and see if you can be longer a stranger to a meaning so obvious.

I read it to myself—Indeed, Madam, I can find nothing but that you are going down to Harlowe-place to be reconciled to your father and other friends: And Mr. Lovelace presumed that a letter from your sister, which he saw brought when he was at Mr. Smith's, gave you the welcome news of it.

She then explained all to me, and that, as I may say, in six words—A *religious* meaning is couched under it, and that's the reason that neither you nor I could find it out.

Read but for my *father's house*, *Heaven*, said she, and for the interposition of my dear blessed friend, suppose the *Mediation* of my *Saviour;* which I humbly rely upon; and all the rest of the letter will be accounted for.

I read it so, and stood astonished for a minute at her invention, her piety, her charity, and at thine and mine own stupidity, to be thus taken in.

And now, thou vile Lovelace, what hast thou to do (the lady all consistent with herself, and no hopes left for thee) but to hang, drown, or shoot thyself?

My surprize being a little over, she proceeded: As to the letter that came from my sister while your friend was here, you will *soon* see, Sir, that it is the cruellest letter she ever wrote me.

And then she expressed a deep concern for what might be the consequence of Col. Morden's intended visit to you; and besought me, that if now, or at any time hereafter, I had opportunity to prevent any further mischief, without detriment or danger to myself, I would do it.

I assured her of the most particular attention to this and to all her commands; and that in a manner so agreeable to her, that she invoked a blessing upon me for my goodness, as she called it, to a desolate creature who suffered under the worst of orphanage; those were her words.

She then went back to her first subject, her uneasiness for fear of your molesting her again; and said, If you have any influence over him, Mr. Belford, prevail upon him, that he will give me the assurance, that the short remainder of my time shall be all my own. I have need of it. Indeed I have. Why will he wish to interrupt me in my duty? Has he not punished me enough for my preference of him to all his sex? Has he not destroyed my fame and my fortune? And will not his causeless vengeance upon me be complete, unless he ruins my soul too?

I assured her, that I would make such a representation of the matter to you, and of the state of her health, that I would undertake to *answer for you*, that you would not attempt to come near her.

This conversation, I found, as well from the length, as the nature of it, had fatigued her; and seeing her change colour once or twice, I made that my excuse, and took leave of her: Desiring her permission to attend her in the evening; and as often as possible; for I could not help telling her, that every time I saw her, I more and more considered her as a beatified spirit; and as one sent from heaven to draw me after her out of the miry gulph in which I had been so long immersed.

And laugh at me if thou wilt; but it is true, that every time I approach her, I cannot but look upon her, as one just entering into a companionship with saints and angels. This thought so wholly possessed me, that I could not help begging, as I went away, her prayers and her blessing.

In the evening, she was so low and weak, that I took my leave of her, in less than a quarter of an hour. I went directly home. Where, to the pleasure and wonder of my cousin and her family, I now pass many honest evenings: Which they impute to your being out of town.

I long for the particulars of the conversation between you and Mr. Morden: The lady, as I have hinted, is full of apprehensions about it. Send me back this packet when perused; for I have not had either time or patience to take a copy of it.—And I beseech you enable me to make good my engagements to the poor lady that you will not invade her again.

Colonel Morden
To Miss Clarissa Harlowe

Tuesday, Aug. 29.

PERMIT me to condole those misfortunes, which have occasioned so unhappy a difference between you, and the rest of your family: And to offer my assistance, to enable you to make the best of what has happened.

But, forgetting past things, let us look forward. I have been with Mr. Lovelace and Lord M. I need not tell *you*, it seems, how very desirous the whole family are of the honour of an alliance with you; nor how exceedingly earnest the former is to make you all the reparation in his power.

I think, my dear cousin, that you cannot now do better than to give him the honour of your hand. He says such just and great things of your virtue, and so heartily condemns himself, that I think there is honourable room for your forgiving him: And the more, as it seems you are determined against a legal prosecution.

Your effectual forgiveness of him, it is evident to me, will accelerate a general reconciliation: For, at present, my other cousins cannot persuade themselves, that he is in earnest to do you justice; or that you would refuse him, if you believed he was.

But, my dear cousin, there may possibly be something in this affair, to which I may be a stranger. If there be, and you will acquaint me with it, all that a *naturally* warm heart can do in your behalf, shall be done.

Nothing but my endeavour to serve you here has hitherto prevented me from assuring you of this by word of mouth: For I long to see you, after so many years absence. I hope I shall be able, in my next visits to my several cousins, to set all right. Proud spirits, when convinced that they have carried resentments too high, want but a good excuse to condescend: And parents must *always* love the child they once loved.

Mean while, I beg the favour of a few lines, to know if you have reason to doubt Mr. Lovelace's sincerity. For my part, I can have none, if I am to judge from the conversation that passed yesterday between him and me, in presence of Lord M.

You will be pleased to direct for me at your uncle Antony's.

Permit me, my dearest cousin, till I can procure a happy reconciliation between you and your father, and brother, and uncles, to supply the place to you of all those near relations, as well as that of

Your affectionate kinsman, and humble servant,

Wm. Morden

Miss Clarissa Harlowe
To William Morden, Esq;

Thursday, Aug. 31.

I MOST heartily congratulate you, dear Sir, on your return to your native country.

I heard with much pleasure that you were come; but I was both afraid and ashamed, till you encouraged me by a first notice, to address myself to you.

How consoling is it to my wounded heart to find, that you have not been carried away by that tide of resentment and displeasure, with which I have been so unhappily overwhelmed— But that, while my still nearer relations have not thought fit to examine into the truth of vile reports raised against me, you have informed yourself (and generously *credited* the information), that my error was owing more to my misfortune than my fault.

I have not the least reason to doubt Mr. Lovelace's sincerity in his offers of marriage: Nor that all his relations are heartily desirous of ranking me among them. I have had noble instances of their esteem for me, on their apprehending that my father's displeasure must have subjected me to difficulties: And this, after I had absolutely refused *their* pressing solicitations in their kinsman's favour, as well as *his own*.

Nor think me, my dear cousin, blameable for refusing him. I had given Mr. Lovelace no reason to think me a weak creature. If I *had*, a man of his character might have thought himself warranted to endeavour to make ungenerous advantage of the weakness he had been able to inspire. The consciousness of *my own* weakness (in that case) might have brought me to a composition with *his* wickedness.

I can indeed forgive him. But that is, because I think his crimes have set me above him. Can I be above the man, Sir, to whom I shall give my hand and my vows; and with them a sanction to the most premeditated baseness? No, Sir, let me say, that your cousin Clarissa, were she likely to live many years, and *that* (if she married not this man) in penury or want, despised and forsaken by all her friends, puts not so high a value upon the conveniencies of life, nor upon life itself, as to seek to re-obtain the one, or to preserve the other, by giving *such* a sanction: A sanction, which *(were she to perform her duty)* would reward the violator.

Nor is it so much from Pride as from Principle, that I say this. What, Sir! when Virtue, when Chastity, is the crown of a woman, and particularly of a Wife, shall your cousin stoop to marry the man who could not form an attempt upon *hers*, but upon a presumption, that she was capable of receiving his offered hand, when he had found himself mistaken in the vile opinion he had conceived of her?

One day, Sir, you will perhaps know all my story. But, whenever it is known, I beg, that the author of my calamities may not be vindictively sought after. He could not have been the author of them, but for a strange concurrence of unhappy

causes. As the Law will not be able to reach him when I am
gone, any other sort of vengeance terrifies me to think of it:
For is such a case, should my friends be *safe*, what honour would
his death bring to my memory?—If any of them should come
to misfortune, how would my fault be aggravated!

God long preserve you, my dearest cousin, and bless you but in
proportion to the consolation you have given me, in letting
me know that you still love me; and that I have One near and
dear relation who can pity and forgive me (and then will you
be *greatly* blessed); is the prayer of

> *Your ever-grateful and affectionate*
>
> Clarissa Harlowe

Mr. Belford
To Robert Lovelace, Esq;

Thursday Night, Aug. 31.

WHEN I concluded my last, I hoped, that my next attendance upon this surprising lady would furnish me with
some particulars as agreeable as now could be hoped for from
the declining way she is in, by reason of the welcome letter she
had received from her cousin Morden. But it proved quite otherwise to *me*, tho' not to *herself*; for I think I never was more
shocked in my life than on the occasion I shall mention presently.

When I attended her about seven in the evening, she told
me, that she had found herself in a very petulant way. Strange,
she said, that the pleasure I received from my cousin's letter
should have such an effect upon her. But she had given way to
a *comparative* humour, as she might call it, and thought it very
hard, that her nearer relations did not take the methods with
her, which her cousin Morden had begun with; by inquiring
into my merit or demerit, and giving her cause a fair audit
before they proceeded to condemnation.

the coffin!

She had hardly said this, when she started, and a blush overspread her face, on hearing, as I also did, a sort of lumbering noise upon the stairs, as if a large trunk were bringing up between two people: And, looking upon me with an eye of concern, Blunderers! said she, they have brought in something two hours before the time.—Don't be surprised, Sir—It is all to save *you* trouble.

Before I could speak, in came Mrs. Smith: O Madam, said she, What have you done?—Mrs. Lovick, entering, made the same exclamation. Lord have mercy upon me, Madam, cried I, what have you done!—For, she stepping at the instant to the door, the women told me, it was a coffin.—O Lovelace! that thou hadst been there at the moment!—Thou, the causer of all these shocking Scenes! Surely thou couldst not have been less affected than I, who have no guilt, as to *her*, to answer for.

With an intrepidity of a piece with the preparation, having directed them to carry it into her bed-chamber, she returned to us: They were not to have brought it in till after dark, said she—Pray, excuse me, Mr. Belford: And don't you, Mrs. Lovick, be concerned: Nor you, Mrs. Smith.—Why should you? There is nothing more in it, than the unusualness of the thing. Why may we not be as reasonably shocked at going to the church where are the monuments of our ancestors, with whose dust we even *hope* our dust shall be one day mingled, as to be moved at such a sight as this?

We all remaining silent, the women having their aprons at their eyes—Why this concern for nothing at all, said she?—If I am to be blamed for any-thing, it is for shewing too much solicitude, as it may be thought, for this earthly part. I have no mother, no sister, no Mrs. Norton, no Miss Howe, near me. Some of you must have seen *this* in a few days, if not now; perhaps have had the friendly trouble of directing it. And what is the difference of a few days to *you*, when *I* am gratified, rather than discomposed by it?—I shall not die the sooner for such a preparation.—Should not everybody make their will, that has any-thing to bequeath? And who, that makes a will, should be afraid of a coffin?

How reasonable was all this!—It shewed, indeed, that she

herself had well considered it. But yet we could not help being shocked at the thoughts of the coffin thus brought in: The lovely person before our eyes, who is in all likelihood so soon to fill it.

We were all silent still, the women in grief, I in a manner stunned. She would not ask *me*, she said; but would be glad, since it had thus earlier than she had intended been brought in, that her two good friends would walk in and look upon it. They would be less shocked, when it was made more familiar to their eye.

I took my leave; telling her she had done wrong, very wrong; and ought not, by any means, to have such an object before her.

The women followed her in.—'Tis a strange Sex! Nothing is too shocking for them to look upon, or see acted, that has but Novelty and Curiosity in it.

Down I posted; got a chair; and was carried home, extremely shocked and discomposed: Yet, weighing the lady's arguments, I know not why I was so affected—except, as she said, at the unusualness of the thing.

While I waited for a chair, Mrs. Smith came down, and told me, that there were devices and inscriptions upon the lid. Lord bless me! Is a coffin a proper subject to display fancy upon?—But these great minds cannot avoid doing extraordinary things!

Mr. Belford
To Robert Lovelace, Esq;

Friday Morn. Sept. 1.

IT is surprising, that I, a *man*, should be so much affected as I was, at such an object as is the subject of my former letter; when she, a *woman*, of so weak and tender a frame, who was to fill it (so soon perhaps to fill it!) could give orders about it, and draw out the devices upon it, and explain them with so little concern as the women tell me she did to them last night after I was gone.

I really was ill, and restless all night. Thou wert the subject of my execration, as she of my admiration, all the time I was quite awake: And, when I dozed, I dreamt of nothing but of flying hour-glasses, deaths-heads, spades, mattocks, and eternity; the hint of her devices (as given me by Mrs. Smith) running in my head.

However, not being able to keep away from Smith's, I went thither about seven. The lady was just gone out: She had slept better, I found, than I, tho' her solemn repository was under her window not far from her bedside.

I was prevailed upon by Mrs. Smith and her nurse Shelburne (Mrs. Lovick being abroad with her) to go up and look at the devices. Mrs. Lovick has since shewn me a copy of the draught by which all was ordered. And I will give thee a sketch of the symbols.

The principal device, neatly etched on a plate of white metal, is a crowned serpent, with its tail in its mouth, forming a ring, the emblem of Eternity: And in the circle made by it is this inscription:

> Clarissa Harlowe. April X. [*Then the year*]
> aetat. XIX.

For ornaments: At top, an Hour-glass winged. At bottom, an Urn.

Under the Hour-glass, on another plate this inscription:

> Here *the wicked cease from troubling: And* Here *The weary be at rest.* Job iii. 17.

Over the urn, near the bottom:

> *Turn again unto thy rest, O my soul! For the Lord hath rewarded thee: And why? Thou hast delivered my soul from death; mine eyes from tears; and my feet from falling.* Ps. cxvi. 7, 8.

Over this text is the head of a white Lily snapt short off, and just falling from the stalk; and this inscription over that, between the principal plate and the lily:

> *The days of man are but as grass. For he flourisheth as a flower of the field: For, as soon as the wind goeth over it, it is gone; and the place thereof shall know it no more. Ps. ciii. 15, 16.*

She excused herself to the women, on the score of her youth, and being used to draw for her needleworks, for having shewn more fancy than would perhaps be thought suitable on so solemn an occasion.

The date, April 10. she accounted for, as not being able to tell what her closing-day would be; and as That was the fatal day of her leaving her father's house.

She discharged the undertaker's bill, after I was gone, with as much chearfulness as she could ever have paid for the cloaths she sold to purchase this her *palace:* For such she called it; reflecting upon herself for the expensiveness of it, saying, That they might observe in *her*, that pride left not poor mortals to the last: But indeed she did not know but her father would permit it, when furnished, to be carried down to be deposited with her ancestors; and, in that case, she ought not to discredit them in her *last appearance.*

It is covered with fine black cloth, and lined with white satten; soon, she said, to be tarnished by viler earth than any it could be covered by.

The burial-dress was brought home with it. The women had curiosity enough, I suppose, to see her open That, if she did open it.—And, perhaps, thou wouldst have been glad to have been present, to have admired it too!

Mrs. Lovick said, she took the liberty to blame her; and wished the removal of such an object—from her *bed-chamber*, at least: And was so affected with the noble answer she made upon it, that she entered it down the moment she left her.

To persons in health, said she, this sight may be shocking; and the preparation, and my unconcernedness in it, may appear affected: But to me, who have had so gradual a weaning-time from the world, and so much reason not to love it, I must say, I dwell on, I indulge (and, strictly speaking, I enjoy) the thoughts of death. For, believe me (looking stedfastly at the awful receptacle): Believe what at this instant I feel to be most true, That there is such a vast superiority of weight and importance in the thoughts of death, and its hoped for happy consequences, that it in a manner annihilates all other considerations and concerns. Believe me, my good friends, it does what nothing else can do; It teaches me, by strengthening in me the force of the divinest example, to forgive the injuries I have received; and shuts out the remembrance of past evils from my soul.

And now let me ask thee, Lovelace, Dost thou think, that, when the time shall come that thou shalt be obliged to launch into the boundless ocean of Eternity, thou wilt be able to act thy part with such true heroism, as this sweet and tender blossom of a woman has manifested, and continues to manifest!

Dr. H.
To James Harlow Senior, Esq;

London, Sept. 4.

Sir,

IF I may judge of the hearts of other parents by my own, I cannot doubt but you will take it well to be informed, that you have yet an opportunity to save yourself and family great future regret, by dispatching hither some one of it, with your last blessing, and your lady's, to the most excellent of her sex.

I have some reason to believe, Sir, that she has been represented to you in a very different light from the true one. And this it is that induces me to acquaint you, that I think her, on the best grounds, absolutely irreproachable in all her conduct which has passed under my eye, or come to my ear; and that her very misfortunes are made glorious to her, and honourable to all that are related to her, by the use she has made of them; and by the patience and resignation with which she supports herself in a painful, lingering, and dispiriting decay; and by the greatness of mind with which she views her approaching dissolution.

I hope I shall not be thought an officious man on this occasion: But if I am, I cannot help it; being driven to write, by a kind of *parental* and irresistible impulse.

But, Sir, whatever you do, or permit to be done, must be speedily done; for she cannot, I verily think, live a week: And how long of that short space she may enjoy her admirable intellects, to take comfort in the favours you may think proper to confer upon her, cannot be said. I am, Sir,

Your most humble servant,

R. H.

Mr. Belford
To William Morden, Esq;

London, Sept. 4.

Sir,

THE urgency of the case, and the opportunity by your servant, will sufficiently apologize for this trouble from a stranger to your person; who, however, is not a stranger to your merit.

I understand you are employing your good offices with Miss Clarissa Harlowe's parents, and other relations, to reconcile them to the most meritorious daughter and kinswoman, that ever family had to boast of.

Generously as this is intended by you, we *here* have too much reason to think all your solicitudes on this head will be unnecessary: For, it is the opinion of every one who has the honour of being admitted to her presence, that she cannot live

over three days: So that if you wish to see her alive you must
lose no time to come up.

She knows not that I write. I had done it sooner, if I had
had the least doubt that before now she would not have received
from you some news of the happy effects of your kind mediation in her behalf. I am, Sir,

Your most humble servant,

J. *Belford*

Mr. Lovelace
To John Belford, Esq;

Uxbridge, Tuesday Morn. between 4 and 5.

A ND can it be, that this admirable creature will so soon
leave this cursed world? For cursed I shall think it, and
more cursed myself, when she is gone. O Jack! thou, who canst
sit so cool, and, like Addison's Angel, *direct*, and even *enjoy*,
the storm, that tears up my happiness by the roots, blame me
not for my impatience, however unreasonable! If thou knewest,
that already I feel the torments of the damned, in the remorse
that wrings my heart, on looking back upon my past actions
by her, thou wouldst not be the devil thou art, to halloo on a
worrying conscience, which, without thy merciless aggravations,
is altogether intolerable.

Shall I give thee a faint picture of the horrible uneasiness
with which my mind struggles? And faint indeed it must be;
for nothing but outrageous madness can exceed it; and *that*
only in the apprehension of others; since, as to the sufferer, it
is certain, that actual distraction (take it out of its lucid intervals) must be an infinitely more happy state than the state of
suspense and anxieties that bring it on.

Forbidden to attend the dear creature, yet longing to see
her, I would give the world to be admitted once more to her

beloved presence. I ride towards London three or four times
a day, resolving *pro* and *con.* twenty times in two or three
miles; and at last ride back; and, in view of Uxbridge, loathing
even the kind friend and hospitable house, turn my horse's head
again towards the town, and resolve to gratify my humour, let
her take it as she will; but, at the very entrance of it, after
infinite canvasings, once more alter my mind, dreading to offend
and shock her, lest, by that means, I should curtail a life so
precious.

Yesterday, I had no sooner dispatched Will, than I took
horse to meet him on his return. When at distance I saw any
man galloping towards me, my resemblance-forming fancy
immediately made it to be him; and then my heart bounded to
my mouth, as if it would have choaked me. But when the person's nearer approach undeceived me, how did I curse the varlet's delay, and thee by turns.

And hence, as I conceive, it is, that all pleasures are greater
in the *expectation*, or in the *reflection*, than in *fruition;* as all
pains, which press heavy upon both parts of that unequal union
by which frail mortality holds its precarious tenure, are ever
most acute in the *present tense:* For how easy sit upon the *reflection* the heaviest misfortunes, when surmounted!—But *most*
easy, I confess, those in which Body has more concern than
Soul. This, however, is a point of philosophy I have neither
time nor head just now to weigh: So take it as it falls from a
madman's pen.

Woe be to either of the wretches who shall bring me the
fatal news that she is no more! For it is but too likely that a
shriek-owl so hated will never whoot or scream again; unless the
shock, that will probably disorder my whole frame on so sad
an occasion (by *unsteadying* my hand) shall divert my aim from
his head, heart, or bowels, if it turn not against my own.

But, surely, she will not, she cannot yet die! Such a matchless excellence,

> —whose mind
> Contains a world, and seems for all things fram'd,

could not be lent to be so soon demanded back again!

Mr. Belford
To Robert Lovelace, Esq;

Tuesday, Sept. 5. Six o'clock.

THE Lady remains exceedingly weak and ill. Her intellects, nevertheless, continue clear and strong, and her piety and patience are without example. Every one thinks this night will be her last. What a shocking thing is that to say of such an excellence! She will not however send away her letter to her Norton, as yet. She endeavoured in vain to superscribe it: So desired me to do it. Her fingers will not hold her pen with the requisite steadiness. She has, I fear, written and read her last!

Eight o'clock.

She is somewhat better than she was. The Doctor has been here, and thinks she will hold out yet a day or two. He has ordered her, as for some time past, only some little cordials to take when ready to faint. She seemed disappointed, when he told her, she might yet live two or three days; and said, She longed for dismission!—Life was not so easily extinguished, she saw, as some imagine.—*Death from grief*, was, she believed, *the slowest of deaths*. But God's will must be done!—Her only prayer was now for submission to it: For she doubted not but by the Divine goodness she should be an happy creature, as soon as she could be divested of these *rags of mortality*.

Of her own accord she mentioned you; which, till then she had avoided to do. She asked, with great serenity, where you were?

I told her where; and your motives of being so near; and read to her a few lines of yours of this morning, in which you mention your wishes to see her, your sincere affliction, and your resolution not to approach her without her consent.

I would have read more; but she said, Enough, Mr. Belford, enough!—Poor man! Does his conscience begin to find him!—

492

Then need not any-body to wish him a greater punishment!—
May it work upon him to a happy purpose!

Just as she had done speaking, the minister, who had so
often attended her, sent up his name; and was admitted.

The good man urged, That some condescensions were
usually expected, on these solemn occasions, from pious souls
like hers, however satisfied with *themselves*, for the sake of
shewing the *world*, and for *example-sake*, that all resentments
against those who had most injured them were subdued: And
if she would vouchsafe to a heart so truly penitent, as I had
represented Mr. Lovelace's to be, that *personal* pardon, which
I had been pleading for, there would be no room to suppose the
least lurking resentment remained; and it might have very happy
effects upon the gentleman.

I have no lurking resentment, Sir, said she.—This is not a
time for resentment. Tell, therefore, the *world*, if you please,
and tell the poor man, that I not only forgive him, but have
such earnest wishes for the good of his soul, and that from considerations of its immortality, that could my penitence avail
for more sins than my own, my last tear should fall for Him by
whom I die!

Our eyes and hands expressed for us both, what our lips
could not utter.

Mr. Lovelace
To John Belford, Esq;

Wedn. Morn. Sept. 6.

AND is she somewhat better?—Blessings upon thee without
number or measure! Let her still be better and better!
Tell me so at least, if she be *not* so: For thou knowest now what
a joy that poor temporary reprieve, that she will hold out yet
a day or two, gave me.

But who told this hard-hearted and death-pronouncing

Doctor, that she will hold it no longer? By what warrant says he this? What presumption in these parading solemn fellows of a college, which will be my contempt to the latest hour of my life, if this brother of it (eminent as he is deemed to be) cannot work an ordinary miracle in *her* favour, or rather in *mine*.

Let me tell thee Belford, that already he deserves the *utmost* contempt, for suffering this charming clock to run down so low. What must be his art, if it could not wind it up in a quarter of the time he has attended her, when, at his first visits, the springs and wheels of life and motion were so good, that they seemed only to want common care and oiling!

I am obliged to you for endeavouring to engage her to see me. 'Twas acting like a friend. If she had vouchsafed me that favour, she should have seen at her feet the most abject adorer that ever kneeled to justly offended beauty.

What she bid you, and what she *forbid* you, to tell me (the latter for *tender* considerations); That she forgives me; and that, could she have made me a *good* man, she could have made me a *happy* one!—O Belford, Belford! I cannot bear it!—What a dog, what a devil, have I been to so superlative a goodness!— Why does she not inveigh against me?—Why does she not execrate me?—O the triumphant subduer! Ever above me!—And now to leave me so infinitely below her!

Marry and repair, at any time; This (wretch that I was!) was my plea to myself. To give her a lowering sensibility; to bring her down from among the stars which her beamy head was surrounded by, that my wife, so greatly above me, might not despise me—This was part of my reptile envy, owing to my more reptile apprehension of inferiority.—Yet she, from step to step, from distress to distress, to maintain her superiority; and, like the sun, to break out upon me with the greater refulgence for the clouds that I had contrived to cast about her— And now to escape me thus!—No power left me to repair her wrongs!—No alleviation to my self-reproach!—No dividing of blame with her!—

Tell her, O tell her, Belford, that her prayers and wishes, her superlatively generous prayers and wishes, shall *not* be vain: That I *can*, and *do* repent—and *long* have repented:—Yet she must not leave me—She must live, if she would wish to have my contrition perfect—For what can despair produce?—

Mr. Belford
To Robert Lovelace, Esq;

Soho, Six o'clock, Sept. 7.

THE Lady is still alive. The Colonel having just sent his servant to let me know that she inquired after me about an hour ago, I am dressing to attend her. Joel begs of me to dispatch him back, tho' but with one line to gratify your present impatience. I therefore dispatch this; and will have another ready as soon as I can, with particulars. But you must have a little patience; for how can I withdraw every half-hour to write, if I am admitted to the Lady's presence, or if I am with the Colonel?

Ten o'clock.

The Colonel being earnest to see his cousin as soon as she awaked, we were both admitted. We observed in her, as soon as we entered, strong symptoms of her approaching dissolution, notwithstanding what the women had flattered us with, from her last night's tranquillity. The Colonel and I, each loth to say what we thought, looked upon one another with melancholy countenances.

Her breath being very short, she desired another pillow; and having two before, this made her in a manner sit up in her bed; and she spoke then with more distinctness; and, seeing us greatly concerned, forgot her own sufferings to comfort us; and a charming lecture she gave us, tho' a brief one, upon the happiness of a timely preparation, and upon the hazards of a late repentance, when the mind, as she observed, was so much weakened, as well as the body, as to render a poor soul hardly able to contend with its natural infirmities.

I beseech ye, my good friends, proceeded she, mourn not
for one who mourns not, nor has cause to mourn, for herself.
On the contrary, rejoice with me, that all my worldly troubles
are so near their end. Believe me, Sirs, that I would not, if I
might, choose to live, altho' the pleasantest part of my life were
to come over again: And yet Eighteen years of it, out of Nineteen, have been *very* pleasant. To be so much exposed to temptation, and to be so liable to fail in the trial, who would not rejoice, that all her dangers are over!—All I wished was pardon
and blessing from my dear parents. Easy as my departure seems
to promise to be, it would have been still easier, had I had that
pleasure. But God Almighty would not let me depend for comfort upon any but Himself.

She then repeated her request, in the most earnest manner,
to her *cousin*, that he would not *heighten* her fault, by seeking
to avenge her death; to *me*, that I would endeavour to make
up all breaches, and use the power I had with my friend, to prevent all future mischiefs *from* him, as well as that which this
trust might give me, to prevent any *to* him.

She had fatigued herself so much (growing sensibly weaker)
that she sunk her head upon her pillows, ready to faint; and
we withdrew to the window, looking upon one another; but
could not tell what to say; and yet both seemed inclinable to
speak: But the motion passed over in silence. Our eyes only
spoke; and that in a manner neither's were used to; mine, at
least, not till I knew this admirable creature.

The Colonel withdrew to dismiss his messenger, and send
away the letter to Mrs. Norton. I took the opportunity to retire
likewise; and to write thus far. And Joel returning to take it;
I now close here.

Eleven o'Clock.

C. dead

Mr. Lovelace
To John Belford, Esq;

CURSE upon the Colonel, and curse upon the writer of the last letter I received, and upon all the world! Thou to pretend to be as much interested in my Clarissa's fate as myself! 'Tis well for one of us, that this was not said to me, instead of written—Living or dying, she is mine—and only mine. Have I not earned her dearly?—Is not Damnation likely to be the purchase to me, tho' a happy Eternity will be hers?

An eternal separation! O God! O God!—How can I bear that thought!—But yet there is Life!—Yet, therefore, hope—Inlarge my Hope, and thou shalt be my good genius, and I will forgive thee every-thing.

For this last time—But it must not, shall not, be the *last*—Let me hear, the moment thou receivest this—what I *am* to be—For, at present, I am

The most miserable of men.
Rose, at Knightsbridge, 5 o'Clock.

My fellow tells me, that thou art sending Mowbray and Tourville to me. I want them not. My soul's sick of them, and of all the world; but most of myself.—Yet, as they send me word they will come to me immediately, I will wait for them, and for thy next. O Belford! let it not be—But hasten it, hasten it, be it what it may!

Mr. Belford
To Robert Lovelace, Esq;

Thursday Night.

I MAY as well try to write; since, were I to go to bed, I shall not sleep. I never had such a weight of grief upon my mind in my life, as upon the demise of this admirable woman; whose soul is now rejoicing in the regions of light.

497

You may be glad to know the particulars of her happy exit. I will try to proceed; for all is hush and still; the family retired; but not one of them, and least of all her poor cousin, I dare say, to rest.

At Four o'clock, as I mentioned in my last, I was sent for down; and, as thou usedst to like my descriptions, I will give thee the woeful scene that presented itself to me, as I approached the bed.

The Colonel was the first that took my attention, kneeling on the side of the bed, the lady's right-hand in both his, which his face covered, bathing it with his tears; altho' she had been comforting him, as the women since told me, in elevated strains, but broken accents.

On the other side of the bed sat the good Widow; her face overwhelmed with tears, leaning her head against the bed's head in a most disconsolate manner; and turning her face to me, as soon as she saw me, O Mr. Belford, cried she, with folded hands — The dear Lady — A heavy sob permitted her not to say more.

Mrs. Smith, with clasped fingers, and uplifted eyes, as if imploring help from the Only Power which could give it, was kneeling down at the bed's feet, tears in large drops trickling down her cheeks.

Her Nurse was kneeling between the widow and Mrs. Smith, her arms extended. In one hand she held an ineffectual cordial, which she had just been offering to her dying mistress; her face was swoln with weeping (tho' used to such scenes as this) and she turned her eyes towards me, as if she called upon me by them to join in the helpless sorrow; a fresh stream bursting from them as I approached the bed.

The lady had been silent a few minutes, and speechless as they thought, moving her lips without uttering a word; one hand, as I said, in her cousin's. But when Mrs. Lovick on my approach pronounced my name, Oh! Mr. Belford, said she, in broken periods; and with a faint inward voice, but very distinct nevertheless — Now! — Now! — (I bless God for his mercies to his poor creature) will all soon be over — A few — A very few moments — will end this strife — And I shall be happy!

Here, she stopt, for two or three minutes, earnestly looking upon him: Then resuming, my dearest cousin, said she, be comforted—What is dying but the common lot?—The mortal frame may *seem* to labour—But that is all!—It is not so hard to die, as I believed it to be!—The preparation is the difficulty—I bless God, I have had time for That—The rest is worse to beholders, than to me!—I am all blessed hope—Hope itself.

She *looked* what she said, a sweet smile beaming over her countenance.

She was silent for a few moments, lifting up her eyes, and the hand her Cousin held not between his. Then, O *death!* said she, *where is thy sting!* [The words I remember to have heard in the Burial-service read over my Uncle and poor Belton]. And after a pause—*It is good for me that I was afflicted!*—Words of Scripture, I suppose.

Then turning her head towards me—Do *you*, Sir, tell your friend, that I forgive him! And I pray to God to forgive him!—Again pausing, and lifting up her eyes, as if praying that He would—Let him know how happily I die.—And that such as my own, I wish to be his last hour.

She was again silent for a few moments: And then resuming—My sight fails me!—Your voices only—[for we both applauded her christian, her divine frame, tho' in accents as broken as her own] And the voice of grief is alike in all. Is not this Mr. Morden's hand? pressing one of his with that he had just let go. Which is Mr. Belford's? holding out the other. I gave her mine. God Almighty bless you both, said she, and make you both—in your last hour—for you *must* come to this—happy as I am.

She paused again, her breath growing shorter; and, after a few minutes, And now, my dearest cousin, give me your hand—nearer—still nearer—drawing it towards her; and she pressed it with her dying lips—God protect you, dear, dear Sir.

Her sweet voice and broken periods methinks still fill my ears, and never will be out of my memory.

After a short silence, in a more broken and faint accent;—

dies

And you, Mr. Belford, pressing my hand, may God preserve
you and make you sensible of all your errors—You see, in me,
how All ends—May *you* be—And down sunk her head upon her
pillow, she fainting away, and drawing from us her hands.

We thought she was then gone; and each gave way to a
violent burst of grief.

But soon shewing signs of returning life, our attention was
again engaged; and I besought her, when a little recovered, to
complete in my favour her half-pronounced blessing. She waved
her hand to us both, and bowed her head six several times, as
we have since recollected, as if distinguishing every person
present; not forgetting the nurse and the maid-servant; the latter
having approached the bed, weeping, as if crouding in for the
divine lady's last blessing; and she spoke faltering and inwardly,
—Bless—bless—bless—you All—And now—And now—(hold-
ing up her almost lifeless hands for the last time) Come—O
come—Blessed Lord—Jesus!

And with these words, the last but half-pronounced, expired: Such a smile, such a charming serenity overspreading
her sweet face at the instant as seemed to manifest her eternal
happiness already begun.

O Lovelace!—But I can write no more!

I resume my pen to add a few lines.

While warm, tho' pulseless, we pressed each her hand with
our lips; and then retired into the next room.

The Colonel sighed as if his heart would burst: At last, his
face and hands uplifted, his back towards me, Good Heaven!
said he to himself, support me!—And is it thus, O Flower of
Nature!—Then pausing—And must we no more—*Never more!*
—My blessed, blessed cousin! uttering some other words, which
his sighs made inarticulate:—And then, as if recollecting himself—Forgive me, Sir!—Excuse me, Mr. Belford; and, sliding by
me; anon I hope to see you, Sir—And down-stairs he went, and
out of the house, leaving me a statue.

When I recovered myself, it was almost to repine at what

I *then* called an unequal dispensation; forgetting her happy preparation, and still happier departure; and that she had but drawn a common lot; triumphing in it, and leaving behind her, every one less assured of happiness, tho' equally certain that it would one day be their own lot.

She departed exactly at 40 minutes after Six o'clock, as by her watch on the table.

And thus died Miss Clarissa Harlowe, in the blossom of her youth and beauty: And who, her tender years considered, has not left behind her her superior in extensive knowlege, and watchful prudence; nor hardly her equal for unblemished virtue, exemplary piety, sweetness of manners, discreet generosity, and true christian charity: And these all set off by the most graceful modesty and humility; yet on all proper occasions manifesting a noble presence of mind and true magnanimity: So that she may be said to have been not only an ornament to her Sex, but to Human nature.

A better pen than mine may do her fuller justice. Thine, I mean, O Lovelace! For well dost thou know how much she excelled in the graces both of mind and person, natural and acquired, all that is woman. And thou also canst best account for the causes of her immature death, thro' those calamities which in so short a space of time from the highest pitch of felicity (every one in a manner adoring her) brought her to an exit so happy for herself, but, that it was so *early*, so much to be deplored by all who had the honour of her acquaintance.

This task, then, I leave to thee: But now I can write no more, only that I am a sympathizer in every part of thy distress, except (and yet it is cruel to say it) in That which arises from thy guilt.

One o'clock, Friday morning.

Mrs. Norton
To Miss Clarissa Harlowe

Wednesday, Sept. 6.

AT length, my best beloved Miss Clary, everything is in the wished train.—For all your relations are unanimous in your favour—Even your brother and sister are with the foremost to be reconciled to you.

I know it must end thus!—By patience, and persevering sweetness, what a triumph have you gained!

This happy change is owing to letters received from your physician and from your cousin Morden.

Colonel Morden will be with you no doubt before this can reach you, with his pocket-book filled with money-bills, that nothing may be wanting to make you easy.

And *now*, all our hopes, all our prayers are, that this good news may restore you to spirits and health; and that (so long with-held) it may not come too late.

I know how much your dutiful heart will be raised with the joyful tidings I write you, and still shall more particularly tell you of, when I have the happiness to see you: Which will be by next Saturday, at farthest; perhaps on Friday afternoon, by the time you can receive this.

For this day, by the general voice, being sent for, I was received by every one with great goodness and condescension, and *intreated* (for that was the word they were pleased to use, when I needed *no* entreaty, I am sure) to hasten up to you, and to assure you of all their affectionate regards to you: And your father bid me say all the kind things that were in my *heart* to say, in order to comfort and raise you up; and they would hold themselves bound to make them good.

How agreeable is this commission to your Norton! My heart will overflow with kind speeches, never fear!—I am already meditating what I shall say, to chear and raise you up, in the names of every one dear and near to you. And sorry I am, that I cannot this moment set out, as I might, instead of writing, would they favour my eager impatience with their chariot; but as it was not offered, it would be presumption to have asked for it: And to-morrow a hired chaise and pair will be ready; but at what hour I know not.

Your Sister will write to you, and send her letter, with This, by a particular hand.

Your uncle Harlowe will also write, and (I doubt not) in the kindest terms: For they are all extremely alarmed and troubled at the dangerous way your doctor represents you to be in; as well as delighted with the character he gives you. Would to heaven the good gentleman had written *sooner!*

They will prescribe no conditions to you, my dear young lady; but will leave all to your own duty and discretion. Only your brother and sister declare, they will never yield to call Mr. Lovelace brother: Nor will your father, I believe, be easily brought to think of him for a son.

I am to bring you down with me as soon as your health and inclination will permit. You will be received with open arms. Every one longs to see you. All the servants please themselves, that they shall be permitted to kiss your hands.

God preserve you to our happy meeting! And I will, if I may say so, weary Heaven with my incessant prayers to preserve and restore you afterwards!

I need not say how much I am, my dear young lady,

Your ever-affectionate and devoted

Judith Norton

Miss Arabella Harlowe To Miss Clarissa Harlowe

Wed. morning, Sept. 6.

Dear Sister,

WE have just heard that you are exceedingly ill. We all loved you as never young creature was loved: You are sensible of That, Sister Clary. And you have been very naughty —But we could not be angry always.

We are indeed more afflicted with the news of your being so very ill than I can express: For I see not but, after this separation (as we understand that your misfortune has been greater than your fault, and that, however unhappy, you have demeaned yourself like the good young creature you used to be) we shall love you better, if possible, than ever.

Take comfort therefore, Sister Clary; and don't be too much cast down—Whatever your mortifications may be from such noble prospects over-clouded, and from the reflections you will have from within on your faulty step, and from the sullying of such a charming character by it, you will receive none from any of us: And, as an earnest of your Papa's and Mamma's favour and reconciliation, they assure you by me of their Blessing and hourly prayers.

I hope you'll rejoice at this good news. Pray let us hear that you do. Your next grateful letter on this occasion, especially if it gives us the pleasure of hearing you are better upon this news, will be received with the same (if not greater) delight, that we used to have in all your prettily-penn'd epistles. Adieu, my dear Clary! I am

Your loving sister, and true friend,
Arabella Harlowe

To his dear Niece
Miss Clarissa Harlowe

Wedn. Sept. 6.

WE were greatly grieved, my beloved Miss Clary, at your fault; but we are still more, if possible, to hear you are so very ill; and we are sorry things have been carried so far.

We know your talents, my dear, and how movingly you could write, whenever you pleased; so that nobody could ever deny you anything; and, believing you depended on your pen, and little thinking you were so ill, and that you had lived so regular a life, and were so truly penitent, are much troubled every one of us, your brother and all, for being so severe. Forgive my part in it, my dearest Clary. I am your *Second-Papa*, you know. And you *used* to love me.

I hope you'll soon be able to come down, and, after a while, when your indulgent parents can spare you, that you will come to me for a whole month, and rejoice my heart, as you used to do. But if, thro' illness, you cannot so soon come down as we wish, I will go up to you: For I long to see you. I never more longed to see you in my life; and you was always the darling of my heart, you know.

My brother Antony desires his hearty commendations to you, and joins with me in the tenderest assurance, that all shall be well, and, if possible, better than ever; for we now have been so long without you, that we know the miss of you, and even hunger and thirst, as I may say, to see you, and to take you once more to our hearts.

God restore your health, if it be his will: Else, I know not what will become of

Your truly loving Uncle, and Second Papa,

John Harlowe

Mr. Belford
To Robert Lovelace, Esq;

Sat. Ten o'Clock.

POOR Mrs. Norton is come. She was set down at the door; and would have gone up-stairs directly. But Mrs. Smith and Mrs. Lovick being together and in tears, and the former hinting too suddenly to the truly-venerable woman the fatal news, she sunk down at her feet, in fits; so that they were forced to breathe a vein, to bring her to herself; and to a capacity of exclamation: And then she ran on to Mrs. Lovick and to me, who entered just as she recovered, in praise of the lady, in lamentations for her, and invectives against you: But yet so circumscribed were her invectives, that I could observe in them the woman well educated, and in her lamentations the passion christianized, as I may say.

She was impatient to see the corpse. The women went up with her. But they owned, that they were too much affected themselves on this occasion to describe her extremely affecting behaviour.

With trembling impatience she pushed aside the coffin-lid. She bathed the face with her tears, and kissed her cheeks and forehead, as if she were living. It was *Her* indeed, she said! Her sweet young lady! Her very self! Nor had death, which changed all things, a power to alter her lovely features! She admired the serenity of her aspect. She no doubt was happy, she said, as she had written to her she should be: But how many miserable creatures had she left behind her!

It was with difficulty they prevailed upon her to quit the corpse; and when they went into the next apartment, I joined them, and acquainted her with the kind legacy her beloved young Lady had left her: But This rather augmented, than diminished her concern. She ought, she said, to have attended her in person. What was the world to her, wringing her hands, now the child of her bosom, and of her heart, was no more? Her principal consolation, however, was, that she should not long survive her. She hoped, she said, that she did not sin, in wishing she might not.

The Colonel proposes to attend the herse, if his kindred give him not fresh cause of displeasure; and will take with him a copy of the Will. And being intent to give the family some favorable impressions of me, he will also, at his own desire, take with him the copy of the posthumous letter to me.

He is so kind as to promise me a minute account of all that shall pass on the melancholy occasion. And we have begun a friendship and settled a correspondence, which but one incident can possibly happen to interrupt to the end of our lives. And that I hope will not happen.

But what must be the grief, the remorse, that will seize upon the hearts of this hitherto inexorable family, on the receiving of the posthumous letters, and that of the Colonel apprising them of what has happened!

Mr. Belford To Robert Lovelace, Esq;

Sat. Afternoon, Sept. 9.

I UNDERSTAND, that thou breathest nothing but revenge against *me,* for treating thee with so much freedom; and against the accursed woman and her infernal crew. I am not at all concerned for thy menaces against myself. It is my design to make thee *feel*. It gives me pleasure to find my intention answered. And I congratulate thee, that thou hast not lost that sense.

As to the cursed crew, well do they deserve the fire *here* that thou threatenest them with, and the fire here*after* that seems to await them. But I have this moment received news which will, in all likelihood, save thee the guilt of punishing the old wretch for her share of wickedness as thy agent. But if that happens to her which is likely to happen, wilt thou not tremble for what may befal the principal?

Not to keep thee longer in suspense; last night, it seems, the infamous woman got so heartily intoxicated with her beloved liquor, arrack punch, at the expence of Colonel Salter, that, mistaking her way, she fell down a pair of stairs, and broke her leg: And now, after a dreadful night, she lies foaming, raving, roaring, in a burning fever, that wants not any other fire to scorch her into a feeling more exquisite and durable than any thy vengeance could make her suffer.

The wretch has requested me to come to her: And lest I should refuse a common messenger, sent her vile associate Sally Martin; who not finding me at Soho, came hither; another part of her business being to procure the divine lady's pardon for the old creature's wickedness to her.

This devil incarnate Sally was never so shocked in her life, as when I told her the lady was dead.

She took out her salts to keep her from fainting; and when a little recovered, she accused herself for her part of the injuries the lady had sustained; as she said Polly Horton would do for hers; and shedding tears, declared, that the world never produced such another woman. She called her the ornament and glory of her Sex.

This wretch would fain have been admitted to a sight of the corpse. But I refused her request with execrations.

At going away, she told me, that the old monster's bruises are of more dangerous consequence than the fracture: That a mortification is apprehended: And that the vile wretch has so much compunction of heart, on recollecting her treatment of Miss Harlowe, and is so much set upon procuring her forgiveness, that she is sure the news she has to carry her, will hasten her end.

Mr. Lovelace
To John Belford, Esq;

Uxbridge, Sat. Sept. 9.

Jack,

I THINK it absolutely right that my ever-dear and beloved lady should be opened and embalmed. It must be done out of hand—this very afternoon. Your acquaintance Tomkins and old Anderson of this place, whom I will bring with me, shall be the surgeons. I have talked to the latter about it.

I will see every-thing done with that decorum which the case, and the sacred person of my beloved require.

Every thing that can be done to preserve the charmer from decay, shall also be done. And when she *will* descend to her original dust, or cannot be kept longer, I will then have her laid in my family-vault between my own father and mother. Myself, as I am in my soul, so in person, chief mourner. But her heart, to which I have such unquestionable pretensions, in which once I had so large a share, and which I will prize above my own, I *will* have. I will keep it in spirits. It shall never be out of my sight. And all the charges of sepulture too shall be mine.

Surely nobody will dispute my right to her. Whose was she living? Whose is she dead, but mine? — Her cursed parents, whose barbarity to her, no doubt, was the *true* cause of her death, have long since renounced her. She left *them* for *me*. She chose *me* therefore: And I was her husband. What tho' I treated her like a villain? Do I not pay for it now? Would she not have been mine had I not? Nobody will dispute but she would.

Take notice, Belford, that I do hereby actually discharge you, and every body, from all cares and troubles relating to her. And as to her last testament, I will execute it myself.

There were no articles between us, no settlements; and she is mine, as you see I have proved to a demonstration: Nor could she dispose of herself but as I pleased. D—nation seize me then if I make not good my right against all opposers!

Her bowels, if her friends are very solicitous about them, and very humble and sorrowful (and none have they of their own) shall be sent down to them — To be laid with *her* ancestors — unless she has ordered otherwise. For, except that she shall not be committed to the unworthy earth so long as she can be kept out of it, her Will shall be performed in every-thing.

I send in the mean time for a lock of her hair.

Let me know if the damn'd mother be yet the subject of the devil's own vengeance — if the old wretch be dead or alive? Some exemplary mischief I must yet do. My revenge shall sweep away that devil, and all my opposers of the cruel Harlowe family, from the face of the earth. Whole hecatombs ought to be offered up to the Manes of my Clarissa Lovelace.

Altho' her Will may in some respects cross mine, yet I expect to be observed. I will be the interpreter of hers.

Next to mine, hers shall be observed; for she is my wife; and shall be to all eternity. I will never have another.

R. Lovelace

Mr. Belford
To Mr. Robert Lovelace, Esq;

O LOVELACE! I have a scene to paint in relation to the wretched Sinclair, that, if I do it justice, will make thee seriously ponder and reflect, or nothing can. I will lead to it in order; and that in my usual hand, that thy compeers may be able to read it as well as thyself.

When I had written the preceding letter; not knowing what to do with myself; recollecting, and in vain wishing for that delightful and improving conversation, which I had now for ever lost; I thought I had as good begin the task, which I had for some time past *resolved* to begin; that is to say, To go to church; and see if I could not reap some benefit from what I should hear there. Accordingly I determined to go to hear the celebrated preacher at St. James's church. But, as if the devil thought himself concerned to prevent my intention, a visit was made me just as I was dressed, which took me off from my purpose.

Whom should this be from, but from Sally Martin, accompanied by Mrs. Carter, the sister of the infamous Sinclair! the same, I suppose I need not tell you, who keeps the Bagnio near Bloomsbury.

These told me that the surgeon, apothecary, and physician, had all given the wretched woman over; but that she said, She could not die, nor be at rest, till she saw me: And they besought me to accompany them in the coach they came in, if I had one spark of charity, of *Christian* charity, as they called it, left.

I was very loth to be diverted from my purpose by a request so unwelcome, and from people so hated; but at last went, and we got thither by ten.

The old wretch had once put her leg out by her rage and violence, and had been crying, scolding, cursing, ever since the preceding evening, that the surgeon had told her it was impossible to save her; and that a mortification had begun to shew itself; insomuch that purely in compassion to their own *ears*,

510

they had been forced to send for another surgeon, purposely to tell her, tho' against his judgment, and (being a friend of the other) to seem to convince *him*, that he mistook her case; and that, if she would be patient, she might recover. But, nevertheless her apprehensions of death and her antipathy to the thoughts of dying, were so strong, that their imposture had not the intended effect, and she was raving, crying, cursing, and even howling, more like a wolf than a human creature, when I came.

There were no less than Eight of her cursed daughters surrounding her bed when I entered; one of her partners, Polly Horton, at their head; and now Sally, her other partner, and *Madam* Carter, as they called her (for they are all *Madams* with one another) made the number Ten: All in shocking dishabille, and without stays, except Sally, Carter, and Polly; who, not daring to leave her, had not been in bed all night.

The other seven seemed to have been but just up, risen perhaps from their customers in the fore-house, and their nocturnal Orgies, with faces, three or four of them, that had run, the paint lying in streaky seams not half blowz'd off, discovering coarse wrinkled skins: The hair of some of them of divers colours, obliged to the blacklead comb where black was affected; the artificial jet, however, yielding apace to the natural brindle: That of others plastered with oil and powder; the oil predominating: But every one's hanging about her ears and neck in broken curls, or ragged ends; and each at my entrance taken with one motion, stroaking their matted locks with both hands under their coifs, mobs, or pinners, every one of which was awry. They were all slip-shoed; stockenless some; only under-petticoated all; their gowns, made to cover straddling hoops, hanging trolloppy, and tangling about their heels; but hastily wrapt round them, as soon as I came up-stairs. And half of them (unpadded, shoulder-bent, pallid-lipp'd, limber-jointed wretches) appearing from a blooming Nineteen or Twenty perhaps overnight, haggard well-worn strumpets of Thirty-eight or Forty.

I am the more particular in describing to thee the appearance these creatures made in my eyes when I came into the room, because I believe thou never sawest any of them, much less a group of them, thus unprepared for being seen[a]. I, for my part, never did before; nor had I now, but upon this occcasion, been thus *favoured*. If thou *hadst*, I believe thou wouldst hate a profligate woman, as one of Swift's Yahoos, or Virgil's obscene Harpyes, squirting their ordure upon the Trojan trenchers; since the persons of such in their retirements are as filthy as their minds—Hate them as much as I do; and as much as I admire, and next to adore a truly virtuous and elegant woman: For to me it is evident, that as a neat and clean woman must be an angel of a creature, so a sluttish one is the impurest animal in nature.

But these were the veterans, the chosen band; for now-and-then flitted in, to the number of half a dozen or more, by turns, subordinate sinners, under-graduates, younger than some of the chosen phalanx, but not less obscene in their appearance, tho' indeed not so much beholden to the plastering fucus; yet unpropt by stays, squalid, loose in attire, sluggish-haired, under-petticoated only as the former, eyes half-opened, winking and pinking, mispatched, yawning, stretching, as if from the unworn-off effects of the midnight revel; all armed in succession with supplies of cordials (of which every one present was either taster or partaker) under the direction of the Praetorian Dorcas, who now-and-then popp'd in to see her slops duly given and taken.

But when I approached the *old wretch*, what a spectacle presented itself to my eyes!

Her misfortune has not at all sunk, but rather, as I thought, increased her flesh; rage and violence perhaps swelling her muscular features. Behold her then, spreading the whole tumbled bed with her huge quaggy carcase: Her mill-post arms held up; her broad hands clenched with violence; her big eyes, goggling and flaming-red as we may suppose those of a salamander; her matted griesly hair, made irreverend by her wickedness (her clouted head-dress being half off) spread about her fat ears and brawny neck; her livid lips parched, and working violently;

[a] Whoever has seen Dean Swift's Lady's Dressing-Room, will think this description of Mr. Belford not only more natural, but more decent painting, as well as better justified by the design, and by the *use* that may be made of it.

her broad chin in convulsive motion; her wide mouth, by reason
of the contraction of her forehead (which seemed to be half-
lost in its own frightful furrows) splitting her face, as it were,
into two parts; and her huge tongue hideously rolling in it;
heaving, puffing, as if for breath; her bellows-shaped and
various-coloured breasts ascending by turns to her chin, and
descending out of sight, with the violence of her gaspings.

As soon as she saw me, her naturally-big voice, more
hoarsened by her ravings, broke upon me: O Mr. Belford! O
Sir! see what I am come to!—See what I am brought to!—To
have such a cursed crew about me, and not one of them to take
care of me!—But to let me tumble down *stairs* so distant from
the room I went from! so distant from the room I meant to go
to! O cursed be every careless devil!—May this or worse be
their fate every one of them!

As soon as she had cleared the passage of her throat by the
oaths and curses which her wild impatience made her utter, she
began in a more hollow and whining strain to bemoan herself.
And here, said she—Heaven grant me patience! (clenching and
unclenching her hands) am I to die thus miserably!—of a broken
leg in my old age!—snatch'd away by means of my own intemperance! Self-do! Self-undone!—No time for my affairs! No
time to repent!—And in a few hours (Oh!—Oh!—with another
long howling O—h!—U—gh!—o! a kind of screaming key
terminating it) who knows, who can tell *where* I shall be?—Oh!
that indeed I never, never, had had a being!

What could one say to such a wretch as this! whose whole
life had been spent in the most diffusive wickedness, and who
no doubt has more souls to answer for, of both sexes, than the
best Divine in England ever saved?—Yet I told her, She must
be patient: That her violence made her worse: And that, if she
would compose herself, she might get into a frame more proper
for her present circumstances.

Who, I? interrupted she: *I* get into a better frame! *I*, who can
neither cry, nor pray! Yet already feel the torments of the
damn'd! What mercy can I expect? What hope is left for me?—
Then, that sweet creature! That incomparable Miss Harlowe!—
She, it seems, is dead and gone! O that cursed Man! Had it not

been for *him!* I had never had This, the most crying of all my sins, to answer for! And then she set up another howl.

I still advised patience. I said, that if her time were to be so short as she apprehended it to be, the more ought she to endeavour to compose herself: And then she would at least die with more ease to herself—and satisfaction to her friends, I was *going* to say—But the word *die* put her into a violent raving, and thus she broke in upon me.

Die, did you say, Sir?—*Die!*—I will not, I cannot die!—I know not *how* to die!—*Die*, Sir!—And *must* I then die?—Leave this world?—I cannot bear it!—And who brought *You* hither, Sir, (her eyes striking fire at me) Who brought you hither to tell me I must *die*, Sir?—I cannot, I will not leave this world. Let others die, who wish for another! who expect a better!—I have had my plagues in This: but would compound for all future hopes, so as I may be nothing after This! And then she howled and bellowed by turns.

Sally—Polly—Sister Carter! said she, did you not tell me I might *recover?* Did not the *surgeon* tell me I might?

And so you *may*, cry'd Sally; Mr. Garon says you may, if you'll be patient. But, as I have often told you this blessed morning, you are readier to take despair from your own fears, than comfort from all the hope we can give you.

Yet cry'd the wretch, interrupting, does not Mr. Belford (and to *him* you have told the truth, tho' you won't to *me;* Does not he) tell me I shall *die?*—I cannot bear it! I cannot bear the *thoughts* of dying!—

Well, but to what purpose, said I (turning aside to her Sister, and to Sally and Polly) are these hopes given her, if the gentlemen of the faculty give her over? You should let her know the worst, and then she *must* submit; for there is no running away from death. If she has any matters to settle, put her upon settling them; and do not, by telling her she will live when there is no room to expect it, take from her the opportunity of doing needful things. Do the surgeons actually give her over?

They do, whispered they. Her gross habit, they say, gives no hopes. We have sent for both surgeons, whom we expect every minute.

Both the surgeons (who are French, for Mrs. Sinclair has heard Tourville launch out in the praise of French Surgeons) came in while we were thus talking. I retired to the further end of the room, and threw up a window for a little air, being half-poisoned by the effluvia arising from so many contaminated carcases; which gave me no imperfect idea of the stench of gaols, which corrupting the ambient air, give what is called the prison-distemper.

I came back to the bed-side when the surgeons had inspected the fracture; and asked them, If there were any expectation of her life?

One of them whispered me, There was none: That she had a strong fever upon her, which alone, in such a habit, would probably do the business; and that the mortification had visibly gained upon her since they were there six hours ago.

Will amputation save her? Her affairs and her mind want settling. A few days added to her life may be of service to her in both respects.

They told me the fracture was high in her leg; that the knee was greatly bruised; that the mortification, in all probability, had spread half-way of the *Femur:*—But at last both the gentlemen declared, That if she and her friends would consent to amputation, they would whip off her leg in a moment.

Mrs. Carter asked, To what purpose, if the operation would not save her?

Very true, they said; but it might be a satisfaction to the patient's friends, that all was done that could be done.

And so the poor wretch was to be lanced and quartered, as I may say, for an experiment only! And, without any hope of benefit from the operation, was to pay the surgeons for tormenting her!

As nobody cared to tell the unhappy wretch what every one apprehended must follow, and what the surgeons convinced me soon would, I undertook to be the denouncer of her doom. Accordingly, the operators being withdrawn, I sat down by the bed-side, and said, Come, Mrs. Sinclair, let me advise you to forbear these ravings at the carelessness of those, who, I find, at the time, could take no care of themselves; and since

the accident *has* happened, and cannot be remedied, to resolve
to make the best of the matter: For all this violence but enrages
the malady, and you will probably fall into a delirium, if you
give way to it, which will deprive you of that reason which
you ought to make the best of, for the time it may be lent you.

She turned her head towards me, and hearing me speak
with a determined *voice*, and seeing me assume as determined
an *air*, became more calm and attentive.

I went on, telling her, that I was glad, from the hints she
had given, to find her concerned for her past mis-spent life, and
particularly for the part she had had in the ruin of the most
excellent woman on earth; That if she would compose herself,
and patiently submit to the consequence of an evil she had
brought upon herself; it might possibly be happy for her yet.
Mean time, continued I, tell me, with temper and calmness,
Why you was so desirous to see me?

She seemed to be in great confusion of thought, and turned
her head this way and that; and at last, after much hesitation,
said, Alas for me! I hardly know *what* I wanted with you. When
I awoke from my intemperate trance, and found what a cursed
way I was in, my conscience smote me, and I was for catching,
like a drowning wretch, at every straw. I wanted to see every-
body and any-body but those I did see; every-body who I
thought could give me comfort. Yet could I expect none from
You neither; for you had declared yourself my enemy, altho'
I had never done you harm: For what, Jackey, in her old tone,
whining thro' her nose, was Miss Harlowe to you?—But *she* is
happy!—But oh! what will become of *me*?—Yet tell me, Shall
I do well again? May I recover? If I *may*, I will begin a new
course of life: As I hope to be saved, I will. Good God of heaven
and earth, but this once! this once! repeating those words five
or six times, spare thy poor creature, and every hour of my
life shall be penitence and atonement: Upon my soul it shall!

Less vehement! a little less vehement! said I—It is not for
me, who have led so free a life, as you but too well know, to talk
to you in a reproaching strain, and to set before you the iniquity
you have lived in, and the many souls you have helped to des-

troy. But as you are in so penitent a way, if I might advise,
it should be to send for a good Clergyman, the purity of whose
life and manners may make all these things come from him with
a better grace than they can from me.

How, Sir! What, Sir! interrupting me; Send for a Parson!—
Then you indeed think I shall die! Then you think there is no
room for hope!—A Parson, Sir!—Who sends for a Parson, while
there is any hope left?—Never tell me of it!—What! die!—What!
cut off in the midst of my sins!

I cannot bear, said I, rising from my seat with a stern air,
to see a reasonable creature behave so outrageously!—Will this
vehemence, think you, mend the matter? Will it avail you any
thing? Will it not rather shorten the life you are so desirous to
have lengthened, and deprive you of the only opportunity you
can ever have to settle your affairs for both worlds? You have
reason to be thankful, that you did not perish in that act of
intemperance which brought you to this: For it might have been
your neck, as *well* as your leg; and then you had not had the
opportunity you now have for repentance—And the Lord have
mercy upon you! into what a State might you have awoke?

Then did the poor wretch set up an inarticulate frightful
howl, such a one as I never before heard uttered, as if already
pangs infernal had taken hold of her; and seeing every one
half-frighted, and me motioning to withdraw, O pity me, pity
me, Mr. Belford, cried she, her words interrupted by groans.
I find you think I shall die! And *what* I may be, and *where*, in a
very few hours—Who can tell?

I told her it was in vain to flatter her: It was my opinion
she would not recover.

I was going to re-advise her to calm her spirits, and endeavour to resign herself, and to make the best of the opportunity yet left her; but this declaration set her into a most outrageous raving. She would have torn her hair and beaten her
breast, had not some of the wretches held her hands by force,
while others kept her as steady as they could, lest she should
again put out her new-set leg: So that, seeing her thus incapable
of advice, and in a perfect phrensy, I told Sally Martin, that

there was no bearing the room; and that their best way was to send for a Minister to pray by her, and to reason with her, as soon as she should be capable of it.

And so I left them; and never was so sensible of the benefit of fresh air, as I was the moment I entered the street.

Nor is it to be wondered at, when it is considered, that to the various ill smells, that will be always found in a close sick-bed room (since generally, when the Physician comes, the Air is shut out) *This* of Mrs. Sinclair was the more particularly offensive, as, to the scent of plaisters, embrocations, and ointments, were added the stenches of spirituous liquors, burnt and unburnt, of all denominations: For one or other of the creatures, under pretence of colics, gripes, qualms or insurrections, were continually calling for supplies of these, all the time I was there. And yet this is thought to be a genteel house of the sort: And all the prostitutes in it are prostitutes of price, and their visitors people of note.

O Lovelace! what lives do most of us Rakes and Libertines lead! What company do we keep! And, for *such* company, what society renounce, or endeavour to make like these!

What woman, nice in her person, and of purity in her mind and manners, did she know what miry wallowers the generality of men of our class are in themselves, and constantly trough and sty with, but would detest the thoughts of associating with such filthy sensualists, whose favourite taste carries them to mingle with the dregs of stews, brothels, and common-sewers?

Yet, to such a choice are many worthy women betrayed, by that false and inconsiderate notion, raised and propagated, no doubt, by the author of all delusions, *That a reformed Rake makes the best husband.* We Rakes, indeed, are bold enough to suppose, that women in general are as much Rakes in their *hearts*, as the Libertines some of them suffer themselves to be taken with, are in their *practice*. A supposition therefore, which, it behoves persons of true honour of that Sex, to discountenance, by rejecting the address of every man, whose character will not stand the test of that virtue which is the glory of a woman: And indeed, I may say, of a man too.

Don't be disgusted, that I mingle such grave reflections as these with my narratives. It becomes me, in my present way of thinking, to do so, when I see in Miss Harlowe, how all human excellence, and am near seeing in this abandon'd woman, how all diabolical profligateness, end. And glad should I be for your own sake, for your splendid family's sake, and for the sake of all your intimates and acquaintance, that you were labouring under the same impressions, that so *we*, who have been companions in (and promoters of one another's) wickedness, might join in a general atonement to the utmost of our power.

I came home reflecting upon all these things, more edifying to me than any Sermon I could have heard preached: And I shall conclude this long letter with observing, that altho' I left the wretched howler in a high phrensy-fit, which was excessively shocking to the by-standers; yet her phrensy is the happiest part of her dreadful condition: For when she is *herself*, as it is called, what must be her reflections upon her past profligate life, throughout which it has been her constant delight and business, devil-like, to make others as wicked as herself! What must her terrors be (a Hell already begun in her mind!) on looking forward to the dreadful State she is now upon the verge of!—But I drop my trembling pen.

To have done with so shocking a subject at once, we shall take notice, That Mr. Belford, in a future letter, writes, that the miserable woman, to the surprize of the operators themselves (thro' hourly encreasing tortures of body and mind) held out so long as till Thursday Sept. 21. And then died in such agonies as terrified into a transitory penitence all the wretches about her.

Colonel Morden
To John Belford, Esq;

Sunday Night, Sept. 10.

Dear Sir,

A CCORDING to my promise, I send you an account of
matters here. Poor Mrs. Norton was so very ill upon the
road, that, slowly as the herse moved, and the chariot followed,
I was afraid we should not have got her to St. Alban's. We put
up there as I had intended. I was in hopes that she would have
been better for the stop: But I was forced to leave her behind
me. I ordered the servant-maid you was so considerately kind
as to send down with her, to be very careful of her; and left
the chariot to attend her. She deserves all the regard that can
be paid her; not only upon my cousin's account, but on her
own. She is an excellent woman.

When we were within five miles of Harlowe-Place, I put on
a hand-gallop. I ordered the herse to proceed more slowly still,
the cross-road we were in being rough, and having more time
before us than I wanted; for I wished not the herse to be in till
near dusk.

I got to my cousin's about four o'clock. You may believe
I found a mournful house. You desire me to be very minute.

At my entrance into the court, they were all in motion.
Every servant whom I saw had swelled eyes, and looked with
so much concern, that at first I apprehended some new disaster
had happened in the family.

Mr. John and Mr. Antony Harlowe and Mrs. Hervey were
there. They all helped on one another's grief, as they had before
done each other's hardness of heart.

My cousin James met me at the entrance of the hall. His
countenance expressed a fixed concern; and he desired me to
excuse his behaviour the last time I was there.

My cousin Arabella came to me full of tears and grief.

O cousin! said she, hanging upon my arm, I dare not ask

520

you any questions!—About the approach of the herse, I suppose she meant.

I myself was full of grief; and without going farther or speaking, sat down in the hall, in the first chair.

Mr. Antony Harlowe came to me soon after. His face was overspread with all the appearance of woe. He requested me to walk into the parlour; where, as he said, were all his fellow-mourners.

I attended him in. My cousins James and Arabella followed me.

A perfect concert of grief, as I may say, broke out the moment I entered the parlour.

My cousin Harlowe, the dear creature's Father, as soon as he saw me, said, O cousin, cousin, of all our family, you are the only one who have nothing to reproach yourself with!— You are a happy man!

The poor Mother, bowing her head to me in speechless grief, sat with her handkerchief held to her eyes, with one hand. The other hand was held by her sister Hervey, between both hers; Mrs. Hervey weeping upon it.

Near the window sat Mr. John Harlowe, his face and his body turned from the sorrowing company. His eyes were red and swelled.

My cousin Antony, at his re-entering the parlour, went towards Mrs. Harlowe—Don't—dear sister, said he!—Then towards my cousin Harlowe—Don't—dear Brother!—Don't thus give way—And without being able to say another word, went to a corner of the parlour, and, wanting himself the comfort he would fain have given, sunk into a chair, and audibly sobbed.

Miss Arabella followed her uncle Antony, as he walked in before me; and seemed as if she would have spoken to the pierced mother some words of comfort. But she was unable to utter them, and got behind her mother's chair; and inclining her face over it on the unhappy lady's shoulder, seemed to claim the consolation that indulgent parent used, but then was unable to afford her.

Young Mr. Harlowe with all his vehemence of spirit, was

now subdued. His self-reproaching conscience, no doubt, was the cause of it.

And what, Sir, must their thoughts be, which, at that moment, in a manner deprived them all of motion, and turned their speech into sighs and groans!—How to be pitied, how greatly to be pitied, all of them! But how much to be cursed that abhorred Lovelace, who, as it seems, by arts uncommon, and a villainy without example, has been the sole author of a woe so complicated and extensive!—God judge me, as—But I stop— The man is your friend!—He already suffers, you tell me, in his intellect—Restore him heaven to That—If I find the matter come out, as I *apprehend* it will—Indeed her own hint of his usage of her, as in her Will, and in her first Letter to me, are enough—Nor think, my beloved cousin, thou darling of my heart! that thy gentle spirit, breathing charity and forgiveness to the vilest of men, shall avail him!

As I was the only person (grieved as I was myself) from whom any of them, at that instant, could derive comfort; Let us not, said I, my dear cousin, approaching the inconsolable Mother, give way to a grief, which however just, can now avail us nothing. We hurt ourselves, and cannot recall the dear creature for whom we mourn. Nor would you wish it, if you knew with what assurances of eternal happiness she left the world. —She is happy, Madam!—Depend upon it, she is happy! And comfort yourselves with that assurance.

O cousin, cousin! cried the unhappy mother, withdrawing her hand from that of her sister Hervey, and pressing mine with it, You know not what a child I have lost!—Then in a lower voice, And *how* lost!—That it is that makes the loss insupportable.

Then they set up another general lamentation. We see, said her father, Enough we see in her heart-piercing letters to us, what a happy frame she was in a few days before her death: But did it hold to the last? Had she no repinings? Had the dear child no heart-burnings?

None at all!—I never saw, and never shall see, so blessed a *departure:* And no wonder, for I never heard of such a *prepara-*

tion. Every hour for weeks together was taken up in it. Let this be our comfort—We need only to wish for so happy an end for ourselves and for those who are nearest to our hearts. We may any of us be grieved for acts of unkindness to her. But had all happened that once she wished for, she could not have made a happier, perhaps not so happy, an end.

Dear soul! and dear sweet soul! the Father, Uncles, Sister, my cousin Hervey cried out all at once in accents of anguish inexpressibly affecting.

We must for ever be disturbed for those acts of unkindness to so sweet a child, cried the unhappy Mother!—Indeed, indeed (softly to her Sister Hervey) I have been too passive, much too passive, in this case!—The temporary quiet I have been so studious all my life to preserve, has cost me everlasting disquiet!—

There she stopt.

Dear Sister! was all Mrs. Hervey could say.

My *dearest, dearest Sister!* again was all Mrs. Hervey could say.

Would to Heaven, proceeded, exclaiming, the poor mother, I had but *once* seen her! Then turning to my Cousin James and his Sister—O my Son! O my Arabella! If WE were to receive as little mercy—

And there again she stopt, her tears interrupting her further speech: Every one, all the time, remaining silent; their countenances shewing a grief in their hearts too big for expression.

Now you see, Mr. Belford, that my dearest cousin could be allowed all her merit!—What a dreadful thing is after-reflection upon a conduct so perverse and unnatural?

O this cursed friend of yours, Mr. Belford! This detested Lovelace!—To him, To him is owing—

Pardon me, Sir. I will lay down my pen till I have recovered my temper.

Mr. Lovelace
To John Belford, Esq;

M. Hall, Thursday, Sept. 14.

EVER since the fatal seventh of this month, I have been lost to myself, and to all the joys of life. Methinks something has been working strangely retributive. I never was such a fool as to disbelieve a Providence: Yet am I not for resolving into judgments every-thing that temporarily chances to wear an avenging face. Yet if we must be punished either here or hereafter for our misdeeds, better *here*, say I, than *hereafter*. Have I not then an interest to think my punishment already not only begun, but completed; since what I have suffered, and do suffer, passes all description?

To give but one instance of the *retributive*—Here I, who was the barbarous cause of the loss of senses for a week together to the most inimitable of women, have been punished with the loss of my own—Preparative to—Who knows what?—When, O when, shall I know a joyful hour?

I am kept excessively low; and excessively low I *am*. This sweet creature's posthumous letter sticks close to me. All her excellencies rise up hourly to my remembrance.

Yet dare I not indulge in these melancholy reflections. I find my head strangely working again?—Pen, begone!

I will soon quit this kingdom. For now my Clarissa is no more, what is there in it (in the world indeed) worth living for?—But should I not first, by some masterly mischief, avenge her and myself upon her cursed family?

The accursed woman, they tell me, has broken her leg. Why was it not her neck?—All, all, but what is owing to her relations, is the fault of that woman, and of her hell-born nymphs. *The* *greater the virtue, the nobler the triumph*, was a sentence for ever in their mouths.—I have had it several times in my head to set fire to the execrable house; and to watch at the doors and windows, that not a devil in it escape the consuming flames. Had the house stood by itself, I had certainly done it.

524 *his kingdom is worldly*

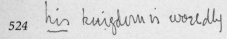

But, it seems, the old wretch is in the way to be rewarded, without my help. A shocking letter is received of somebody's, in relation to her—Yours, I suppose—Too shocking for me, they say, to see at present.

They govern me as a child in strings: Yet did I suffer so much in my fever, that I am willing to bear with them, till I can get tolerably well.

At present I can neither eat, drink, nor sleep. Yet are my disorders nothing to what they were: For, Jack, my brain was on fire day and night: And had it not been of the *asbestos* kind, it had all been consumed.

I had no distinct ideas, but of dark and confused misery: *It was all conscience and horror* indeed! Thoughts of hanging, drowning, shooting; then rage, violence, mischief, and despair, took their turns with me. My lucid intervals still worse, giving me to reflect upon what I *was* the hour before, and what I was likely to be the next, and perhaps for life—The sport of enemies! the laughter of fools! and the hanging-sleev'd, go-carted property of hired slaves; who were perhaps to find their account in manacling, and (abhorred thought!) in personally abusing me by blows and stripes!

Who can bear such reflections as these? To be made to *fear* only, to such a one as me, and to fear such wretches too!—What a thing was this, but *remotely* to apprehend! And yet, for a man to be in such a state as to render it necessary for his dearest friends to suffer this to be done for his own sake, and in order to prevent further mischief!—There is no thinking of these things!

I will *not* think of them, therefore: But will either get a train of chearful ideas, or hang myself, by to-morrow morning.

—To be a dog, and dead,
Were paradise, to such a life as mine.

Mr. Lovelace
To John Belford, Esq;

I AM preparing to leave this kingdom. Mowbray and Tourville promise to give me their company in a month or two.

Thou hast made good resolutions. If thou keepest them not, thou wilt never be able to keep any. But, nevertheless, the devil and thy time of life are against thee: And six to one thou failest. Were it only that thou hast *resolved*, six to one thou failest. And if thou dost, thou wilt become the scoff of men, and the triumph of devils.—Then how will I laugh at thee! For this warning is not from principle. Perhaps I wish it were: But I never lyed to man, and hardly ever said truth to woman. The first is what all free livers cannot say: The second, what every one can.

I am mad again, by Jupiter!—But thank my stars, not gloomily so!—Farewel, farewel, farewel, for the third or fourth time, concludes

Thy Lovelace

Mr. Belford
To Colonel Morden

Thursday, Sept. 21.

GIVE me leave, dear Sir, to address myself to you in a very serious and solemn manner on a subject that I must not, cannot, dispense with; as I promised the divine lady, that I would do every-thing in my power to prevent that further mischief which she was so very apprehensive of.

I will not content myself with distant hints. It is with very great concern that I have just now heard of a declaration which you are said to have made to your relations at Harlowe-Place, That you will not rest till you have avenged your cousin's wrongs upon Mr. Lovelace.

I have just now read over the *copies* of the dear lady's

posthumous letters. I send them all to you, except that directed for Mr. Lovelace; which I reserve till I have the pleasure of seeing you. Let me entreat you to read once more *that* written to yourself; and *that* to her Brother; which latter I now send you; as they are in point to the present subject.

My dear Colonel Morden, the highest injury was to *her:* Her family all have a share in the *cause: She* forgives it: Why should we not endeavour to imitate what we admire?

You asked me, Sir, when in town, If a brave man could be a premeditatedly base one?—*Generally speaking*, I believe Bravery and Baseness are incompatible. But Mr. Lovelace's character, in the instance before us, affords a proof of the truth of the common observation, That there is no general rule but has its exceptions: For England, I believe, as gallant a nation as it is deemed to be, has not in it a braver spirit than his; nor a man who has greater skill at his weapons; nor more *calmness* with his skill.

I mention not this with a thought that it can affect Col. Morden; who, if he be not with-held by superior Motives, as well as influenced by those I have reminded him of, will tell me, That this skill, and this bravery, will make him the more worthy of being called upon by him.

To these superior motives then I refer myself: And with the greater confidence; as a pursuit ending in blood would not, at *this time*, have the plea lie for it with *anybody*, which sudden passion might have with *some:* But would be construed by *all*, to be a cool and deliberate act of revenge for an evil absolutely irretrievable: An act, which a brave and noble spirit, such as is the gentleman's to whom I now write, is not capable.

Excuse me, Sir, for the sake of my executorial duty and promise, keeping in eye the dear lady's *personal injunctions*, as well as *written will*, inforced by *letters posthumous*. Every article of which (solicitous as we *both* are to see it duly performed) she would have dispensed with, rather than farther mischief should happen on her account. I am,

> Dear sir,
> Your affectionate and faithful servant,

> > > J. Belford

The following is the posthumous Letter to
Col. Morden, referred to in the above.

Superscribed,

To my beloved Cousin
William Morden, Esq;

To be delivered after my death.

My dearest Cousin,

A S it is uncertain, from my present weak state, whether, if living, I may be in a condition to receive as I ought the favour you intend me of a visit, when you come to London, I take this opportunity to return you, while able, the humble acknowlegements of a grateful heart, for all your goodness to me from childhood till now: And more particularly for your present kind interposition in my favour — God Almighty for ever bless you, dear Sir, for the kindness you endeavoured to procure for me.

One principal end of my writing to you in this solemn manner, is, to beg of you, which I do with the utmost earnestness, that when you come to hear the particulars of my story, you will not suffer *active* resentment to take place in your generous breast on my account.

Remember, my dear cousin, that vengeance is God's province; and he has undertaken to repay it; nor will you, I hope, invade that province:—Especially as there is no necessity for you to attempt to vindicate my fame; since the offender himself (before he is called upon) has stood forth, and offered to do me all the justice that you could have extorted from him, had I lived: And when your own person may be endangered by running an *equal* risque with a *guilty man.*

 Duelling, Sir, I need not tell *you*, who have adorned a

public character, is not only an usurpation of the Divine prerogative; but it is an insult upon magistracy and good government. 'Tis an impious act. 'Tis an attempt to take away a life that ought not to depend upon a private sword: An act, the consequence of which is to hurry a soul (all its sins upon its head) into perdition; endangering that of the poor triumpher—Since neither intend to give to the other that *chance*, as I may call it, for the Divine mercy, in an opportunity for repentance, which each presumes to hope for himself.

Seek not then, I beseech you, Sir, to aggravate my fault, by a pursuit of blood, which must necessarily be deemed a consequence of it. Give not the unhappy man the merit (were you assuredly to be the victor) of falling by your hand. At present he is the perfidious, the ingrateful deceiver; but will not the forfeiture of his life, and the probable loss of his soul, be a dreadful expiation for having made me miserable for *a few months* only, and thro' that misery, by the Divine favour, happy to all Eternity?

In such a case, my cousin, where shall the evil stop? And who shall avenge on you?—And who on your avenger?

Let the poor man's conscience then, dear Sir, avenge me. He will one day find punishment more than enough from that. Leave him to the chance of repentance. If the Almighty will give him time for it, why should you deny it him?—Let him still be the guilty aggressor; and let no one say, Clarissa Harlowe is now amply revenged in his fall; or, in the case of yours (which Heaven avert!) that her fault, instead of being buried in her grave, is perpetuated, and aggravated, by a loss far greater than that of herself.

May Heaven protect you, Sir, in all your ways; and, once more I pray, reward you for all your kindness to me: A kindness so worthy of *your* heart, and so exceedingly grateful to *mine:* That of seeking to make peace, and to reconcile parents to a once beloved child; uncles to a niece late their favourite; and a brother and sister to a sister whom once they thought not unworthy of that tender relation. A kindness so greatly preferable to the vengeance of the murdering sword.

Be a comforter, dear Sir, to my honoured parents, as you

have been to me: And may we, thro' the Divine goodness to us both, meet in that blessed Eternity, into which, as I humbly trust, I shall have entered when you read This.

So prays, and to her latest hour will pray, my dear cousin Morden, my Friend, my Guardian, but not my Avenger—[Dear Sir! remember That!—]

Your ever-affectionate and obliged

Clarissa Harlowe

Colonel Morden To John Belford, Esq;

Sat. Sept. 23.

Dear Sir,

I AM very sorry that any-thing you have heard I have said should give you uneasiness.

I am obliged to you for the Letters you have communicated to me; and still further for your promise to favour me with others occasionally.

All that relates to my dear Cousin I shall be glad to see, be it from whom it will.

Fear not, however, that your communications shall put me upon any measures that otherwise I should not have taken. The wickedness, Sir, is of such a nature, as admits not of aggravation.

Yet I do assure you, that I have not made any resolutions that will be a tie upon me.

I have indeed expressed myself with vehemence upon the occasion. Who could forbear to do so? But it is not my way to resolve in matters of moment, till opportunity brings the execution of my purposes within my reach. We shall see by what manner of spirit this young man will be acted, on his recovery. If he continue to brave and defy a family, which he has so irreparably injured—If—But resolutions depending upon future

Mr. Belford
To Lord M.

I T may be some satisfaction to your Lordship, to have a brief account of what has just now passed between Colonel Morden and me.

We had a good deal of discourse about the Harlowe-family, and those parts of the Lady's Will which still remain unexecuted; after which the Colonel addressed himself to me in a manner which gave me some surprize.

He flattered himself, he said, from my present happy turn, and from my good constitution, that I should live a great many years. It was therefore his request, that I would consent to be *his* Executor; since it was impossible for him to make a better choice, or pursue a better example, than his cousin had set.

He took my hand, seeing me under some surprize: You must not hesitate, much less deny me, Mr. Belford. Indeed you must not. Two things I will assure you of: That I have, as I hope, made every-thing so clear, that you cannot have any litigation: And that I have done so justly, and I hope it will be thought so generously, by all my relations, that a mind like yours will rather have pleasure than pain in the Execution of this Trust. And this is what I think every honest man, who hopes to find an honest man for his Executor, should do.

I told him, that I was greatly obliged to him for his good opinion of me: That it was so much every man's *duty* to be an honest man, that it could not be interpreted as vanity to say, that I had no doubt to be found so. But if I accepted of this Trust, it must be on condition—

I could name no condition, he said, interrupting me, which he would refuse to comply with.

This condition, I told him, was, that as there was as great a probability of his being *my* survivor, as I *his*, he would permit me to name *him* for mine; and, in that case, a week should not pass before I made my Will.

With all his heart, he said; and the readier, as he had no apprehensions of suddenly dying; for what he had done and requested was really the effect of the satisfaction he had taken in the part I had already acted as his cousin's Executor; and in my ability, he was pleased to add.

I told him, that I was pleased to hear him say, that he was not in any apprehension of suddenly dying; as this gave me assurance that he had laid aside all thoughts of acting contrary to his beloved cousin's dying request.

Does it argue, said he, smiling, that if I were to pursue a vengeance so justifiable in my own opinion, I must be in apprehension of falling by Mr. Lovelace's hand?—I will assure you, that I have no fears of that sort.—But I know this is an ingrateful subject to you. Mr. Lovelace is your friend; and I will allow, that a *good* man may have a friendship for a *bad one*, so far as to wish him well, without countenancing him in his evil.

I will assure you, added he, that I have not yet made any resolutions either way. I have told you what force my cousin's repeated requests have with me. Hitherto they have with-held me—But let us quit this subject.

This, Sir (giving me a sealed-up parcel), is my Will. It is witnessed. I made no doubt of prevailing upon you to do me the requested favour. And so God protect you, Mr. Belford! You will soon hear of me again.

He then very solemnly embraced me, as I did him: And we parted.

I heartily congratulate your Lordship on the narrow escape each gentleman has had from the other: For I apprehend, that they could have not met without fatal consequences.

Time, I hope, which subdues all things, will subdue their resentments. I am, my Lord,

Your Lordship's most faithful and obedient servant,

J. Belford

Mr. Belford
To Mr. Robert Lovelace, Esq;

London, Oct. 26.

I CANNOT think, my dear Lovelace, that Colonel Morden has either threatened you or intends to follow you. They are the words of people of that fellow's class; and not of a gentleman: Not of Colonel Morden, I am sure. You'll observe, that Joseph pretends not to say that he heard him speak them.

I have been very solicitous to sound the Colonel, for your sake, and for his own, and for the sake of the injunctions of the excellent lady to me, as well as to him, on that subject. He is (and you will not wonder that he should be) extremely affected; and owns, that he has expressed himself in terms of resentment on the occasion. Once he said to me, That had his beloved cousin's case been that of a common seduction (her own credulity or weakness contributing to her fall) he could have forgiven you. But, in so many words, He assured me, that he had not taken any resolutions; nor had he declared himself to the family in such a way as should bind him to resent: On the contrary, he has owned, that his cousin's injunctions have hitherto had the force upon him which I could wish they should have.

He went abroad in a week after you. When he took his leave of me, he told me, That his design was to go to Florence; and that he would settle his affairs there; and then return to England, and here pass the remainder of his days.

I was indeed apprehensive that if you and he were to meet, something unhappy might fall out: And as I knew that you proposed to take Italy, and very likely Florence, in your return to France, I was very solicitous to prevail upon you to take the Court of Spain into your plan. I am still so. And if you are not to be prevailed upon to do that, let me entreat you to avoid Florence or Leghorn in your return, as you have visited both heretofore. At least, let not the proposal of a meeting come from you.

537

Let *me* therefore (and thro' me all your friends) have the satisfaction to hear, that you are resolved to avoid this gentleman. Time will subdue all things. No-body doubts your bravery. Nor will it be known, that your plan is changed thro' persuasion.

Young Harlowe talks of calling you to account. This is a plain evidence, that Mr. Morden has not taken the quarrel upon himself for their family.

I am in no apprehension of any-body but Colonel Morden. I know it will not be a means to prevail upon you to oblige me, to say, that I am well assured, that this gentleman is a skilful swordsman; and that he is as cool and sedate as skilful. But yet I will add, that if I had a value for my life, he should be the last man, except yourself, with whom I would chuse to have a contention.

I have, as you required, been very candid and sincere with you. I have not aimed at palliation. If you seek not Colonel Morden, it is my opinion he will not seek you: For he is a man of principle. But if you seek him, I believe he will not shun you.

Adieu therefore! Mayst thou repent of the past: And may no new violences add to thy heavy reflections, and overwhelm thy future hopes, is the wish of

Thy true friend,

John Belford

Mr. Lovelace
To John Belford, Esq;

Munich, Nov. 11–22.

I RECEIVED yours this moment, just as I was setting out for Vienna.

As to going to Madrid, or one single step out of the way, to avoid Colonel Morden, let me perish, if I do!—You cannot think me so mean a wretch.

And so you own, that he *has* threatened me; but not in gross and ungentlemanly terms, you say. If he has threatened me like a gentleman, I will resent his threats like a gentleman. But he has not done as a man of honour, if he has threatened me at all behind my back. I would scorn to threaten any man to whom I *knew* how to address myself either personally or by pen and ink.

He had not taken any resolutions, you say, when you saw him. He *must* and *will* take resolutions, one way or other, very quickly; for I wrote to him yesterday, without waiting for this your answer to my last. I could not avoid it. I could not (as I told you in that) live in suspense. I have directed my letter to Florence. Nor could I suffer my friends to live in suspense as to my safety or otherwise. But I have couched it in such moderate terms, that he has fairly his option. He will be the challenger, if he take it in the sense in which he may so handsomely avoid taking it. And if he does, it will demonstrate that malice and revenge were the predominant passions with him; and that he was determined but to settle his affairs, and then *take his resolutions*, as you phrase it. — Yet, if we are to meet (for I know what *my* option would be, in *his* case, on *such a letter*, complaisant as it is) I wish *he* had a worse, *I* a better cause. It would be sweet revenge to him, were I to fall by his hand. But what should I be the better for killing him?

I will inclose the copy of the letter I sent him.

To William Morden, Esq;

[*Inclosed in the above.*]

Munich, Nov. 10–21.

Sir,

I HAVE heard, with a great deal of surprize, that you have thought fit to throw out some menacing expressions against me.

I should have been very glad, that you had thought I had punishment enough in my own mind, for the wrongs I have done to the most excellent of women; and that it had been possible for two persons so ardently joining in one love (especially as I was desirous, to the utmost of my power, to repair those wrongs) to have lived, if not on amicable terms, in such a way, as not to put either to the pain of hearing of threatenings thrown out in absence, which either ought to be despised for, if he had not spirit to take notice of them.

Now, Sir, if what I have heard be owing only to warmth of temper, or to sudden passion, while the loss of all other losses the most deplorable to me was recent, I not only excuse, but commend you for it. But if you are really *determined* to meet me on any other account (which, I own to you, is not however what I wish) it would be very blameable, and very unworthy of the character I desire to maintain as well with you as with every other gentleman, to give you a difficulty in doing it.

Being uncertain when this letter may meet you, I shall set out to-morrow for Vienna; where any letter directed to the post-house in that city, or to Baron Windisgratz's (at the Favorita) to whom I have commendations, will come to hand.

Mean time, believing you to be a man too generous to make a wrong construction of what I am going to declare, and knowing the value which the dearest of all creatures had for you, and your relation to her; I will not scruple to assure you, that the most acceptable return will be, that Colonel Morden chooses to be upon an amicable, rather than upon any other footing, with

His sincere admirer, and humble servant,

R. Lovelace

Mr. Lovelace
To John Belford, Esq;

Trent, Dec. 3–14.

TO-MORROW is to be the Day, that will, in all probability, send either one or two ghosts to attend the Manes of my Clarissa.

I arrived here yesterday; and inquiring for an English gentleman of the name of Morden, soon found out the Colonel's lodgings. He had been in town two days; and left his name at every probable place.

He was gone to ride out; and I left *my* name, and where to be found: And in the evening he made me a visit.

He was plaguy gloomy. That was not I. But yet he told me, that I had acted like a man of true spirit in my first letter; and with honour, in giving him so readily this meeting. He wished I had in other respects; and then we might have seen each other upon better terms than now we did.

I said, there was no recalling what was pass'd; and that I wished some things had not been done, as well as he.

To recriminate now, he said, would be as exasperateing as unavailable. And as I had so chearfully given him this opportunity, words should give place to business. — *Your* choice, Mr. Lovelace, of Time, of Place, of Weapon, shall be *my* choice.

The two latter be yours, Mr. Morden. The Time to-morrow, or next day, as you please.

Next day, then, Mr. Lovelace; and we'll ride out to-morrow, to fix the place.

Agreed, Sir.

Well; now, Mr. Lovelace, do you choose the Weapon.

I said, I believed we might be upon an equal foot with the Single Rapier; but, if he thought otherwise, I had no objection to a Pistol.

I will only say, replied he, that the chances may be more equal by the Sword, because we can neither of us be to seek in

541

that: And you'd stand, says he, a worse chance, as I apprehend, with a Pistol; and yet I have brought two; that you may take your choice of either: For, added he, I never missed a mark at pistol-distance, since I knew how to hold one.

I told him, that he spoke like himself: That I was expert enough that way, to embrace it, if he chose it; tho' not so sure of my mark as he pretended to be. Yet the devil's in't, Colonel, if I, who have slit a bullet in two upon a knife's edge, hit not my man. So I have no objection to a Pistol, if it be *your* choice. No man, I'll venture to say, has a steadier Hand or Eye than I have.

They may both be of use to you, Sir, at the Sword, as well as at the Pistol: The Sword therefore be the thing, if you please.

With all my heart.

We parted with a solemn sort of ceremonious civilty: And this day I called upon Him; and we rode out together to fix upon the place: And both being of one mind, and hating to put off for the morrow what could be done to-day, would have decided it then: But De la Tour, and the Colonel's valet, who attended us, being unavoidably let into the secret, joined to beg we would have with us a Surgeon from Brixen, whom La Tour had fallen in with there, and who had told him he was to ride next morning to bleed a person in a fever, at a lone cottage, which, by the Surgeon's description, was not far from the place where we then were, if it were not that very cottage within sight of us.

They undertook so to manage it, that the Surgeon should know nothing of the matter till his assistance was called in. And La Tour being, as I assured the Colonel, a ready-contriving fellow (whom I ordered to obey him as myself were the chance to be in *his* favour) we both agreed to defer the decision till to-morrow, and to leave the whole about the Surgeon to the management of our two valets; injoining them absolute secrecy: And so rode back again by different ways.

We fixed upon a little lone valley for the Spot—Ten to-morrow morning the Time—And Single Rapier the Word. Yet I repeatedly told him, that I value myself so much upon my skill in that weapon, that I would wish him to choose any other.

He said, It was a gentleman's weapon; and he who understood it not, wanted a qualification that he ought to suffer for not having: But that, as to him, one weapon was as good as another throughout all the instruments of offence.

So, Jack, you see I take no advantage of him: But my devil must deceive me, if he take not his life or his death, at my hands, before eleven to-morrow morning.

His valet and mine are to be present; but both strictly injoined to be impartial and inactive: And, in return for my civility of the like nature, he commanded *his* to be assisting to me, if he fell.

We are to ride thither, and to dismount when at the place; and his footman and mine are to wait at an appointed distance, with a chaise to carry off to the borders of the Venetian territories the survivor, if one drop; or to assist either or both, as occasion may demand.

And thus, Belford, is the matter settled.

A shower of rain has left me nothing else to do: And therefore I write this letter; tho' I might as well have deferred it till to-morrow twelve o'clock, when I doubt not to be able to write again, to assure you how much I am

Yours, &c.

Lovelace

Translation of a Letter from F. J. De la Tour

To John Belford, Esq;

near Soho-Square, London.

Trent, Dec. 18, N.S.

Sir,

I HAVE melancholy news to inform you of, by order of the Chevalier Lovelace. He shewed me his letter to you before he sealed it; signifying, that he was to meet the Chevalier Mor-

the duel

den on the 15th. Wherefore, as the occasion of the meeting is so well known to you, I shall say nothing of it here.

I had taken care to have ready, within a little distance, a Surgeon and his assistant, to whom, under an oath of secrecy, I had revealed the matter (tho' I did not own it to the two gentlemen); so that they were prepared with bandages, and all things proper. For well was I acquainted with the bravery and skill of my Chevalier; and had heard the character of the other; and knew the animosity of both. A post-chaise was ready, with each of their footmen, at a little distance.

The two Chevaliers came exactly at their time: They were attended by Monsieur Margate (the colonel's gentleman) and myself. They had given orders over-night, and now repeated them in each other's presence, that we should observe a strict impartiality between them: And that, if one fell, each of us should look upon himself, as to any needful help, or retreat, as the servant of the survivor, and take his commands accordingly.

After a few compliments, both the gentlemen, with the greatest presence of mind that I ever beheld in men, stript to their shirts, and drew.

They parried with equal judgment several passes. My Chevalier drew the first blood, making a desperate push, which, by a sudden turn of his antagonist, missed going clear thro' him, and wounded him on the fleshy part of the ribs of his right side; which part the sword tore out, being on the extremity of the body: But, before he could recover himself, his adversary, in return, pushed him into the inside of the left arm, near the shoulder: And the sword, by raking his breast as it passed, being followed by a great effusion of blood, the Colonel said, Sir, I believe you have enough.

My Chevalier swore by G—d, he was not hurt: 'Twas a pin's point: And so made another pass at his antagonist; which he, with a surprising dexterity, received under his arm, and run my dear Chevalier into the body: Who immediately fell; saying, The luck is your's, Sir—O my beloved Clarissa!—Now art thou—Inwardly he spoke three or four words more. His sword dropt from his hand. Mr. Morden threw his down, and

ran to him, saying in French—Ah Monsieur, you are a dead man!
—Call to God for mercy!

We gave the signal agreed upon to the footmen; and they
to the Surgeons; who instantly came up.

Colonel Morden, I found, was too well used to the bloody
work; for he was as cool as if nothing so extraordinary had
happened, assisting the Surgeons, tho' his own wound bled
much. But my dear Chevalier fainted away two or three times
running, and vomited blood besides.

However, they stopped the bleeding for the present; and
we helped him into the voiture; and then the Colonel suffered
his own wound to be dressed; and appeared concerned that my
Chevalier was between whiles (when he could speak, and struggle) extremely outrageous.—Poor gentleman! he had made
quite sure of victory!

The Colonel, against the Surgeons advice, would mount
on horseback to pass into the Venetian territories; and generously gave me a purse of gold to pay the Surgeons; desiring
me to make a present to the footman; and to accept of the remainder, as a mark of his satisfaction in my conduct; and in
my care and tenderness of my master.

The Surgeons told him, that my Chevalier could not live
over the day.

When the Colonel took leave of him, Mr. Lovelace said in
French, You have well revenged the dear creature.

I have, Sir, said Mr. Morden, in the same language: And
perhaps shall be sorry that you called upon me to this work,
while I was balancing whether to obey, or disobey, the dear
angel.

There is a fate in it! replied my Chevalier—A cursed fate!
—Or this could not have been!—But be ye all witnesses, that I
have provoked my destiny, and acknowlege, that I fall by a
Man of Honour.

Sir, said the Colonel, with the piety of a confessor, (wringing Mr. Lovelace's hand) snatch these few fleeting moments,
and commend yourself to God.

And so he rode off.

The voiture proceeded slowly with my Chevalier; yet the motion set both his wounds bleeding afresh; and it was with difficulty they again stopped the blood.

We brought him alive to the nearest cottage; and he gave orders to me to dispatch to you the packet I herewith send sealed up; and bid me write to you the particulars of this most unhappy affair; and give you thanks, in his name, for all your favours and friendship to him.

Contrary to all expectation, he lived over the night: But suffered much, as well from his impatience and disappointment, as from his wounds; for he seemed very unwilling to die.

He was delirious, at times, in the two last hours; and then several times cried out, Take her away! Take her away! but named no-body. And sometimes praised some Lady (that Clarissa, I suppose, whom he had called upon when he received his death's wound) calling her, Sweet Excellence! Divine Creature! Fair Sufferer!—And once he said, Look down, blessed Spirit, look down!—And there stopt;—his lips however moving.

At nine in the morning, he was seized with convulsions, and fainted away; and it was a quarter of an hour before he came out of them.

His few last words I must not omit, as they shew an ultimate composure; which may administer some consolation to his honourable friends.

Blessed—said he, addressing himself no doubt to Heaven; for his dying eyes were lifted up—A strong convulsion prevented him for a few moments saying more—But recovering, he again with great fervor (lifting up his eyes, and his spread hands) pronounced the word _Blessed:_—Then, in a seeming ejaculation, he spoke inwardly so as not to be understood: At last, he distinctly pronounced these three words,

LET THIS EXPIATE!

And then, his head sinking on his pillow, he expired; at about half an hour after ten.

He little thought, poor gentleman! his End so near: So had given no direction about his body. I have caused it to be embowelled, and deposited in a vault, till I have orders from England.

This is a favour that was procured with difficulty; and would have been refused, had he not been an Englishman of rank: A nation with reason respected in every Austrian government—For he had refused ghostly attendance, and the Sacraments in the Catholic way. May his Soul be happy, I pray God!

I have had some trouble also on account of the manner of his death, from the Magistracy here: Who have taken the requisite informations in the affair. And it has cost me some money. Of which, and of my dear Chevalier's effects, I will give you a faithful account in my next. And so, waiting at this place your commands, I am, Sir,

Your most faithful and obedient servant,

F. J. De La Tour

Richardson here adds a Conclusion, "Supposed to be written by MR. BELFORD." Mrs. Harlowe lives for two and a half years, Mr. Harlowe for half a year. James and Arabella marry into unhappy matches. Solmes remains single, his addresses being rejected "by several women of far inferior fortunes . . . to those of the Lady to whom he was encouraged to aspire." All of the minor characters' fates are revealed. Joseph Leman, for example, dies, consumptive, in less than a year. Miss Howe marries Hickman and Belford himself marries Charlotte Montague, niece of Lord M. [Ed.]

Thus virtue again rewarded

appendix A

selections from Richardson's
Familiar Letters *(1741)**

Letter Fifteen

From a young Lady to her Father, acquainting him with a Proposal of Marriage made to her.

Nottingham, April 4.

Honoured Sir,

I THINK it my Duty to acquaint you, that a gentleman of this Town, by Name *Derham*, and by Business a Linen draper, has made some Overtures to my Cousin *Morgan*, in the way of Courtship to me. My Cousin has brought him once or twice into my Company, which he could not well decline doing, because he has Dealings with him, and has an high Opinion of him and his Circumstances. He has been set up Three Years, and has very good Business, and lives in Credit and Fashion. He is about Twenty-seven Years old, and a likely Man enough: He seems not to want Sense or Manners; and is come of a good Family. He has broken his Mind to me, and boasts how well he can maintain me: But, I assure you, Sir, I have given him no En-

---

* The full title is *Letters Written To and For Particular Friends, On the Most Important Occasions, Directing Not Only the Requisite Style and Forms to be Observed in Writing Familiar Letters; But How to Think and Act Justly and Prudently, in the Common Concerns of Human Life.*

couragement; and told him, that I had no Thoughts of changing
my Condition, yet-a-while; and should never think of it but in
Obedience to my Parents; and I desired him to talk no more on
that Subject to me. Yet he resolves to persevere, and pretends
extraordinary Affection and Esteem. I would not, Sir, by any
means, omit to acquaint you with the *Beginnings* of an Affair
that would be want of Duty in me to conceal from you, and
shew a Guilt and Disobedience unworthy of the kind Indulgence
and Affection you have always shewn to, Sir,

> *Your most dutiful daughter.*

> My humble Duty to my honour'd Mother; Love to my
> Brother and Sister; and Respects to all Friends. Cousin
> *Morgan*, and his Wife and Sister, desire their kind Re-
> spects. I cannot speak enough of their Civility to me.

Letter Sixteen

*The Father's Answer, on a Supposition that
he approves not of the young Man's Addresses.*

Northampton, Apr. 10.

Dear Polly,

I HAVE received your Letter dated the 4th Instant, wherein
you acquaint me of the Proposals made to you, thro' your
Cousin *Morgan's* Recommendation, by one Mr. *Derham*. I hope,
as you assure me, that you have given no Encouragement to
him: For I by no means approve of him for your Husband. I
have enquired of one of his Townsmen, who knows him and
his Circumstances very well; and I am neither pleased with them,
nor with his Character; and wonder my Cousin would so incon-
siderately recommend him to you. Indeed, I doubt not Mr.
Morgan's good Intentions; but I insist upon it, that you think
nothing of the Matter, if you would oblige

> *Your indulgent father.*

Your Mother gives her Blessing to you, and joins with me
in the above Advice. Your Brother and Sister, and all
Friends, send their Love and Respects to you.

Letter Seventeen

*The Father's Answer, on a Supposition that
he does not disapprove of the young Man's
Addresses.*

Northampt. Apr. 10.

My dear Daughter,

I N Answer to yours of the 4th Instant, relating to the Addresses of Mr. *Derham*, I would have you neither wholly
encourage nor discourage his Suit; for if, on Inquiry into his
Character and Circumstances, I shall find, that they are answerable to your Cousin's good Opinion of them, and his own Assurances, I know not but his suit may be worthy of Attention.
But, my Dear, consider, that Men are deceitful, and always
put the best Side outwards; and it may possibly, on the strict
Inquiry, which the Nature and Importance of the Case demands,
come out far otherwise than it at present appears. Let me advise
you, therefore, to act in this Matter with great Prudence, and
that you make not yourself too cheap; for Men are apt to slight
what is too easily obtained. Your Cousin will give him Hope
enough, while you don't absolutely deny him; and, in the mean
time, he may be told, that you are not at your own Disposal,
but intirely resolved to abide by my Determination and Direction, in an Affair of this great Importance: And this will put
him upon applying to me, who, you need not doubt, will in
this Case, as in all others, study your Good; as becomes

Your indulgent father.

Your Mother gives her Blessing to you, and joins with me
in the above Advice. Your Brother and Sister, and all
Friends, send their Love and Respects to you.

Letter Eighteen

The young Gentleman's Letter to the Father, apprising him of his Affection for his Daughter.

Nottingham, Apr. 12.

Sir,

I TAKE the Liberty, tho' personally unknown to you, to declare the great Value and Affection I have for your worthy Daughter, whom I have had the Honour to see at my good Friend Mr. *Morgan's.* I should think myself intirely unworthy of *her* Favour, and of *your* Approbation, if I could have a thought of influencing her Resolution but in Obedience to your Pleasure; as I should, on such a Supposition, offer an Injury likewise to that Prudence in *herself,* which, I flatter myself, is not the least of her amiable Perfections. If I might have the Honour of your Countenance, Sir, on this Occasion, I would open myself and Circumstances to you, in that frank and honest Manner which should convince you of the Sincerity of my Affection for your Daughter, and at the same time of the Honourableness of my Intentions. In the mean time I will in general say, That I have been set up in my Business in the Linen-drapery Way, upwards of three Years; that I have a very good Trade for the time: That I had 1000 *l.* to begin with, which I have improved to 1500 *l.* as I am ready to make appear to your Satisfaction: That I am descended of a creditable Family; have done nothing to stain my Character; and that my Trade is still farther improveable, as I shall, I hope, inlarge my Bottom. This, Sir, I thought but honest and fair to acquaint you with, that you might know something of a Person, who sues to you for your Countenance, and that of your good Lady, in an Affair that I hope may prove one Day the greatest Happiness of my Life; as it *must* be, if I can be blessed with that, and your Daughter's Approbation. In hope of which, and the Favour of a Line, I take the Liberty to subscribe myself, good sir,

Your most obedient humble servant.

Letter Thirty-Four

Recommending a Chamber-maid.

Madam,

THE bearer, *Jane Adams*, is well recommended to me as a diligent, faithful Body, who understands her Needle well, is very neat and housewifely, and, as you desired, no Gossip or Make-bate; and has had a tolerable Education, being descended from good Friends. I make no doubt of her answering this Character. Of which I will satisfy you farther, when I have the Honour to see you. Till when I remain

Your most obedient humble servant.

Letter Thirty-Five

Recommending a Nursery-maid.

Madam,

THE bearer, *Sarah Williams*, is a housewifely genteel Body, who has been used to attend Children, and has a great Tenderness for them. She is very careful and watchful over them in all their little pretty Ways; and is a very proper Person to encourage their good Inclinations, or mildly to check their little Perversenesses, so far as you shall permit her to do the one or the other. She is come of good Friends, who have had Misfortunes; is very honest; and will, I dare say, please you much, if you are not provided; which I hope you are not, for both your Sakes; for I love the Girl, and am, with great Respect, Madam,

Your obliged humble servant.

Letter Sixty-Two

A young Woman in Town to her Sister in the Country, recounting her narrow Escape from a Snare laid for her, on her first Arrival, by a wicked Procuress.

Dear Sister,

WE have often, by our good Mother, been warned against the Dangers that would too probably attend us on coming to *London;* tho' I must own, her Admonitions had not always the Weight I am now convinced they deserved.

I have had a Deliverance from such a Snare, as I never could have believed would have been laid for a Person free from all Thought of Ill, or been so near succeeding upon one so strongly on her Guard as I imagined myself: And thus, my dear Sister, the Matter happened:

Returning, on *Tuesday*, from seeing my Cousin *Atkins*, in *Cheapside*, I was overtaken by an elderly Gentlewoman of a sober and creditable Appearance, who walked by my Side some little time before she spoke to me; and then guessing (by my asking the Name of the Street), that I was a Stranger to the Town, she very courteously began a Discourse with me; and after some other Talk, and Questions about my Country, and the like, desired to know, If I did not come to Town with a Design of going into some genteel Place? I told her, If I could meet with a Place to my Mind, to wait upon a single Lady, I should be very willing to embrace it. She said, I look'd like a creditable, sober, and modest Body; and at that very time she knew one of the best Gentlewomen that ever lived, who was in great want of a Maid to attend upon her own Person; and that if she liked me, and I her, it would be a lucky Incident for us both.

I expressed myself so thankfully, and she was so very much in my Interest, as to intreat me to go instantly to the Lady, lest she should be provided, and acquaint her I was recommended by Mrs. *Jones;* not doubting, as she said, but, on Inquiry, my Character would answer my Appearance.

As that, you know, was partly my View in coming to Town, I thought this a happy Incident, and determined not to lose the Opportunity; and so, according to the Direction she gave me, I went to inquire for Mrs. C— in J—n's Court, *Fleet-street*. The Neighbourhood look'd genteel, and I soon found the House. I ask'd for Mrs. C—; she came to me, dress'd in a splendid manner; I told her what I came about; she immediately desir'd me to walk into the Parlour, which was elegantly furnished; and after asking me several Questions, with my Answers to which she seemed very well pleased, a Servant soon brought in a bowl of warm Liquor which she called *Negus*, consisting of Wine, Water, Orange, &c. which, she said, was for a Friend or two she expected presently; but as I was warm with walking, she would have me drink some of it, telling me it was a pleasant innocent Liquor, and she always used her Waiting-maids, as she did herself. I thought this was very kind and condescending, and being warm and thirsty, and she encouraging me, I took a pretty free Draught of it, and thought it very pleasant, as it really was. She made me sit down by her, saying Pride was not her Talent, and that she should always indulge me in like manner, if I behaved well, when she had not Company; and then slightly ask'd, What I could do, and the Wages I required? With my Answers she seemed well satisfied, and granted the Wages I asked, without any Offer of Abatement.

And then I rose up, in order to take my Leave, telling her I would, any day she pleased, of the ensuing Week, bring my Cloaths, and wait upon her.

She said, that her own Maid being gone away, she was in the utmost Want of another, and would take it kindly if I would stay with her till next Day, because she was to have some Ladies to pass the Evening with her. I said this would be pretty inconvenient to me; but as she was so situated, I would oblige her, after I had been with my Aunt, and acquainted her with it. To this she reply'd, That there was no manner of occasion for that, because she could send the Cook for what I wanted, who could, at the same time, tell my Aunt how Matters stood.

I thought this looked a little odd; but she did it with so much Civility, and seemed so pleased with her new Maid, that

I scarcely knew how to withstand her: But the Apprehension
I had of my Aunt's Anger for not asking her Advice, in what so
nearly concern'd me, made me insist upon going, though I could
perceive Displeasure in her Countenance when she saw me re-
solv'd.

She then ply'd me very close with the Liquor, which she
again said was innocent and weak; but I believe it was far otherwise; for my Head began to turn round, and my Stomach felt
a little disordered. I intreated the Favour of her to permit me
to go, on a firm Promise of returning immediately; but then my
new Mistress began to raise her Voice a little, assuring me I
should on no Account stir out of her House. She left the Room,
in a sort of a Pet; but said she would send the Cook to take my
Directions to my Aunt; and I heard her take the Key out of the
outward Door.

This alarmed me very much; and, in the Instant of my
Surprize, a young Gentlewoman enter'd the Parlour, dress'd
in white Sattin, and every way genteel: She sat down in a Chair
next me, looked earnestly at me a while, and seemed going to
speak several times, but did not. At length she rose from her
Chair, bolted the Parlour-door, and, breaking into a Flood of
Tears, express'd herself as follows:

"Dear young Woman, I cannot tell you the Pain I feel on
your Account; and from an Inclination to serve you, I run an
Hazard of involving myself in greater Misery than I have yet
experienced, if that can be. But my Heart is yet too honest to
draw others, as I am desir'd to do, into a Snare which I have
fallen into myself. You are now in as notorious a Brothel, as
is in London; and if you escape not in a few Hours, you are
inevitably undone. I was once as innocent as you now seem to
be. No Apprehension you can be under for your Virtue, but I
felt as much: My Reputation was as unspotted, and my Heart
as unvers'd in ill, when I first enter'd these guilty Doors, whither
I was sent on an Errand, much like what I understand has
brought you hither. I was by Force detained the whole Night,
as you are designed to be; was robbed of my Virtue; and knowing I should hardly be forgiven by my Friends for staying out
without their Knowledge, and in the Morning being at a Loss,

all in Confusion as I was, what to do, before I could resolve on any thing, I was obliged to repeat my Guilt, and had hardly time afforded me to reflect on its fatal Consequences. My Liberty I intreated to no purpose, and my Grief serv'd for the cruel Sport of all around me. In short, I have been now so long confined, that I am ashamed to appear among my Friends and Acquaintance. In this dreadful Situation, I have been perplexed with the hateful Importunities of different Men every Day; and tho' I long resisted to my utmost, yet downright Force never failed to overcome. Thus, in a shameful Round of Guilt and Horror, have I lingered out ten Months; subject to more Miseries than Tongue can express. The same sad Lot is intended you, nor will it be easy to shun it: However, as I cannot well be more miserable than I am, I will assist you what I can; and not, as the wretched Procuress hopes, contribute to make you as unhappy as myself."

You may guess at the Terror that seized my Heart on this sad Story, and my own Danger: I trembled in every Joint, nor was I able to speak for some time; at last, in the best manner I could, I thanked my unhappy new Friend, and begg'd she would kindly give me the Assistance she offered: Which she did; for the first Gentleman that came to the Door, she stept up herself for the Key to let him in, which the wretched Procuress gave her; and I took that Opportunity, as she directed, to run out of the House, and that in so much Hurry and Confusion, as to leave my Hood, Fan, and Gloves, behind me.

I told my Aunt every Circumstance of my Danger and Escape, and received a severe Reprimand for my following so inconsiderately, in so wicked a Town as this, the Direction of an entire Stranger.

I am sure, Sister, you rejoice with me for my Deliverance. And this Accident may serve to teach us to be upon our guard for the future, as well against the viler Part of our own Sex, as that of the other. I am, dear Sister,

Your truly affectionate sister.

N. B. This shocking Story is taken from the Mouth of the young Woman herself, who so narrowly escaped the

Snare of the vile Procuress; and is Fact in every Circumstance.

Letter Seventy

From a Father to a Daughter, against a frothy
French *Lover.*

Dear Polly,

I CANNOT say I look upon Mr. *La Farriere* in the same favourable Light that you seem to do. His frothy Behaviour may divert well enough as an Acquaintance; but is very unsuitable, I think, to the Character of an Husband, especially an *English* husband, which I take to be a graver Character than a *French* one. There is a Difference in these gay Gentlemen, while they *strive to please,* and when they *expect to be obliged.* In all Men this is too apparent; but in those of a light Turn it is more visible than in others. If after Marriage his present Temper should continue, when *you* are a careful Mother, *he* will look more like a Son than a Husband: If entering into the World should change his Disposition, expect no Medium; he will be the most insipid Mortal you can imagine: If his Spirits should be depressed by the Accidents of Life, he is such a Stranger to Reflection (the best Counsellor of the Wife), that from thence he will be unable to draw Relief. And Adversity to such Men is the more intolerable, as their Deportment is suited only to the Smiles of Success.

He *dances* well; *writes* very indifferently: Is an artist at *Cards;* but cannot cast *Accompts:* Understands all the Laws of *Chance;* but not one of the *Land:* Has shewn great Skill in the Improvement of his *Person;* yet none at all, that I hear, of his *Estate:* And tho' he makes a good Figure in *Company,* has never yet studied the Art of living at *Home:* He *sings* well; but knows nothing of *Business:* He has long acted the Part of a *Lover;* but may not find the same Variety and Entertainment in acting the *Husband:* Is very *gallant;* but may not be over *affectionate:*

And is so tender of *himself,* that he will have little time to indulge *any body else.* — These, Child, are my sentiments of him. You are not wholly ignorant of the World: I desire to *guide,* not to *force,* your Inclinations; and hope your calm Reason will banish all farther Thoughts of this Gentleman, who, however you may like him for a Partner at a *Ball,* seems not so well qualified for a Journey through the various Trials, from which no Station can exempt the *married State.* I am

Your affectionate father.

Letter One Hundred and Thirty -Eight

A Father to a Daughter in Service, on hearing of her Master's attempting her Virtue.

My dear Daughter,

I UNDERSTAND, with great Grief of Heart, that your Master has made some Attempts on your Virtue, and yet that you stay with him. God grant that you have not already yielded to his base Desires! For when once a Person has so far forgotten what belongs to himself, or his Character, as to make such an attempt, the very Continuance with him, and in his Power, and under the same Roof, is an Encouragement to him to prosecute his Designs. And if he carries it better, and more civil, at present, it is only the more certainly to undo you when he attacks you next. Consider, my dear Child, your Reputation is all you have to trust to. And if you have not already, which God forbid! yielded to him, leave it not to the Hazard of another Temptation; but come away directly (as you ought to have done on your own Motion) at the command of

Your grieved and indulgent Father.

Letter One Hundred and Thirty-Nine

The Daughter's Answer.

Honoured Sir,

I RECEIVED your Letter Yesterday, and am sorry I stay'd a Moment in my Master's House after his vile Attempt. But he was so full of his Promises of never offering the like again, that I hoped I might believe him; nor have I yet seen any thing to the contrary: But am so much convinced, that I ought to have done as you say, that I have this Day left the House; and hope to be with you soon after you will have receiv'd the Letter. I am

Your dutiful daughter.

Letter One Hundred and Sixty

From a Country Gentleman in Town, to his Brother in the Country, describing a public Execution in London.

Dear Brother,

I HAVE this Day been satisfying a curiosity, I believe natural to most People, by seeing an Execution at *Tyburn:* The Sight has had an extraordinary Effect upon me, which is more owing to the unexpected Oddness of the Scene, than the affecting Concern which is unavoidable in a thinking Person, at a Spectacle, so awful, and so interesting, to all who consider themselves of the same Species with the unhappy Sufferers.

That I might the better view the Prisoners, and escape the Pressure of the Mob, which is prodigious, nay, almost incredible, if we consider the Frequency of these Executions in *London,*

which is once a Month; I mounted my Horse, and accompanied
the melancholy Cavalcade from *Newgate* to the fatal Tree. The
Criminals were five in Number. I was much disappointed at
the Unconcern and Carelessness that appeared in the faces of
three of the unhappy Wretches: The Countenances of the other
two were spread with that Horror and Despair which is not to
be wonder'd at in Men whose Period of Life is so near, with the
terrible Aggravation of its being hastened by their own voluntary Indiscretion and Misdeeds. The Exhortation spoken by the
Bell-man, from the wall of *St. Sepulchre's* Churchyard, is well
intended; but the Noise of the Officers, and the Mob, was so
great, and the silly Curiosity of people climbing into the Cart
to take Leave of the Criminals, made such a confused Noise,
that I could not hear the Words of the Exhortation when spoken:
tho' they are as follow:

"All good People pray heartily to God for these poor Sinners, who now are going to their Deaths; for whom this great
Bell doth toll.

You that are condemned to die, repent with lamentable
Tears. Ask Mercy of the Lord for the Salvation of your own
Souls, thro' the Merits, Death, and Passion, of Jesus Christ,
who now sits at the righthand of God, to make Intercession
for as many of you as penitently return unto him.

Lord have mercy upon you! Christ have mercy upon you!"
—Which last Words the Bell-man repeats three times.

All the way up *Holborn* the Croud was so great, as, at
every twenty or thirty Yards, to obstruct the Passage; and Wine,
notwithstanding a late good Order against that Practice, was
brought the Malefactors, who drank greedily of it, which I
thought did not suit well with their deplorable Circumstances:
After this, the three thoughtless young Men, who at *first* seemed
not enough concerned, grew most shamefully daring and wan-
ton; behaving themselves in a manner that would have been
ridiculous in Men in any Circumstances whatever: They swore,
laugh'd, and talked obscenely; and wish'd their wicked Com-

panions good Luck, with as much Assurance as if their Employment had been the most lawful.

At the Place of Execution, the Scene grew still more shocking; and the Clergyman who attended was more the Subject
of Ridicule, than of their serious Attention. The Psalm was
sung amidst the Curses and Quarrelling of Hundreds of the
most abandon'd and profligate of Mankind: Upon whom (so
stupid are they to any Sense of Decency) all the Preparation
of the unhappy Wretches seems to serve only for the Subject
of a barbarous kind of Mirth, altogether inconsistent with
Humanity. And as soon as the poor Creatures were half-dead,
I was much surprised, before such a Number of Peace-Officers,
to see the Populace fall to haling and pulling the Carcases with
so much Earnestness, as to occasion several warm Rencounters,
and broken Heads. These, I was told, were the Friends of the
Persons executed, or such as for the sake of Tumult, chose to
appear so, and some Persons sent by private Surgeons to obtain
Bodies for Dissection. The Contests between these were fierce
and bloody, and frightful to look at: so that I made the best
of my Way out of the Croud, and, with some Difficulty, rode
back among a large Number of People, who had been upon the
same Errand with myself. The Face of every one spoke a kind
of Mirth, as if the Spectacle they had beheld had afforded
Pleasure instead of Pain, which I am wholly unable to account
for.

In other Nations, common criminal Executions are said to
be little attended by any beside the necessary Officers, and the
mournful Friends; but here, all was Hurry and Confusion, Racket
and Noise, Praying and Oaths, Swearing and Singing Psalms;
I am unwilling to impute this Difference in our own from the
Practice of other Nations, to the Cruelty of our Natures; to
which, Foreigners, however, to our Dishonour, ascribe it. In
most Instances, let them say what they will, we are humane
beyond what other Nations can boast; but in this, the Behaviour
of my Countrymen is past my accounting for; every Street and
Lane I passed through, bearing rather the Face of a Holiday,
than of that Sorrow which I expected to see, for the untimely
Deaths of five Members of the Community.

One of their Bodies was carried to the Lodging of his Wife, who not being in the way to receive it, they immediately hawked it about to every Surgeon they could think of, and when none would buy it, they rubb'd Tar all over it, and left it in a Field hardly cover'd with Earth.

This is the best Description I can give you of a scene that was no way entertaining to me, and which I shall not again take so much Pains to see. I am, dear Brother,

Yours affectionately.

appendix B

from the preface to the first edition of Clarissa *(1747)*

The following History is given in a Series of Letters, written principally in a double, yet separate, Correspondence;

Between Two young Ladies of Virtue and Honour, bearing an inviolable Friendship for each other, and writing upon the most interesting Subjects: And

Between Two Gentlemen of free Lives; one of them glorying in his Talents for Stratagem and Invention, and communicating to the other, in Confidence, all the secret Purposes of an intriguing Head, and resolute Heart.

But it is not amiss to premise, for the sake of such as may apprehend Hurt to the Morals of Youth from the more freely-written Letters, That the Gentlemen, tho' professed Libertines as to the Fair Sex, and making it one of their wicked Maxims, to keep no Faith with any of the Individuals of it who throw themselves into their Power, are not, however, either Infidels or Scoffers: Nor yet such as think themselves freed from the Observance of those moral Obligations, which bind Man to Man.

Length will be naturally expected, not only from what has been said, but from the following Considerations:

That the Letters on both Sides are written while the Hearts of the Writers must be supposed to be wholly engaged in their Subjects: The Events at the Time generally dubious:—So that

they abound, not only with critical Situations; but with what
may be called *instantaneous* Descriptions and Reflections; which
may be brought home to the Breast of the Youthful Reader:
—As also, with Affecting Conversations; many of them written
in the Dialogue or Dramatic Way.

To which may be added, that the Collection contains not
only the History of the excellent Person whose Name it bears,
but includes The Lives, Characters, and Catastrophes, of several
others, either principally or incidentally concerned in the Story.

But yet the Editor [to whom it was referred to publish the
Whole in such a Way as he should think would be most acceptable to the Public] was so diffident in relation to this Article
of *Length*, that he thought proper to submit the Letters to the
Perusal of several judicious Friends; whose Opinion he desired
of what might be best spared.

One Gentleman, in particular, of whose Knowledge, Judgment, and Experience, as well as Candor, the Editor has the
Highest Opinion, advised him to give a Narrative Turn to the
Letters; and to publish only what concerned the principal
Heroine;—striking off the collateral Incidents, and all that
related to the Second Characters; tho' he allowed the Parts which
would have been by this means excluded, to be both instructive
and entertaining. But being extremely fond of the affecting
Story, he was desirous to have every-thing parted with, which
he thought retarded its Progress.

This Advice was not relished by other Gentlemen. They
insisted, that the Story could not be reduced to a Dramatic
Unity, nor thrown into the Narrative Way, without divesting
it of its Warmth; and of a great Part of its Efficacy; as very few
of the Reflections and Observations, which they looked upon
as the most useful Part of the Collection, would, then, find a
Place.

They were of Opinion, That in all Works of This, and of
the Dramatic Kind, STORY, or AMUSEMENT, should be considered as little more than the *Vehicle* to the more necessary
INSTRUCTION: That many of the Scenes would be render'd

languid, were they to be made less busy: And that the Whole would be thereby deprived of that Variety, which is deemed the Soul of a Feast, whether *mensal* or *mental*.

Others, likewise gave *their* Opinions. But no Two being of the same Mind, as to the Parts which could be omitted, it was resolved to present to the World, the Two First Volumes, by way of Specimen; and to be determined with regard to the rest by the Reception those should meet with.

If that be favourable, Two others may soon follow; the whole Collection being ready for the Press: That is to say, If it be not found necessary to abstract or mit some of the Letters, in order to reduce the Bulk of the Whole.

Thus much in general. But it may not be amiss to add, in particular, that in the great Variety of Subjects which this Collection contains, it is one of the principal Views of the Publication,

> To caution Parents against the *undue* Exertion of their natural Authority over their Children, in the great Article of Marriage:

> And Children against preferring a Man of Pleasure to a Man of Probity, upon that dangerous, but too commonly received Notion, *That a Reformed Rake makes the best Husband*.

SAMUEL RICHARDSON

In the Preface to the Third Edition, Richardson drops the apologetics for the length of *Clarissa* and expands the descriptive passages in which he attempts to guide his readers' response. The following paragraph is representative.

The principal of these two young Ladies is proposed as an Exemplar to her Sex. Nor is it any objection to her being so, that she is not in

all respects a perfect character. It was not only natural, but it was
necessary, that she should have some faults, were it only to shew
the Reader, how laudably she could mistrust and blame herself,
and carry to her own heart, divested of self-partiality, the censure
which arose from her own convictions, and that even to the acquit-
tal of those, because revered characters, whom no one else would
acquit, and to whose much greater faults her errors were owing,
and not to a weak or reproachable heart. As far as is consistent
with human fraility, and as far as she could be perfect, considering
the people she had to deal with, and those with whom she was
inseparably connected, she *is* perfect. To have been impeccable,
must have left nothing for the Divine Grace and a Purified State to
do, and carried our idea of her from woman to angel. As such is
she often esteemed by the man whose *heart* was so corrupt, that he
could hardly believe human nature capable of the purity, which,
on every trial or temptation, shone out in *hers*.

Richardson appended a Postscript to the novel which was
also revised and expanded for the later editions. Most of the
Postscript is concerned with answering the criticism of readers
who had wished his novel to end happily for Clarissa. The vigor
of the defense and the range of citations used to buttress the
argument make the Postscript a document of some value to
literary history, even though the ideas are unremarkable. But
what is likely to interest the modern reader most is the part of
the Postscript, near the end, in which Richardson describes
his craft.

Some have wished that the Story had been told in the usual
narrative way of telling Stories designed to amuse and divert,
and not in Letters written by the respective persons whose history is given in them. The author thinks he ought not to prescribe to the taste of others; but imagined himself at liberty
to follow his own. He perhaps mistrusted his talents for the
narrative kind of writing. He had the good fortune to succeed
in the Epistolary way once before. A Story in which so many
persons were concerned either principally or collaterally, and
of characters and dispositions so various, carried on with tolerable connexion and perspicuity, in a series of Letters from different persons, without the aid of digressions and episodes for-

eign to the principal end and design, he thought had *novelty* to be pleaded for it: And that, in the present age, he supposed would not be a slight recommendation.

The Length of the piece has been objected to by some, who perhaps looked upon it as a mere *Novel* or *Romance;* and yet of *these* there are not wanting works of equal length.

They were of opinion, that the Story moved too slowly, particularly in the first and second Volumes, which are chiefly taken up with the Altercations between Clarissa and the several persons of her Family.

But is it not true, that those Altercations are the Foundation of the whole, and therefore a necessary part of the work? The Letters and Conversations, where the Story makes the slowest progress, are presumed to be *characteristic.* They give occasion likewise to suggest many interesting *Personalities*, which a good deal of the instruction essential to a work of this nature is conveyed. And it will, moreover, be remembered, that the Author, at his first setting out, apprised the Reader, that the Story (interesting as it is generally allowed to be) was to be principally looked upon as the Vehicle to the Instruction.

To all which we may add, that there was frequently a necessity to be very circumstantial and minute, in order to preserve and maintain that Air of Probability, which is necessary to be maintained in a Story designed to represent real Life; and which is rendered extremely busy and active by the plots and contrivances formed and carried on by one of the principal Characters.

Some there are, and Ladies too! who have suuposed that the excellencies of the Heroine are carried to an improbable, and even to impracticable height, in this History. But the education of Clarissa from *early childhood* ought to be considered, as one of her very great advantages; as, indeed, the foundation of *all* her excellencies: And it is hoped, for the sake of the doctrine designed to be inculcated by it, that it will.

It must be confessed, that we are not to look for *Clarissa's* among the *constant frequenters* of Ranelagh and Vaux-hall, nor among those who may be called *Daughters of the Card-table.* If we do, the character of our Heroine may then indeed be justly thought not only improbable, but unattainable. But we have neither room in this place, nor inclination, to pursue a subject so invidious. We quit it therefore, after we have *repeated*, that we *know* there are *some*, and we *hope* there are *many*, in the British dominions [or they are hardly any-where in the European world] who, as far as *occasion* has called upon them to exert the like *humble* and *modest*, yet *steady* and *useful*, virtues, have reached the perfections of a Clarissa.

PHILIP STEVICK